£1-50

Pr

'Very funny, h
antidote for anyor
ladder they've achieved is a run in their tights'
Fiona Walker on *Lizzie Jordan's Secret Life*

'It's a great idea for a plot, and Manby's writing
more than does it justice'
Marie Claire on *Getting Personal*

'Manby will have you in fits once again'
OK! Magazine on *Getting Personal*

'The perfect antidote to the cold winter weather . . .
light-hearted romp of sun, sea, sand and sex . . .
This merry novel should blow away the winter blues'
Hello! on *Seven Sunny Days*

'A girl's night out in book form – brilliant'
Company on *Ready or Not?*

'A laugh-every-page, romping read. Excellent!'
B Magazine on *Running Away from Richard*

About the author

Chris Manby is editor/contributor to the *Girls' Night In* anthologies, which have so far raised more than £1,000,000 for humanitarian organisation War Child and No Strings, and topped book charts all over the world. Raised in Gloucester, Chris now lives in London.

CHRIS MANBY

Lizzie Jordan's Secret Life

Getting Personal

HODDER

Lizzie Jordan's Secret Life Copyright © 2000 by Chris Manby
Getting Personal Copyright © 2002 by Chris Manby

Lizzie Jordan's Secret Life first published in Great Britain
in 2000 by Hodder and Stoughton
Getting Personal first published in Great Britain in 2002
by Hodder and Stoughton
This omnibus edition first publiushed in 2006 by Hodder and Stoughton

A division of Hodder Headline

A Hodder paperback

2

A CIP catalogue record for this title
is available from the British Library

ISBN 0 340 92218 4

Printed and bound by
Mackays of Chatham Ltd, Chatham, Kent

Hodder Headline's policy is to use papers that are natural,
renewable and recyclable products and made from wood grown
in sustainable forests. The logging and manufacturing processes
are expected to conform to the environmental regulations
of the country of origin

Hodder and Stoughton Ltd
A division of Hodder Headline
338 Euston Road
London NW1 3BH

Lizzie Jordan's Secret Life

Author's Note

16 December 1999

Dear reader,

Please excuse me while I do a quick Gwyneth Paltrow . . .
This book is dedicated to the people who supported me in
so many different ways during my very own *annus horribilis*.
Sometimes I feel quite giddy when I think about how lucky I
am to have such a special and steadfast circle of family and
friends. Here goes . . .

To Mum, Dad, Kate and Lee with thanks for their constant
love and support. To Ryan 'cake for questions' Law. To
Jane and Ian Wright for putting up with the world's worst
bridesmaid. To Jane Brown for pretending we had a great
time in Ibiza. To Peter Hamilton and Kate Fell (you know
you've got room for a marquee, so use it!). To Mark Love
and Jacqui Saunders for the 'love cupboard' and their love.
To Geraldine and Dylan Gray for making my birthday so
special. To Mike Elms and Trudy Kelleher for letting me live
with them. To Alex Lay for listening. To Vicki Fisher and
Pam Rutherford for the girls-only moans. To Jools Simner
(that draw was rigged!). To Tom Callaghan (if I was ten
years older . . .). To Malcolm Alsop, Philip Allard and
Lisa Webb for putting up with my erratic appearances and

typing. To Jessica Adams for the hopeful horoscopes (draw more boxer shorts!). To Fiona Walker, Brit-Lit Queen for Groucho gossip and being such a professional in Glasgow!!! To Helen Lederer for restoring my faith in the possibility of true love. To Julie Wright and Jon Stroud for having faith in *Deep Heat*. To Nick Rhodes for the best advice. To Steve Barnham for having the misfortune to be in when Nick wasn't!!! To Bill Sillery for making me feel fanciable at 8.30a.m. on the Fulham Road. To Dr Anna Trigell for being perpetually sunny. To Sian Kelley for giving me the opportunity to have a near-death experience in front of sixty fourteen-year-old boys. To Mike Gayle and Zelda West Meads for the Borders gigs. To Rachel Huggard, ditto plus the dissections!!! To Elaine Noone and Claire Edgar. To Graham Joyce. To Solomon for being wise! To Nick Davies for the vitriol! To Roz Chissick for her endless patience. To Ant and the team at Gillon Aitken Associates for showing me the money. To David Garnett for keeping me on my toes. To Ian Percival for being the best best man. To Nikki Jones. To Nick 'Bombshell' Cornwell and Toby Stone. To Jo Medcroft and Helena Roberts.

To the Americans! To Chris Hobbs and Marty 'Bea-vil' Beal. And to Jenn Matherly, a truly special friend. To the real Brian – Brian Rabin – though of course this book isn't about you . . . And to Collin Madden – my all-time favourite Yank. It isn't about you either, my dear!!!!

Finally, I owe a huge debt of gratitude to everyone at Hodder and Stoughton for their tremendous efforts on my behalf. Especially to Kate Lyall Grant, an editor of great vision (obviously) and a valued friend, who not only corrects my punctuation but has also variously found me a place to live, a clutch of great party invitations and even the occasional hot date. For author care beyond the call of duty (rivalled only by Jon 'discreet' Wood's attention to my coat on *that night*), this book is dedicated in particular to her.

Couldn't have done it without you . . .

Love,
Chris Manby

I

Brian.

Hardly the kind of name you'd give a romantic hero, is it? But he was mine.

Brian Coren.

Quite tall. Quite dark. Quite handsome. Brad Pitt had nothing to worry about. But somehow Brian Coren stole my heart.

I met him during my second year at university. I was reading English Literature at Oxford. I wasn't sure how I'd managed to get on to the course in the first place but it might have been because the college I was accepted by – St Judith's – had a quota of poor people to fill. For pretty much the whole of my first term, I was totally overwhelmed by it all. The hard work. The tradition. All that cutlery.

Meanwhile, Brian Coren had been studying economics at some small but exclusive college in a pretty part of New York State. In his senior year, he was sent over to the UK on an exchange programme to increase his understanding of the London Stock Exchange amongst other things. His mother at least hoped that a year at Oxford might give him a certain '*je ne sais* what' that would set him apart from his less well-travelled peers when he returned.

I can still remember the very first time I saw him as clearly as if it were only an hour ago. It was the beginning of the autumn term, still just about sunny and warm enough to sit on the Mediterranean-style mezzanine outside the experimental psychology block for a quick fag between tutorials. I was sitting on a step with my best friends at the time: Bicycle Bill, who was always on his bicycle, and Miserable Mary, a gothic psychology student who was always looking miserable, in case you hadn't guessed.

We were comparing boring summer vacations. Mine in a lens-grinding factory that reminded me of the outer circles of hell. Bill's on a fruit farm somewhere in the West Country and Mary's on the cheese counter at some West London deli. None of us could ever afford to go travelling in the breaks. Well, we probably could have done if we'd really wanted to. But I didn't fancy doing the backpack and diarrhoea thing, so I pretended that travelling was for the idle rich and that I was underprivileged rather than plain chicken.

'Shame God didn't invent the volume control before he invented Americans,' Miserable Mary said suddenly, jerking her head in the direction of two guys and a girl who looked unusually smart for students. The trio were veritably *bouncing* towards the psychology block (which was the only department that served pecan pie for elevenses) in their shiny new leather shoes. *Polished* leather shoes. The girl tossed her glossy brown hair as if she were auditioning for a shampoo ad and the guys punched each other jovially in a jock mock fight. Even without hearing their voices, it was clear that they weren't locals. They stood out like three gaudy tropical parrots in the midst of the flock of hungover pigeons that were the British students in their uniformly 'alternative' grey and black rags.

'Jesus, it's the Brady Bunch,' hissed Mary, as the Americans briefly broke into song.

'More like the Osmonds, I say,' said Bill, adjusting his

crotch. Bill was a geography student with a fine line in cycling shorts with reinforced gussets. 'I've got one of them in the room next door to me in halls this year. Americans – I swear they don't even know how to breathe quietly,' he sighed. Just loud enough so that the Brady Bunch who had now drawn up beside us went suddenly silent and stared.

Mary, Bill and I studied the grimy paving stones until we thought they might have passed us. But I looked up first and that is when he caught my eye. Brian Coren caught my eye and smiled right at me for the very first time.

'Hi,' he said.

'Bloody Americans,' muttered Bill, totally missing the greeting.

'Yeah,' said Mary. 'So full of themselves. Get back to Disneyland.'

'Nice to meet you too,' said Brian.

You can imagine how embarrassed I was when I next saw the Americans. It was later on in the same day, in fact, and I was sitting on another step. This time I was outside the college dining hall, waiting for Mary and Bill to return from their lectures.

I rarely bothered with going to my own lectures unless I was in love with the lecturer. In such circumstances I would suddenly be fired with enthusiasm for my subject, which was great until I started to think that the lecturer in question might have noticed my crush and then I wouldn't be able to go to his lectures any more because I was too embarrassed. It was a really vicious circle and as a result, in my first year, I had only been to half my Middle English lectures (Dr Law looked a bit like Indiana Jones, I thought), three lectures on Hardy (Dr Sillery could have been Rupert Everett's twin) and a single symposium on Sylvia Plath (Dr

Trigell looked like Gerard Depardieu. That crush didn't last long).

Anyway, college dinner was at seven sharp, but the queue outside the dining block usually began to gather from half-past six onwards. It wasn't that the canteen food was so fantastic, you understand. It was simply that if you got to the dining hall the minute the vile stuff was served, you had a much better chance of getting your hands on a packet of cream crackers and a Dairylea triangle instead of a dubious gelatinous pudding. The crackers were hermetically sealed in clear plastic wrappers and hence the theory was that the college chef couldn't possibly have rendered them inedible with his idiosyncratic gastronomic touch. Five days out of six, however, I seemed to get a packet of crackers that had gone very stale.

'Is this the right place for dinner?' Brian asked. In a whisper, I noticed right away.

'Sorry?' I muttered.

'I said,' he said, even more quietly than before, and having to lean up close to my ear to say it, 'is this the right place for dinner?'

'Yes,' I said, as confidently as I could. He was obviously taking the piss about the volume control crack that Mary had made earlier, so I spoke up extra clearly and slowly – as if I were speaking to somebody French. 'You have to queue up here,' I told him. 'It's an English thing,' I added with a smirk. 'A queue.'

'A queue? Really? So many things to learn,' sighed Brian, taking up a position on the steps beside me while his happy shiny friends perused the club notice boards and signed up for all those things that English students rarely bother with, such as counselling rotas and netball.

Ignoring my new companion, I tried to read the book I

hadn't opened since I'd picked it up in Blackwells, Oxford's cavernous book superstore. I could spend days in Blackwells – reading the self-help manuals mostly – but this book was *Far From the Madding Crowd*. One of that term's set texts in fact. I hated it when we had to do actual novels instead of plays and poems. So much more to read. Too much like hard work, which rather defeated the point of having chosen English as a degree in the first place.

'You're reading Thomas Hardy,' Brian observed observantly.

'Yes. Well, I would be if I could concentrate,' I said testily, starting the first sentence of the preface again.

'He's one of my favourite authors actually,' Brian persisted. 'Have you read *Tess*?'

'I've seen the film,' I told him.

'Pretty good adaptation of the book, don't you think?'

I really had no idea. I hadn't actually *read the book* back then. Didn't even know it wasn't just called *Tess* at the time. But I nodded anyway.

'I like the girl in it,' said Brian. 'My name's Brian Coren, by the way.'

'Bw-yan,' I said automatically. I couldn't help myself doing a quick impression of Michael Palin's Roman emperor. We had watched Monty Python's *Life of Brian* at least twice a week in the first year (the Junior Common Room video cupboard had only two films – the other one was *Die Hard*). I clapped my hand to my mouth when I realised what I was saying.

Brian laughed in a pained sort of way. 'Monty Py-thon, right? That film has been the bane of my life. *My life of Bw-yan*,' he added lamely.

'I'm sorry,' I snorted into a tissue. I always had a cold in those days. 'It's sort of automatic. An in-joke around college.'

'I see. So, what's yours?'

'Uh?'

'Your name?' he asked patiently.

'Oh! Elizabeth Jordan.' I stuffed the tissue back into my pocket and extended my hand automatically.

'Pleased to meet you. Is that Elizabeth after the Queen of England?' he asked, shaking my hand rather stiffly.

'No,' I laughed at the thought. 'My parents aren't exactly royalists. I was named after Liz Taylor, I think.'

'The film star? Wow. You know, I think I can see that,' he nodded. 'You have similar eyes.'

'To Liz Taylor?' I breathed. Didn't she have the most beautiful eyes in the world? 'Do you really think so?' I asked eagerly.

'Well, you both have two,' said Brian, putting a pin in my bubble. But he did it with a smile. A really nice smile that told me that perhaps he was just trying out a bit of English sarcasm.

'I also have my own teeth,' I added to let him know I hadn't taken offence.

'Hey, here come your friends,' said Brian then, making as if to get up from the step. 'I'd better go. I think they took quite a dislike to me early on and I wouldn't want to get you into trouble for talking to the enemy.'

Bill and Mary were indeed mooching along the corridor towards us. Bill was wearing his prized *Tour de France* cycling ensemble (which the rest of us suspected hadn't been washed since it crossed the finish line on a British contender's back and Bill won it in a raffle at the university cycle club) and Mary looked as though she had just lost her pet dog to a ravenous crocodile (which actually meant she was in a relatively good mood for Mary). When they spotted me, Mary turned to Bill and whispered something that was doubtless fairly poisonous. She frequently lamented the fact that we never met any new people, but her tendency to hate almost everyone on sight hardly helped our cause. Some of the most socially confident people in college would hide in shady doorways when Mary came into the quad.

'Has someone in your friend's family died?' Brian asked me. 'Only she looks really miserable all the time.'

'She's a gothic,' I explained. 'It's part of her look.'

'Really. Some friends of mine had to dress up like that to be extras on *Interview with a Vampire*. Scary. Well, I guess I'll see you around, Miss Elizabeth Jordan. Better get back to Disneyland.'

'No,' I insisted. Hearing the Disneyland crack again made my cheeks flame automatically. But suddenly I didn't want him to go. Suddenly I wanted to prove that we weren't the biggest xenophobic dorks in the United Kingdom before every foreign student in the university started to avoid us. I wasn't sure why it was so important at that moment but perhaps I had an inkling even then that if I talked to Brian for a bit longer, I might actually discover something interesting. 'Stay and meet them properly,' I begged him. 'I'm sure they're sorry things got off to such a bad start too. Their barks are far worse than their bites, I promise.'

'Well, as long as his bite isn't as bad as his snore,' said Brian, cocking his head towards Bill. 'I've got the room next to him. You know, he should really think about having his adenoids out.'

'Made a new friend?' purred Mary, looking down on us through false lashes that looked like big black spiders stuck to her lids with thick glue.

'Bill and Mary, this is Brian.'

'Bw-yan!' they chorused automatically. Mary even smiled at him. Sort of.

'Er, we've already been through that,' I said.

'*He's not the Messiah – he's a very naughty boy!*' said Bill, in a high-pitched impression of Terry Jones playing Brian's ugly mother. 'That film is so funny.' He slapped his lycra-ed thigh at the thought.

'Actually,' said Brian very seriously, 'where I come from, *The Life of Brian* is considered blasphemous and I don't find it very funny at all.'

Two mouths dropped open.

'Wow. Are you from Utah or something?' Mary asked in awe.

'Nah! I'm from New Jersey originally. Though I live in New York now. And I'm Jewish. So I don't really give a shit. We don't believe he was the Messiah anyway.'

'What? Brian?' asked Bill.

'Jesus,' I corrected before Bill started to explain to Brian that it was 'only a film'. 'But enough about that. We need to get in there.' I jerked my head towards the dining-room door. The queue had started to move and we had somehow managed to lose our coveted place at the head of it.

'Shit!' said Mary. 'I only wanted cream crackers and now they'll all have gone. I don't believe it. I'm going to starve to death.' She could never resist the opportunity for a spot of hyperbole and right then she sounded like a shipwreck survivor who had just discovered that the last of the weevil-studded biscuits has fallen overboard. 'What is it supposed to be tonight anyway?' she added, just a little more calmly.

Bill sniffed the air floating out from the kitchen like a wolf scenting its prey. 'Mmm, I'd say we're having celery soup to start, followed by a delicious celery *en croûte* with boiled celery as an accompaniment. And for dessert, puréed celery with custard.'

Brian looked faintly disgusted.

'Why so much celery?' he asked.

It was just another in-joke. The college chef had a thing about celery. Either that, or a very cheap supply of the stuff. He put celery into almost everything, including, it was rumoured, the tutti-frutti ice-cream. Mary didn't mind, because she was a firm believer in the theory that eating celery burns off more calories than it contains. But I was heartily sick of the stuff. Besides, have you ever heard of anyone serving up boiled celery instead of proper vegetables like potatoes or carrots? Where are the vitamins when it's been simmered for four days? That's what my mother wanted to know whenever she visited.

Anyway, Mary was reading the menu pinned up by the college door. 'Well, it's actually meant to be egg mayonnaise on lettuce followed by spaghetti bolognese with treacle sponge for afters. Great,' she snorted. 'I can't eat any of that. Eggs bring me out in a rash and spaghetti bolognese has got tomatoes in it.'

'Not at this college,' Bill reminded her.

'I'll give it a try,' said Brian bravely.

But instead he was quickly introduced to the joys of the kebab van which parked outside the college gates every night. For the first year, I had thought of the kebab van man as a saviour; the only thing standing between me and malnutrition. However, when he put his prices up three times in one term at well over the rate of inflation I began to wonder whether the chef was making college food deliberately bad and taking a cut of the kebab van's earnings.

'Any pork in this?' Brian asked, as he took his cold pitta bread filled with slivers of dubious brown meat analogue and those twisty green pickled chillies that you find all the way up and down the High Street in Oxford on a Sunday morning.

'I don't think there's actually any meat of any description in it at all,' said Mary. She was supposed to be a vegetarian, but she made an exception for kebabs. Brian took a cautious bite of the brown matter and spat it out again instantaneously.

'What *is* this stuff?' he asked us.

'Welcome to Oxford,' said Mary.

His initiation was done.

After that, Brian quickly became a regular fixture in our college lives. He zoomed up in Mary's estimation when he revealed that the two corn-fed kids we had seen him with on that first day, and hated at first sight, were simply the people he had travelled over with on the plane, not people he particularly liked hanging out with. He didn't play baseball, or basketball, or live all year just to watch the Superbowl. Though he wore proper lace-up shoes and not disgraceful tattered workmen's boots like the rest of us, it turned out that he didn't have terrible taste in anything but his preppy clothes (all chosen by his mother – he had too many things to think about apart from changing his image, he claimed, and Mary said she actually respected him for that).

He also had several albums of dirge-like goth music unavailable in the UK that Mary borrowed at once and couldn't be persuaded to return for almost three terms. He connected with Bill over long nights of Led Zeppelin and the revelation that his parents, like Bill's (or so Bill constantly claimed), had been at the original Woodstock.

But Brian didn't have to listen to the right music or wear the right clothes to impress me. I just adored his sense of humour. It was so – well, so English actually. Mostly sarcastic and ever so slightly sick. I loved to hear crazy stories about his New York childhood. Before I met Brian, I had harboured no inclination to visit America whatsoever. All Disney and obesity, as far as I was concerned. But listening to his stories, I quickly realised that there were so many other things that I would be missing out on if I never crossed the pond.

I screamed with laughter at his impressions of bolshie *Noo Yoik* taxi drivers ordering *quaffee*. I listened with due reverence when he told me about his experiences as a fresh-faced waiter in a Manhattan Pizza Hut frequented by the Mob.

And when I couldn't stop gazing at his big brown eyes while he told me about the time his grandmother had taken her apricot toy poodle, *Spencer Tracey the Second,* to the orthodontist to fix its overbite, I knew that I was falling in love.

2

The thunderbolt really hit one day about a month after we first met.

We were hanging about in the undergraduate students' common room, Bill, Brian, Mary and I, drinking the vile coffee that we were each obliged to pay three pounds a term into a kitty for. The common room was always chock-full at about eleven o'clock in the morning with people trying to get their money's worth of the stuff without gagging.

'There's a performance of *Antony and Cleopatra* on tomorrow night, in the crypt at St Edmund Hall,' said Brian suddenly. We had been lamenting the fact that we never really got any culture (without admitting that we never really tried). 'Do you think it will be any good?' he asked.

Mary snorted into her cup. 'Why don't you ask Liz?' she said.

'Have you been to see it already?' asked Brian.

I blushed hard and stared into my coffee. What had Mary done to me?

'Actually, I'm going to be in it,' I had to admit. 'So I don't know whether I'm qualified to say whether it'll be good or not,' I waffled. 'I mean, it's probably not, if they let me on to the stage.'

'Lizzie, this is brilliant,' said Brian excitedly. 'How come you didn't tell us?' He turned to Bill and Mary. 'Isn't this great? Our friend Liz is an actress. We're definitely going to have to go now.'

'Uh-uh,' said Mary, shaking her head smugly.

'She won't actually let us go and see her act,' Bill explained before he added in a squeaky approximation of my voice, 'She says that it makes her shy and then she fumbles her words.'

It did. Knowing that people I knew were in the audience made me fumble my words.

'Liz, I didn't even know you did act,' said Brian in surprise. 'And here you were agreeing with us that you didn't do anything cultural. Now I discover you're doing Shakespeare on the quiet!'

I shrugged.

'Who are you playing?' he asked me.

'She's probably just a spear carrier,' said Mary quite dismissively.

'I'm playing Cleopatra actually,' I corrected.

'Wow,' Brian almost clapped his hands. 'That's a major part. Wait, that's like *the* major part in this play. You're the leading lady and you didn't tell us?'

'Isn't Cleopatra supposed to be all beautiful and dusky?' said Mary, examining her nails like a cat considering unsheathing its claws on the family budgie. 'She didn't have freckles, for a start.'

'I will be wearing make-up,' I reminded her. 'And I haven't got freckles anyway. What are you talking about?'

'Must be a blackhead then.'

'Stop teasing her, Mary,' Brian interrupted. 'I'll bet Liz is perfect for the part.'

'I don't know about that,' I said. Truthfully.

'She's so embarrassed that she practises her lines in the shower,' said Mary. 'So that no one can hear her over the sound of the water.'

'I do not,' I protested. Though in actual fact I had, after Graham the mathematics student in the room next door to me complained that my constant talking to myself while learning my lines was interfering with his ability to concentrate on logarithms. He also got the student dean to break into my bedroom after I practised the bit with the asp a little too loudly. I took it as a compliment at first. My death scene must have been hyper-realistic to warrant such concern. But the dean soon burst that bubble when he warned me that any repeat performance would result not in applause but in a hefty fine.

'I still can't believe I didn't know this was going on. Why hide your talents from your friends?' asked Brian.

'Because I'm not sure that I actually have a talent,' I explained. 'Anyway, I'm not hiding anything. I just don't want to bore you all with my thesping. It's a private thing.'

'But you're doing a play,' Brian reminded me. 'That's not very private.'

'I was press-ganged into it,' I lied. 'And it's a set text. It saves me having to do too much revision if I learn the part to play it.'

'You must want to do it a little bit,' he persisted.

I shrugged again. But oh, I *had* wanted to play Cleopatra. Until Mary let loose the fact. I was actually really excited to have wangled such a great part. But I still wasn't convinced that I entirely deserved it and I didn't want to get a reaction to my acting ability from people I would have to see on a daily basis afterwards. That meant Mary, Bill and Brian. What if they hated my performance? What if they couldn't even look me in the eye afterwards because I was so bad? I would never be able to act again if I had to face my biggest critics over breakfast every day.

Until Mary forced me to admit my part in the play

prematurely, I had made a bargain with myself that I would wait for at least five good reviews before I invited my mates along to watch me. Five *good* reviews. It sounded reasonable but the likelihood of that happening was actually pretty slim. Not least because I knew only four student critics would bother to see the play.

'I'd really like to see you on stage,' said Brian, trying to be all persuasive.

'We want to too,' chorused Mary and Bill in irritating harmony. 'If you let Brian see the play, we've got to see it as well. It's only fair.'

'Well, you definitely can't,' I said, all exasperated. 'Do you want me to go wrong? Please don't come. You're not really interested. I'd die of embarrassment.'

'Don't hide your light under a bushel,' said Brian jewishly.

'I'm not. I just want to hide it from you guys. At least for the moment. Look, I know what it would be like. Mary and Bill would make faces at me all the way through. I let them watch me act once before. I was playing the nurse in *Romeo and Juliet* and nearly choked to death trying not to laugh when Bill mooned at me from the back of the hall in the final act. Luckily it looked as though my shoulders were shaking with grief and the snobby git from *Isis* was impressed. But how can I expect to be taken seriously when I'm corpsing through the sad parts?'

'I won't do it again,' promised Bill but I never took Bill's word for anything; not since he made a New Year's resolution to change out of his cycling shorts as soon as he returned from the gym each day so that no one had to look at his finely tuned musculature unless they specifically asked to. He had made that resolution last until, oh, at least the fifteenth of January.

'I wish I could believe you. Does anyone want another

coffee?' I asked, desperate to move the conversation on to another topic. Anything other than me. Luckily Brian stepped to my rescue.

'I'll fetch them,' he said. 'But only if you let us all come and watch you do the nurse thing tomorrow night.'

'No way!' I shrieked. 'I've told you why I can't.'

'I was only joking,' Brian said, backing off with his hands in a gesture of surrender. 'If you really don't want us to be there, we won't be. Wouldn't want to disturb your creative genius.'

'Aw,' Mary moaned. 'I really wanted to watch you pulling that funny face you pull when you're being all serious again.'

'Don't pick on her, Mary,' warned Brian.

I sighed in relief.

But I won't pretend that I wasn't ever so slightly disappointed when the time came for the play to begin the next night and I couldn't see any of them in the audience. I'd met Bill in the dining room earlier that evening and he told me that they were going for a curry straight after dinner (I've already explained to you about college dinners as a slimming aid). But I thought that was just a cunning bluff. I still fully expected to see all three of them sitting at the back of the hall with their programmes across their grinning faces in a pathetic attempt at disguise. But they weren't. At least not as far as I could see, because before I could finish checking the audience really thoroughly from the safety of behind the curtains, the spotlights came on and I couldn't see a thing except the stage in front of me.

There were hundreds of theatrical groups at the university. I had signed up for most of them during Freshers' Week but ended up with the minute Crypt Company because they were the only group who actually let me finish my audition piece. All the other groups had cut me short in my portrayal of *Twelfth Night*'s plucky Viola arriving shipwrecked in Illyria, and suggested that I might like to help out behind the scenes instead. Perhaps I could operate the curtains? Did I know how to sew a tunic? The members of the Crypt Company were altogether more sympathetic to my acting ambitions. Most of them were on Prozac, which probably helped.

I had wanted to tread the boards from a very early age. I think the bug bit when my brother Colin and I were taken to see a West End production of *Annie* as a special Christmas treat back in 1981. Colin had hated the musical about a plucky orphan. Too much singing and far too many girls as far as he was concerned. But I had been entranced and spent the next six months belting out all the songs at the top of my voice in the hope that someone influential would hear me singing in the street and drag me off to stage school. It didn't happen of course. That kind of thing doesn't happen in Solihull. But my mother did enrol me in a local church-based amateur dramatic group, who were putting on their own production of my beloved *Annie*. I auditioned my heart out, but the title role went to the church warden's daughter (she couldn't sing a note but she had the right hair). Reluctantly I took up the part of one of the other orphanage girls but feigned tonsillitis on the opening night and never actually performed.

After that, puberty struck and the thought of having too many people looking at me while I tried to hide my spotty forehead behind a ridiculously long fringe kept me firmly backstage. I acted as stage manager for my school house in three house drama competitions in a row. Nobody thought to ask me whether I would like to be on stage because I must have seemed so contented pulling the curtain strings;

but I found myself watching the leading ladies and thinking that I could do better. I learned all their lines and performed them in front of my bedroom mirror just in case both star and understudy should fall ill. One day, I told myself, I would no longer be so shy.

By the time I got to university, I hadn't entirely got over my shyness but I forced myself to audition for the theatre groups because I had read an article in *Cosmo*, or some worthy tome like that, about confronting your biggest fears. Get back on to the horse, they said. The irony was, I don't think that the idea of an audience in itself bothered me. What bothered me was the opinion of my peers – specifically the people I knew. I wouldn't have minded if Sir Dickie Attenborough saw my Cleo and thought my performance was rubbish. At school, it had been the thought of my classmates thinking I was rubbish that had scuppered my acting career. Now it was the thought of my closest college friends thinking the same.

I had acted my heart out in front of the Crypt Company because I didn't know any of them and they all looked as ordinary and uninspiring as me. They practically begged me to join them, assuming that I must have been inundated with offers from every theatre group going. In fact, only one other group had recalled me to audition again – for the part of a spear carrier in *Julius Caesar*. The Crypt Company offered me the part of Juliet's nurse in *Romeo and Juliet*, and so I took the option of being a big fish in a small pond instead.

Rod, the company's floppy-haired, fringe-flicking director, had decided that we would do *Antony and Cleopatra* after his insistence on producing a disastrous Catalan play about the secret language of sentence structure (at least I think that's what it was about) over the summer had earned damning reviews from every university publication and the subsequent lack of interest had almost wiped out the company's finances.

We needed to do a crowd pleaser and *Antony and Cleopatra* was pretty much guaranteed to draw the crowds with its tale of love and death in equal measure. I thought we had chosen the right play this time, but I wasn't convinced that we had chosen the right venue. Though the crypt at St Edmund Hall was great for all the interior scenes (and had given the company its name), there wasn't enough room for a really impressive crowd and scene changes were a nightmare in the confined space and crepuscular darkness. I forgot to mention that the Crypt Company was so small that we frequently doubled up on parts and even the most important actors had to shift scenery as well. It was particularly difficult for me since my costume had a large amount of padding at the front and on the backside that seemed to get bigger with every performance. I knew that I wasn't exactly womanly in my natural state, while Cleopatra was already a mother by the time she met her man, but I was beginning to wonder whether I was playing the Queen of Egypt or one of the Teletubbies.

Phylidda, who would be playing my handmaiden Charmian, was in charge of the costumes. It was a bit of a step down for her to be playing my maid, since when we'd played *Romeo and Juliet*, she had been Juliet to my nurse. I had auditioned for Juliet too and think I might have got the part if Phylidda's boyfriend hadn't been chosen to play Romeo. When it was announced that Greg was playing the romantic hero, I knew that my chances of swooning across the balcony were over. If Phylidda didn't get Juliet, everyone suspected she would walk; and with her would go the extremely valuable lighting equipment that she had bought with an interest-free loan from her terrifyingly rich step-daddy.

'Don't forget to put your warts on,' said Phylidda as I was applying my make-up that first night.

'I'm not sure Cleopatra would actually have had warts,' I ventured.

'Oh, but they all did,' she assured me. 'Have you any idea what kind of nasties you can get bitten by in the desert? And what about that plague of boils they had?'

'Was that in Cleopatra's time?' I asked.

'Probably.'

'I still don't see why we have to have them. They're a bit distracting.'

'Rod wants this to be the most realistic production of *Antony and Cleopatra* ever seen at the university,' she explained patiently. 'The warts were his suggestion.'

'Fine.' I was dubious about that but I stuck one right on the end of my nose to keep her happy and was momentarily doubly relieved that my friends wouldn't be in the audience that night.

'Aren't you having warts too?' I asked her as she sketched thick black lines around her eyes, transforming herself from Home Counties to houri in a stroke. 'If Cleopatra had warts, her handmaiden would definitely have had them too.'

'I've got one,' said Phylidda, showing me a minute bump on her chin. 'Now sit perfectly still while I do your eye make-up.'

I closed my eyes and tilted my head backwards.

'Sit still,' reminded Phylidda as she drew nearer, holding the eye-liner pencil like a dagger. 'If you move I'll have your eye out.'

'I'm not moving,' I promised.

'No, you are moving, Lizzie,' she said, before she poked me right in the eye.

'Ow!' I sat up very suddenly, clapping my hands to my face. 'You've stabbed me!'

'I told you not to move, didn't I? Does it hurt?' she asked. Her voice was strangely excited. 'Do you want me to call Rod and tell him that you won't be performing tonight?'

'I want you to check that I'm not going blind first!'

'Open your eye!' Phylidda wrenched my eyelids apart. 'Can you see?'

'No. You've got your thumb in it now.'

'God, I'm sorry,' she said, not moving her thumb at all. 'Oh, Lizzie, this is terrible. Your first night playing Cleopatra and now you won't be able to go on.'

'I will go on,' I insisted, batting her hands away blindly. My vision was terribly blurred. Though she had stabbed me in the left eye, they were both filled with tears and seemed to be stinging equally badly. 'What does my bloody eye look like?' I begged her.

'Oh, it's awful, Lizzie. Really, really awful. I don't know what to say to you.'

'Just pass me the mirror.'

'I don't think you ought to look.'

'Pass me the mirror!'

The bell rang to warn the audience that it was time for them to take their seats. I had less than two minutes after the curtain went up to be on stage looking serenely foxy and in control, and there I was with my mascara streaming down my face like an oil spill at Niagara Falls.

'That's the bell for the audience,' shrieked Phylidda, as if I hadn't heard. 'Oh, God, Lizzie. What can we do? I'm going to have to go on as Cleopatra, aren't I? You can do Charmian. The fringe on my wig is longer than yours and you won't need to concentrate so hard if you've got fewer lines.'

'What's going on?'

It was Rod, come to see why we weren't at the pre-performance meditation circle he always insisted on. 'We're doing the mantra.'

'Lizzie's had a terrible accident,' Phylidda explained. 'I'm going to have to go on as Cleopatra instead. It's so awful.'

But it wasn't so awful for her. It suddenly came to me that Phylidda might have stabbed me deliberately so that she could go on in my place. After all, her boyfriend Greg was playing Antony and we all knew that Phylidda didn't entirely believe in Greg's ability to 'act' a love scene.

'I can go on,' I insisted to Rod. Through my blurred vision I saw Phylidda's face take on a look of deep disapproval.

'You're not well enough, Lizzie,' she said quietly.

'I am well enough. I can see perfectly well out of my right eye and I'm sure the left one will be fine by the time we get to the second act.'

'Tell her she's not well enough, Rodney,' said Phylidda, only just managing to keep the edge of hysteria out of her voice. 'What if a delayed reaction makes her forget her lines? What if she falls over or something?'

'Then you can take over,' I told her. 'But I am going on. Have you got any idea how hard it has been for me to get this far? Make me an eyepatch.'

Realising that she wasn't going to keep me off the stage that night, Phylidda set to her task grudgingly. I had intended that she make a discreet little patch that could be hidden beneath the long beaded fringe of my Egyptian-style wig, but when the curtain was finally raised on the first night of my Cleopatra, it was a Cleopatra with a great wad of cotton wool stuck against her eye with sellotape. At least it detracted attention from the warts.

I just tried to forget that I looked like I'd done ten rounds with Frank Bruno. In fact, I felt that the sting in my eye helped me to focus and be extra fiery when I needed to be. Not that the performance went without hitch from then on. Antony nearly met an early death when one of the heavy spotlights came loose from the rig and fell crashing to the floor right next to his feet as he spoke with Caesar. Between scenes it became clear that Charmian suspected Antony of having a fling with a fresher at their college and the poor boy took on a harassed look that must have made the audience wonder why he was bothering with women at all.

I managed to raise a few gasps and murmurs. I hoped it was my acting and not the eyepatch or the wart on my nose which dropped off on to Charmian's lap while she sat at my feet and listened to me dribbling on about Antony. When we broke off for an interval after the scene, Phylidda returned the detached wart to me with such disgust in her expression you might have thought it was a real one.

'This totally detracted from one of my best lines,' she snarled.

'I won't put it on again then,' I told her.

'No, you must. For continuity's sake. But try putting it on your cheek this time.'

'Won't people find it funny that I have a migrating wart?'

'I'm the wardrobe mistress.'

'I think it suits you,' said Greg, Phylidda's feckless Antony. 'Physical defects can be strangely cute on the right girl.'

'Do you think so?' I asked.

'Of course he doesn't,' Phylidda snapped.

'Is there any money to split tonight?' Greg asked to change the subject.

'No. In fact, you all owe me three pounds apiece for the hire of the venue.'

'What?' said Greg. 'I bet this never happened to Laurence Olivier.'

'I bet Laurence Olivier never fluffed his lines because he was too busy hamming it up for the girl in the front row,' Phylidda snapped.

'What girl in the front row?' Greg asked innocently.

'You know very well who I mean. Her with the nipples from Pembroke.'

'Eh?' said Greg.

'Either she's very pleased to see you or it's very cold in here. Can't she afford to buy a bra, for heaven's sake?'

'It is actually very cold in here,' I said, in an attempt to save Greg's bacon. 'My nipples feel like bloody thimbles.'

That was a mistake. Greg instantly fixed his eyes on my chest. Phylidda fixed her death rays on my remaining healthy eye.

'I can't believe you let her come here on my opening night,' she continued, spinning Greg around and marching him away from my chest. 'How can I lose myself in the lyrical glory of Shakespeare when *she*'s sitting in the front row reminding me of what you've been up to while I've been revising for my finals.'

'Don't you think we ought to be ringing the bell for the second act?' I suggested. I'd had enough of being caught in the crossfire and in any case I wanted to get to the curry house for a last poppadom. In between arbitrating for their argument, I'd taken a quick peek out into the audience again to see if anyone I knew had sneaked in. No one. I knew I should be relieved, what with the warty make-up and all,

24

but for some reason I wasn't. So they really hadn't bothered to turn up. Why did I feel so let down?

'I just might kill myself for real in the final scene,' Phylidda sobbed dramatically.

'Phylidda, don't be so ridiculous!' begged Greg.

I made a mental note to make extra sure that the basket full of snakes that would be instrumental in Cleopatra's end contained only rubber ones (it wasn't an entirely stupid notion – Phylidda was studying zoology and I knew she had access to poisonous lizards at least). I was in charge of the props.

Thankfully the play ended without a real suicide. After Caesar had spoken his final word on the dignity of the Egyptian queen and her Roman lover, those members of the cast who had not died in the snake frenzy all bowed their heads, as if to signify that everyone should remain silent until Rod, who was playing the great Roman emperor, looked up and gave the signal for rapturous applause (not that I expected that with so few people in the audience) and my sudden return from death to take a curtain call. Usually the audience understood and waited until the resonance of the final phrase had completely died away before they began to applaud our efforts . . . but not tonight. The carefully measured period of silence was smashed by much clapping of hands and cat-calling from the previously empty back row.

'Bravo! Encore! Three cheers for the one-eyed Queen of Egypt.'

A single red rose came whizzing over my head where I still lay pretending to be dead. That flower was followed by another and another until there must have been – oh, at least half a dozen roses on my body. I sat up and squinted out into the audience. We hadn't even gathered to take our curtain call yet. Many of the cast were still off-stage. This was unprecedented behaviour from a usually sedate-to-the-point-of-comatose Shakespeare-loving crowd.

'Well, they're nothing to do with me,' said Phylidda, struggling to her feet, as suddenly a pair of y-fronts joined the flowers on the stage, followed by a wolf whistle so loud I'm sure I nearly lost both ear-drums. Unfortunately I had already guessed that the rowdy element could only be something to do with me.

I slowly picked up the stray pants and turned them over in my hands. Purple y-fronts. I knew of only one person in the world who could possibly bring himself to wear purple y-fronts except as a dare. More specifically, white y-fronts that had been dyed deep purple in the college washing machine and given everyone else in college lilac-coloured clothes for about a month afterwards.

It was Bill.

Now that the spotlights were off I could see him clearly at the back of the hall, sticking his fingers into his mouth for another raucous whistle. To one side of him Mary was clapping relatively sedately. And to the other side, Brian held the last of the bunch of long-stemmed red roses he had been throwing with such an impressive aim. Now they ran to the stage, as if we actors were a rock band and they were planning to mob us. Phylidda turned to me with raised eyebrows. 'I'll make a note of that three pounds you owe me,' she said. She was the club treasurer as well as the wardrobe girl. Then she left without saying goodbye.

'That was so fantastic,' Brian said, grabbing my hand and kissing it extravagantly. 'You were wonderful, marvellous, you were all the superlatives a man could possibly think of if only he was doing an English degree and not economics.'

'You were pretty good,' said Bill.

'Yeah, not bad,' said Mary. 'Particularly liked the migrating warts. And what on earth happened to your eye?'

'Phylidda. Eye-liner.'

'Nasty. I thought she might have given you a punch because you were too realistic when you kissed Antony.'

'Way too realistic. I know I was jealous,' said Brian, causing me to flush to the bone marrow. 'You were sooo hot, Queen Cleo.' I certainly was right then. I covered my reddening cheeks with my straight black wig.

'But, but I didn't see you in the audience,' I stuttered.

'Ah-ha!' said Bill. 'That was Brian's idea. We ducked down behind the seats in front of us as soon as you first came on and stayed there until the end of your first scene so that you wouldn't see us and think we'd come to make you muck up your lines.'

'You really were brilliant,' said Brian incredulously.

'Yeah. Shall we go for that curry now?' Mary interrupted. She was either very hungry or getting sick of having to congratulate me on my performance. Whatever her motives, it seemed like a great idea. I couldn't take much more flattery and I was dying to take off that terrible wig.

'I didn't think you'd come tonight,' I told Brian as we headed for Tandoori Nights, Oxford's best, and cheapest, curry emporium.

'Did you really think I'd miss it?' he said. 'A chance to see such a good friend tread the boards? You were triumphant, Lizzie.'

'I can't believe you managed to keep Bill and Mary in check,' I added gratefully.

'They knew I'd be mad at them if they didn't behave on your big night. You know, I really admire people who spend their free time learning how to act like that,' he told me. 'You were even better than Liz Taylor in the movie.

You're a very special, very talented and endlessly surprising girl, Lizzie Jordan.'

'You don't really mean that,' I stuttered.

'You know I really do,' he said.

'Oh.'

He looked me straight in one eye and the patch.

Special, talented and endlessly surprising?

No one had ever said anything like that to me before and I'm afraid I had to punch him. Only in the arm . . . And only very lightly. But I did have to punch him just the same. Didn't Brian realise that the English way to pay a compliment was with sarcasm or a joke? I felt hot all over for the rest of the walk to the restaurant and was bright fuchsia even before I tasted my first mouthful of the chef's legendary chicken tikka makhani. In fact, I was much less embarrassed when Bill pointed out that I had forgotten to take my warts off.

Special, talented and endlessly surprising.

Brian Coren might just as well have told me that he loved me.

3

'Do you think he has a girlfriend waiting for him back in America?' Mary asked the next day as we pushed a trolley around Tesco's in search of marked-down food only just past its sell-by date to supplement our diet of cream cheese and crackers.

'He's never talked about one if he has,' I told her.

'That's true. I bet he gets overlooked in favour of all those big football-playing jocks, anyway,' she said. 'American women have no taste in men whatsoever. Just look at all those big-haired girls throwing themselves at Bill Clinton.'

'That's more about power and book deals than physical attraction,' I reminded her. 'There's something inherently attractive about shagging the most powerful man in the world however gross he is in physical terms.'

'Mmmm. I wonder what he looks like without his clothes on,' Mary mused.

'Bill Clinton? Not overly fat, but not too toned. Flabby round the midriff? Better with a tan, I should imagine.'

'Not him, stupid. I meant Brian,' said Mary impatiently.

'Brian? What? *Our* Brian? Oh, I don't know,' I laughed nervously. 'I can't say I've ever really thought about it.'

'You liar.'

'I am not lying. He's a friend of ours!' I protested. 'Not just some piece of boy-meat to drool about while we're walking round the supermarket.'

'So? Are you telling me you've never imagined Bicycle Bill without his clothes on either?' Mary asked, pointing at me menacingly with a green banana.

'Too right I haven't,' I shuddered, holding my hands up. 'That all-in-one lycra bodysuit he wears to go training in hardly leaves much room for imagining anyway. But I try very hard not to. In fact, I like to try and imagine what Bill would look like with a proper pair of trousers on. Nice thick ones made of tweed with a proper fly for modesty and a crease right down the front of each leg. And a shirt that buttons all the way up to his neck so that you can't see that nasty bit of chest hair that looks like it could just reach out and entangle you while you're not looking.'

'Ugh. You've noticed that clump of hair too?' Mary whispered. 'I hate it. But sometimes I just can't take my eyes off it.'

'I know exactly what you mean. It's like not being able to stop yourself looking at a hedgehog that's been killed on the road with its guts spilled all over the place, isn't it?' I elaborated unnecessarily. 'And you do know that he's got hair like that on his back as well?'

'How do you know?' Mary shrieked. 'I would have to scream if I saw that. When did you see that? You didn't actually *sleep* with him without telling me, did you? Did you? Liz, I can't believe you . . .'

'No!' I protested loudly. 'There's a perfectly innocent reason. It was in the summer. He was sunbathing out by the cricket pitch. He put his shirt on again before you came out to join us.'

'Well, thank God for that. I might have fainted if I'd seen him semi-naked. What a nightmare. Do you think Brian has chest hair too?' she asked to change the subject.

'I swear I've never really thought about it,' I lied again.

'He's bound to. The hair on his head is so thick and dark. He looks like he needs to shave at least twice a day. Then there's the fact that he's Jewish of course,' said Mary, raising her eyebrows meaningfully.

'What do you mean by that? Are Jewish men generally more hairy?'

'No! I mean. You know,' she looked groin-wards. 'I mean, he's not going to be a cavalier, is he? *Comprendez?*'

'No? What do you mean?' I asked in exasperation as I threw a canister of UHT squirty cream into our trolley. Well, I didn't know what I hoped to do with it either, but it was only just out of date and had been reduced by sixty pence.

'I mean, he's a roundhead, dumbo. No hood to pull up.' She mimed putting a hood on, which left me none the wiser.

'Eh?'

'I mean, he's circumcised, of course,' she whispered.

'Oh, right,' I said slowly. She had left me behind with the chest hair.

'Don't tell me you've never thought about that either!' she said, giving me a shove in the arm. 'Have you ever seen one? One that's been done? How far do they cut it off to, do you think?'

'I don't know.' But my mind's eye was suddenly unavoidably full of truncated little penises with bandages wrapped around their ends like so many wounded soldiers. 'They don't actually make *it* any shorter when they do it, do they?' I asked.

'Not sure,' said Mary. 'It's only the foreskin that goes, I think. But is it the whole foreskin, d'you reckon? Or just a bit?'

'Wouldn't be much point taking just half of it off,' I suggested. 'I suppose they must chop it right back to the shaft.'

We had reached the refrigerated cabinets. A man choosing thinly sliced luncheon meat suddenly changed his mind about what he wanted for his supper.

'Well, it's about cleanliness, apparently,' Mary told me, as she picked out an anaemic-looking sausage and began to use it as a teaching aid. 'That's why it started. Historically. Stops a chap from getting any infections under the hood.'

'But doesn't it make the whole thing more vulnerable not to have the hood there in the first place?' I countered. We loved an intellectual argument, Mary and me.

'Obviously not,' Mary said firmly. 'And that's not the only advantage apparently. Jemima from my neurophysiology class says that they're much better for blow jobs. For a start, it doesn't take so bloody long, because an exposed tip is that much more sensitive to oral stimulation. And secondly . . .'

'Because you don't have to make the guy a bacon sandwich afterwards?' I quipped, examining a packet of streaky.

'Nice one,' Mary cackled. 'But it's really because you don't have to worry about crusty rim cheese.'

'Ugh!'

We looked at each other and grimaced. I knew exactly what she meant. Sadly, most girls would.

Mary put the sausage back sharpish. And not just because she'd remembered that she was supposed to be a vegetarian for the very highest moral reasons.

'Oh no, I've just had the worst possible thought,' she said then, going all pale and wobbly. She grasped my arm to hold herself up as she said to me in a horrified whisper, 'What if you had to give Bill a blow job? What if you had to give him a blow job or your entire family would be shot dead by fanatical religious terrorists at dawn?'

'Don't!' I pleaded.

'Can you even imagine it?'

'I'm trying my hardest not to.'

'You've got to, Liz. I can't bear the burden on my own. Imagine it. You'd have to peel him out of that funny-coloured jock strap that's always hanging from the back of his bedroom door for a start. Imagine he's just done a twelve-mile jog and then been rowing on the river for a couple of hours and . . . and . . .' She gagged. She actually gagged at the thought of it!

'Come on, Liz. Let's get out of here,' she said, dragging me towards the exit.

'But what about our shopping?' I asked her.

'I can't even think about it now. I think I'm going to hurl.'

Since we only had one can of squirty cream and three green bananas as it was, we abandoned our trolley by the chiller cabinets and fled to the safety of the street and fresh air.

'Are you OK?' I asked Mary, who was doubled over by the bus stop with a horrible mixture of nausea and hysterics by the time I caught up with her.

'I'll be fine in a minute,' she promised, straightening up but unable to stop guffawing. 'You know what, I think I've just invented a new diet. It's called the *Blow Job Diet*. You get all the protein you need by swallowing when you give blow jobs to the guys you really fancy and stave off hunger pangs by imagining having to give a blow job to someone who never washes his knob.'

'Nice theory, Dr Bagshot, but what about the fibre?'

'Oh, you get that from chewing the pillows while Leonardo di Caprio is performing cunnilingus beneath the duvet.'

'Ugh, please,' I laughed. 'That's practically lesbianism. It has to be a man who can grow facial hair at least.'

'Mmm. Perhaps you're right,' she mused. 'OK. How about

this? You can take your pick of gorgeous men. Just imagine your very own heart-throb. The beauty of this diet is that it can be tailored to suit the individual.' She sounded as if she were writing the blurb for the back of the book already.

'Well, I'm going for Brad Pitt,' I told her. 'Little bit of stubble, but not too much.'

We started the walk back to college, stopping off *en route* at the chip shop since our food shopping expedition had failed so miserably. 'Brian could grow a good beard,' said Mary thoughtfully, as she speared the fattest chip in the bag with her wooden chip fork and popped it between her cherry-red lips. 'You know, Jemima said that she quite fancied him but I told her that she couldn't have him because he's strictly ours.'

'Platonically ours,' I reminded her.

'Yes, of course only platonically. It would ruin things, wouldn't it, if one of us had to have him any other way?'

'Absolutely ruin things.'

'Absolutely. So all bets on Brian Coren are off unless one of us falls totally head over heels in love with someone else outside our gang entirely, in which case the other one can have a go with Brian. Agreed?'

She held out her hand to shake on it.

'I suppose. As if he would want either of us anyway,' I sighed.

'Speak for yourself, Ms Low Self-esteem,' said Mary.

4

As you can imagine, when we saw Brian that evening I could think of little else but the conversation that Mary and I had shared in the frozen food aisles of Tesco and the deal that had been made in the chip shop.

I wondered if, as he sat there drinking Guinness and pretending that he really liked it, Brian had any idea at all how much we girls actually fancied him – unlike Bill, who, by the way he always sat with his legs wide open to accentuate his not inconsiderable lycra-sheathed manhood, clearly thought every girl in college fancied him when in reality we would rather have licked dog hair off a dirty carpet than have to kiss him on the lips. Especially since Bill was in the middle of telling us all, rather proudly, how many fillings he had. There were seven in his top teeth, he explained, and just six in the bottom. I could tell that Brian was trying not to wince when Bill invited him to inspect the mercury in his mouth.

'Yes, you probably could pick up radio signals with that,' Brian told him seriously.

Brian, of course, had zero fillings. His teeth were movie-star straight and whiter than Tippex. As were the teeth of just about everyone in America, from the president to parking attendants – at least the ones I had seen on TV. When he had finished cooing over Bill's extensive bridgework, Brian turned to me and said, 'You know, you have very nice teeth for an English girl, Liz.' I immediately stopped grinning and looked at my hands. For a start, I wasn't sure it was a compliment and secondly, because I could sense Mary's envious stare boring into the top of my head as she kept her chipped front tooth (the result of a particularly raucous Freshers' Week drinks party, followed by kissing the pavement) firmly hidden.

'So,' said Bill, slamming his empty glass down on the table to regain our full attention now that everyone had finished looking into his mouth. 'Are we going to the Two Items of Clothing party at the Union tonight or what? You get free drinks if one of your items is a hat,' he added, as if that was an incentive to strip off in the middle of winter.

Two Items of Clothing parties were Bill's idea of a dream night out. He often said he would like to shake the hand of the man (and it just had to be a man) who first thought of the idea. The principle was simple. You could get into the party only if you were wearing two items of clothing, or less. For Bill it was heaven. Lots of half-frozen girls wearing nothing but skimpy bikinis while he got to maintain his dignity (almost) by wearing his all-in-one lycra bodysuit with hefty gusset reinforcement (bought for rowing in, you understand) and a fedora he had picked up on a field trip to Spain.

'I'm game,' said Brian, surprisingly. 'Look what I bought today.' Then he pulled up his perfectly respectable t-shirt to reveal something that appeared to have been sprayed on underneath. An electric-blue lycra bodysuit. 'I got this for rowing in, you understand,' he assured me. He had just been chosen for the college's second rowing team and had been getting up at six a.m. to go training every morning. The nutter. That wouldn't last long. 'You get too much drag if you wear something baggy,' he explained. Bill nodded vigorously in agreement.

'Way too much drag.'

I looked to see what Mary thought of the idea but her eyes were firmly fixed on Brian's pectoral muscles. His not unimpressive pectoral muscles. I had never noticed quite how well-defined he was before. Though, let's face it – I had never seen him in a jumped-up leotard before either.

'It's pretty cold out there,' I tried. 'It is November.'

'So wear your biggest knickers and a fur coat,' said Brian wickedly.

'Come on, Liz,' Mary pleaded suddenly. 'It'll be a laugh.'

I looked at her in absolute horror. A 'laugh'? Mary Bagshot had never before referred to Two Items of Clothing parties as a 'laugh', preferring instead to refer to them as 'pathetic juvenile enterprises' and 'just an excuse for disgusting perverts like Bill to wear their bloody sweaty lycra in public while they ogle semi-naked girls'. Now she was asking whether shoes counted as items of clothing at all. Apparently they didn't.

'You don't have to come, Liz,' Brian told me with a shrug. 'But it would be so much nicer if you did. You can wear your jumper and your jeans. That's two things. You'll be quite warm. I've just got to go to one of these crazy Bacchanalian parties before I go home to America. They simply don't happen in the States in case someone cries sexual harassment.'

'Oh, I don't consider myself to have had a good night unless I've managed to get some of that,' said Mary irresponsibly. And coquettishly, to boot. She really needed slapping with a frying pan that night.

'I don't know if I'm on for it,' I muttered. I had hitherto thought that the whole idea was disgraceful, childish and unnecessarily harrowing for would-be party-goers who didn't tan well. I had managed to get thus far in my university career without ever going to one and didn't feel as though

I had particularly missed out. I couldn't believe that Mary wasn't backing me up now. She was usually so humourless about these things. She was a girl who once thought Andrea Dworkin wore too much make-up. What was wrong with her now?

'Oh, come on. Don't be such a party pooper,' Mary teased me with a pinch. 'You can wear your elasticated staprest slacks and a woolly jumper when you're fifty. Might as well make the most of your youthful body now before you get fat and frumpy.'

That swung it. The twin spectres of 'fat' and 'frumpy' reminding me that I ought to be having a good time while I could still wear a tubi-grip as a boob tube if I wanted to rather than strictly as support for knees overburdened by carrying around a ton and a half of cellulite.

'I can't strip off. I haven't shaved my armpits for nearly a fortnight,' I groaned.

'We'll wait for you,' said Mary, sensing that I'd given in.

So, we ended up going to the Two Items of Clothing party after all and thankfully the two rugby team boys organising the event were already too drunk to bother checking how many items we really had on once they had stamped our hands with the smiley face stamp that said we had paid to get in. I was actually wearing three items. I mean, have you ever tried to wear jeans without the protection of a nice cotton gusset between you and the rivets? To escape from the misery of nasty chafing, I was happy to risk being caught bending the rules and losing my entrance fee.

Mary wore a *risqué* lycra dress (a dress that I thought she had thrown out after reading Naomi Wolf's *The Beauty Myth*) and Brian's baseball cap, grabbing me every two minutes to have me reassure her that no one could see up her skirt. Fact was, no one could really see anything of anybody anyway, since the room the party was being held in was so dark you couldn't even be sure whether the pert g-strung buttocks in front of you were male or female.

Brian and I fought our way to the bar, evading the graze of naked limbs which made me feel as though I were in some kind of virtual reality anonymous pleasure palace straight out of a seventies film. Bill was in his element however. And strangely, so was Mary. When Brian and I returned with the drinks in those flimsy plastic glasses, Mary was resting one slender hand on Bill's hairy shoulder and sliding her naked thigh up and down his silky lycra-ed leg as they grooved to the theme tune from *Shaft*. About three minutes later, they were snogging like two fourteen-year-olds who have just had their train-track braces taken off.

'Yuk!'

'Now that is a surprise,' said Brian, as we edged away to give them some privacy. Well, as much privacy as they seemed to want in a room that was so full I expected the walls to give way at any moment. Brian was surprised that Mary was tongue-wrestling Bill and he hadn't even heard our supermarket conversation about knob-cheese!

'Mmm, I certainly didn't think they fancied each other that much,' I told him. 'In fact, to hear them talk you'd have thought they found each other repulsive.'

'Yes,' Brian agreed. 'But isn't that always the way? People who are deeply, uncontrollably attracted to each other often try to protect themselves from the possibility of disappointment and rejection by pretending that they hate each other's guts in public. They were obviously just crazy about each other all along. You know, I think I'd be willing to lay money on a long and very passionate affair starting tonight.'

'Nah, this is just an aberration,' I said confidently, though by now Mary had been examining Bill's fillings for three whole songs.

'Perhaps you've been too close to them to see it happening,' mused Brian. 'I've never said anything about this before, but I had a gut feeling from the very first time I met Bill and Mary that they might get together one day. She's always touching him. Haven't you noticed that? Just little touches. But they're clearly signals of possession.'

'Do you really think so?' I said, screwing up my nose doubtfully. But when I came to think of it, Mary *was* always touching Bill. Though she had pretty successfully passed off those little signals of possession as hearty thumps of exasperation for as long as I'd known her.

'Yep. They're absolutely nuts about each other,' Brian concluded.

'And how do you know all this stuff?' I asked him.

'You can learn a lot from listening to your big sisters. These days I reckon I can spot just about any embryonic relationship forming at least two weeks before the people involved actually know it's happening.'

We had been walking as we talked and found ourselves outside the party now, passing through the peeling lobby of the students' Union that smelled permanently of spilled beer and sick.

'At least two weeks before it happens, eh?' I mused. 'I wish I had a gift like that. It might come in very useful.'

'Well,' said Brian, slipping his arm around my shoulders in what I assumed was a friendly manner, 'it's not actually that useful to me. You see, this gift I have for spotting fatal attraction is a bit like being able to tell people's fortunes. Clairvoyants can't actually use their fortune-telling powers to predict the future for themselves, you know.'

'I didn't know that,' I admitted.

'Well, it's true. You can't use the gift for yourself. Only for the good of others. That's the law of the universe. I felt sure that the moment Bill actually plucked up the courage to make his move, he would be pleasantly surprised to find his feelings reciprocated. But when it comes to me . . .' He raised his shoulders dismissively. 'When I decide that I've met someone I really like and want to get it on with them, I can watch them all I want to and still have no clue whatsoever whether they feel the same way about me in return.'

We sat down on a low wall outside the Union to ponder the mysteries of the world. And then had to move when we discovered that a couple who had clearly just met at the Two Items of Clothing Party were getting to know each other rather better on the grass right behind us. No wonder we students were so resented by the local taxpayers.

'I find myself falling madly in lust and have no idea at all whether my advances will be reciprocated or rebuffed,' Brian continued to a soundtrack of the courting couple's enthusiastic sighs and grunts. Suddenly, he turned to face me, his heavy arm still around my shoulders, keeping me nice and warm.

'That's a bit of a bummer,' I said with a nervous giggle.

'Isn't it just?'

'Mmm,' I mumbled. 'It really is. A bummer.'

I was burbling. Another giggle. Almost hysterical this time. Brian was looking at me in a very funny way. Was he moving in on me, I asked myself? Surely not. It just wasn't possible. I mean, I was *me*. Lizzie Jordan. He couldn't possibly fancy me, could he? I had bigger spots than tits in those days. It simply wasn't an option. I held my breath in anticipation of the moment when he would tell me that he really fancied Jemima from Mary's neurophysiology class and ask my advice to help him sort the matter out.

'I suppose that the only thing I can do is be brave and throw myself into this scary thing head first,' he murmured. 'Will she or won't she? I'm really not sure. But I'm beginning to think she just might.'

He was so close to me now that his face had gone out of focus and I had to close my eyes to stop them from crossing. But before I could open them again, I felt the soft brush of his lips upon mine. Ohmigod! He was kissing me. It *was* me. He had been talking about me!

'Bri-urghh!'

He wasn't stopping.

Chiming bells and crashing waves! A heavenly choir struck up a quick chorus between my ears. A herd of wildebeest stampeded frantically through my stomach, annihilating the butterflies that usually lived there as they went.

The arm that had been draped so casually around my shoulders moved down towards my waist as Brian pulled me on to his shiny lycra-ed lap. As I relaxed, I let his tongue slip inside my mouth. Brian's hand slid smoothly up the back of my jumper and pressed against my chilly flesh. I searched for a way into his bodysuit but couldn't find one, so I had to wait until we were back in my room before I found out whether he had a hairy back or not. Mercifully, he didn't.

I don't know how we even got back to college that night. We kissed all the way and I didn't notice the route we took. But we ended up in my room somehow and despite it being just a little cramped for the two of us in my single bed with its lethal mattress (the broken springs were forever getting me in the kidneys), Brian and I were dead to the world when Mary hammered on the door at eight the next morning.

'Liz,' she shouted. 'Lizzie. Open the door, quickly. I've

done a terrible thing. A really, really terrible thing! I feel awful!'

'Then go to confession!' shouted Brian, before I could put my hand over his mouth.

There was a moment of horrible, loaded silence as I imagined my visitor registering the strange man's voice coming from inside my room.

'Have you got someone in there?' asked Mary at top volume. I pictured her with her eye to the keyhole now. Only thank goodness there wasn't a keyhole in my door because we had some kind of new fangled magnetic key system in the halls that was forever going wrong. 'Who have you got in there, Liz? Are you with a man? It's not Brian, is it?'

'The very same,' Brian obliged, not sensing, as I had, that it was that time of the day when he should just shut up, climb out through the window and wait on the little concrete balcony outside until summoned back in; so that I could open the door to Mary and pretend that no one had been in the bed with me all along. So much for his psychological insights into people's real feelings for each other.

'Let me in!' Mary demanded. She sounded half-hysterical now. 'Let me in there at once, Lizzie Jordan.'

'We've got to put our clothes on first,' Brian told her, digging me in even deeper. I was already racing around the room picking up random bras, pants and socks and flinging them on in no particular order. At one point I found myself wearing two pairs of knickers. Brian only had his ridiculous lycra cat-suit to get into, so he was dressed in half the time and opened the door to Mary while I still had only one leg in my jeans.

'Morning, Mary.'

'I don't believe it!' she shrieked, catching me *in flagrante*. 'I really don't believe it. How could you?'

Then she disappeared down the hall without waiting for any kind of explanation at all.

'What's wrong with her?' asked Brian.

Mary avoided me for the rest of the day. And it turned out, as I had sort of guessed, she was avoiding Bill as well. So much for Brian's theory about hidden passions running deep. As far as Mary was concerned, when that long-suppressed passion for Bicycle Bill finally broke through the surface of her chilly disdain like an oil drill hitting paydirt, someone should have stuck a finger in the hole before too much spilled over. She later told me she had screamed when she saw the hair on Bill's back despite the fact that I had warned her more than once what she would find if she ever got him out of his lycra.

'And all the time you were getting off with Brian,' she said accusingly, when I finally caught up with her in the queue for the kebab van. 'You made MPL with Brian Coren after what you said to me in the chip shop.'

MPL. Mad passionate love. It had been pretty much like that. I blushed at the very thought of it.

'But . . .' I tried to explain Brian's theory to her, that he had told me that she and Bill had been burning to get together and find out that theirs was true love. Wasn't there a part of the bargain we had made in the chippy that excused my behaviour if she found true love first?

'True love? With Bill? Oh, for goodness' sake, Liz. I was pissed,' she spat. 'You would have tried to stop me. If you were really my friend.'

'I didn't realise,' I said all meekly. 'And I swear I didn't know that Brian was going to make a move on me either until he actually did it. I tried to stop him. Well, didn't try to stop him,' I admitted. 'But I swear I didn't start it.'

'Oh, forget it,' she said eventually. 'Brian obviously wanted you. He's wanted you all along. And it's not even about that anyway,' she added hurriedly. 'I'm not jealous of *you* getting off with Brian, Lizzie. I'm just confused about Bill and a bit pissed off that our happy little gang has to be broken up now. Everything is ruined.'

'What? Why should it be broken up? We can still all hang out together. You, me, Bill and Brian. We can all still be friends.'

'Not now that Bill has seen my bottom, we can't. The balance has shifted, Lizzie.'

And so it had. Though I didn't really notice it then.

In fact, later that night, we were all in the bar together again, exactly as we had been twenty-four hours earlier, before the life-shattering events of the Two Items of Clothing Night, as it later came to be known. Mary was sitting next to Bill and I was sitting next to Brian. The only real difference I could see was that when Jim the one-eyed barman called time, Brian walked me back to my room and stayed there all night making mad, passionate love.

Until I met Brian, I'd never really known what the fuss was about when it came to sex. My experience of this great international pastime had been limited to a single-figured number of inexpert drunken fumbles. Even in the long-term (i.e. three-month-long) relationship I had had the year before Brian's arrival at Oxford, with a rather *naice* boy called James, it seemed that we always had to be completely pissed before we could have sex. And it had to be with the lights out (not at my insistence). And I was categorically *not* allowed to look at him while he did it *to* me as I lay completely still without touching him unless *he* asked me to. I later discovered on the college grapevine that this was a trait peculiar to boys who had been to his internationally renowned public school.

Anyway, with experiences such as that behind me, it was hardly surprising that I was one of the few people who agreed with miserable old Boy George and Morrissey that a cup of tea was probably better than a night's worth of horizontal aerobics. Brian changed all that. He turned me on by pressing buttons I had previously suspected were broken. His obvious adoration of my body eventually even managed to strip away all the shyness I carried about with my cellulite.

I had never imagined that having sex could make me feel so sexy even when I wasn't actually in bed with my new transatlantic lover. I wondered if other people could sense the Ready-Brek glow I felt lingering about me hours after a night in Brian's hunky arms. Could other people see the difference in my walk as I stepped out of the lecture hall? (I'm talking about a newly confident wiggle in my step, not a waddle brought on by friction, by the way.)

The only pity about the whole thing was that I felt I couldn't tell Mary all about it. Before the whole Bill/Brian Two Items of Clothing Night debacle, there hadn't been anything Mary and I didn't talk about. Her secrets were mine and mine were hers. We spoke about our love lives in no-holds-barred detail. The people, the positions, the *smells*. Honestly, we were disgusting. Now, however, I sensed that it wouldn't exactly be appreciated if I burst into Mary's room full of tales about my wonderful new love life. Hers wasn't exactly steaming at that point.

After the Bill episode, which had her swearing that she would join a convent straight after graduating, Mary set her heart on a post-graduate student called Ralph who had five earrings in each ear, a sapphire nose stud and a tattoo of a dolphin on his backside (according to the rumour).

Ralph had been assigned to be Mary's supervisor while she undertook the cruel and unusual experiments that formed part of her psychology dissertation.

The idea was that Ralph, being young and funky, would stimulate her interest in the subject she had chosen (the acquisition of spider phobias in children – she told me with a yawn) but in fact the quality of her work went rapidly downhill as she spent fruitless hours in the psychology library pondering whether this post-grad with his pierced tongue also had a Prince Albert (Mary had a thing about foreskins). I never did get to the bottom of whether she actually wanted him to have a barbell through the end of his penis or not. And it didn't seem as though Mary would be finding out anytime soon either – all her attempts to find herself locked in a lab with him overnight had failed – hence, I didn't want to incur her wrath by appearing to crow that my love life was going swimmingly.

But we did all hang out together. Bill, Brian, Mary and I. And though it was never quite as jolly and easy as it had been before now that Bill's every *double entendre* was inevitably taken personally by Mary, it was almost as good. Besides, I wasn't too worried, because things between Brian and me were much better than before, of course. I felt guilty about breaking the pact I had made with Mary in the chip shop, but hoped that she would understand. She said she did, after the 'one-night thing' I had with Brian had lasted for over three months.

'I'm over it,' she said. 'Back then, I thought it would be quite nice to get off with Brian myself, but seeing how soft and soppy he is over you, I realise I would have found his overly affectionate nature quite cloying actually.'

OK, so it wasn't exactly complimentary, but I took it as my green card to keep hanging in there.

5

We had a wonderful winter and spring term together, Brian and I, but as summer approached, the quiet evenings we had once enjoyed – sometimes just sitting in each other's company reading out of boring text-books – began to be tinged with melancholy.

At the end of the spring term, I had tried to remain disinterested as Brian typed out his amazingly impressive curriculum vitae on my computer and sent letters to companies in America asking them for work experience during the long vacation. I persuaded him to apply to companies in London too, so that we could at least have a slim chance of spending the whole summer together. And he did. But it was an American company which eventually offered him the most interesting internship, not to mention a free flight back home to take up the position.

Six weeks before Brian left for the States, I found a flight number and departure time scribbled on a pad by his bedside and suddenly knew the exact moment when he would be flying away from me. Of course, his return to America didn't necessarily mean that I wouldn't ever see him again, but it did mean the end of 'us' as I had come to think of us. I knew that much. I wasn't stupid. Brian and I had had a conversation about that aspect of things very early on. About how hard it could be to keep long-distance relationships going, especially when the people involved were still so young and had so much to be getting on with back in their respective countries. Back when we had had that conversation, however, I didn't really expect our dalliance to last long enough for the question finally to come up for real.

A week before he had to go home to the United States, Brian and I hired a car and drove out of Oxford for the day. We took pictures of each other outside Blenheim Palace. Brian assured me that one day he would be back to buy the place. We had lunch in an oak-beamed tea-room. Brian bought a little model of a thatched cottage for his mother – 'She's nuts about English stuff,' he said – and discovered later that it had not only been made of china but in China as well. We did a whirlwind tour of Cotswold villages. As whirlwind as you can get when you're stuck in a Renault Clio behind a Massey Ferguson and a flock of sheep.

And we ended the day at the Rollright Stones. Bill, Mary and I had discovered this little-known stone circle in our first year. Mary had seen the circle marked on a map and thought we should have a spiritual picnic there one Sunday afternoon. We packed peanut butter and banana sandwiches and set off from college in Bill's battered Mini. With Mary navigating we were quickly lost. Bill said it didn't matter since he could navigate using the power of the local ley lines.

'I can feel the stones,' he assured us. 'I'll just go with my instincts and we'll be there in no time.'

We ended up going twenty miles in the exact opposite direction.

Brian and I arrived at the Rollright Stones for our own adventure just as the sun was setting. We walked around them reverently at first – we'd got into a bit of a coach-tour mentality that day – while I told him the legend of the Stones, that it was impossible to count them. We counted round three times and came up with three different numbers. I told him about the Rollright Stones expedition I had taken with Bill and Mary. The thunderstorm that broke when we finally found them. We took it as a sign from the heavens and got drenched instead of staying in the car.

'I can feel the spirit of the stones washing all the negativity out of me,' Mary had said at the time.

A busload of Japanese tourists took pictures of us driving back to Oxford in our sodden underwear.

'Sounds like a pretty special trip,' Brian said.

I couldn't begin to tell him how much more special it felt to be there alone with him that afternoon. We tried to count the stones one more time. Then Brian and I chose the comfiest-looking rock and settled down against it to watch the sun slip away behind the hills. Brian took my hand and brought it to his lips for a kiss.

'You will always be special to me,' he murmured.

That almost made me cry right away. Suddenly the sun seemed to be setting on something more than a Tuesday in the middle of June.

'I love you,' I told him. It seemed like the only thing to say.

'I know,' said Brian. He didn't say he loved me back but I took his reply as a 'ditto' and squeezed his hand hard. 'But you know how hard it would be for us to keep this going once I'm back in the States,' he continued. 'And I do have to go back to the States.'

There was silence for a beat.

'You could still change your mind and work in London, couldn't you?' I tried. 'There are big banks in London too. American banks even. I bet the one you're going to work for has a branch here somewhere. Can't they arrange a transfer? It would save them the cost of a flight.'

'London isn't New York, Liz. That's where my family is. And you know I love my family. I've missed them while I've been here.'

'I love my family too, but I would go to New York like a shot. If someone asked me,' I hinted.

'We have to finish our degrees,' he said, conspicuously missing the opportunity to make that invitation.

'Do you think,' I asked him then, 'if we had met after finishing our degrees. If we were both, say, twenty-five or thirty now instead of just twenty-one . . . Do you think that we might have made a proper go of it?'

'We have made a proper go of it,' he told me firmly. 'I will remember this special year I've shared with you for the rest of my life.' His fingers tightened around mine.

I tried to smile, but my eyes were stinging with the effort of holding back the tears. It seemed so unfair, yet oddly incredibly romantic at the same time. Forces beyond our control were tearing us apart. We said nothing while the sun finally sank from view, then we got to our feet, still holding hands, and walked in silence to the car.

When we went to bed that night I felt like Shakespeare's Juliet, who only has until dawn with her Romeo, and knows that the love to be squeezed into that short spell of darkness has to last a lifetime. Even though Brian and I actually had another week until we said goodbye for good, that sunset was our final act.

On the day that Brian finally left for America, I didn't go with him to the airport. He asked if I would but I'm afraid I can't stand goodbyes at the best of times. There's something about waving someone off too extravagantly at a train station or an airport that seems to tempt the gods to prevent them from ever coming back again. And I wanted Brian to come back.

I wanted it more than anything in the world. I would have given the rest of my life for another year in his company.

For at least twenty-four hours after I closed my door on the unhappy sight of his retreating back and slumped, sad shoulders, I expected to hear a knock and find him standing in the hallway with a bunch of flowers, desperate to tell me that he realised he loved me after all and simply could not go away again. Not ever. How on earth could he have pretended that he could?

But there was no knock. Not until Mary dropped by at six o'clock to ask why no one had seen me for over a day and to find out whether I wanted to go to the kebab van with her. She was leaving for home next morning and said she couldn't wait to go back to London this time. The post-graduate with the tongue-ring had rebuffed her advances at an end of term party and she wanted to get out of his way. Bill had already left for the holidays. He would be cycling in the Himalayas this time. No more fruit-farming for him.

I had made vague plans to stay behind for a while and catch up with some coursework in the library (I'd done bugger all real work that year – too busy snogging), but suddenly being alone in college didn't seem such a great idea. Far from being free from distractions, with my friends all gone home to their families, I knew it was more likely that instead of working I would only be able to sit in the library and gaze into space while I remembered being in the exact same place a week before, or a fortnight before, scribbling silly soppy notes to push beneath Brian's nose while he pretended to be immersed in some dry text on economics; fondling his knee under the cover of a table; secret trysts in the library toilets. I knew it would be too much to be surrounded by all those memories. I would have to get away too.

I shrugged on my jacket and followed Mary down to the

dining hall without even bothering to brush my hair. I knew I looked a real state and I didn't feel like saying much, but Mary hardly seemed to notice. She was too busy chatting about the plans she had for the holidays, which included a serious diet that would miraculously turn her into a supermodel and make the foolish post-graduate rue the day he had ever refused to kiss her with his nasty pierced tongue.

'Next year is going to be great,' she said, uncharacteristic-ally positively for Mary. 'You know, I'm thinking of getting my belly-button pierced as soon as I get back to London.'

'Next year there won't be any Brian,' I murmured. It was the first thing I had said for about half an hour.

'Yes, well,' she said dryly. 'It's a shame he had to go home, but life does go on, Lizzie. Perhaps next year you won't neglect your other friends as much as you have done.'

'I'm sorry if you think I've neglected you,' I said, feeling rather surprised.

'That's OK,' she said softly. I wondered whether she thought she had been just a bit harsh. She put her arm around my shoulders and gave me a half-hearted hug. 'I know what it's like to be in love.'

I nodded, thinking that perhaps she was slightly over-estimating the strength of her feelings for Ralph the post-grad, but grateful for her empathy all the same.

6

I spent the summer working at the same lens-grinding factory where I had spent my summer holiday a year before. Apart from the itinerant holiday workers – other unfortunate students like myself who couldn't afford to flee the country till September – the staff at Greville's Lenses was largely unchanged. In fact, everything at Greville's Lenses was unchanged. Irene the tea lady even remembered how I liked my coffee.

'Had a good year at university, have you?' she asked. 'Don't look like you've learned all that much to me.'

She said that every time I saw her. Twice a day. Every day. But oh, I told my melancholy self as I mooned about the office, if only she knew how much I *had* learned since I last carried a clipboard around that stinking, screaming factory. I was a totally different person now. I was no longer content to while away my precious free time ticking off numbers on a clipboard in a factory where the windows had been white-washed to stop the inmates from staring out at the real world and getting ideas above their station. In fact, I had never been content to do it, but now it was even worse than before.

I spent my days in a kind of trance, trying to block out the reality of my grand vacation in hell. When the factory bell rang to signify that it was time to down tools at five o'clock, I tried not to think of Brian in New York, five hours behind me, perhaps just going out for lunch with his high-flying boss. When I staggered home from the stinking pub where I went drinking each night with punk-haired Paula, who was working at the factory to fund her degree in religion and dance studies, I tried doubly hard not to think of Brian just setting out for a night on the town with new friends I had a dreadful feeling I would never meet. Our lives were worlds apart now. Literally and figuratively.

The following September, Mary, Bill and I returned to college as finalists. Our tutors gave us all the predictable lectures about how much harder we were going to have to work in this last year for those all-important exams that would help map out the rest of our lives. The job-seekers 'milk round' had started. My pigeon-hole was already stuffed full of leaflets from accountancy firms eager to sign up the best graduates in return for a pitiful starting salary and a free ballpoint pen. We finalists were given bigger rooms in the halls of residence to spread our numerous books about in. New freshers wandered around the quad making friends and swapping A-level results.

'We're the dinosaurs now,' commented Mary, as we watched two freshers get excited about the prospect of another college dinner (they'd learn – even if it did take a bout of e-coli). *Dinosaurs*. It was what we had called the third years when we were new in town. Bill even looked like a dinosaur now. He had spent his summer cycling up and down mountains and came back tanned like a mummified corpse and with his lower intestine infested by a strange worm that meant he could eat his body weight in chocolate and still not get fat. Mary was spittingly jealous (she had decided to put off having her belly-button pierced until she lost half a stone, though perhaps it was more to do with the fact that Ralph the post-grad had suffered a nervous breakdown over the long vacation and ended up joining a buddhist monastery).

There were new Americans in college too. Another batch of economics students from the very college Brian had attended wandered round the ancient halls I had grown so used to and said things like 'How quaint,' when they banged their heads on a low oak beam. I couldn't help but be interested in them. I even looked one out on my hallway and asked her if she needed any help settling in. Her name was Megan Sanderson. She was from New York too. She had a comfortingly familiar accent and an orthodontically enhanced smile a mile wide. But had she any news of Brian Coren? No, she didn't think she knew him. 'It's a big place, New York,' she laughed. I didn't bother with her much after that and she quickly found friends of her own.

When he first went back home, Brian had written at least twice a week and I wrote twice a week back. Which one of us tailed off first, I'm not quite sure. But three weeks into the new term I realised that I hadn't written to Brian at all that week. I'd been busy. Meeting a new man.

Phil was everything that Brian hadn't been. English. Tall (Brian was only just taller than me). And as blond as Brian was dark. Phil played on the college rugby team. Brian was only interested in indoor sports. Bearing all this in mind, you can probably understand why, when I met Phil, it seemed like a good idea to get off with him to help exorcise the painful memory of the love of my life (so far). And Mary was seeing his best mate, so it meant that we could go out on foursome dates. I would now admit that Bill and Mary had drifted apart since the Two Items of Clothing incident. Bill now chose to hang out with a bunch of guys from his department who were intent on hacking their way into the Pentagon before they finished their degrees.

Ironically, I got together with Phil at another 'Two Items of Clothing party'. He was wearing lycra cycling shorts and a ready-tied bow-tie with red polka dots. I was wearing a fleecy all-in-one sleep-suit that I had brought to college that term just in case such an event should arise, and a bobble hat – so I was getting free drinks. The whole affair might not have happened at all if Phil and I hadn't both been getting free drinks. I knew I hardly looked alluring in my overgrown baby-gro with a bunny on the pocket. And he wasn't looking all that hot either, having thrown up six pints into a wastepaper basket shortly before I arrived. But Mary's advice was ringing in my ears. I needed to move on from Brian and she had convinced me that there is no better cure for a broken heart than getting your talons into a fresh one. So I cornered Phil as he emerged from the gents and thus began a very sorry period in the history of my love life.

He was sweet. He was generous. But if he ever picked up a newspaper at all, it was only to read the sport and the cartoons, and our intellectual discussions were strictly of the 'If a polar bear and an African lion met on neutral ground, which one would win the fight?' variety. Not at all surprisingly, I still felt as though something was missing from my life. Brian had obviously left a hole that was not going to be filled with just any old warm-blooded body.

Which makes it all the more peculiar that when Phil finally pulled the plug on our dalliance two terms later I reacted quite so strongly. Seven days of solid weeping, followed by a fortnight when I would only get out of bed to limp down to the canteen for some cream crackers, and another long month or so of trying to corner Phil whenever he came into college for a rugby match, or dinner, or to pick up some returned coursework.

Phil told everyone that I was a psycho, although I suspect that he was secretly quite delighted by my over-emotional reaction to his departure. My friends couldn't understand it.

'He's an ape,' said Mary. Again and again and again. She was getting rather fed up of finding me sobbing on her doorstep night after night, waiting to ask her if John, her boyfriend, had told her anything that Phil, my ex-boyfriend, might have said about me.

'He said he's thinking of getting you sectioned,' she said, one night.

'That must mean he cares about me,' I translated. 'If he's so concerned about my mental health that he wants to have me taken into hospital against my will.'

'I think he's more concerned that your continuous weeping presence outside his room isn't doing much for his pulling power,' said Mary dryly. 'You know, Liz. I just can't understand what's going on in your head. All the time that you were actually with him, you did nothing but complain about what a neanderthal he is. You used to nod off when he talked to you, for heaven's sake. And don't you remember telling me that he thought foreplay was something to do with golf?'

'He's really sensitive,' I assured her. 'He said he could tell that I was the kind of girl who liked clitoral stimulation.'

'All girls like clitoral stimulation,' sighed Mary. 'But did he ever try it? Look, all the time you were together, you wanted something different. But now he's chucked you, you've gone all *Fatal Attraction* on him.'

'I would never hurt an animal,' I retorted, thinking of the rabbit.

'So what is it then? What's wrong with you these days?'

'I think I must have loved him.'

'Rubbish. You were much happier with Brian, but you didn't cry this much when he left.'

At the time, the implication of Mary's words went in one ear and out the other. But now, looking back, I can see that I made an utter tit of myself when Phil chucked me, not because Phil chucked me, but because the experience had opened up the scar left by Brian's return to the States. I wasn't mourning Phil, I was mourning the loss of Brian. I think I was also far happier to be in romantic misery than having to think about my finals, which were the bane of all our lives at the time.

Needless to say, I did no revision – in fact, the night before my first exam, I could be found, not cramming for my Middle English paper with the other finalists in the library as I should have been, but sitting on the windowsill outside Phil's fourth-floor room, threatening to jump out on to the High Street if he didn't get back together with me. I failed most of the papers I took but, miraculously, so did almost everyone else on my course (it must have been a very bad year), and so I actually managed to limp away from college with a mediocre 2:2. A Desmond, as Bill frequently quipped.

'Desmond Tutu?' he nudged me. 'Tu-tu? Geddit?'

I got it all right.

The last time I saw Phil was when we went to fetch our results. All that heartache he had caused me (or so I thought at the time) and he got a bloody 2:1.

Next time I heard from Brian, he too had completed his degree (first class, *naturellement*) and had taken up a pretty junior (so he modestly said) position with a Japanese bank in

New York City. Meanwhile, I went straight back to Solihull and spent six months living at home and getting under my parents' feet while I 'found myself' and decided what I really wanted to do with my life. Or rather, what anyone would let me do with a mediocre 2:2 in English Literature. Teach, perhaps? suggested my sarcastic tutor.

Perhaps I should have taken his advice, but I couldn't motivate myself to fill out a single application form. Every night before I went to sleep I would promise myself that the next day I would set to job hunting in earnest. And every morning I would hit the snooze button for an extra half hour every half hour until eleven o'clock, getting up just in time to catch *Richard and Judy* on daytime TV, getting dressed just before Mum and Dad came home from work.

At Christmas, Brian wrote to tell me that he had already been promoted to a more senior position at the bank and given a hefty raise. My parents warned me that if I didn't get myself a job (any job at all) in the New Year I might be needing the cardboard boxes that my Christmas presents had come in.

In January, Brian wrote to tell me about his sparkling new warehouse apartment in New York's trendy Soho district. I, having finally worn out my welcome at home, packed my green army surplus rucksack and moved into a filthy squat in the somewhat less trendy East End of London, where nobody really cared whether I got a job or not, as long as I rolled a good joint. I was still getting up at eleven o'clock, still watching *Richard and Judy*, but never getting dressed at all some days.

Occasionally I would get a phone call from an old college pal. A half hour of torture filled with their high-flying news and promises that one day we would 'do lunch'. It seemed that everyone but me was going into accountancy. I told myself that they were selling out. Meanwhile I was blazing a trail for individuality. I told myself that I was actually exercising my creativity by making up jobs I was supposed to have applied for on the form I had to fill in fortnightly to qualify for my Job Seeker's Allowance.

A year after graduating, Brian was in charge of six people in his office. I was typing letters and doing the filing for seven different people (six of whom were considerably younger and probably thicker than me) as a temp at an East End packaging factory. On good days I managed to spend up to an hour on loo breaks. I don't know whether this had something to do with why my colleagues never asked me to go to the pub with them.

Two years later, Brian was responsible for a staff of fourteen and spent his working week jetting between smart city offices in New York and Los Angeles. I had at least moved out of the squat (didn't have much choice. My squatmates and I came home from a club one cold winter's night to discover that the squat's owner had made a bonfire out of all our belongings on the front lawn); though the flat I now legitimately paid rent on would have given the squat a good run for its money in the squalor stakes, and my new flatmates – Dizzy Seema and Fat Joe (he introduced himself as that, can you believe it – though he may have meant 'phat' as in 'cool' rather than tubby) – seemed to be quite the weirdest people I had ever met.

But at least I was no longer doing the typing for seven people in packaging either – they had the temp agency replace me with a bubbly Australian because they *didn't like my attitude*. (I think it might have been my constant depressive monologues about the best way to kill oneself with implements found about the average office that finally helped them make the decision to *downshift* me.) I tried to seem grateful when the temp agency offered me one more chance and sent me on a two-week assignment at Corbett and Daughter Estate Agency. I tried to feel lucky when I found myself on a rolling contract there when Harriet Corbett's stinky lap-dog took a tail-wagging, leg-humping liking to me. I can think of no other reason at all for my successful sideways (and slightly downwards wage-wise) move into property management.

Not that I said any of this in my letters to Brian. I confined comments on my miserable new life of data input and cold baked beans straight from the tin to: 'I'm well. I'm working hard. I've just moved into a new flat.' He didn't have to know that my new room was the size of an airing cupboard and that the plumbing in the bathroom never worked so we had to fill the bath from a kettle. Or more specifically, from a big saucepan of water that had to be boiled on the hob since none of the plug points in the kitchen worked either so we couldn't actually use the kettle.

Every time Brian wrote back he begged me to go into more detail about my life in London. He said he knew that I must be up to something interesting. I started to confine my correspondence to postcards that allowed me just enough space to write (in massive handwriting): 'Too busy to write. Sorry. Will call soon. I promise.' Except that I never called. I hoped Brian would imagine that my high-flying new job was taking up too much of my time to allow me to write long letters to old friends, without taking offence and stopping his much-appreciated letters to me.

'Sounds like you've come a long way,' he wrote in one particularly lovely letter – four pages chock-full of amazing events and funny anecdotes about his life in response to my half a postcard of fact-free drivel.

Oh yeah, I'd come a long, long way since we were both fresh-faced students at college. Unfortunately, I'd been travelling in quite the wrong direction.

7

Yep. My London life. What a bloody whirl.

Dear Reader,

You will no doubt be relieved to know that, after many months of fruitless searching, I have finally found the perfect handbag. What a relief! My little sac *of joy arrived just in time for top designer (and close personal friend) Sebastian Heron's birthday party at Marco Pierre White's new eaterie, The Taj Mahal. I had been sick with worry about what I might wear for such a momentous occasion, but with the bag in hand, my conundrum was solved. The bag is a perfect little strapless number in the softest pink leather from Hermes. I popped into Alexander McQueen's and had him whip up a cat-suit to match.*

The party was a gas, as you can probably imagine, though the new Chanel lipstick I had been on a waiting list for since February was all but kissed off by the time I got to the birthday boy. As usual, Sebastian's guest list read like a Who's Who of the media world. I got stuck in the corner with the younger one from Oasis (him of the mono-brow), who asked me if I thought I could get his lovely wife a job like mine (he's feeling the pinch since big brother went solo). But it's not all fun, fun, fun, I had to tell him. In fact, I had to leave the fabulous party early to fly to Mauritius at the crack of dawn to report on a new hotel for this very paper.

Anyway, I was in such a hurry to get to the airport without breaking any traffic bye-laws that I forgot to pack my suncream and had to spend my first day in the shade while the lovely receptionist sent to Paris for my favourite brand. I was most upset to lose out on a whole day's sunbathing but decided that I would just have to make do with being pale and mysterious. Almost as good. At least Jack Nicholson seemed to think so when he took me to dinner that very night . . .

I put down my newspaper and picked up my sandwiches.

No Jack Nicholson for me that day. Just tuna mayonnaise. Again. Even though it was my birthday.

As I bit into the thin white sliced and a blob of tuna mayo landed on the newspaper, right on the smirking picture of Arabella Gilbert that accompanied her nauseating column in *The Daily*, I wondered why I tortured myself by reading it. Every time I picked up the glossy supplement she wrote for, I had the sort of shaky feeling of anticipation that a drug addict must get before a fix. I knew I didn't 'need' to read her column. I knew that for at least an hour after I had read her column I would be overcome by feelings of social inadequacy and bottomless depression. But I just couldn't seem to help myself.

I could hardly believe that Arabella Gilbert and I lived in the same city. The places she went to – the most fashionable new restaurants, the private drinking clubs that charged more than a month's worth of my skimpy wages for membership – I didn't even know where they were. While Arabella Gilbert had a fistful of golden credit cards, I wasn't even in credit on my Sainsburys' Reward points.

I was about to sink into a serious blue mood when the telephone rang. I cursed the caller through a mouthful of mayo. I was on my own in the office. My boss, Mad Harriet, the once-gorgeous sixties debutante now gone to seed, was getting her hair done in preparation for a clandestine meeting with her married lover, Bunny. Rupert, the 'property valuer' and the only other employee at Corbett and Daughter Estate Agents but me, had taken the opportunity to go and browse through classic car showrooms with his imaginary bonus (and anything else he could reach through his trouser pockets) in hand. So it was I who had to abandon lunch and answer the phone. As usual. I hoped it was a wrong number and not someone who actually wanted to buy a house because that might entail paperwork and I didn't want to have to do paperwork – not on a Friday afternoon. But I needn't have worried. It was just Seema, my flatmate, who had been off sick all week from her job at the video shop with the kind of cystitis you deserve after a particularly dirty weekend with a Marine.

'Do I look like I'm your secretary?' she asked me irritably, without bothering with such niceties as 'hello' or 'happy birthday'. She had still been in bed when I'd left the house that morning, although she had left a suitably rude birthday card propped up against the toaster for me to find over breakfast.

'Eh?'

'I said, do I look like I'm your secretary, Lizzie Jordan? Some idiot just called here for you and when I said that you weren't in, he asked if I was your blinkin' secretary. Honestly. The bloody cheek of it.'

I was just as surprised as she was. 'Did he say who he was?'

'I didn't ask him, did I? But he had an American accent if that means anything to you. East coast, I think, though I can't really be sure. All sound the same to me. Anyway, if you've been going round telling people that I'm your secretary, Elizabeth Jordan . . .' She went on.

But I was already on another planet. An American planet. The caller had an American accent. I only really knew one American, so, unless I had been unexpectedly invited to appear on *The Jerry Springer Show* to talk about why I couldn't hold down a relationship, a job, my drink, I had a pretty good idea who had called.

'And you can get a pint of milk on the way home,' Seema continued. 'Fat Joe finished the last of it this morning but he says he's having one of his attacks and can't go out to get another one. I certainly can't go out either. I've got to be within three feet of a loo at all times. I'm still in agony, in case you're interested.'

I wasn't.

'Did he say he'd call back?'

'What?' Seema snapped.

'The American? Did he say he'd call back or leave a message for me or anything?' I asked in hope.

'I don't know. I had to hang up on him to run to the bathroom. But I'm sure he'll call back if it was really important. I didn't know you knew any exotic foreigners anyway,' she added with just the faintest spark of interest in her voice.

'Just the one,' I told her.

'Yeah. Well, don't forget to get the milk on your way home. Semi-skimmed. And a carton of cranberry juice if you can afford it.'

She hung up.

I replaced the receiver slowly and pushed my chair away from my desk. I knew one exotic foreigner. It was Brian. Brian had called.

I felt suddenly very hot. A blush crept over my body as though he had just walked into the room. I pushed away the remains of my tuna mayo sandwich. All thoughts of lunch left me as my stomach contracted in a peculiar mix of anticipation and apprehension. Brian never called. But he had called. Good news or bad news? What did he want?

That evening, back in Balham, I was on tenterhooks as I waited for *the call*.

Brian would call back. I knew he would. And every time Fat Joe or Seema went anywhere near the telephone I would plead to know for how long they expected to talk. When Seema's mother phoned, I almost told her that her beloved only daughter wasn't in, in order to free up the phone for my far more important call. But I didn't, and they seemed to talk for ever just to punish me for my impatience. I paced the room, rolling my eyes in desperation every time Seema tried and failed to cut short the conversation with her mama.

'Why don't you just phone him?' Seema asked me reasonably, when she had finally managed to convince her mother that: a) she was eating properly, and b) yes, she was wrapped up warm against the bitter August weather – Seema's mother wore two buttoned-up cardigans over her sari at all times.

'Because I'm already way over my overdraft limit this month,' I told her. 'I can't afford to go making long-distance calls to America and I can't call him and hang up after ten seconds, can I? What would that look like? We haven't actually spoken to each other in years. Just letters and e-mails. We'll have loads to talk about. If he calls me, we can talk all night long and I won't have to worry about the cost.'

'But we've only just had a phone bill,' Seema reminded me. 'It's three months until the next one comes. You might have had a windfall by then. I say you should call him. He might want you to jet out to the States, all expenses paid, for a surprise birthday present but if he doesn't hear from you tonight, the invitation's off.'

'He might do, mightn't he?' I said stupidly. It was my birthday. So I picked up the phone and started to dial the massively long number that would put me straight through to him in his Wall Street office. It was picked up at the other end by an answering service. I put the phone down straight away. No point wasting money to talk to a machine.

'Oh, you should have left a message,' Seema sighed. 'So that he's reminded to call you back. I love it when I get a machine instead of the person I'm trying to get hold of. It means that you've done your bit but they then have to pay to call you back.'

'Good point,' I said. I dialled again. I held my breath as the connection was made. The phone was picked up. This time, by Brian.

'Brian Coren.'

I said nothing. I was still waiting for the beep.

'Hello? This is Brian Coren. Who's calling?'

'Oh,' I suddenly realised that my call had been picked up. 'Oh, Brian. I didn't expect to get you. I was calling to talk to your machine.'

'Is that Liz?' he asked excitedly. 'Lizzie Jordan? Is it really you?'

'Er. Yes. It's me. It's Liz. You called me this morning?'

'Oh, Liz. It's so good to hear your voice again,' he said. 'It's been so long. I'd forgotten how English you sound.'

'Oh, everybody speaks like this over here,' I joked. 'Was there something you wanted, Brian?'

'Sorry?'

'When you called today. Did you want something?'

'To wish you a Happy Birthday of course, my darling.'

'Thanks for remembering. Is that all?'

'And to touch base,' he said defensively. 'You sound flustered, Liz. Do you have to get off the phone to go someplace in a hurry? I don't want to keep you talking if you do. I know how busy you must be with your thriving property business and all.'

I could hardly tell him that I didn't think I could afford to pay the resulting phone bill.

'Er, no. No. It's just that you usually e-mail me when you've got something to say.'

'Yeah. But don't you think that's just a bit impersonal sometimes?'

Sure it was impersonal. But it was charged at local rate, I said to myself.

'And I wanted to wish you a Happy Birthday *personally*. How are you?' Brian continued jovially. 'Working hard?'

'Oh, yes. Much too hard. You know how it is.'

'I certainly do. Lots of new projects?'

'Oh yes. Lots of new projects on the go. But how about you, Brian?' I didn't want to have to make up one of those new projects so I quickly changed the focus.

'Well,' he exhaled slowly. 'For the first time in my career, I actually seem to have things pretty much under control here at the bank. I've been going home before midnight lately,' he laughed. 'Can you believe it? I'm practically taking half days as far as my workmates are concerned.'

'You always worked too hard.'

'Yeah, like you. But that's what my physician said too. She said I ought to take a holiday and shake my muscles out a bit or I'll be an old man before my time.'

'Wouldn't want that,' I told him.

'No. Definitely not. So I'm going to.'

'Going to what?'

'Take a holiday, dufus. Next week. Just like my physician suggested.'

'That's nice. Where are you going?' I asked naively. 'Somewhere sunny? Nice and hot?'

'Well, I was rather hoping,' he began. 'You know how it is, Liz . . . You get so wrapped up in your work that you don't have time to meet nice people you could go to nice places with. I don't want to go somewhere exotic but just end up spending the whole week on my own, catching up on my reading, so I was hoping that perhaps I might be welcome in London.'

I must have been quiet for too long.

'Are you still there, Liz? Lizzie?' he called. 'Has the line gone dead or something?'

'Of course I'm still here,' I squeaked.

'Oh, good. Look, it'd just be for three days or so. I may have to go to Zurich for business anyway, so I thought I'd leave the States a little bit early and drop by to see you *en route* to Switzerland.'

'Uh!' I squeaked.

'I guess you're probably pretty tied up with work, and this is very short notice, so I'd stay at a hotel, of course. Perhaps you could recommend somewhere nice that's not too far from your place so we can meet up in the evenings.'

'What?'

'A hotel? Can you suggest a nice hotel where I could stay? My budget's pretty flexible. I can charge it to the firm.'

I don't know where my common sense went right then, but I said, 'Hotel? You don't have to stay in a hotel, Brian. You should come and stay with me.'

'No, Liz. I couldn't possibly. You don't want to have to

worry about me,' he assured me. 'I'll stay in a nice hotel and as long as we get to go out to dinner together a couple of times, I'll be more than happy.'

'No, Brian, I insist. I couldn't possibly let you stay in a hotel if you're coming all the way to England to see me.'

'Liz, don't put yourself out. Really. It's such short notice. I didn't even expect you to be around for the whole of my visit. And I don't want to be any bother.'

'You wouldn't be a bother, Brian.'

'I like staying in hotels,' he said.

'I really couldn't forgive myself if you did.'

There was a short pause before he said, 'OK then.'

Then there was another short pause while the words filtered through to my stupid dumb-ass brain. OK then?

Well, he wasn't supposed to say that, was he?!! I was going to let him suggest a hotel just one more time for appearances' sake before I agreed that it was a great idea and packed him off to the Metropolitan.

'What?' I said.

'OK then. It's fixed. I'll stay with you, if you really insist that you can't be without me,' he laughed. 'Next week? Friday afternoon through Tuesday? Just e-mail me the directions and I'll find my own way there when I get to the airport.'

'No!' I cried.

'No?' he asked.

'I mean, no. Don't find your own way here. I'll meet you at the airport. My place is quite tricky to find. It's in a mews, you know.'

Seema gave me a very odd look when she overheard that.

'Well, if you're sure I won't be interrupting your busy schedule. In that case I'll e-mail you my flight details instead.

Liz,' he said softly. 'It's been way too long since we were last together. You know I really can't wait to see you again.'

'Same here,' I murmured.

'It'll be great fun, won't it?'

'Brilliant,' I said, with about as much enthusiasm as I reserved for emptying the wastepaper bins at work. 'I'll see you next Friday then.'

'Looking forward to it. Bye.' He put the phone down, leaving me staring at the receiver wondering what on earth I had done.

'Did I just hear you inviting someone to stay here?' Seema asked, all excited. 'The American guy who called this morning? I must say I liked the sound of his voice. Is he rich and hunky as well as gorgeous-sounding?'

'Oh, yes,' I sighed. 'He's all that and more.'

'Yippee. We could use some fresh blood around here. Unless you've got first dibs on him, of course. But you haven't, have you, Liz? I mean, you haven't even mentioned him before. He's not an old squeeze of yours, is he?'

'I don't think there's any possibility of action on that front any more,' I said disconsolately.

'So, I'm in with a chance, am I?'

'Seema, you're man-mad,' I exclaimed in exasperation. 'But he's not staying here, in any case.'

'But you just said . . .' Seema began.

'Forget what I just said to him. Look at this place,' I exploded. 'Haven't you guys heard of a vacuum cleaner?' I picked up a cushion and shook out a snowstorm of cheese and onion crisp crumbs. At least I thought I could smell cheese and onion. It may just have been the aroma of Fat Joe's feet that seemed to linger constantly around the place. 'And I found half a lamb chop in the sink this morning.'

'You know I don't eat lamb,' Seema said defensively.

'So? You could have moved it before I had to. You have been at home all day, haven't you?'

'Studying!' she protested.

'Yeah, *studying*,' I sneered. 'I was a student once myself, remember. Do you realise there are things growing in the fridge that might hold the key to a cure for cancer? You could grow bloody potatoes in the ring around the bath. And as for the toilet – don't even get me started on that disgusting article. I would rather go to that little cubicle thingy outside Safeway than use our own loo. Didn't you know we had a loo brush?'

'We don't. Not any more. Joe used it to try to unblock the drain last October and somehow lost it in the process.'

'Well? Didn't anyone think to buy another one?' I walked around the room, picking up stray items of clothing (largely of the intimate variety) and a handful of fast-food wrappers. A pair of dirty tights was inextricably entwined with the wrapper from a year-old pepperami.

'I did mean to throw those away,' said Seema, hot-cheeked with embarrassment, snatching both tights and pepperami packet from my hand.

I found three single socks that didn't have mates to go home to. A pair of men's trainers that were so rank and rancid they curled up at the toes like Ali Baba's slippers. I found two CDs beneath the sofa that I had thought were gone for ever after a particularly ugly birthday party. Both CDs had been used as coasters. One for coffee. One for red wine. When I shifted the sofa to see if I could find that tenner I had lost about the same time, I found an even bigger red wine stain on the cream/dust-grey carpet.

'Did you know about this?' I shouted at my flatmate. 'How on earth can we shift this stain now? It's dried in. We're never going to get our deposit back!'

Seema ran behind me, running one of the spare socks along the book shelves in lieu of a duster, retrieving knickers from a plant pot, and diligently emptying an over-flowing ashtray into a wastepaper bin before remembering that the wastepaper bin was always empty because some careless smoker had burned a big hole through its raffia bottom with an improperly extinguished cigarette a couple of weekends before.

Struggling with a pint glass that actually seemed to be glued to the mantelpiece, I found a white towel covered in a huge blood-red stain draped along the useless radiator. 'What is this?' I asked, picking it up by a corner.

'It's just henna,' explained Seema quickly. 'I'm sure it will wash out. This isn't *your* towel, is it?' she added cautiously, snatching the offending item from my hands.

'No, thank God. But Brian definitely can't stay here,' I groaned, sinking on to the sofa and feeling the pointy end of a discarded biro jab right in the base of my spine. 'Absolutely no way on earth.'

'It'll be OK,' said Seema, cheerfully. 'Look, this place is much better already with all those empty glasses gone.' She made an expansive arm gesture as though she had just transformed the house into something from *Homes and Gardens* with the flick of a filthy old sock. 'We've got a whole week before he comes here. We can go out right now and buy some Jif, if you like. And dusters. We'll have a house meeting to divide up chores just as soon as Fat Joe thinks he's able to come out of his bedroom again and by the time your mate turns up, this place will be as good as any Hilton. Well, as good as the Bangkok Hilton in any case.'

'No, Seema!' I told her. 'You don't understand. Brian couldn't stay here even if we cleaned the place from now until Christmas. He can't stay here because whichever way you look at it this house is a filthy three bedroom terrace in Balham. And as far as Brian is concerned, I live in a gorgeous penthouse that overlooks Hyde Park.'

The truth was out.

I've already told you that I had become brief to the point of dishonesty in my letters to my old boyfriend. Problem was, since the advent of e-mail, I no longer had an excuse for the once a year postcard that just said ambiguously that everything was 'fine'.

It was Fat Joe who introduced me to the World Wide Web, back in the days when I was still making an effort to get to know my new flatmates and sometimes ventured into his pit of a room to take him a cup of tea. He was only too pleased to take time off from making a tape recording of the sounds he had downloaded from the Jubilee Extension Line website to set me up my very own e-mail address. He showed me how to track people down over the Net. And I quickly tracked down Brian.

Since then Brian and I had become e-mail pals, corresponding almost every day on the information superhighway (when I could get into Joe's bedroom – fortunately he was quite regular in his habits and I usually got fifteen minutes after his first cup of coffee of the day). And with so much cyberspace to fill each day I had quickly progressed from little lies of omission to those old-fashioned big black lies that your mother always warned would land you in strife.

Well, what could I do when Brian e-mailed me to say that he had just had lunch at a table next to Madonna's at New York's most fashionable new eaterie? E-mail him back with a list of the sandwich fillings to be avoided at Greasy Fred's Café in Battersea? No, I'm afraid I had to e-mail him with the revelation that I had once worked out next to Madonna at my exclusive women-only gym in Covent Garden. And it all went pretty much pear-shaped from there.

When Brian e-mailed me to say that he was going to the Hamptons for a weekend with a minor Kennedy, I told him that I was just about to jet off to the south of France to stay with a besotted Arab princeling I'd met in the posh folks' nightclub Annabelle's. When Brian regaled me with tales of a crazy shopping spree at Ralph Lauren, I'm afraid I sent an e-mail straight back saying that Dolce and Gabbana were designing something exclusive for my twenty-sixth birthday party which was to be held in the ballroom at the Grosvenor House Hotel.

But it was when he e-mailed me with details of his latest swanky address that I made my biggest mistake . . .

As far as Brian was concerned, I had moved out of the pit in Balham as soon as we gave up pen and paper for electronic mail. These days I had my very own gorgeous apartment overlooking Hyde Park, bought with the proceeds from a multi-million-pound property deal I had clinched all by myself as a senior partner at Corbett and Daughter Estates – which was of course one of the biggest commercial property companies in England rather than a one-room operation with three vaguely human staff and an incontinent Cavalier King Charles Spaniel on the team.

My e-mails were littered with the names of the in-places to be and the right people to be there with. In my secret cyber-life, I was forever picking up a little sparkling something from Tiffany or Cartier to treat myself for working so hard and to set off that exclusive dress from Donna Karan when I went out to meet movie-star clients who would trust only me to find them that special London *pied à terre*.

My friends were artists, writers, models and princes. Not a penniless business student with a part-time job at Blockbuster

(Seema) and a wannabe computer hacker who never came out of his bedroom (Fat Joe). As far as Brian was concerned, I entertained megastars of the stage and screen nightly with recipes I had created myself under the supervision of Michelin-starred chefs and never, ever ate cold alphabetti spaghetti straight from a rusty tin in the company of no one but a flickering black and white television screen.

It had all seemed so harmless. In fact, it was almost good fun. Sometimes I just lifted my stories straight from Arabella Gilbert's *Daily* column with no real editing at all. I never imagined for a moment that one day I would have to prove that all the rubbish I had written over the course of three years on-line was true. Brian was such a dedicated workaholic. He never took any time off, probably didn't even go to the loo during working hours if he could possibly help it. There was no danger that he would suddenly decide to drop by and see me in London on a whim. Oh no.

'Oh no. Oh no. Oh no,' I wailed into the filthy sleeve of my threadbare towelling dressing-gown.

'What are you going to do?' asked Seema, when I had finished my tale of woe.

'I really do not have a clue,' I admitted most unhappily.

'Oh, dear,' she said. 'Oh dear.'

We sat down side by side on the sofa and gazed at the fireplace as if we might see the answer to my dilemma in the orange flickering of the singed electric bars that always smelled as if they were about to burst into real flame.

'What did you want to go and tell him all those silly lies for anyway?' she asked me suddenly.

'Why do you think? He's out there living the high life in New York City while my status in London is about one up from a one-legged pigeon in Trafalgar Square. No. Make that one down. At least those pigeons are a protected species now. I had to tell Brian all those lies because I didn't want him to know how badly I've failed since leaving college.'

Seema put an arm around my shoulders. Sometimes, when she wasn't borrowing my favourite Estée Lauder body lotion without asking or washing her netball socks with my Stergene, she was really quite incredibly sweet.

'Why on earth do you think you've failed?' she asked me seriously.

'Why do you think?' I replied. I waved my arm around the shabby, sorry room we were sitting in in almost the same manner she had used moments earlier in her attempt to convince me that the house was quite fab underneath the baked-on filth.

'Well,' she began in her most positive, junior counsellor voice. 'I live in the same house as you – your real house – and I don't think that I'm a failure because of it. Taking a bit longer than I hoped to move up to that gold card status, sure, but not a failure. Not by any means. You're only twenty-seven, Liz. Cut yourself some slack. You've got a good job, haven't you?'

'Huh! I'm a secretary at an estate agency. I'm not even on a permanent contract. I type labels for a living, for God's sake. I did a degree in English Literature, you know.'

'So? I'm doing a *master's* degree in business and I work at Blockbuster,' she reminded me quite gently.

'Well, my social life is rubbish,' I tried again.

'But you've got some great friends,' she said, not showing if any offence had been taken. 'We could go out together more often if you want to. We could go clubbing tonight. Do some dancing. Drink some cocktails.'

'I can't afford to go out.'

'Look, Liz,' Seema almost lost her patience because, skint as I was, I nearly always had more money than she did. 'Stop beating yourself up. I think you're doing really well, OK? Why should you have a penthouse by now anyway?'

'Brian does.'

'Have you seen it?'

'No.'

'Exactly. For all you know he could be living in a New Jersey trailer park, surviving off the immoral earnings of his two little sisters.' That raised a faint smile to my lips. But only a very faint one.

'His sisters are both older than him,' I corrected her mercilessly.

'OK. His two *big* sisters. All I'm saying is that you shouldn't worry so much about impressing him. Everyone exaggerates on e-mail from time to time. I wasted two weeks giving it my all over the internet for someone who claimed to be Bill Gates's brother but he turned out to be a data inputter for *Dalton's Weekly*. Fat Joe is upstairs right now, probably telling some schoolgirl who's supposed to be downloading facts for her homework that he's a six-foot-four Adonis with a torso like Michelangelo's *David*.'

'I know. I know . . . But Brian doesn't need to lie. Believe me, if Brian says he's done something amazing, then he most certainly has.'

'Is he really such a paragon of virtue that he's never added a few inches or dropped a couple of years?'

'Oh, Seema,' I sighed. 'He really is. He's probably the most scrupulously honest person I've ever met. He even admitted to smelling his own farts when we played "truth or dare" in the college bar, for heaven's sake.'

'That is honest,' Seema had to agree. 'In which case, perhaps you should just come clean, Liz. I'm sure he'll think the whole thing is incredibly funny and even be mightily relieved that you won't expect him to go dutch on Cristal champagne at the Mirabelle every night while he's here on his visit.'

'No,' I shook my head solemnly. 'If it was anyone else I would come clean straight away. Honestly I would. But not Brian. I just can't do it. You don't know him, Seema. He'd be mortally wounded if he knew that I had lied to him and in such a big way. He's American, remember. They've got a different moral code out there. Some of them still abide by the Ten Commandments. I could hardly pass the whole thing off as a grand exercise in irony. He'd think I'd gone completely bonkers.'

'Well, that's me clean out of suggestions then,' said Seema, as she shifted to pull a soft cream cracker from beneath the cushion she was sitting on. 'I'm afraid I don't think I can magic a penthouse out of thin air. You really are a complete tit, Liz.'

Didn't I know it. We gazed at the electric fire for a bit longer. Me, contemplating the only honourable way out of the situation – which seemed at that moment to be hari-kiri with a kitchen knife (if only all our cutlery wasn't so blunt). Seema contemplating I knew not what. Until she came up with this gem. 'I know, why don't you say that you had a terrible fire at the penthouse and have had to move in here with me – your secretary, if you like – on a temporary basis until the cleaning up and repair works are finished. Perfect, don't you think?'

Yes, it did seem perfect. For about ten seconds, until Fat Joe waddled into the sitting room looking like a giant maggot, wearing, as usual, his arctic fox print combat gear beneath his duvet (which never sported a cover over its faint yellow stains). He squashed himself into the sofa between us, not taking his eyes off the readers' letters at the back of the latest edition of *What Hi-fi?* he was carrying, until he spotted the stale cream cracker that Seema had just retrieved with the intention of binning it and crammed it into his mouth.

'Anything interesting in that?' asked Seema conversationally, pointing towards the mag.

'Well, this stupid bloke here has written in to say that he can't find a measurable difference between the Audiolab and equivalent F3-branded products,' Joe spluttered, spraying crumbs all over the carpet. 'What a moron. Ha!'

'Ha, indeed!' said Seema.

We very rarely expected to actually understand something Fat Joe said.

'Anyone mind if I put the television on?' Joe asked then, simultaneously letting out the most resonant fart you can possibly imagine. Seema and I shook our heads, but I knew at that instant that the penthouse fire plan was out of the question too. Brian couldn't possibly stay in our dump of a house while the human slug was in residence. He would be repulsed. I knew I generally was.

Seema and I popped out from our sofa corners and headed for the kitchen to continue our conflab. 'I can't have Brian here while Fat Joe is,' I told her.

'I see your point. We'll have to ask him to move out for a while.'

'Seema, you know as well as I do that even coming downstairs is a major breakthrough for Fat Joe these days. There's no way we're going to be able to make him take an enforced vacation without armed assistance.'

Seema frowned. 'Oh, this is so unfair. I really wanted to meet your American friend. He sounds so nice . . . and rich.'

I plopped three pyramid tea-bags into three chipped and dubiously stained mugs. 'If anyone gets first dibs on him, it's me,' I reminded her. 'You're getting an arranged marriage.'

'But you've already got a boyfriend,' she whined. 'You can't have two.'

And just at that moment the boyfriend shouted from the sitting room. 'Better make that four cups of tea if you're doing a brew, Lizzie.'

Richard had arrived.

8

Richard. My boyfriend. I'd completely forgotten that he was supposed to be coming round to deliver my birthday present that evening. When I heard him call out from the sitting room, my stomach lurched as if I had been caught betraying him by my need to impress Brian. Fact was, I suppose I already had betrayed Richard. Never mind telling Brian that I had a great flat, what I hadn't told him was that I really did have a reasonably great boyfriend.

A week earlier I had been happy to refer to Richard as my 'new boyfriend'. We had been seeing each other for about seven months. Well, it was seven months since we had first locked tongues in the back of a taxi anyway and he'd been round to our house almost every night since then so I had simply assumed that we were seeing each other properly by now. When you're in your mid-twenties, you can't really ask 'Are we going out, then?' as you would have done aged twelve, however much you itch to do so.

I met Richard at an infamous backpackers' bar in central London, the kind of place where homesick Aussies and Kiwis, who are almost too drunk to see, gather together to recite old beer adverts wholesale in lieu of chat-up lines. I wouldn't have been there at all but it was Seema's birthday and she was determined that she would start her twenty-second year on earth with a casual shag – especially as her parents had announced in a postscript at the bottom of their birthday card to her that if Seema didn't find herself a suitable husband by her twenty-third birthday, they would be finding one for her.

Anyway, we had been drinking tequila since six o'clock in the evening, had eaten nothing but a bowlful of stale pistachio nuts between us, and were well on our way to a couple of spectacular alcohol-induced blackouts when we stumbled into Richard and his gang.

I say stumbled, because that is literally what we did. Seema and I were standing at the top of a short flight of stairs, arms locked around each other to help us stay steady. Seema leaned too far forward while attempting to adjust the straps on her ankle-breaker silver platform sandals. She still had her other arm around my waist and when she went over, so did I. Arse over tit, as my father used to say (though not in front of my mother). Talk about making an entrance. Thank God there were only four steps between the top of the flight and the humiliating landing with my skirt up round my waist and most of Richard's pint on my head.

I quickly offered to buy him a new pint but he said that he would buy me a drink instead, for being the first woman ever to throw herself at his feet. After that, it would have been churlish not to snog him. Plus, he and his flatmate Paul (who was using all the exact same lines on Seema at the time, I later discovered) lived in Balham too and it seemed sensible to share a taxi back home when the bar closed. Not to mention cheap, as Seema and I had both run out of money by that point.

Richard leapt on me in the taxi, which was quite embarrassing as I was sitting on the jump seat with my back to the driver at the time and Richard somehow ended up on his knees on the floor between me and the proper seat. Luckily Paul and Seema were too busy with their own bout of tongue-wrestling to see Richard tumble. The taxi driver tutted loudly and turned up the Talk Radio show he was listening to in an attempt to drown out the sucking noises. Taxi drivers – they can be a right pain in the backside, can't they? But I can't say that I envy them doing the Saturday night shift. All spew and strangers snogging. What a job!

Paul and Richard never made it back to their own flat that night. In the morning, Seema and I bumped into each other on the way to the bathroom, both hoping to have a chance to clean our teeth and prettify ourselves before our respective catches woke up.

'What do you think?' Seema asked in a whisper, as she struggled with the love knots in her gorgeous long black hair. 'Is it breakfast in bed, or an urgent early morning appointment with the chiropodist?'

An urgent early morning appointment with the chiropodist was a great excuse to use when you needed to get someone out of your way after a big mistake of a night. Firstly, because it meant that the unwelcome visitor had to leave right away and secondly, because the thought of a young girl having her corns done seemed to prevent any further telephone calls from unwanted admirers pretty damn effectively in most cases.

I was having breakfast in bed. Two days later, Richard asked me to ask Seema how her corns were on behalf of Paul. She hadn't returned his phonecalls. But I was ready for love. I was ready to hitch up with someone I could spend my Sunday afternoons with, drifting around London's parks and galleries, gazing into his eyes; making all those poor single suckers deeply aware of how empty their Marks and Spencer's ready-meals-for-one existence was, just as all those smug couples had been doing to me for the past four years on and off . . .

And Richard fitted the description of the man who would help me do my bit to annoy all those irritating people who had told me how much they envied the freedom of my single life when they were cuddled up on life's sofa with a complementary bod. He was passably handsome – well, he had all the requisite features that go to make up what we refer to as a human face – and his trousers were just about long enough for his skinny legs. He occasionally wore a shirt that didn't have a number on the back and he also had a full-time job (very important that – upon arriving in London with dreams of becoming the next Marianne Faithfull, I had gone through a period of exclusively dating musicians and painters. I discovered that creative 'artistes' are all very well until you have to get up to go to work on a Monday morning, leaving him lying there in bed, and return on Monday evening to find him exactly where you left him. Creative thinking – my arse! It's just plain rude). No, I wanted a man who had to leave the house before I did. And Richard did, to go to his job in the City.

OK, so he was an accountant and not some super-rich bonds trader who drank Bollinger like I drank Perrier, but there comes a point in every girl's life when she realises that there is a point to comfy knickers and stops hankering after a pop star for a mate. My mother had informed me only the weekend before, seven days before the watershed that was to be my twenty-seventh birthday, that that big knicker time had come for Lizzie Jordan.

'Weren't we supposed to be going out tonight?' said Richard now observing me standing by the kitchen door in my dad's old pyjamas and a dressing-gown that was getting as thin as a cobweb around the elbows.

I looked down at my slippered feet. In the excitement of Brian's impending visit, I had completely forgotten that I had agreed to go out for a pint and a pub quiz that night and got ready for bed straight after my bath.

'Don't you want to celebrate your birthday?'

'What's to celebrate?' interrupted Seema gleefully. 'Lizzie's nearly thirty now.'

'I am not,' I protested. 'I'm still in my mid-twenties.'

'Mid-twenties?' Seema snorted. 'Not at twenty-seven, you're not. Mid-twenties is from twenty-four to twenty-six only. Any older than that and you're officially into your pre-thirties.' She poked out her tongue to underline the insult.

'So we're not going out because you've gone all middle-aged on me? Never mind,' said Richard, settling himself into the one and only armchair so that Seema and I had to squish back in beside Fat Joe. 'I haven't got any money on me anyway. You haven't got any beer in the house have you, by any chance?'

'I'll just go and have a look,' I said, secretly relieved to have an excuse not to sit next to the farting bag of soft upholstery that was my flatmate. 'We've probably only got that French crap we brought back from the booze cruise to Calais.'

'That's fine,' said Richard. 'And I suppose it's a bit cheeky of me to ask if you could whip me up something on toast while you're out there? Cheese or beans. I don't mind which. I did mean to go food shopping myself on my way back from work but the cashpoint sucked up my card again.'

'I thought your wages went through last Friday,' I said in surprise.

'They did. But I was so overdrawn anyway that by the time I took out a tenner for my football subs on Saturday morning I was already up to my limit again. I'll just tighten my belt this month and have it sorted by the end of next. Promise.'

Seema shot me a doubtful look when she heard that.

Humanitarian organisations the Third World over were campaigning to put an end to her horrendous overdraft at the National Westminster but she still wouldn't consider dating anyone with a matching one.

'Hope your card got eaten *after* you bought Lizzie's birthday present,' she said, arching one imperious eyebrow meaningfully.

Richard shuffled uncomfortably. 'Actually, Lizzie, I was going to talk to you about that. I had an idea of what I wanted to buy you but I decided that it might be a better idea if you chose your present yourself and I just paid for it. That way you'll definitely get something you want. What do you think?'

Seema rolled her eyes in disapproval. 'How romantic is that?' she sneered. 'You'd better be prepared for some serious damage to your plastic, Richard.'

'I'll be kind to you,' I reassured him.

That was the difference between me and Seema. If one of her suitors foolishly offered to take her shopping on his plastic, he would find himself remortgaging his flat before she had finished emptying the racks at Joseph. If anyone offered to take me shopping, on the other hand, I would come back with a one-sleeved jacket that had been left over in the sale, muttering that it was exactly what I wanted and that making another sleeve would be no trouble at all. I told myself that my approach marked me out as the nicer person but Seema told me that I needed to sort out my attitude. 'Your approach may not be greedy,' she conceded. 'But it is insulting in another way. Men like to feel that they can provide for their woman. By refusing to take their cash, you're effectively castrating them.'

What a nice idea.

Seema was a perfect example of the Zoe Ball backlash.

She didn't want to be one of the lads. She wanted the right to wear pink tulle and feathers and flutter her eyelashes and when she did gifts fell into her lap left, right and centre. Whereas me, I did all the other traditional girly things – like cooking the beans on toast, doing the ironing – and yet still refused to take advantage when any man wanted to stretch his economic muscle in my direction. She was right. I was a mug.

'There's a sale on at Top Shop, Lizzie,' was Seema's parting shot as she went to inspect her reflection for the second time that hour.

'Have you seen this letter?' Joe asked Richard when Seema was safely out of the way. 'Some nutter here has written in to say that he doesn't know the difference between Audiolab and an F3-branded equivalent!'

'You're joking,' said Richard, taking the magazine off him to read the apparent heresy for himself.

Ho hum.

My relationship with Richard had been on a kind of fast forward since we met. We'd been through the attraction and lust bit on the first night. Now we were already into that period when I was starting to wonder whether someone who couldn't stay out of the red for a whole week could really provide for the gorgeous girl and boy children I had always imagined myself having. With a rich man.

Nevertheless, I pulled a couple of slices of Mighty White out of the bread bin, scraped off the Fortnum and Mason green mould which was already encroaching on the corners, and went to put them under the grill. The grill-pan was, of course, opaque white with a thick smelly layer of bacon fat. If I had been making toast for myself, this is the point when I would have exploded with fury, scrubbed at the pan with a brillo pad until my hands bled, and called a house meeting to insist that whoever used the grill covered it with silver foil first, so that the fat could be removed quickly and easily to leave a shining clean pan for the house pseudo-vegetarian (I wouldn't eat anything with a *cute* face) to use straight afterwards. But I was making toast for Richard and I figured that he would actually appreciate the flavour a bit of old bacon fat might impart.

I shoved the bread under the grill and leaned back against the sink to wait for it to toast. This wasn't how my life was meant to be, I thought. It was my twenty-seventh birthday! I had planned to be living an instant coffee ad lifestyle by now – all swanky Nicole Farhi separates and polished blond-wood floors. Instead I was making mouldy bread into toast for a skint accountant – did other people *really* trust him to look after their money? I wondered – who was showing disturbingly nerdy tendencies, in a kitchen that would have been closed down by the World Health Organisation if they found it being used in a third world country. Far from wearing head to toe Nicole Farhi, I wished I was wearing wellington boots instead of slippers to protect me from the scum on the floor.

Mould crept along the bottom of the walls like an alien creature waiting to reach out and grab my ankles. A miniature archaeology team were searching for artefacts in the rock-solid remains of a disastrous lemon daal that Seema had cooked to impress her brother (needless to say he hadn't been impressed and reported to his parents that they were going to have trouble getting Seema off their hands). Hell, we didn't even have a toaster. Everybody in the civilised world owns a toaster, I told myself. I bet the lovely Arabella Gilbert had one of those great big Dualit toasters in her interior-designed bachelorette flat. I bet Brian had one too. One of those shining bright silver industrial ones that can even do tea-cakes and crumpets without burning them. I dreamed of unburnt tea-cakes . . . I started to dream of Brian.

At which point the bacon fat that had been left to accumulate in the grill-pan burst into flames and what was meant to be toast quickly became ashes.

'Shit!' I shrieked, pulling the flaming pan out from beneath the grill and waving at it ineffectually with a spoon.

Seema, Richard and Fat Joe instantly appeared at the kitchen door to shout instructions with varying degrees of usefulness.

'Get the fire extinguisher!' cried Seema.

'It's bloody empty,' I reminded her. 'You used it to make snow at last year's Christmas party!'

'Put a damp cloth on it,' said Richard.

'That's what you do for chips, stupid,' Fat Joe replied.

'It's not the chips specifically, dumbo,' Richard informed him. 'It's what you're supposed to do for burning fat.' He strode manfully across to the sink, doused a tea-cloth in water and flung it over the pan which I was still holding like the lemon that I was. There was a damp sounding sizzle and the room filled with noxious, choking smoke. Richard gently prised the pan from my hand and put it down on top of the hob with the damp cloth still draped across it. Then he put his arm around my shoulders and looked at me expectantly while he waited for me to either burst into tears or call him a hero. I did neither.

'Jesus!' cursed Seema. 'Can't you even make toast without nearly causing a fatal disaster, Liz?'

'This wouldn't have happened if someone' – I looked daggers at Fat Joe, the big bacon eater in our house – 'would clean out the grill pan after his Saturday morning fry-up occasionally. There was nearly half an inch of bacon fat in the bottom of that pan.'

'Then why didn't you clean it before you tried to set fire to the flat?' Seema asked.

'Because,' I snarled dramatically, shaking Richard's arm from my shoulder. 'Because I couldn't be bothered. Because I'm fed up of this life of drudgery. I'm fed up of the constant round of clearing up the mess after you lot like I'm your bleeding mother. The dirt. The dust. The grease. It's hideous. Have either of you looked at the kitchen ceiling lately?'

We all gazed ceiling-wards to where little yellow stalactites of grease had been forming over the two years that we had been in residence and deep-fat frying on a daily basis.

'Urgh. That is disgusting,' Seema breathed.

'Well, why doesn't somebody do something about it!' I screamed. 'I don't want to have to live like this any more! I was meant for better things than this!' Then I flounced out of the kitchen and headed for my room with Richard in hot pursuit.

'PMT?' he asked cautiously as I sobbed into my pillow.

'No!' I roared. 'No, I do not have pre-menstrual tension. God, you're so predictable.'

'Sorry I asked,' he said, backing away. 'But "predictable"? That's a bit of a harsh thing to say about me after only seven months together, isn't it?'

He rolled me over to face him. 'Are you depressed because it's your birthday, Liz? Is that it? Is it because of what Seema said? Twenty-seven isn't that old, you know.'

'I know it's not that old!' I snapped. 'I'm not depressed because it's my birthday.'

'Did you have a bad day at work?'

'No, not particularly. But I have been having a bad life

for the last five years. What am I doing here, Richard? Why do I live in a horrible place like this stinking house with two insane flatmates who never lift a finger to help me?'

'I think it's rather nice here,' he replied, admiring my peeling wallpaper. And I suppose that compared to his own place it was quite nice. I mean, at least we had an *indoor* toilet. So did Richard's flat, actually. But it had been sealed off for three years and the landlord refused to get it fixed unless the tenants made up the shortfall for a phone bill which had been run up by three South African backpackers before Richard and his friend even moved into the place.

'Why don't I live somewhere glamorous like New York? Like Manhattan?' I asked him with a sniffle.

'Why would you want to live somewhere like that?' he replied. 'You get lots of rats in New York. Even in the poshest parts of Manhattan, so they tell me. Running in and out of everywhere. Eating your furniture. Biting the babies.'

'You get rats in Balham too,' I interrupted. 'I saw one run out from behind the dustbins last week. It was this big.' I indicated the size of a small terrier.

'OK, so you get rats in New York and Balham but at least you can walk down the High Road in Balham without getting caught in the gun cross-fire of some gang fight,' Richard tried again. 'At least Balham's safer than Harlem.'

'What? Didn't you hear about that chap who got an air-gun pellet shot into his thigh outside McDonalds?' I asked Richard. 'He only went in for a milkshake. He may never dance again.' I was determined not to be persuaded that there was anything great about living in south London at all.

'You really are in a bad mood, aren't you?' he said observantly. 'Do you fancy going for a walk to cheer up?'

'What? In the dark? Where to?'

'Well, I was hoping you might be able to lend me a pound to go to the chip shop, actually. I'm still really hungry. I was sort of desperate for that toast.'

'Oh, come on then,' I groaned, pulling on my jeans over my pyjama bottoms. Anything to get out of the flat, which still smelled like an explosion in a chip factory. In the sitting room, Seema and Joe were watching the television again with handkerchiefs held over their mouths to stop themselves from choking on the smoke which lingered in a thick layer just below the ceiling. A quick glance into the kitchen revealed that nobody had bothered to move the grill-pan yet.

Outside, the drizzle that had coated London all day had at least started to peter out.

'Do you still want me to come and meet your parents on Sunday?' Richard asked as we headed back from the chippy.

Yet another date I had forgotten about. I was due to go home for my monthly appraisal with the parents – not to mention to pick up my birthday present, which would probably be a kettle or an iron – and had, before the Brian saga took over my waking thoughts, gone to great lengths to persuade Richard that he should come too. Since I had made no progress whatsoever on the 'getting a better job' front and my hair was still not entirely its natural colour after a brush with Seema's home-brewed henna, I had hoped that the appearance of a new and, to all intents and purposes, professional boyfriend would at least keep Mum off my back for a couple of hours.

'I've bought a new jacket, especially,' he said, going to great pains to be sweet.

'Well, if you really want to come,' I told him.

'Of course I do. It'll be very interesting to see where you get your temper from.'

'I do not have a temper,' I snapped, as I stabbed at his arm with my chip fork. 'But you had better not show me up all the same. I hope you know how to eat using proper cutlery. I've only ever seen you use a plastic chip fork or chop sticks.'

'I can use a spoon perfectly well,' he retorted. 'Hey, listen, I was thinking, since next weekend will be our seven-month anniversary . . .'

I groaned.

'And since I haven't yet got you a present for your birthday, what do you say to going away for a really dirty weekend to celebrate getting this far?'

'What about your overdraft?' I asked practically.

'I could put the weekend on my credit card instead. If it's still working, that is,' he added. 'We could go to Brighton. Or Bristol. Or Bath. Wherever *you* want to go, Liz. It's your choice. It's your birthday. Let me treat you.'

'Oh, Richard. I'm sorry. But I couldn't go even if you could afford it. I'm busy next weekend.'

'Not washing your armpit hair again?' he joked.

'Actually I've got a friend coming to stay.'

'Great. Has she got a boyfriend? Paul's been a real pain in the proverbial since your heartless mate Seema dumped him after a single night of passion. Perhaps we could set him up with this new girl. Go on a double date. It could save him from going into a decline. He thinks his balls might be atrophying from under-use.'

'Er, Richard,' I stopped him. 'This friend of mine is a guy.'

'Oh. Well, a double date might not be such a good idea then. Old boyfriend?' he asked cautiously.

'A boy who is an old friend, yes,' I admitted that much. 'From America.'

'Oh. Well, I'm sure he's a very nice bloke,' said Richard, sounding utterly unconvinced.

'Oh, he is. Very nice.' I must have looked a bit wistful then because Richard's expression went all odd. He cleared his throat.

'I guess I'll just stay out of your way next weekend then.' We had reached the gate to my flat. I could tell that Richard was waiting to be asked to come in. It would be nice, I thought, to have someone to cuddle up to on my first night as a pre-thirty something. I was feeling pretty wretched. I pulled him in through the gate with me. 'Come on.'

'Actually, I think I might just go back to my place tonight, if that's OK with you,' he surprised me. 'Got to get up early in the morning. Five a side practice. Big match against the boys from Coopers next Wednesday night.'

'Oh.'

'What time do you need me to be ready on Sunday morning?' he asked.

'Ten-ish. I'll pick you up.'

'Yeah.' He kissed me on the cheek. 'See you Sunday morning then.'

I was peeved for about ten seconds. No girl likes to feel as though her charms have been rebuffed, especially on her birthday, and even if she was only using them half-heartedly. But then I found myself feeling strangely relieved. I went upstairs – careful not to look into the kitchen as I passed in case no one had cleared up; I would leave that disappointment for the morning. Once safely behind the locked door of my room, I delved under my bed for the box full of my dearest treasures.

It was just an old shoe-box but its contents were more precious to me than any amount of gold-plated tat from

Tiffany. A daffodil pressed between two yellowed leaves from a note-pad. A scrap of paper on which someone – Brian – had scrawled 'see you at lunch time' (it was the first note he ever pinned to the little cork notice board on my college room door – two weeks before he kissed me). Half a dozen longer notes from Brian, finished with love and kisses. A little Valentine's card with a heart-carrying teddy bear on the front – signed on the inside (Americans do that – seemed strange at the time but now I'm glad). A button from his favourite blue shirt, which I found on the floor of my college room after he had gone back to New York. A handful of photographs taken over nine glorious months together.

I pulled out my favourite. It was a photograph of me and Brian at the end of term ball that also marked the end of his all too short stay in England. I was wearing a red velvet dress that had cost me almost half my student grant for that year. My thin hair was pinned up on top of my head in an extravagant style that I had never before or since managed to achieve. Brian was in a smart black tux. He had even bought me a corsage to pin to my dress. None of the girls with an English date that night had a corsage. I had a white lily flecked with red that matched my oufit perfectly – Brian had asked Mary to tell him what I was going to wear.

The corsage had dropped off when we were dancing to the act the ball committee had hired for the night – some ska band that had been big when we were kids and inspired lots of pushing and shoving on the dancefloor. It had been trampled underfoot and by the time I realised it was missing I could only retrieve the piece of pink ribbon which still lay at the bottom of my box of treasures.

Now I lay down on my bed and just looked at that photograph of the ball for hours. Brian had been so gorgeous.

His bright white smile seemed to light up his perfect brown face. Looking at that photograph, I could almost remember how he smelled that night. Davidoff Cool Water – that was his aftershave.

At the bottom of the box I also found a slightly battered tape. It was a tape of tunes that Brian had compiled for me. A tape of tunes that had special relevance to us at the time. There was 'Love Cats' by the Cure, which had been playing at the Two Items of Clothing party while we shared our first kiss just outside the Union. 'Everywhere' by Fleetwood Mac – that had been playing as we first made love. (Fleetwood Mac's greatest hits was one of only two CDs I had.) And finally, a scratchy version of 'Let's Call the Whole Thing Off' sung by a long-dead musical star.

I slipped the tape into the tape deck of my tatty old stereo and spooled it forward to the old song about the fatal differences between lovers from the US and the UK sung by a man with a plum in his mouth. I hadn't played the tape for quite a while and goose pimples peppered my spine as the first piano chords sounded.

> *'You say po-tay-to and I say po-ta-to,*
> *You say to-may-to and I say to-ma-to . . .'*

It was *our* song. Absolutely relevant to Brian and me. Brian would burst into the tune spontaneously whenever I picked him up on the way he said 'erb' instead of 'herb' or mistook a pavement for a sidewalk. By the time the singer got to the bit about breaking hearts I couldn't hold back a nostalgic tear.

It hardly seemed possible that I hadn't actually seen Brian in the flesh for almost six years. He was still so much part of my life in that I thought of him so often. Nothing had happened in those six years that could compare with the happy times we spent together. No one had eclipsed him in my memory.

I wondered if he would have changed. Would his smooth black hair still be so thick and wavy or would the stress of his high-flying job have made it drop out in handfuls? Would he still have a stomach you could iron your shirts on, or would he have spread a bit, as the rest of us definitely had since we were students surviving on kebabs and crackers? Would his eyes still crinkle up at the corners while he tried hard not to laugh? Would he still smell the way he used to – good enough to eat? I went to sleep with the photograph next to me on the pillow. When I woke up, it was all creased.

9

And sleeping on my picture of Brian had certainly not solved the problem that he posed by proposing to visit me in my Balham hell-hole.

The grill-pan stood on the kitchen table, still covered by the damp tea-towel that was now brown with singe marks. The sink was piled high with mugs, plates, cutlery and part of a dismantled bicycle. The sock that Seema had been using as a duster still hung listlessly from the end of the mantelpiece as though she was expecting an early Christmas. And all through the house, not a creature was stirring that might have had any intention of doing any housework.

I made myself some sort-of-toast by singeing the mould off the edges of a piece of bread using flames from one of the gas rings on the hob and had a cup of tea without milk. There wasn't even an empty carton in the fridge that morning. I knew that Fat Joe had taken to hoarding milk in his room in case Armageddon came during the night but I didn't feel strong enough to go and look for the missing pint right then. If Fat Joe's feet could stink out the sitting room within five seconds of his walking in, then you can imagine how bad his bedroom was. Saddam Hussein had spent millions on research, trying to perfect a gas so bad that it could kill a man, when just one waft from the doorway of Joe's room would have done the trick on a whole army. Even with gas masks.

Anyway, having finished my 'toast' – that is, having thrown it into the bottomless wastepaper basket after just one bite, I pondered the reality of making the house fit for Brian in less than a week since, having slept on the problem, it seemed that Seema's plan to claim that my penthouse had been destroyed in a fire was the only real option open to me other than simply telling him not to come at all. Glancing about me, I could see a great many things that could be improved instantly by banishment to a dustbin bag. I had heard about incredible carpet cleaning hoovers that could be hired for £50 a day. I had heard about incredible cleaners who could be hired for £50 a day, more to the point. But I didn't really have £50 to spare. I would have to do it myself.

I ventured back into the kitchen and, careful not to disturb the mountain of washing up which certainly wasn't doing itself, I had a search through the cupboard beneath the sink for cleaning materials.

Well, I didn't find any Jif, but I did find my cream Armani-lookalike jacket. The one which Seema said must have been stolen from the washing line, after she borrowed it and, she claimed, diligently washed it for me afterwards. Now I discovered a story which I thought might have been closer to the truth. The jacket had a big hole on its front. A hole which corresponded pretty much exactly with the shape of our iron. Seema may have been good enough to wash the jacket but she had still been cack-handed enough to burn a bloody great hole through it. Thinking back, I could even remember the day she must have hidden it in the cupboard beneath the sink. I had come home from work one evening to find Seema standing awkwardly against the sink, explaining away the faint haze of smoke which hung in the air as the result of an afternoon spent baking bhajis. She told me that Fat Joe had eaten the results of course.

But angry though I was, that had been a long time ago. Well, over a year. And I knew that even if I wanted to wear the jacket again now, I wouldn't have been able to since I had recently been porking out on a diet of KitKats, the only thing that could get me through a day at Corbett and Daughter's without crying. I stuffed the jacket into a dustbin bag and resolved to keep the revelation of its discovery for a later date, when I needed to guilt-trip Seema into doing something really awful.

When I emerged from the cupboard again with a rusty pan scourer and a bottle of cream cleaner that had already haemmorhaged most of its contents into a sticky white puddle on the cupboard floor, I wondered whether that moment to make Seema do something really awful might not have come slightly sooner than I hoped.

Pushing the crockery piled high on the draining board into a sink full of lukewarm, but not soapy (we had run out of washing-up liquid, naturally) water, I poured a little of the cream cleaner on to the scratched aluminium and started to scrub. And scrub. But the hardwater scum showed no signs of wanting to give. Perhaps if I just rinsed the draining board down, I thought. If I knew that it was clean, a little bit of wear and tear wouldn't be too horrifying when Brian arrived.

I pulled the plug out of the sink, intending to drain away the brown water which had been sitting in there for about a week. But it didn't drain away. I started to unload the crockery again, in an attempt to find out what was causing the blockage. Soon I had taken out everything I could feel in the water that I couldn't actually see my hands in. Gingerly, I felt my way towards the plug hole where I had once found a fish's head with staring dead white eyes.

This time, I pulled out a mouse.

I screamed until everyone in the house was awake. It wasn't that it was a mouse, you understand. I'm not one of those girls who has to stand on a chair and wait to be rescued at the first sight of a worm-like tail disappearing under the skirting board. I had even kept mice as a child. Perhaps that was why I was so upset at having to pull a dead one out of the sink. It must have drowned while trying to reach some tasty morsel floating in the dishwater, poor thing. Perhaps it had become trapped beneath one of my own dirty plates. The thought would surely haunt me for the rest of my life.

It certainly put me off cleaning anything else that day. All I needed right then was a swift drink as soon as the pubs opened. Luckily, there was someone who would oblige. Miserable Mary was meeting me in town for lunch. She was always game for a swift gin and tonic whatever the time of day. And she was going to pay. Birthday treat. She'd promised.

Though we had been like two peas in a pod while at college, these days I hardly saw my old best friend, despite the fact that we lived less than four miles apart. But that's four miles across the river Thames and, as anyone who has ever lived in London knows, you can't guarantee that you'll get anywhere – from Clapham South to Clapham North even (just two tube stops apart) – in less than an hour by public transport. (Not that Mary ever took public transport these days.) If you're talking about taking a trip from low-rent Balham (so far south it's been nicknamed the Gateway to France) to lovely trendy Belsize Park in the north, you might as well be talking about flying to New York for the night. It's that easy.

So, my relationship with Mary, like the relationship I

had been having with Brian, had become confined to hasty e-mail messages two or three times a week. Though Mary genuinely didn't have time to write anything more interesting than 'How are you? Sorry I haven't e-mailed you in ages.' Because, while my life had been on a strictly downward trajectory ever since we threw our mortar boards into the air in graduation glee, Mary's life had gone into interstellar orbit. Honestly, if I hadn't seen her five times a year or so in the five years since that last day and thus had some idea of the processes which had been in motion since college ended, I wouldn't have believed that the new look Miserable Mary, who was always putting me on hold to take a far more important call, could possibly have been made of the same genetic material as the one who refused to come out of her bedroom for a week when that chap from the Manic Street Preachers went missing near the Severn Bridge.

Her hair wasn't even dyed black any more. Her mother, who turned out to be a PR guru with a massive firm that did public relations for anyone who was anybody from soft drinks manufacturers to Arabian arms dealers (Mary had kept that very quiet during the college years), managed to persuade Mary to both fix her broken tooth and go back to her natural hair colour (honey blonde) before her first job interview and Mary's hair had been getting lighter ever since. When I popped my head around the door of the Mezzo café, I wasn't sure whether I was seeing my old pal Mary or some breakfast TV presenter sitting at her usual table, such was the telegenic sheen on her coiffured golden waves. She was wearing a cream trouser suit over a chocolate silk vest with expensive chocolate leather accessories to match. She looked as though she had been dressed by Thorntons – in the nicest possible way. It was a real champagne truffle of an outfit. I, on the other hand, looked distinctly inedible in my paint-flecked jeans and a jumper I had retrieved from the laundry basket. I wasn't even sure it was my jumper, to be honest.

'Well, we won't be going anywhere nice for lunch, obviously,' she said when she saw me. 'Get yourself a coffee or something, darling. I've just got to make a few more calls before I can give you my full and undivided attention.' She pushed a fiver across the table to pay for my coffee and spent the next quarter of an hour persuading the editor of the *Daily Mail* or some other worthy rag that another arms crisis in Iraq wasn't the kind of story he needed on his front page on a Monday morning.

'Dahling,' she told him in her most flirtatious voice (the one that hadn't worked on the pierced post-grad). 'You run that story all the time. It's just such a depressing way to start the week. People will be topping themselves all over the home counties. How about this instead? A little bird told me that if Anthea Turner's new boyfriend doesn't have an engagement ring on her finger by the end of next week, she's going to join a convent of Carmelite nuns. I can get you the pictures. Now don't you think that deserves a front page headline?' Amazingly, he did.

Mary had moved sideways from her first job in fashion PR into artist management (or *artiste* management, as she liked to call it) and had quickly risen to the top of her chosen career. Her father had bankrolled Mary's very own talent agency when it became clear that she had her own talent for schmoozing celebrities, but that wasn't something she liked to talk about. Now, anyone who was anyone had her business card in their wallet for media emergencies. She was on first-name terms with everyone from mega heavyweight foreign correspondents, whose idea of travelling light was to pack just one bullet-proof vest, to the Spice Girls' toddling children who never went anywhere without a gross of Gucci nappies.

'So how's it going with you?' she finally asked, when she had finished regaling me with the story of a glamour model she had just taken on. (Mary had got her promising new client a date with a gay MP who wasn't New Labour enough to exit the closet. They went to a sushi bar and the model drank the finger bowl, etcetera. The MP took a sip himself to save her from embarrassment.) 'Did you have a lovely birthday?' Mary sighed.

I shrugged.

'Get any decent presents?'

'Definitely not.'

'Well, I hope you like this one,' she said, pushing a package across the table towards me. I fell upon the blue-wrapped parcel eagerly. At least there was some hope that Mary would have got me something I wanted. And she had. The box inside the paper was also pale blue and stamped with the legend 'Tiffany and Co.' The second best phrase in the English language after 'will you marry me' from the mouth of Joseph Fiennes.

'Don't get too excited,' Mary warned me. 'It's only a key-ring.'

It was still the best present I had had all year. And it was engraved with my initials. How thoughtful. 'Thanks,' I said, remembering the cheapo Body Shop bubble bath I had given Mary on her own birthday. 'I wish I could get you something half as good.'

'Perhaps you will one day. You could find me a nice little flat for a start and waive your commission.'

'Nobody ever puts their nice little flats through Corbett and Daughter Estate Agents,' I reminded her. 'Though having said that, there's somewhere in Eaton Place that might come up if Harriet's aunt doesn't pull through from the heart attack she had last week.'

'Eaton Place?' Mary sneered. 'Horribly dark round there unless you're on the top floor.'

'I wouldn't say no.' It was one of the best addresses in Belgravia. Possibly in the whole of London.

'I don't suppose you would,' she said, a little meanly. 'How are your flatmates?'

'One still fat and annoying, one just annoying.'

'Honestly, Lizzie,' Mary laughed. 'You should get yourself out of there before some of their unique charm rubs off on you.'

'I can't afford to move,' I reminded her. The landlord is putting the rent up again at the end of the month and there's still no sign of the new hot-water tank he promised us. I've looked at our contract, but all it really says is that he can throw us out pretty much whenever he wants to with about three minutes' notice.' I could see Mary's eyes starting to glaze over as she listened to my tale of domestic terror.

'Love life?' she asked, quickly moving on to something she might be able to relate to.

'Still that Richard chap I told you about in my e-mail,' I said.

'What?' she raised her eyebrows in amusement. 'That's been . . .'

'Seven months.'

'Is he the one?' she asked me conspiratorially. 'Do you think it's MPL?'

'He's an accountant,' I replied.

'Oh. Well, don't get too attached then,' she sighed.

'I'm not,' I only half-lied. 'How's your love life?'

'Didn't you see the picture in *Hello!* last week, darling? It was only a small one admittedly, on the party pages at the back, but at least it was in colour this time. Mitchell and I went to a bash for Ivana Trump's fiftieth. Again,' she added wickedly.

'I didn't know you knew Ivana Trump,' I told her.

'I don't really. Well, perhaps well enough to say "hello" if I see her in San Lorenzo. But I owed her agent a massive favour and he was terrified that Ivana's birthday party would be a media washout. I just had to turn up with Mitchell for half an hour and get him to smile for some photos. It won't have done his career any harm to be in *Hello!* again either. It was a two-way thing.'

'I see. How's his new album going?'

'In the studio from dusk till dawn. Sleeps all day. Works all night. It's been like having a relationship with a bloody vampire.'

Not only was Mary doing meteorically well in her career, in case you hadn't guessed she had managed to bag herself a pretty impressive trophy boyfriend into the bargain.

Mitchell – he only had one name (like the name the 'Artist who was formerly known as' was once known by, if you know what I mean) – was the only surviving member of a boy band called Teenage Crush who had been the big thing of 1999. They had split to pursue solo projects at the height of their popularity, but so far Mitchell was the only one of the foursome who had managed to scale the charts alone – albeit with a number of offensively inoffensive cover versions. Anyway, Mitchell had always been considered to be the handsome one of the band with his movie-star looks and action man body, though he was also rumoured to be slightly soft between the ears (I mean, thick, of course. Not just soppy about animals). But I guessed that Mary must have had a change of heart since she announced that she could never go to bed with anyone who didn't stimulate her mind as well as her clitoris (that was during the pierced post-grad crush). Whatever, I was impressed that Mary was shagging her most fanciable client however appalling his GCSE results had been.

'Is he doing any of his own material on this album?' I asked, relishing the fact that almost everyone in the café was suddenly ear-wigging on our conversation. *Mitchell* was a name everyone knew right then – darling of every publication from *Tatler* to *Take A Break*. But Mary merely rolled her eyes extravagantly at the idea of Mitchell's songwriting.

'Good God, no. He can't afford to retire yet. Though I foolishly let him spend the first week of this latest session in the studio making a demo tape of his own stuff, just to placate him. You've never heard anything like it, Liz, and thankfully no one else ever will. It was so dark. And absolutely rubbish. All bleeding hearts and unattainable love, with a dash of satanism and vampires thrown in for luck. *Très* Ozzy Osbourne.'

'What?'

'That is exactly what I said when I heard it. Anyway, bollocks to that, I told him. We're in the business of making money, not mistakes. So he's going to do a load of new stuff by the talented one from BoyZone, a couple of old Burt Bacharach classics with some Madonna samples and a version of Slade's 'Come on Feel the Noize' instead. I've promised him that I might let him put one of his own tracks on as a bonus track that you only get to hear if you leave your CD in the player for two hours after the last proper track has finished.'

'That doesn't sound like a very good idea to me,' I told her. 'If it's as full of satanic imagery as you say it is, before you know it you'll have people claiming that Mitchell is trying to subliminally subvert the fresh-faced youths who buy his records. Angry parents will be storming the desks at HMV demanding blood. And refunds.'

I had a pretty good idea which demand frightened her more.

'Mmm, I suppose you might be right,' she admitted. 'Though fresh-faced is hardly how I'd describe some of the fourteen-year-old trollops who were throwing themselves at him when he did a signing at Tower Records the other week. Honestly, Liz, you've never heard such language. If anyone was corrupted it was me, by them. One of them asked me for a light for her spliff for heaven's sake! They know no morality, the kids of today. Sex, drugs and rock and roll? These kids were *bored* of that old crap before they got to senior school. Oh, listen to me,' she snorted. 'I sound like I'm ready to retire to Nappy Valley.'

Nappy Valley was the nickname we'd given to the houses around Clapham Common where *naice* people went to have babies once a year or so until their husbands found temptation in au pairs or the gay cottaging hot-spot near the cricket pitches (made very public by the poor one-time Minister for Wales).

'I can't imagine you in Clapham,' I told her. 'Or Mitchell for that matter.'

'I think he'd rather like to be near the Common,' Mary said, her mouth turning down at the corners as if she had just tasted something nasty.

'You're not thinking of tying the knot, are you?' I asked excitedly.

'Get real, Liz. If Mitchell gets married at the moment his record sales will go like that.' She pointed her thumb downwards into the sugar bowl. 'A huge part of his appeal for the hormonal hordes of screaming girlies is the perpetual perception of availability. They need to be able to imagine that they could have him. Remember how Take That weren't even allowed to have girlfriends in case it upset the fans? It was written into their contracts.'

'Then how come Mitchell's allowed to be seen cavorting with you in the illustrious pages of *Hello!*? Aren't you spoiling his aura of availability simply by being around him at all?'

She shook her head. 'There's a balance to be struck,' Mary explained. 'Between having Mitchell appear available and not having him appear to be afraid of women.'

'Oh. So it's not about *true love* then?' I probed.

'Of course it's about love,' Mary retorted tetchily. 'But he's still my client as well as my lover and I can't start picking fabric for the bridesmaids' dresses yet. His career must come before my feelings right now.'

'What a shame.'

'It's my pension too,' she said flatly. 'When he earns, I earn. Besides, you know I don't really believe in marriage and all that *happily ever after* crap. Not after some of the things I've seen.'

'How are your parents?' I asked automatically. I'd never actually met Mary's parents. Well, I'd seen her mother from a distance once, sitting outside the college gates in her silver convertible Mercedes, tapping her manicured fingers on the leather-covered steering wheel while she waited for Mary to bring her trunk down at the end of term. But I knew enough about them to realise that if anyone had put Mary off the idea of marriage it was the two people who had brought her up.

'Dad's having another affair,' she sighed, confirming my suspicions. 'Honestly, Liz, he thinks we don't know about it. Stupid fool. It's bloody obvious. As soon as he gets besotted with some new tart he goes on another crash diet and picks up the gym membership again, then Mum dyes her hair a shade or two lighter and goes hunting for a casual shag of her own in Browns. They're as bad as each other. I don't know why they don't just cut their losses and get a divorce. Well, I do know. They're both too frightened that the other one would end up with all the money and the house in Palma. How are your parents, anyway?'

'Same as ever. Still together. They don't need to get a divorce now that Dad's got a new shed to hide in when Mum's on the war path,' I joked.

'You're so lucky to have parents like yours,' Mary murmured, looking into her coffee as though she expected the froth to start forming words. Mary was always telling me how wonderful my parents were, but then she had only met my mother *after* the menopause (five long years spent waiting for Armageddon to strike every time someone dropped biscuit crumbs on the carpet had rather coloured my own view of Mum).

'Anyway, am I ever going to get to meet this wonderful man of yours before his star drops out of the ascendant and you're finally allowed to marry him or dump him?' I asked her then to get back into more cheerful waters.

'Of course you'll get to meet him,' Mary promised. 'But you know how difficult it is. I mean, you and I hardly ever get to see each other as it is because of my crazy work schedule. Factoring Mitchell into the equation would make it practically impossible to arrange a night out with all the appearances he has to do.'

'Then perhaps I could meet you both at an appearance,' I suggested excitedly. 'In the VIP room at some swanky nightclub. I'd like that. I've always wanted to be a VIP.'

'Yeah. I'll see what I can do,' she said distantly. But she didn't seem keen. Perhaps she was just fed up of people asking to meet him all the time. I was sure I wouldn't have minded having a celebrity boyfriend myself, but I imagine that it must make you feel quite inadequate if you're not also a big celeb yourself. I mean, you'd get to go to loads of sparkling media parties full of superstars, sure; but no one would actually care whether *you* turned up or not. In fact, most people would probably prefer your other half to turn up alone.

'You'll never guess who phoned me yesterday,' I said, to break the silence that had fallen since I dared to ask to meet Mitchell.

'Bill?' she guessed, not even looking up from her coffee. 'I spoke to him last Friday. He said he was going to call you. He's coming through Heathrow *en route* from Chile to Nepal next weekend.'

'No. He didn't call.' And I was slightly offended that he hadn't. I only got the occasional postcard from him since we'd gone our separate ways after college but he and Mary always seemed to be in touch by phone.

'Oh. I don't know then,' Mary continued guessing. 'Andrew?'

'Andrew? Who's Andrew?' I asked. I didn't know anyone called Andrew. 'No, Brian called.'

She looked at me blankly for a moment.

'Brian Coren? You must remember Brian?' I said incredulously. 'Brian from America. Our second year? Cute arse. Big smile. The one true love of my life?'

For a moment, Mary's jaw dropped and we were suddenly six years back in time, sitting on the steps outside the experimental psychology block, cringing with embarrassment that the Brady Bunch had heard us bitching. 'Not Brian Coren from New York?' she breathed.

'The very same. He called me last night to say that he's coming to visit.'

'Oh my God.' Mary put down her cappuccino and ran

an elegant hand through her perfect hair. I noticed she had given up biting her fingernails (or had some very expensive falsies). 'When's he coming?' she asked.

'End of the week. Friday afternoon, can you believe?'

'Oh my double God, Liz. That's a bit short notice, isn't it?'

'You're telling me. He says he's just got to snatch some time off work while he can.'

'I can appreciate that,' she muttered. 'I haven't had a proper holiday in three years. Where's he staying? Somewhere central?'

'Well, I actually said he could stay with me.'

'What? In Balham? You are joking, Liz,' she exclaimed with a grimace.

'If only. He said he would be happy to stay in a hotel, but I said I wouldn't hear of it. Then he said that he really didn't mind staying in a hotel because it is such short notice but I insisted that I couldn't live with myself if I let him. I told him that I wouldn't even consider it. I had to be his host. He insisted one more time that he'd be happy to stay somewhere else, then I insisted one more time that he shouldn't and this time I won.'

'You idiot!' said Mary. 'You can't possibly have Brian to stay at Fleapit Towers.'

'Fleapit Towers? What are you saying? It's not that bad.'

'You think so? Look, I didn't want to have to say this to you, Lizzie, but you remember that night I crashed at your place after . . . you know, that incident . . .'

When she was dumped by Mr Rich, Handsome and Eligible Mark Four, she meant (I think he was the psychotic heir to some supermarket chain – never actually met him) and turned up on my doorstep at three in the morning wearing nothing but her pyjamas and looking as though she should be sectioned. I remembered it well. We were up until four on a work-night drinking neat gin with vodka chasers. It was the first and only time Mary had visited my house in Balham. All our other meetings had taken place in far more salubrious Soho. Only severe desperation could have brought Mary south of the river these days.

'Well, when I woke up the next morning after sleeping on your sofa, I swear I had little red bites all over my legs. Flea bites,' she added in a half-whisper. But not so much of a whisper that everyone in the café didn't turn round to see who was the unclean one with an infestation in the house.

'You did not,' I said indignantly.

'I'm afraid I did. I looked like someone had been at me with a pin cushion. But I'm not blaming you, Liz. I didn't even want to have to tell you about the incident. I'm sure it's not your fault. I mean, you've never even really liked cats, have you? Must have been left over from a moggy that belonged to the previous tenants or something – fleas can live in the carpet for years if they're not treated straight away. All I'm saying is, you can't risk that happening to Brian, can you? You know what Americans are like about hygiene.'

'I know,' I said miserably. I remembered with a sinking heart Brian's vitriolic views on the subject of English plumbing. He couldn't understand the logic of sitting in a bath without having showered first. He was the type of man who wore clean underpants every day and washed his bedclothes at least once a week. He wouldn't be overly impressed to find himself boarding with Fat Joe, who thought that changing his skanky underpants might weaken his spirit, or something sick like that.

'Even though I don't believe you about the fleas,' I continued. 'I know I can't have Brian staying with me in Balham.

Particularly as . . .' Then I spilled out the whole sorry tale about the mendacious e-mails from cycling next to Ginger Spice to partying with Arabella Gilbert.

'Oh my God,' breathed Mary when I had finished. She was approximating a shocked expression but I could tell that she was really just struggling not to laugh. 'Oh my God! You told him you live in a flat that overlooks Hyde Park? Well, perhaps if you took a step-ladder up on to your flat roof and a pair of really good binoculars you might be able to see Tooting Common. But Hyde Park? That's hilarious, Liz.'

'I wish I could agree with you.'

'It's the funniest thing I've heard in a fortnight. Whatever possessed you?'

'I wanted him to think I was making a success of things,' I sighed, looking down into my coffee.

Mary pursed her lips disapprovingly.

'Oh Lizzie. You should never, ever tell lies,' she said, still biting back a snigger. 'Unless you really think you can pull them off.'

'Well, I did, didn't I?' I snapped back. 'Whoever told a lie they didn't think they could pull off, for heaven's sake?'

'Keep your hair on. I was only offering some friendly advice.'

'Right. The kind of friendly advice I could have got from my mother, thanks all the same. Mary,' I said weakly. 'I was rather hoping that you might be able to help me in a slightly more practical way.'

She smiled at that. 'I'll do anything I can, darling. Of course I will. You know that.'

'Like, could I stay at your flat while Brian is in town?'

A slow grin spread across her face.

'Please. Pretty please. I'd pay you whatever the going

rate is,' I begged, though I was taking the big smile on her face to mean that she was already considering the idea in a positive way.

'You don't have to pay me, Liz,' she said magnanimously as she patted my hand. 'You're my best friend. Of course I'd be happy to help you. And of course you can stay at my flat for just as long as you need. I'll be delighted to have you both. When I was in your position,' she said, as though she were fifty years my senior instead of a couple of months, 'I couldn't wait to live on my own and get out of the whole washing-up rota thing, but now that I have my own luxury flat with a dishwasher to worry about that for me, I actually get quite lonely from time to time. You must call Brian and tell him that I can't wait to play hostess. I'll even throw a party for you both if you want me to. We could hire a room at one of my clubs. Soho House or Groucho? Just let me know who needs inviting. Wouldn't it be great if Bill could be in town too? I think he's flying in on Monday. Perhaps they'll overlap . . .'

I gritted my teeth to tell her, 'Actually, I was also hoping that you might make yourself scarce for the duration.'

'What?' She looked at me uncomprehendingly.

'Please, Mary. It's only for four days. Two of those are over the weekend. You could stay with Mitchell, couldn't you? In that fantastic luxury bachelor pad he was photographed in for *Hello!*,' I added with an appealing smile.

'For God's sake, Liz, he doesn't actually own that flat,' said Mary sharply. 'Besides, I never stay at Mitchell's.'

'Why not?'

'Because . . . because I just don't ever stay there, OK. We like to maintain our own space. Keep our own identities. I don't want him living in my pocket and he doesn't want me hanging round him all the time either.'

'Yeah, but sometimes you must stay round there for a night or two. At weekends.'

'Liz, I can't stay with Mitchell next weekend,' she said firmly. 'Just forget that.'

'Well, you must have a health farm or something you'd like to go to. What about Champneys? You're always saying how much you like it at Champneys. All those lovely masseurs. Perhaps they've still got that Czech one who asked if he could marry you.' (He was after a visa.) 'I'll pay for you to spend the four days there. How about that?'

'Why do you want me out of my own bloody flat so badly?' she snapped.

'Because . . . because I need to pretend that your flat is mine, Mary. You know I do.'

'Why?' she whined.

'Why?' I echoed sarcastically. Hadn't she been listening? 'Because I don't want to have to tell Brian the truth about my e-mails, that's why. He's only coming to England for four days. After that I probably won't see him again for another six years by which time even I might just have a place of my own. Please, Mary. I just can't stand the thought of having to tell him the truth next week. He'll think so badly of me. We're only going to have four days together as it is. I don't want to have to spend half my time with him making up for the fact that I've been telling him a whopping big pile of lies about my life for the past three years.'

'You should have thought of that before you decided to audition for a job on *Jackanory*,' she said disdainfully. 'I know you've always had pretensions to being an actress, Liz, but this really is ridiculous. You've been a total idiot.'

'Mary, I know that. And I know that I'm asking a great deal of you. But this visit means so much to me . . .'

'So it seems. You're not planning to pick up where you

left off, are you?' she asked. 'Six years ago?' she added with a little snort.

'I suppose so. I mean, yes. I am.' I hoped the idea that I was pursuing true love might soften her into agreeing to help me on my terms.

'Well, I think you're expecting a bit much there,' she said instead.

'Perhaps I am. But you'll help me out. Won't you?'

She straightened her mouth into a firm, thin line before she told me, 'No. No, I bloody won't. I have to be in London for the whole of next weekend. I'm afraid I can't mess up my plans just because you've got yourself into another ridiculous situation. I thought I was being bloody generous offering you both a decent, flea-free place to stay at all, considering the amount of work I've got going on at the moment. When one really deals with celebrities, as opposed to pretending that you've jogged on the treadmill next to Ginger Spice at the Sanctuary, one doesn't have time to engage in elaborate and downright pathetic charades for people who aren't decent enough to accept their rotten lot in life and admit to it.'

She took a triumphant sip of her cappuccino and waited for my reaction.

The cow. She had the answer to my problems at her fingertips and she would not let me have it.

'Mary?' I said pleadingly.

'Absolutely not,' she smiled. 'If you don't want to stay in my flat with me in it simultaneously, you can forget the whole thing.'

Double cow. She had been my best friend all through college. I was the person she turned to when an attempt to dye her facial hair a lighter colour gave her a bright red rash of a moustache. I was the person she turned to when she went through a very nasty case of haemorrhoids and thought that she was dying of something undiagnosable. Once I had known more about her than anyone in the world. I wondered if I should remind her of all those little things we'd shared in the years that we had known one another. The good times and the bad. But no. She'd changed. She'd probably deny that most of them had even happened.

'Shall we get some lunch now?' she asked to close the discussion. 'I know a lovely Italian place just around the corner where they might let you in looking like that. I'm not drinking today though. Empty calories. I need to shift some weight for the start of the party season. You know I got my first Christmas party invitation yesterday?'

'Well, I'm not eating anyway,' I told her frostily. 'I've got to go to the supermarket and pick up some flea powder for my stinking flat, haven't I?' Then I left.

Well, I walked out of that café with my head held quite high, all things considered. But I was no nearer to finding a solution to the Brian problem and I had fallen out with one of my best friends to boot. Why wouldn't she help me? When had Mary been hit with the bitch stick? I had a sudden, awful vision of her sitting at the aluminium table in the café, ultra-powerful lap-top in front of her, tapping out an e-mail to Brian which she would send via the modem on her mobile phone. As far as I knew, she didn't have Brian's e-mail address, but I was sure it wouldn't be difficult for her to track him down and spew out the whole story before I got to him.

And I'd forgotten to pick up my one and only decent birthday present before making my dramatic exit.

On the way to the tube I thought of ways to get my revenge on Mary. If we had still been at college, I could have written something terrible about her on the back of a toilet cubicle door, or forged her spidery handwriting and left a note in the college geek's pigeon-hole saying that she really, really fancied him but was too shy to ask for a date. As it was, I couldn't think of anything I could do that would inflict a suitable amount of psychological pain on her right then, without me winding up in prison as a consequence.

Meandering through Soho towards the nearest underground station, I passed gay couples (in both senses of the word), sitting together outside chi-chi cafés, enjoying the late summer sunshine and each other's company. Everyone seemed to be laughing brightly at private jokes. Touching each other secretly beneath the tables. Kissing openly over their cappuccinos. Everyone was happy. Everyone had someone special. Everyone was in love. If she wasn't already getting hold of Brian, Mary was probably calling Mitchell, arranging a hot date for that evening. Whispering sweet nothings to him over the Nokia. Funny nicknames. Stupid jokes.

Was it so much to ask to be like these happy shiny people? All I wanted was someone I could feel passionate for, who felt the same way about me. Yes, I know I was supposed to be seeing Richard. I should have been feeling passionate about him but the fact was, I imagined that Richard, like me, would feel an outsider if he walked past these ultra-trendy people now. He was just an accountant after all. He thought that the height of individuality was wearing odd cartoon character socks to the office. A Bart Simpson tie when he felt particularly daring. He probably had ambitions to own a Ford Sierra Cosworth and spend his Saturday afternoons cleaning it rather than canoodling outside a café anyway.

But I wanted to be a part of a 'scene'. The kind of scene that they write about in the colour supplements to all the Sunday papers. I wanted to be able to walk into a café and order a latte without feeling as though the girl behind the counter thought I was being pretentious. I knew that Brian could order a latte without wincing. I knew that Brian was part of a glamorous scene somewhere. With someone ordinary like Richard I would always be just a registry office ceremony away from the purgatory of suburbia and I would never reach my true potential. With Brian, I could be my wacky individual creative self. I did have a wacky self somewhere, I was sure. I could feel it sometimes, when I'd had a couple of bacardis.

A girl with bright yellow hair clipped up into fifty or so tiny spiky bunches suddenly stepped out of a domination gear shop doorway and straight on to my foot in her gravity-defying patent stilettos. She didn't even say 'sorry'. I did, however. I said 'sorry' to someone who had just stepped on me! As I watched her stagger down the footpath in her pink mini-skirt and stripy tights, greeting other funky people outside every café she passed, I bristled with frustration and wondered if she had even seen me standing there in my army regulation jumper and jeans.

'I'm easily as good as you are underneath all that slap,' I said in an imaginary conversation with the confident girl. 'I could be working for some Soho television company. I could be making the coffee in a recording studio, 'cos I bet that's all you're doing even with your high heels and your hair. I'm cultured. I'm educated. I could be anything I want to be. I'm just working as a secretary at Corbett's and wearing these crappy clothes while I decide what I really want to do. And when I do find out, then you'll notice me. I could be a famous actress one day. Then everyone will recognise me. No one would dare step on my feet in the street again without saying sorry to me.'

But before I could catch up with her, or grow the courage to say such a thing to her face, she had slipped inside the doorway to a members-only club. *Soho House*, said the plaque on the door. It was one of the trendy media clubs that I had read about in the *Evening Standard*, or Arabella Gilbert's society column, and written about in my stupid lying e-mails to Brian. I think I had described myself sitting inside on a red banquette, listening to the brothers from Oasis have an impromptu jamming session with the kooky lead singer from The Cardigans. Looking up at the windows, I was reminded with heart-stopping misery that I had no idea what the furniture in that club looked like at all, or whether the Gallagher boys were even members.

'I could be a member too,' I said half out loud. 'If I really wanted to be.'

'Cheer up, love,' said a man lurking in the shadows. When he stepped forward I saw that he was one of the many people who slept rough in Soho doorways. His hair was matted into a single squidgy dreadlock on one side. My guess was that it wasn't a fashion statement. If he had been an animal, Rolf Harris might have picked him up and taken him back to the dog's home for a good bath and some loving grooming.

'You can have some of this if you like. You waiting for a giro too?' He thrust a can of Special Brew into my hand. I thrust it quickly back into his grimy fingers. Once upon a time, I might have been touched by a gesture of such generosity, but right then I was simply mortified that he might have seen me as a kindred spirit. Someone he had something in common with. Another of life's failures. A bottom-feeder in life's big fishtank. A piece of the base metal beneath London's thin layer of gilt. He thought that I was one of them. One of the losers. It must have been because I was talking to myself so passionately.

'Spare any change?' he asked me then.

And, indignity of all indignities, when I reached into my

pocket to oblige, I discovered that I couldn't spare any at all. I had just enough money to get the tube home.

When I got home, the burnt grill-pan was still sitting on the kitchen table. My flatmates were nowhere to be seen. But an envelope had arrived for me. Inside was my copy of the college magazine. *The St Judith's Chronicle*. I had no idea why I still subscribed, since it served only to depress me in much the same way as Arabella Gilbert's glittering social column.

But that day I tore the envelope open eagerly, wanting to make a full-blown tragedy out of my miserable morning. I read the news of other alumni. Ryan Fisher had set up his own internet café company. Anna Simner had written a book. Jemima Shad-Chequebook, the college's most renowned slapper, was engaged to be married to one of the directors of the vast bank she had gone to work for as a trader (a nice early retirement for her, I thought). Name after name that I recognised. All doing something exciting with their lives. All starting companies, or getting promotions, getting married or moving abroad. One of my Freshers' Week flings had already married and was father to a six-month-old daughter. Even Janie Spright, the college girl-geek, had started to publish her own alternative style magazine and was hoping to be able to float it on the stock exchange within a year. I remembered with a wry smile a conversation I had once had with Mary about whether the thick-rimmed glasses Janie wore in the library were a fashion statement or a necessity. I thought they were merely for her myopia but Mary had obviously been right. Again.

At the bottom of the column, another list asked 'Where are they now?'; and there I found my own name, right next to a request to write in with an update on my achievements and my whereabouts. Everyone was simply *dying* to hear how I was getting on . . .

'Where am I now?' I asked myself. Twenty-seven years old. No career to speak of – I didn't even have a permanent job, although Harriet was constantly promising me a proper contract when her solicitor cousin came out of the clinic. Where was I? Reading the college magazine on a springless sofa surrounded by the pathetic detritus of a life gone horribly wrong. That's where I was.

'Feeling better?' Seema trilled when she came in loaded down with library books and shopping bags.

I couldn't even bring myself to moan in disagreement.

'Look at this,' she pulled a green bottle out of one of the plastic bags. 'Californian Chardonnay is on special offer at Habib's. Probably full of anti-freeze. Do you think it will be nice?'

It was only just past two but I helped her drink three bottles to be sure.

10

Having drunk so much on an empty stomach, I fell into such a deep sleep that I could only be woken the next morning by the rather horrible sensation of Richard knocking on my forehead with his knuckles.

'Wake up! Wake up!' I heard him say through the mists of a hangover to rival the one I got after the end of the last Millennium. 'It's half-past eleven. We've got to be at your mother's in half an hour.'

'What? What!!!'

I sat up and banged my head on the angle-poise spotlight which I had taped to my bed-head for perfect in-bed reading. Great idea that had been.

'She's already called to see if you've left yet,' said Seema, who was standing in the doorway. 'I told her you left at ten. Even then she said that she couldn't see how you could possibly make it to Solihull before she burned the beef.'

'Oh, bollocks,' I shouted.

I jumped out of bed and began to pull on socks and shoes. Then I had to take my shoes off again to put my jeans on. 'Are you wearing that?' I asked Richard as I sniffed my *Pulp in concert* t-shirt to see if I could get away with it. He was wearing a smart Mandarin collared shirt and a pair of fairly reasonably well-pressed trousers. 'Where's your tie?'

'I wear a tie all week. Isn't this smart enough for you?'

'Not really. No. Seema, do you think Fat Joe has got a tie?'

'He's got one,' she told me. 'But I think he's been using it to hold his trousers up since he broke his belt.'

'Phone my mum,' I instructed my flatmate as I hopped into my shoes. 'Phone my mum and tell her you've just seen me outside the house trying to change the wheel on my car. Oh, and make sure you tell her Richard's helping or she'll only want to know why.'

A minute later, Seema returned. 'She wants to know why Richard hasn't got a car you could use instead of your old Fiesta.'

'Oh, just tell her I'm on my way. But not to put the Yorkshire puddings in yet.'

'Too late,' said Seema. 'She's already done that. She says everything is going to be ruined because of your selfishness. She said that she doesn't suppose I'd give *my* mother such a runaround. Certainly not, I told her. If I did, I'd have been sent to live with my aunty in Mumbai. She asked if my aunty had a spare room for you.'

'Oh, shut up, perfect daughter,' I snapped. 'Or I'll write and tell your parents about the lap-dancing audition at Stringfellow's.'

'I did that for a dare,' Seema protested. 'I was raising money for Rag Week.'

'Tell that to your aunty in Mumbai.'

Richard sat on the end of my bed and watched with amusement as, having decided that the t-shirt was probably a health hazard, I started flinging the entire contents of my wardrobe on to the floor, rejecting skirt after shirt after jumper until Seema came back from her room with the suit she saved for interviews.

'You can wear this,' she told me. 'If you swear you'll keep

quiet about the dancing thing. But promise not to get it dirty, won't you?'

'Thanks,' I said. 'Do I look like the kind of girl who can't get a forkful of food from her plate to her mouth without dropping it?'

Richard and Seema both focused on the tea-stains that patterned the front of my pyjamas but said nothing.

Poor Richard. It was bad enough that he was going to have to meet the two extra-terrestrials that had been pretending to be my parents for the past twenty-seven years, but when we finally pulled into the street where they lived (only two hours late), I realised that even more horrors awaited him. My brother Colin's car was already in the driveway.

Colin and I are twins. But you wouldn't believe it unless you saw our birth certificates or did a blood test. Obviously we were never going to be identical – after all, I'm a girl and he's a boy. But you'd think that we would have something in common at least. As it was, we didn't even have the same kind of hair. Somehow he managed to end up with the jaunty blond curls that should have been mine, while I got the mousy rats' tails and receding hairline. OK, so the receding hairline bit is a slight exaggeration, but what kind of cruel witch is mother nature to keep doling out the best hair and eyelashes to the boys? Tell me that the person with the best eyelashes you've ever seen wasn't a member of the un-fair sex and we'll ask that girl where she got her lash-building protein-enhanced mascara from.

So, we weren't in the least bit alike, Colin and I. He was blond. I was mousy. He had blue eyes. Mine were like shallow pools of stagnant green mud. He was athletic. I was pathetic. And on and on and on. By the time we were six he was so much more physically advanced than me that most people assumed he was at least two years my senior when in fact I predated him by a good eight minutes. But the fact that we were so different didn't stop people making fruitless comparisons once they knew that we were buns from the same oven.

All through junior school, the sadistic teachers (who ought to have been working as dominatrixes in Soho rather than moulding such tiny hearts and minds) would say to me every time I made a mistake: 'Why can't you do maths? Your brother Colin can do maths. Why can't you spell "misappropriation"? Your brother Colin can spell any word up to eight syllables long.' I wondered if anyone ever asked him why he couldn't do a decent French plait? Or name all the members of Bucks Fizz *and* remember their birthdays? I don't think so.

'Nice car,' breathed Richard when he clocked Colin's egg-shell blue Ford Focus in the driveway. It would be, wouldn't it? My Ford Fiesta (red from rust, not a paint job – it was supposed to be yellow) looked as though it had seen active service in the Crimean War. It stood to reason that Colin could only have turned up in a vehicle so spanking new it was still smarting.

'That's my brother's car,' I told him despondently.

'You never said you had a brother,' said Richard.

'Twin actually.'

Richard looked at me in a very peculiar way. 'Then I'm doubly surprised you didn't tell me about him. I thought twins were supposed to be really close. Don't you have a telepathic bond or something?'

'It got cut off when I forgot to pay the bill,' I said dryly. I turned off the juddering engine of my poor little car and pulled the handbrake up so hard it sounded as though I had done something an injury. 'Are you ready for this?' I asked Richard, giving him one last chance to escape. But Richard already had one hand on the door handle on his side of the car, a bunch of service-station flowers clutched in the other.

'I'm ready,' he said, giving me the thumbs up like a Second World War fighter pilot about to go into action.

'Well, I just need a few more seconds,' I told him. But it was too late anyway. Mum had spotted us turning into the driveway and was already opening the front door while deftly removing her apron like some superwoman from the 1960s who could flit between kitchen and dining room boiling spuds and drinking cocktails while simultaneously holding a coherent conversation about the lunar landings.

She was upon the car before we could get out of it.

'Was the traffic terrible?' she asked as she kissed my cheeks off. 'I could only think that that was why you're so late,' she added pointedly.

'I overslept,' I told her.

'Oh, late night was it?' she tutted. 'Been out partying so hard that you forgot you were coming to see your poor old mother?'

'Mum, this is Richard,' I said, reminding her that I had brought a guest before she brought up the time that I dawdled on the way home from Brownies and she called out the entire South Midlands police force to look for me. They even dredged the local pond, apparently. I'd only been missed for ten minutes. When I walked through the garden gate to see Mum dabbing at her eyes with a tea-towel while a big policeman took notes on my distinguishing marks, she threw herself upon me and smothered me with kisses as though I had been missing for a month. As soon as the policemen had gone however, I got a stinging wallop across the back of the legs and was sent to bed early for making a show of us all. I can still see Colin's face, eyes glittering with amusement, as he watched me get a slapping from the safety of the first-floor landing. I had actually been dawdling home from Brownies because *he* had told me that there were fairies living in the hedge behind the community hall.

'Richard, I'm Lizzie's Mum,' Mum was saying.

'I think he might have guessed.' It was Colin. He stood behind Mum now in a sleeveless Fair Isle patterned jumper and stiffly ironed trousers. If he had been smoking a pipe I wouldn't have been in the least bit surprised. Twenty-seven going on fifty, my brother.

'Hey, little sis,' he said when he saw me. 'How's life in bedsit land?'

He helped me out of the car. I had been so tense on the drive up that I was finding it difficult to straighten out again. 'I am not your little sister,' I reminded him. 'I'm a good eight minutes older than you are. And I don't live in a bedsit. But other than that, life in the Metropolis is fine, thanks for asking. How's tricks in the sticks, Col? Must be about that time of year when you get to do interesting things with silage.'

Colin opened his mouth while he tried to think of a suitably witty retort, but Richard was out of the car too now and he was obviously waiting to be introduced. 'Richard, this is my brother Colin.'

'You don't look like twins,' Richard said reflexively.

'Good job,' said Colin. 'Imagine the looks I'd get down at the golf club. You play golf do you, Richard?'

I hurried him inside.

There's only one thing worse than an unexpected encounter with my brother and that's an unexpected encounter with his wife. My sister-in-law Sally was stirring gravy in the kitchen.

When we came in, she didn't even leave the hob, so scared was she of letting her Bisto go lumpy. I introduced Richard, who, clearly very nervous, reiterated his surprise that Colin and I didn't look more like twins.

'Mmmm,' Sally simpered. 'It is funny, isn't it? You know, lots of people have actually said that if they saw the three of us in a room – me, Colin and Lizzie, that is – they would probably think that I was his twin instead!' She giggled uproariously at that. She always said it when meeting someone new. I don't know why she thought it was so cute, though. I thought it was just plain weird to fall in love with someone who people often mistook for your blood relative.

'How are you getting on in your bedsit, Lizzie?' she asked me then.

'It's not a bedsit,' I reminded her too.

'Oh, I remember when I lived in shared accommodation,' she said with a far-away smile, as if she were a hundred years old. She was actually two years younger than me. 'No one ever doing the washing up. People forgetting to buy the milk. It was like something out of a television programme sometimes.'

But less *Men Behaving Badly* than a temporary holding hostel for apprentice *Stepford Wives*, I should imagine. I had been to Sally's spinster flat once, for her hen night – held, very sensibly, a whole month before she was to be married to Colin so that there would be no danger of her not having recovered from the hangover before she took her vows. For a start, what kind of girl has her hen night at home instead of in the seediest nightclub in town? And secondly, what kind of hen bakes three hundred cheesy scones for the occasion? What kind of twenty-four-year-old girl even knows how to bake cheesy scones, for heaven's sake? Or has a baking tray, before she puts one on the wedding list because she thinks she ought to?

That was a hen night to remember all right. There were two bottles of wine. The red one got kicked over by Sally's great-aunty Gina who couldn't get out of her chair without the aid of two sticks and a Chippendale (though needless to say, there were to be no male strippers that night). The white bottle was wasted on trying to get the red stain out of the carpet. Then we watched *Four Weddings and a Funeral* and had an in-depth discussion on how Hugh Grant's character really missed out by not forcing Andie MacDowell to the altar in the end.

'Such a shame you're not getting married at the same time as Colin,' Sally said to me at the end of that evening, as I helped her pick sausage roll crumbs off the previously pristine carpet. 'Colin would have loved for the pair of you to have had a joint wedding. If only I'd had a twin brother too,' she added wistfully. 'He would have been your ideal man . . .'

Now she was sizing Richard up to see if he would do instead.

'What do you do?' she asked him after they'd had a bit of a dance about while she tried to shake his hand with her oven gloves still on.

'I'm an accountant,' he told her.

'Oh, really? That must be exciting,' she smiled warmly, and not at all ironically.

'Come and sit down in here, Richard,' Colin shouted from the sitting room. 'The girls can get on with the dinner. Sally likes me to stay out of the kitchen. Don't you, Sally?'

'I do,' said Sally to me in a conspiratorial whisper. 'He's absolutely hopeless, you know. If I let him try to help with the housework, I always end up having to do everything again as soon as he's gone out of the house. I don't tell him that, of course. I mean, I don't want to belittle him for doing his best to help me.'

Colin grinned at her wolfishly from the kitchen door. If he had heard her belittling his abortive attempts to make gravy, he didn't seem to care. In fact, I had a sneaking suspicion that it was all part of his master plan. Burn the Sunday roast once and you'll never be asked to do it again. Most cunning. Though it had never worked for me. I burned whatever I touched in the kitchen. Even the washing up. And yet I was always being asked back for more.

'Come on, Richard,' Colin boomed. 'You're missing the match. You do like rugby, of course.' He physically dragged Richard away while Sally filled my empty hands with a potato masher and a packet of butter.

'You do know how to mash parsnips, don't you?' she asked me. 'It's almost exactly the same as mashing potatoes.'

'I think I've got it. How's your job?' I asked.

'Oh. So, so. They've given me a little promotion to deputy head of the entire personnel department and wanted me to go to a trade fair in Frankfurt next week but Colin had already asked me to cook for his boss on Friday night so I had to turn it down.'

'Is this the twenty-first century?' I asked no one in particular as I started to mash the parsnips as if I were mashing Sally's silly head.

Mum appeared at my shoulder and told me I was doing the mashing wrong.

'Not so roughly . . . I've left your new boyfriend with the other boys. I must say he seems very nice, but then I noticed that he has a tattoo on his knuckles.' Mum sucked in her breath.

'Tattoo? What tattoo?' I asked.

'Right there,' she said, indicating the back of her left hand.

'Mum,' I sighed. 'That's not a tattoo. It's just a note in biro, to remind him that we were coming here today. Richard wouldn't get a tattoo.'

'A note in biro? On the back of his hand? Can't he remember what he's supposed to be doing from one day to the next? Honestly, Liz. Where do you find them?'

Of course, Brian Coren had been a major hit with the family. I had taken him to visit the folks shortly before the end of the spring term of that heady year we shared, when he expressed a desire to see the countryside I had grown up around. The thought of introducing him to my parents hadn't really crossed my mind until he suggested it. Well, it had, but I didn't want the relationship to end prematurely and that's what always seemed to happen when the family got involved. Perhaps it was the way my Mum would leave *Bride and Home* magazine lying casually open on the coffee table whenever I brought someone round for dinner.

I tried to dissuade him by telling him that Solihull was hardly the countryside and in any case, it was too far from Oxford for a weekend away. But Brian wasn't having any of that. He, after all, had grown up in a country where people think nothing of having to drive for three hours to the nearest corner shop, and so he insisted that we take the trip. He thought it would be fun to have a real English Sunday lunch with a real English family. I tried to explain that I had spent a good eighteen years of my life trying to avoid such a torture.

I nearly died of shock when Mum opened the door to us both and Brian immediately kissed her 'hello' on both cheeks. Such behaviour was quite different to the way things happened in our family and Mum was so taken aback she completely forgot to ask me why I wasn't wearing the scarf she had given me for Christmas.

Brian also came bearing gifts, which is a good move if you're meeting someone's parents for the first time. Mum made a great show of getting out her best cut-glass vase for the huge pink roses tied in a raffia bow Brian had bought, not at a garage *en route*, but at the swankiest florists in Oxford (I noticed that she had stuck Richard's roadside bunch into a tupperware juice holder). And to top it all, the conversation with Brian flowed so easily. My past experiences of introducing man to *mater* had been text-book examples of great failures in communication. One sixth form crush of mine had read a book about vampirism all the time my mother tried to talk to him. But not Brian.

'Lovely weather, Mrs Jordan,' said Brian. Cue monologue on sunny day that belied the late frosts that were ruining all the daffs, running into questions about the weather in New Jersey. Does it really snow every Thanksgiving? Into weather in California. How can they stand it being so hot when they go jogging? There wasn't an awkward pause all day.

After that visit, Brian Coren became the boyfriend benchmark. Every man I brought home – and in six years, I'd managed two or three more – was compared to Brian. Did he bring flowers? Did he kiss Mum 'hello' with exuberant confidence or cower behind me at the front door as if he expected my mother to be a fire-breathing dragon in pantyhose? How were his table manners? Would he eat her roast pork even if he wasn't strictly supposed to? Brian's successors failed all of these important tests. One of them, a media analyst I had somehow flukily managed to pick up in Soho and get past the third date mark, wouldn't even eat Mum's roast potatoes because he was a vegetarian and the spuds had been cooked in animal fat. It didn't impress him that Brian had set aside his entire religion to please my mum by eating her pork and we split up on the drive back to London.

'Now, do you think Richard will eat everything?' Mum asked as she dished out the rock-hard Yorkshire puddings. 'Do you remember that American boyfriend Lizzie had?' she asked Sally. The one who was Jewish but still ate my pork? What a lovely boy he was. Probably got himself kicked out of Jewish heaven for having such lovely manners.'

'He did have lovely manners,' agreed Sally.

We processed into the dining room like three serving wenches with two plates apiece. Colin was sitting at the head of the table, knife and fork upended in a manner which would once have earned him a slap on the hands.

'Who did the gravy?' he asked as he took the first mouthful. 'Looks a bit lumpy.'

Sally suddenly went a bit lumpy herself, and I thought she might be about to cry.

'Only joking, my treacle,' Colin said to reassure her. 'It's gravy fit for a king. Made by my princess.'

I noticed that I had been seated as far away from Richard as possible. Too far even to share a look of exasperation without it being intercepted by someone else. He wasn't saying much. But then he didn't really need to. Colin was holding court. He started a long monologue about the new responsibilities he had taken on with his promotion, without seeming to stop to draw breath once and yet managing to eat everything on his plate at the same time.

'We ought to have a toast; for the twins' birthdays,' Dad dared to interrupt. 'Happy twenty-seventh birthdays, Colin and Liz.'

'Twenty-seven,' Mum sighed as we all raised our glasses. 'Seems like only yesterday when my waters broke in the back of your father's new Morris Traveller. But now you're both adults.'

'Well, one of us is definitely an adult,' Colin smirked in my direction.

'What do you mean by that?' I asked.

'Well, what do you think I mean? You're nearly thirty now, Lizzie Jordan. It's about time you started to do something with your life.'

I was just about to eat the last of my mashed parsnip but I put down my fork to get on the defensive.

'Can't believe we came from the same place, you and I,' he continued blithely. 'You just don't seem to want to go anywhere with your life. And you haven't even got the excuse of being a student any more.'

'At least I've gone further than the outskirts of Birmingham,' I told him angrily, when I had recovered from the shock of his sudden attack. 'How dare you say I'm not doing anything with my life. I've been to university and I'm actually working really hard right now with a view to running my own estate agency in a couple of years' time.'

'I can't imagine you being able to sell an igloo to an eskimo,' Colin laughed.

'One day you'll eat your words,' I promised him.

'Mmm. I'll have lost a lot of weight if I have to wait until then for my next meal. Have you finished that?' he asked Sally, whisking the remains of her meal from under her nose even as he asked her. She nodded and Colin finished the best roast potato she had been saving till last, in one bite.

'You see,' he said, still chewing. 'You people have got it all wrong thinking that London is the centre of the universe and that everyone who goes there is automatically a success.

Commuting on that stinking tube day after day? I wouldn't force that trip on a sheep. Liz, if you ask me . . .'

'I'm not asking you,' I told him.

'If you ask me,' he continued regardless, 'what you really want to do is cut your losses and move back to Solihull before it really grinds you down. I can tell you're not happy there. You're not made of the right stuff for the big city. You're not getting anywhere in London, little sis. I could get you a job with some estate agency here and perhaps in ten years or so you could start thinking about branching out on your own again. I'll help you if you like.'

'I don't want to come back to Solihull,' I said petulantly. 'I am never moving back to Solihull.'

'You talk some sense into her,' Colin said with a wink to Richard. Richard smiled treacherously in return. 'If you've got a couple of weeks to spare, that is. You know, you were always the dreamer, Liz. Always having your big dreams for the future and making your incredible plans. Rushing about pretending you were going to be the next unknown to play little orphan Annie or get spotted in the supermarket by Quentin Tarantino. You'd never listen when someone told you that it couldn't be done. Always had to find out something was wrong for yourself.'

He said it in such a way that someone listening might have thought he was paying me a clumsy compliment, but I knew better than that.

'Yep, you were always the dreamer but dreams can't come true until you wake up. Dreams are nothing unless you can put them into practice. And I was always the practical one. Your stories always made me laugh though, sis. Perhaps you should think about being a novelist.'

'You could come back to Birmingham then,' Sally piped up. 'I mean, you can write anywhere, can't you? And you've got an English degree so you should be quite good at it.'

'Another waste of time that was,' Colin interrupted. 'I may not have gone to such a fancy college as you to get my qualifications in business studies but at least I've got a proper job.'

'Lizzie, could you stack the plates,' said my mother, trying to mediate in her peculiarly passive-aggressive way. I followed her into the kitchen before I gave in to the temptation to throw a punch. 'Evan, tell your son not to pick on his sister,' she called to Dad before closing the kitchen door behind us. Dad just laughed.

'Don't take too much notice of your brother,' Mum told me as I slid the plates into a bowl of soapy water. 'You know he loves you really. He just loves to pick a fight.'

'But all those things he said. They're so unfair. So what if I'm a dreamer.'

'So what indeed,' agreed Mum. 'Dreamers are the people who have the ideas that make the world a more interesting place. If they act on the dreams that they have.'

'I do,' I protested at her insinuation.

'Mmmm. I'm not so sure. What about that time you got the part in *Annie*?' she said. 'You pretended you had tonsillitis because you weren't the leading girl. I don't call that following your dreams.'

'For heaven's sake. I was only seven.'

'But you've been a bit like that ever since, sweetheart. You know, all the time you were growing up I used to wish that Colin had a little bit more of your imagination and you had a bit more of his pig-headedness. Whatever you say about your brother, and I know as well as you do that he isn't always right, when he decides to do something he does it.

He follows through and he doesn't let little things get him down. He's a trier.'

'He's certainly been trying my patience today,' I quipped.

'Well, if you're serious about starting your own estate agency, why don't you turn your annoyance on its head and do your best to prove him wrong? Use upsetting Colin as an incentive.'

'I don't want to start my own estate agency,' I admitted.

'I didn't think so,' Mum replied, sitting down on a stool and folding her arms in a way I had seen so often. How did she know? How do mothers know everything?

'So what are you hoping to do with yourself, Lizzie? Whenever I call you these days you sound like you've just had some terrible news. When you first went up to London I thought your life sounded so exciting. Now it just sounds awful. Nasty job. Nasty flat.'

'Well, perhaps it's about to pick up again,' I told her. 'Brian's coming to visit.'

'Not Brian? Lovely Jewish Brian from America?'

'That's the one.'

She clapped her hands delightedly. It seemed that everyone I told about the impending visit was almost as excited as I would have been were it not for the complications.

'You know, I always had a feeling he'd come back for you,' Mum whispered, squeezing my arm.

'He's not coming back *for* me, Mum. He's just coming to visit.'

'Yes, to visit *you*. I could tell the first time I met him that he was besotted with my only daughter.'

It was what I wanted to hear, I suppose, but it didn't make my predicament any easier. I pondered telling her about the whole e-mail fiasco, but she was already off on another unstoppable train of thought.

'You know,' she said. 'Some mothers would hold their daughters back from running off with someone who's of a different religion who lives in a different country, but your father and I, we just want you to be happy.'

'Mum, don't you think you might be jumping the gun? Brian's only stopping here for four nights. I'm not sure if that will be long enough to plan an elopement to Las Vegas.'

'But you've kept in touch all these years. I knew from the moment I saw him that he felt very deeply for you, darling. Shall I get a roast in? Chicken, of course. I know he ate pork last time but it wouldn't be respectful of me to expect him to do it again.'

'Don't get anything in,' I told her. 'I don't think we'll have time to visit.'

'Oh. Well, your father and I could come up to London and see you both while he's in the country. There's room in your house. Though, I wouldn't want to show Brian that house of yours if it's in the same kind of state as it was last time we visited.'

Which, as far as our dump went, had been spotless. I'd cleaned for three weeks before Mum's last visit.

'Perhaps you should bring him straight here from the airport. He's only coming to see you. It doesn't matter whether you're in London or Birmingham. But what about him?' Mum jerked her head towards the sitting room where I had left Richard to fend for himself. I could hear Dad laughing. Very few of my boyfriends had ever made Dad laugh.

'I've told him I'm going to be busy next weekend.'

'Good. Don't blow it, Lizzie. All I've ever wanted for you has been a life full of the excitement that mine never had. I dreamed all my teenage years of going to America, of New York and Hollywood, of standing in front of the White House in Washington. And I saved as hard as I could to make that dream happen. But then I met your dad, and three months later I was putting my America money towards a registry office wedding and a two-week honeymoon in Scarborough.'

'But you do love Dad, don't you?'

'Of course I love your dad. It's just that, sometimes, I wonder what would have happened if I hadn't got on that 137 bus that day and stood on his foot in my stilettos. I wouldn't change him for anything now. Unless Robert Redford suddenly becomes available,' she laughed. 'But if you don't do everything that you've wanted to do before you settle down, you won't ever stop wondering about those dreams. If I'd gone to America, I'm sure I would have been frightened and lonely and back home again within a week, but because I didn't go, there will forever be a part of me that thinks I would have walked down Sunset Boulevard and stepped on to Robert De Niro's foot instead of your father's.'

'Then how come, when I asked you for money to go to America straight after I graduated, you wouldn't let me have any?' I asked. 'That was my dream then too.'

'Rubbish. You just wanted to get out of having to go to work,' said Mum, getting a new tea-towel out of the drawer.

'Well, thanks a lot.'

'But now you've got your own money,' she continued. (Eh? I wondered where it was hidden.) 'You can do whatever you like now. If Brian asks you to go back to America with him, don't you hesitate, my girl. Just chuck that job in, say goodbye to that filthy house and go. Your father and I won't mind a bit as long as we get some phonecalls.'

Chuck my crappy job in? Leave my stinking flat? I couldn't believe she was encouraging me to be quite so impulsive.

'You're twenty-seven now,' she said ominously. 'You can't keep waiting for something to happen. You've got to start grabbing whatever opportunities you get by the throat. And this is one huge opportunity.'

'He's only coming to visit,' I reiterated.

'Perhaps that's what he thinks now but you could make him change his mind about going back alone. Men don't know what they want. Not really. If Sally hadn't taken the initiative with your brother, he'd have been happy to go on living here and seeing her on Wednesday nights and at weekends until I got too old to do his ironing for him.'

I was trying to imagine Sally taking the initiative. 'What on earth did she do?'

'She made him think she was the only woman worth having. She had her hair done differently and started to make out like she was having a great time without him on every night except Wednesdays. Next thing you know, Colin suddenly announced that he'd proposed. She trapped him.'

'And you're suggesting that I do something like that with Brian?' I said indignantly, as if I hadn't already been pretending that I'd been having a great time without him. 'It's not obligatory for a girl to bag a man these days, you know,' I told her contrarily, as if I hadn't spent all my days as a singleton praying for a knight in shining armour to take the responsibility out of my life.

'No, but it makes life easier,' said Mum pragmatically. 'I don't know where I went wrong to bring up a daughter who could let a millionaire slip through her fingers.'

'I don't think Brian is a millionaire.'

'Not yet perhaps. But he's a damn sight more likely to become one than the boy you've brought home with you today. That Richard's a dreamer like you, Lizzie. I can tell.

And you know what you get when you put two dreamers together, don't you?' she asked me.

'Tell me,' I begged her.

'Mortgage arrears.'

Just then, Richard poked his head around the kitchen door. He was carrying the mint-sauce boat.

'That was a top roast dinner, Mrs Jordan,' he said, with his best cheeky chappy smile. 'Don't think even my mum could have done it better.'

Mum allowed herself a proud little smile.

'Is there anything I can do to help out here?' he asked.

'Oh no,' said Mum, in very strange overtones. 'I don't think there's anything you can do any more.'

When Richard had retreated again, Mum grabbed my hands. 'I think it's destiny, you know. When I was about your age, I went to see a fortune teller on the pier at Brighton who told me that one day, one of my children would leave these shores and go abroad. Brian is coming back to take you with him. I know it.'

'But what if she meant Colin?' I protested. 'He's already left these shores once.' It was true. My brother had worked in Germany for almost two years.

'Oh, that's hardly abroad, is it?' said Mum. Despite the fact that she had cried for two weeks solid when Colin first announced that he was off, and packed him enough sandwiches to keep him going for a fortnight in case he found he couldn't eat the foreign food. For the first month he was away, I overheard several amazed conversations where my mother would sigh, 'It sounds as if you're just down the road,' marvelling that Germany had half-decent telecommunications.

'Well, I'd better get this apple crumble on the table before it goes cold,' Mum said suddenly. 'Let me know how it goes,' she added with a conspiratorial wink before returning to the dining room singing 'My bonnie lies over the ocean' as she went.

11

I got Richard out of there as quickly as was humanly possible. Luckily it was Sunday, so we had the excuse of needing to get back to London to prepare for another week at work.

'What did you think of my brother?' I asked as soon as I was sure that the car was out of sight.

'Nice bloke,' said Richard non-committally. Then he added, 'Did you two have some kind of big rivalry going on when you were kids?'

'Not really,' I lied.

'Only he seemed pretty intent on keeping you in your place today. All that stuff about going back to Solihull. And telling me to talk some sense into you!'

'Are you going to?' I asked him dryly.

'Of course not. I want you to stay in London, don't I? I've got to after all.' He squeezed my knee. 'And I'll be right behind you if you want to become a property mogul. Perhaps you can get me a decent flat while you're about it.'

'I don't really want to become a property mogul,' I told him. 'It's just that if I told Colin that I wanted to become an actress or a journalist, he might have choked to death on his Yorkshire pudding.'

'Do you want to be either of those things?' asked Richard in surprise.

'Yeah. Well, I'd certainly like to be an actress.'

'Seriously?'

'Sort of seriously. It's always been my dream.'

'Then why are you working in an estate agency?'

'I need to pay my rent, of course. And keep you in chips,' I added, just a little cruelly considering that Richard had promised to pay me back as soon as he could, but an afternoon with Colin always left me feeling cruel.

'Well, I never would have thought it,' Richard mused. 'You've never told me that you wanted to become an actress. Was that what the *Annie* crack was about? Did you do lots of drama as a child?'

'Yep. I always wanted to be little orphan Annie. Mum and Dad took us to see the show when we were seven. But I gave up dreaming about that when I was only offered "third orphan" in a church-group play.'

'It was probably only because you had the wrong hair,' said Richard, running his fingers wistfully through my mousy bob.

'Praise the Lord for that,' I cracked.

'Have you done any acting since then?' Richard probed.

'I did a bit. At college.'

'What did you play?'

'Cleopatra, Juliet's nurse, Viola in *Twelfth Night*, one of Chekhov's sisters.'

We had stopped at the traffic lights as I counted off on my fingers the rest of the parts I had taken. When I had finished, Richard looked at me in shock.

'Wow. I had no idea,' he said. 'You've done loads.'

'I don't like to talk about my glory days now,' I smiled ruefully as I put my foot down to move forward again.

'But you must have been pretty good to get all those parts.'

'Anyone could act at college. There were certainly more drama groups than revision ones.'

'You must have enjoyed it too.'

'I did. Even thought about going to drama school when I finished my degree.'

'Then what happened?'

I shrugged. 'Real life. Student loans. Overdrafts.'

'They're easily overcome. You've got to take your ambitions a bit more seriously if you actually want to fulfil them,' said Richard rather heavily. 'You say that you want to be an actress and yet you've never talked about it to me before.'

'Seems a bit of a pipe-dream now.'

'Rubbish. If Michael Caine can make a brilliant career out of playing himself, I'm sure you can earn a living. Hollywood here we come. I bet you're really good.'

'Thanks.'

'Why haven't you joined a drama group since you've been in London?'

'I just don't seem to have had time.'

'Maybe you should make some time,' he suggested, giving my knee another squeeze. So hard this time that I nearly accidentally changed gear and the clutch made a terrible crunching sound.

'Maybe,' I said disconsolately.

Oh, Richard, I sighed to myself. He was trying to be so nice. He was a nice guy. Not exciting perhaps. But very nice. A dreamer like me? Mum's accusation ran through my head. I felt horribly mean for wondering whether she had been right and squeezed his knee back out of guilt.

'Don't let other people's expectations of you become your own expectations of yourself,' he continued. 'Because nine times out of ten, they don't know what's best for you. If you ask me, your brother only ridicules the fact that you used to be a bit of a dreamer because he doesn't understand the real power of dreams. He's a worker ant. He always will be. And he wants to drag you down to his level because he knows that you're a caterpillar waiting to turn into a butterfly and he finds that rather frightening.'

We had stopped at a set of traffic lights and I looked at Richard askance. 'Where did you come up with that?'

'I studied English literature too once,' he told me.

'But you're an accountant.'

'I didn't always want to be an accountant,' he sighed. 'No one does. But I lost sight of my own dreams and got sucked in by the status and the money instead.'

'The status?' I laughed somewhat disdainfully. I had never thought of accountants as having that much standing in the scheme of things.

'You may laugh, but my family are pretty proud of me for doing what I've done. I'm a professional, you see.' He adopted a weird squeaky nerd voice to tell me that. 'I may not be living out my dream existence but at least I'm not giving my poor mother nightmares.'

'Like I am,' I snorted. 'My mother thinks my only possible route to salvation is to marry out of my situation now. She's like something out of a Jane Austen novel sometimes.'

'I expect she wants you to find yourself a nice professional,' said Richard straightening an imaginary tie.

'I expect so,' I agreed. 'With an income of at least two thousand pounds a year,' I added, mimicking Austen's money-mad Mrs Bennet.

'I think I can manage that.'

'But it's rubbish, isn't it?' I sighed then.

'What? Your impression of a Jane Austen character?'

'No. Being a grown-up. All through your childhood you can't wait for the day you hit eighteen. You tell yourself that as soon as you're officially an adult you can stay out as late as you like, with whoever you like, and go out in the morning to do whatever you want to do all day. Like eat sweets and play Nintendo. Except that it doesn't happen. You don't often find vacancies for filmstars and poets in the *Evening Standard*, so you end up getting a boring job like yours and mine to pay the rent, which means that you can't stay out late because you've got to be presentable for work in the morning. No wonder people were always telling me that schooldays are the best of your life.'

'Stop before I burst into tears,' Richard begged me. 'They don't have to be the best days, Liz. It is possible to continue having a good time well into your eighties if you work at it. You've just got to be determined not to let other people chip away at your efforts for happiness. If you want to be a professional actress, you'll have to start doing more practice and actually do some auditions. Join a bloody drama group for a start. If I want to be an artist, I'll have to spend some of my drinking money on paints.'

'Do you want to be an artist?' I asked in surprise.

'I've dabbled with the idea in the past. When I was eight, I did a really great picture of a spaceship and my teacher told me that I was good at drawing. After that, I drew on every bit of paper that came to hand until I got into trouble for drawing a horse when I should have been doing long multiplication. That was when my teacher explained to me that even though I was good at drawing, I was wasting my time, because drawing would never pay my wages. Unlike maths . . .'

'Hence accountancy?'

'Hence accountancy. I reckon there are a lot of secret artists out there,' he said, gazing out through the car window at the tall blocks of flats we were passing on the way into London, 'who abandoned all hope of ever making a living from it because some teacher with no idea told them that art wasn't a career but a hobby. If anyone said that to a child of mine, I'd tell the teacher concerned to have a look at Damien Hirst.'

'Do I need to turn down here if I'm dropping you off at your flat?' I asked, interrupting him before he could go into a rant.

'Oh, yeah. We're here already. Time really flies when I'm with you.'

'Yeah. Makes Monday come that much more quickly though,' I replied. I was on a downer to end all downers. 'Thanks for coming home with me today. I promise I'll never ever inflict such torture upon you again.'

'I had a good time,' he assured me. 'Relatively speaking. So, shall I give you a call some time this week? We could go out on Thursday night. Cinema or something?'

'Er,' I gripped the steering wheel extra hard. 'Thursday's not good. You know. I told you about Thursday. I've got a friend coming to stay.'

'Oh, yeah. I remember. So I'm not going to get to meet this friend of yours?'

I played a little drum roll with my fingernails on the steering wheel. 'I . . . er, I . . . don't really know. He's here for such a short time and he may already have made plans of his own. There are probably other people he wants to catch up with. He's got lots of old college friends for a start. People I haven't seen for years either. We'll only talk about the old days all night and you'd be bored rigid with all the in-jokes.'

'I get the message,' said Richard.

'Look, I don't . . . I don't mean any of this in a nasty way,' I tried to reassure him.

'I know,' he said, planting a dry kiss on my cheek before he let himself out of my car. 'Have a good time.' He turned to go inside, but suddenly swivelled back to look at me. I wound down the window to hear what he had to say.

'What's up?' I asked.

'I was going to ask you exactly the same question,' he countered. 'You still look really sad. Is it just because of the things that your brother was saying today?'

'No. I always get depressed when I come back to London after a day out of town,' I told him. 'It's only the thought of having to go back to that awful house again. No matter how long I stay away, it's always a complete pit when I return.'

'I know that feeling,' Richard sympathised. 'But perhaps they'll have washed up this time.'

'What? Sloppy Seema and Filthy Joe? Want to make a bet on it?'

'How about all the money I owe you?' he smiled.

I smiled back. Disdainful as I had been of Richard lately, he knew how to get a smile out of me. But then his face seemed to settle into a more serious expression and I stopped smiling too when I realised that he was about to go all soppy on me again.

'What is it?' I asked.

'My lease comes up for renewal at the end of next month,' he began. 'Stop me if you think this sounds a bit mad, but I was wondering . . .'

Oh no, I knew instantly what he was wondering. I clenched my hands into fists and dug my fingernails into my palms as I silently begged him not to say it out loud.

'Perhaps you and I could look for a place to live together? We could get somewhere nice and I promise I'd always do my share of the housework.'

'Richard,' I began.

'I know it seems like a massive step to take but we've known each other for seven months now. We get on really well. I swear I'd be asking you exactly the same question if you were just a friend, you know, instead of my girlfriend. I think of you as my best friend too.' His voice tailed off and I could see in his eyes that he wished he hadn't just said all that.

I tried to smile again but it must have been obvious by then that I wasn't going to leap into his arms and shout 'Yes, yes, yes!' As I would have done only a week before. When I was in the mood to settle for anything. Before Brian called.

I wanted to hide beneath my car seat now. I wondered if Richard could tell just by looking at me that I wasn't going to object on grounds of morality or the fact that we hadn't known each other long enough but rather the fact that Brian was about to come back into my life. Could he tell that I had spent the last few days hoping I could rekindle my old relationship and wondering whether I should chuck him before Brian came to the UK or wait to see if Brian still wanted me first?

'I'll have to think about it,' I said pathetically.

'Of course,' Richard agreed. 'I didn't expect you to give me an answer right away. It's not something to be rushed into.'

'I might not have time to think about it this week though. You know, with my friend coming.'

'Call me when he's gone. Yeah?'

'I will,' I promised him.

'I'll look forward to it,' he said, as if he didn't mean it at all.

I drove off as quickly as was safely possible. When I got to my own house I stopped the car outside and thumped my fists on the steering wheel. It wasn't fair. Richard had just made me an offer I had been waiting for for months but instead of being a source of great joy it was simply a source of further complication. Before Brian's call I might have accepted such an offer very happily. Now I felt like a swimmer who, having got just over half-way across the Channel, has suddenly been offered a lift back to Dover in a dinghy. At one time I would have climbed on board happily, but now I had the smell of croissants in my nose and was determined to try for a better life. Know what I mean?

I went up to bed as soon as I got in. I was shattered. A combination of an almighty day-long hangover, an afternoon with the family and Richard's unexpected proposal of co-habitation had left me hanging in rags.

Families, I muttered to myself as I dragged on my tea-stained pyjamas. They were supposed to be the people who gave you the most support and yet I always came away from a visit to my childhood home feeling wretched and hopeless; my head spinning with all the subtle and not-so-subtle pressure that families inflict. All those questions about my future! Did I even have a future?

But I could be in the same position as Colin, I told myself. If I wanted to. I could have a house of my own on some awful estate. A nice boring husband. A flat-screen TV and a washing machine. Colin had all those things because he didn't ever take risks like I did. When futures were being dished out, he chose the box labelled 'assured but boring'. All he had to do was work at the same firm for thirty years and be content to holiday in Weston-super-Mare for two weeks every summer.

I had chosen a different path. I had chosen to follow a route that definitely seemed less comfortable at first, but might eventually lead to far greater rewards than Colin would find if he spent the rest of his life within three miles of our parents.

I had to be in London. I told myself that London was the only place for people like me who no longer quite fitted in the places they had grown up in. I mean, in Solihull, people stared if you wore a hat when it was seventy degrees below. In London, you could walk through the streets naked but for your body piercings and attract about as much attention as the numerous pigeons. In London, I told myself, everyone was accepted and everyone had an equal chance of success. There was no one around to say, for example, you weren't any good at painting as a child so you can't be an artist now. The galleries were full of exhibitions which proved that thesis wrong. There was no one to say: 'Yo-yos will never catch on again.' Or in-line roller skates. Or whatever it was that I wanted to invent. London was where the black sheep of every family went to join a massive flock where every sheep was black and proud of it.

I had left Solihull to follow a dream and I was going to follow it. That was the thought that had run through my mind as I squared up to my brother across the dining-room table. Seeing him grow red with indignation at the very suggestion that there was life outside the Midlands, I could almost convince myself that I was right.

But back in London, sitting in the middle of the reality of my dream, wondering whether that nasty patch of mould on the ceiling was bigger than it had been a week before, I didn't feel so sure that I was doing the right thing at all.

In reality, I knew that when Monday morning rolled around I wouldn't be brimming with positivity as I strode off to the office to get on with building my empire in my spanking new trainers bought on a shopping weekend in New York. Nothing about my so-called cosmopolitan life thrilled me any more. The *frisson* of excitement that used to run through me when I got off the tube at Knightsbridge had been replaced by a sinking feeling of annoyance that I would have to force my way through the tide of tourists heading for Harrods before I could get to the office. The office where I was junior to a Cavalier King Charles Spaniel. Perhaps Colin was right. Perhaps I really needed to go home and stick with the pond life I knew.

How stupid of me to think that I would be able to make myself into something special just by going to London. Far from being paved with gold, the streets were thronged with evidence of just how far apart the dream and the reality were. The dead-eyed people at the café near the station who slopped my coffee into a polystyrene cup each morning; the miserable tube workers who never even looked at their customers, let alone said 'hello'; the other commuters who studiously avoided each other's gaze in an attempt to convince themselves that they weren't crammed more tightly into a metal box than veal calves as they made the two-mile, hour-long commute to offices where the windows were sealed shut and the air conditioning circulated nothing but fag smoke and germs. Then there were the people who actually had to sleep in the tube underpass and asked me for money each day. All of them had come to London expecting something better than this. Lured happily to bed-sit land by the bright party pictures in the back of *Hello!*.

I closed my eyes and tried to sleep. I tried to block out the negative thoughts in the hope that I might wake up and find them gone. Eventually I did manage to fall asleep, but I was soon awoken by Seema, who was shaking me by the arm.

'I think the house is on fire,' she told me urgently. 'There's smoke coming from beneath the door of Fat Joe's room.'

I leapt from my bed to follow her out on to the landing. There was indeed a fine mist of smoke emerging from beneath Joe's door. 'Well, what are we waiting for?' she asked me. 'He could be dead already.'

I made to crash through the door in true fireman style. But just as I made contact with the wood, Joe swung the door open and I careered straight into his unmade bed. When I came round, he was looking at me as though I was the mad one, even though he was wearing plastic safety goggles and a polystyrene bicycle helmet at one o'clock in the morning.

'What are you two up to?' he asked. 'Making so much noise in the middle of the night?'

'What are we up to? What are you doing, you idiot?' Seema asked. 'Why was there smoke coming out from beneath your door?'

'I'm making a radio transmitter,' Joe said, picking up his soldering iron and brandishing it in Seema's direction. 'So that when I go out you can keep a track on my movements.'

'Why on earth would we want to do that?'

'You never know when they're going to come for me,' said Joe seriously.

'They?' I asked.

'I think my activities are being watched,' Joe told me earnestly. 'Ever since I hacked into Barclays Bank.'

'You mean ever since you found their website,' Seema sneered.

'Ah yes, but there are things in that website. Encrypted messages that only the initiated can understand.'

'You're bonkers, Joe,' said Seema. 'I'm going back to bed and you had better not burn the house down while I'm asleep.'

Seema shuffled back to her bedroom but I remained sitting on the edge of Joe's bed, rubbing at my shin. It had taken quite a bashing when my commando-style rescue went wrong.

'Do you want to see how it works?' he asked me, handing me what appeared to be one of my old plastic Alice bands with a battery glued on to it.

'OK,' I said. I couldn't sleep after all.

'You walk around the room and I'll keep my back to you but tell you exactly where you are by looking at your position on the computer screen.'

I dutifully wandered around the room with Joe's new contraption in my hand.

'You're by the bed,' he said excitedly.

'Yes,' I said in amazement, although in Joe's room, which wasn't terribly big (Seema and I had convinced him that girls *needed* more room as we bagged the bigger ones) you couldn't really be anywhere but by the bed.

'It's great,' I told him however. 'I'm sure this will be really useful.'

'Could save my life,' he said earnestly.

'Mmm, could do. Perhaps you ought to make it a bit less obvious though. Disguise it in some way.'

'I've been thinking of covering it with a ribbon,' he said.

I nodded slowly. 'Yes, that would be good. No reason why anyone should get suspicious if they see you wearing a ribbon in your hair.'

Joe nodded enthusiastically and turned back to his flickering screen.

'Joe,' I said softly. 'Are you happy with your life?'

He swivelled on his chair and fixed me with his big brown eyes.

'What's that, Lizzie?'

'I mean, do you like it here in London? Are you doing everything you've ever wanted to do?'

His gaze wandered to the far side of his room where an ancient and dubiously creased picture of Pamela Anderson fought for wall space with a number of cut-away layouts of the spaceships used in *Star Wars*. He was thinking about my question. I hoped.

'I suppose so,' he said. 'Obviously I may not be able to stay here for much longer though. When the net starts closing in – as it very well may – I will probably have to flee the country. Go to Rio, I expect.'

'God, how dreadful,' I said. 'Makes my life seem much more manageable,' I added.

Joe nodded and smiled. 'Sleep tight,' he said. 'If they come for me, I'll make sure they don't touch you at all.'

I plodded back to my room. I had hoped that Joe and I would be able to have a heart to heart about the meaning of life. I had hoped that he would say something which might make me think I wasn't doing too badly for a twenty-seven-year-old. I had hoped he would tell me that things get better when you hit twenty-eight. He was two years older than me and I had hoped he might have some insider knowledge about coping with late-twenties angst. But he didn't come up with the goods.

I couldn't even laugh at the fact that he was clearly a nutter.

12

Well, I didn't sleep tight that night and Monday morning dawned before I could finish counting the mould patches on the wall.

I wasn't usually in much of a hurry to get to the office on a Monday morning. Rupert certainly wouldn't be in until twelve at the earliest. He got away with this every single week by pencilling a lot of bogus house visits into his diary for Monday morning and claiming that all the people he was supposed to have visited had stood him up when Harriet wanted to know what the flats were like. Not that Harriet ever made it in on a Monday morning either. But she was the boss, so she didn't even have to pretend that she didn't have the hangover from hell when she eventually turned up on a Monday afternoon just as I was about ready to go home again.

That Monday however, I wanted to guarantee some time to myself before the others came in. I had decided that I needed to send Brian an urgent e-mail from the office. A damage limitation one. I would have to tell Brian the whole truth about my situation and offer him the option to come over and stay at Fleapit Towers in Balham or just write the whole incident and our friendship off to experience and forget that he ever even met me.

It seemed the only thing to do. The decent thing. I trudged towards the office that morning with my head down and my heart in my boots (as if I ever actually skipped there!) and was at my desk by half-past eight.

'Lizzie, darling. What on earth are you doing here so early?'

I couldn't believe it. It was Mad Harriet. On a Monday morning? She was usually recovering from a heavy night at Annabelle's. She looked terrifically flustered as she flung her lovely Maxmara coat haphazardly on to a peg and began to rake frantically through the cluttered drawers in her desk, while I racked my brain for a reason why I was in the office so early in case she suspected industrial espionage.

'Had a bit of typing to finish off,' I said. But she wasn't really even interested.

'Good. Good,' she muttered. 'Heavens! You haven't seen my car keys have you, darling? I can't seem to find them at home, though I could have sworn I drove home from the restaurant last night. But then I couldn't find the bloody car either so perhaps I actually parked it up somewhere around here and took a taxi home after all. Do you remember?'

I shook my head.

'Ah-ha!' She emerged triumphant from the wastepaper basket. 'Found them. Great. Wonder how they got in there?'

It was a mystery.

'Now just got to find the car,' she said. 'Any clues?'

I shook my head again.

'Blast. I've got to be at the airport in less than an hour. Flying to Majorca at ten this morning. All a bit last minute, I'm afraid. Bunny's wife has taken herself for a fat-blitzing week at Champneys so he's taking me to the villa while she's safely out of the way.'

She grinned excitedly. I tried to grin back in return but my cheeks just weren't having it.

'Why don't you just get a taxi to the airport and I'll go and look for the car?' I suggested. 'I'm sure it's safe wherever you parked it.' It certainly wouldn't be moving, I thought wryly. The nice bright yellow clamps of Chelsea and Westminster's parking authorities might as well have been fitted as standard to the wheels of Harriet's neat little Mercedes coupé.

'Oh, darling. Would you really do that? I'd be ever so grateful if you could.'

I nodded.

She showed me the car keys on their solid silver Tiffany key-ring. A key-ring identical to the one Mary had bought me for my birthday, I noticed with more than a *frisson* of annoyance. Mary still hadn't called to apologise for being such a cow.

This one is for the driver's door and this one is for the ignition. No. Hang on,' Harriet hesitated. 'Perhaps this one is for the door and this one is for the ignition. Oh, God. I just can't seem to remember. What will you do?'

'I'm sure I'll work it out.'

'Oh, you're such a clever little angel. I promise I'll make you permanent staff as soon as I get back.'

She was always promising to make me permanent staff when she got back. From Spain. From the corner shop. From the bathroom.

'Now, a cab,' she grimaced. 'How on earth can I get a cab to come and meet me here at the office?'

I lifted the telephone receiver and began to call one for her.

'Easy when you know how,' I said sarcastically.

'Splendid. You are so clever,' she added, as though I were some kind of magician. 'Now, have I got everything I need? Suitcase. Passport. Spermicidal jelly. You will be OK here in the office, won't you, darling? After all, nothing ever happens much, does it? You can get people to call me on my mobile if they're absolutely desperate. Oh, hang on. No, you can't. I think I must have left it on the roof of the car when I drove in yesterday morning. Could be anywhere between my house and Sloane Square, I reckon. If you could possibly have a look for that while you look for the car . . . Tell Rupert I'm really sorry to leave you both in the lurch like this but you do understand the need, don't you, sweetheart? Do you think he'll mind awfully?'

'I'm sure he'll understand.'

I imagined Rupert's gleeful face as he arranged a round of golf for every afternoon she was away.

'I'll be flying back into Gatwick on Wednesday week. Is that taxi coming yet? Do you think I should have had my hair done first?'

'You look wonderful,' I assured her. In a dragged through the haystack backwards sort of way. She was wearing her white Jil Sander t-shirt inside out. Doggy pawprints made a muddy pattern half-way up the shins of her expensive black jeans.

'Thank you so much. Now. Have I remembered everything? Look, there's the cab already. That was pretty speedy. Come on, Hercules. We're going for a nice long walkies. All the way to Spain.' She made for the door, with her passport, her Louis Vuitton . . . and her dog.

'Harriet!' I ran after her. 'Harriet! What about Hercules?' I pointed at the stinky little Cavalier King Charles, all wet nose and runny eyes. 'You can't take Hercules on an aeroplane.'

She looked at me uncomprehendingly.

'What's the matter, darling? Why ever not?'

'Hercules? Because he's a dog, Harriet. And dogs aren't allowed to fly. Well, they are. But they have to go in the luggage hold.'

She clasped poor Hercules so close that his eyes stuck out further than ever.

'And I don't know what the rules are about taking a dog into Majorca,' I continued. 'But you certainly won't be able to bring him straight back to England afterwards. He'll have to go into quarantine.'

'Quarantine?' breathed Harriet in horror.

The taxi driver confirmed that I was right.

'At least six months in a bare-walled cage,' he nodded.

'Then what can I do?' she asked me desperately.

'Leave him in a kennel?' said the taxi driver helpfully. 'That's what we normal people do with our pets when we go on holiday, love.'

'I couldn't possibly do that,' she snorted, looking at the driver as if he had just suggested having the dog put down. 'Are you trying to tell me that I should leave my precious baby with someone he doesn't know for a whole week? I'll have to phone Bunny and tell him that I can't go.' She started to get out of the cab again.

I pushed her back in and wrestled Hercules from her arms.

'Harriet,' I said firmly. 'You must go to Majorca. I know how much you're looking forward to it. Hercules can stay with me. He knows me. I'll look after him.'

'Oh, would you?' her face brightened. 'Oh, darling. That would be so kind. But do you know what you're doing?'

'I've met dogs before. And I'm sure my landlord won't mind. He can stay in my bedroom.'

'Oh no,' Harriet said firmly. 'Hercules can't sleep if he's not surrounded by his own bits and bobs.' She fiddled with her key-ring and handed me the front-door key to her apartment in Notting Hill Gate. 'Look, he can stay with you in the office all day, but you'll have to take him home at night and go back there to let him out again each morning. It has to be before seven or he'll widdle on the Persian carpet. It is on your way in, isn't it, darling? Oh, and when you do take him out, you'll have to carry him between the house and the park. He doesn't like the feel of tarmac on his delicate feet. He quite simply refuses to walk on it.'

'You should buy him some shoes,' said the cabbie, with a wry smile in my direction.

'What a wonderful idea,' said Harriet. 'Do you think anybody makes little shoes for dogs? Lizzie, could you possibly find that out for me as well? I'm sure they probably stock them on the internet.'

'Look, do you want to catch this plane or not?' the cabbie asked.

Harriet gave Hercules one last kiss on his wet black nose before reluctantly handing him over to me once more. 'What an impatient man,' she whispered. 'You will look after my baby for me, won't you?'

I promised that I would and at last the taxi sped away. Putting Hercules down on the pavement, I turned to go back into the office. Hercules didn't follow me. When I looked to see what had become of him, he was standing exactly where I had set him down on the paving stones, shaking like a hairy white-and-ginger leaf.

'Come on, Herky,' I called in a jovial doggy sort of voice. 'Come on. Let's go inside.'

Hercules's skinny body seemed to strain towards me but his little feet did not move at all. Harriet had not been joking. This was one pampered pup who did not like the feel of tarmacadam beneath his toes. Three whistles later, I gave up and picked him up. He licked my face in pathetic gratitude. It was like being kissed by an insole from one of Fat Joe's trainers.

'We're going to have to get you out of that little habit for a start,' I warned the pampered dog, as he happily took a turn around the shag-pile carpet before widdling against one leg of my desk.

The e-mail I had been writing to Brian was still on the screen waiting to be sent. I hadn't got very far with it. 'Dear Brian, there's something I need to tell you,' it began. Where did I go beyond that? Should I make a joke of the whole thing, or take a repentant tone from the very beginning? I guessed Brian's reaction to the affair would very much depend on the light in which I myself presented my horribly extensive catalogue of lies. Perhaps he would laugh it off too if I myself seemed to think of it as no more than a game that had got out of hand.

Perhaps I should sleep on it, I decided eventually, and I switched the computer off. Besides, there was still a vague chance that Brian would never need to know. He had warned me when calling to announce his troublesome visit, that he would not be able to confirm his plans until he'd seen how that month's end of period figures were received at some big meeting or other. If it was decided that his team had not performed well enough, he might have to cancel his holiday plans altogether. He had promised to let me know as soon as he knew himself, which would be first thing on Tuesday morning – his time. Tuesday lunch time, mine. Yes, I told myself. I should hold off sending any bombshells in his direction until then. No point making myself look an idiot unless I absolutely had to.

The phone rang. It was Rupert calling from his bedroom no doubt. 'Hello, is that Harriet?' he croaked in his 'might be laryngitis' voice.

'It's Liz,' I told him.

'Is she in yet?' he asked me, sounding altogether healthier at once.

'Been and gone. To Majorca.'

'What?' he spluttered. 'What do you mean?'

'Bunny's wife has gone to Champneys, so he's taking Harriet to the villa in Majorca while the cat's away.'

'Way-hey. Good old Bunny,' said Rupert chauvinistically. 'One day I would like to meet that guy and shake him warmly by the hand. He's a good sort.'

'He's an adulterer,' I snorted. 'And Harriet spends far too much of her time waiting for moments like this – putting her life on hold for some balding old man who'll never leave his missus for her. I don't know why she bothers.'

'Because there are far fewer eligible men about than women, my dear,' Rupert reminded me. 'Some of you will have to double up and lump it. It's inevitable.'

'Then how come you're still single?' I retorted.

'Who says I am? For all you know, I might have spent the whole weekend in bed with a very lovely lady.'

I winced at the thought. I hated it when he referred to his lovely 'ladies' since he clearly treated them as anything but. As far as Rupert was concerned, it was a matter of honour that he collected girls' phone numbers but never actually used them.

'What time are you coming in?' I asked before he could elaborate on his lost weekend.

'Coming in? Are you mad? How long is Harriet away for?'

'Until next Wednesday.'

'Well, I'll see you then,' he said. 'You know I'd love to help you hold the fort, but I think I must be coming down with a terrible bout of that summer flu that's been going around. Wouldn't want to give it to you, would I?'

'Yeah right. Thanks a lot. I was hoping you might be able to help me look after Hercules. She's just dumped the bloody mutt in the office. Had no idea that she couldn't take him with her.'

'Lizzie, you know how much I'd love to help you with that too,' Rupert smarmed. 'But I'm allergic to dogs.'

'No you are not,' I protested. 'You sit in an office with him just about every day of the week.'

'And it makes my eyes stream. Haven't you noticed me sniffling?'

'I can't say I have.'

'Look, Lizzie. Just be a good girl and keep the old office ticking over for me. I promise you I'll make it up to you one day, but in the meantime, why don't you just kick back and have a bit of fun on the internet like you usually do? Send some e-mails. Surf some porn sites. Download any good ones. I'll see you next Tuesday.' And that was that.

The pig.

Well, if Rupert wasn't coming in, then I sure as hell wasn't going to hang around either. Besides, I was hungry. There were no biscuits left in the office biscuit tin but I knew I had half a packet of fairly fresh garlic mushroom tortelloni in the fridge at home. It had been there that morning at least. I knew I couldn't guarantee its continued existence with Fat Joe and Seema both at home. I had once caught Fat Joe eating a bagful of frozen croissants, uncooked, for breakfast. He said they weren't up to much. A bit too hard for his tastes.

'Come on, Hercules. It's lunch time.'

It was almost half-past nine by now.

Hercules trotted happily behind me to the office door and stepped out on to the welcome mat at the top of the steps to wait for me to lock up. I locked the door behind us and headed down the steps to the pavement. Hercules stood at the top of the steps and watched.

I had already forgotten his little, but mightily incapacitating, phobia.

'You are joking?' I said to the canine swine. 'You don't really want me to carry you whenever we have to cross a pavement? It's a twenty-minute walk to the tube station and there's no grass between here and there. And I bet you don't even go on public transport anyway! Well, I'm not having it. Harriet's in Spain and I'm your mummy until she comes back. So you're going to bloody well heel and walk like a proper dog. Come here.'

Hercules whimpered. He tried to put one paw in front of the other but just couldn't do it.

'Heel!' I demanded, patting my shin with authority.

Once again, the little front paw hesitated over taking a step on to concrete. He looked at me with his big wet eyes.

'He-el!' I tried again. I wasn't going to be taken in by the lost puppy look – it had already landed me in too many hopeless human relationships. I patted both my shins this time.

But still no dog biscuit.

'He-el. Please, Hercules. Pur-leese. Look. I'll carry you when we get to Balham, I promise. But round here, the pavement is probably quite safe even for your paws. We're in Knightsbridge. Lovely. Look,' I patted the pavement. 'Knightsbridge! Lovely and clean. I'm sure they sweep the roads here every day. Posh people live here. Let's go for a lovely walk.' Hercules remained unconvinced.

'Oh, for heaven's sake.' I stomped back up the stairs and snatched him up. He licked me pathetically again and then lay in my arms like a baby on the longer than usual walk to the tube.

'Why is that lady carrying her dog?' a little boy asked his mother.

'Why indeed?' I replied.

But thankfully, Hercules didn't mind public transport. As long as I didn't try to put him down on the floor. Which was OK until we got to Charing Cross and had to change on to a packed Northern Line train. Have you ever tried to strap-hang with a wriggling King Charles Spaniel tucked under one arm? Then I almost dropped him on the escalator at Clapham South, only managing to save him from sure oblivion by grabbing his pedigree tail. A nation's worth of animal lovers tutted loudly behind me while Hercules squeaked his annoyance.

I was met by another barrage of tutting when Hercules did his business just outside the station.

'Haven't you got a pooper scooper?' asked a rather grand old man who had caught us in the act.

'No I haven't,' I told him, picking Hercules up again. I had only just managed to put the dog down in time to avoid having the mess go straight into my coat pocket. I was hot and bothered from having carried him all the way from Knightsbridge in the first place. I was in no mood to do any scooping.

'There's an automatic five-hundred-pound fine for people who let their dogs foul the pavement round here,' the gentleman boomed. 'I suggest you clear that mess up or I will report you to the council.'

'What?' I snapped.

'Scoop the poop,' he told me. 'If your dog fouls the pavement, you are legally and morally obliged to clean up after him.'

'Right,' I said sarcastically.

'Right,' said the grand old man. Only he was serious.

But what could I clear the mess up with anyway? I wasn't in the habit of carrying plastic bags around. If I had had a bag in my pocket, I told myself, I would have sorted the matter out right away, but as I didn't, I tried to walk on, eyes forward, ignoring the public-spirited chap who had stopped me. But he wasn't about to let the matter drop.

'Young lady. I want you to know that I am making a note of your description and a description of your dog to hand in at the police station. I can assure you that they will not take this matter lightly.'

I have to say, I couldn't imagine the police dropping a triple murder inquiry to investigate a case of serious dog mess but the old man seemed to think otherwise and was indeed making notes.

'Look. I haven't got anything to clean the stuff up with,' I told him. 'This isn't even my dog. I'm just looking after him for a friend.'

'Then the dog is your temporary responsibility and therefore his mess must be too. You can use this.' The man handed me a rather flimsy blue and white striped plastic bag.

'What's this?' I asked.

'It's a bag.'

I took it from him and said thanks, hoping that would be the end of it, but he still wouldn't leave me alone.

'Go on then.' He jerked his head towards the mess. He was going to watch me.

'Oh, you're joking,' I protested. 'It's all runny.'

'Dog ownership has its pleasures and its problems,' he told me.

'I've already told you, this is not my dog.'

'Tell that to the court, young lady,' the man said, actually grasping me by the top of the arm and pushing me towards Hercules's calling card.

'Take your hands off me. I could have you for assault,' I warned him.

'And who do you think they'd believe?' he asked me. 'An upstanding member of the community with an illustrious career in the army behind him and ten years' involvement in the neighbourhood watch? Or some kind of illegal refugee dog-stealer?'

'Now hang on. I'm not an illegal refugee and while this dog isn't mine, I certainly didn't steal it.'

'Then perhaps you would be so kind as to give me the name and address of the dog's real owner so that I can check up on that detail later on. Don't think the police don't know about the dog-stealing racket in these parts, young girl. They know all about it. You drugged-up teenagers stealing people's pets to be sold into animal experimentation labs so that you can get a fix of marijuana to inject.'

'What?'

'You heard me. I've got your number, missie. Don't you pretend that I haven't.'

Drug abusers stealing dogs? I pondered asking the man if he'd been at the kaolin and morphine himself.

'Look, I'll clean it up, OK,' I sighed. 'Just leave me alone. Why don't you go to the library and check up on your obscure bye-laws or something?'

'I'll just stand here to make sure you do the job properly, if you don't mind.'

'Actually, I do mind,' I told him.

'Well, I don't mind whether you mind or not. I'm staying.'

'Fine,' I snarled and set Hercules down on the grass verge while I sorted the mess out using the plastic bag like a makeshift glove. 'You're going to have to learn to be more careful,' I hissed at the mutt.

'Are you talking about me?' said the deaf brigadier.

'No, if I'd been talking about you, I would have been using more swear words. Sir,' I added, for facetious good measure. The poo was in the bag now and I waved it in front of his nose so that he could see. 'Good enough for you?'

'Hmm. Well, don't let me catch you at it again,' he snorted, before striking off in the direction of the tube station.

'Thanks so much,' I said to Hercules. 'That really made my day.'

I looked around for somewhere to dump my dainty plastic bag of doggy doings, but couldn't find one.

'Bugger.'

I was about to drop the bag behind someone's garden wall when I noticed that while he was not standing over me any more, the conscientious colonel was still watching from the end of the street.

'What?' I muttered under my breath. He was definitely waiting to see what I would do with the bag, so I had to carry Hercules under one arm, and the bag of shit in the other hand until I could be sure I was no longer being observed. But every time I looked over my shoulder, the neighbourhood watcher was still there. I could hear the metal cap on the end of his stick as he tapped along at a safe distance behind me.

Could my life get any worse? Now I was carrying a plastic bag full of shit to add to my sack-load of worries. I decided I would have to try to lose the old codger. But there were no dark alleyways between the tube station and the house. Next thing I knew, I was at the top of our street, standing outside the corner shop. The colonel was on the other side of the road, nonchalantly examining the black fly on someone's wilted roses as he pretended not to be watching me.

I didn't want him to know my address in case he really did send the council round, so I had to try some delaying tactics which I hoped would make him tire of his pursuit. I needed to go into the shop anyway. We always needed milk. (Having said that, we always seemed to have either no milk at all or three pints of the stuff.) And I also needed dog food. Harriet hadn't left any at the office and I was pretty sure we wouldn't have any at home. (Though Fat Joe probably had some somewhere. All those pies he ate straight from their polythene wrappers certainly smelled as though they were filled with the stuff and I knew that he was hoarding all manner of tins for Armageddon.) Anyway, Habib's – the twenty-four-hour corner shop – would have a varied and cheap selection. Emphasis on the cheap. I walked straight in, Hercules still tucked under my arm (poo bag dangling gracefully from my wrist like an elegant evening purse), and was surprised when Habib, who was usually so nice and friendly whether it was six in the morning or half-past eleven at night, demanded that I go straight back out in a not very friendly way at all.

'No dogs!' he said.

'Habib!' I pleaded. 'I only want some milk, some bread and some dog food. I'll be thirty seconds.'

'No dogs. That's the rule. Leave him outside.'

'OK,' I said, backing out into another pensioner. Why did people have dogs, I wondered? I'd been in charge of Hercules for less than an hour and already I felt like I had leprosy as well as a mutt. Dog owners were clearly that popular. I set Hercules down outside the shop and fastened his lead to the drainpipe. At which point, of course, he started to whimper and the colonel narrowed his eyes as if he suspected terrible cruelty. 'Can't I bring him in?' I begged Habib through the half-open door. 'He's a pedigree. He just won't stand on tarmac.'

'What is this silly nonsense about tarmac? You cannot bring him into the shop. What about hygiene?'

'What about it?' I was tempted to say as I looked at a dust-covered row of Roses chocolate boxes that hadn't been renewed in the two years I'd been living on that street. But Hercules looked at me as though he might have a heart attack if I left him standing on the pavement while I disappeared from his sight for a moment to buy him a tin of Pedigree. What could I do? I took off my coat, spread it on the floor, and Hercules climbed on. The whimpering stopped and I bought the dog food. Unfortunately there wasn't any Pedigree Chum so I bought something with a nice orange label instead, Cheapster's Own brand, illustrated with a dog that bore an uncanny resemblance to a polar bear. Perhaps polar bear was what the stuff was made of.

'Since when are you getting a dog, Lizzie Jordan?' Habib asked as he wrapped up my purchases in another one of those practically see-through plastic bags.

'Never,' I replied.

He looked at me strangely.

'Oh, you mean, when did I get the dog I brought in just now? Well, he belongs to my boss. And I'm looking after him until she comes back from her holidays next Wednesday. As if I didn't have enough to worry about as it is.'

'Worrying about what?' asked Habib. 'Do you want to talk about it?' He could never resist a good gossip. And somehow I felt that if I told him what was going on, he might just have enough wide experience of life to come up with a decent solution. He had probably spoken to someone with a similar problem only that morning. I spilled the story out again.

'You should always be telling the truth,' he sighed when I had finished.

'I had a feeling you might say that,' I said. 'But what do you think I should do about it?'

'You could put some money in here,' he rattled the brightly coloured collecting tin for his Hare Krishna temple. 'And we will pray for you.'

'Thanks all the same, but I'd probably be better off selling my soul to my own devil. How much do I owe you for the dog food?' I asked. Outside, Hercules was keening like a spirit damned to hell.

'Just one moment,' said Habib. 'I'll just weigh this.'

I watched in horror as Habib picked up the bag of shit that I had absent-mindedly put down on the counter as we talked, and put it on to his shiny electronic scales. 'This is mince, is it?' he asked.

I snatched it back. 'Stewing steak,' I told him quickly. 'But I bought it in town.'

'This is looking very much like one of my shop bags,' he said doubtfully.

'I know. All the small shops are using them these days. Perhaps you should change the design you buy to make your shop more distinctive.'

'But blue and white are my shop's colours,' he said, looking most put out.

'I'll never buy anything from anywhere else again,' I assured him, taking my change and making for the door.

'Just one minute. Do you want to know what I really think you should do about your problem?' Habib began, but before he could even get started, I noticed that Hercules was looking all tremble-legged on my jacket and leg trembling usually meant only one thing.

'See you tomorrow, I expect,' I said, rushing out just in

time to save my jacket from a soaking, but not able to get Hercules away in time to save the paper sack full of potatoes which formed an integral part of an artful display of veg outside the shop. I made a note to tell Seema to go to Safeway for her veg for the next couple of weeks.

'Done my shopping. Going home now!' I shouted across the road to the old git who was still following me. 'I expect my boyfriend's waiting for me. He's a big guy. Gets violent if he doesn't eat regular, like.'

It worked. The colonel nodded curtly and set off in the opposite direction.

I threw the poo bag straight over the next garden wall.

Trying hard not to gag on the fatty, meaty smell, I forked Hercules's dinner out on to a saucer as soon as we got into the house. I gave him a whistle to say that dinner would be served in the kitchen, but it transpired that he was as funny about the shiny tiles in the kitchen as he was about tarmac and refused to cross the threshold from the sitting room. I couldn't really blame him. Since getting a bare foot covered in spilt honey which subsequently picked up three pubic hairs and a couple of price tags, I never went into the kitchen without shoes myself. I took the saucer to the doorway and placed it just within Hercules's reach so that, while spillages would hopefully be confined to the tiles, Hercules's feet could remain safely on the shag pile.

He sniffed the bowl of dog food disdainfully, like he wasn't a spaniel but A.A. bloody Gill.

'I knew that would happen,' I told Seema, who had appeared behind Hercules *en route* to make a cup of tea.

'What?'

'I knew he wouldn't eat that bloody dog food. Honestly. They're all the same,' I told him. 'Whatever brand you get.

They're all made at the same factory out of bits of the same old racehorse. Don't you try to tell me that by paying an extra quid a tin you're getting a bit of a Derby winner as opposed to the one that came in second.'

'Why is there a dog in the house?' Seema asked suddenly. She had been upstairs doing coursework for the Business Spanish module she was taking as part of her MBA and this was her first sight of the little mutt.

'It's Harriet's. She's gone to Majorca for a week and I've been left holding the dog. He's called Hercules.'

'Oh. wow. Hercules? What a nice name. Oh, isn't he sweet?' Seema said, getting down on her knees to ruffle his fur. 'Aren't you a bootiful little bwoy?' she said to him. He responded by licking her nose.

'Seema. Please. He's just a bloody dog.'

'Aaah.' She had Hercules on her lap by now and was cuddling him close. 'Don't be so mean to him. Here he is without his mummy and you're trying to feed him some awful crap that even Fat Joe wouldn't touch. It's not his fault he doesn't want to eat cows' lips – that's what it's really made of, you know, not horses. You got that wrong. I've got some chicken in the fridge. He can have that instead.' With Hercules still in her arms she made for the fridge and brought out a juicy piece of roast chicken breast.

'Hey,' I said. 'If you don't want that, I could have put it in a sandwich for myself.'

'Get your own,' she replied, putting Hercules down on the work surface next to the sink while she cut the chicken into little bite sized pieces and put them into a plastic bowl. I thought for a moment that she was going to add some kind of garnish. Or perhaps whip up a masala sauce. (Not that she could cook.) 'There you go, sweetheart,' she murmured as she set the new dish down. 'None of that nasty processed rubbish for you. You're a pedigree dog, I can tell.'

But Hercules still wasn't interested. Well, he took perhaps a slightly deeper sniff at his lunch but quickly recoiled again with one limp paw lifted in ever such a pathetic gesture.

'See. He doesn't like your chicken either,' I told her, not without a slight sense of triumph. 'He's just a spoiled mutt, Seema. Leave that saucer on the floor there and he'll eat it when he's hungry.'

'He's hungry now. I can tell. Look at his sorrowful eyes.'

'Hark at Rolf Harris.'

'His tummy is rumbling. I think he might be feeling dizzy. Perhaps he'll only eat out of his own bowl. My parents had a neighbour whose Yorkshire Terrier was incredibly particular like that. He would have starved to death before he ate anything out of a bowl that didn't have his name on it.'

I rolled my eyes heavenwards. 'I do hope you're joking.'

''Fraid not. He lost nearly half his body weight when the bowl got broken and it took two weeks to find an identical replacement. Didn't Harriet give you all Hercules's bits and bobs to make him feel at home?'

'She was in such a bloody hurry to get to the airport that she almost forgot she couldn't take him with her anyway,' I explained. 'She just gave me the keys to her flat and said I should put him to bed there every night and pick him up again on my way into work in the morning but I'm buggered if I'm going to go out of my way to do anything for this flea-bag. He's a dog. He can sleep in the kitchen and he'll eat out of anything when he's really hungry.'

Seema set her mouth in a straight, disapproving line. 'Well, if you really can't be bothered to take him home, you could at least go over there to get him his own bowl and his blanket. How would you like it if your parents had dumped you with some strange family with not even your favourite teddy bear for company?'

'They frequently did. Look, I am not schlepping all the way over to Harriet's flat to pick up a piece of stinky blanket. If he really needs a stinky blanket, he can have one of Fat Joe's. I'm going to check my national lottery numbers on Ceefax and see if I've won enough money to get me out of the mess I'm in over Brian.'

'I see. I take it Mary still won't let you borrow her flat for the weekend then? Did you call her and grovel like I suggested?'

'No, I did not. It's she who should be grovelling, anyway. She's the one who was so bloody mean. After everything I've done for her.'

'Success changes people,' Seema told me gravely.

'Is that why I'm still the same lovable person I used to be?' I muttered.

'So, who's looking after Harriet's flat while she's away?' Seema asked as she tried to handfeed Hercules some chicken. He wasn't having that either.

I shrugged. Three lottery numbers that I didn't have later, the penny dropped. 'No one,' I said, sitting up. 'There's no one in Harriet's flat all week.'

'Are you thinking what I'm thinking?' I could almost hear the cogs in Seema's brain whirring into action.

'Hercules really does need his own blanket, doesn't he?' I said, suddenly very enthusiastic. 'Come on. Let's go to Harriet's place and fetch it.'

'Bags I carry the dog,' said Seema. I wasn't going to argue with that. She'd learn soon enough.

Though I had been at Corbett and Daughter's Estate Agency for so long that I had almost broken a chair leg by carving notches for the passing days into it like some prisoner on a life sentence, I had never been to Harriet's flat before. When Seema and I finally found the block that matched the address she had given me (Harriet's handwriting was beyond dreadful – she should have been a doctor), I looked up in disbelief. It seemed to go up for ever. An elegant red brick Victorian building with a huge front door flanked by seven brass nameplates and corresponding shiny doorbells.

'This is fantastic!' said Seema, throwing herself down on to an overstuffed leather sofa in Harriet's sitting room moments later. 'How much money must she make at that agency to be able to afford a place like this?'

'Nothing,' I assured Seema. 'I type up the accounts. But I think she may have had a thing with a Saudi prince when she was younger. And there's family money, of course. I think her family own some village on the south coast.'

I looked closely at a pencil sketch of a little girl which stood on the marble mantelpiece. I didn't know much about art, but I was pretty sure that it was a genuine Picasso. Harriet had once mentioned that her father had met the great man in Paris and swapped stock market advice for some speedy sketches.

'There's nothing in the fridge except chicken breasts for the dog and Cristal champagne,' Seema announced. She was now skulking around the kitchen. 'Oh my God, Liz, you've got to see this. She's got one of those gorgeous Dualit toasters. I've always wanted a Dualit toaster. And a cappuccino machine. Bloody hell, she's even got a juicer.' She looked inside it. 'Never used. Of course. This is a dream flat,' she sighed. 'What a lucky cow.'

We left Hercules eating his chicken from bone china and took in the rest of the flat. There were two huge bathrooms leading off from the hall. One in black marble. One in white.

The white one had a massive double shower so that two people could rinse off at once. Fluffy fresh towels hung on the towel rail. Seema buried her face in their fabric-conditioner softness and laughed at the opulence of it. The towels in our house had probably been dishcloths in a house like this in a past life.

The bedrooms were vast too. All four of them. And in the master bedroom, to Seema's utter glee, we found a four-poster bed with thick red curtains. It was like something out of a costume drama on the life of Elizabeth the First. You couldn't fail to get laid if you slept in a bed like that.

'Harriet was probably born in that bed,' I told Seema. 'Her family used to own half of Scotland.'

Seema was already bouncing on it. 'Well, the mattress is a bit soft, which isn't much good for your back. But imagine having a four-poster! Liz, this is magic. Come on in.'

'Later. Later,' I told her. 'I want to finish exploring first.'

Harriet had the top-floor flat and a spiral staircase led up from the middle of the sitting room to a roof garden. I climbed slowly up the wrought iron steps and out into a little glasshouse which covered the opening. Stepping out of the glasshouse I managed to put my size six trainers straight into one of Hercules's delicate little turds but I didn't care, because, when I had finished wiping the muck off on the edge of some terracotta planter, I looked up to see the most amazing view.

Far into the distance London lay before me like a toy town. Turning to the east I could see the British Telecom tower sticking out of Bloomsbury like an upended baby's rattle. Further east still, the futuristic pyramid of Canary Wharf, the tallest building in the country, glittered in the sunlight and I could just make out the faint flash of the white light to warn passing aircraft that the tower was bigger than you might expect. That was wonderful in itself, but when I turned to the south, the view was even better. Because looking south from Harriet's roof garden I could see the tops of the tallest trees in one of the country's greatest parks. Hyde Park.

'She's got a view of Hyde Park!' I cried, almost overcome with emotion. Relief flooded through me. 'She's got a bloody view of Hyde Park!' I shouted down the staircase to Seema. 'Come up. Come quickly. It's perfect!'

'So, are you looking forward to Brian's visit now?' Seema asked me, as she emerged from the glasshouse that covered the stairs behind me.

'Looking forward to it? I can't bloody wait. Hooray for Harriet.'

'Hooray for Hercules too,' said Seema soppily, just before she too put her trainers in some of his unattended mess.

The decision was made. I would pretend that Harriet's flat was mine. We spent the whole of that afternoon scouring the place for anything that would suggest otherwise, in between bouts of sunbathing up in the roof garden which was, of course, a perfectly designed sun-trap.

Harriet's family photographs in their shining silver frames were consigned to the backs of drawers and cupboards. It would be far too tricky to try to pass off her relatives as my own since many of Harriet's relatives were faces that Brian might have recognised from the BBC's coverage of the House of Lords which he occasionally liked to watch on satellite. Bundles of unopened post (mostly bills from Harrods and Harvey Nichols) addressed to The Lady Harriet Corbett were consigned to an almost empty cornflakes box on the top of the fridge.

Seema decided that rather than change the message on

Harriet's answering machine, we should just unplug the whole thing and stash it in a cupboard.

'Now all you've got to do is bring a couple of pictures of your family round and replace her clothes in the wardrobe with yours.'

'Seems a shame to have to do that,' I said, fingering a beautiful red silk tunic. But I knew that none of it would fit me. Harriet had the figure of a baby bird. A baby bird that has been dead for a couple of weeks and nibbled by maggots. Yep, the cow was too rich and too thin, can you believe it?

'Does this look like the kind of flat that I would live in?' I asked Seema seriously when we had finished making the place 'my own'.

'I certainly think so,' she nodded. 'To the manor born.'

'I can't help thinking we shouldn't really be doing this, though,' I said, having a momentary pang of conscience as I hid a photograph of Harriet as a plump-cheeked debutante face down in a drawer. 'Should we be doing this?'

'Of course we shouldn't. Not really. But they do say that what you don't know can't hurt you and how will Harriet ever find out? If you don't do anything about the dust we can see exactly where the photos need to go when we put them back. And if she does catch you out, you can always say that Hercules refused to sleep in the flat on his own so you had to stay over to comfort him.'

'It is foolproof, isn't it?'

'Like a tetrapak,' said Seema.

It wasn't an analogy I would have chosen, considering the trouble I had opening milk cartons.

'Relax,' she added, sensing that she hadn't dispelled my nervousness. 'If you ask me, this is fate. You needed a fabulous flat and Harriet has provided you with the keys to one.'

'Yeah, you're right,' I conceded. 'Thank you Bunny for taking Harriet away for the week. And thank you Hercules for having to eat out of bone china.' I gave the dog an affectionate little pat. 'My skin has been saved.'

I looked out of the window one more time, in the direction of Mary's flat. A considerably smaller flat, as it happened. 'And up yours, Miserable Mary.'

When we got back to Balham however, I found a message from Mary on the answer machine that almost made me feel guilty for taking her name in vain like that. I called her back right away.

'Look, I'm really sorry about Saturday lunch time,' she said, all sugary unctuousness. 'I wasn't much of a friend to you, was I, sweetheart?'

I resisted the temptation to say anything too sharp in reply.

'And I really missed having a good old gossip over lunch. I had been looking forward to it for ages.'

'Me too,' I admitted.

'We don't get to see each other often enough as it is. So I was thinking, perhaps I could make it up to you. Perhaps we could go out this evening instead. You've got to pick up your birthday present anyway and I've been invited to a party. Why don't you come? I know it's a bit short notice and it'll probably be deathly dull but at least we won't have to pay for the drink.'

'Where is it?' I asked, trying not to sound too eager. Strictly speaking it was a work night, but with Harriet out of the way, I decided it would be stupid to turn down any invitations when no one would know whether I made it to the office next day for nine or half eleven. If at all.

'It's at the Hyperion,' Mary sighed, as if she was telling

me that a gang of our mates had decided to meet up at Burger King on Balham High Road.

'The Hyperion?'

'It's an after-show party for the Golden Brothers.'

'Wow.' I couldn't help myself. The Golden Brothers were fast taking over from Versace empire as purveyors of glittery Euro-tat to the rich and famous. Then it hit me. 'A fashion party?' I groaned. 'I've got nothing to wear.'

'Don't worry about that,' laughed Mary. 'Come over to my place. I'll sort you out. I just had a bundle of goodies delivered. Something is bound to fit you.'

A bundle of goodies? Sounded great. It was the kind of offer I couldn't be expected to refuse. And although I probably should have been wondering what Mary's ulterior motive was for suddenly being so nice, I agreed to be at her flat as fast as London transport would carry me.

'Oh, no,' she said. 'I can't wait that long to see you. Take a cab.' And she gave me her account number to charge it to. Mary Bagshot was number one friend again.

13

When I arrived at Mary's gorgeous flat, she buzzed me into the building from the bathroom. She was still lying in her tub, up to her neck in bubbles, looking horribly comfortable as she got all soft and fragrant. I had only had time for a quick flannel wash before I came out and felt rather grubby as I sat down on a cream velvet upholstered stool.

'I've missed you,' she purred.

'You only saw me on Saturday morning.'

'I know. But it's a long time to be angry with someone, isn't it?'

'Were you angry with me?' I asked in surprise.

'A little bit,' she admitted. 'But only because I had PMT. When I got home and took a few Feminax, I realised what a cow I'd been. You weren't asking for all that much really. So I've decided that I want to help you after all. With the flat,' she announced. I could sense that she was waiting for me to look suddenly grateful. I smiled. I should have said thank you. But although she had come up with the old PMT excuse, she hadn't actually, officially, apologised to my face as I suddenly felt she needed to.

'Actually,' I told her, wickedly relishing my sudden upper hand. 'I don't need your help on that front any more anyway.'

She raised an eyebrow. 'Really? Did you tell Brian that you'd been lying? Is he still coming over?'

'No and yes. Yes, he is still coming. And no, I don't need to tell him the full story because a friend has lent me her flat in Grantchester Square.'

Mary, who had been in the process of taking a sip from the glass of white wine on the bathrack almost choked. 'Grantchester Square? Who on earth do you know who can afford to have a flat there? That's Arab sheik land.'

'I've got lots of well-connected friends that you don't know about,' I said mysteriously.

'Obviously,' she sneered.

'And one of them is going to be out of town this weekend.'

'How very fortunate,' said Mary, unable to avoid sounding just a little bit peeved.

'But I suppose I still need your help,' I added, casting my eyes downwards. 'I mean, you won't go telling Brian the truth, will you? You won't send him an e-mail or anything that might drop me in it.'

'What kind of bitch do you think I am, Lizzie?' she asked me. 'I've just told you that I wanted to be able to help you. I've been thinking about what I could do for you all weekend,' she continued. 'It's just that, when you said you wanted me out of my own flat and assumed I could just go and stay with Mitchell, you touched on a rather sore point.'

'I did?' I was all ears.

'Yes. You know I'd love to go and stay with Mitchell. It's just that he doesn't want me to. I think I love him a lot more than he loves me.'

'Oh, Mary,' I said, leaning over the bath to put my arm around her and getting soaked in the process. 'You should have said. I would have understood.'

'I know,' she pouted out her lower lip like a baby. 'I just get so used to all the bullshitting and putting on this inscrutable face for work that I don't seem to be able to switch it off sometimes. Can you forgive me?'

'Of course I can.'

'I really want to help you make a go of things with Brian. I was going to let you have the flat and stay at the Metropolitan so that I wouldn't be in the way while you got things going again, but now that someone else has stepped in and helped you with that, is there anything else I can do?'

I bit my lower lip and allowed the thought that perhaps I shouldn't let Mary get involved at all to pass across my mind for just a second. Then I said, 'You could perhaps lend me a couple of decent outfits. I mean, I'm going to look a bit out of place sitting in my penthouse in my Top Shop specials.' I wasn't indebting myself too much with that, surely. If Mary hadn't had a wardrobe full of Armani, if all her clothes had been from Oasis, I wouldn't have thought twice about borrowing something. It was a natural thing, wasn't it? Girls swapped clothes all the time. It didn't mean that she would have anything over me.

'Help yourself to anything in my wardrobe,' she said generously.

'Anything?'

'Anything,' she said. 'You are my best friend.'

'I'm so glad we've made it up,' I told her. 'I really hate falling out with you.'

'I hate arguing with you too, Liz. It makes me so unhappy. Now help yourself to anything you need for Brian's visit from my bedroom. Except the red Armani,' she added as I raced to raid her cupboards.

Her wardrobe was like every girl's dream. Mary had made a lot of designer friends during her days in fashion PR and they were still keen to keep in touch now that she had the ear of some of the world's most beautiful men and women as a talent agent. I was green as a gherkin when she told me that she rarely bothered to go shopping any more since sooner or later someone would bike over the ideal outfit in exactly her size, gratis.

They biked over a lot of outfits that weren't exactly her size too, I noted with a grin. Mary wasn't terribly good at passing on the dresses she received for some of her skinny actress clients, preferring to keep them for herself in anticipation of 'thin days' ahead.

I pulled out a gorgeous green sequinned dress that looked like it had been pinched from a mermaid's suitcase.

'That'd look lovely with your hair,' said Mary, who had emerged from her bath and was now wrapped in a big fluffy robe. 'But it's only a size eight.'

'Size eight?' I gasped. 'Who on earth is a size eight?'

'I might be one day soon,' she said hopefully. 'I've signed up with a personal trainer.'

'Is that good?' I asked.

'I don't know. I haven't had time to see him yet. Why don't you try the brown dress instead?'

'Brown? That's not really my colour.'

'No? I think it might be.'

She held a brown dress up in front of me. All the colour seemed to drain from my face. 'Lovely,' she said.

'I don't think so.'

'Well, at least try it on. A bit of make-up will soon stop you from looking so pallid.'

'Only a year in the sun would stop me from looking pallid now.'

'I know,' she said, opening her industrial sized box of make-up tricks. 'I keep meaning to book myself into that spa in Malta again, but I can never seem to find the time.'

'I'd make time if I had the money,' I told her, as I shrugged on the brown silk shift.

'I don't think you'd really want to go there.'

Mary cocked her head to admire me in her dress. 'I think that looks classy.'

'Mmm. I think I look like one of those sausages wrapped in bacon that you get at parties.'

'Not at any parties I've been to recently,' she said, but I could tell she was trying hard not to agree. 'Anyway, you're wearing that tonight.'

'Are you sure? I look so pasty.'

'Once you've got a bit of slap on you'll look like a star. Let me put some of this new eye-liner on you,' she said, stepping forward with a pencil. 'It's not available over here yet. That travel show girl I've been looking after brought me a couple of sticks back from a trip to the States. It's supposed to tighten your eyelids and brighten your eyes as it decorates.'

'How on earth can it do all that?' I asked sceptically.

'It contains some extract of emu oil but don't let that put you off.'

'Emu oil? Is that?' I decided not to ask her to elaborate but she had already decided she would.

'Mmm, it's rendered from emu fat. Boiled down in huge vats. It's the new miracle cosmetic ingredient. Incredibly moisturising and yet non-comodogenic,' she added, as she poked the pencil right into my eye.

'Ow.' I stumbled backwards on to the bed.

'Oh, shit, Liz,' said Mary, rushing forward with a tissue. 'I didn't mean to do that. Look, the line's gone all smudgy. Do you want me to do it again?'

'I think I'll do it myself, thanks all the same,' I told her, safely removing the pencil from her unsteady hand.

'Are you OK?'

'I think so.'

'You don't think we should rush you to the accident unit and see if you need an eyepatch like you did that time at college? What was the name of the girl who stabbed you when you were getting ready for that play?'

'Phylidda Crawley.'

'That's it. Phylidda Crawley. God, she was really jealous of you, wasn't she? Probably wanted to make you have to have a glass eye,' she added with a laugh. 'Wasn't she mad at you because she thought you were trying to steal her boyfriend?'

'Well, I wasn't,' I said, struggling to open my eye so that I could look at the damage in the mirror. 'And I'm not after Mitchell either, if that's what you were thinking.'

'I just slipped,' said Mary, rather seriously.

Fortunately, no major surgery was needed. By the look of the streak of blue liner on my lid, I had managed to close my eye before too much harm was done. But I was still squinting just a little when we got to the party an hour later. Mary handed me her sunglasses.

'I'll look a prat,' I told her.

'You'll look just like everyone else,' she said.

She was right, of course. The lobby of the hotel was full of people wearing sunglasses, though the sun had long since set; all conspicuously trying to look inconspicuous. While I waited in the long queue to hand our coats in at the cloakroom (Mary had people she simply had to talk to – and as she thought I might be bored she promised to get all business out of the way while I dealt with the coats), I watched more new arrivals, all hovering for slightly longer than necessary by the door, in case the paparazzi hadn't had time to get their best sides.

The stinging pain in my eye had somewhat taken the edge off the anticipation I had felt when Mary called to invite me to the party – the only bash she had ever taken me to before was an afternoon launch for a new brand of tights. But now that we had actually arrived, I felt the bubbles of excitement begin to rise inside me again like the bubbles in the champagne that was being handed out all around me. And, if the truth be known, I was still reeling from the fact that as I had walked through the huge double doors of the Hyperion, a paparazzo had actually focused his camera on me, even if he did stop clicking as soon as his blunt Australian colleague told him, 'That's no one, mate.'

But no one or not, that night I had an invitation to what was clearly the hottest party in town. For once I was not one of the pale-faced girls in the crush on the wrong side of the red rope, trying to ignore the rain, hoping to catch a glimpse of some children's TV presenter or a minor British film star as they raced from limo to lobby. Nor was I one of the people walking back to the tube from some awful smoky pub who would pass events such as these and try to convince themselves, even as they craned their necks to look inside, that they had been having a better time at the Slug and Lettuce. I *was* on the inside. Even if I was being largely ignored in the queue to hang up coats.

Every face I cared to focus on seemed familiar. I found myself saying 'hello' in ever such a familiar way to a friendly looking man before his blank gaze reminded me that I didn't know him from anywhere but a cough sweet commercial.

The gregarious star of a West End musical, his face still orange from that evening's greasepaint, helped a former soap actress with her jacket. I couldn't help staring at her – I was used to seeing her playing the battered wife in a tatty nylon cardigan but here she was in a strappy blue dress, her glossy hairstyle very much more London than Liverpool. And when I heard her cut-glass vowels float across the lobby towards me as she shared a joke with the hotel's manager, I felt even more strongly that I had been admitted to an inner sanctum. How many of those poor sad people outside would ever guess she spoke like that, for example?

'Hello again,' said a man behind me. He put his hand on my bare shoulder and turned me towards him for a kiss. But his face echoed mine in surprise when he saw who I was. Or rather who I wasn't.

'God, I'm sorry,' he said. 'Man-handling you like that. I thought you were Arabella Gilbert, for a minute there. God, I'm so embarrassed.'

'Don't be,' I said.

'I'm really sorry.'

'You've made my night,' I told him.

But he had already gone in search of the real McCoy.

As he scuttled away though, the words sank in. Arabella Gilbert? He thought *I* was Arabella Gilbert. Did that mean she might be here? At the same party as me? My heroine. I searched the crowd for her face but couldn't see her.

'D'you want me to take that or what?'

I had finally reached the front of the queue and the coat-check girl grudgingly took my coat without even meeting my eye. She was under no illusions. She knew I was a no-namer. And probably a no-tipper, as a result.

But the surly coat-check girl couldn't ruin my night. Moving back into the room, I searched the thickening crowd for Mary, hoping to ask her whether the social columnist would be there. Would Arabella Gilbert be there reporting on the party for her column? If I could just get myself into the background of the little picture that usually accompanied her party diary I would be happy for a million years. I felt as though I were in the presence of some kind of magic. At last I was part of *Cool Britannia*. Or whatever they were calling it now . . .

Even if I was part of it without another part to talk to. I couldn't see Mary anywhere.

'Do you have your invitation?' asked a stick-thin girl on the door that led from the lobby to the room where the party proper was being held. The girl, who was flanked by two huge security guys with headsets, was dressed from head to toe in black and her matching black hair was pulled so tightly back from her face that it made her eyes look oriental even though she was clearly pure home counties.

'No, I don't,' I said. 'I'm here with my friend. She must have gone on inside without me. I think she's got the invitations.'

'Who's your friend?' she asked disinterestedly.

'Mary Bagshot,' I said.

'I'd like to believe you,' she replied with a totally warmth-free smile. 'But I'm sure you can appreciate that quite a few people claim to be friends with Mary Bagshot. She's the hottest new agent in town.'

'Yes,' I said. 'But I really am her friend. We were at college together.'

'Which college?'

'St Judith's. Oxford.'

'Wrong,' said the door girl triumphantly, crossing her arms to underline her point and nodding me back in the direction I'd come from. 'You can find your own way out.'

'Now, hang on,' I protested. 'I should bloody know which college she was at. I was at St Judith's with her.'

'She didn't go there.'

'She did,' I insisted.

'Look, I'm not even going to argue about this with you,' said Stick-girl. 'I don't recognise you. You don't have an invitation to this party. You can't come in.'

'Are you looking for this?'

Suddenly Mary appeared behind the anorexic Cerberus on the door and handed me my gilt-edged invitation. 'She's with me, Amaryllis.'

'Oh, hi Mary,' Amaryllis blushed. 'Did you get a chance to look at my show reel yet? You know I'm really keen to do anything. Even adverts. Have you had a minute?'

I couldn't believe it. The hard-faced bitch was suddenly rolling over to have her tummy tickled by my best friend.

'Not yet,' Mary said sweetly to the aspiring star. 'Nor will I ever,' she whispered to me as she dragged me into the party proper. 'That girl's tape is going straight in the Westminster Council filing cabinet.' (Which was what Mary called the wheely bin.) 'Where did you go? I waited for you *for ever*.'

'I was trying to put our coats in the cloakroom,' I reminded her impatiently.

'Oh, yeah. Thanks for that.'

I knew I'd been waiting in the queue for the cloakroom for a long time, but in the meantime Mary appeared to have necked enough champagne to make a Gladiator tipsy. At least, that's what I assumed she'd been doing because, considering the moaning and groaning she had done in the cab about hating this kind of party but needing to see and be seen, she looked pretty relaxed and sparky now. Her eyes glittered and she laughed as if she'd just heard that one of Pamela Anderson's boobs had exploded when I told her that the girl on the door had tried to tell me that Mary hadn't been at our college.

'It wasn't that funny,' I found myself saying when she couldn't seem to control herself. 'But while I was in the queue for the cloakroom, a man mistook me for Arabella Gilbert,' I told her then.

'That's quite possible,' said Mary. 'She does have the saggiest arse in the business.'

'Thanks a lot.'

'I was only joking,' said Mary, really stretching out her words. 'Now, do you want to meet some interesting people?'

Did I ever! Just as she said that, Jed Thunderton – the guitarist of Mental Strain, an early nineties grunge band of which I had once been a massive fan – appeared to Mary's left and reached out to tap her on the shoulder. Was she going to introduce me to him? It was almost as good as Christmas! Jed Thunderton! That hair! Those eyes! I pulled in my stomach and prepared my best smile.

But no.

Mary didn't even seem to notice the man who wanted to make himself known and before I could protest and draw him to her attention, she was dragging me by the arm in the direction of the ladies'.

'Come to the loos with me,' said Mary. Nothing unusual in that. Girls always go to the loo in pairs, on account of the fact that we always have to wait so long for a cubicle to become free that we'd miss valuable gossiping time if we didn't.

'I thought we were going to meet some interesting people,' I reminded her.

'We are,' she said. 'All the best people hang out in the loos at these parties.'

14

There were certainly enough people hanging out in the loos that night. Girls and boys. The elegant gold scrolled gender notice on the door didn't seem to have bothered anyone. The subtly lit ante-room was full of animated chatter as people reapplied their make-up and adjusted stray hair. Mary nodded 'hello' to a few familiar faces but she didn't seem to want to introduce me to them. Then, when one finally became free, she asked me to go into a cubicle with her.

'What?'

'Come in here with me. Quick.'

I'd noticed it while we were waiting. Pairs and even threesomes of girls slipping in and out of the toilet cubicles together as if it was the most natural thing in the world to watch your close friends having a pee. I hesitated but Mary dragged me inside and locked the door behind us.

'Er, I don't think I really need to go after all,' I said.

'Me neither,' she replied cheerfully. She closed the lid of the loo down and put her handbag on top of it.

'Then what are we doing in here?'

We may have been at one of London's best hotels, but still the ladies' wasn't exactly the most salubrious place to while away a week-night.

'You're so naive, Lizzie,' Mary laughed, as she opened her purse and took out a tiny little envelope of white paper. 'I don't know about you, but I was really starting to flag out there. All that social obligation. All that kissing and creeping. I need a little livener to help me carry on.'

She opened the handmade envelope to reveal a minuscule amount of dense white powder which looked like finely ground flour. She took a piece of loo paper and wiped the top of the cistern clean, then she tipped some of the powder straight out on to the enamel. 'Pass me my platinum card,' she ordered, handing me her bag. Then she set about chopping the little pile of powder into two neat and equal lines.

'What is that?' I asked in a whisper. 'Speed?'

She pulled an amused face. 'Oh, please. That's hardly my style. Any more,' she added with a chuckle. 'It's Charlie. Really good stuff too. Mitchell knows this really great little man in Highgate who can get him as much as he wants.'

'Charlie?' I whispered.

'Cocaine,' she explained.

The words swam about my head. Why wasn't she speaking more quietly? She rolled a crisp twenty-pound note into a narrow tube and held it out towards me. 'You do want some of this, don't you?'

I shook my head. 'I'm not sure.'

'Why not?'

'It's just . . .'

'You've never had any before, have you?' she asked acutely. I shook my head again. 'Seriously? Not in all the time you've been in London? Not once? I thought estate agents were at it all the time, stuffing their fat commissions up their big fat noses. One of my clients told me that one estate agent showing her round a flat actually nipped off to do a line in the middle of the viewing.'

'I'm not an estate agent,' I reminded her. 'I'm just the

secretary and I don't get any commission to waste on Class A narcotics!'

'Well, you won't be wasting any of *your* money tonight,' she reminded me. 'This is on Mitchell.' She bent over the cistern and hoovered up her share of the two thin lines. 'Look, I've done it. I'm fine.'

'You've only just done the stuff,' I hissed. 'You could die any minute. What would I tell your mum?'

'This is OK. I had some of it before you came round tonight too. And I'm not dead yet, am I? Just do half a line. I'll finish the rest. But do it quickly because there are people queuing up out there. Desperate people no doubt.'

I took the rolled-up note from her hand and tried to remember which end had just been up her nostril. Apart from anything else, I remember thinking that taking cocaine was just so, well, so inelegant. Stuffing a paper tube up your hooter and snorting the stuff to your brain? Half of me wanted to hand the rolled note back and tell her I wasn't interested. But the other half of me was very interested indeed. I wasn't entirely innocent of these things after all. I'd smoked plenty of blow at college and even done an 'e' once. (Unfortunately I had a very bad trip and had diarrhoea for a week after that.) So it wasn't as though I was a life-long member of the 'just say no' brigade. And cocaine was just so glamorous compared to those little printed ecstasy tablets that made you want to make love to men you wouldn't look twice at if they were standing next to you at a bus stop.

It also seemed to be yet another perfect detail for my perfect night. Cocaine. In a top London hotel. While outside the cubicle famous faces from the worlds of TV, film and fashion adjusted their hair and body-sculpting tights in front of the brightly lit mirrors. My mother would never believe it. Not that I'd ever actually be able to tell her, of course.

But the cocaine just seemed to fit the bill. And the bill fitted right up my nose.

I bent over the cistern, just as Mary had done. When I glanced up at her, she seemed to be shining. Her eyes were wide open. Her grin was a mile across.

'Go for it,' she whispered. 'It makes life so much more interesting.'

I inhaled hard and was surprised that when I looked down, all the little line had gone. Absolutely all of it. Right up my nostril.

'Like a pro,' commented Mary. 'You must have good lungs.'

I shook back my hair. Then suddenly the innocuous-looking powder hit the back of my nose like sherbet. I could taste it in my throat too. A weird metallic taste. But nothing amazing had happened yet. At best, I felt like I was choking on a sherbet fountain.

'Let's get back to the party, shall we?' Mary asked.

We squeezed out of the cubicle at the same time. Another pair of girls squeezed in after us, talking intently. Mary started to tell me a story about one of her clients. A washed-up soap actor who had been stitched up by a journalist. He had procured a minuscule amount of dope for the journo and ended up doing six months in prison for his pains.

'Got made an example of. But it will probably improve his work prospects no end when he comes out,' she assured me. 'People like a bit of "history". And it wasn't as if he was ever going to present *Blue Peter* anyway. Champagne?' I took a glass from a tray that seemed to be floating past. 'Now what are we going to do about that nuisance, Brian?'

'I'm just going to have to do some pretending.'

'Darling, you'll be perfect at it. Just look at you tonight. You fit right in.'

'Do you think so?'

'Absolutely,' she said, through a mouthful of bubbly. 'Nobody would know you're just an estate agency secretary. And I do hope it all goes well. You've had a rough time of it lately and you deserve to have a wonderful time while Brian's around. Besides, I can't wait to hear the gossip. If he asks you to fly back to New York and marry him, you have to promise that you won't ask me to be the bridesmaid.'

'I'm really glad we've patched things up between us,' I told her.

'I'm glad too,' she said.

We hugged.

'So what are you going to do about that new boyfriend of yours while Brian's in town?' Mary continued.

'I've told him I've got a friend coming to stay over the weekend.'

'Doesn't he want to meet him?'

'Yes. But I've told him that Brian and I will want to spend time with mutual friends. I told Richard he'd probably find it boring, to dissuade him from coming along.'

'Nice touch. But if I know anything about men, he'll probably tag along to check up on you anyway. Perhaps you should have chucked him to make sure he didn't get in the way.'

'That seems a bit harsh.'

'Of course it's harsh. But you do want to get things on with Brian again, don't you? You don't want some sad accountant hanging about and spoiling your chances.'

'But what if Brian doesn't want to get back together with me? I'll have chucked Richard for nothing and I'll end up with no one at all.'

Mary shrugged. 'That's always been your problem, Liz.

Hedging your bets. You're never going to get the glittering prize if you don't point your arrow right at it.'

'That's very profound,' I said.

'I know. Coming to the loo again?'

It couldn't have been more than two minutes since we had last been, but I let myself be led.

This time, Mary saw someone she recognised touching up her make-up in the mirror. The woman's sharp brown bob hid most of her profile but she was still unmistakably familiar. In fact, the back of her head was almost as familiar to me as the back of my own.

'Is that?' I asked. But before she could answer, Mary was enveloping Arabella Gilbert in her arms. Arabella Gilbert. My heroine. Sort of. And Mary knew her. I was open-mouthed with awe.

'Hello, darling.' Mary and Arabella air-kissed extravagantly.

'How are you?' Mary purred. 'You look fantastic.'

'Shame I don't feel too fantastic,' she sighed. 'Do you find coke has a laxative effect, Mary?'

'Only if that's what it's been cut with, sweetheart. Any time you want some really good stuff you know who to call. Call me about anything in fact.' She handed Arabella one of her little Smythson business cards.

'Who's this?' Arabella said suddenly, jerking her head towards me. 'Do I know you from somewhere?' she asked, addressing me directly. 'You used to write for the *Mirror*, didn't you?' Her eyes narrowed suspiciously.

Sensing her concern, Mary wrapped her arm around Arabella's shoulder and assured her that I most definitely wasn't a journalist. 'She's just an old friend of mine. Lizzie and I were at college together,' she explained. 'I've brought her out this evening to show her a bit of the glamorous world of showbiz. Lizzie works for an estate agency. This really crappy agency in one of the tattier parts of Knightsbridge. She's actually not even an estate agent, just a secretary really.'

Thanks a lot, I thought.

'She's a big fan of yours, Arabella.'

'That's nice.'

'Do you want to get Bella's autograph?' Mary asked me.

'I don't have my album with me,' I smiled.

'I'll get my secretary to send you a photo in the post,' said Arabella, totally sincere.

'Thanks,' I said flatly.

'Well, enjoy yourself this evening,' Arabella told me. 'If anyone can show you the social ropes, Mary Bagshot can. She's the A-list party queen. Gets almost as many invitations as I do. Is Mitchell coming this evening, by the way?'

'He's in the studio,' Mary told her.

'Still? I didn't think he actually had to record anything himself. You will give him my regards, won't you?'

'Of course I will.'

'I'll expect an invitation to the launch party of course.'

'Yours is the first name on the guest list.'

'Then I take it you've forgiven me for that little debacle at the video shoot,' Arabella smiled with her eyes downcast.

'A simple misunderstanding, I'm sure.'

'Good. Er, Mary. I don't suppose you've got any powder I could borrow for my nose? I seem to have run out.'

'Of course,' Mary handed over her handbag. 'Don't use it all at once,' she told her as Arabella disappeared into a cubicle. 'It's incredibly rarefied stuff.'

'What happened at the video shoot?' I couldn't resist asking in a whisper as soon as Arabella closed the cubicle door.

'What indeed?' sniffed Mary. 'I found her in the bedroom of Mitchell's winnebago with no clothes on.'

'Was he with her?' I asked agog.

'No, he was sitting by the catering van at the time, stuffing his face with sausages.'

'But had he? You know. With her?'

'I very much doubt it. Though that didn't stop her implying the opposite in her bloody column.'

'It must be very hard going out with someone so many people want to get their hooks into,' I said.

'You can't blame Arabella for wanting to raise her profile.'

'Well, I know you're in the business of raising profiles yourself, but I still think you seem very calm about it. I would have kicked her arse.'

'I know I can trust Mitchell not to mess around with the likes of her.'

Just then Arabella emerged from the cubicle and gave Mary her bag back. 'Great stuff,' she said, wide-eyed. 'Really great. You know what, I think I will give you a ring tomorrow morning after all.'

'You do that,' said Mary. 'We could do lunch if you want to. Enjoy the rest of the evening.'

Arabella gave her a dazzling smile. Her eyes, I noticed, were so dark you couldn't see where iris ended and pupil began.

'I can't believe I've been standing in the ladies' with all these celebs drifting in and out,' I sighed when Mary and I were alone again.

'The trick is to act like you're used to it.'

'Well, you are. Do you know Arabella Gilbert really well? Are you friends?'

'No. She's not the kind of girl I'd be friends with. Though my cousin Edward had a brief thing with her once after some Benenden/Eton disco. She was gutted when he chucked her for her brother. And I must say, her rise and rise has certainly surprised me. She's thicker than double cream but potentially worth a fortune,' Mary assured me.

'Thick? How can she be thick if she's a journalist?'

'She doesn't actually write her column, stupid. She wouldn't have got the job at all if her parents hadn't been involved in that pot-holing accident with Prince What's-his-face of Sweden.'

'Oh.'

'But whatever the obscure reason she rose to fame she seems to be hot property all the same. She's been on the panel for every game show imaginable and now she wants to move into presenting herself. There's a lot of interest. And not all of it from Channel 5. Her current agent is about to retire to Tuscany and I want to be standing underneath the tree when that particular apple drops. Arabella Gilbert is on the up and up and I am going to be right behind her.'

'Sounds a bit mercenary.'

'Sounds business-like to me.'

'Hi, Mary.'

Another familiar face appeared. A weather girl. One who had been on the panel game scene for rather longer than Arabella. She was just the wrong side of thirty and had probably even reported on the great storm of 1987. 'Did you hear that Michael is going to retire next month? I'm devastated.'

'Janie shares an agent with Arabella Gilbert,' Mary explained for my benefit.

'I'm fishing for a new agent if you're interested.'

'Oh, Janie,' Mary sighed extravagantly. 'You know I'd be

after you like a shot but my artist roster is totally full for the foreseeable. You know my theory. Stay small and personal for the very best results.'

'Surely you could squeeze me in?' Janie protested. 'I'm only very little.'

Mary winced at Janie's baby voice before telling her, 'I wouldn't want to take you on knowing that I might not be able to give you the time and attention you deserve, sweetheart.'

'Perhaps we could do lunch one day in any case?'

'I'll get my assistant to call you.'

The weather girl left without powdering her nose.

'I don't understand. You just told Arabella you were after new clients,' I said.

'I am after new clients like Arabella,' Mary explained to me. 'But dear old Janie should be thinking about having kids and presenting a daytime animal rescue show. Television presenters are a very highly strung bunch. I'm willing to take terrible tantrums from someone like Arabella because I've got a feeling that one day her fees will keep me in anti-stress massage and aromatherapy oils permanently. But I don't want someone like Janie. She's a charity case and I already have a direct debit donation going to the RSPCA.'

I couldn't help chuckling at that.

'I'm glad to see you haven't totally lost sight of the old Mary,' I told her. 'Still looking out for helpless animals, eh?'

'It's a tax break,' she said flatly.

I followed her back out into the party, marvelling at the professional businesswoman she had become. She could barely move through the room for people trying to air kiss her and ask her out to lunch. She introduced me to most of them, but I saw their eyes glaze over when she explained that I was a friend from college and that no, I wasn't in the business myself. The feel-good factor of the little line of coke Mary had given me soon wore off and I found myself wishing the fire alarm would go off, or there'd be an earthquake – anything to get me out of that ballroom – when I found myself in conversation with a television producer who never met my eye but was constantly looking over my shoulder for someone more useful to talk to.

In the end, I didn't bother to look at him either. Over his shoulder I had the most wonderful view of Arabella Gilbert. She was standing at the centre of a circle of equally glittering admirers and from the way they were laughing, it seemed she was telling them all a joke. When it came to the punchline, she had to put down her handbag. It was the very same pink leather strapless Hermes number she had written about in her column. Exquisite.

Anyway, whatever joke she was telling, Arabella had to get down in a squat to illustrate the last bit. She puffed out her alabaster cheeks and made flapping movements with her arms. Anyone else attempting such an inelegant move would have looked like an idiot but to me she still looked ridiculously glamorous. When she had finished, she straightened up and flicked her shiny hair back over her shoulder. Then, as if she had sensed my gaze upon her, she turned in my direction and smiled at me. Straight at me. I shifted to my left as subtly as I could, so that the TV producer obscured her view of me.

Oh, dear. I had been star-struck. Seeing Arabella Gilbert in the flesh had made me feel twenty times as inadequate as reading her bloody column.

Unfortunately, Mary didn't seem to want to leave the bash and end my agony any time soon. Occasionally she glanced over at me and gave me a little thumbs up sign or a smile that asked 'How are you?' but she never actually paused for long enough in her important conversations for me to say that I wanted to go home.

In fact, when the party ended, Mary was keen to follow a particularly select group of people upstairs to the suite the Golden Brothers had hired for the duration of their stay in London for Fashion Week. I tagged along because, while I hadn't been having such a great time since my celebrity moment in the loos, I felt I still ought to make the effort to join the inner sanctum while the opportunity was being offered to me. I had often tried to hint to Mary that I would love to go to a VIP party with her. Now I was being taken upstairs to the best suite at the Hyperion to raid the mini-bar with three supermodels, two top fashion designers, an up-and-coming Hollywood actor and one of my best friends.

Mary linked arms with the Hollywood supernova-in-waiting, Rad Bradbourne – he had just made a film about the Second World War in which he played a GI who single-handedly saved an entire French village from the Nazis without even messing up his hair. I can't say I had ever thought much of him as an actor, but seeing him in the flesh, I could understand why he had been the darling of the casting couches since his voice broke. Even his back view was extra special. Imagine the buttocks of Michelangelo's *David* made flesh.

Just as we reached the door to the suite, Mary turned to me and said, 'Do you think you could be a darling and pop downstairs to get a bottle of something nice? We could ring room service but they'll take for ever. Tell them to put it on the room bill.'

Then she slipped in through the half-open door and closed it behind her leaving me in the hallway outside. There was nothing I could do except do as I was told.

I had made my way to the twelfth floor with my eyes firmly on Rad Bradbourne's buttocks. Without such a good view to keep me occupied on the journey back downstairs I waited impatiently for the lift; but when it finally arrived the door opened to reveal a couple who were getting to know each other rather intimately and before I could get in – as if I would have wanted to at that point – the girl reached out one elegant foot in a very pointy heeled shoe and pressed the button that closed the lift door again.

I waited for another two minutes while the floor counter indicated that the happy couple had become stuck between the fifth and sixth floors. I doubted very much that the lift had actually broken. How selfish was that? Making love in the lift of a high-rise building? I pressed the up button one more time, hoping to dislodge them, but I couldn't.

So I had to walk down the stairs. All the long walk down I met people walking up who were clearly a lot more disgruntled by the lift failure than I. Someone had given up altogether half-way between the tenth and ninth floors and lay slumped against the wall looking like she had just had a coronary.

It was Arabella Gilbert. She didn't look quite as polished as she had done at the beginning of the party. Her pale face was red with puffing her way up so many stairs. Her slinky cat-suit was looking decidedly crumpled. She carried a bottle of champage in each hand.

'Are you OK?' I asked her as she tried to stand up but swayed backwards violently and looked in real danger of tumbling all the way back down the stairs.

'I'm fine,' she slurred. 'Weally, we-ally fine.'

'You don't look it,' I observed.

'I don't feel it,' she admitted then, sliding down the wall to find herself sitting on the stairs. She looked totally bewildered. As if she didn't have a clue where she was.

'Do I know you?' she asked. 'You're not that girl who used to write for the *Sun*, are you?'

'No,' I said. 'And I'm not the girl who used to write for the *Mirror* either. We've been through this before. My name's Lizzie Jordan. We met in the loos earlier on.'

'Oh, Lizzie. You're the one with the leaking boob job, right? That's too awful. I can see it leaking now.'

'Er, no,' I said, looking down at my chest nervously. 'You've got the wrong girl.' Though there was a wet mark on my chest where an energetically camp make-up artist had stumbled into me and spilled his drink earlier on. 'I was with Mary.'

'Oh, Mary. Mary, Mary quite contrary. Is she still sleeping with that gorgeous brother of hers? I've had a crush on him for ages, you know.'

I raised an eyebrow. 'Think you might have the wrong girl. Again. I'm talking about Mary Bagshot the agent. She gave you her card.'

'Oh, Mary the agent!' cried Arabella, as if enlightenment was thumping her between the eyes. 'Mary the agent one. What's your name again?'

'Lizzie.'

'Well, Lucy,' she wiped a string of dribble from her expensively powdered chin. 'Why don't you sit down here with me for a little while? Talk to me until I get my breath back.'

'Where were you trying to get to?'

'To the party upstairs. I know Rad Bradbourne is in there with those supermodel sluts and I've simply got to talk to him. He told me that I drink too much to be his girlfriend. I've got to tell him that's he's wrong.'

'I don't think you'll have all that much luck trying to convince him of that right now,' I warned her. 'Can I take one of those bottles for you?' She was waving her arms about and occasionally thumping me in the side. She gave up the bottle fairly easily though, then started to wrestle with the cork in the top of the other one. She tried for several minutes, resisting all my attempts to help her, before giving up with conventional methods of opening a champagne bottle and smashing the neck of the heavy green bottle against the wall. It took two whacks to break the top off, but when it did break we were both soaked with champagne and bits of broken glass.

I snatched the bottle away from her just as she was about to put the jagged neck to her mouth.

'Are you mad?' I asked.

'That's what he said to me,' she sighed.

'You could have cut half your face off, drinking out of this.'

'I don't care.'

'I'm sure you would in the morning,' I told her.

'I just want him to know I'm not mad. I'm just sad. I'm really sad.'

'What about?' I was fascinated to know.

'Don't know,' she sniffled. She leaned her head momentarily on my shoulder. 'Just very sad.'

'But you've got such a great life,' I told her. 'You seemed very happy earlier on. I heard you telling a joke. Everyone was laughing.'

'That's just it. I seemed very happy. But I'm not, you know. Rad will never love me.'

'I'm sure he does.'

She turned her face towards me. Her eyes were red. Tears edged towards the corners of her lower lids, ready to spill down her increasingly puffy face.

'My life is in ruins.'

She was crying properly now.

'You've just won columnist of the year,' I said.

'And I've just been told that I'm too fat to be on TV.'

Too fat? She was like a pepperami. And hadn't she ever heard of Vanessa Feltz?

'I've just found out that I've got to have liposuction and a tummy tuck if I want to make it in television. It doesn't matter when I'm writing a column but television adds ten pounds and I know exactly where it would be added.'

'I don't think you look fat,' I said.

'Of course you don't,' she said. 'I'm thinner than you.'

'Thanks.'

'But compared to the other girls I'm up against in the television world I might as well be an elephant. I've tried everything. Amphetamines. Cocaine. I even went to India for a week and drank water straight out of a toilet bowl in the hope of getting amoebic dysentery but it didn't happen and I came back weighing three pounds more than I did before I went because I'm so fond of tikka masala and gulab jamun.'

'Maybe you should try exercising more?' I suggested.

'What if someone snaps me looking all hot and sweaty on the way out of an exercise class?' she replied as if that were a perfectly logical objection to working out.

'Well, at least they couldn't accuse you of doing anything other than looking after yourself,' I said. 'Which has to be better than accusing you of having had liposuction.'

'God, I wish I were you,' said Arabella. 'You really have no idea how easy your life is, do you? You get up in the morning, you look a wreck and you don't have to care about it. You don't have to worry if your hair looks awful day after day.' She picked up one limp side of my bob to illustrate her comment. 'No one cares if they can see your knickers through your dress.'

I looked for a knicker line nervously.

'Your life is perfect.'

'And yet I've been pretending to be you,' I told her.

'Yeah, well, I've been pretending to be me too,' she said, waving her arm in my face. 'I don't write that column, you know.'

'Don't you?' I said in mock surprise.

'I don't even know how to type. If my parents weren't who my parents are, I wouldn't be anybody either. I'd be just like you. Do you have any idea how scary that thought is? What do your parents do, Lucy?'

'Lizzie,' I corrected.

'I bet your dad wears a flat cap and your mother goes to the shop in her slippers.'

I opened my mouth to protest. Shop in her slippers? My mother would have gone purple to hear such an accusation.

'I bet she has his tea on the table every night when he gets home from work. Or the dole office. I bet they drink cans of lager while they watch *Brookside*.'

'Actually—' I wanted to tell her that she was wrong.

But she was on a roll.

'I bet that your dad used to take you to football matches.'

He hated football.

'And you used to eat chips every single day.'

If only.

'I hardly ever saw my parents when I was a child,' she continued. 'They packed me off to boarding school aged three and a half and I didn't see my father again until I turned sixteen.'

'That sounds awful.'

'I think that's why I'm like I am.'

'I think you're really nice,' I said comfortingly.

'Of course you do. Lots of ordinary people think I'm nice. But how can they possibly know? The girl who writes the column – that's not me. I mean, obviously it's not me. It's some secretary at the paper. I don't have the time. But the girl they think I am because they read my column, that really isn't me either. Are you following?'

'I think so.'

'I've got a horrible feeling that underneath it all, I'm ordinary too. I'm just the sum of my expensive outfits. That's the only difference between me and you.' She poked me in the chest. 'I wear nice clothes and you . . . don't.'

I knew the brown shift had been a mistake.

'But that's actually Calvin Klein, isn't it?' she added, momentarily sounding as if she wasn't completely out of her head on booze and drugs.

'It is,' I told her. And even though she had just made one of the most offensive remarks about me I had heard in a long while, I suddenly felt rather elated. The only difference between me and Arabella Gilbert, as heard from the horsey-girl's mouth itself, was a matter of superficial appearance. It was a great comfort to me.

'You know, you should be careful of that Mary,' Arabella slurred. 'She seems to be your friend, but really she just wants something you've got. When she has got it, she'll dump you. All agents are like that.'

'Well, I'm happy to say that she's not my agent. And I can't think what I've got that she could possibly want. We've been friends for a hundred years. Well, at least nine.'

'I still say you should watch your back,' said Arabella. 'Always watch your back and never trust anyone ever.'

'Thanks for the advice,' I said.

'Watch out below!'

Talk of the devil. Mary suddenly tumbled down the stairs and came to a stop right next to me and Arabella.

'I've got to go home,' she said to Arabella. 'It's getting too crazy up there. One of the supermodels produced a bottle of absinthe – it went down the wrong way and I think she may have choked to death. Hey, Arabella. You haven't seen that mousy girl I came here with tonight?'

'Hi, Mary,' I said, hoping that she had known I was there all along and that she had been having a joke.

'Oh, hi, Liz. Do you mind if we get a taxi home now?'

'I've been waiting for you to say that for about the last two hours,' I admitted.

'What's up with you, Arabella?' Mary asked the society girl who had finally abandoned the idea of sitting up under her own steam and was now slumped against the bannister like a puppet with its stuffing knocked out.

'Had a few too many, I think?' I suggested.

'Well, we'd better take her home with us,' said Mary, getting to her feet and very quickly recovering her sober self. 'The last thing I need is for one of my clients to be found drowned in a pool of her own vomit.'

'But she's not one of your clients.'

'She will be after tonight. Easy as tickling trout. Take her other arm, will you?'

I dutifully slung one of Arabella's arms around my shoulders and helped to lift her to her feet. I soon learnt what Arabella had meant when she said she was 'deceptively slim'. She weighed a ton.

15

What a night! All the way back from the West End I prayed that Seema would still be up when I got in. I was ready to burst with the news of my night with the stars and I especially wanted to tell her in blow by blow detail how *the* Arabella Gilbert had cried on my shoulder and told *me* about her impending liposuction. I wanted to tell Seema about the champagne, the canapés, the cocaine.

But Seema wasn't up – I had a vague recollection of her having said that she had an early shift at the video shop next day – and neither was Fat Joe to be found outside the confines of his bedroom-come-bunker. He would have been a passable ear to bend in Seema's absence even if he had no interest in canapés whatsoever and no idea who Arabella Gilbert was either. So I had to hold my magical stories inside me for another night.

Instead I went to my bedroom and sat down on the end of my bed to admire myself in Mary's designer dress. I still couldn't see the knicker line that Arabella had so cruelly referred to.

I stood up and sashayed across to the full-length mirror on the back of my wardrobe door in a fairly close approximation of Arabella's model-style wobble. I could do the walk all right. But would Brian be impressed with what he saw when he stepped off that plane at Heathrow? That was *the* question.

I looked pretty good from the front at least, I thought. Though I had ballooned from a ridiculously skinny size eight at the age of eighteen to a size twelve now (ten at Marks and Spencer) my body still curved in all the right places. I still had a pretty narrow waist between my bigger boobs (I was happy with those) and my bigger hips (not so sure about that). I mean, I didn't need them to be quite so *childbearing* yet.

But then I turned sideways to get a profile view. Not so good. The girl in the mirror now definitely wasn't one that I wanted to recognise as me. My back was so hunched and curved with slouching over a computer keyboard at Corbett and Daughter all week long that my head jutted out from my shoulders like a tortoise's from its shell. I looked like an eighty-year-old lady. And worst of all, my belly jutted out almost as far as my chin did.

Shocked and horrified by the thought that other people had seen me standing like that, I pulled myself up straight and instantly looked as though I had lost twelve pounds. Well, that wasn't so awful. I would just have to stand up straight while Brian was around. But I had spent so long slouching that it felt weird to stand up straight again and by the time I had walked around my room picking up the clothes I had thrown off and on to the floor after getting home from work every night the previous week, and looked in the mirror again, my body had reverted to its previous shape.

If only Brian had given me more notice, I sighed. If I'd had, say, a whole month to prepare for his visit, I could have greeted him with a body like Anthea Turner's in her workout video (not the face or manic grin, of course). If I'd had six months . . . Well, I could have achieved anything in six months! It just wasn't fair that he should spring a visit on me like this.

But would extra time really have made such a difference? I leaned over to pick up a stray sock and discovered a leaflet I had picked up from a new health club in town three months earlier on one of my cyclical 'must get fit' kicks (which generally kicked in on one of those days when I couldn't get my jeans done up). I had circled in thick black felt tip all the classes I promised myself I would attend starting with water aerobics on Mondays (ideal for the elderly, pregnant women and people who have not been near a gym for a very very long time) and working up to advanced kick-boxing on Friday nights (ideal for SAS-trained PE teachers and Gladiators).

I snorted when I saw all those optimistic little circles. I had ringed six classes. Six a week!! Can you imagine it? In reality, on the evening when I was supposed to get the ball rolling with a little light water aerobics, I had arrived at the health club to discover that I had completely forgotten to pack a towel. The girl on the desk told me that I could hire one of the club's own towels for fifty pence but much as she insisted that they were boil-washed clean every evening and nice and fluffy from the tumble drier, I just couldn't bring myself to rub my body down with a towel that might have been used by someone with impetigo or body lice the night before.

Well, that was my excuse.

It would have been so easy to stay fit if I had been one of those weird people who actually enjoy exercise, I told myself. You know, the type who claim they get a natural high from jogging around the block avoiding the dog shit. Unfortunately for me, much as I wanted to get fit, I couldn't get over the psychological hurdle of seeing exercise not as pleasure but as a punishment. I blame the PE teachers I had at school. When your PE teacher lands you with the nickname 'Crash Bang Wallop' (Wallop for short) at the impressionable age of four and a half, you haven't really got much hope of growing up to be the kind of adult who regards the prospect of raising a pulse rate with anything other than trepidation.

But how much weight can you lose in four days anyway? All the diet books I had amassed over my years as a woman (i.e. all my years of being weight-obsessed and longing to be in control of my body), didn't promise anything in less than a month. Take things slowly, they all said. Sudden weight loss usually only indicates dehydration. A total fast was cheating and would only lead to dangerous binge eating later on. Did I want to be a yo-yo dieter? the gurus threatened. If the Yo-Yo diet involved eating nothing but those chocolate covered minty biscuits, then the answer was probably yes.

Seema, stick thin on three Mars Bars a day, would surely have the answer. I collared her next morning as she was shovelling in a Snickers bar for breakfast. The answer was, she suggested, three Mars Bars a day and absolutely nothing else. Put that way it wasn't quite such an appealing regime.

'You've left it a bit late to worry about losing weight anyway, haven't you?' she said.

'I would have started the moment he called but I was too depressed by the prospect of having to tell him the truth about the flat. Now that I've got the flat sorted out, I've only got to look as though I've been working out at the Harbour Club for six years to complete the illusion.'

'Did you tell him that?'

'As far as Brian's concerned, the gym is my home from home.'

'I can only see you being a regular at a gym if you have to get a job cleaning one,' said Seema. 'You could buy him a blindfold. Or you could try the cabbage soup diet,' she suggested only slightly more usefully. 'That has very quick results or so I've heard, so you could lose half a stone by the weekend. You just make a huge vat of cabbage soup at the beginning of the week and you can eat as much of that as you like but nothing else. Only problem is, it makes you a tad unsociable, if you know what I mean. It's all right now, while Brian isn't here and you're with us in Balham, because we won't be able to tell if it's you or Hercules, but when Brian turns up, you don't want to be farting like a shire horse.'

'I'll probably be farting through fear anyway,' I told her.

'Yeah, but not cabbage farts.'

That was a good point.

'Then if the cabbage diet is out, what do you suggest?'

'How about a pair of those big knickers from Marks and Spencer? The industrial-strength lycra ones that hold you in all over.'

'They're hardly very sexy,' I replied. 'And besides, all the fat that's meant to be held in is really just squashed out over the waist band or even worse through the leg holes. All this so-called amazing underwear is hopeless. And if you look good while you've got your clothes on, you've still got the problem of how to breathe without fainting or explode discreetly when you get your kit off.'

'I know,' Seema sympathised. 'I've given up on Wonder-bras ever since one of my pads fell out on the dancefloor at the Ritzy leaving me with one peak and one valley at the crucial moment. I was so embarrassed. I could see the pad lying on the floor between me and the bloke I was cruising at the time but I could hardly just bend over and pick it up, could I? Then he stepped on it and picked it up himself.'

'What did you do?'

Chris Manby

'I crossed my arms over my chest, told him it was probably someone's shoulder pad come loose and got out of the club before he came in for a grope. He could have had me under the Trades Description Act. Anyway, does all this panic mean that Brian's visit is definitely going ahead? Has he called to confirm?'

I opened my mouth to say 'not yet' but as if by telepathy, the telephone rang.

'Good news,' said Brian. 'I've just come back from a great night out with my boss.' It was four in the morning his time. 'He's had a sneak preview of the figures for this month and he was ecstatic. I'm definitely coming to see you. Who knows, I might even be able to stay for longer than I thought.'

Eeek!

'Er, that's great,' I said. 'But I've got to be in Jersey on Tuesday for a business meeting so I don't know if I can put you up for longer than four days.' Seema gave me the thumbs up for my quick thinking.

'That's OK,' said Brian. 'I'm sure four days will be plenty of time for us to get to know each other all over again.'

'I'm glad your figures looked good,' I told him.

'Not as good as your figure has always looked to me,' he flirted. 'I'll see you Friday.'

I put down the phone with a freefalling feeling that was midway between ecstatic anticipation and bottomless misery.

'He commented on my good-looking figure,' I told Seema. 'I used to have one, once.'

'Oh, for God's sake. You don't look that bad,' Seema tutted. 'Get your hair done. Get some streaks. Have a manicure. Brian won't notice that you've put on three pounds if you get your eyelashes dyed.'

224

Mmm. Perhaps she was right. Perhaps the bodywork wouldn't look too bad if the paintwork was up to scratch.

I had to get my hair done in any case. My chic city bob was no longer quite as sharp as it had been and was instead getting to that length where it wouldn't do anything but part in the middle like it belonged on the head of a hippie unless I plastered it with enough lacquer to waterproof a yacht.

Since Harriet was away and I didn't have to go into the office, I could get an appointment with the best stylist in town in the morning. It cost so much money – my bank manager would have passed out – but once you factored in the money saved by not having to buy the glossy magazines I could read for free while I was waiting, it almost seemed reasonable. I even found a mag with a picture of Arabella Gilbert in it, snapped grinning in Armani as she attended the opening of another envelope.

'I'd like to look like that,' I told Guido the stylist, waving the picture in front of him.

'OK,' he said, flicking back his own blond Princess Di layered job. I expected him to say 'dream on' but instead he put his fingers to his chin in a pensive gesture and said, 'I think we can do that. You know what? You even look a bit like her already. Same jaw-line.'

To hear that comment alone I would have paid the price of two haircuts. *I* had the same jaw-line as Arabella Gilbert? Suddenly I was proud of my slightly soft chin.

Anyway, it was while I was reading one of those magazines that I also happened upon the miracle weight-loss cure. *Want to lose weight instantly?* the article asked. *Why not try colonic irrigation?*

Mmm. Sounded scientific. By the time I'd finished reading the article it also sounded quite horrific, but the magazine's game guinea pig claimed she lost five pounds in her first session. That was it. I decided my excess weight was in fact due entirely to the volume of compacted red meat in my colon – although apart from my Mum's Sunday lunch I hadn't actually eaten red meat in five years, not since the BSE crisis (and a final Oxford kebab that nearly landed me in hospital). But there were other benefits too. Bright eyes and clear skin. A feeling of total well-being that lasted for – ooh, I don't know – minutes!! The humiliation of a backless gown and a hose-pipe up the jacksy was a small price to pay for such side-effects, I thought.

The actual price to pay for the humiliation however, was far from small.

Guido the hairdresser recommended a clinic where he had undergone the treatment himself.

'Tell them I sent you,' he said. 'You might get a discount.'

'Guido who?' asked the receptionist before quoting a three-figure sum.

'Have you ever had colonic irrigation before?' the clinician asked moments later, as she led me into a small room which was not unlike the room where I got my legs waxed in Balham. (Which was yet another torture I needed to fit in before Brian's arrival, I reminded myself.)

'Where did you hear about the clinic?' the white-coated woman asked me in her bright, put-at-easy voice.

'In the back of *Complete Woman*,' I piped up.

'I see. So would you like me to tell you a little bit about what actually happens before we start?'

'I think I got the general idea from the article,' I assured her. As with ear-piercing, I figured that the best approach to take with a colonic was to pretend it wasn't happening and hope that the therapist took you by surprise.

'Well, feel free to ask any questions,' my therapist said, getting what looked like a pot of vaseline out of the cupboard. 'You might want to change out of your clothes now and put this on.' She handed me one of those paper gowns that are split right the way down the back and fastened with totally ineffectual ribbons. I slipped behind a curtain and changed into it. It was just like a hospital gown – exactly as I had expected. And by the time I emerged from behind the curtain and saw her greasing up her fingers, I might as well have been going in for major surgery, so nervous did I feel at the prospect.

'Can you tell me when you last had an evacuation?' she asked me.

'Excuse me?' I said. I wondered for a moment whether she wanted me to tell her about the evacuation of children living in London to the safety of the countryside during the Second World War to concentrate my mind elsewhere while she started to do the business down below. She didn't.

'A poo, dear,' she said impatiently. 'When did you last do a poo?'

'Er, this morning, I suppose.'

'And are you regular?'

'I've never really thought about it before.'

'Not a lot of people do think about their bowels,' she said, fixing me with a sad and serious look. She crossed her rubber-gloved arms across the front of her apron and started a lecture I sensed she had delivered several times before. 'Just because a part of your body is hidden away doesn't mean that it's not important,' she warned me. 'People care so much about their hearts and their lungs and their kidneys. All the *popular* organs. Even their spleens get a look in. Everybody forgets about the good old bowel. But can you imagine what would happen if it suddenly decided to stop working?'

I shook my head like a school-girl caught smoking by the bike sheds.

'Well, how about if all the bin men in London suddenly decided to go on strike?' she asked me. 'Tomorrow? In this weather? Putrid, that's how it would be. Putrid.'

She prodded my belly accusingly. Was that going putrid too?

'As it is, you've probably been abusing your bowels for far too long,' she sighed. 'It may be too late for you already. Lie on that couch and roll over.'

As the little tube went up my bum, I asked in an anguished whisper, 'Brian Coren, are you worth it?'

'What was that?' the therapist enquired. She could hardly hear me because she was cranking up some kind of machine that made alternate whooshing and sucking sounds.

'Oh, nothing. I was just swearing.'

'Swear away,' the therapist said. 'Everybody does. And let me tell you that no man is ever worth it.'

Perhaps not. But colonic irrigation was certainly a faster method to a flat stomach than sit-ups. I hoped.

'I'm going to start introducing the warm water into your body now,' the therapist continued. 'In a short while you will be able to see all that nasty debris flowing from your body into this pipe. You can watch if you like. You might find it interesting.'

'I think I'll just close my eyes,' I said.

After the irrigation I was so worried about seepage that I spent the rest of the day wearing three pairs of pants.

Of course, I didn't look as though I'd lost an ounce – though the therapist had assured me that all sorts of stuff had come out through the tube (I didn't like to look when she invited me to). And far from being filled with a sense of well-being, I felt totally grotty. Not to mention slightly sore.

I may have had a spotless backside but I certainly wasn't in the mood for visitors, so I was slightly less than welcoming when Richard came round uninvited that evening. He must have guessed that I wasn't all that pleased to see him, because he remained on the doorstep until I invited him in, instead of bounding straight into the sitting room, stealing my place on the sofa and demanding a cup of tea as he usually did.

'You've had your hair done,' he said.

'No one else has noticed. Did Seema tip you off?' I asked.

'No,' he said indignantly. 'I noticed it immediately. You look different somehow. Radiant. What have you been doing with yourself since the weekend?'

I didn't tell him I had been spending that month's rent money on having someone stick a tube up my bum to suck out the solidified contents of my guts.

'Oh, nothing much,' I said instead. 'Do I really look different?'

'Yeah. You look really lovely.'

'Thanks.'

'Look, I don't want to keep you long. I know we didn't arrange to see each other tonight, but I just wanted to see you again before your mate comes to stay. I'll really miss you, Lizzie.'

'It'll only be a few days,' I snorted.

'I know but I think I'll still miss you all the same.'

'Don't be so soft. Go and practise your football or something.'

'Well, it probably needs it. Look, if you change your mind about bringing your mate out to meet us lot at any time, just give me a ring. I mean, if you get fed up of him and want to pack him off to play football with the boys or something. To give you a bit of a break. I'll be happy to look after him.'

'Thanks. But I don't think I'll need a break from Brian,' I said. 'And he doesn't play football anyway.'

He hovered by the door, hand still on the handle. 'Brian. That's his name, is it?'

'Yes.'

'Funny name.'

'I suppose so.'

There was a pause. Normally I would have said something to get the conversation going again – something silly and affectionate – but that night I wanted to get back to painting my fingernails. It was Richard who broke the silence.

'Er, Lizzie, have you, er, have you thought any more about what I said on Sunday?'

'About what?'

'About getting a flat? You and me together.'

Oh, no, I sighed inwardly. I had completely forgotten. I felt my heart make a quick trip towards my feet.

'I've been sort of busy,' I blustered to Richard. 'I'm holding fort at the office on my own. Harriet's gone away for the week, but she's left the dog behind.'

As if on cue, Hercules came to investigate the visitor. Richard crouched down to pat him on the head.

'He's sweet,' he said.

'He's a complete pain in the proverbial.'

'Could we take him out for a walk perhaps? Have a bit of a chat?'

'He doesn't like going for walks very much. He's pretty highly strung.'

'OK,' Richard nodded. 'Well, look, I guess I'll see you when your friend's gone back home then. I just wanted to say "hello" tonight. And let you know that . . .'

'What?'

'Oh, just that you look really lovely and all that. You always do, of course.'

I put a hand to my hair self-consciously, then I planted a little kiss on Richard's cheek and encouraged him back towards the street. 'I've got to be in work early tomorrow morning to open up the office,' I lied.

'And just one more thing,' he started again.

'What?' I said, finding it very hard not to be snappish.

'I know I haven't got you anything for your birthday yet but I'd like you to have this in the meantime. Until we can go shopping.'

He handed me an envelope.

'You've already given me a card,' I said.

'Yeah, but I did this one myself.'

I opened the envelope and pulled out a piece of thin paper that had been folded in half to make a card. On the front was a pencil sketch. Of me. I recognised the pose at once. Richard had drawn me from a photograph taken on a trip we'd made to Brighton. Back when I was still too excited by the novelty of having a boyfriend to be churlish enough to want to change him. To make him, say, richer.

'Thanks. It's very good,' I said.

It was.

'You're easy to draw,' said Richard. 'I'd like to draw you from life one day.'

'Yeah,' I said, non-committally, putting the card back into its envelope and putting the envelope on the plant stand just inside the door, where it would stay for quite some time.

Richard was finally on the pavement outside the house. 'I'll see you then,' he said again. 'When your friend's gone.'

'Yeah. See you. Look, I'm going to close the door now

because we're letting all the heat out of the house standing here like this.'

Richard nodded. And I closed the door to save the heat, even though it was possibly the hottest day of the year so far outside. I raced up to my room and, hiding myself behind the curtains, I watched Richard walk down the street, kicking at stones and lamp-posts until I couldn't see him any more. Then I sat down in front of the mirror and gave myself a long hard staring at, again.

But I wasn't staring at myself because I was filled with disgust for the coldness with which I had treated my boyfriend – letting him wander off like some poor kicked puppy – instead I was dwelling on something he had said.

Did I look unusually lovely? I was reasonably impressed. My hair certainly looked much tidier since Guido had done his miracle work and my skin suddenly seemed much clearer too. Perhaps the colonic irrigation had done the trick. I struck poses like a fourteen-year-old whose only ambition in life is to be a supermodel. I was trying to imagine Brian's first sight of me after so long apart.

Did I have a best side that he should see first? Should I be pouting moodily like a hopeful starlet when he first caught sight of me, or grinning like a looney? Did my friendly smile make my face look fat as my cheeks bunched up beneath my eyes? I pouted again, suddenly deciding that smiling too broadly made me look like a demented hamster.

'Hello, Brian,' I murmured in my most seductive voice. 'Long time no see. Did you have a nice flight?'

More questions. Should I wear the shimmery lipstick that made my lips look bigger but my teeth slightly yellow? Or the dark red pout that made me look slightly tight-lipped but with teeth that were pearly white?

I tried on some of the outfits I had borrowed from Mary for the adventure ahead.

'I am drop-dead gorgeous,' I said, reading from the post-it note that Mary had advised I stick on the mirror to remind me of my priceless worth every time I went to inspect my blackheads. 'I am the most wonderful, unique and beautiful woman in the whole damn world.'

Well, near enough.

Upsetting Richard was suddenly as far from my mind as pension schemes. Right then I knew that what I really wanted could be mine.

'Brian Coren,' I murmured to the fox in the mirror. 'Meet your destiny.'

16

I couldn't sleep at all the night before Brian's plane arrived, even though I went to bed at eight o'clock with two slices of cucumber sellotaped to my eyes as a last-minute rescue remedy for my panda rings and my hair slathered in conditioner and wrapped in a plastic bag.

I had decided to spend the evening before Brian's arrival in Harriet's flat, with the intention of getting to know it a little better so that I might seem a more likely resident when he became my guest. But it certainly didn't help me to get any rest. When I turned the expensive-looking bedside lamp out, the flat began to creak and yawn as flats in old houses do and the unfamiliar sounds of beams expanding and water-heating systems making knocking noises as they cooled sent me racing to turn the lights back on.

I even managed to convince myself that the antique four-poster bed in which I had installed myself for the night was possessed by some ancient Corbett family ghost that would exact a terrible revenge on me as soon as I drifted off. I just couldn't seem to get comfortable and when I finally did, the sensation of cold fingers resting on my cheek awoke me just after midnight. I banged my knee on a chest of drawers as I stumbled across the room with the cucumber slices still on my eyes, only to discover when I could see again that the cold fingers had in fact been Hercules's wet black nose. He had climbed into the bed beside me and from his contented snores as he snuggled down into a pillow, I guessed he must always have slept with Harriet in that way.

I moved my pillow to the other end of the bed and lay top to tail with the pampered mongrel until dawn brightened the room. My mind raced throughout the early hours, playing out the precious nine months I had spent with Brian scene by giddy scene. I hadn't imagined how good it had been, had I? We had been incredibly well-suited, hadn't we? Considering we came from such different backgrounds. I wasn't setting myself up for the most embarrassing knock-back of my life, was I? I tried to resummon the faith in my remarkable attributes I had experienced six hours after getting my guts sluiced.

The glowering antique clock in the hallway began to strike the hour. I had lost track of the exact time and told myself that if the hour was an even one, everything would go according to my complicated plan. The clock struck five. I even got out of bed again to check that the chime hadn't become stuck in some way when it should in fact have struck six. But the clock was in perfect working order. I told myself that if I could get back into bed without waking Hercules up, then the clock deal didn't count. As I slipped beneath the covers, Hercules opened a lazy eye and licked my pedicured toes.

I closed my eyes tightly and offered up a little prayer. If I could pull this off, if Brian would only fall for my charms once again and invite me to accompany him back to New York, I promised whoever might be listening to my pleadings that I would dedicate the rest of my life to helping other people – preferably by organising charity balls for my rich American husband's banking colleagues to attend – but I would be good whatever. I deserved this break, I told myself. I deserved to be rescued from my lowly London life and elevated to the Empire State heights of Manhattan society. I had done five years in London after all. Surely I must be up for parole by now.

And miracles did happen, didn't they? How else had Arabella Gilbert got her column in *The Daily*? And what about the time when Seema had her credit cards cut up by her bank manager one day and won three hundred pounds on the lottery the next? She wasn't even being particularly good or nice at the time, but her prayers had been answered – although she had been praying to Ganesh, the elephant-headed Hindu money god whose effigy she kept on her dressing table next to her Jolen creme bleach. I hoped I hadn't been praying to the wrong god for romantic miracles. Was there a god for romantic miracles?

Dawn was definitely with us by then. I looked out of Harriet's bedroom window in the direction of the park. Down below, the main road into central London was already busy with commuters hurrying to beat the worst of the traffic on their way to work. The dustbin van made its halting way with them. It was an ordinary day for everybody. Everybody except me. I felt as though it was the most important day of my life. Far more important than the day I sat my finals. Infinitely more important than the day I started my first job.

Even as I scrubbed at my face in Harriet's en-suite bathroom, my destiny was winging its way towards me. He was passing over Greenland even as I brushed my teeth.

'Please let this go well,' I muttered beneath my breath. 'Please let that psychic who talked to Mum be right about me going abroad. Please let Brian Coren fall for me again. Please let Seema be right about this cream suit.'

I had booked a limousine to bring us back from the airport to Grantchester Square on Harriet's private account, hoping that when the bill arrived she would assume she had booked the car herself and forgotten all about it – she was forever booking cars that she denied all knowledge of when they turned up at the office. I travelled *to* the airport, however, on the tube, trying hard not to get any muck on the cream trouser suit that Mary had lent me for the occasion of my joyous reunion with the love of my life. It was the suit Mary had been wearing in the café that awful morning when she refused to let me borrow her flat. I had actually promised that I would get the suit dry-cleaned after wearing it, but I was hoping I would be able to get away with giving it a quick press with the iron and handing it back unwashed.

As the train sped through the tunnels to the west, I studied my reflection in the dark glass of the window opposite. A sleek-haired, smooth-cheeked face gazed back. I could hardly believe that the calm face framed by such a sophisticated hairdo belonged to me, but when I fingered the gold chain around my neck (another loan from Mary – a firm believer in the power of small but chic accessories) the reflection did the same. I couldn't take my eyes off myself between Green Park and Gloucester Road, as if I were worried my composure might disappear if I didn't keep an eye on it. But at Gloucester Road a tourist wearing a stetson sat down opposite me and blocked out my view.

All went well until we got to Hounslow, then some kind of security alert at the airport meant that the tube train was kept waiting on the tracks between stations. I tried not to panic as the extra time I had factored into my journey for emergency make-up touch-ups in the airport loos started to ebb away. Londoners are so used to security alerts that they don't worry about being blown away by terrorists, only about being late for work or last orders. After twenty minutes the train began to move again, limping towards the terminals at Heathrow.

When I arrived at the airport, I raced to the arrivals lounge, only to discover that Brian's flight was expected to arrive half an hour late anyway, which gave me half an hour longer to study my reflection in a murky mirror in the ladies'.

As the moment when Brian's plane was due to touch down approached, the butterflies which had taken up residence in my stomach upon hearing his voice again in that first phonecall, went into a frenzy. At one point I was convinced I would be sick with nerves the minute he walked out through customs and so I spent five minutes attempting to chuck up manually so that if I did heave with nerves when I finally saw him, there would be nothing left to heave out all over whatever fantastic suit he was bound to be wearing. As it was, I hadn't eaten anything that day anyway. My stomach had been looking flatter since the colonic . . . *Hadn't it?*

But then the landing of Brian's flight suddenly flashed up on the arrivals board, and I raced to find my place at the barrier where the families and friends of the people who had just flown in on flight 607 were gathering in anticipation. The guard at the exit to immigration control however told me that it would take at least another twenty minutes before the first passenger came through. Twenty more minutes. Everything seemed to be conspiring to make me wait, wait, wait. I was sooo nervous. My stomach groaned. My palms were sweating. I suddenly needed to hurl.

Would he recognise me? I began to worry. Would I recognise him? Should I have brought a piece of card with his name written on it just in case? All these things were going through my head as I stared at the empty doorway that led to immigration. Finally, after numerous baseball-capped disappointments had caught my eye and raised my spirits unnecessarily, Brian emerged into the hall pushing a trolley.

He blinked in the bright lights as if he had just spent a year underground. The room faded into a blur around me. He was the only thing in my sight. The noise of the other people milling about the arrivals lounge retreated into a distant hum as my mind was filled with a romantic fanfare more suited to this wonderful moment. Brian scanned the crowd for me, starting at the wrong end of the barrier and taking for ever to spot me while all the time I shouted, 'Brian, Brian! I'm over here!' At least two other guys looked up before Brian finally saw me and made his way across to the barrier where I stood shaking so hard that my legs felt about to give way.

I thought I would definitely pass out then. If it hadn't been for the sheer pressure of the eager people behind me – waiting for a flight of pilgrims to come back from Mecca – I probably would have fallen over. But they held me pressed up against the barrier until Brian took my hand, leaned over the flimsy rail and planted a huge smacker right on my mouth.

Instantly, it was as if he had never been away. He smelled the same. He tasted the same. He was the same. I swayed backwards dangerously.

'Brian,' I murmured.

Then he took both my hands in his and just looked at me, with the barrier still between us. He stared deep into my eyes, saying nothing but communicating everything with a look. He *was* as glad to see me as I was to see him. That much was clear from his eyes. My heart soared towards the high ceiling of the arrivals lounge then swooped down to wing about our heads in ecstasy.

'We got a bit delayed,' was the first thing he said to me. The first thing he said to my face after six whole years.

'I would have waited for ever,' I assured him.

'I hope not,' he said, passing me his suit bag before jumping over the barrier instead of going round it like he was supposed to. 'I don't like to think of you sitting here all night. Is there somewhere we can go to get a coffee before we catch the tube to your place?'

'We're not catching the tube back to my place,' I told him. 'Follow me.' I linked my arm through his and pulled him towards the exit, eager for part one of *Operation Impress Brian* to start.

'You look fantastic,' he chattered as I looked for the limo I had hired for us on Harriet's account. 'I feel so untidy compared to you in that wonderful suit.' He was wearing jeans and a faded blue sweatshirt but I thought he looked delicious. He wasn't any fatter. If anything he looked much fitter and leaner than the Brian I had kissed goodbye. His thick black hair still fell across one eye, begging to be brushed out of the way. I reached across and did just that, hoping that he didn't notice as my hands shook.

'Still, not much point getting dressed up to cross the Atlantic,' he continued. 'I hate travelling cattle class. It's such a nightmare having to sit with your knees under your chin for six hours. You just don't appreciate business class until you have to be at the back of the plane again. Still, I don't suppose that'll ever happen to you. First class all the way from here for you, Lizzie Jordan. You high-flyer, you.'

'What?'

'With your business doing so well,' he elaborated.

'Oh, I sometimes fly cattle class too,' I said modestly.

In fact, I hadn't flown anywhere at all for almost six years. My life had been strictly National Express since college. But I was almost flying then as we waited outside Terminal Two. In a brief moment of silence, Brian squeezed my hand. The feel of his palm against mine after all that time apart sent me sky-rocketing. It was for exactly this reason that I had requested a hire car. I could have driven to and from the airport in Harriet's Mercedes – which I had rescued from the car pound (it had been towed away after she left it at a bus stop on Oxford Street) – but I didn't trust myself to be able to drive in a straight line in my excitement.

'So, are we waiting for a taxi?' Brian asked.

'Not a taxi,' I smiled, as a smooth grey car finally slid forward into the taxi rank with my name on the card in the window. 'A limousine.'

The limousine driver, like most professional drivers in London who don't drive a black cab, had never been to London before. In fact, he told me proudly, we were his first ever pick-up since leaving Newcastle for an even bigger smoke.

'You'll have to start directing me once we get inside the M25,' he said as we cruised back into the city.

'Er, aren't we inside the M25 already?' I asked. 'Just follow the signs for London.'

'And you'll give me the directions to your place once we get a bit closer?'

I nodded irritably. I had wanted to be able to enjoy this journey without worrying about how to get to our destination. Brian and I were sitting at either end of a leather back seat that was almost as big as my bed in Balham. Brian told me it was great to be able to stretch out after six hours with only nineteen inches of leg room, but I hoped he would soon cuddle up. Perhaps some booze would loosen his reserve.

'There should be champagne in here,' I told him, flipping open a neatly upholstered stool that contained a secret fridge.

But when I looked inside I discovered that there was no champagne, just three cans of Stella.

'Where's the champagne?' I buzzed the driver via his intercom.

'Champagne?' he asked with a blank look on his face. 'Was there meant to be some?'

'Yes. I ordered it specially.'

'Well, no one told me,' he shrugged. 'You can have one of my cans of Stella if you like.'

I raised an eyebrow towards Brian. 'It's hardly the same. Would you like a beer?'

'I think I can manage until we get back to your place. I'm just intoxicated by you,' he smiled.

I dissolved into my own puppyish grin.

'Are we getting anywhere near your place by the way?' the driver interrupted.

'Where are we now?' I asked. I hadn't really been following our progress. I'd been too interested in looking at Brian. 'Have we passed Hyde Park?'

'About ten minutes ago. I think.'

Looking out of the darkened windows, I tried to spot a landmark I recognised but the street along which we were cruising was totally unfamiliar.

'Well, I don't think this is the right way,' I said.

'Well, what is the right way?' said the driver, mimicking my voice.

'Haven't you got an *A to Z*?' asked Brian.

Of course he hadn't. Not for London anyway. The driver pulled out a map of Manchester instead. 'Bugger,' he muttered. 'Picked the wrong one up. Don't you know the way to your own house, lady?' the driver asked me when I expressed my consternation. It was clearly my fault as far as he was concerned.

'Well, I don't usually drive around London,' I told him. 'I usually take public transport. More eco-friendly. I only know London from the underground.'

'Seems an awful waste to have a Mercedes and not drive it all the time,' Brian commented.

'Sorry?' I was confused. I'd forgotten that as far as Brian was concerned I did actually have a Mercedes.

'Your car. The silver soft-top you bought last month.'

'Oh, right,' I laughed nervously. '*My* car. Yes, well it's a wonderful drive, but who wants to sit in this traffic in a car when they could be whizzing along in the bus lane on the top of a double decker instead?'

In fact, I did. Almost every night. When the bus lane was parked up with Mercedes Benz coupés carrying diplomatic numberplates, I wished that I owned one of them very much indeed.

'You always were such a green fiend,' Brian joked. 'It's kinda odd that you ended up in the evil world of property development given the way you always felt about the environment. I have to say, I almost choked when I read you had a Mercedes. A huge great gas guzzler like that? I thought you'd get one of those 2CV things if you ever got a car at all. Do you remember those pram-cars we used to see around Oxford from time to time? I guess it would hardly go with your image now.'

'No. In any case, those are about the only cars that can't take unleaded petrol,' I reminded him. The driver still hadn't reset our course and now we were sailing out into a no-man's land of lock-ups and railway arches.

'Er, I think we need to turn around and head back towards the City again,' I suggested. 'Then the West End.' A sign for Docklands whizzed by. 'Docklands is definitely not right,' I told the driver hurriedly. 'I'm really sorry about this, Brian.'

'That's OK,' he assured me. 'I'm enjoying the ride.'

And so was I, at last, with his warm thigh finally against mine. At one point, when I said something that made him laugh – probably something sarcastic about our driver's map-reading abilities, Brian even covered my knee with his hand and squeezed it. The rush of excitement that shot through my body then was enough to make me want to pass out. But before I had a chance to swoon, the driver pulled the car into the kerb and addressed me via the intercom again.

'Is it the Street, the Square or the Mews? Only there's all three here and I can't remember what you said.'

'Mews,' I replied confidently. But almost before I had finished the word, I changed my mind. Mews. That didn't sound right. 'I meant Street,' I said.

'Well, make your mind up. They're in two completely different places.'

'No, hang on. It's the Square. Yes, definitely the Square. Grantchester Square. I haven't lived there long,' I said by way of an excuse.

'I thought you moved into this place in January,' said Brian in surprise.

'January?' What? What had I said about moving flats in January? 'Oh no,' I stumbled. 'That was my last place. Didn't like it much at all. Put it on the market almost as soon as I moved in and I've been in this place for about, oh, two days.'

'Two days?' Brian exclaimed. 'Liz, you should have told me you were moving. I would never have imposed myself upon you if I'd known you were in the middle of moving house.'

'That's OK. You can be my first house guest. Like a house warming.'

'I'm honoured.'

I smiled with my teeth clenched. I had promised myself that I would tell the absolute minimum number of lies needed to get through Brian's visit with the minimum of embarrassment and no more. Already the untruths were spilling from my lips more easily than my two-times table. Just moved in? I cursed myself. That would have been easier to pull off if I'd taken the precaution of passing a duster over everything in Harriet's flat first.

'We're here,' said the driver, proudly. He stopped the car and got out to open the passenger doors. 'Grantchester Square.'

Well, it looked right. I climbed out on to the pavement and realised that I had remembered the square, but in my nervousness at seeing Brian again the house number had since escaped me. I knew it was on the left-hand side of the square and somewhere towards the middle, but every block looked exactly the same and I was suddenly very unsure whether Harriet lived in block seven or block five.

'Where to?' The driver had lifted Brian's lighter bag out of the trunk, leaving Brian to carry the heavier one. 'Only I can't carry too much with my back and I've got to be in Maida Vale at two o'clock to pick up Chaka Khan. Remember her?'

Brian looked towards me expectantly. I scanned the upper windows of blocks five and seven for clues. Of which there were none, of course. I prayed that Hercules would jump up against a window pane in a desperate attempt to follow Harriet to Spain. Bloody mutt must have been asleep again.

I made my way forward as confidently as possible, considering I didn't feel very confident at all, towards block number five and tried to jam my key into the lock. It went all the way in, but refused to turn.

'Let me have a go,' said the driver, after I had twisted it

pathetically for what felt like half an hour. 'You women,' he sighed. I wondered if he meant it in a kind way, but guessed he probably didn't. 'Got no upper body strength, have you?' He gave the key an almighty twist but still the door did not budge. Brian and I looked on with some amusement. 'Just gonna give it one more.' He put his boot against the door and tried again, just as a rather smart woman with a dog almost identical to Hercules appeared behind us and harumphed in an annoyed sort of way.

'Can I help you?' she asked, in that way which does not mean 'Can I help you?' at all, in the sense that friendly shop-keepers mean it. What she meant was, in any other language, 'Should I be calling the police to have you removed?'

'Hercules?' I asked the spaniel, which was looking at me almost as intently as his boss. I was going to be in big trouble if this was some close friend of Harriet's come to check up on the dog because Harriet had called from Majorca when she remembered how canine unfriendly I really was. 'Is that you, Hercules?'

Everyone, including the dog, looked at me as if I were mad.

'This is Camelot,' said the woman archly. 'Hercules lives next door.'

'Oh, my God,' I exclaimed in as light a manner as I could muster. 'I'm awfully sorry. That's it. Next door every-body. I've got completely the wrong block of flats. Silly me.'

Three pairs of eyebrows dipped in confused amusement.

The posh woman put her key into the front door of number five and it opened effortlessly. She went inside and shut the door behind her, but I could see her peeking out through the letter box as I rallied my troops and hustled them on to the next doorstep.

'You really haven't lived here long, have you?' said the driver sarcastically.

'Who's Hercules?' asked Brian.

'My dog.'

'You've got a dog?'

'Didn't I tell you that I'd bought a dog? Well, not bought it exactly. Inherited him really. From the lady who used to own my flat.'

'I thought you hated dogs,' said Brian with a note of rising concern.

'So did I. Until I met Hercules. Top floor,' I said to the driver, who had by now let himself into the hall.

'You must be joking, love,' he replied, putting Brian's suit bag down on the front step. 'I can't go up all those stairs with my back. I'm going to have to love you and leave you, my darling.' And yet he didn't. Leave, that is. He just stood there, looking expectant. I started to climb the stairs. He coughed. Brian, realising what the man was waiting for, dug into his pocket and pulled out his wallet. 'I haven't changed much money yet. Will a twenty do you?'

He handed the driver a twenty-pound note! A twenty-pound note! That was just about my weekly food budget. 'Twenty?' I said, when the driver had gone. 'A twenty-pound tip for someone who didn't even know the way here?'

'Hey, compared to New York taxi drivers, I thought he was rather nice. And at least he spoke English. You know, a guy in New York got killed last week when he didn't realise that his taxi driver was only asking him not to smoke in the cab. The driver asked him to quit puffing in some bizarre language from Kazaksthan or something. The passenger thought the driver-guy had insulted him and threw an insult back and then all hell broke loose. Next thing you know, the passenger's lying on the pavement with his brains blown out.

Witnesses saw him fall out of the back of a yellow taxi, but how many of those do you see around town?'

'I guess we'll count ourselves lucky that he was just an imbecile and not a gun-toting imbecile then.'

'Hey, you really have got snotty since you joined the working world. The old Lizzie Jordan would have been pushing tenners on to every beggar we passed, even when she didn't have one to spare.'

I hesitated to tell him that the old Liz probably had more disposable income when she was on a student loan.

'Come on,' I said, eager to get off the subject. 'Let's go on in.'

'Er, Liz,' Brian stopped me by putting his hand on my arm. 'I just have to ask you one thing before we go inside. What kind of dog is this Hercules?'

'He's a Cavalier King Charles,' I told him. 'Bloody smelly breed but he's reasonably well house-trained.' I had opened the door to the flat and stepped through with a welcoming smile. Brian waited outside.

'Come on in,' I beckoned.

'Oh no,' he said, looking rather wobbly.

'What's up with you?'

'Liz, did I ever tell you about the time I was bitten on the neck by a King Charles Spaniel when I was just two years old?'

Oh God. He had! I remembered the story very well – the creature had almost severed Brian's jugular – and yet it hadn't even crossed my mind when inviting him to stay in a flat with Hercules.

'You know, if it was any other kind of dog . . . Any other kind at all. Rottweilers, dobermans, Irish wolfhounds. I could sleep in the same bed as one of those. But King Charles Cavaliers? I can't explain it, Liz. I mean, it's been almost twenty-five years since it happened, but I still can't be in the same room as a King Charles. They give me panic attacks. Even if I just walk by one in Central Park, even if it's on a lead, it can bring me out in a sweat that lasts for hours.' He mopped his forehead with his cuff. 'See.' He was indeed already sweating.

'Well, what are we going to do?' I asked. 'You must try to come in. He's very nice. Very gentle. Ever so small. If you don't show him you're afraid I'm sure everything will be fine.'

'You might trust that dog to babysit your children, Liz, but I know I can't be in the same flat as a King Charles. I know it's ridiculous. I know I'm a grown man and I shouldn't let a little pooch stop me from going anywhere. But nobody really knows why phobias are so persistent and my therapist advised me that the best way I can deal with my fear is simply by avoiding the focus of that fear.'

'You've been seeing a therapist?' I asked disbelievingly.

'Everyone in America sees a therapist. You know I don't really think they're up to much but I decided I had to go to one when I started to date a girl who kept a King Charles in her apartment. She was a great girl. Fantastic girl. And I was really fond of her. But she had this dog so we could never go to her place and she couldn't stay over at mine because she couldn't leave the dog on its own all night.' He shrugged his shoulders. 'You look shocked, Lizzie.'

I was. But not about the strength of his dog phobia. I was reeling from the fact that he was telling me he had *dated* someone. Someone he really liked? Though I hadn't exactly been celibate since we last saw each other, I hadn't let it cross my mind that Brian might still be in the dating game. I didn't think he had the time to date from what he said in his letters and e-mails. And I had liked it that way.

Now he was telling me, 'I was so disappointed that it had to end. I tried everything to get through my fear. Therapy. Hypnosis. Got myself stuck all over with acupuncture needles. I wanted so badly to overcome my phobia so the relationship could work but I just couldn't do it. Every time I saw her dog I ended up having a panic attack. Once I even fainted.' He smiled a little wistfully. 'She took it very well considering. And we're still friends. How long does this type of dog tend to live for?'

'Hundreds of years,' I found myself telling him testily. 'She should have had it put down.' I wouldn't have let a pooch stand in the way of my future with Brian Coren.

'Well, listen, Liz. I'm really sorry about this but if the dog's in the flat I'm going to have to stay in a hotel tonight.'

'No,' I almost shouted. I wasn't going to let that mutt spoil my plans. Not now that I had come so close. 'I'll sort something out. Perhaps if I just locked Hercules in one of the spare bedrooms? You wouldn't even have to see him.'

'What if he escaped in the middle of the night?'

'He won't escape,' I sighed.

'He might. He'll smell my fear and get out to find me.'

'You really are scared, aren't you?' I groaned.

'I'm afraid so. Can you think of a good hotel?'

'No,' I told him. 'But I can think of a very good kennel.'

'I couldn't possibly ask you to put your dog in a kennel for me. It's not really fair. It's his home.'

'Brian, you're much more important to me than some bloody dog!' I nearly snapped.

'I thought you English were mad about your animals?'

'Pur-leese. Anyway, I'm not really going to send him to a kennel. I'm just going to call someone I know and see if she would like to look after Hercules for the weekend. She's a dog lover without a dog of her own so she'll probably jump at the chance. I'll get her to come over at once. In the meantime, I suppose we'll have to wait over the road.'

So, at the precise moment when I had hoped that Brian and I would be re-acquainting ourselves on Harriet's fat leather Chesterfield sofa, we were instead sitting on two rather less alluring red plastic seats in a greasy café, waiting for Seema to come and take Hercules out of the way.

She came as quickly as she could, bless her. But I was still ready to cry when almost an hour after I'd called her, Seema burst through the café door wearing a ridiculously skimpy pink sari top under her denim jacket. She was also wearing lipstick, which wasn't a good sign. She never wore lipstick unless she thought she had a chance of pulling somebody and she looked gorgeous. Every man in the café was transfixed. Including mine.

'Brian, this is Seema.'

'Liz's secretary,' she added quickly as she pumped Brian's hand to a cacophony of jangles from her real Indian gold bangles and slid on to a plastic seat beside him, eyelashes fluttering all the while.

'Her secretary? Did I speak to you the other day?'

'Yeah, that's right,' said Seema, putting on a coquettish accent that I had never heard her do before. One that made it seem utterly impossible that she was in fact studying for an MBA part-time. 'I can't believe how lucky I am working for Lizzie. She's such a good boss to have, more like a friend than a boss really. And my work is *so* varied. One minute I'm doing her typing. Next, I'm looking after her lovely little dog.'

'Sounds like she takes advantage of you,' Brian joked.

Seema laughed a tinkling laugh and patted Brian on the arm, lingering way too long as she did so. 'Oh, I hope I'm not giving you the wrong impression of her. She doesn't work me *too* hard. Wouldn't dare to on my salary.'

I shot her a look which I hoped she would interpret as 'don't overdo it, Gwyneth Paltrow'.

'Would you care to join us for a coffee before you go to the flat and fetch the dreaded hound?' Brian asked her chivalrously. 'It's the least I can offer after putting you to so much trouble over my silly phobia.'

'Oh, that would be lovely,' Seema said, slipping off her jacket.

'Brian, wouldn't you prefer to have another coffee in the privacy of the flat?' I asked him before he could attract the waiter's attention. 'You've had a long day already, with the flight from New York. And I'm sure Seema has got plenty to be getting on with. The office doesn't close until five on a Friday, remember, Seema?'

The last thing I wanted was for her to stick around for a chat. The more Brian saw of the people from my real life, the more likely someone was to make the remark that would unleash the sorry truth. And Seema was hardly the best liar I had ever met. She was forever clapping her hand to her mouth moments after a careless remark of hers had flown across the table and slapped someone about the face. I remembered particularly vividly the time she had greeted Mary with the immortal line, 'You sound so much thinner on the phone.'

'I suppose I have got tonnes of filing to do,' she said then, rolling her eyes in my direction. 'That's the problem with working for such a high flyer, Brian. Lizzie generates so much more work than anybody else in the office. Has she told you about the 20:20 project yet?'

The what?

'I bet she hasn't,' Seema continued as a smug grin spread

across her plum-coloured, irritatingly beautiful lips. 'She's so modest about her achievements. But don't let her gloss over this particular coup, will you, Brian?'

Brian smiled at me. 'I won't. What was that again? The 20:20 project.'

'That's right.'

I glared at Seema. 'Shall we fetch the dog now?'

'If you insist,' she said.

'Oh, I insist most strongly.'

Brian stayed behind in the café. I would fetch him when the dog had gone. On the way to the flat, I linked my arm through Seema's in what I hoped would seem a friendly gesture from behind in case Brian was watching, but I was using my other hand to pinch her on the front of her arm. Hard.

'What was that for?'

'Coming out looking like that, you cow.'

'Like what?'

'Like you're about to go clubbing.'

'Perhaps I was.'

'On a Friday afternoon? You can see your bra through that top by the way.'

'Perhaps that was the intention.'

I pinched her again.

'Ow.'

'And what was all that crap about the bleeding 20:20 project?' I asked.

'Didn't you like that?' asked Seema. 'I thought it added a very authentic touch, mentioning a specific deal. I made up the name while I was sitting on the tube.'

'I asked you to come and pick up the dog, not audition for a part in *EastEnders*. You're such a bloody bitch.'

'Well, how about you? Treating me like I'm your servant. *Packing me off back to the office* indeed?'

'I had to. What if you'd blown my cover? Well, you probably already have with that 20:20 project crap,' I grumbled. 'What am I going to say when he asks me about it?'

'You'll think of something. You're always telling me you used to be an actress so improvise! Tell you what though,' she sighed. 'I can see why you're going to such ridiculous lengths to impress him. What a babe! He's amazing. Those eyes.'

'Yep,' I agreed. 'He is still truly delicious. I felt like a teeny bopper spotting the lead singer of BoyZone when Brian walked into the arrivals lounge.'

Seema and I both inclined our heads at the thought of Brian's loveliness.

'His eyes are so penetrating,' Seema sighed. 'It's as if he can see into your soul when he looks at you.'

'He was looking at you like that?' I said, suddenly snapping back out of my swoon.

Seema sensed my annoyance and muttered, 'No, of course not. I was just imagining . . . So, do you think you've got a chance with him?' she added to change the subject. 'I mean, to get it back together in the sexual sense?'

'I certainly hope so. He kept putting his hand on my knee on the way back from the airport.'

'You lucky cow. That's a pretty good sign.'

I couldn't help grinning. 'Guess you wasted your lipstick.'

'Damn. I even broke out a new pair of pants.'

'Don't even try it,' I warned.

'I won't,' she sighed.

'Thanks for agreeing to take Hercules,' I softened.

'My pleasure. It's the only male company I'm going to get this weekend. Besides, I like dogs. Especially Hercules.

Did you remember to give him his tablets this morning?'

'What tablets?'

I just hoped that Hercules was still alive and hadn't made too much of a mess in his loneliness. When I opened the door to the sitting room he was chewing on a shoe. One of my favourite Pied a Terre loafers, I noted angrily, and not one of the hundreds of pairs of Manolo Blahniks belonging to Harriet that lay around the flat waiting for someone to break their neck either by wearing the damn things, or by tripping over them. As you can imagine, I had tried a few pairs on. Unfortunately, Harriet had size three feet to go with her size three frame.

I pulled my shoe from Hercules's mouth and hissed, 'I thought you only liked to eat exclusive things.' He'd also had a little go at my imitation Hermes handbag. It was covered with doggy slobber.

When he saw Seema behind me, Hercules went into ecstasies, wagging his tail so hard that his entire backside wagged with it. He wasn't bothered about letting me know exactly where his affections lay when it came to me and my flatmate. She crouched down to greet him with her baby voice and he leapt into her arms, slobbering half her make-up off with his big pink tongue.

'How can Brian not love a wonderful dog like you?' she said with a motherly cluck.

'Well, thanks for the vote of confidence,' I replied. 'But I wouldn't have called myself a dog. I'm not that bad if I get enough beauty sleep.'

'I wasn't talking to you,' she rolled her eyes in exasperation. 'Now, you'd better get Hercules's things together. He'll need his bowl and his blanket. His coat-conditioning tablets were on the windowsill when I last saw them. And you'd better bag up some of that chicken from the fridge.'

'Yes, sir. No, sir,' I whizzed around the flat collecting Hercules's stuff. I couldn't wait to get rid of him. Or Seema. 'Remember he won't walk on tarmac or paving stones,' I reminded her.

'I wasn't going to make him walk on paving stones,' she exclaimed as if she were horrified by the very suggestion of such cruelty. 'You're going to have a lovely weekend with me, aren't you, Herc? Oh, and you owe me big time, by the way.'

'Are you talking to me or the dog this time?'

'You, stupid.'

'What is it you want?'

'I'll think of something. Something that fits the enormity of this favour.'

'Anything you want. But can we just get the dog out of the flat now? Brian has been waiting in that café for almost two hours.'

'And you want to get him into bed,' Seema smiled.

'Only to get over his jet lag,' I insisted.

'Yeah, right. Give him one for me while you're at it.'

'Seema!'

I walked back in the direction of the café with Seema and the dog. We parted ways at the café door. Seema couldn't come inside again, for obvious reasons, but she caught Brian's eye through the glass and waved at him. He waved back, trying hard not to look at Hercules.

'She's nice, your secretary. Very sharp. But why was she carrying the dog instead of walking it?' Brian asked.

'He has bad feet,' I explained. Harriet may not have been embarrassed to own a phobic dog but I was. 'Well, that's sorted out now. Shall we go back to the flat?'

*   *   *

'Wow.'

At last Brian was standing in the middle of Harriet's living room, taking in the view.

'Wow. This is great. Considering you've only been here for a couple of days, you've really made this place look like home. Wow, Liz. It's fantastic. Where did you get all this wonderful stuff?'

'You know,' I shrugged. 'On my travels.'

'Do you mind if I take a closer look at this?' he asked, picking up a vase that I guessed would probably cost me more than a year's salary to replace.

'Er—' My heart stopped as he turned the vase over and looked at the mark on its bottom.

'Oh. It's not what I thought it was,' he told me as he deciphered the little sign. 'Did you know it's not what it looks like it is?'

I nodded, dumbfounded. I didn't know what it looked like, other than a vase.

'Pretty though,' Brian conceded. 'Hope you didn't pay too much for it.'

'Put it down,' I ordered, unable to contain my panic.

'OK.' He put the vase down again abruptly. 'Guess that's pretty rude of me isn't it? Coming round here and appraising your antiques before I've even got my coat off. Blame it on being American. I can't get over all this old stuff. I just love antiques.'

He wandered over and threw his arms around me then, picking me up and swinging me around and around on the Persian rug, with me petrified the whole time that my feet might take out something that was real.

'Alone at last. I am so glad to see you again,' he sighed, finally placing me back on my feet and gazing tenderly into my eyes.

'I'm glad to see you too,' I told him. Our lips hovered so close for a moment, I felt sure that he was going to kiss me. Properly.

'I have a present for you in my bag,' he said instead, breaking away to hunt through his luggage for my gift. 'It's only a little something but I hope it might mean more than a little to you.'

He handed me a flat square parcel, carefully wrapped in layers of silver and gold tissue paper, tied with a metallic gold ribbon.

'I found it yesterday,' he explained. 'In an antiquarian bookshop in the Village. Bearing in mind that I was coming to see you, it seemed like an omen. I had to get it. Open it up.'

I peeled away the tissue paper. Obviously it was going to be a book, but an omen? I wondered what on earth it could be.

'It's a really old edition of *Antony and Cleopatra*. Obviously, it's not a first edition, but look inside. Look at what it says on the nameplate. I couldn't believe it.'

I opened the book up. A nameplate was pasted to the inside cover and in swirly black, somewhat faded, old-fashioned handwriting, the book's previous owner had written her name.

'Elizabeth Taylor,' I breathed reverently. 'Do you think this belonged to the real one?'

'Maybe. Maybe not. But I thought you'd like to have it anyway. Do you like it?'

'I love it,' I assured him, turning the little book over in my hands and admiring the gilt lettering on its hard red cover.

'Perhaps you'll give me a solo performance later on. You were the best one-eyed Cleopatra I ever saw.'

'I think I'm probably the only woman who ever played Cleopatra with one eye,' I reminded him.

'But you were still magical,' he told me. 'Really moving. You know, I think I fell in love with you that night. While you were playing with your asp.'

We shared a meaningful gaze for a moment before I had to look away, cheeks flushing furiously.

'Well, where do you want me to put these bags?' Brian asked me, and the moment was broken.

I took him not to Harriet's bedroom but to one of the other bedrooms. Although I hoped he wouldn't actually be sleeping in there, I didn't want to make an idiot of myself by putting his bags in the room I had been sleeping in and having him ask for them to be moved. I had however also taken the precaution of choosing the most uncomfortable bed to help him make his mind up in the way I hoped he would.

Looking at the inscription he had added to his gift to me, I had every reason to think I would be getting my way.

'To my own darling Lizzie,' he had written. 'To old times and new. All my love, Brian.' He had underlined the 'all' three times and signed off with five big kisses.

'Would you mind if I had a little nap now?' Brian asked me. 'Only I'm starting to feel real tired. Wake me for dinner?'

I assured him that I would. He disappeared into the bedroom and I returned to the sitting room where I sat reading his inscription in the front of the book again and again and again. I was in heaven. Mission almost accomplished. Brian Coren was back in my life.

17

I insisted that we went somewhere really special for dinner that night, despite Brian's protestations that he was very jet-lagged and would be happy with Marmite on toast – a taste he had acquired during his year in Oxford. But I had it all planned out and wasn't going to let Brian waste a moment of his visit on sleep if I wasn't in the bed with him.

I had picked the Capricorn restaurant from *Tatler*'s best restaurant list for its reputation as being a wonderful place to impress and seduce. Besides, Mary had lent me the most amazing Donna Karan dress imaginable and I could hardly change into it to make toast, could I?

'Come on, Brian,' I jollied him. 'You're not here for long. I want you to make the most of your trip to London. We're going out.'

'Couldn't we go tomorrow instead?' he pleaded.

'No. You have no idea how difficult it was for me to get a reservation at this restaurant. It's only just opened. Last time I was there I found myself sitting between Michael Caine and Sly Stallone. Sly is terribly short, you know.' At least the first part of that spiel wasn't a lie. It had been difficult to get a reservation. In fact, I'd had to use Mary's name simply to get a look in.

'OK,' he said. 'Point me in the direction of the bathroom again.'

I pointed him in the direction of the broom closet. Absolutely accidentally, of course. But I think he thought I was joking.

I, meanwhile, retired to Harriet's bedroom to deck myself out in the DKNY. I had put Brian in the 'spare' room but I had no intention that this arrangement should actually persist when we got home from the restaurant. I had splashed out on the most incredible set of underwear imaginable. From Rigby and Peller – corsetiers to the Queen, no less. I had seen the set I wanted on a model in *Cosmopolitan* and Rupert from the office had agreed that if anything could persuade a man to give up a pair of Rugby World Cup tickets it would be the prospect of an evening at home with a girl in burgundy-coloured lacy half-cups with a matching g-string and suspender belt. Well, if it could persuade rotten Rupert away from the rugby, it would definitely work on a man with no obvious need to suspend real life whenever twenty-odd grown men started kicking around a leather sac full of air.

My most expensive knickers yet gave me just the confidence I needed not to trip over with surprise when the doorman at the Capricorn actually opened the door for us.

'Have whatever you want,' I insisted just before I opened the menu and clocked the astronomical prices. Brian's menu didn't even have any prices on it. We were in that kind of place. 'Mmm. Doesn't this look wonderful,' I said, scanning the menu for anything under a tenner. Bread rolls perhaps. I could have two of those.

'Pick whatever you like,' I bumbled on. 'I'll be putting it on my expense account.' If only. 'I'm going to say that you're a potential customer so we can go as mad as we like.'

'Excellent,' said Brian. 'Shall we start with some champagne in that case?'

The wine waiter was already hovering. Meanwhile, two waiters appeared with something they termed an *amuse bouche*. I was confused and told them that they must have got the wrong table because we hadn't ordered our meals yet.

'Madame. These are complimentary,' the waiter smiled. Bloody condescendingly, I thought, for someone who cleared plates for a living. 'This is a quail's egg in caramel. This is seared tuna on sushi rice. And that,' he said, as I popped something that looked like a mushroom vol-au-vent into my mouth, 'is escargot in a garlic sauce.'

'Snails,' Brian translated obligingly.

My hand went to my mouth instinctively, but I just about managed not to hurl.

'I wonder if we might have some champagne to wash this lot down?' I asked as I choked my mouthful down.

'Certainly. And which champagne?'

'Cristal,' I said confidently.

Brian raised an eyebrow – subtly. As did the sommelier – not so subtly. And I would raise both of mine when I finally saw how much the bloody stuff had set me back.

'I was drinking Cristal by the bucketload only the other night,' I said, loudly enough for the sommelier to hear as he minced off to fetch some. 'At an after-show party for the Golden Brothers. You know the Golden Brothers?'

'The designers?' said Brian.

'Yes. The hottest duo in town.'

'Even I've heard of those guys. How did you get to meet them?'

'Oh, through Mary,' I had to admit.

'Mary?' Brian leaned forward, looking altogether more interested than he had been at the mention of the Golden Brothers. 'Not Miserable Mary? Do you still see much of her?'

'From time to time.'

'What's she doing now?'

'Oh, she runs a little business of her own,' I glossed.

'Really? What as?'

'Agent,' I said briefly. 'You know, you really should try these quail eggs.'

'What kind of agent?' Brian wasn't about to give up.

'A sort of talent agent for actors and footballers and things,' I muttered. 'Sorts out deals for lots of adverts. Voice-overs.'

'That sounds interesting.'

'I'm sure it is. Would you like half of this egg with me?' I tried again.

'Have you told her about my visit?' Brian asked. 'Because I'd really love to catch up with her if that were possible.'

'I think she's pretty busy.'

'Not all the time, surely. We could call her.'

I frowned.

'What's up? Have you two fallen out?'

'No,' I smiled. 'Nothing's up at all. I'm just wondering how Mary will be able to fit in seeing us.'

'She'll make time when she hears that I'm over in England. Mary would do anything for her old friends.'

I tried not to snort into the glass of champagne that had just been placed in my hand by the diligent sommelier. Anything for her friends. Ha! If only Brian knew. Having said that, I was actually spilling my drink down *her* dress at the time.

'Good old Mary,' Brian sighed. 'Tell you what, let's make the first toast of the evening to old friends. To Mary and Bill, in fact.'

I raised my glass. 'To Mary and Bill.'

'We must call her as soon as we get home,' said Brian.

★   ★   ★

For the whole of the meal, I couldn't stop worrying that Brian really would insist on calling Mary when we got back to the flat. It was the last thing I wanted, for him to see just how successful and sophisticated Miserable Mary had become. And though she had promised she would not tell my secret to anyone – except any of her glitterati friends who might find it amusing – I had decided that keeping Mary and Brian apart was the only way to guarantee that she didn't drop me in it with some careless comment about how good I looked in her dress, or her necklace, or someone else's flat.

But Brian was on a real nostalgia kick. He wanted to talk about the past, to go over the times we had shared in Oxford; and I suppose I should have been grateful that it saved me from having to elaborate on my fictional present. However, I wasn't too happy that he wanted to talk not just about the time that he and I had spent together snuggled up in our bedrooms, but the times we had spent as a foursome, Brian, Bill, Mary and I.

'Do you remember the night when Bill and Mary got off with one another?' he laughed.

Anyway, the thought that he wanted to see Mary so badly rather distracted from the calamari I had ordered. I couldn't even relax and enjoy my mousse au chocolat.

When the bill came, I didn't even look at it. I knew that looking at it would in no way diminish the horror. Instead, I threw my RSPCA-sponsoring Mastercard on top of the bill with as much nonchalance as I could muster. I had given up counting after the first course, but I had probably just agreed to write off the best part of a month's salary on less than two hours' enjoyment. Not as well enjoyed as it could have been considering the amount of time Brian spent talking about Mary. And I still felt hungry, having avoided eating any of the petit fours because I wasn't sure if they were actually supposed to be edible with all that gold leaf.

'Er, I'm afraid there seems to be some kind of problem with madame's card,' said the maître d', bending close so that he could whisper subtly in my ear. My expression must have let Brian know almost instantly that there was a problem. And I knew exactly what the problem was. I must have been up to my limit.

'What's up?' he asked.

'My card,' I said, in a very little voice.

'It often happens, madame,' said the maître d'. 'The magnetic strip gets damaged and then the card won't scan through our machine. We would have punched the number in manually, but the last digit seems to have been . . .'

Chewed off.

I took the card and looked at it in wonder. Hercules must have put a tooth through it when he got hold of my handbag.

'I'll deal with this,' said Brian, throwing his own card on to the plate.

'I'll pay you back,' I said weakly.

'No,' he said. 'This can be my treat.'

Thank God I hadn't drunk so much that I went into the 'No, I will' type of scenario that had preceded this whole debacle.

'Anyway,' said Brian, as he signed the receipt with a flourish. 'At least this way I come away with some of my male pride still intact. It's a bit disheartening for an old-fashioned guy like me to be taken out by a really successful career girl like you . . .'

★   ★   ★

I was about to ask the maître d' to call a taxi, all the better to take me quickly home for a lie down after that narrow shave with the credit card, when Brian suggested, 'Let's walk back across the park.'

'What? Hyde Park?' I asked.

'Yes. It's not too far is it?'

'No. But it's dark.'

'Are you scared? You'll be with me.'

I could hardly tell him that the thing I was most scared of right then was stepping in something unspeakable in a pair of Mary's expensive shoes. Brian took my worried smile to mean that I thought he had proposed a wonderful idea and soon we had crossed Park Lane – at a gallop through the traffic instead of taking the sensible underpass – and we were climbing over the fence into Hyde Park.

'Doesn't this feel like old times?' Brian asked. 'Do you remember that time when we climbed over that gate to get down to Christchurch meadow after dusk?'

'Of course I do. I ripped a hole in my one and only jumper.'

'I'd forgotten that. But it was romantic, wasn't it? With the moonlight glittering on the river and the mist rolling across the fields.'

'Very romantic,' I had to agree. It wasn't quite the same to be looking at the moonlight on the Serpentine, where empty plastic bottles floated like ghostly submarines, but that was where Brian chose for us to sit down and take in the night air.

'That was a great restaurant,' he said. 'But you know what, I'd have been just as happy to get a bag of fish and chips and eat them out here, with you.'

Now he tells me, I thought.

'I mean,' Brian continued, 'that restaurant was clearly very well-designed and decorated but no matter how much money we throw at things, we can never quite recreate the beauty of the things that surround us anyway. Nature's beauty. What could be better than the reflection of tall trees on water? The sound of night birds calling to one another.'

I tilted my face up towards his in case he thought it was about time he kissed me. But he hadn't finished talking.

'You know,' said Brian, 'it doesn't feel like I haven't seen you in six years at all. You're almost exactly the same, once you take into account the accoutrements of your incredible success, of course. But it's nice that you haven't let success go to your head. All the women I meet in New York are successful, sure, but they're so hardened by it. Always thinking about the money. Always listening out for the hot tip that will make them their next million. Never relaxing and being themselves. Not like you. You still let the old Lizzie Jordan come out to play. It makes me feel like we're at college again. Transported back in time.'

'It's as if we're back where we left off?' I suggested eagerly.

'Exactly.'

He turned so that he was facing me more squarely and stretched his arm along the back of the bench. Next, he started to play with the hair on the back of my neck.

'This haircut really suits you,' he told me. 'I love this bit at the back.' And he ran his fingers up the back of my neck, sending shivers running down my body in the opposite direction. 'It feels so fluffy. So soft. Like you.'

My internal organs gave a collective shudder.

'I've thought about you often,' he said, leaning a little closer. 'Sometimes I would see a girl who looked like you on the subway, or coming out of a store and then I wouldn't be able to get you out of my head for hours.'

'I know exactly how that feels,' I murmured.

'I even followed a girl for half a mile once because she looked so much like you. I thought she was you. But when I caught her up, she was nothing like you. She didn't have your eminently kissable lips.'

Kissable lips? Were they really? I licked them to make sure.

'Kissable, missable lips,' Brian whispered as finally his own lips landed on mine.

'Let's go back to the flat,' I said urgently, once I'd come up for air.

'That's the best idea I've heard all day.'

He got up and pulled me to my feet after him. I stumbled on the grass in my borrowed high heels. Brian reached out to steady me but even when I was steady again, he didn't let me go. Instead, he wrapped his arm around my waist and held me tight all the way to the next perimeter fence. And when we got back to the flat, he still didn't let me go.

18

Oh, magical morning! When I woke up and rolled over in bed to find Brian beside me, all the disappointments of the past six years seemed to have faded away with my quickly forgotten dreams.

Even the weather was with me. Outside, London was already bathing in the early sunlight of another beautiful day. The sky above us was pure baby blue but for a handful of cotton-puff clouds. Stepping out on to the roof garden while Brian slept on below, I was wonderfully surprised to discover that it was already warm. A few of Harriet's badly neglected flowers were slowly unfurling to turn their faces to the sun. I picked a miniature pink rose, not quite open yet, from a straggling rose bush that had long since outgrown its peeling trellis. I carried the rose into the kitchen, where I placed it in an egg-cup full of water to decorate Brian's breakfast tray. A better fate had no flower, I thought poetically as I made some toast. In a proper toaster for once.

But Brian was already up before I could take the tray to him. He walked across the polished wooden floor of Harriet's sitting room, pushing his fringe from his eyes and looking as though at any moment we might hear a voice-over artist boom out a slogan for a new brand of instant coffee. It was perfect. A snapshot from the perfect life I had always hoped for. We smiled shyly at each other across the breakfast bar as if we had just spent our very first night together.

'I was going to bring you breakfast in bed,' I told him.

'Perhaps we should go back there,' he said, taking my hand and kissing me on the palm. 'Wow, you look beautiful in the mornings.'

I took the compliment gracefully. He didn't have to know that I had spent a good half hour making repairs to my face in the bathroom before he woke up.

'Come on, let's go,' he said, taking me by the hand and leading me back to the bedroom. Our breakfast remained uneaten until lunch time.

'We must call Mary,' Brian said as we finally ate our toast. Cold and hard, it was by then. Just like the toast at college.

Brian took me by surprise. I was rather hoping he had forgotten about our other old friend.

'I can't come to London and not see Mary,' he continued. 'I'd be gutted if I found out she came to the States and didn't drop by to see me.'

He picked up the fake antique telephone on Harriet's bedside table. 'What's her number?'

I wondered whether I could get away with pretending that I didn't have it. But I knew that Brian would only look in the telephone directory and Mary was in the phone book, of course. Blast her. I trotted out the number and Brian dialled.

'Let's hope she's in,' he said to me.

'Be out,' I prayed silently. 'Be out.'

But she was in.

'Brian! Darling!'

Brian held the receiver between us so that I could hear Mary too as she shrieked her hellos.

'What do you think of Lizzie's lovely new flat?' was the first thing she asked.

'It's great. Really beautiful. And I've been having a wonderful time. But it doesn't feel right to be in England and not see you. Liz feels the same. We need to have a reunion. Get the whole old gang together.'

'What a fabulous idea!' she said. She would.

'How about tonight? If you're not too busy.'

Be busy, I prayed. She was always too busy when I called and tried to get to see her, but . . .

'I'm never too busy for you, Brian,' she flirted. 'You know I'd drop anything for my friends in any case.'

The cow. That wasn't the way it had seemed when I last asked her for a favour.

'Tell you what,' she said excitedly. 'I'll throw a party for you. Just a small one. My apartment isn't as sumptuous as Lizzie's, of course,' she smarmed. 'But I'm sure I can get four around my little kitchen table.'

'Sounds wonderful,' said Brian. Genuinely.

'Are you up for that, Liz?' Mary shouted for my benefit.

'Of course,' I said.

Brian handed the phone to me so that I could make the arrangements. A rendezvous was fixed for seven.

'You don't mind coming to my place tonight, do you, Lizzie?' Mary asked.

I grunted my assent.

'You should wear that gorgeous white dress of yours. You know the one.'

I did indeed. It was one she had lent me, naturally.

'Isn't that great of Mary to go to the trouble of having us over for dinner?' said Brian when she finally hung up.

I nodded. And it was good of her really, if I was honest with myself. I had been selfish in hoping that Brian and I would get to spend our four days together entirely alone. He hadn't seen Mary for six years either. I shouldn't begrudge her one night of his company with me to chaperone. And it wasn't as if I wouldn't benefit too from a night in with Mary. It would give my credit card a break. It was a good idea.

The dress which Mary had suggested I wear for this particular occasion was particularly gorgeous. Versace, she claimed, though the label had been cut out so I couldn't confirm whether that was really true. Whatever it was, it was beautiful. Possibly the most beautiful dress I had ever worn. A column of glittering white pleated silk encrusted with crystal and gold beads. I felt as if I was on my way to the Oscars. Not round to Mary's for spag bol and chianti. Except that Mary threw a very different kind of dinner party now.

On the way to her flat, Brian reminisced about Mary's infamous spaghetti, cooked in an old kettle in the overflowing pedal-bin extension that passed for a kitchen in our halls of residence. But when the door to her flat was opened by an unfamiliar young boy in a smart white shirt and a black bow tie, I guessed that whatever we were having, it wasn't going to be Ragu.

Though it was August, and an unusually hot British August at that, Mary had lit the fire (living flame gas – this was a smoke-free zone) to complete the ambience which she had clearly been throwing a cheque book at all afternoon. She stood by the fireplace, staring into the flames as though she were looking for omens. When we walked into the room she took an age to turn round and I cursed her for trying to create some kind of tableau. It was something she used to do while we were still at college. She would spend ages arranging herself in her room just before someone she fancied came round. She told me it was about making a grand entrance without having to be the one who was doing the entering. And that night she was doing it considerably more successfully than when she used to lounge half-naked on a bean-bag with The Doors playing *sotto voce* in the background.

If I had thought the dress she lent me was great, it now became clear that Mary had been giving me her cast-offs. The red dress she was wearing now had a scooped-out back that dipped almost to her knicker line (not that she had a VPL, of course). To emphasise the perfection of her rear view, a long string of pearls dangled from a knot between her shoulder blades to her waist.

I glanced nervously from Mary's back to Brian and back again. Brian's mouth was ever so slightly ajar. When I looked at him he smiled as if he had just been caught picking his nose.

At last Mary turned around.

'I didn't hear you come in,' she said.

'Yeah, right,' I muttered.

'Brian,' Mary purred, advancing towards him with her arms wide open. 'It's been so long.' She embraced him in a glittering bear hug and shot me a wolfish smile over his shoulder. 'I'm so glad you could make it. You look wonderful. You look nice too, Liz. Is that Armani?'

'Versace apparently,' I corrected the cow.

Mary left off the boa constrictor act for a moment and held Brian at arm's length to get a better look at him.

'I can't believe you're really here,' she almost whispered.

Brian put his hand to his tie, nervously I thought. I wondered if he was even sure who he was talking to. As far as I knew, the last time he'd seen Mary, she had been doing an impression of a hobo, a particularly dirty one at that, in a huge hairy black coat that covered her from neck to feet even though it was high summer. He had certainly never seen her with her natural hair colour.

'You . . . You've changed,' he stuttered.

'I know,' she said, smiling broadly, confident that she had changed for the better. 'But you haven't. Still so slim! Are you working out?'

'I don't really get a lot of time for that right now, but thanks. Er, are you?'

Mary ran a lazy hand down across her hip. 'I try to take care of myself.'

'I've never seen you in anything but black before. Red suits you.'

'Doesn't it? I hardly ever wear black these days. I can't believe I spent so much time looking like an undertaker's moll.'

'You were going through a phase,' Brian laughed. 'Lots of creative people make themselves deliberately ugly so that people concentrate on what they can do, rather than what they look like.'

Mary agreed. But I could tell by the way her eyebrows dipped together ever so slightly that she wasn't entirely happy with the implication that she had actually looked ugly during her gothic years.

'Well, let's get you two some champagne,' she trilled.

'Good idea,' Brian agreed.

Mary clicked her fingers and the young man who had opened the door to us appeared with a bottle of bubbly and three glasses.

'You got staff in,' I said incredulously.

'Don't you?' she replied. 'Well, here's to us,' Mary raised her glass ever so slightly. 'Old friends.'

'Such a shame Bill isn't with us as well,' said Brian. 'Then it could have been exactly like old times.'

'Not exactly,' Mary laughed. 'Dear old Bill. Can you imagine him here? He'd have to wear gold lamé cycling shorts or something. I think he's best where he is, looking for rocks in the mud somewhere hot.'

'Come on,' Brian nudged her with his elbow. 'Don't be so cruel. We all know that you love Bill really. What about that night at the Two Items of Clothing party?'

'What about that night?' said Mary with a piranha grin and a naughty wink.

'Is Mitchell going to be joining us tonight?' I asked. Somehow, during the course of their conversation, Mary had insinuated herself between Brian and me. Now, she had her long bare arm linked through his and somehow she managed to end up sitting next to him on a very small white sofa.

'Oh, I don't know. Maybe. He's very busy.'

'Is this a boyfriend?' Brian asked.

'Depends who's asking,' Mary replied with another wink.

'Got something in your eye?' I asked her.

We sipped champagne in Mary's recently feng shui-ed sitting room for what seemed like an age. But even though I must have had at least half a bottle to myself, I simply couldn't relax. Without a fourth person to bounce conversation off, our banter was strictly limited to reminiscing about college and talking about what we were doing now. Brian was keen to hear all about Mary's business but Mary kept throwing his questions back at me.

'You don't want to hear about my boring little agency,' she smiled. 'Lizzie's the big business woman around here these days.'

'That's very generous of you,' I retorted. 'But I've been boring Brian about my work all day. Why don't you tell him about the time you met Michael Jackson?'

I had another, very momentary, reprieve while she told

the tale about her meeting with the man himself and, even more interestingly, I thought, the man's pet monkey. But she wasn't about to let me off the hook.

'Didn't you once look for a little flat for Michael Jackson?' she asked me when she had finished.

I shook my head and stuck my nose into my glass.

'I'm sure you told me that,' Mary persisted. 'Honestly, Brian, she's so modest. Liz gets to meet even more celebs than I do in her business. In fact, nine out of ten celebrity house-hunters wouldn't trust anybody else.'

Brian looked at me expectantly. I shrugged.

'You know,' he said, 'come to think of it, I'm sure you e-mailed me to say that you were flat-hunting for Michael Jackson . . .'

I felt like a drowning sailor whose life is flashing in front of his eyes. Flat-hunting for Michael Jackson? Was that to be the lie that put the puncture in my dinghy? Please, no. I looked from Mary to Brian. Both of them were smiling at me. Brian in a nice way – hoping to hear a juicy story he could take back to New York. Mary however was smiling like the cat that's got the fieldmouse running backwards into a milk bottle.

Then, inexplicably, she snatched me back to safety.

'Come into the kitchen, Liz. I want to ask your advice about the bouillabaisse.'

'But you're not cooking,' said Brian. He was right. There were two further serfs in the kitchen doing battle with Mary's unpredictable Smeg hob.

'Brian, don't be such a tease,' said Mary, waving his objection away with a flick of her red-nailed hand while simultaneously hauling me to my feet. I followed her mutely. I was so shocked by my brush with the truth that I didn't even complain that Mary had been the cause of it.

In the kitchen, Mary strolled about dipping a tea-spoon into various bubbling pots like a home counties missus. The hired help addressed her as 'madam'. She complained that there wasn't enough salt in the sauce.

'It's meant to be like that. Besides, too much salt is bad for your blood pressure,' said the fresh-faced young chef.

'I think my blood pressure's about to shoot the top of my head off,' I said.

'You did look a bit stressed in there,' Mary commented. 'Everything all right?'

'Oh yeah,' I started to say. No thanks to her. But before I could add that I was all right compared to someone who's just been bitten by a scorpion or discovered that their house has been blown away by Hurricane Mitch, Mary was finding fault with the vegetables.

'Did you go anywhere good last night?' she asked, when she had finished explaining the right way to cook peas.

'Capricorn,' I told her.

'I'm surprised you got a table,' she replied.

'Not half as surprised as I was. I'm afraid I had to use your name.'

She snorted in an amused sort of way. 'Well, you might have asked me first, Liz. What if I'd decided to go to the same restaurant last night and hadn't been able to get a table because the *real* Mary Bagshot had already booked? What if I'd needed to wine and dine an important client? It might have been very embarrassing.'

'I didn't think of that.'

'Seems to me like you've given up thinking ahead altogether lately. Have you had any serious discussions with Brian about your glittering career yet?' she asked sarcastically.

'I can't say we have,' I admitted. 'For obvious reasons.'

'I suppose your biggest worry must be other people dropping you in it,' she added, with just a glint of malice beneath her blue eyeshadow. 'Have to keep him well away from your usual haunts, eh? Just in case one of your friends asks how the place in Balham is, or something.'

'Mary, you won't, will you?'

She blinked her eyes innocently. As if the thought had never crossed her mind. 'Liz! How could you suggest such a thing! I'm throwing a dinner party for you. I even lent you my favourite dress for the occasion. I've been trying to help you pull this whole stunt off.'

'And I am so grateful,' I said warily. 'You know I am.'

'Is it exactly as it used to be or better?' Mary asked suddenly.

'It's all exactly as it was before he left to go back to the States. Which is fabulous,' I sighed.

'How wonderful. I'm very pleased for you. Seems like everything is going according to your plan.'

'Do you think Mitchell will be coming tonight?' I asked. I can't tell you how much I wanted him to be there too. I thought if Mary and I both had men to hang on to that night I might feel a little more secure about her promises.

'He might do,' she sighed. 'He's trying to put the new album to bed before he runs into another week's studio time.'

'You deserve more attention,' I told her, hoping to butter her up. 'Isn't he worried that you might run off with someone else if he leaves you on your own all the time?'

Mary shook her head. 'Who else would I run off with? All the men I know are attached or gay. Besides, why would they be interested in me? Good old Mary Bagshot?'

'Why? Because you're beautiful. Witty. Hugely successful. Why wouldn't everybody be interested in you?'

She nodded modestly. 'Some men are threatened by all that.'

'Brian isn't.'

'Mmm. Funny isn't it? And really rather ironic. Brian's absolutely mad about you and you're basically pretending to have my kind of life.'

She pulled a Chanel lipstick out from her delicate velvet pochette and smeared on a deep-red smile. When she had finished, she offered the lipstick to me.

'Put some of this on. Then I can almost pretend that I've kissed him myself. He is looking incredibly gorgeous tonight.'

I had taken the lipstick from her before the significance of her words hit home. 'Mary, you're not . . . I mean, you don't want to be with Brian, do you? Not after all these years.'

'God, no,' she laughed. 'I was joking. I haven't thought about Brian in a romantic way since the night that you first got off with him. After we had that long conversation in Tesco's about how neither of us should ever get off with him because it would break up our happy little social scene, remember?'

'I thought we made the actual pact in the chip shop.'

'Well, there you go. Perhaps we did. You see, it's all so unimportant to me that I can't even remember where we had such a supposedly pivotal conversation. So much has happened since those days, Liz. We were practically children back then. I was attracted by Brian because he seemed so glamorous and cultured compared to the likes of boring old Bill. Now that I meet cultural icons on a daily basis, I'm rather bored by all that sophistication. Perhaps if Bill were to walk through the door tonight dressed in his muddy archaeology gear I might actually be tempted to give him another go.'

'You never really did tell me what happened between the pair of you that night,' I probed.

'Well, what do you think happened? We were students, we were drunk, we got our kit off and had the worst sex imaginable. After which he sat back with a cigar, singing along to his bloody *Led Zeppelin Live* album like he had just performed for his country. I had barely felt a thing. Except the bloody hair on his back. Tell me,' she linked her arm through mine, 'has Brian got any hairier since your last encounter?'

'If he has, he must get them waxed.'

'That's another thing I like about American men. So fastidious. Did I ever tell you about the American guy I met who made me sit in a bath of hot water and baking soda before he would come anywhere near me?'

'Jeez! And you did what he asked?' I said, wrinkling up my nose. The hired girl who was shelling a fresh pile of peas cocked her head in our direction and wrinkled her nose too.

'I was in love,' Mary told us. 'And I actually quite liked the smell of the stuff. Sure I must have had plenty of baking soda up my hooter without knowing it since then anyway.'

She looked at the young waiter meaningfully. He pretended he hadn't been listening and carried on folding napkins.

'We should get back to Brian,' I said, heading out of the kitchen.

'No, wait,' she grabbed my arm. 'I've got a secret to tell you first.'

She pulled me close. 'You've got to promise that this won't go any further. If I want press leaks, I'll arrange them myself.'

'Why would I talk to the press? What have you done?'

'I'm sorry, Lizzie. I'm just so used to everyone I know knowing someone worth knowing. I keep forgetting that you don't really know anybody except students and penniless loonies.'

'Thanks for reminding me. So, what's the big surprise?'

She didn't seem unduly bothered that there were three hired hands in the room so it couldn't have been that incredible, I figured.

'Mitchell and I have decided to get married,' she said in a stage whisper.

My mouth dropped open. The girl on pea duty stopped shelling.

'But I thought you said that he couldn't. I thought you said that it would ruin his career to get hitched,' I protested.

'Well, I did think that last week. But Mitchell is absolutely desperate to make us official and so I've decided to let him have his way. It might help him to work more effectively and I don't think marriage will be too much of a turn-off to his fans. Heaven knows, the fact that my father is married has never stopped women throwing themselves at him and he doesn't have Mitchell's abs or his bank balance.'

'I'm really pleased for you,' I told her sincerely. Although, oddly, she didn't look as though she was bubbling over at the prospect herself.

'I hope you won't mind if I don't ask you to be a brides-maid,' she added matter-of-factly.

'Mind? I was dreading it,' I said, before it hit me that much as I had always complained that I would hate to don a puff-sleeved satin number for any of my friends, I was actually quite offended not to be considered. 'Are you going to ask your nieces?' I suggested. She had two gorgeous nieces, aged seven and five.

'Er, no. I'm going to ask Arabella Gilbert actually.'

Now my mouth dropped open again.

'Obviously the wedding will be covered in all the big gossip mags and Arabella could do with the exposure.'

'But . . . I mean, you hardly know her. Not really.'

'We've become very close since that party last Monday.'

'Right,' I snorted.

'Anyway, the Golden Brothers have promised to make my dress and something nice for Arabella too so that we won't look like a pair of meringues. I was thinking red. Do you think that will go with her hair?'

'The Golden Brothers are designing the dresses?' I whimpered. Not only was my best friend telling me that I wasn't to be her bridesmaid, she was also torturing me with the thought of a gorgeous designer dress that might have been made especially for me instead of for Arabella Gilbert who was a girl with plenty of amazing dresses already.

'You do understand, don't you?' Mary asked.

'I understand,' I assured her. 'You can't stop thinking about the opportunities for a front page in the *Mirror* even on your wedding day.'

'Don't say it like that,' she chided. 'You make it sound as though I'm *only* doing this for publicity. I'm talking about my wedding day. You know how seriously I take the institution of marriage. It's taken me a long time to come to the decision that I should give in to Mitchell's demands and marry him.'

'And to think you thought that he didn't love you as much as you love him,' I commented, remembering the conversation we'd had before the party at the Hyperion.

'Did I say that?' Mary asked. 'I'm always over-reacting when Mitchell goes off into one of his creative huffs. Look, whatever I said, I wanted you to be the first to know about the wedding but you've got to promise to keep it under your hat until I make the official announcement. There are a few things I have to make absolutely certain of first. I mean, if it turns out that Arabella's agent isn't going to retire after all – and I have heard rumours – it might not be such a good idea for me to have her as my bridesmaid. I could be calling you up after all.'

'Thanks a bundle. I'll hold my breath, shall I?'

'Lizzie, don't be bitter, sweetheart. I'll be perfectly understanding if you choose someone over me when it comes to your own big day. And you will have one. Brian's clearly still crazy about you.'

'He is, isn't he?' I said, because I wanted to hear her confirm it.

'Yes,' she assured me. 'I think he is. And I swear I won't mention Michael Jackson again.'

19

'You still haven't told us what happened with Michael Jackson,' said Brian when we joined him once more.

I was saved this time by a far more unexpected knight in shining armour.

The specially hired waiter didn't have time to get to the door to let the new guest in. The young man staggered into the pristine sitting room looking as though he should be instantly ejected, in a suit that, although well cut, had clearly been used as a sleeping bag for more than a couple of nights. His hair stuck up all over with God only knows what kind of sticky substance making it particularly stiff on one side. Brian got to his feet as if he thought he might be called upon to sort the intruder out. Mary's mouth turned down at the corners as she introduced us to the fourth member of our exclusive party.

It was only when he took his broken sunglasses off that I recognised the superstar.

'This is Mitchell,' she said. He stuck out his hand in my direction and gave my hand a cursory shake. Then he took Brian's hand in his and planted a wet kiss on the back of it.

'Wrong way round,' Brian joked.

Mitchell looked at him blankly before snorting with what might have been amusement, might have been a head cold.

'I'm sorry I'm late,' he said, collapsing on to the cream-covered sofa.

I could tell that Mary was already computing the dry-cleaning bill. Her smile tightened.

'Running late at the studio. Bloody drummer couldn't get anything right.'

'I thought you were using a drum machine,' said Mary.

'Yeah, right. Well, that wasn't working properly either, was it?'

'I don't know,' she said. 'You tell me.'

'Aren't you going to get me some champagne?' Mitchell asked her.

'When you've tidied yourself up a bit,' Mary told him, guiding him expertly in the direction of the shower. 'We've got guests.'

'Creative types, eh?' she laughed in a brittle way when he was out of earshot. 'Gets a bit out of it sometimes. One of the hazards of the business.'

Brian and I said nothing.

'Of course, once he's finished recording the album he'll be fine again. Doesn't touch a drop between recording sessions. It's just the studio atmosphere. Everyone gets a bit tense.'

'You don't have to explain,' Brian said kindly.

But Mary clearly felt otherwise. 'I only put up with it because I know how difficult these times are for him. If he couldn't have a couple of drinks he might, quite literally, dry up. It's a small price to pay for the end product.'

I resisted the temptation to raise my eyebrows at the thought of Mitchell's creative output to date.

'He'll be fine in a minute,' said Mary. 'Shower should sober him up.'

'Well, he's arrived just in time to eat,' said Brian cheerfully. 'That should soak up some of the alcohol.'

Mary smiled at him gratefully.

But Mitchell still hadn't emerged from the shower when we

were getting to grips with the towering meringue confection that might have been made into a listed building if you left it in the centre of London for long enough. The conversation was rapidly going the way of the wine – that is to say, it was running out.

None of us could help glancing towards the hall that led to the bathroom between each mouthful. Mitchell had been in the shower for at least an hour. If he wasn't clean by now, then he had probably drowned. Finally, Mary excused herself to check. Her expression upon her return at least told us that he wasn't dead.

'He wasn't even in the shower,' she said. 'He must have fallen asleep with his head on the loo seat.'

Brian and I smiled and nodded as if that was perfectly reasonable.

'I just put a towel under his head to make him more comfortable. Though he'll probably still have a stiff neck when he wakes up. I hope you don't mind if I leave him there for a while.'

'Not at all,' we said politely.

'Good job I've got two bathrooms, eh? Coffee, anyone?'

I would have hurled myself through her plate-glass window to get out of that room right then, but instead Brian and I agreed to coffee and continued to sit there in silence. Every so often, a peal of laughter would ring out from the kitchen and remind us that we weren't alone. Eventually, Mary asked the help she had hired to leave and promised to send their cheques after them.

When the doorbell rang again seconds after the waiters left, I assumed they must have forgotten something. Mary went to inspect the entry system, but this visitor had already got past the main entrance to the block, bypassing the snoozy porter. He was standing right outside Mary's door.

Brian and I tried to talk amongst ourselves but pretty soon it was impossible not to be drawn to the events taking place at the door. Mary hadn't let her visitor in. She stood with the door between their bodies like a shield, chain on.

Mary was whispering, but her visitor was less concerned about keeping quiet for the sake of the neighbours.

'I want to see him,' the visitor said.

'You can't see him. He's passed out in the bathroom. I assume it's your fault he got into such a state in the first place.'

'I want to see him,' the visitor insisted.

'I'll call the police and have you removed.'

Brian started to get out of his chair and, for the second time that evening, prepared to throw his weight behind Mary's problem. But she glanced back into the sitting room, saw him getting up and motioned him to sit again.

Brian and I returned to our coffee. Conversation was impossible. I clinked my cup against saucer loudly as if to show that I wasn't ear-wigging.

'Well, that's fine,' said Mary, suddenly talking at full volume again. 'If you're prepared for him to turn up on your doorstep in Rio with his Louis Vuitton suitcase and nothing else ever again, you can have him. I'll tell him you called.'

At last she slammed the door in her visitor's face. She waited a few beats before returning to the table, grinning manically, and handed round a plate of handmade Belgian chocolates as if she had just popped out to the kitchen to fetch them and not spent the last five minutes rowing with someone through a half-closed door.

I ached to ask her what was going on. And would have done too if Brian hadn't gone into gentlemanly overdrive and changed the subject to an excruciating discussion about the best way to clean silver. I thought we should leave, but when I suggested as much, Mary looked distraught. We stayed for another hour. Mitchell never came out of the bathroom. The other visitor wasn't discussed.

The evening had ended on such a strange note that I wasn't even sure I could talk about it safely in the cab back to Harriet's house.

'She's done really well for herself, hasn't she?' I began just as we reached Grantchester Square. Brian looked at me doubtfully.

'I mean the flat and everything,' I clarified.

'Oh, yes. It's a great apartment. Really great.'

We went back to staring out of our respective windows.

'That was really tense, wasn't it?' said Brian when we got into Harriet's flat.

'Terrible,' I admitted. 'Poor Mary.'

'I was dreading having to take a shot at some massive guy for her. My shoulders are in agony from the anticipation.'

'You sound like you need a massage.'

'Naked,' he said.

I stopped thinking about Mary's mystery guest pretty soon after Brian suggested that.

20

I thought about calling Mary the next morning to check that she was OK. And also to check that Mitchell had come round after his night on the tiles. The bathroom tiles.

I decided I would call her after breakfast. But after breakfast I went back to bed with Brian. And then it was lunch time. The fact that I hadn't called Mary either to check up on her or to thank her ran through the front of my mind at high speed as I dipped a carrot stick into some guacamole and then into Brian's gorgeous mouth. But I decided she would have called me if anything really awful had happened. If something really *really* awful had happened to Mitchell, we would have heard about it on the news. If we had turned the TV or radio on. Which we didn't.

Fact was, I didn't want to have to think about anything but Brian and myself.

'Don't you want to call and see how your dog is getting on?' Brian asked me at one point.

'He'll be fine,' I assured him. Brian was feeling a hell of a lot more guilty about Hercules than I was. Besides which, I didn't want to know what was going on in Balham. I hadn't told Richard that I wouldn't be at home for the duration of Brian's visit and I didn't want to call Seema about the dog only to have her tell me that Richard had been mooning about the place demanding to know where I was hiding with my mysterious visitor.

Richard. I felt only slightly more guilty when I thought of him than when I thought of Hercules, but having Brian back in my life threw even clearer light on to the things that had always bothered me about my accountant boyfriend.

For a start, there was the way Brian could throw his credit card at everything like some magical talisman that melted away all problems. Just that morning he had called the local deli and had them deliver breakfast so that I didn't even have to boil the water to make a cup of tea. By contrast Richard was always counting up pennies and trying to persuade Habib at the corner shop to change them into silver so that he could catch the bus to work.

Then there were the little things – like the way Brian would walk on the roadside edge of the pavement to protect me from drivers splashing through puddles. The way he opened doors for me and insisted on carrying anything heavier than a lipstick. There had been plenty of occasions when Richard had let me struggle back from Safeway with loaded shopping bags, let the front door swing shut in my face as he let himself into the house first, and then started bleating for a cup of tea before I had even unpacked the milk. I know it's old-fashioned, and I'm all for sexual equality and that, but I liked the way that Brian treated me as if I were ever so slightly fragile. As far as Richard was concerned, it seemed that equality of the sexes simply meant that he no longer had to offer me any help with the heavy lifting work at all.

But it wasn't all superficial money and manners. Brian was so much sexier too. And it was a self-perpetuating energy. His obvious interest in all my hitherto slightly underestimated charms filled me with self-confidence that in turn made me feel sexier as well. With Brian complimenting me at every turn, I began to feel as though I really could achieve some of the things I was pretending I had achieved already. (And he didn't go to bed with his socks on either as if the stench emanating from them might ward off any things that go bump in the night.)

I could never go back to Richard after this, I thought, as Brian massaged my feet. It would be like putting UHT milk in my coffee after getting used to drinking it with double cream. But how could I carry on affording the cream once Brian had gone back to the States and Harriet had come back for her flat? While Brian sucked my toes under the breakfast table, I plotted my escape to America. I could ask Mary to lend me the money for a flight. Brian would be happy to have me to stay with him. I would make a pretence at setting up a property business in New York but before I actually had to do anything, Brian would have asked me to marry him for fear that he would lose me when my visa ran out. Once Brian had agreed to marry me, I could give up the pretence. It would be too late for him to change his mind.

I even managed to convince myself that it wasn't entirely an evil plan because Brian would have realised that he loved me whether I was a successful businesswoman or not by then. I would be just as good at bringing up the little Brians as anyone who actually understood the financial pages.

Brian looked up from sucking my toes. 'You are so gorgeous,' he told me. 'Even your toe jam tastes good.'

I swatted him round the head with a newspaper, folded to the travel page for flight prices.

'I wish you lived in New York,' Brian said.

Oh, Brian, I thought. Your wish is my command.

21

When she called later that day, Mary didn't seem at all bothered that her dinner party had turned into something that resembled a made-for-television film by Mike Leigh. When I apologised for not having called to thank her or enquire after Mitchell's health, she assured me that it didn't matter. She had some exciting news that had really cheered her up.

'I've got a new client,' she said proudly. 'Guess who?'

It had to be Arabella Gilbert.

'She called at my flat at four o'clock this morning looking for some decent Charlie. I said I'd sort it out for her on condition she signed on the dotted line before she left my doorstep.'

'And she did?'

'She did. She was completely out of it. But I think she'll find it legally binding. Anyway, it was just the push that she needed to fall into my lap. We had lunch on Friday and she'd near as dammit agreed to move to my agency then anyway. And I've already got a job for her lined up.'

'What job?' I asked.

'Do you ever watch that talk show at tea time where ordinary people pour their hearts out in front of a live studio audience? Like Jerry Springer only not quite so grubby.'

'How would I have seen it?' I asked. 'I'm at work at tea time.'

'Come on, Liz. You're forever taking sickies. But since you claim you haven't seen it, it's called *Lorinda*. At least, it was called *Lorinda* until she checked herself into the drying-out clinic last weekend. For the next three weeks it's going to be called *Arabella* and the Arabella in question just happens to be my new client. Ta-daa.'

'Well done,' I said. 'That's really good news.'

'Thank you,' said Mary. 'The competition for the spot was amazing. I am rather delighted.'

She sounded more delighted than she had done when telling me about her forthcoming wedding.

'I have never lunched so hard in my life,' she continued. 'But I think Arabella knows a professional when she meets one. Anyway, I've got you two tickets for a pilot recording tomorrow afternoon.'

'You mean you've got us tickets to see the show?'

'Uh-huh. I thought Brian might be interested. See how the English deal with the skeletons in their closets? I'm not sure what the topic will be, but I can guarantee some scandal and a punch-up. Shall I bike them over to you at your love-nest?'

'I'll just ask Brian.'

His eyes practically popped out of his head. Though his day-to-day life in Manhattan seemed incredibly glamorous to boring old me, he was still totally over-awed by everything to do with that little glowing tube in the corner of the sitting room.

'A TV show? Like, can we really do that?'

'Mary's got us some tickets. One of her clients is the presenter.'

'Wow. I'd love to. And thank her for me.'

I took my hand back off the mouthpiece. 'Brian says he would love to see the show and thanks you for sorting it out. Thanks from me, too.'

'Oh, believe me. It's my pleasure entirely,' she purred. 'Absolutely my pleasure. Now, you will wear something special, won't you? They show the whole audience in the opening credits and I don't want my best friend to show up my fave new client by appearing in her tatty jeans. Why don't you wear that suit I loaned you? The cream one? Cream always looks good on TV.'

'OK. Though I'm going to try to sit at the back if at all possible. I don't want to get caught in the cross-fire when some poor bugger finds out that his girlfriend is really a man.'

Mary laughed. 'Oh, Lizzie,' she said. 'Getting caught in the cross-fire is all part of the fun.'

Brian and I decided to spend the rest of that day doing some sightseeing. Brian put on a baseball cap for the occasion, and when I winced he told me that he had to wear it or people wouldn't know he was an American. I didn't like to tell him that his grey silk blouson jacket had already marked him out. I vowed one day I would bin that jacket and buy him something truly gorgeous to wear instead – with his credit card, of course.

We went to the Tate Gallery first. Brian had read about that year's Turner Prize nominees in the newspaper that week and was eager to see two works in particular. One was a giant sculpture of a vagina that incorporated (don't ask me how) two tonnes of melted chocolate; the other was a triptych of the crucifixion painted entirely in horseshit.

'I expect it will all be horseshit,' said Brian as we climbed the steps to the Tate's grand entrance.

The gallery lobby with its impressive vaulted ceiling was buzzing with tourists and art lovers. The shop was even busier, I noted, as we walked through into the first big hall.

A row of magnificent sculptures led the eye down the cool white room to a gigantic illuminated cross. It didn't look much better than the cross they erected outside the Baptist Church in Balham each Easter, but this one, being in the Tate, was obviously art.

Brian and I drifted down the long room, pausing momentarily to look at each sculpture. Brian even ran his hand over the liquid curves of a Henry Moore, which brought one of the gallery curators scuttling out from her corner to tut.

'The moisture from your hand may damage the surface of the sculpture,' the uniformed woman explained.

'Don't think it would make much difference to some of this stuff,' Brian sneered to me when the curator was safely out of the way. 'Where are the real paintings? All this stuff is like something my nephew does in his remedial pottery class.'

We drifted into the permanent exhibition of Turner paintings. Brian liked the sea-scapes but commented that Turner couldn't draw people. He preferred the pre-Raphaelites, and I got rather jealous of poor Ophelia, lying drowned in her flower-strewn stream when Brian said that he thought she was the most beautiful woman ever painted. But even she couldn't hold his attention for very long and we soon found ourselves back in the echoing white hall where we had started our whistle-stop tour of art.

'Isn't that your secretary?' Brian asked me suddenly.

At first, I didn't know what he was talking about. It took a while before I remembered that as far as Brian was concerned I did actually have a secretary.

'Where?' I asked worriedly.

'Over there, by that painting of the two seventies types?'

The two seventies types were Ossie Clark and Celia Birtwell, immortalised with their pet cat by David Hockney as *Mr and Mrs Clark and Percy*. The secretary to whom

Brian was referring was obviously my erstwhile flatmate Seema, but when I looked over towards the place where Hockney's masterpiece hung in a dimly lit alcove, I couldn't see Seema anywhere. I could however see Richard. Richard my boyfriend. The boyfriend I'd neglected to mention. He was right in front of the Hockney, tapping his lower lip thoughtfully as he took the painting in.

I dragged Brian behind the Henry Moore he had laid his hands on earlier.

'Was that her?' he asked innocently.

'I couldn't see her,' I shrugged. 'Would you like to go to the Natural History Museum now? I hear they have a fascinating exhibition of maggots.'

'We haven't seen the Turner Prize exhibition yet,' he protested.

'Well, you said yourself that it's probably all horseshit. I don't think we should waste our time.'

'Sure,' said Brian, giving in. 'But don't you think you should say "hi" to your secretary before we leave?'

'I couldn't see her when I looked. You must have been mistaken.'

'No. I'm sure I'm not. See! There she is again.'

This time when I glanced back towards the alcove where Mr and Mrs Clark kept their cool-eyed watch, I did see Seema. She must have been obscured by the crowds taking illicit photos last time I looked. And there too was Richard. My boyfriend. And Seema was linking her arm through his!

I tried not to look in the least bit surprised as I popped back behind the Henry Moore to gather myself and come up with an escape route. Suddenly the hole in his famous reclining nude's midriff didn't seem such an enchanting feature.

'Was I right?' Brian asked me.

'Yes, you were right. It's Seema. But she's with someone. Someone I've never met before,' I added in a hurry. 'She might be on a date or something. It doesn't seem right to go barging up and interrupt. She sees enough of me at the office.'

'You're only going to say hello,' Brian protested. 'We're not going to play gooseberry.'

'I don't think she'll be too upset if she finds out that I left her in peace instead.'

'Sure. But aren't you a little concerned to find out where she's left your dog while she's out on this hot date?'

'I'm sure he's fine.' I linked my arm through Brian's in an echo of Seema's gesture with *my* man. 'Let's go.'

'We can't leave now. They're coming towards us.'

And to my absolute horror, they were. Seema and Richard had finished looking at the painting and were heading in our direction though as yet they didn't appear to have spotted Brian and me.

'Look at this,' I said, falling to my knees behind the Henry Moore and dragging Brian down with me. 'Have you ever looked at a piece of granite really closely?'

'Lizzie? What are you doing?' he asked in a voice of pure exasperation, brushing the dust from his knees and attempting to straighten up again.

'Brian, I don't want to spoil my secretary's date,' I hissed, keeping him close to the floor.

I began a close inspection of a strand of lucite flecks in the base of the reclining nude. I would be OK as long as Richard didn't stop to look at the sculpture too. Through the hole in its midriff I saw him pass by without pausing, clearly intent on an exhibit on the other side of the hall. But they passed by so closely that Brian and I could clearly hear their conversation, or rather, we could hear Seema simpering like some brainless eighteenth-century socialite as Richard explained some of the finer points of art.

'The composition of Mr and Mrs Clark is particularly interesting,' he told her. 'Normally, the woman would be in the sitting position, but in Hockney's painting, it is the man who takes the chair. And his direct, challenging gaze is all the more pertinent when you realise that he probably knew at the time that the artist was screwing his wife.'

'Really?' Seema gushed.

'Yes. Celia Birtwell was about the only woman who ever slept with Hockney. It broke poor Ossie Clark's heart.'

'Infidelity's a terrible thing, isn't it?' observed Seema and although I couldn't see from behind the Henry Moore, I could well imagine her batting her eyelashes to devastating effect.

'Sounds like her man knows a bit about art,' said Brian as we straightened up in time to see Seema and Richard disappearing into the Turner Prize exhibition. Still arm in arm.

It certainly did. So how come Richard had never taken me to an art gallery to benefit from his superior knowledge of all things cultural?

'You know about art though too, don't you, Brian?' I asked, suddenly needing to be reassured that anything Richard could do, Brian could do better.

'Never really seen the point of it. Not this modern stuff. Except perhaps as an investment. A friend of mine bought an unsigned sketch in Paris once. Turned out to be a Monet. Doubled his money like that.' He clicked his fingers.

'What was it a picture of?'

'I don't know. Hell, it hardly matters if it was a Monet.' He pronounced it 'Moan-ey'. 'But when he found out what it was he sure wished that he'd bought the matching pair.

Monet equals Money. That's all I need to know about art.'

'That's a terrible story,' I said. 'Let's get some lunch.'

'We could eat in the café here?' Brian suggested.

No. No, we couldn't. I needed to get Brian at least three tube stops away from the Tate before Richard and Seema came out of the Turner Prize exhibition again.

I chose an Italian place in Soho. We were the only customers. The whole of Soho is pretty much deserted on a Sunday afternoon while the type of people who normally frequent the noisy bars on Old Compton Street are at home sleeping off a good twenty-four hours' clubbing before the working week starts again. Away from Oxford Street none of the shops were open either. I can't say it was a particularly great time to be in Soho. It felt like the morning after a bomb has been dropped, but I felt secure that it was one of the few places where I could guarantee that we wouldn't bump into Richard and Seema.

'Are you sure you want to have lunch here?' asked Brian as we stepped out of the balmy afternoon sunshine into the chilly shadows of a restaurant that was far better suited to the night. The languid French waiter seemed equally unimpressed with my choice of lunch-time venue since it meant that he had to abandon the Sunday papers to attend to us. He practically threw a basket of ciabatta towards us when we sat down at the table nearest the kitchen.

'You've gone all quiet,' Brian observed.

'I have not,' I almost snapped at him.

'You have. You've been all quiet ever since I told you I'd seen your secretary in the gallery. And now you've brought us to this dark and gloomy place. Is there something wrong?'

'Nothing at all. Do you want to go somewhere else?'

'I'm not bothered about where we eat, Lizzie. I only want to know what's eating you?'

'It's just . . . it's just that sometimes art overwhelms me,' I burbled. 'Don't you ever feel that way?'

'Can't say I do,' he said, biting down on a chunk of bread. 'You shouldn't let yourself get worked up about a few old pictures. Heaven knows the artists didn't.'

'How can you say that?'

'Do you think Picasso's heart bled when he painted those weeping women? No way! He was laughing all the way to the bank. Don't let it bother you. Let the latest market crash in Asia bother you. Let earthquakes in California bother you. Something really serious. Buck up, Lizzie. I've only got a couple more days.'

'I'll try,' I said, forcing a smile, as the waiter slapped a menu into my hand.

Of course the irony of my situation had struck me. Here I was, being eaten from the inside out by with jealousy at the fact that Richard was out at a gallery with my flatmate Seema while I was having lunch with Brian, having made mad passionate love to him, and not to Richard, my official boyfriend, for the past two nights. Richard hadn't technically done anything wrong. He was merely enjoying a Sunday trip to an art gallery with a friend. It was probably utterly platonic. Definitely, in fact, since I could be absolutely sure that Seema wouldn't even consider dating a lowly accountant. On the other hand, I knew I had been doing wrong. I had definitely been unfaithful. For heaven's sake, the only reason I hadn't chucked Richard the very second that Brian announced his impending visit was that I was too much of a slimeball to risk losing out on a birthday present unnecessarily. I was the emotional pond scum. Not him.

And hadn't I decided that it was all over between me and

Richard now anyway? I would have to tell him it was over in order to go to America with Brian. I should have been pleased that Seema was prepared to help him lick his wounds in my absence. Nope, I could find no justification whatsoever for the unreasonable feelings of having been betrayed that were currently keeping me from eating my olive ciabatta and instead making me tear the bread into a pile of little chunks.

'You going for a Turner Prize nomination?' asked Brian, cocking his head towards the heap of crumbs. 'Something is wrong, isn't it? Don't you think you'd better tell me what's going through your mind before the waiter brings you a bib?'

Brian took my sideplate away from me, depriving me of more bread on which to vent my anger.

'Tell me,' he demanded, while simultaneously rubbing my thigh beneath the table to help coax out an answer.

'OK,' I said, thinking quickly. 'There is something wrong. I was having a wonderful day out but now I can't stop thinking about work and the 20:20 project. I know I should be able to trust Seema in my absence but seeing her at the gallery today has made me wonder if I was right to trust her with so much. Perhaps she's too young for all the responsibility I've been giving her lately. I think I've been relying on her good nature just a little too much.'

At least the last part of what I had said was true. I was certainly beginning to wonder if Seema had decided to take her reward for looking after Hercules already. And she had decided that the reward in question was to be *my* boyfriend.

Brian reached across the table to take my hand. 'Lizzie, it's a Sunday. Even if Seema is ruining your business while you're looking after me, there isn't a great deal you can do about it now. But since we're on the subject, just what is this 20:20 project I keep hearing about? You promised to tell me all about it.'

Great. I hadn't bothered to make anything up, hoping that I might be able to get away with never mentioning Seema's damn invention again.

'You don't want to hear about it,' I tried. 'It's boring. Seema's just excited because it's the first real project she's had responsibility on.'

'But why 20:20? That's a great title,' Brian continued. 'Like 20:20 vision.'

'That's it,' I said; a lightbulb had suddenly been switched on between my ears. 'It's a project for a national chain of opticians.'

'Oh.'

'See? I told you you'd find it boring.'

He nodded.

Phew.

We ate our lunch quickly, with the waiter standing over us to snatch away our plates as soon as we had scraped up a last mouthful. Brian wanted to go to another museum. The British Museum this time, to see the Egyptian mummies and to marvel at the stolen marbles.

I followed him through the room stuffed with Egyptian antiquities, making suitably impressed noises when we saw a carved hand big enough to make a pretty comfortable armchair. But I still couldn't block the sight of Seema linking her arm through Richard's out of my mind. I tried to tell myself that I should be glad for them both. I liked Richard, and Seema was one of the best women I knew. But though I had made the decision to throw my hand in with Brian, I couldn't help feeling just a faint twinge of regret at the thought of the other budding relationship which now had to end.

To make matters worse, Brian was now standing in front of a statue that Richard had admired when he and I had bunked off work to spend an afternoon trawling the museum in the heady early days of our acquaintance. When Brian reached out to take my hand, I was reminded of Richard making exactly the same gesture seven months ago. I felt happier with Brian's hand in mine, though. Didn't I?

Of course I was happier with Brian, I told myself firmly as we gazed at each other over another spectacular dinner that night.

I had spent the early evening making a mental list. Brian versus Richard. Pros and cons for both.

In Richard's favour: he was a nice bloke, he made me laugh and he knew a bit about art. On the other hand, he was an accountant, which is international shorthand for boring, and yet he never had any money. He would make a nice friend. But he was hardly husband material, was he? Not if I was intending to be a lady who did nothing but lunch from the moment I had that gold band on my finger.

The list in Brian's favour was clearly very much longer. He was a nice bloke too, he made me laugh and he knew enough about art to make money from it, money that he could use to buy me presents. He was also handsome. And he made me do things in bed that I had hitherto only imagined in a very abstract way.

The only disadvantage to being with Brian was that he lived in New York. New York. An advantage and a disadvantage. I wanted desperately to get out of London. I wanted to go somewhere even more exciting. But I also wondered whether I would miss my family and friends.

'Did you miss your family and friends when you came to spend a year at Oxford?' I asked him now.

Brian shrugged. 'I made new friends. And hey, there was always the telephone. I've missed you though since I went back to NYC.'

That was what I needed to hear. I decided to take the plunge. 'I'd like to come and stay with you in New York.'

'I'd like that too,' he said.

'I mean, stay for a long time, Brian.'

There. I had said it. And Brian didn't say no.

22

We stayed up late discussing the possibilities. Brian suggested that I entrust my business to Seema's capable hands while I checked out the situation in America. I would need a working visa and other paperwork, but Brian would be more than happy to have me stay with him for as long as I needed to.

As long as I *needed* to? I wasn't sure I liked the sound of that since it seemed to imply that at some stage I would be moving into a place on my own, but I told myself that Brian was just being polite. Perhaps he thought I might be put off if he offered me a home for life right away.

We decided that I would follow Brian out to the States about a week or so after he returned. That would give me a chance to hand the business over to Seema properly, I told him. In reality, it would give me enough time to earn one more week's wages at Corbett and Daughter to pay for my air fare.

'Of course, you'll have to find somewhere for Hercules to stay while you're away,' Brian said. 'Are you sure you can bear to leave your dog behind?'

If Harriet didn't come back to collect her pooch that week, he would be straight off to Battersea Dogs Home. I didn't tell Brian that, naturally.

'I can't believe this is really happening,' I said. 'Crazy, isn't it?'

'Crazy, but wonderful too,' he replied.

I couldn't wait to get to the TV recording the next day. Mary would be shocked to hear that I had pulled off my grand plan, but I hoped she would be pleased as well. When we got to the studio, however, Mary was nowhere to be seen. I guessed she would be backstage with her new client but thought better of interrupting pre-recording preparations even if I did have the most incredible piece of gossip to impart in the entire world.

Brian and I chose to sit somewhere near the middle. He wanted to sit right at the front but to my immense relief, we discovered that all the seats down there had been allocated prior to our arrival. Next to us was a man with the name 'Melinda' tattooed on his forearm. His wife introduced herself. She was called Anita.

Despite Mary's warning that we ought to dress up, I have to say I felt distinctly over-dressed as the rest of the crowd took their seats wearing tracksuit bottoms and tattered denims. I slipped off my jacket and went to hang it casually over the back of my seat but the man behind me was eating a packet of Maltesers rather messily and the thought of sticky chocolate fingers on Mary's silk soon had me putting the jacket back on again.

To get things warmed up, one of the production team came on to the stage and sparked off a little debate in the first couple of rows by asking one woman what she would do if she discovered that her husband habitually dressed up in her underwear while she was out on the town with the girls. She said she'd be disgusted and that it meant he was probably gay – which went down very well with the six-foot-tall plumber beside her who was dressed as Joan Collins's big sister.

'This is fun,' Brian whispered to me, as we watched the row unfold. 'I had no idea that English people could get so passionate.' I punched him in the arm. But before the rest of the audience could come to fisticuffs, another member of the production team, wearing headphones and one of those funny-looking mikes, emerged to announce that Arabella was on her way up to the studio from her dressing room.

An awed silence fell over the room as we waited for the woman herself to arrive. It seemed like aeons before the production assistant who had started the transvestite row stepped out briefly in front of the cameras and raised her arms to signal that it was time for everyone to cheer and clap as Arabella finally appeared from behind a curtain at the top of the auditorium and made her way down to the stage, shaking hands as she went like every other talk-show host you've ever seen.

'Arabella! Arabella!' the crowd chanted in time with the theme tune. Well, nearly in time. There were too many syllables. I wondered if Mary would make them change the theme tune.

Arabella shook seven people by the hand then headed straight for a cross which was painted on the studio floor, ignoring anyone else who pleaded to press her flesh. She flicked back her glossy brown hair and fixed the nearest camera with a glitteringly expensive smile. She looked fantastic, although I couldn't help wondering idly how much better she might look when the liposuction was done.

'Thank you for coming, everybody,' she said straight to the camera, including the audience at home. 'It means so much to me.'

'At least she's got better legs than Jerry Springer,' Brian commented. Anita glared at him to be quiet. She'd come a long way to have her fifteen minutes that day and she was taking proceedings very seriously.

'On today's programme we're going to be talking about secrets,' Arabella continued. 'Secrets or lies. What's the difference? When does a secret become a lie? Are we right to keep secrets from people who love us or are we only storing up trouble for the future when what we thought was just a teensy little thing we wanted to keep to ourselves becomes a huge explosive problem that tears families apart?' She looked deeply serious for a moment. Frighteningly so, in fact. The audience was gripped.

'My guests today all have a secret that they finally want to tell. They need to unburden themselves, admit to their dishonesty and get things off their chests. But how will that feel to the people they have to admit something to? By unburdening themselves, will my guests be doing the right thing or will they simply be passing their problems on for someone else to handle? My first guest is Jane from Worcestershire. She's been keeping her secret for almost five years. Let's have a big hand for Jane.'

The audience erupted dutifully and Jane crept out on to the stage, looking as if she had already changed her mind. The crowd whooped its approval as she found her way to a pink velvet upholstered chair and sat down blinking like a deer caught in headlights.

'You're looking lovely today, Jane,' Arabella told the girl in a red dress that was way too small and left nothing to the imagination. Especially the control top on her tights. Jane blinked her thank you.

'Now, Jane. You've taken a very long time to come to the decision to tell your secret, haven't you?'

'That's right,' said Jane, inaudibly. She cleared her throat and said, 'That's right,' again. This time she angled her chin down so that her words boomed from her mike.

'Just talk naturally,' Arabella coached. 'Just imagine that

there's no one here in the studio today except you and me. Imagine you're having a one-to-one chat with your closest friend.'

'I bet she'd feel more comfortable having a one-to-one chat with General Pinochet,' I whispered to Brian. 'She looks terrified.'

And little wonder. For Jane from Worcestershire had chosen that day's episode of *Arabella* to make the announcement to her husband, in front of heaven knows how many millions of people (about three – Mary had estimated), that the boy he thought was his son, was in fact his nephew. Brian peeped through his fingers when Jane delivered the blow. It was like road-kill. I didn't want to look myself, but my eyes were forever being drawn back to that poor girl's face as she spilled her beans on national TV.

'Do you think you'll be able to work this out?' Arabella asked sincerely. Jane and her dazed husband nodded, but despite the promises of counsellors behind the scenes, I couldn't imagine that any fate awaited poor Jane back in Worcestershire but a pair of suitcases dumped on the front step.

'Why do they do it?' Brian asked me. 'Why do they let themselves get so set up?'

'Everyone wants their fifteen minutes,' I said wisely.

'Fifteen of fame and a lifetime of pain,' agreed Brian.

After Jane's revelation, the next guest up was practically light relief. Norman wanted to admit to his great-aunt that it was he who had broken her favourite vase fifteen years before. The old woman was so profoundly deaf, I was certain that she left the show none the wiser, but she seemed happy to have had her fifteen minutes too. As was Deirdra, who discovered that the secret her boyfriend Mark had been keeping from her was a whopping great diamond engagement ring.

'That's sweet,' said Brian, squeezing my hand in a way which seemed loaded with meaning to me. Deirdra's boyfriend got down on his knees to make the proposal and had to be helped to his feet afterwards as the emotion of the moment overcame him.

'Jesus,' said Brian. 'What happened to the good old British Stiff Upper Lip?'

'It's not good to suppress your emotions,' said Anita. 'The death of Diana the Queen of all our Hearts showed us how important it is to feel and show what we're feeling without embarrassment.'

'Is that so?' Brian asked her.

'Holding everything in has been proven to cause cancer,' she nodded.

'Are we in California?' Brian asked me.

Three guests down. I was sure we must be coming to the end of the show when Arabella stepped in front of the row of seats where Jane and her husband sat staring into space like strangers while Deirdra and Mark canoodled.

'I hope she's not going to do one of those cheesy summing-ups,' Brian muttered.

If only she had been. Arabella gazed deeply into the camera on her left. 'We've got one more person here today,' she began. 'Someone who's been keeping quite a big secret from her friend. Several big secrets in fact. Or perhaps you might prefer to call them lies. Let's see what you think when we ask Lizzie Jordan to come clean on *Arabella*.'

I looked around expectantly as the spotlight turned on to the audience. Which poor sucker had been caught out this time? It was only when I saw Brian's amused expression that I realised it was me.

'Lizzie Jordan?' Arabella smiled. She was suddenly standing right beside me. A spotlight cast a circle around my head.

'Yes,' I squeaked. 'Er, yes,' I said a little more deeply into Arabella's microphone.

'Have you got any idea what secrets we might be referring to here?' she asked me.

What could she be talking about? That my friend Amy Weskey and I had cheated in the maths GCSE exam twelve years before? That I saw the family dog lick a jam tart but didn't tell my brother before he bit into it? I didn't have any other secrets that I could think of right then.

'Nope,' I said, grinning nervously. 'I'm afraid I really don't have a clue.'

'Oh, come on now,' tutted Arabella. 'Don't play the innocent with us. Try one more time. Have a really good think. What big secret have you been keeping from your handsome friend here?'

She looked at Brian. Brian looked at me expectantly. And then the penny dropped.

'No,' I breathed. 'Noooo.'

'Perhaps you'd like to tell your friend Brian, who's come all the way from America to visit you, who it is who actually owns the flat in Grantchester Square and that flash sports car you've been driving around in? What you really do when you say you're going out in the morning to broker some high-powered property deal? Who owns the designer suit you're wearing today on my show? Who owns those shoes you're wearing? Don't you think that Brian deserves to know?'

'Know what?' asked Brian, looking faintly bemused.

'The truth,' boomed Arabella.

'Are you going to tell him, Lizzie? Or shall I tell him what

I heard in the ladies' room at the Dorchester less than a week ago? That you had actually been typing up tales lifted straight from *my* social column and sending them to your former lover in e-mails on the pretence that *you* were in fact living *my* exciting life?'

Suddenly, Arabella's face seemed to grow clown-like, looming in and out of my vision as the room started to blur. I got to my feet and pushed past the painted presenter as I headed for a door – any door. I got as far as the stage. Production hands leapt out from behind the backdrop to restrain me. Jane and her downtrodden husband looked momentarily distracted from their own pain as mine began.

'You see, Brian, Lizzie Jordan isn't quite the high-flying executive she led you to believe she was during the course of your torrid internet affair. In fact she is a lowly secretary at an unsuccessful estate agency. The flat that you've been staying in belongs to her kindly boss. That suit she's wearing belongs to her friend Mary. Lizzie's been lying to you, Brian, in an attempt to persuade you to fall in love with her again and rescue her from her dire situation. And by the look of the pair of you sitting so closely together before you heard this revelation, I would have said she was succeeding. But how do you feel about her now, Brian? Can you ever feel the same again now that you know she's been lying to you?'

Without saying anything, Brian got to his feet and walked from the studio. He had the sense to choose the back entrance however and made it away from the camera's gaze before anyone could stop him. I remained rooted to the middle of the studio floor as Arabella summed the programme up and then disappeared to her changing room without so much as a backward glance at the people who had humiliated themselves so spectacularly for her career advancement.

* * *

Not knowing whether to laugh or cry, I stood on the stage until everybody had gone but the production staff.

'I have to see Arabella,' I told someone.

'Arabella won't see anybody. You'll have to leave now,' the stage manager told me. 'Unless you're also in the audience for *Kilroy*.'

'But she knows me. And so she must know how much she's humiliated me.'

'Arabella meets a lot of people,' the stage manager said to humour me. 'She doesn't remember them all. You'll have to go now.'

I followed the stragglers down the corridor to the car park. I felt in my pockets for Harriet's car keys but I was still shaking so hard, I wasn't sure I would be able to drive anyway. And where had Brian gone? I couldn't see him anywhere.

He wasn't in the car park. He wasn't leaning on the car with a grin on his face, waiting for me to explain the joke. He must have left the studio complex altogether and got a taxi somewhere. But did he know anyone in London other than me who he could stay with until his plane left the next day? Would I get a chance to explain to him why I had been such an almighty fool?

I let myself into the borrowed Mercedes and collapsed into a sob with my head on the steering wheel. I couldn't believe what had happened. Another twenty-four hours and everything would have been perfect. Mission accomplished. But Mary Bagshot had clearly set me up. Set me up and ruined my life.

23

After briefly going back to the flat and discovering that he hadn't made his own way back there either, I headed straight for Mary's. Mary was the only other person Brian knew in London so perhaps he was at her place, getting the whole story from her. And even if he wasn't, I was after her blood anyway.

I parked Harriet's car at a forty-five-degree angle to the kerb outside Mary's plush portered block and stormed up to the door. I jabbed at the doorbell and kept my finger on it until she answered. She sounded pretty groggy on the entryphone, and came to the door wearing her dressing-gown, which was odd, since it was only six in the evening. She looked a little red around the eyes but I put that down to some kind of herbal facial treatment. She spent more on the surface of her skin than NASA spent getting to the surface of the moon.

'I hope I haven't interrupted anything,' I said sarcastically. 'Having your moustache bleached?'

'Actually, I think I'm coming down with the flu,' she told me flatly.

'Well, don't expect me to feel sorry for you. What did you think you were playing at, Mary, sending me to that studio to be humiliated?'

'What?' she asked.

'Don't play the innocent. You know what happened to me this afternoon.'

'No. I don't.'

'Right.' I squared up against her on the doorstep. 'Are you telling me that your precious new client decided off her own pretty, empty head to spew out all the lies I've been telling Brian for the benefit of a live studio audience? You set me up. I could knock your bloody head right off.'

'Lizzie, what are you talking about?' Mary sighed.

'Arabella told Brian that I'd been lying to him! More precisely, she tried to force me to own up on national TV.'

'Don't panic. It was only a pilot.'

'Do you think that makes it better?'

A woman with a King Charles walked past and gave us a very disapproving stare. In fact, I think it was the exact same woman with a King Charles who had caught me trying to break into her mansion block with Harriet's key three days before.

'Liz, I think you'd better come inside.' Mary grabbed me by the collar and yanked me in off the step. 'I promise I don't know what you're talking about.'

'Don't even try to pretend,' I shouted as Mary dragged me up the stairs to her apartment. 'Your client told Brian I had been lying to him in front of an entire studio audience. The only way she could have known is because you told her.'

Mary twisted her Cartier watch around her wrist. 'I wouldn't do that.'

'God, you're such a liar. I thought you were my friend.'

'I am your friend.'

'You *were*.'

'Where's Brian now?' she asked.

'I don't bloody know. He walked out of the studio in front of everybody. I thought he might have come here. Just admit it, Mary. Admit you set me up.'

I'm ashamed to say that I grabbed her by the arms and shook her. She cracked instantly.

'Oh, all right. I did set you up,' she squeaked. I let her go. 'But it's not as though you didn't deserve it.'

'What?' I grabbed her again. 'Why? What have I ever done to you, Mary Bagshot? You've got everything,' I spat. 'You've got everything and you had to go and spoil the best thing that's ever happened to me.'

'I haven't got everything,' Mary sneered. 'You don't know what you're talking about.'

'You have,' I insisted, counting off the reasons on my fingers. 'You've got a great job, a nice place to live, a fast car and a bloody pop star for a fiancé. What more could you possibly want, Mary? All I wanted was one great weekend with the love of my life. One single weekend. Why did you have to have the satisfaction of seeing me trip up as well?'

'Because you were getting the one thing I wasn't. Brian loves you. It's obvious. Mitchell doesn't love me.'

'Of course he does. You're getting married.'

'He doesn't.'

'Stop feeling sorry for yourself.'

'Look, he really doesn't. Mitchell's gay.'

'What?'

'You heard me, Liz. Mitchell's gay. Our whole relationship is bollocks. I don't love him and he certainly doesn't love me. Mitchell loves a male model from Rio with a 44-inch chest and a handlebar moustache he can swing off. He wanted to marry me so that the journalist who's been speaking to his boyfriend would be put off the scent until the new album hit the shelves. I was just Mitchell's beard.'

'But why would you do that?'

'What did I have to lose? It wasn't as if I was ever likely to have a real relationship, was it? I've never managed to have a decent one so far. No one has ever fallen in love with me,' she cried dramatically. 'You've always attracted the decent blokes, Liz. The ones I attract are either married or mad or both. All I want, all I've ever wanted, is someone to love me the way Brian loves you. Preferably Brian. He wasn't just the love of your life, Liz, he was the love of my life too.'

'What?'

'He was the love of my life,' she repeated haltingly. 'I was in love with him too. Brian. All the time you were together.'

'No, you weren't. What about that post-grad?'

'What about him? He was just a distraction.'

'Why didn't you say something?'

'I did. I said it all those years ago in the chip shop, remember? I told you that I fancied Brian. But he chose you. And you chose him over me, too. After that, there didn't seem to be much point protesting about it. You wanted each other. Not me. I had a miserable year while you two swanned around like love's young dream, kissing and cuddling and making me sick to the very pit of my stomach every time I had to stop and be civil to you while you were holding hands. When Brian went back to America, I cried almost as much as you did. I watched him walk out of the quad from my bedroom window and then I threw myself down on my pillow and cried until I thought I would die. After that, I felt a bit better. I was almost relieved not to have him around any more because at least I wouldn't have to watch him getting all loved up with you.'

'I didn't know,' I promised her. 'You didn't make it clear enough.'

'Would it have made a difference? Anyway, you might

have guessed, if you hadn't been so wrapped up in yourself. If you'd given a damn about me you'd have known that I was unhappy.'

'But that was so long ago, Mary. Six years.'

'Yes. And I thought I'd got over it. I thought I'd put that whole stupid crush out of my mind. I thought I'd see him with you again, see that he'd got fat and old like the rest of us, and put all the feelings I once had for him behind me. But it didn't happen like that. He was just the same as ever and just as mad about you. I saw you standing there looking like a goddess in a dress that I had hoped would make you look like a sack of potatoes tied up with string, and Brian couldn't take his eyes off you. I knew that it didn't matter how much *I* had changed since he went away. I still couldn't compete with you in the one area of my life that I'll never be a success in. Men fall in love with you all the time. No one loves me. No one.'

She looked at me with a strangely smug look, as if she had just delivered a foolproof excuse. I was dumbfounded. 'So that's why you dropped me in it. Because you're jealous. You are really, really sick.'

'I know.' She clutched my sleeve desperately. 'And getting Arabella to do what she did to you this afternoon must have been a cry for help. Yes, that's exactly what it was. Can't you see? A cry for help.'

'Then keep on crying,' I snarled. I shook my arm free of her grasp. 'Because you needn't ever expect me to help you again. You were supposed to be my best friend, Mary. But best friends would never do what you did to me, no matter how big a crush they once had on someone about a million years ago. As far as I'm concerned, I don't even know you any more. You tried to ruin my life just because yours isn't exactly how you want it to be. Even though your life is exactly the way I'd like mine to be. You're a spoilt, selfish brat. You've had every advantage in life with your private schools and your loaded parents. They even bought you your company. You've never had to work for anything. Perhaps that's why you're such a hopeless case. Perhaps that's why nobody loves you.'

Her jaw quivered and I knew she was about to cry, but I walked towards the door with my head held high. I wasn't going to take anything back right then. No mercy.

'Well, if that's how you feel,' she shouted after me, momentarily regaining her legendary poise, 'you can take off that bloody suit you borrowed and go home in your underwear.'

'OK then. I will.' And I did. I took the suit off, stepping all over it with my dirty shoes as I did so.

'And that necklace,' she shrieked at me. 'Don't forget that necklace belongs to me too!'

'Have it,' I spat. 'I never liked it anyway.'

I dropped the simple gold chain on top of the crumpled suit. 'You're pathetic.'

'You're the one who's pathetic round here,' Mary muttered as she picked up the chain.

'No, you are,' I retorted. 'You're the one who can't face the world without your drugs. Snort, snort, snort. You can't even put your knickers on in the morning these days without having a quick line first.'

'I can,' she protested. 'My drug use is purely recreational.'

'Right. And so the line you had before I came up here today was just because you thought we were going to have some fun together?'

She glanced back at the coffee table where one of her many credit cards lay beside a little white paper package. 'It's none of your business. Anyway, you know you'd be doing it too. If you weren't such a loser. If you could afford it.'

'And how do you afford it?'

'I, in case you've forgotten, run my own successful artiste management business.'

'Bought for you by your daddy,' I sneered.

'I did it all on my own,' she told me indignantly.

'You never did anything on your own, Mary. You've always had someone to give you a leg up in life. If I came from your background I'd be running the bloody country by now not some stupid poncey agency.'

'Oh yeah,' she spat back. ''Cos you've never had any advantages in life, have you? You haven't had the stable family background I would have killed for. If I had your background, perhaps I wouldn't need these drugs.'

'You're so sad,' I mocked, as I put on my coat and wrapped it tightly around me.

'No, you are. I'm not the one who doesn't even own the clothes I stand up in.'

'I don't need to hide a fat arse behind designer trousers,' I said with extra spite.

'Well, I'm not the one who's going to be walking back across Notting Hill naked,' she sobbed, as she buried her face in the jacket of the borrowed suit and finally let the floodgates go.

'I am not naked,' was my parting shot. But I did leave Mary's flat wearing nothing but my underwear and the coat I had borrowed from Harriet. I might as well have been completely naked though, since the coat was more a novelty silk kimono than a sensible mac and I was bloody freezing despite the fact that it was supposed to be August (a very British August). But at least I left that flat with my pride.

'Yeah!' I shook my fist up at Mary's panoramic window. 'I've still got my pride.'

What I didn't realise at that point was that I also had the small problem of retrieving Harriet's car which, having been parked so badly in my hurry to get to Mary before Brian did, was even now being loaded on to the back of a council tow-truck.

'What are you doing?' I squeaked at the balding man who was watching Harriet's Mercedes being lifted into the air with no regard for its expensive paintwork at the mercy of the rusty towing chains.

'Is this your car, darling?' the man asked me, clearly amused by my outfit. I wrapped the coat tightly around me.

'No. I mean, yes. Yes, it is my car. Put it down at once.'

'Can't do that, love. We've already started to lift it, see. Once we've started to lift the car we can't put it down again until we get it to the pound. If you'd got down here just a couple of minutes ago you could have sat in it and stopped us. We couldn't have touched it. Not with you in it, see. In case you had an accident and sued us. But you're just a bit too slow today, ain't ya?'

'But you haven't even clamped it! How can you be towing it away if you haven't even clamped it? I was only upstairs for ten minutes. Why didn't you give me a ticket first? You didn't give me any warning.'

'We don't have to give a warning if we find a car this badly parked. Two foot out from a double yellow line. Not to mention the fact that it's right across a bus lane. You passed your test yet have you, love? You're lucky we don't have the power to arrest you for dangerous driving.'

'Great. Thanks for that,' I said sarcastically. 'Look, can't you put it down again? Please? It's hardly off the ground yet. It's easier to put it down than pull it up. Put it down. Just this once. Just for me. I won't tell anyone you did it.'

He let his eyes run lazily down the length of my body which only made me pull the coat about me more tightly.

'Now, what possible reason could I have for wanting to put your car back down for you? What would make it worth my while?' He licked his lips. I crossed my arms. 'I could get into trouble for helping you. Why should I want to risk that?'

'It'll give you a feel-good feeling?' I tried. 'Look, I've got to get to the hospital,' I said, thinking quickly. 'My aunt has just been admitted to the Chelsea and Westminster with chronic appendicitis and I'm the only relative she has in town.'

'Yeah. Like I haven't heard that one before,' said the traffic warden, crossing his arms to match mine.

'Please. She really has. What if she dies or something while I'm standing here arguing with you? I could never forgive myself,' I sobbed. My eyes were starting to fill with tears, which must have helped my story because the speccy chap who had been working the hydraulics from inside the van popped his head out of the driver's window and said, 'We could do it, Bob. I could call the control room and say that the car had been moved before we got here. I haven't told them that we've started to shift it yet.'

'And then you'd owe me a favour,' said Bob, pressing his fat finger hard into my breastbone. 'So I'd have to take your phone number so that I could collect it.'

'Yeah. Of course,' I replied blithely, figuring that I would give him Mary's number just as soon as the wheels of Harriet's Mercedes hit tarmac again. That'd teach her to be such a good friend. Not.

'But we'll need to see your driver's documents first,' said

the speccy one. 'I need proof that this car belongs to you before we can release it.'

I bit my lip. 'I haven't got anything like that with me. But I've got the keys so obviously it's my car, isn't it? Can't I send that other stuff on?'

'I'm afraid not. No proof. No car. Go back into your flat and get the papers and we'll put the car down while you run upstairs.' He clearly thought I had just come out of my own flat.

'But I don't live here. I was visiting a friend.'

'Call you out of your bath to visit him, did he?' snorted the fatter guy.

'She, actually. Look, can't you just put the bloody car down and pick on someone else!' I shouted, unable to wait any longer.

Bob's face hardened. 'You posh girls,' he said, poking me in the breastbone again. 'Seem to think that all you have to do is shout loud enough and everyone will step to it. Well, I'm here today to teach you a lesson in working class manners. You shout. You don't get. You don't got no papers for this car, you don't get. Now why don't you just call yourself a taxi to see your imaginary Auntie and get Daddy to drop by the car pound with his cheque book later on. Finish lifting her up, Phil. The girl ain't got no documents.'

'Please!' I begged. I even tried loosening the front of my coat a little to entice him into mercy. But to no avail. The creaking hydraulics steamed into action again and moments later Harriet's Mercedes settled on to the back of the van with an ominous clunk.

'See you at the car pound,' said the fat guy Bob as he clambered back into the tow-truck cab.

'You! You! You fat, ugly bastard,' I yelled. 'You mean, fat ugly bastard. You must be descended from Hitler. Your

mother must have been Stalin. Do you get a kick out
of picking on helpless women, is that it? You must be
bloody gay!'

Bob the fat warden merely raised his eyebrows in an
absurdly genteel gesture and wound up his window. I went
to kick the tyre of the tow-truck and they nearly ran over
my foot.

'I'll sue you. You bastards!' I screamed after their fast
disappearing tail-lights.

'You damn right, they bastards,' said a rasta guy who was
walking past. 'You should have got in the car. They can't
take the car with you in it.'

'I know that now,' I snarled at him. You've never seen
a six-foot-four man walk away from a five-foot-two girl
so fast.

'Bastards,' I said once more, kicking a stone on the pavement and getting it wedged in the open toe of my stupid
silver shoe. 'Bastards,' I muttered as I hopped on one foot
while pulling the sharp-ended stone back out. My big toe
was bleeding. As if it wasn't going to be hard enough to
walk home as it was in my stupid too-small Manolo Blahniks.
Call a taxi? I had, of course, no money on me at all. I had
left my handbag in the glove compartment of the car. The
only minute chink of silver lining was that I still had the
keys to Harriet's flat in my hand. But only because I had
been clutching them with the intention of gouging Mary's
eyes out.

I looked up at the window of her flat now and was sure
that I saw the tartily swagged curtains twitch. I imagined her
watching with glee as I tried in vain to stop the car being
towed away. Bitch. I flicked a finger at her empty window
just in case she could still see me. Double bitch.

I took off my ridiculous sandals and began the long walk

back to Harriet's flat. It wasn't too long before I started to see Hercules's point about pavements and bare feet, I can tell you. Never had less than half a mile seemed so bloody far.

And all the time I was having the worst possible inner dialogue with myself about Brian. Where had he gone? If he hadn't gone to Mary's flat, then I was really left without a clue as to his possible whereabouts. Perhaps he had got the next plane back home. Perhaps even as I felt I was doing serious penance on the streets of London, he was sitting in a coffee shop at Heathrow waiting to board a flight back to JFK.

I had blown things so badly.

24

Brian was sitting on the doorstep of Harriet's flat when I finally limped into the square.

'Oh, Brian!' I cried, flinging my arms around his neck. 'Oh, Brian. You've come back to me. I was so worried.'

'Don't get excited,' he warned me. 'I'm only back here because when I went to check into a hotel I discovered that I left my wallet in my other jacket which is up there in your ... or whoever's it is, flat. Otherwise, I was just going to get you to send my luggage over, believe me.'

'But you're here now. You will stay, won't you? You'll give me a chance to explain.'

'I don't know if I want you to explain, Lizzie.'

'Oh, but you'll laugh so much when I do,' I said, as playfully as possible. 'It was all a set-up. Hilarious really.'

'I certainly feel as though I've been set up,' he snorted.

'You know that the girl presenting that show was one of Mary's clients?'

'Yes,' he said cautiously.

'Well, she's new to the business and she's got so much competition that Mary wanted to make sure that her first show really went with a bang. She needed some scandal, you see. But you know what English people are like. Even when an English girl is telling her fiancé that she's pregnant by his brother, everyone keeps their cool and no one throws any punches. It's not like Jerry Springer, where you can get punched for saying that you dislike your neighbour's choice of net curtains. Mary was afraid that the show wouldn't be very interesting, which is why she called me yesterday morning.'

Brian looked doubtful.

'I said I'd be a stooge for her, you see. I said I'd pretend to have done something awful to get the show going a bit. All that stuff about me not owning the flat is rubbish. Mary and I came up with the idea while we were in the kitchen at her dinner party. I do really own this flat. I was just pretending not to for the cameras.'

'You did a very realistic impression of someone who had just been rumbled,' Brian commented.

'I was petrified of being on TV. I think that helped my performance.'

'And if it was a set-up, why didn't you tell me?'

Good question. But the long walk across Hyde Park had given me time to come up with an answer.

'I felt really awful about having to do that to you. But if you'd known what was coming, you wouldn't have reacted half as spectacularly as you did. You've never been much of an actor, have you? If you'd known, it would have been so obvious that the scene was set up. Mary would have killed me. But as it was, she's already seen the edited version of the show and she's absolutely ecstatic with the results. Sends her love,' I added for authenticity.

'Does she?' said Brian. 'Well, in future you can tell her that I don't appreciate being made to look a fool for someone else's career enhancement. That show won't be going out in the States, will it?'

'I don't think so,' I assured him.

'Good.' His frown relaxed a little. Had he gone for it?

'But what I don't understand,' he continued, 'is why you

didn't try to stop me when I stormed out of the studio? Or why none of the production staff stopped me and took me aside to explain the real situation?'

'That was a major oversight,' I told him. 'And I'm sure heads will roll. Do you want a drink?' I certainly needed one. All this rubbish about having been acting was the most difficult role I had played for a long while.

'Do you think we were really convincing on the small screen?' Brian asked, as he accepted a large whisky with ice from Harriet's cabinet.

'Absolutely. I'm expecting contracts to pour in,' I added with a forced laugh. 'Now, what do you want to do on your last night in London?'

'Find out what happened to your suit,' he said.

'Oh, that old thing? I took it to the cleaners.'

'You're bizarre, he said affectionately.

'And after that?'

'Perhaps we should catch up with Mary,' he suggested. 'After this afternoon's performance I think she owes the pair of us dinner. Shall we call her?'

'Er, I don't think so,' I said hurriedly. 'When I popped by after the recording to see if you'd gone there, she was up to her eyes in paperwork. One of her clients is just about to sign a new recording deal with a record company in America so she's got to stay in and call people in Los Angeles all evening. Time difference, you know.'

'I know about the time difference,' said Brian. 'So why don't we pick up a take-away and keep her company while she makes her calls?'

'She wouldn't like that. These calls are confidential.'

'We could promise not to listen.'

'Look,' I said, my tension coming out in a little snap. 'She said that she really needs to work tonight. She's sorry to have to miss you on your last night in the UK but she's sure she'll see you in America very very soon. OK?'

'OK,' said Brian apologetically.

'So we'll go out on our own, shall we? And get an early night so that you're ready for your flight home,' I added coquettishly, as I twisted a curl of his thick black hair around my forefinger.

'I'm not flying until the afternoon, so we can stay out as late as you like.'

'I don't want to stay out late,' I told him, planting a kiss on his mouth.

When I pulled away, he was smiling like a baby. I muttered a silent thank you to whoever it was who was watching over me. Lizzie Jordan, the Teflon girl, gets out of a sticky situation yet again.

We didn't make it to the restaurant. We were lying top to tail on Harriet's leather sofa having watched the sky turn red with the sunset before London was plunged into inky black night as I told Brian how unhappy I had been on the last occasion when we spent a 'last night' together.

'But you won't have to wait six years to see me again this time,' he told me.

Then the doorbell rang. I had never heard the doorbell to Harriet's flat before so it didn't immediately register that someone was trying to attract my attention.

'Isn't that the doorbell?' Brian asked as I continued to reminisce while apparently taking no notice of the visitor.

'It can't have been,' I said, looking towards the ringer as if it had just sounded the bell for Armageddon.

'I could have sworn it was,' said Brian, as the bell sounded again.

'I don't know who it could be. It's very late.'

'Maybe it's the pizza guy,' said Brian.

'I haven't ordered a pizza.'

'I was trying to be funny.'

But he wasn't making me laugh.

The doorbell requested my attention again. Urgently, this time. But what would I do if it was one of Harriet's busy-body friends? What if it was Harriet herself, having forgotten her keys?

'Aren't you going to answer it?'

'I don't know. I mean, I'm not expecting anyone. What if it's an armed robber?' I said, hoping I didn't sound too ridiculous. 'There've been quite a few incidents lately. A lot of single women live in these flats. The robbers come round in the middle of the night posing as people from the gas board in search of a leak.'

'Then why don't you have a look through this,' Brian said, pointing out the little screen that would show me who was waiting in the lobby. 'We'll see if it's a robber who won't let off ringing the bell.' His voice rose very slightly in exasperation because the bell was now ringing without ceasing, as if the caller was leaning upon it and had forgotten that somewhere the bell would be making a terrible noise. Brian pressed the button that would show the caller's face.

'I don't know him,' I said automatically.

But Brian said, 'It's Bill.'

25

'Bill? It can't be.'

But indeed it was. Now that he turned towards the camera I could see him clearly. He was a little thinner perhaps. He definitely had less hair than when I last saw him. But it was unmistakably Bill. He put the flea-bitten fedora he had been carrying back on his head and made as if to leave.

'Wait, wait,' said Brian excitedly, pressing on the button that would allow Bill into the hall. 'Wait. Bill!'

But Bill was already back on the street. Brian flew to the window, threw it open and let out an ear-splitting whistle. 'Bill! Hang on. We're up here!'

Like Clint Eastwood taking one last look at a town where he has just left all the menfolk dead or dying, Bill turned slowly and looked up towards the flat, tipping back the brim of his hat with one finger in lieu of a smoking gun.

'Hey, Brian-man!' he shouted back. 'I'm coming on up.'

What a disaster! My last night with Brian and Bill had turned up to play gooseberry. Who had given him the address? Well, that was easily answered. Mary had obviously sent him round, knowing that any plans I had would be ruined while Brian spent the rest of the night slumped on the leather sofa with his other old buddy, smoking gigantic doobs as Bill regaled us with long and rambling stories about hill-tribes in the Andes or rampant diarrhoea in south-east Asia. A

331

night with Bill was the most effective contraceptive money couldn't buy.

'This is so lucky,' said Brian. Unlike me, he was very excited. Totally thrilled in fact. 'This is fantastic. I'm going to get to see the whole gang after all. I haven't seen Bill for six years. This is incredible.'

I nodded in half-hearted agreement. It was incredible. I hadn't seen Bill for six years either, but I wouldn't have minded too much if I'd had to wait just one more day for the pleasure.

Brian opened the door to Harriet's flat and shouted encouragement to Bill as he climbed the four flights of stairs to the penthouse. For someone who could be found jogging up Kilimanjaro at least twice a year, he was taking an awfully long time to cover a climb that even I had become quite used to over the past few days. Finally, his fedora came into view. He was walking terribly slowly, with his head bent low.

'Must be stoned,' I commented in annoyance.

'He's not the Messiah! He's a very naughty boy!' Brian shrieked à la Monty Python's Terry Jones when Bill lifted his face and tried to smile at us. But the old in-joke didn't help him to crack into his familiar grin. Instead of punching Brian on the arm as he might once have done, Bill shook Brian's hand in a very formal way.

'Hello, Brian. Hello, Lizzie,' he said, turning his big black eyes towards me. When he took off his hat, I saw at once that he had been crying.

'I'm really sorry to disturb you guys in the middle of the night, but I didn't know who else to go to. I found your new address scribbled on a pad by Mary's phone, Liz. She's been taken into hospital. They think she's taken an overdose.'

I felt as though someone had taken one of those big

rubberised hammers to the back of my knees and taken my feet out from under me. I backed into the flat and collapsed on to the leather sofa.

'Which hospital?' Brian was asking. 'What did she take? Why?'

As Bill told his story, I could hear only snatches of what he said. The conversation racing through my mind was the showdown Mary and I had after the television recording. It *had* been a terrible argument. She had told me that she wasn't happy. But Mary had never been really happy, not in all the years I had known her. It was part of her personality, wasn't it? If she won a million pounds, she would complain that her purse wasn't big enough to carry it in. Miserable was her natural state. There had been no reason at all for me to suspect that this time she really did feel suicidal.

'Why would she try to kill herself?' Brian asked again. 'We saw her just the other night. She was on top of the world.'

'She was always good at hiding her true feelings,' Bill said solemnly.

'No, she wasn't,' I protested. 'She never pretended that she was happy. Miserable was her middle name. But she never wanted to kill herself.'

'Perhaps she didn't tonight. She didn't leave a note.'

Bill had found her. He had been passing through London *en route* to Nepal and called in at her flat to wash some shorts and eat her food. When she didn't answer the door, he got someone else in the building to let him in, intending to sit on the landing outside Mary's flat until she came home. But the door to her flat was open.

'I found her face down on the coffee table,' he said. 'The door to her flat wasn't locked. I just walked in and there she was, lying on the coffee table with a rolled up tenner in her nose.'

'God, how awful,' Brian breathed. 'You mean she over-dosed on *that* sort of drug?'

Bill nodded. 'Last time I saw her she promised me she was going to get cleaned up. She even went to some secret clinic in Malta.'

'I thought she was having anti-cellulite treatment in Malta,' I interrupted, and was immediately aware how stupid that must sound. Bill snorted, though not too unkindly consider-ing. 'I didn't know she was using so much,' I added quietly. 'I thought she just took coke when she went out. She told me it was purely for recreational purposes.'

'I'm sure it was. At first. That's how every addict starts. Will you come to the hospital with me? Her family are on their way but I don't know when they'll arrive. I'd hate for Mary to wake up and find herself all alone.' Brian had already fetched my coat.

'So, she will wake up?' I said hopefully. 'She is going to be OK, isn't she?'

'I think it will be a while before we find out just how many internal organs she's fried this time.'

In the cab to the hospital (I hadn't even considered how I was going to afford to get Harriet's car out of the pound again) both Bill and Brian were silent. I sat between them, holding hands with both. Every so often, Bill or Brian would squeeze my hand as if to remind me that we were all still together. United and reunited.

But I couldn't help being sure that they knew Mary's overdose was my fault. The television show fiasco had been a cry for help. She wanted to stop me on my road to happiness before I waltzed out of sight and left her alone in her despair. She had wanted to stop me and ask me to help her. But I hadn't been able to see beyond my own embarrassment and anger. My refusal to help her had pushed her to a suicide attempt.

I couldn't stop going over all the conversations Mary and I had had over the past week. Were there clues before she broke down when confronted about Arabella's stupid TV show? She had definitely been snappish at my birthday lunch but she had explained that away as PMT. She hadn't seemed on the edge of a nervous breakdown when she had told me in such a matter-of-fact manner that Arabella would be her bridesmaid at her wedding to Mitchell.

'She was supposed to be getting married,' I squeaked, as the taxi pulled up under the brightly lit canopy where ambulances discharged their limping passengers.

Bill and Brian looked at me as if I had told them that Mary was a victim of extra-terrestrial abduction.

'She was. She told me on Saturday night. She's supposed to be getting married to Mitchell.'

'What? The gay one?' asked Bill.

'Yes. The gay one,' said Brian.

The gay one. Was I the only person who hadn't noticed that?

Bill led us straight to the ward where Mary had been taken. The nurse, recognising him, stopped us and said, 'She's woken up. But her parents are with her now.'

I breathed a secret sigh of relief. It seemed as though now that her parents had arrived, the responsibility had been taken from us.

Two people emerged from the room where Mary was being kept under observation. The man, tanned from a holiday someplace warm, kept trying to put his arm around the woman's shoulders but she refused all his advances. She was crying openly. He was red around the eyes.

'She did it because of you,' the woman sobbed as they

passed by. 'Because you keep going off and having stupid affairs the whole time.'

'You've had your affairs too.'

'Only in retaliation. God, Bunny, you're so selfish.'

'Me, selfish? You're her mother. Where were you when she needed someone to talk to?'

'She had my mobile number. She knew she could have called me at any time of the day or night.'

I could see that Bill was wondering whether he ought to interrupt the fight to ask Mr and Mrs Bagshot how their daughter was, but he thought better of it and instead made his way to the door of Mary's room.

'Are you coming?' he asked me. 'Two of us can go in at a time.'

'Take Brian with you. I'd quite like to see her on my own.'

Brian followed Bill, leaving me alone to read the poster advertising the Samaritans which was starting to peel away from the wall. Bit late if they're reading it in here, I thought.

Why had Mary tried to top herself? When I took off her borrowed suit and left it on the floor of her apartment, she had been giving at least as good as she got from me in terms of blind fury. She didn't seem like someone who would be attempting to commit suicide just eight hours later. What she said about my having it all while she was emotionally bereft was just another one of her set pieces intended to make me feel guilty enough to forgive her for having humiliated me so utterly on national TV, wasn't it?

I mean, ever since I first met Mary she seemed to be determined to see the dark side to everything; no silver linings for her, but there had never been any hint that she would try to take her own life. There was always some new skinny goth to lust after or a Bauhaus reunion concert around the corner to look forward to. And she was so squeamish. She couldn't take a single aspirin without gagging, let alone enough to kill her. And then there was the time she had fainted when I trapped my fingers in a door and had to have a fingernail cut off. That was hardly the kind of attitude that was going to help her top herself. No, Mary had always seemed more likely to be one of those people who would bore the rest of the planet to death with her problems before she took any action about them, positive or otherwise.

Now Brian and Bill were coming out of her hospital bedroom, joking nervously like two small boys who have just got off a ghost train. They've spent the whole ride holding on to each other tightly through fear and now they have to pretend that they weren't really that afraid.

'Is she OK?'

'She's fine. Physically. They think she'll be going home tomorrow. But she's got to see a shrink first.'

'Did she say why she did it?'

'I don't think she really knows,' said Brian. 'Look. She's waiting for you. You'd better go on in.'

The walk to her room seemed interminable.

She was like a tiny china doll propped up against the big white pillows in a ridiculously frilled nightdress that her mother had supplied. Her wrists, from which opaque plastic tubes led to bags of saline, were crossed neatly on her lap in front of her. Her face was white, but for the big black rings around her eyes where fatigue and old mascara had joined forces to make her into a passable panda.

'Hello, Lizzie,' she said. Her voice seemed incredibly small and far away.

I sat down on the chair next to her bed. For a moment, we just looked at each other. It was unreal, seeing the girl I had been rowing with so violently that afternoon suddenly looking so breakable. So broken.

'I'm sorry to do this to you all,' she began. 'I know you wanted to have a special last evening with Brian.' She sniffed away a tear.

'Why did you do it?' I asked her in a whisper. 'Why did you try to kill yourself?'

'I wasn't trying to kill myself,' she protested. 'I just felt so lonely. I was trying to make myself feel better with a couple of lines.'

'A couple? Bill said you had a novel's worth of lines chopped out on the coffee table.'

'I only managed three. But I'd been drinking as well. I think that's what did it. They had to pump out my stomach with some horrible charcoal stuff. I feel terrible. Imagine your worst ever hangover times twenty.'

I nodded sympathetically.

'Twenty million that is.'

'You'll soon start to feel better,' I promised her banally.

'I've got a feeling that the nightmare has only just begun. This is bound to get into the papers.'

'Why should it?'

'Because Mitchell is going to come out of the closet tomorrow. Coupled with my suicide attempt, it's a perfect story for the silly season.'

'You once told me there's no such thing as bad publicity.'

'That's what I say to my clients. I'm not sure it's actually true.'

'Look, I'm sorry for what happened earlier on. For the argument. I've spent the whole night thinking that this is my fault. Is it?' My voice came out whiny and I hated myself for having to ask. But I needed to know all the same.

Mary shook her head. 'No. Not really.'

'Is that the truth?'

'You know it is. In fact, I had a good laugh when the car got towed away.'

'You saw that?'

'I called the tow-truck. But it wasn't your fault, Lizzie. You've been the best friend ever. It's me who should be apologising to you.'

I grabbed her hands gratefully, nearly yanking out one of her drips.

'Careful,' she winced but she squeezed my hands back.

'You're my best friend too,' I told her. 'I want to do anything I can to help you get better.'

'I think I'm starting to realise that there are some things I'm going to have to work on by myself,' she half-smiled.

'We can work on them together.'

She squeezed my hands again, then let me go. 'Look, you don't have to stay here all night. I know that Brian is going home tomorrow. I swear I didn't do this deliberately to keep you from getting your oats.'

'Thank you for not telling him.'

'I think I can keep my mouth shut for another twenty-four hours. Come and see me when he's gone. You can give me all the gory details then.'

I promised I would. Then I left. I wondered if I should stay for longer, but Mary told me that she felt exhausted and wanted to be alone.

Brian and Bill were still sitting in the waiting room, swapping reminiscences. They looked up at me expectantly.

'She says we should go. She wants to get some sleep.'

Bill had to go anyway to catch his flight to Nepal, leaving me and Brian alone to watch the sun come up over the hospital car park as we had a coffee in the visitors' cafeteria.

He was quiet. As you can probably imagine. He had just seen one of his oldest friends looking like a barely animated corpse.

'Liz, what is going on?' he asked.

I shuddered. Before I realised that it was a rhetorical question.

Back at Harriet's flat, Brian took my hand and led me into the bedroom. He had been stroking my hair in the taxi back from the hospital and now he continued in the dark gloom beneath the canopies of Harriet's four-poster bed. I curled my body against his, breathing in the warm smell of him. He tilted my face towards his and kissed me tenderly.

Slowly, he unbuttoned my shirt and slid it from my shoulders. He kissed a path down across my neck to my breastbone. He cupped my breasts and murmured loving words into my burning ears.

The years we had spent apart had done nothing to diminish the heat between us when we found ourselves together again. We made love as gracefully and easily as old dancing partners, responding to each other's moves as though they had been choreographed. Brian knew exactly what to do to make me melt in his arms. When we came that early morning, we came together of course.

Afterwards, we resolved to get a couple of hours' sleep before Brian had to get ready to catch his flight, but I was actually awake when I heard the sound of a key turning in the front door of Harriet's flat. I had been lying on my side, looking at Brian's profile as though I was trying to burn the image of him into my memory for the lonely Balham nights ahead. Except I was planning that there wouldn't be too many of those. As soon as I had paid off the damage Brian's visit had done to my credit card, I would buy a one-way ticket to New York and my brilliant future. I really thought I had just about pulled the scam off.

Even as the front door was creaking open, I planted a kiss on Brian's sleeping forehead.

'Herky? Herky?'

The landing light clicked on. Though it was morning, some parts of Harriet's flat were still terribly dark and shady. 'Herky? Where are you, darling? Mummy's home.'

I sat bolt upright in bed. The clock on the bedside table told me in big luminous numbers that it was quarter past ten in the morning. Harriet was not due back for another twenty-four hours at least.

'Herky? Are you hiding from me? Where are you hiding from your mummy, sweetheart? Are you having a little sulk because I've been away for so long?'

I didn't know what to do. What should I do? Should I race out into the hallway and intercept her before she got as far as the bedroom? I didn't have time to decide. Before I could pull on anything to cover my modesty, Harriet had opened the bedroom door and turned on the light.

'I bet you're in he-re!' she sang.

Brian woke up instantly.

'Hey!' he shouted. 'Who the fuck are you?'

Harriet went white.

'Well, who the . . . who the blinking heck are you?' she replied.

Brian jumped out of bed with a pillow across his privates and before I could stop him, he was striding menacingly towards Harriet with the nearest thing to hand he thought he might be able to clock her one with. Her, undoubtedly priceless, rose vase.

'Brian,' I shouted. 'No.'

'Lizzie,' Harriet shouted.

And the world went into slow motion as pieces fell into place all round.

26

'I am Lady Harriet Corbett and this is my flat.'

'You're mistaken, old lady,' said Brian.

'I'm afraid she's not,' I had to admit.

Harriet looked as if she had swallowed a goldfish. I wasn't sure whether it was the shock of catching us in her bed or the indignity of being called 'old'.

But that was how it finally caught up with me. To cut a long story short, I told Brian simply to take everything I had told him and know that the opposite was true. There was no point in trying to give my admissions and apologies in any further detail now. My best friend was in hospital and my boss was back in her flat.

So what did Brian do? Well, at first he had a weird, weary sort of smile on his face as he waited for me to say that this was just another of my crazy, hilarious set-ups, all designed to make his holiday in London more interesting. When it became clear that wasn't going to happen this time, that finally he had heard the truth, the weather over Brian's expression turned first cloudy and then thunderous.

'You really have been lying to me all the time,' he said slowly.

I couldn't do anything but nod.

'Do you take me for some kind of fool?'

He spoke very quietly and somehow that was even more frightening than hearing him shout.

'I can't believe this.'

He reached to pick up his boxer shorts from the floor and tugged them on.

'I think we ought to get up, don't you?'

He threw me my dressing-gown. Well, it was actually Harriet's dressing-gown, as he would soon find out.

Harriet remained in the doorway, not knowing where to look and yet seeming unable to leave us alone. It was like something out of a seventies farce. I toyed with the idea of jumping through the window to make my escape. Four floors up. It wasn't such a great idea. Instead, I pulled the dressing-gown tightly around me and followed Brian and Harriet into the sitting room where they stood on either side of the fireplace while I, in the hot seat that was the sofa, wilted beneath their hostile glares.

Impossible to believe that only hours before Harriet had turned up early, Brian and I had been making plans for a future together. If I had been an employee he would have sacked me. If I had been his child, he would have had me adopted. As his girlfriend, I was definitely finished.

'Why?' he asked.

Good question.

'Because I love you,' I began hopefully. 'Because I wanted things to be just like they used to be. Because I didn't think you'd want to know the real me. The girl with the dead-end job . . .'

'In my company,' Harriet added helpfully.

'With a horrible flat.'

'In Balham,' said Harriet. 'Not here in Notting Hill. This is mine.'

'And the Mercedes?' Brian asked.

'That's mine too. Where is it, incidentally?'

'In the pound where it was when you left for Spain,' I snapped. Brian shot me a look. I was lying again. 'OK. So I borrowed that too and I parked it illegally,' I had to admit. 'It got towed away yesterday but I'll pay to get it back.'

'I don't want to hear any more of this,' said Brian. 'I'm going to get my stuff together and go straight to the airport. I might be able to get an earlier flight.'

'Brian. No.' I reached out to touch his arm as he passed but he brushed me off quite brutally.

'I'm very sorry about all this, Lady Corbett,' he said. 'You have my word that had I known we were trespassing on your property, I would not have come here at all.'

'Apology accepted,' Harriet nodded graciously and Brian left the room to pack. I strained to follow him but Harriet, who was surprisingly strong for someone so dizzy, held me back in the sitting room.

'I think you had better tell me,' she began in a voice trembling with anticipation of the awful, 'just what you have done with my dog.'

As I opened my mouth to tell her, I heard the front door to the flat slam shut. I raced to the window just in time to see Brian emerge from the building into the sunlight. He must have thrown his clothes into his bag any old how. He wanted to be gone. He wanted to be gone right away. And he didn't want to say goodbye.

A hot tear inched its way on to my cheek. My lover, my true love, my future, was driving away from me in a London cab.

'Brian!!!'

But Harriet wouldn't let me follow him. She told me that if I didn't take her to see Hercules right away she would call the police and have me arrested for squatting in her flat and stealing her car. She was like a lioness in defence of her cubs when it came to Hercules.

'Brian!!!' I yelled one more time in vain. He didn't look up.

'No use shouting after him,' Harriet told me. 'I think you've really cooked your goose with that one.'

In the cab to Balham she softened up a little when she realised just how inconsolable I was.

'Lover's tantrum,' she told me then. 'He'll be back when he's had a chance to calm down.'

I sniffed and nodded but I knew that Harriet wasn't right.

By the time we were within a mile of her beloved dog. Harriet was actually apologising for having blown my gaff.

'I'm sorry I had to come back early,' she told me. 'Bunny and I were having an absolutely wonderful time. He even told me that he would leave his wife and set up home with me. I know he's said that before, but this time, I think I believed him. Anyway, all that's gone out of the window now.'

'What happened?' I asked. Though I really didn't care.

'He got a phone call from his wife, who was at the Chelsea and Westminster hospital with their daughter. Apparently, she'd tried to commit suicide, the little fool. And of course Bunny's wife expected him to rush back right away. I told him that when I was a girl I tried to kill myself at least once a fortnight. She's just seeking attention, I told him. But he wouldn't listen to a word of it. And before I knew what was happening, he was on the next flight home. I had to wait seven hours for the next available flight home.'

'Poor Harriet,' I said sympathetically. 'Still, I'm sure he'll call you as soon as he knows his daughter is OK.'

'I wouldn't count on it. He'll have to play happy families

for at least a month now. The selfish girl. It's not even as though she's a child any more. She was twenty-seven last birthday. You'd think she'd have got over the histrionics by now.'

Which was very funny coming from Harriet, who could throw a tantrum over a difficult-to-dislodge staple.

'Bunny was forever telling me what a success his little girl is. Runs some kind of agency for footballers and pop stars. MB PR. Ever heard of it?'

Mary Bagshot Public Relations. You bet. Bunny was Mary's father. How on earth was it possible that of all the married men in London, Harriet had picked Mary's father?

'I think I know the firm,' I groaned.

'Well, she's ruined my life,' said Harriet.

Ditto, I thought.

'I don't suppose I'll ever find a man like Bunny again. I don't know what I'd do if I didn't have Hercules. Are you sure he's safe in Balham?'

'What could possibly have happened to him in Balham?' I said.

'Hercules has gone.'

Seema's eyes were ringed with worry.

'Gone potties?' said Harriet hopefully.

'Gone walkies,' said Seema. 'On his own.'

The smile on Harriet's face hardened as she waited for an explanation. A good one.

'It's not my fault,' Seema began. 'I didn't let him out. Fat Joe did it. I told him not to. He attached that bloody chip thing to Hercules's collar and left him in the middle of Clapham Common to see if he could find his way home.'

The chip thing. The tracking device that Joe had been making in the middle of the night. He had attached it to

Hercules's collar with the intention of seeing whether he could plot the dog's route home. Except that home to Hercules was not a stinking terraced house in Balham. As soon as he was off the lead, the daft pooch set his internal compass in the direction of Harriet's flat overlooking Hyde Park. Within half an hour – despite the pavements he would have to cross – Hercules and the tracking device were out of Fat Joe's range. When Seema got back from her visit to the Tate with Richard, Joe told her what had happened right away. They'd searched the Common all evening. Seema, Joe and Richard. They gave up when it got really dark but began again as soon as dawn broke.

Harriet exploded into tears.

'My baby. My poor baby!' she wailed, punctuated by Seema's chorus of 'It's not my fault.' It was like all the worst parts of a Gilbert and Sullivan operetta made flesh.

I dragged Seema into the kitchen, leaving Harriet sobbing on the only patch of the sofa that was remotely sanitary, and closed the door that had never quite fitted behind us.

'I trusted you,' I snarled at her as soon as we were out of sight.

'I told Fat Joe not to let him out,' she whined.

'Is Fat Joe out there looking for Hercules now?' I asked.

'I think Fat Joe's under his bed at the moment.'

'You had better sort this out, Seema. Because I hold you totally responsible. This wouldn't have happened if you hadn't been out with my boyfriend!'

'What?' she stopped whining and stared at me. 'What did you just say?'

'Don't pretend you don't know what I'm talking about. I saw you, on Sunday. At the Tate. With Richard. And you were all over him.'

'Well, I won't deny that I was in the Tate with your

boyfriend,' she said defensively. 'But I was certainly not all over him.'

'You were. You had your arm through his arm and you were batting your eyelashes so hard you could have turned back the tide.'

'I was not.'

'You were wearing your leather trousers,' I said, which was the ultimate accusation. Seema's leather trousers were her official first-date garb, especially when she had a first date with someone she wanted more than a free dinner out of. 'What do you have to say about that?'

I thought I had her bang to rights. But instead of admitting her guilt she squared up to me.

'I have to say that just about everything else I own was covered in dog hairs. From the dog that *you* were supposed to be looking after, remember? Except that you couldn't do what you had been asked to do because your ex-boyfriend, who you wanted to get back together with, is allergic to King Charles Spaniels. Ring any bells?'

'Phobic. Not allergic,' I quibbled.

'Whatever. *I* was doing *you* a favour. And I was doing you another favour by trying to keep *your* boyfriend occupied while you had a dirty weekend with someone else. I wasn't flirting with him. Far from it. He spent the whole day talking about nothing but you.'

'He wasn't talking about me when I saw you in the Tate,' I persisted.

'God, Lizzie, what did you want him to be doing, pulling out clumps of his hair while he wails your name from the top of the British Telecom tower? Trust me, he was really pissed off that you refused to let him meet your American friend. I think he guessed what was going on. He said that he was having second thoughts about how you felt about him. He said he was thinking about telling you that he didn't want to carry on with your relationship. It was me who persuaded him that he was being ridiculously suspicious. I persuaded him that he should just wait until Brian went home and everything would be great again. I was trying to help you out. Keeping all your bets hedged. That's what I was doing in the Tate on Sunday afternoon. Though God only knows why I bothered. Richard's too nice a bloke to be messed around.'

I snorted.

'I didn't know it until I spent the afternoon with him. I always thought he was just another bog-standard bloke with no interests except Denise Van Outen and lager. But he's not like that at all. He's really knowledgeable. He's interested in art and music and architecture. Do you know that he knows the names of all the people who designed the most famous buildings in London? He's amazingly well-read. And he's very funny too.'

'I know,' I groaned.

'And he's not so bad-looking either. When we'd finished at the Tate I dragged him to Harvey Nicks and made him try on some decent clothes. I've made him promise that he's going to buy some next time he gets paid.'

'He could do with a haircut too.'

'Yeah. But what's most important, Liz, is that he really loves you. He says he's never met anyone to compare with you. He'd do anything to make you happy. Including take a day off work to search for that bloody dog.'

'What?'

'When Hercules didn't turn up last night, I called Richard at work. He booked himself out of the office and promised to start searching right away. He should be here soon. Are you going to make yourself scarce before he arrives? Only

I don't think it's fair that he should have to find out the truth about Brian now, not when he's gone to such efforts to help you out. You are going to chuck Richard now that everything's back on with Brian, I assume?'

'It's not. Brian's gone. When Harriet came home early I had to tell him the truth and he's gone.'

Seema sighed. 'It was inevitable, I suppose.'

'No, it wasn't. I nearly did it. If Harriet hadn't come back early. If bloody Mary hadn't overdosed on coke and booze so that Harriet's lover had to fly back from Spain to be with her, I would have got away with it. Why did Mary's dad have to be Harriet's bit on the side? They've ruined things for me.'

'For heaven's sake, I don't think you can blame them,' said Seema.

'Well, who should I blame?' I asked her.

'I can't believe you're asking me that. You set up a ridiculous number of lies and you're blaming everybody else for getting on with their lives around you. Aren't you in the least bit concerned that your friend nearly died last night?'

'She wouldn't have died.'

'Well, if she had, at least you wouldn't have had to worry about her telling Brian the truth about you, would you? That seems to be all you care about. You've used everybody. You used Harriet's flat, Mary's clothes, even me as your dog-sitter. You've lied to everybody. Not just Brian. You lied to Harriet and to Richard.'

'I didn't lie to Harriet.'

'You would have done if she hadn't come home to find you in her bed,' Seema pointed out.

'I just wanted to be happy,' I shouted. 'Why shouldn't I get what I want for once?'

'Because you didn't deserve it this time?'

'Why not? What's deserving got to do with anything? Does Mary deserve to be so bloody rich? Does Harriet? Why should they have such great lives for doing absolutely nothing?'

'Great lives? Mary's so lonely she tries to kill herself and Harriet has to make do with another woman's man. Lizzie, you don't know when you're on to a good thing. You've got a family who loves you. You had a boyfriend who worshipped you. The real you.'

She put her arm around my shoulders, sure that she had made a point I would understand. It was like the night when she had tried to convince me that our flat was all right really. She wanted me to be happy with what I had. Look, she was telling me, count your blessings. But right then, I still wasn't ready to.

'I'm sick of this existence,' I snarled. 'I'm better than this fucking flat. I deserve a better life.'

Seema pulled her arm away from me again. 'What you deserve, Lizzie Jordan,' she hissed, 'is a bloody hard slap.'

'Why don't you just shut up?' I said inadvisedly.

And she gave me the slap I deserved.

'Ow!' I balled up my fist and thumped her in return.

But while I had scrapped with my brother Colin throughout my childhood, Seema had had sisters to fight with. Before I could get another thump in, she had grabbed hold of my hair and twisted it hard.

'Don't even think about it,' she roared.

'Are you going to help me find my dog?' Harriet interrupted. When she saw Seema holding me in a headlock she got an instant migraine.

'Put each other down!' she shouted. 'How can you girls fight like children when nobody knows where poor Hercules has gone?!'

Seema let go of my hair and shoved me away.

'Well, now are you going to help me find my dog?' asked Harriet again. The look on her face told me that if I didn't, she would have my skin flayed off my back and made into a collar for her winter coat.

'I don't know where to start,' I admitted.

Suddenly the house was filled with a whirring and crackling noise.

'I've done it!' Fat Joe yelled at the top of his voice. 'Come in number seven, your time is up.'

Harriet clutched her throat in horror again as Fat Joe came thundering towards us in his sky-cam gear, cap pulled down over his eyes, a pair of swimming goggles that he liked to think gave him night-vision over the top of the cap.

'Operation Hercules is back on line,' he told us. His face was deeply, deadly serious and yet more animated than I had seen it in a long time. 'I stayed up all night to increase the range of my signal receiver,' he chattered. 'They said it couldn't be done, but I took the . . .'

There followed something which sounded like 'I took the doo-berry out of the what-sit and stuck it in the eugynon' but the upshot of this nonsense was that Joe had picked up a signal from Hercules's tracker collar again. And what's more, it wasn't moving.

Was that a good sign or a bad one? Perhaps the collar had just fallen off. But perhaps the dog was dead. Whatever, with Fat Joe's portable tracking system to guide us, we set out to follow the signal and to find out whether there was still a live pedigree dog attached to it.

We crossed the Common and raced down streets that I had never been down before, quickening our step as the bleeps got closer together. As the streets became less salubrious as we neared Clapham Junction, Seema clutched her tail-ended comb like a dagger in case we had to attempt a daring rescue from a mean dog-smuggling gang.

Harriet clipped along in her high heels beside Joe, saying nothing, her mouth set in a determined line. She had only one thing on her mind.

As did I. Every time a plane passed overhead I wondered if Brian was on it. I wanted to tell Harriet to stuff this stupid dog hunt and race to the airport. I might still have time to see Brian before he left. I might have time to explain. But Harriet had threatened to make me explain all to the police already.

And it was outside the police station that we found ourselves now.

'It's the police station,' said Seema. She was very quick.

'The signal's coming from inside,' Fat Joe insisted.

'You think Hercules is in here?' Harriet asked him.

A helmet-less bobby was already peering through the station window at our unlikely gathering. A looney in combat gear, two girls dressed for a night at Stringfellows and a faintly shabby aristocrat in high-heeled toe-less sandals. None of us were dressed for a Tuesday afternoon on Lavender Hill.

'Can I help you?' the bobby asked.

'My dog has been kidnapped!' Harriet told him.

'Oh, so it's *your* dog.'

27

Harriet pushed past the policeman and raced into the station like a mother who has just discovered that the son she thought she had lost at sea may still in fact be alive.

'Where is he?' she begged the woman behind the desk, who was trying to take down details of a car theft at the time. 'Where is he? I've lost my baby,' Harriet explained to the man she had pushed in front of.

'Well, in that case,' he said, stepping out of her way. He was rather less sympathetic when the duty sergeant brought Harriet's 'baby' round from the back.

The sergeant put Hercules down on the tiled floor, where the little dog stood with shaking legs. Hercules looked at Harriet and blinked, as if he too couldn't believe that they were really about to be reunited.

'Is that him?' the sergeant asked.

'Oh, yes. It's him.' Cue that movie moment. Hercules suddenly leapt into Harriet's arms and smothered her face with sloppy pink-tongued kisses. 'I'm sorry I left you with that nasty lady,' she told him, referring, I guessed, to me. 'I'll never ever ever leave you again.'

'Where did you find him?' asked Seema.

'This gentleman here brought him in.'

As if that day couldn't get any worse. In the corner of the waiting room sat the man who had tried to nick me for not pooper scooping when I first brought Hercules home.

'And the man who was trying to kidnap him,' the sergeant continued.

Someone was really trying to kidnap Harriet's dog?

'That's her!' shouted the colonel when he caught me staring at him. 'She's the ring-leader. You should be taking her into custody too.'

'What?'

'Perhaps you might be of some use to our inquiries,' the sergeant nodded. 'What do you know about a drug addict called Richard Adams? He's the man that the colonel here caught trying to kidnap this dog.'

Drug addict Richard Adams? Not my Richard Adams?

'Richard Adams is my boyfriend,' I squeaked. 'Sort of.'

'I told you,' said the colonel. 'There's a whole ring of them stealing pedigree dogs for animal experimentation.'

'I was looking after him for Harriet.'

'You were trying to sell my dog into animal experimentation?' Harriet breathed in horror.

'No, I wasn't. And neither was Richard. Probably.'

'I think you'd better come in here,' said the sergeant opening the door to interview room number one.

We were led into an interview room where Harriet finally confirmed that I had indeed been *in loco parentis* as far as Hercules was concerned. I hadn't been living up to my responsibilities very well, but Harriet had entrusted her dog to me. That much was true.

It turned out that the interfering colonel had made a citizen's arrest on Richard when he saw him trying to coax Hercules into his rucksack with a piece of Belgian sausage (which would never have worked, confirmed Harriet, since Hercules wouldn't touch anything processed). Anyway, when Richard made a grab for Hercules, the colonel made a grab for Richard. He brought Richard down with a flying rugby tackle to the legs and sat on him bodily until the park warden happened by.

Now Richard was being held in custody on suspicion of dog-napping.

'You can drop the charge now,' said Harriet.

But the sergeant couldn't drop the fact that Richard had been found to have a half-smoked spliff in his pocket when he was searched. Hence the drug addict bit.

I dropped my head in despair.

'This is all your fault,' hissed Seema.

As if I didn't know.

No one needed to remind me that if I hadn't wanted to be with Brian so badly, Seema wouldn't have been put in charge of Hercules. Neither would Seema have found herself having to spend a Sunday afternoon consoling my boyfriend while I went ahead with my dirty weekend, giving Fat Joe the time and opportunity to incorporate Hercules in one of his experiments, which resulted in Hercules being lost, which resulted in Richard going out to look for him, which resulted in Richard suddenly finding himself drawn to the attention of the police by the strong arm of the local neighbourhood watch.

Richard didn't even smoke dope. At least, I hadn't known about it, if he did.

'He bought a spliff off his flatmate because he thought it would help him forget about you,' Seema told me later. 'He smoked half of it round here, had a coughing fit and gave up. He was never even going to finish the damn thing. He was going to throw it away.'

But now it seemed that little ill-timed spliff was going to be with him for the rest of his life. And it was all my fault.

I felt like holding my hands out to the sergeant and telling him to cuff me there and then. I was the villain. Because of me, my boyfriend was in the cells, my best friend was in hospital and the love of my life was spending the last day of his vacation at Heathrow Terminal Two.

It's little wonder that no one was talking to me on the walk back from the station.

28

I left several messages for Richard to call me when they finally let him go home. But he didn't. I called Mary at her flat. The phone there was picked up by her mother who informed me curtly that Mary's office was dealing with any enquiries that day. There hardly seemed to be any point in calling Brian on his mobile. But I did.

'Hello.'

I don't know why I was surprised that Brian answered his own phone. I think I believed that everyone was screening their calls in case they heard from me that day.

'Who is this?' he said.

I hadn't yet breathed a word.

'OK,' he sighed. 'Lizzie, is that you?'

He should have been half-way over the Atlantic Ocean, but Brian was still sitting outside Burger King in Terminal Two. His plane had been delayed by some technical hitch he didn't particularly want to think about – he'd always been a nervous flyer. He'd read all that day's papers, including the classified ads. And yes, he could use some company. Even if it was mine.

I was there in an hour, looking rather less polished than I had done for our last airport assignation but grateful for the chance to see him all the same.

'I hate saying goodbye to people at airports,' I reminded him.

'Isn't it better than not saying goodbye at all?'

Considering the terrible fallout from my lies, I know I didn't deserve a chance to explain why I had told them. But Brian listened. It was getting on for ten in the evening and his plane still wasn't fit to depart. He'd been at Heathrow for a whole day, which I suppose can leave you rather desperate for quality entertainment.

In the corner of the airport lounge I told him about my real life since college. I told him the truth about the crappy degree, the dead-end jobs I'd found myself as a result and the squats that I had lived in. I told him about the nights Seema and I had spent sneakily finishing the dregs of other people's expensive cocktails in bars we couldn't really afford to drink in. I told him about customising clothes from Oxfam and telling Mary that I had picked them up at Voyage. I even told him about the *night of the fleas* – though I stressed that I had seen no evidence of the infestation myself.

I told him that nothing had worked out as I planned it after university and as soon as I started to waver, I couldn't seem to steer a path back towards those plans. At first I'd sent off job applications by the post-box full. But with every rejection my confidence slipped a little further away until there came a point when I was almost grateful for my temp job at Harriet's firm. That feeling didn't last long though and soon I was looking for an escape route. At first it had been lottery tickets, but then it had been Brian.

'I don't understand how this happened to you,' Brian said. 'You were one of the most talented people I ever met.'

'I guess I must have had my moment of greatness when I

played my one-eyed Cleopatra. I couldn't really have hoped to repeat that kind of success in the real world.'

'Sounds like you've given up trying.'

'Wouldn't you? With all the rejections I've had . . .' I began.

Brian grabbed my hands and started passionately, 'But the rejections you had were for jobs in accountancy, for fuck's sake. Jobs punching figures into a spreadsheet. What about the auditions you should have been going for? You didn't get any of those office jobs because anyone with half a brain could tell within seconds of meeting you that it's not what you were designed for. You'd be bored within days.'

He kissed my fingers and rubbed them as if he was trying to keep them warm. 'When I met you,' he continued, 'I knew at once that there was something different and special about you. I knew that you could never be mediocre. But with that blessing comes the curse that you could end up at one of two extremes. In the stars or in the gutter.'

'I can see the stars from where I'm lying in the gutter now,' I joked.

'I know. It looks bad. But what I'm trying to say is, you can be either rubbish or brilliant, Lizzie Jordan. It's up to you which one. And you won't have to put all that much effort in to be brilliant.'

'How?' I asked in a tiny voice.

'Channel some of the energy you've put into making such a pantomime of your real life into showing someone that you'd be just as convincing on stage. Hell, you could even use this whole debacle as an interview piece if you like. I'll vouch that I was utterly taken in. But join a drama group. Do some auditions. Do it properly. If you let your dreams go, you can't expect anyone else to catch them for you.'

Déjà-vu. I could hear Richard on the drive back from my parents' house saying almost exactly the same words.

'I'll try,' I promised. 'But I'm really sorry, Brian. I made a fool of you.'

'It doesn't matter now. Especially as I haven't been exactly straight with you either,' said Brian.

I waited for him to tell me that he was really a post-boy rather than a rising star at his bank. But he didn't.

'See, the thing is, Lizzie, I've sort of been using you too.'

'Using me?'

'I don't know how else to put it. I've been using you to help me sort out a few things in my life. You know I told you about that girl, the one I was going out with, with the King Charles Spaniel?'

I had an awful feeling that I wasn't about to be relieved by what I would hear.

'Well, she and I haven't split up. Not altogether. In fact, I want to ask her to marry me.'

'Marry you?' I squeaked, like an unhappy echo.

'Yes. But before I came over here I wasn't sure. And it wasn't just the issue of the dog. I wasn't sure that I had finished being on my own. Worse than that, I wasn't sure that I was completely over you. You probably won't believe this – I mean, I'm sure you've met loads of guys since I went back to the States and some of them must have given you a good time, but it hasn't been like that for me. Since I waved you goodbye, I haven't met anyone who could live up to the memory of you. Except perhaps Angelica.'

'That's her name?'

'Angelica Pironi. You know, I think you'd like her. She's a lot like you.'

'What? A failure? A loser? An incurable liar?'

'No,' he hugged me. 'She's funny, generous, lovable. In fact, she's so much like you that she brought back all the memories of the time we had together. I found myself running every minute we had together over and over. I used to wait all day for your e-mails to arrive. I started to think that I could never love anyone the way I loved you.'

'You loved me?'

He was saying all the right things, but in absolutely the wrong context.

'That's why I had to come to London. I didn't really suddenly get time off. In fact, when I go back, the bank will probably have gone belly up in my absence. But it was getting ridiculous. I was trying to pluck up the courage to ask Angelica to be my wife, but all I could think about was you. I needed to know the reality behind the dream. I needed to see you again and find out if we had a future. I figured that if I came to England I'd know for sure. I was going crazy; hesitating over the biggest thing in my life so far in case you still wanted me. I didn't really think I had a chance but I needed to be certain. You never spoke about your love life in your e-mails.

'So I got on that plane. And I spent the whole flight wishing you'd got fat or dyed your hair some awful colour. Anything to make me find you less attractive and help me make my mind up.'

'I was wishing pretty much the same thing of you,' I half laughed.

'But you looked better than ever.'

'And so did you.'

'And it seemed like the friendship between us hadn't altered much either.'

'I felt the same.'

'By the time we found ourselves sitting by the Serpentine

on that first night together I felt sure that I would be telling Angelica that it was over between us as soon as I got back home.'

'But I cocked up. You found out about all my lies and decided that it wouldn't work.'

'No. No, it wasn't exactly like that. I made my mind up that we weren't going anywhere last night, Lizzie. When we were sitting in the hospital. I was playing one of those silly mind games where I was thinking about what I would do if it were you instead of Mary in that bed. Then I got to thinking about what I would do if it was Angelica, and my heart almost exploded. I realised that I loved her after all. I've never had a fear of her dog. I've just had a fear of commitment.'

'When were you going to tell me?' I asked.

'I was going to send you an e-mail as soon as I got home.'

I tried to feel indignant, but I couldn't.

'Cheers,' I said.

'But it wasn't only that, Liz. I sensed that your heart wasn't in it either. That afternoon at the Tate, and later at the British Museum. When you were preoccupied. I guessed that it wasn't just about the office.'

'But . . .' I started.

'You called me Richard when we made love last night.'

I coloured from the toenails up. 'You're joking?'

Brian shook his head. 'You definitely called me Richard. Is he someone special?'

I looked down at the floor and though I couldn't bring myself to admit them, my feelings must have been obvious.

'If this Angelica girl says yes to your proposal, will you invite me to the wedding?' I asked.

'You're top of my guest list. But you've got to promise to do the same in return.'

'Who am I going to end up with now?' I snorted.

'There's already someone special for you.'

The loud-speaker system announced the imminent departure of Brian's flight back to New York.

'I had the best holiday,' Brian said, squeezing my hand. 'Despite everything. Really good fun.'

'And things are still the same between us, aren't they?' I said, hopefully.

'No,' he said. 'They're better. I think we've reached a new stage in our relationship, don't you? I hope you think you can trust me now when I tell you that you're doing fine. Though you're going to work hard at doing better, aren't you?'

'I am.'

'Good.'

The silky-voiced airport announcer announced once more that Brian's flight was boarding. My heart contracted in anguish.

'Thanks for coming to say goodbye,' he said. 'I know how much you hate goodbyes. But it won't be for so long this time. You will visit, won't you?'

'Try and keep me away.'

'I've got to go. I've got to be back in the office tomorrow morning, can you believe?'

'You work too hard.'

'I've had a wonderful holiday.' He leaned forward and kissed me. On the cheek. I didn't know whether I felt disappointed. But then he wrapped his arms around me and pulled me in for a long hard hug. When he pulled away, I wondered whether I saw the glitter of tears in his chocolate eyes.

'I'll see you soon.' He picked up his carry-on bag and made for the gateway to passport control.

I stood where he left me and waved until I couldn't see him

any more. When he had disappeared through the gate, I went upstairs to the café from where you can see the planes taking off through big picture-windows. I watched three American Airlines flights take off. I didn't have a clue which one he was on, but I wanted to feel as though I had seen him safely out of British skies. Then I turned and joined the rest of the heavy-hearted people who had just said goodbye to someone they loved and made my way to the tube.

I was sad for about three stops, but by the time I changed from the Piccadilly to the Northern Line, I was feeling altogether better. Perhaps it was because I was mentally writing my letter of resignation to Harriet and filling out forms for a course that would change the direction of my life. I could do it. I knew that now. In the end, Brian's visit had been a strange success.

I realised that I had never really wanted Brian after all. I had merely wanted what he represented. Escape. Escape from the life I had found myself in five years after leaving university. The boring job. The awful flat. The social life that revolved around pub quizzes and promising each other that the very next week we would all sign up to do a line-dancing class.

I had wanted Brian to take me away from all that. To fly into the UK on a white charger of a 747 and return to New York with me riding beside him, to find my rightful place in Manhattan's glittering social whirl. Never mind whether Brian wanted to take me there or not. Never mind whether it would actually be so much better than my life in London anyway. It was simply easy to imagine that there was a magic bullet that would solve all my problems and Brian was it.

I finally realised that I had done exactly the same thing during my finals, mooning about over that fat-headed rugby player, spending too much time thinking that things were going wrong because I wasn't the centre of his universe, when I would have been better off doing a bit of revision instead. I had projected everything, my future, the apex of my ambitions, on to him. A mere man. I had effectively tried to make him responsible for my happiness because it was easier to be unhappy when I thought it was someone else's fault that things were not going as well as they should have been.

Well, all that was going to change. At long last I realised that the fact that my life was not the life I had always wanted for myself was something only I could remedy. I could change my life. Me, alone. But I had to clear up Harriet's flat first . . . And get her car back from the pound . . . And start making a lot of apologies.

Epilogue

It's almost a year since Brian's visit and at last I've got a life I'm happy to e-mail him about. I took his advice and started to make an effort to change things rather than cover the bad parts up. I even sent an article about my experiences on that painful television programme to a magazine who published it and paid me. I sent off a few more about various dilemmas I had known and before I knew it, people were actually calling me and asking me to write about this or that.

Harriet was sorry to see me leave Corbett and Daughter to devote myself to becoming a freelance writer while I wait to take up a place at drama school, but soon after I quit she decided that she wasn't all that bothered with keeping the estate agency going anyway and has set up a high class dog-sitting company instead. She has also started seeing a real bona fide bachelor since Bunny resolved to make one last attempt to rebuild his shambolic marriage to Mary's mum.

I kept my head down when the colonel who had been so ruthless about Hercules's dog mess came to take Harriet to dinner on my last day as chief paper pusher at Corbett & Co. Harriet had made the rather kindly gentleman's acquaintance properly when she thanked him for his part in rescuing her dog. The colonel was instantly smitten. Good old Hercules acting Cupid. I knew he'd come in useful for something.

Unable to see himself as a highly paid dog-walker, Randy Rupert has moved to an estate agency where he is actually expected to do some work. He says he is very unhappy. Now that he has to work weekends, there's less time left to woo 'lovely ladies' and improve his skills at golf. I wish that I could feel sorry for him, but I told him to his face that the women of the United Kingdom should be relieved that he was no longer free to pursue them so rabidly. I think he may have taken that as a compliment.

Mary and I are on better terms again. After her cocaine crisis, she spent a month detoxing in Malta and came back with a clear head and five new celebrity clients from her exclusive therapy group. Her talent agency goes from strength to strength, specialising in launching the media careers of ex-wives and fiancées of the rich and famous. Mitchell, however, has disappeared. Last seen dancing to 'Copacabana' in some seedy Rio nightclub. Mary isn't terribly bothered about that though. Mitchell's records are actually selling in larger quantities than ever, thanks to a whole tribe of misguided teenage girls who think his sudden disappearance rather romantic. Mary still has her percentage points on his royalties, of course.

She also has Bill. For the time being, he's taking a break from his mission to see the four corners of the earth by bicycle and has moved himself and his dirty lycra into her hitherto pristine flat. He was always in love with her. We all knew that. And she just needed to be woken up to the fact that it is possible to love someone who isn't intent on running away. Her days of lusting after the unreliable and unavailable are over now. She's realised that she actually deserves better.

'But you have to have had a few pigs in your life to help you recognise the truffles,' she told me last time we had lunch. That made sense to me.

She also said that she even adores the hair on Bill's back

these days. That didn't quite make so much sense but I didn't press her for more details.

Ace tracker Fat Joe bought an exercise bike with a view to getting slim and getting himself a relationship. He spent two weeks fiddling with the heart-monitor cum speedometer cum microwave oven thing that came attached to the handlebars but then he met 'Venus' in a chat room on the internet and now he comes out of his room even less frequently than before. He says that he's definitely in love with her. Assuming that Venus is a 'her'. One day they're going to meet up in real time, he told me. He's been talking about mailing her a marriage proposal. Needless to say I have warned him about the dangers of losing perspective in cyberspace.

As for Seema. She finished her business studies course and left sunny Balham for sophisticated Harvard to do a PhD in something terribly complicated in an attempt to stave off marriage to a rich second cousin from Madras. She's been given until she's twenty-nine to find herself a husband now. Doesn't even have to be a Hindu boy any more as long as he's prepared to eat curry.

Shortly after she arrived in the States, Seema took a trip to New York to spend a weekend with Brian and his fiancée, Angelica. She had a wonderful time in their company and sent me a postcard of the Statue of Liberty confirming that Brian does indeed have a gorgeous apartment in one of the best parts of Manhattan. But guess what? She said that he doesn't have a view of Central Park after all! I had to smile when I read that.

The fiancée, Angelica Pironi, wrote to me herself to thank me for helping Brian to overcome the debilitating 'phobia' that had kept them apart. Apparently Brian's even been taking her dog for walkies. She told me I should visit too, but I think I'll give it another six years. Hopefully by that time Brian and I really will be able to laugh about the web of lies that surrounded his visit to England.

Looking at how things have turned out, I can't imagine the frame of mind I must have been in back then. What low self-esteem I must have had. Not only that, my actions also implied that I had a very low opinion of Brian to think that he wouldn't have wanted to know me if I didn't put on that high-flying act. The implication was such an insult to his broadmindedness and generosity. Sometimes I think back and shudder with the realisation that I'm very lucky I still have my American friend.

Which leaves only Richard. Of all the people I treated so badly, he took the longest to come round to even thinking about forgiving me. After the ridiculous dog-napping incident, he was cautioned for his possession of a minuscule amount of the evil weed and that caution was enough to lose him his job as an accountant. Drug conviction equals the sack. His bosses weren't interested in any mitigating circumstances, and it was a long time before Richard would start to see his enforced resignation as a positive thing. Naturally, he felt that I was in some small way responsible for his having to disappoint his mother and sign on the dole. He sent me a stinging letter to that effect, enclosing the Blur CD I had bought him for Valentine's Day and asking for the return of his *Fawlty Towers* video collection forthwith. That was the end of us, of course. And there was no way I could pretend that I didn't deserve his utter contempt.

But one day, while I was mooning over the fact that he wasn't ever likely to phone me again, I showed Mary the picture that Richard had drawn for me as my birthday present. I had been beating myself about the head with the memory of how disdainfully I had discarded the drawing back then, anxious to get rid of Richard so that I could prepare for Brian's arrival and even slightly irritated that he hadn't given me a 'proper' present, that is, something I could wear.

Mary held the picture up and compared likeness against reality.

'It's really very good,' she told me.

'I know it's good,' I half-sobbed back at her. 'He's an incredibly talented man. And I lost him!!!'

'Yeah, well,' said Mary brusquely. 'I think you've learned your lesson. Can I take this?' she asked.

'What for? It's the last piece I have of him.'

'I'll give it back,' she promised. And she did. But not until she had shown it to Arabella Gilbert and Arabella, who had begun to fancy herself as a bit of a Renaissance-style patron of the arts since a guest appearance on the *South Bank Show*, gave Richard his first commission as a society portrait artist. The result – a stunning painting of Arabella Gilbert as Diana the Huntress – made the cover of the *Sunday Times* Style supplement. Richard was hailed as a rare new talent, lauded by art critics who felt that it was about time young artists started using proper paint instead of elephant dung. He was the talk of the country. And my mother couldn't believe that I'd let him slip from my grasp.

'I knew he'd make something of himself,' she said, with a stunning display of selective memory. 'You could have been going to all those society parties with him.'

'I know. But I blew it.'

'Why don't you give it one more try?'

I'd done more stupid things in my life.

I got Mary to stand over me when I picked up the

phone, ready to cut me off if the conversation started to get ridiculous.

'Take a deep breath and smile before you start talking,' she advised me, as though I was one of her clients. 'Let him hear the smile in your voice. Talk to him as though you were talking to any other friend.'

I pulled a rictus grin and dialled Richard's number. 'Act as though I'm talking to any other friend.' But I wasn't. I was calling the love of my life. The real love of my life. The one I'd lost. Even before he picked up at the other end, I had almost started blubbing.

'Richard, I really miss you. And I don't think that feeling's ever going to change.'

There was silence at the other end of the line.

After that, he agreed to see me for one cup of coffee as a thank you for the roundabout way in which Arabella Gilbert had made contact with him and kick-started his glittering career. Three bottles of wine later, I agreed to pose nude for his re-working of *The Birth of Venus*. I'm sure I don't need to tell you what happened then but when we woke up on the pile of cushions on the floor of his studio next morning, covered only by a paint-splattered dust-sheet, our grand romance was back on.

Two months later, Richard's looking for a new flat. A flat with lots of light and room for *two* struggling creative types. And I'll never tell even the littlest white lie again. I won't have to.

If you enjoyed *Lizzie Jordan's Secret Life* read on for an extract of *The Matchbreaker*. This latest hilarious novel by Chris Manby is out in January 2006, published by Hodder & Stoughton.

CHRIS MANBY

The Matchbreaker

HODDER

I

I could think of far better ways to spend a Saturday afternoon in June than trying on bridesmaids' dresses. However, that is exactly what I found myself doing one day last summer; sweating like a French cheese in a changing room without air-conditioning in one of London's biggest department stores; trying not to swear out loud as I stepped into a dress specifically designed to bring out the red in my spots. It was a gold dress. Who on earth does a gold dress suit? Not an ash-blonde like me, that's for sure.

Still, the bridesmaid doesn't really get much choice what she's going to wear, does she? And if the bride's special colour scheme for her big day decrees that her attendants look like they're suffering from a bad case of jaundice, there's not much the average bridesmaid can do about it but slap on some extra blusher. Not that there was enough blusher in the world to save me from looking like a convalescent right then. Karen's colour scheme decreed that her bridesmaids look as though they had just been disinterred . . .

'Oh, Lindsey, you look beautiful,' Karen gushed as I emerged from the changing room. I prayed as I did so that no one I knew would walk past. I would have dropped dead for real if anyone I respected caught me looking so grim.

'That empire line is super-feminine,' the shop assistant chipped in. 'And it really does suit you.'

'Try this head-dress with it,' Karen suggested.

She plonked a garland of gold polyester roses on my head and the village idiot effect was complete.

Karen had already changed into her wedding dress. The best one could possibly say was that the dress she had chosen was *complicated*. It had more swags and flounces than a set of theatre drapes. And it was pure-as-the-driven-snow *virgin* white. I mean, let's be realistic . . .

Karen resembled nothing so much as Marie Antoinette pretending to be a milkmaid – a train crash of low class meets too much cash, right down to the little white silk and bugle-beaded pouch that dangled from her wrist for those all-important wedding day accessories. Like her mobile phone. Meanwhile, the shop assistant tugged at the back of my balloon of a skirt and held the waist in tightly so I could see how I might look once alterations to the gold sack had been made.

Hideous. Still hideous.

'Doesn't Lindsey look beautiful?' Karen asked her mother.

Marilyn, Karen's mother, paused long enough in searching through her handbag for nicotine patches to agree.

'She looks lovely,' she said without looking up.

'See, I knew you'd look fantastic,' Karen persisted. 'Gold really is your colour, Linz.'

'You'll look better in the church. The lighting in here isn't terribly flattering,' said the assistant, noticing my frown.

Didn't I know it?

I'd been in that changing room before, you see. Three times in fact. And each time trying on a dress more spectacularly loathsome than the last. Melanie, the personal assistant, had wanted to see me in peach. Heather, the 'model', thought yellow would go with my hair. Trisha, the yoga teacher, had my 'colours done' and stuck me in mauve.

They were all wrong.

Fortunately, I wasn't to be seen in public in any of those disaster outfits. For years afterwards, the dresses hung unworn in my wardrobe like taffeta scalps. And the gold dress Karen wanted me to wear was going to join them there, I promised my unhappy reflection.

'You'll look like a princess on the day,' said the shop assistant cheerfully.

If the day ever came, I would look like one of the Hanson boys in drag.

'Your dad is going to be so proud of you, Linz,' Karen – the woman who wanted to be my stepmother – assured me.

That's right. Karen had wangled herself a pretty spectacular catch. She was my father's fourth fiancée. Fifth if you count my mother, his first and only wife.

Sounds bad, doesn't it? Like Dad was addicted to engagement ring shopping or was the kind of man who didn't follow through on his promises. That's not the case. He just made some unfortunate choices.

Really, I can think of no better man than my father. I know pretty much every daughter says that – whether the dad in question is a prince or a train robber – but I also know I am telling the truth. Give me any fatherhood scale you care to mention and my dad would be right at the top of it.

You see, I grew up without a mother and, with Mum gone, Dad worked harder than you can possibly imagine being two parents' worth of father to me. In fact, he was as steadfast and supportive, protective and loving as two parents, four grandparents and an entire extended family of aunts, uncles and irritating younger cousins.

He certainly didn't have it easy, raising me all on his own. When he found himself in the role of single parent, Dad soon came to sympathize with those articles you read in women's magazines about the difficulty of juggling work and family life. Dad was a high-flyer at university and had a serious career in advertising with all the attendant serious career stresses before he was twenty-five. He was the youngest ever account manager in his firm. He was a partner by the age of twenty-eight. But although he quickly reached the top of his career tree, it definitely wasn't at the expense of our relationship.

Dad was there at every important moment in my life. He saw me take my first steps. He heard my very first word (which, somewhat strangely, was 'Mama'). He sewed nametags into my first school uniform and cried like a girl with the real mums at the gate as he watched me walk into the playground for the very first time.

He taught me to ride a bike. He taught me to swim. He was never too busy to help with my homework. He made it to every school concert, even if it meant having to slip away early from a meeting (in fact, he once brought an entire commercial film crew to see me play an Oompaloompa in a musical version of *Charlie and the Chocolate Factory*). He took a weekend cookery class so he could bake a cake for me to take into school at harvest festival time (the other 'mums' were gently patronizing until Dad's Chocolate Yule Log won first prize at the Christmas Fayre).

Dad was always there for me. When the time came, he even took me aside and told me about periods and puberty. I don't know which of us was more embarrassed.

But my favourite memory of Dad comes from when I was four years old. As I think about it, I can still smell the fallen leaves mouldering on the ground, the delicate hint of a bonfire for Guy Fawkes' on the air. It's an autumnal smell that makes me smile even now.

We were walking across Hampstead Heath on our way home from the playground. Dad always took me to the swings on a Sunday afternoon. He was holding my hand in his big, fatherly paw. It was almost dark, though it can only have been five o'clock.

And then I heard my first firework. It exploded with a bang that seemed impossibly big and dangerous to a four-year-old girl. Immediately, I burst into tears. I wrapped myself around Dad's leg, almost bringing him to the ground. He scooped me up and lifted me on to his shoulders. He pressed his bristly cheek against mine and kissed the end of my nose. I buried my face in his neck.

But Dad gently took my face and turned it towards the sky, directing my eyes to where the fireworks still glittered on the horizon above London like shattering stars. He wouldn't let me hide.

'Look,' he said. 'There's nothing to be frightened of. There will never be anything to be frightened of. Not while I'm here.'

Gradually, I loosened my grip around his neck and relaxed. We stood on the Heath for a long time after that, me on Dad's shoulders, watching the graceful arc of dozens of Roman candles as they lit up the November sky. From terrified to mesmerized in a matter of minutes. I knew then that he was right. I didn't need to be afraid. Dad would open my eyes to the good things in life and I would never be afraid or unhappy as long as he was there.

As I was growing up, whenever people found out what had happened with Mum, they would pull a sympathetic face or reach out to touch me gently on the arm as though I needed comforting. But I honestly didn't feel I lacked a thing. I had a complete and perfect family in Dad and me. I couldn't have been happier. And that's how it was for a very long time. Just the two of us. Me and Dad against the world.

3

Nineteen years later in that bridal department, I took off the stupid gold bridesmaid's dress and threw it over the back of the chair in the changing room like a fish-packer discarding stinking overalls at the end of a shift. I didn't even bother to pick the dress up when it slithered from the chair on to the frankly filthy floor. Outside, Karen twittered on to her mother and the assistant as they unlaced the ice-white monstrosity she had chosen for her wedding day.

Not that Karen looked much less tacky in her day clothes. She had come out in her usual shopping attire. A pair of velour tracksuit bottoms with something retarded written in big letters across her buttocks (today it was 'Hard Tail': it should have been 'Soft in the Head'). A matching hoodie. Her Ugg boots: at least two years too late. Looking at Karen's mother, Marilyn, it was easy to see where her dress sense came from. Marilyn kept her nicotine patches in a gold-trimmed Fendi baguette. Fake, of course.

Karen's style had been making me wince since the day I first met her. In fact, I think I started wincing in anticipation the moment I heard Karen's name . . .

She was a personal trainer. *A personal trainer!* What kind of job is that? You can imagine how I felt when Dad told me he had been seeing someone new and that she worked in his gym.

Karen had been recommended by my father's GP. Dad had been suffering from chronic backache for a while. All those hours at the office and long-haul flights to shoot commercials all over the world were starting to take their toll. After his doctor patched him up and prescribed anti-inflammatories for the umpteenth time, he insisted that Dad sort out a new exercise routine to strengthen his muscles and prevent him from ending up permanently incapacitated. Something Pilates-based might be a good idea. He knew exactly the woman to help.

Karen had, according to Dad, a wall full of certificates in her office. She had studied sports medicine in the United States, trained in some of the best fitness centres in the world, and knew more about anatomy than the average surgeon. She wasn't just a trainer. She was, to use the American term as she did, a sports physician. That didn't make the revelation that Dad's new 'sports physician' was getting to know his anatomy rather more intimately than the average client's any easier to take.

I found out during the Christmas holidays. I came home from a very difficult term at university – feeling quite guilty that I hadn't managed to make it back to London at all until then – and found an unfamiliar hairbrush in *my* ensuite bathroom. Dad didn't look at all embarrassed when I confronted him about the pink plastic bristles covered in long dark hair. Instead, he grinned widely at the memory of something I really didn't want to guess at and said, 'Ah, yes. I've been meaning to tell you. We're going to be three for Christmas this year.'

'Three?'

'That's right,' he confirmed. 'I've met someone fabulous.'

'Someone serious?' I asked, heart in mouth.

He merely grinned.

Oh dear, I thought. 'Where did you find her?'

'I met her at the gym. She's my trainer. She's called Karen.'

Everything – the cheap hairbrush by my bathroom basin, the job description, that horrible name – told me this was a terrible idea.

Getting Personal

This one's for Harrison Arnold.
See, Harry, once upon a time your auntie
was quite cool!

Acknowledgements

With love and thanks to Mum, Dad, Kate and Lee. To everyone at Hodder, especially Carolyn Mays and Sara Hulse who didn't ask for their money back when they read the first draft. To Ant and James at Antony Harwood Limited, Sally Riley and Joanna Kaliszewska at Aitken Associates and Sheryl Petersen at Diverse Talent Group for their continued support and the spondulicks. To Ryan Law and Jenn Matherly for being such steadfast friends. And finally, to Rob Yorke, who bore the brunt again. *See, I told you you should have gone fishing!*

Prologue

Intelligent, attractive and inexplicably unat-
tached. Three London friends seek some serious
summer loving . . .

'Will I ever be somebody's Whoopsie?'

That was the question on Ruby Taylor's mind as she
watched the new Mrs Winky Foreman smash a lump of
chocolate wedding cake into her brand-new husband's
mouth. If there really is someone for everyone, Ruby
thought, then her old college friend Susannah (known
affectionately to her husband as Whoopsie) and Winky –
known to everyone as Winky – it was his real name, must
surely be the proof.

Personally, Ruby would have run screaming from a
man who looked like the original model for Humpty
Dumpty, sported sweat patches like small paddy-fields
even in the dead of winter and thought it funny to refer to
the animal noises his new wife makes in bed in his
wedding day speech. But to Susannah, who galumphed
up the aisle as though she was wearing Wellington boots
even in her new Jimmy Choos, Winky Foreman was
perfect. Yin to her yang. Salt to her pepper. *Stinky* to her
Whoopsie. Apparently.

It was the fourth wedding Ruby had attended so far
that year and it wasn't even June. First Jane and Ian. C of
E and canapés in Gloucestershire. Then Mark and Jacqui. Registry office and pizza in South Ken. Then Peter
and Katherine. Pomp and circumstance in Rutland. Now

Winky and Susannah. Full-blown upper crust bad behaviour in Shropshire. Morning coats, pink marquee,
stomachs pumped at dawn.

Lou Capshaw and Martin Ashcroft, who often
seemed to Ruby to be the only single people left in
the world bar herself, sat with her on the 'miscellaneous'
table. There's one at every wedding – usually stuck by
the kitchen door – for the singles, the widowers, the
holiday acquaintances and the barking great-aunt of the
bride. They whiled their time away playing 'Wedding
Disco Bingo' (which involved writing down ten songs
you expected to hear at the reception and ticking them
off as they were played).

Martin was winning. Susannah and Winky started the
dancing to 'Lady in Red', putting him straight into the
lead. Then came 'The Birdie Song' (for the little ones),
'Tainted Love' (for the bitter ones) and 'Oops, Upside
Your Head' (especially for the bride).

'OK, then. Which side is going to start the food fight?'
Lou asked idly.

By now Susannah was wearing less make-up than
cake.

'Bride,' said Martin definitely.

'Groom,' said Lou. She was right. Within seconds, a
profiterole missile issued from a table of louts who
played for Winky's rugby club. They had long since
turned their old school ties into Red Injun-style ban-
dannas and now they were attacking the bridesmaids
in a brutal re-enactment of General 'Custard's' Last
Stand.

'Ladies' room?' Ruby suggested to Lou. Susannah may
not have been bothered about getting icing on her vintage

silk wedding dress but Ruby was rather more precious about her one and only real Donna Karan.

'Aren't they just perfect for each other?' slurred a girl in the queue for the Portakabin that was serving as the ladies' that afternoon.

'Perfect,' Lou agreed. Ruby was grateful that Lou didn't go into her theory about bride and groom sharing a paternal grandmother.

'Of course,' said the girl, as she reapplied her lipstick somewhat haphazardly. 'It's rather funny when you think about how they met.'

'How did they meet?' Ruby wondered aloud, imagining a Scottish reeling ball where Winky whirled Susannah out of a badly stitched ball gown during the Duke of Perth and then offered to help her back into it.

'Through a *personal ad*! Can you believe it? Susannah advertised in *The Telegraph* for a man with GSOH.'

'Good sense of humour?' Ruby translated.

'More like great shag, own helicopter!' Lipstick Girl replied. 'What a catch, eh?'

'I think I would have thrown him back,' muttered Lou.

Just then the bride herself lurched into the queue for the loos.

'Coming through, girls,' she said. 'Wide load approaching.' Her multi-layered skirt would barely fit through the Portakabin door.

'Oh, Suze,' sighed the Lipstick Girl. 'Can you believe you've finally bagged your man?'

'Bit bloody surprised,' Susannah admitted. 'Better get him on honeymoon before the Rohypnol wears off! Haw, haw, haw!!!'

Ruby and Lou shared a worried glance.

'Louisa!' Susannah brayed. 'And Ruby! Thanks for coming, darlings. Set your sights on any dishy guys yet? There's a whole bunch of lads from Winky's rugby club over by the dance floor and most of them are single or in the process of getting divorced. Get your orders in before Finty Chambers has them all!'

'Already have had them all!' brayed Finty, as she emerged, at last, from the cubicle they'd all been waiting for. 'And none of them made *my* first fifteen. Haw haw haw!'

'Somebody hold my skirt,' said Susannah, as she backed onto the lavatory. Ruby closed the door behind her. 'Oh bugger!' cried the bride. 'Got my petticoat caught in the pan.'

'A personal ad,' Ruby mused as soon as they were out of earshot. 'She kept that one quiet.'

'Wouldn't you?' Lou laughed. 'Great shag, own helicopter? She obviously settled for grey shoes, own hair.'

'But they're happy,' said Ruby. 'Which is more than you, me and Martin are.'

Half an hour later, a new Lonely Hearts Club was born.

It was a beautifully simple idea. They were all single. All looking. (Some more actively than others, Ruby sighed.) None of them wanted to spend the summer alone, watching couples smooching on every piece of open parkland, getting sunburn on that part of your back you just can't reach with the sun-cream on your own. Lou proposed that they each place a personal ad in a paper of their choice to see if they could find their very own *Winkys*.

Better than that, Lou elaborated, they should all place ads *for each other*.

Lou would write an ad for Martin, Martin would write one for Ruby and Ruby would write one for Lou. That way there would be no room for false modesty. No tragic undersell.

'And no exaggeration worthy of prosecution under the Trades Description Act,' Ruby added with a nod towards Martin.

When the sacks full of replies came in – because of course, there would be sackfuls – the trio would each choose a likely partner for the person on whose behalf they had advertised. The experiment would culminate in a grand blind date at a venue with suitable cubby-holes from which they could secretly observe their success in choosing mates for their mates, as it were.

'Since we know each other better than we know ourselves,' Lou pointed out, 'there's no reason why it shouldn't work.'

'It's like an arranged marriage!' Martin was horrified when Lou outlined the scheme to him back at the miscellaneous table.

'How do I know he won't pick me a horrible date for a laugh?' Ruby asked, when it sank in that Martin would be writing her ad.

'Don't you trust me?' Martin asked.

'Martin,' said Ruby. 'I trust you with my life. But whether I can trust you with my *love*-life, I'm simply not so sure.'

I

Earlier that week, Ruby gazed out of her office window at a drizzly afternoon, depressing herself with matrimonial maths.

Seven million people in London. Of whom 51 per cent are female. That leaves roughly three million, four hundred thousand men. Of whom 20 per cent will be under eighteen, immediately cutting down the field to two million seven hundred thousand. Of whom at least 30 per cent will be over fifty, narrowing down the number of men in London that Ruby could consider snogging on basis of suitable age alone to one million nine hundred thousand.

Discount from that one million nine hundred thousand the 10 per cent likely to be gay. One million seven hundred thousand. Approximately 50 per cent would be married. Eight hundred and fifty thousand. Fifty per cent of those remaining would be seriously attached, bringing the total of *available* men in London between the ages of eighteen and fifty to four hundred and twenty-five thousand.

Discount from that total the number of London men residing at Her Majesty's pleasure. Twenty-five thousand? Probably more. The number living with their mothers. Another twenty thou perhaps? Divide that by the percentage of men that Ruby might actually fancy (judging by the men of her acquaintance that was in the region of one in thirty-three, or three per cent). And before you take into account matters of religion, political differences and the fact that nine of out of ten men prefer witless teenage sex kittens to thirty-something women of the world, the number of single men in London that Ruby could realistically hope to shack up with was already down from almost three and a half million to less than one hundred thousand. For whom she figured (using a computational method entirely different to that she had used to whittle down the boys) her competition was at least two million girls, all of whom were simply bound to be better-looking, funnier and more successful than she was.

Ho hum.

Ruby hated statistics. Especially the one that said the most likely place to find a partner was at the office. It was a statistic she had held close to her heart when she got her first job as a graduate trainee at Hollingworth Public Relations and set about learning how to convince journalists to run a story on everything from pressed steel to panty liners while she waited for the promised workplace romance to happen.

Unfortunately, Ruby soon realised that one of the most striking things about public relations is that it is full of girls. And most of them are blonde and bubbly and perma-tanned, as though they spend every spare weekend on the ski-slope. In fact, there were so many gorgeous single girls in the Hollingworth Public Relations empire that even the chief accountant, Frank 'Five Bellies' Clark, could be guaranteed a snog come the company conference. Even if he had a cold sore (Ruby Taylor, Bournemouth International Centre, November 1999) . . .

When Ruby read yet another problem page in one of her glossy mags in which some hapless bloke claimed that he couldn't get a girl, she wondered why the agony aunt didn't say 'work in public relations' instead of 'join a club'. For her part, Ruby might as well have signed up for the nuns.

For Emlyn 'The Panter' Cruickshank, however, the glass-walled offices of Hollingworth were like a stream full of salmon to a hungry bear. Emlyn was an account manager who had the cubicle next door to Ruby's. He liked to think that people called him 'The Panther' because of his sleek dark looks and his ability to pounce on a new client before any other account manager in town could say 'lunch'. In reality, the girls all called him the 'Panter' as a reference to his lasciviousness. That said, sleeping with the Panter was practically a rite of passage for all new girls at the firm. *In the kingdom of the blind, the one-eyed man etc. . . .*

Ruby was just glad that the Panter had started at Hollingworth after her. In fact, he had been her assistant once and she'd got over any slight crush she might have had on him when he revealed, over lunch one day, that he was the proud possessor of the 'worst case of athlete's foot the doctor had ever seen'. That in itself was enough to put Ruby off her Boots' own calorie-counted egg mayonnaise sandwich. But when Emlyn went on to elaborate about the flakes of skin that dropped out of his socks like fish-food every time he changed them, Ruby wondered if she'd ever eat again. From that moment onwards, as she explained to Lou and Martin, she found she was strangely immune to his charms.

With her brief 'thing' for Emlyn cured, Ruby resigned herself to the fact that her big office affair would not happen. At least the lack of potential talent at Hollingworth meant that, if she didn't have a meeting, Ruby could roll into work of a morning without bothering to put on her slap (or even wash her face, if she'd woken up that little bit later than she should have done). Then, of course, according to Sod's Law, John Flett walked into her life.

Jonathan Flett. The engineering world's answer to Michael Douglas. ('He wishes,' Lou would later say.) John Flett was acting CEO at Barrington Ball-bearings.

To tell the truth, Ruby had been a little disappointed when her boss chose her to head up the team that would put those little silver balls back in the limelight (she'd been angling for the Two-Faced Cosmetics account at the time). But when she saw Jonathan Flett at their first strategy meeting, he more than made up for Ruby's disappointment at not having unlimited access to free lipstick, blue mascara and glittery purple eyeshadow.

Hell, he was gorgeous. Ruby had been expecting the worst when she rolled up for the meeting at the concrete monstrosity that was Barrington's headquarters in sunny South Croydon. Half an hour later, she was wishing she had worn her Wonderbra, put on some make-up, done anything at all that would render her more memorable than her lacklustre proposals for a campaign to make Barrington 'the new black' of ball-bearings. In his beautifully cut Italian suit, Flett wouldn't have looked out of place on the marketing team at Gucci. When he asked her for her opinion on Barrington's exciting new logo, it was all Ruby could do not to swoon.

Over lunch in the only decent restaurant in the area, Ruby soon discovered that Flett was as interesting as he was good-looking. He was no ordinary ball-bearing engineer, but a top-flight industrial trouble-shooter, hired by Barrington's new American owner to turn the company around. He was forty-two and recently separated. He liked playing squash and listening to opera and a variety of other things that came way down on Ruby's list of good ways to spend a Saturday. Not that she told him that. Instead, she just kept nodding as he expounded on the virtues of Wagner, and, by the time they were on to coffee, Flett said he was glad they had so much in common, since they would be working very *closely* with each other from then on.

They started sleeping together the very next week, when Ruby accompanied Flett to a ball-bearings convention in Leeds with the intention of gaining some useful knowledge about Barrington's competitors. (Needless to say, the only knowledge she picked up at that convention was carnal.) Six months later, however, the Barrington campaign was almost finished and so was their wild affair.

'What did I tell you?' Lou lectured when Ruby phoned to say that Flett had accidentally informed the entire company that he was dumping her and now she had no choice but to leave her job or die of embarrassment. 'You shouldn't . . .'

'Mix business with pleasure? I know . . . !!!!' Ruby wailed.

No one had demanded that she hand her notice in, of

course. Not even Flett himself, though Ruby suspected that if he made such a request, it might well be favourably considered. But how else would Ruby be able to survive the acute and quite unbearable shame of being dumped by an e-mail that the stupid bloody Luddite had somehow managed to forward to everyone at Hollingworth PR, including Ruby's boss? She straight away deleted the two-line e-mail that said he was attaching his comments on the latest draft press release but wouldn't be coming for dinner that night – *or any other night, not even if hell freezes over.* But all day long wellmeaning people in the office kept forwarding the damn thing back to her.

'I've got to quit my job,' she told Lou hopelessly.

'You could just let the new Barrington catalogue go into print with a pithy footnote about the size of his penis at the bottom of one of the pages?' Lou suggested.

'But it's huge!' Ruby wailed.

'For God's sake,' Lou sighed. 'It doesn't have to be the truth.'

2

Unlike Ruby, Lou Capshaw took no rubbish from any
man.

Following a series of early disasters, Lou had developed an in-built bullshit radar that enabled her to spot
trouble in a pair of trousers *before* she ended up sleeping
with it. Ruby was right that it gets harder to meet new
people as you leave college, start work and begin the
process of excising likely candidates from your address
book as they get paired up, get married, or go gay . . . But
Lou knew that the field is also necessarily narrowed
down as you start to know *yourself* better and resolve
to look for a partner who fits every aspect of your
personality rather than settling for someone with the
requisite number of limbs.

Just thinking about some of her loser ex-boyfriends
reminded Lou that there were, as she would assure Ruby
on a daily basis, definitely some advantages to being a
single girl. Lou could only hope that Ruby would look
back on her ridiculous affair with John Flett and feel the
same way. Upon receiving Ruby's desperate phone call
about the 'Dear Jane' e-mail, however, Lou knew she was
in line for at least a good week's worth of extensive and
elaborate whinging, at the end of which, Ruby would
probably take the tosser back.

Lou often joked that since she always had to bear the

brunt of Ruby's love-life dilemmas when Mr Wonderful turned out to be Mr W*nk (again), she should also have the right to veto any budding relationship that had 'doomed' stamped all the way through it like the letters on Danish bacon. Why couldn't Ruby see that her fling with John Flett was always destined to turn out badly, as had her previous liaison with a recently separated accountant called Dave?

John Flett and Dave Evans were practically interchangeable. Both had recently hit forty and dumped their loyal wives (teenage sweethearts) in a fit of midage angst. 'Madolescence', Martin called it. Both left behind two small children. 'Too young to be affected,' they claimed. Both needed Ruby's support to get them through the traumatic early days when their wives called in the solicitors to undermine their confidence and bank balances. Then, six months post-separation, confidence miraculously restored by the mere fact that they were shagging someone born in the 1970s, they were ready to dump mother-substitute Ruby and hit the nightclubs with their ridiculous new haircuts and 'old skool' trainers in search of the 1980s vintage totty they had been after all along.

'Ruby,' sighed Lou, 'you've become a finishing school for newly separated men. Halfway-house between the first wife and the next one. You cook them lovely dinners, when otherwise they'd be eating boiled eggs in the bed-sit. You listen to them whinge about the cost of alimony because it means they can't afford another sports car. You help get them out of their moth-eaten Fair Isles so they don't look a twat when they're clubbing. Then they're off to snare some bimbette using the new, improved dress sense and unwarranted sexual confidence that you helped them develop.'

Ruby nodded as though she understood but, in reality, Lou knew she might as well have tried to explain the rationale behind walking to heel to a poodle. No amount of tugging on the choke chain was going to stop Ruby from racing off after the next interesting scent. Which would inevitably be a shit . . .

Lou was pondering the Ruby problem as she waited in companionable silence with another two hundred or so bleary-eyed commuters for the tube that would take her to her work as a fiction editor at Piper Publishing.

When the train finally appeared, Lou tucked the manuscript she had been working on overnight under her arm and groaned. She had been waiting for the best part of twenty minutes and the train that arrived now was more tightly packed than a jar of anchovies. When the doors opened, a couple of passengers actually fell out of the carriage in front of her, panting for breath. They quickly shoved themselves back in though, like contestants in that Japanese game show, *Endurance*. Which was more ridiculous, Lou wondered. Eating worms or electing to squeeze yourself into a metal tube, buried two hundred feet underground, with five hundred assorted Londoners and their smells?

Taking a last deep breath, Lou barged her way on board. The passengers already on the train gave feeble mutters of indignation, though just as Lou had predicted, no one had actually bothered to take any notice of the platform announcer's advice that they should 'move down inside the cars'. When Lou wriggled her way to the space between the long rows of seats, she actually found an empty strap to hang from.

A few stops later, the train came to a halt so quickly that even Lou, who was used to strap-hanging after six years' commuting to the office on the same hellish route, couldn't stay upright. She landed heavily on the lap of a rather stuffy looking gent. He glared at her as she quickly straightened up again.

'Sorry,' she mouthed sarcastically. 'I mean, it's not as though I would have chosen to sit on your lap.'

The man simply tutted and opened his paper out again aggressively. The *Financial Times*, of course. Obviously the only values in his life were the FTSE and the NAS-DAQ. What was he doing sitting down anyway, Lou thought angrily, when a very obviously pregnant woman was squashed up against the glass partition to his left? When Mr *FT* was safely hidden behind his broadsheet, Lou pulled a hideous face in his direction. She would have added appropriate hand signals too, if she hadn't needed to hold onto that strap. It was a childish gesture, she knew, but it made her feel much better.

And it very much amused the gorgeous commuter in the dark blue suit standing next to the pregnant woman. When she had finished gurning, Lou caught a look across the top of a newspaper and blushed to the roots of her hair. But before she could hide in embarrassment behind the manuscript she was carrying, Lou also caught the stranger grinning a melon-slice smile and giving her a slow, cheeky wink that definitely spoke of approval.

Lou was shocked to feel the unmistakable all-over body flush of attraction rush across her skin so quickly it almost made her knees give way. Then the tube stopped at King's Cross and the stranger got off the train.

Lou strained in vain to get a better look as her new friend stepped out of the carriage but got just a glimpse of fluffy blond hair as the anxious crowds on the platform quickly surged forward. They had locked eyes for a matter of seconds but if Eros still worked with arrows in this age of guided missiles, Lou knew she had got one straight in the heart. That long-neglected muscle in her chest was pumping as if she had just run a marathon. She was sure she must be bright pink with totally inappropriate arousal. For a mad, mad second she considered getting out of the train and following . . . But only for a second.

City Branch trains during the rush hour were more rare than sightings of the Siberian tiger and Lou knew that if she got off this one, she would definitely be late for work. She couldn't be late for work that day. There were phone calls to make. E-mails to answer. Lou took a deep breath to still her thumping heart. She didn't have *time* to follow a stranger onto the platform at King's Cross. What a ridiculous idea.

It was a feeble excuse for lack of daring, she knew, but Lou still bit her lip and let the stranger go. After all, it was just a wink. Not actually an invitation to have dinner. Eros had scored a direct hit with her, but he might have fired straight over her dream lover's head. In fact, under the circumstances, that was more than likely to be the case.

Lou looked at her shoes, as though anyone else in that carriage was able or interested enough to read her racing thoughts. Ridiculous. Just ridiculous. Bloody hell, though, she admitted to herself. She hadn't felt like that in half a decade. Hadn't felt so naked under another's gaze in a very long time indeed. She fanned her face self-consciously.

At the next station, Mr *FT* left the train too. He tripped over Lou's briefcase as he went.

'Sorry . . .' she sang after him, '. . . not. Here, you need this more than I do,' Lou said, gesturing the pregnant woman towards the seat Mr *FT* had just vacated.

'What are you getting at?' the woman asked aggressively.

Lou hid behind her manuscript a second time as she realised that the woman was not pregnant at all. Just chunky.

On long lazy Sundays with Ruby and Martin, the conversation had often turned to the flirting potential of the tube. In general they agreed that it rated zilch on the Metropolitan pull-ometer. There was something about the subterranean light that lent everyone a hell-bound pallor, and even if you did see someone you fancied, there was little hope of catching their eye. It's a well-documented fact that when people find themselves wedged into a space more tightly than veal calves, they attempt to preserve their privacy by looking anywhere but at each other. Staring at a stranger on the tube is as much a breach of London etiquette as flashing.

Pity though. Lou wondered how many embryonic love stories had ended with a scowl when two lovely people who might otherwise have shared a drink, were caught sneaking a mutual peek on the Northern Line and each instantly branded the other a nutter. Why should that moment when you lock eyes and realise that you *know* someone in the sense that you have connected with their soul, be invalidated just because it happens underground? People get talking to complete strangers in nightclubs all the time. Why is the person you meet in the pub less threatening than the one on his way to the office? It didn't make sense. Nothing much was making sense to Lou that morning.

But talking of the pub . . .

Safely in her office, Lou opened her Microsoft Outlook and started to draft an e-mail.

From: Lou.Capshaw@piperpublishing.com
To: Ruby.Taylor@Hollingworthpr.co.uk
        Martin.Ashcroft@Internationalmagazines.com

Re: The meaning of life.

Answers to this and other questions including: what is the capital of Lithuania? And who won the FA Cup in 1974? Tonight at the Hare and Hounds pub quiz. You know you've got nothing better to do. I haven't. Seven-thirty?

3

Martin didn't have time to read Lou's e-mail when he got to his desk. He'd overslept – again – and arrived at the office with seconds to go before that morning's team meeting. God, he hated the Wednesday morning meeting. As a child, mapping his life out, when railway drivers still seemed like heroes, Wednesday morning meetings where a sweaty, balding git called Barry Parsons yelled at him for not achieving an unachievable sales target had definitely not been part of the plan. In fact, there wasn't much about Martin's current situation at all that fitted the dream future he had held for himself as a child. When did it all go wrong?

Martin started in the sales room of International Magazines as a temp; fresh out of university with a 2:2 in English Lit. He had planned to become a journalist, with a view to making Will Self's incisive interviews for the broadsheets look like reader reviews on Amazon.com. At least that was what he told his mother when she started to get fed up of seeing him lazing on the sofa in front of *Ricki Lake* when she got home from work. Unfortunately, the big news corporations wanted something more than a term's editorship of an obscure poetry magazine called *Pudenda* from their candidates . . .

With his mum threatening eviction, Martin told himself that a temporary job at International Magazines would be a stepping-stone to a proper journalistic career. But the sales and editorial departments weren't even in the same building, and six months' experience selling classified ad space on *New Catering Equipment Digest* got him no nearer to a position as foreign correspondent for *The Times* than had the previous six months spent signing on and playing Nintendo.

Eventually, Martin became chief telesales rep for International Magazines' new flagship publication *The Satyr*. It was a men's magazine, a heady mix of ads, topless celebrities and full colour photos of medical anomalies. Its cover gimmick was to have the hottest *totty du jour* dressed in animal costumes – bottom half only – like the part animal deity the magazine took its name from. Martin's personal favourite was Kylie Minogue, half-dressed as a squirrel, issue three.

Martin knew when he signed on the dotted line at International Mags that he was simultaneously kissing goodbye to all hope that he might one day be the dude with the leather chair actually choosing the arse that would grace *The Satyr's* cover so he focused his attention on the money he could earn if he did the job properly. He even won a weekend in San Francisco as salesperson of the year. And it was disappointingly easy to stifle his creative ambitions after that. For a while anyway.

After four years at International Mags, Martin began to wonder once more if he was hiding a great light under his bushel. He had creative talent. He was going to write a novel. He bought himself a laptop that could have controlled a manned mission to Mars with his end-of-year bonus and promised himself that fifty-two weekends later he would have a draft of the next *High Fidelity* to present to astonished agents and salivating publishers alike. Lou assured him there was a gap in the market.

And it started well enough. The first weekend Martin wrote a chapter, obsessively checking the word count after every paragraph because he had figured out by a process of complicated, mathematical deduction based on a selection of classics that the ideal first chapter should be exactly five thousand words long. He spent the next weekend going over the first chapter and editing out the good bits because he had also heard that a great literary genius pronounced you should 'kill your darlings' and get rid of the bits that pleased you most since they were actually most likely to be rubbish. The following weekend, Martin read through the amended first chapter, decided that he had left in all the rubbish parts by mistake and wiped the whole lot from the hard drive of his computer. The weekend after that he had writer's block. And the weekend after that he went to Brighton with Ruby and Lou and didn't fire up his laptop at all.

Now his laptop had an accusing layer of dust all over its high-tech black lid. Lou drew a smiley face in the grime and added the caption 'Use me'. But Martin hadn't made any progress on his novel for the past seven months. It had reached the stage where nobody even asked about it any more.

Not that he could actually have used his laptop if he wanted to. About the same time that Martin was making his brief bid for literary superstardom, he was dating a girl called 'Webecca'. Webecca from Wuislip. Couldn't say her 'R's'. Voice like Bonnie Langford. (Face like Bonnie Langford, if the truth be told.) What on earth had he been thinking?

'You'd been thinking about her tits, of course,' said Lou.

Webecca was a postgraduate student at Birkbeck and, while he was still interested in the extraordinary assets she kept beneath her baggy brown jumper, Martin lent Webecca his laptop's power adaptor when hers blew up days from her dissertation deadline. Unfortunately, the adaptor became a casualty of their break-up. Webecca was so distraught by the end of their relationship that she grabbed hold of Martin's ankles when he tried to leave her flat and clung on for at least half a mile. At the time, losing the power source to his all-singing, all-dancing computer had seemed a small price to pay for never having to see the deranged woman or eat her chick-pea curry ever again.

Lou and Ruby had initially leapt to Webecca's defence, accusing Martin of being shallow by allowing Webecca's external appearance (getting hairier by the day) to put him off her inner beauty. They certainly didn't approve of the next incumbent in his affections. Leah was a 'spokesmodel'. They met while she was handing out free samples of a new nut-filled breakfast bar on the platform at Waterloo Station, dressed in a pair of red hotpants with a squirrel tail attached. (Martin instantly saw the possibility for the realisation of a long-held fantasy there!)

Leah couldn't have been more different from Webecca. She rang him just before their second date to say, 'I don't know if I can come out tonight. My hair's kinda gone wrong.' She had long, straight black hair. How wrong could it possibly go? Leah was more high-maintenance than a thoroughbred Arab pony. 'With possibly less horse-sense,' Ruby commented.

'She's bubbly,' said Martin defensively.

'Only because her head is full of air. I think that botox injection she had in her forehead must have gone through to her brain. What on earth do you have to talk about?'

Not much, it was true. But Martin was not to be put off. He convinced himself that he really did want to know everything about 'leave-in' hair conditioners and gravity-defying face creams. What did it matter if everything that came out through Leah's lips was rubbish when those pink lips were moving so prettily? It didn't even matter that she continued to move her lips while she was reading *Hello*.

It all ended badly of course. Martin was on a corporate jolly to Ireland at the time, pining for his luscious, lovely back in London. When he phoned to tell her that he missed her, she told him that she had some good news and some bad news. The good news was that she got the job she had gone for.

'The bad news is . . .' The long-distance phone line crackled loudly. 'We've got to go to . . .' Another crackle. '. . . herpes . . .'

'Her*mes*,' Martin laughed, assuming his little shopa-holic was pronouncing it wrongly again. This was a girl who wore 'Ver-sash' after all. 'You're not intending to drag me round the sales all weekend, are you?'

Unfortunately, she wasn't. Leah had pronounced *her* latest acquisition perfectly. A parting gift from her ex-boyfriend Mad Mike, the market trader, who gave Leah her 'Guci' – 'with one "c" 'cos it's more exclusive, innit?' – handbag.

Martin tested negatively, thank God, but the aftermath would be with him for eternity, it seemed, with Lou and

Ruby almost wetting themselves with laughter every time they saw the exclusive Hermes logo. Ruby even bought him a Hermes tie for Christmas. Thoughtful, eh?

Since Leah's revelation, Martin had been thoroughly single, barring a couple of dates with hapless temps who wandered through International Mags. But lately, even the thought of the temp controller at Office Angels accidentally sending *Charlie*'s *Angels* to stuff envelopes in *The Satyr*'s airless office had seemed strangely unappealing.

'I am turning into my father,' Martin told himself one morning as he stared at his thirty-something face in the steamy bathroom mirror. It wasn't just the nose hair.

Was this his future? Ogling pretty temps across the open-plan offices? Drifting from one unsatisfactory fling to the next? A life marked out by Arsenal home games, Wednesday morning team meetings and yet another Wednesday evening at the Hare and Hounds' pub quiz?

4

Martin was determined to do something different that Wednesday night, but when Lou and Ruby arrived at the Hare and Hounds he was already waiting for them. He was supposed to have had a 'proper date' that evening, with a fashion department assistant from *Capital Woman*, another title in the International Magazines empire. But the girl in question had cancelled, claiming pressure of work. Martin quickly relegated the evening he had been looking forward to from 'proper date' to 'casual arrangement to hook up' and convinced himself that Geri was just nipping out of the office to get supplies for the long stint of overtime ahead when he saw her leaving the office building in her coat at six o'clock.

'Never mind, Mart,' said Lou. 'You and Ruby can console each other. Do your impression of John Flett for her.'

'What impression?' Ruby asked foolishly.

Martin adopted a mid-Atlantic drawl (despite the fact that Flett hailed originally from Tunbridge Wells and had spent a total of three months on the other side of the Atlantic) and slurred, 'The driving force behind western civilisation is really the humble ball-bearing.' Then he licked his lips like a camel going for the snot up its own nose.

Lou burst out laughing. Ruby looked as though she would burst into tears.

'He doesn't do that!' she protested hotly.

Martin and Lou chorused, 'He does.'

'Aren't you glad you don't have to sleep with him any more?' Lou asked. 'How on earth could you have ended up with a man who had such a bizarre facial tic?'

'He does not have a facial tic,' Ruby persisted. 'I've never seen him do that.'

'He does it all the time,' Lou assured her. 'That would have been my fatal flaw.'

'Mine too,' agreed Martin. 'I mean, apart from the fact that he's a man.'

The Fatal Flaw. When they didn't have a wedding to play 'Reception Disco Bingo' at, Martin, Lou and Ruby had a number of other interesting games to pass the time. 'Fatal Flaw' was based on a game called 'Shag or Die,' as in, 'would you rather shag your secondary school geography teacher – or die?' In Fatal Flaw, the potential shag-ees were better. In fact, under normal circumstances, you wouldn't have kicked any of them out of bed. But, the supermodels and Hollywood actors offered up in Fatal Flaw were not without their catch. Of course you would sleep with Brad Pitt. What red-blooded single girl wouldn't? But what if he was suddenly afflicted by a terrible condition of the saliva glands that meant he couldn't talk without spitting all over you? What if, as Lou often asked Martin, Julia Roberts offered him a blow-job but had a mouthful of needle-sharp teeth?

For Ruby, the fatal flaw was unattractive tootsies. She had a theory that you're never so naked as when you take your socks off. People rarely have ugly eyes. They rarely have ugly hands. Even genitals are generally quite in-offensive to look at. But feet are a different matter. The best you can hope for is that your new lover's feet just look normal. An unexpected encounter with an in-grow-ing toenail could send Ruby into a faint.

'It's the only thing that saved me from sleeping with the Panter,' Ruby reminded her friends that evening. 'His fungal infection. I just can't deal with dodgy feet.'

'Here's one for you then,' Martin interrupted. 'Russell Crowe with athlete's foot. Shag or die?'

'I'd have to stay celibate,' said Ruby.

'Tom Cruise with a single verruca?'

'Stop,' Ruby covered her ears. 'It's making me gag just to think about it. You know, I would have lost my virginity a whole year earlier than I did if Nick Stevens hadn't shown me his in-growing toenail.'

'I still can't believe you ended a relationship because of an in-growing toenail,' said Lou.

'How on earth could I have slept with him after that? What if he'd stroked his foot down my leg while we were at it?'

Now Lou gagged too. 'Fair enough. I lost my virginity to a man who looked like Kermit the frog and I've regretted it ever since. You've got to get it right, eh, Martin? The first time.'

Indeed you should. But Martin didn't elaborate.

The last thing Martin wanted was to get into a round of 'how I lost my virginity' stories, because he couldn't quite remember how he'd last told the girls he lost his. He had a vague feeling that he'd told Lou and Ruby he lost his virginity to a friend of his big sister's when he was just fourteen, but he didn't want to get halfway through the tale and have one of the girls point out that the last time he recounted the tale, the sister's friend's name was different.

Because the truth was that Ruby had been there when Martin lost his virginity. She had no idea. It was during their first term at university. Freshers' week. Martin had noticed Ruby hanging about in the halls of residence, trying to pretend that she wasn't crying when her mum and dad dropped her off at the door of the bleak seventies building with her brand new toaster. He didn't see her again until the Freshers' ball almost a week later. By that time Ruby had paired up with Lou and tears of hilarity had replaced tears of homesickness as she snorted her fourth tequila slammer. High on alcohol and independence, Ruby made a beeline for Martin. They smooched (with some difficulty) to Nirvana's 'Teen Spirit'. And suddenly they were in Ruby's room.

Ruby dragged Martin onto her narrow single bed and threw her treasured teddy bears onto the floor to make room for him. Ten minutes later, Martin was naked and ejaculating into a banana flavoured condom bought from a vending machine in the Union. Ruby pushed him off, retrieved her favourite bear from the pile on the floor and fell into a deep sleep, snoring loudly. Martin spent the night shivering on the edge of her single bed, horribly uncomfortable but vaguely aware that it might be bad manners to disappear right after shagging her. Besides, Ruby had her head on his arm and he didn't dare move it in case he woke her up.

Next morning, clutching a towel around herself as though Martin hadn't already seen her naked, Ruby told him flatly that she had a boyfriend in her home town and added that if Martin told anyone that they had slept together she would tell everyone he was a premature ejaculator. Martin didn't dare tell her that he had been a virgin until she manhandled him. Ruby didn't think to ask. In fact, she didn't even speak to him for another four weeks after that.

Ten years on, the sorry little incident of Martin and Ruby had been relegated to the ranks of those drunken horror stories such as the time Martin fell asleep face down in a kebab and had to go to hospital to have a chilli removed from his nostril or the night Lou snogged the captain of the university women's cricket club. And, thankfully, that evening, the quizmaster intervened before the storytelling really began. Ruby and Lou turned their attention from Ruby's virginity to marking their answers to that week's general knowledge round.

'I told you the capital of California is not Los Angeles,' Ruby complained.

'But did you know it was Sacramento?' Lou retorted.

They got three out of ten.

'You all right, Ruby?' Martin asked as they meandered back to the tube station after closing time. He put his arm round her shoulder and squeezed her against him. 'I'm sorry I took the mickey out of the love of your life,' he added, before flopping his tongue out of his mouth like a half-demented spaniel and doing it over again.

'No,' Ruby laughed this time. 'You were right. John Flett is a loser and I'm much better off without him.' What a difference four vodkas could make. She only hoped that the effect would last until she woke up again next morning. 'You've really cheered me up this evening,' Ruby continued. 'I'm glad I came out after all. At least I've got you two. You're the best friends in the world.'

'Aaaah,' Lou and Martin chorused. 'We love you back.'

'You know, I don't think Flett's actually got any friends any more since he left his wife and their two children with nothing to live on but the proceeds of her part-time job . . .'

Martin winced. The man really was a loser.

'There will be no further references to Jonathan Flett from now on,' Lou proclaimed. 'He's a pathetic little man.'

'But will I ever find a good one?' Ruby asked, drooping against Martin's side.

'Of course you will,' Lou reassured her. 'We'll start looking for you on Saturday. Susannah's wedding is on Saturday. And everyone can score at a wedding. Only thing you need is a pulse.'

5

A pulse, eh? Ruby couldn't be sure that her dancing partner had one.

After the food fight, during which one of the bridesmaids almost lost an eye to a handful of sugared almonds, Susannah and Winky's sophisticated wedding reception had rapidly descended into anarchy. Susannah's millionaire father had generously catered four bottles of vintage champagne for each and every guest and this incredible extravagance was creating an ugly backlash. Four of the rugby players were stark naked on the dance floor. One of them appeared to have stuck the stem of his corsage down the eye of his penis and was using the flower to point suggestively at any girls he fancied. Ruby could only wonder what he might tell the Accident and Emergency staff later on.

Ruby had managed to fend off the rugger buggers' advances, leaving herself at the mercy of an altogether different kind of sexual predator when the slow dances started. Lou dragged Martin off to the centre of the floor as soon as she heard the first strains of Whitney singing 'I Will Always Love You,' which meant that Ruby had nowhere to run and nowhere to hide when Winky's grandfather materialised beside the miscellaneous table and offered her his brittle arm.

'You're a lovely, lovely young lady,' he whispered

hotly into her ear as he ran his hand along her bra strap.

'Thank you,' said Ruby, grateful that etiquette didn't require her to respond in kind with a sincere or truthful compliment of her own. 'You're a dirty old man. Move your hand from my arse,' wouldn't have sounded too friendly.

Ruby just about managed to keep Granddad at a safe distance as the guests took to the floor in a reprise of 'Lady In Red' by adopting a stiff elbow-locked variation on a traditional ballroom dancing hold. It all went horribly wrong when the DJ started to play The Rolling Stones' 'Satisfaction'. Now Ruby hovered between utter revulsion at the old man who was trying to push his pelvis up against hers and abject terror that he would keel over at any moment and cast a rather depressing note upon which to end such a high-spirited wedding. To that effect, she felt obliged to hang on to Granddad while he convulsed against her body in time with the beat, so that if he did flake out unexpectedly, she might at least be able to get him to the edge of the dance floor without the bride noticing that someone had died at her wedding reception.

Meanwhile, Lou and Martin bobbed up and down enthusiastically behind Ruby's septuagenarian partner, cruelly giving Ruby the thumbs-up every time they caught her eye.

'Love your new boyfriend,' mouthed Martin over Lou's shoulder.

'Groovy mover,' said Lou sarcastically when the song ended and Granddad actually went off in search of someone *younger* to play with.

'Great,' said Ruby as she watched her erstwhile dancing partner getting down to 'Come On Eileen' (again) with the bride's seventeen-year-old cousin. 'I can't even keep the attention of a seventy-something any more. I am doomed.'

'Are we ready to go yet?' asked Martin, as he slid gracefully beneath the miscellaneous table like the *Titanic* meeting her iceberg.

'None of us have scored,' said Lou.

'Do you honestly think we're likely to?' Ruby asked.

They surveyed the room like two generals at the end of a particularly bloody battle. Bodies in various states of undress were littered about the furniture. A semi-naked rugger bugger lay where he had fallen in the middle of the dance floor, oblivious to the high-heeled shoes that clattered dangerously about him. There was no blood yet, thank goodness. But a great deal more nudity and vomit than one would have expected for such a grand occasion. In fact, as the girls watched in horrified amazement, a smartly dressed young lady was actually puking in somebody's handbag.

'Hope that's her own,' said Ruby with a wince.

'Let's bail,' said Lou, grabbing a couple of half-finished bottles of champagne for later.

'You don't really want any more of that, surely?' Ruby gasped.

'Hair of the dog,' Lou explained with drunken logic. 'We'll be grateful for this in the morning.'

'Looks like Martin's already getting his.'

Ruby raised the edge of the tablecloth to reveal Martin snoring gently on a pile of discarded shoes and handbags, while Susannah's favourite pet, a Norfolk terrier that had

35

been specially decked out for the day in a dinky bow to match the bridesmaids' dresses, licked the sweat off Martin's forehead with its slobbery pink tongue.

'Shall we leave him there?' asked Lou.

'I don't think that would be friendly,' said Ruby.

'Let's leave him,' said Lou.

The girls made for the door.

They were staying in a bed and breakfast place a couple of miles from the country house in whose grounds Susannah's marquee had been pitched. The sixteenth-century coach-house hotel looked idyllic from the outside. Inside, unfortunately, it wasn't so great. Fifty quid a head and Ruby found a pubic hair stuck to the soap.

Lou and Ruby were sharing a room. Ruby didn't get much sleep. When they got back from the reception, Lou crashed out instantly (on the less knackered of the two single beds, so that Ruby got a bedspring in the kidneys) and spent the first half of the night snoring on her back. She spent the second half groaning as dehydration kicked in.

It's true what they say about hangovers getting worse as you get older. As a sixteen-year-old, Ruby could down twelve assorted shorts on a Friday evening and still get up to do her job at the local garden furniture salesroom next morning, earning just enough money in a day to drink another twelve Bacardi and Cokes on the Saturday night. Lately, she'd given up mixing her drinks (or at least tried to stick to one colour all night), drank two pints of water *and* took a couple of aspirin *before* she went to sleep. Yet she still woke up feeling as though she had used her tongue to clean the carpet.

At least Lou and Martin were similarly afflicted. Far from being pleased that she had remembered to bring home some booze for a 'hair of the dog' as soon as she woke up, when Lou rolled over to see (and smell) the two half-empty champagne bottles on the bedside table in the early hours of the morning, she had to leg it to the bathroom before nature took one of its courses. The day after Susannah's wedding, Martin even turned his nose up at a freshly cooked breakfast. He was as green about the gills as the chipped nineteen-sixties-style crockery upon which the unwanted fry-up was served. Ruby soon realised that, compared to the other two, she had actually fared quite well.

'Did I score?' Martin asked the girls when he surfaced just before lunchtime.

'You fell asleep beneath the table,' Lou replied.

'I could have sworn someone was licking my face,' he muttered.

'Someone was,' Lou assured him. 'Or rather, something was. Susannah's dog.'

'Oh, God,' Martin groaned. 'I ended up with a dog again. I am giving up alcohol,' he added solemnly.

'Where have I heard that one before?' Ruby laughed. 'Hangovers are like pregnancy. At the time, you swear you'll never put yourself through it again. Seven days later you just can't remember the pain.'

'You're always so smug,' Martin complained. 'Haven't you ever lost a weekend through alcohol?'

The waitress drifted past with another plateful of bacon and eggs for another guest. Lou and Martin clutched hands to their mouths and swayed like two victims of seasickness. Over in the corner of the restaurant, the rugger bugger wedding guest who had ordered the breakfast thought better of it too and relieved his nausea by heaving dramatically into a bread-basket.

'Lounge, anybody?' Martin suggested.

They re-seated themselves in the hotel's chintzy day room with the Sunday papers.

'So,' said Ruby, as she settled down into an armchair with a glossy fashion supplement. 'Another wedding over and none of us is any nearer to being the girl in the puffball.'

'I don't want to be the girl in the puffball,' said Martin.

'Me neither, for that matter,' added Lou.

'It would have been nice just to meet someone different,' said Ruby.

'I just want to know that some lovely lady is going to ask to see my penis again before I lose sight of it forever,' said Martin, patting his expanding waistline.

'But you will,' said Lou. 'Remember the pact we made last night? About writing ads for each other?'

Ruby and Martin groaned like a pair of teenagers being reminded of a promised visit to the zoo with great-aunt Sarah.

'I think we should go for it!'

Lou's enthusiasm was met by two blank stares.

'You both thought it was a good idea last night,' she said defensively.

'I can't be held responsible for anything I say under the influence of Bollinger,' said Martin.

'But why shouldn't it work?' Lou persisted. 'Susannah and Winky met through a personal ad.'

'They'd have met at the Kennel Club eventually,' said

Martin. 'It's not going to happen for any of us, Lou. Get real.'

Ruby smiled into her coffee cup, tacitly agreeing with Martin. But that morning Lou was unusually bullish. 'Well, I don't think you should be so quick to dismiss my idea,' she told them. 'We're all single. We all want to meet people, don't we?'

'Yeah, but not *losers*,' Martin sneered.

'You're so pessimistic,' sighed Lou.

'Realistic,' he said, 'is the word.'

Romantic that she was, Ruby wanted to be able to back Lou up, but there wasn't much proof in Lou's favour. Personal ads had long carried the stigma of being the last resort of the desperate. Or the downright deviant. Ruby recalled one of those morning television debates where some poor woman revealed to the audience that she had answered an ad placed by a man who claimed to like 'motorbikes and horse riding' only to discover this was Lonely Hearts' code for sado-masochism and bondage and it wasn't a pony he expected to wear the saddle . . .

Of the thousands of personal ads placed in the papers every Sunday, what percentage really ended with a buffet in a pink and white marquee? A far smaller percentage than those that ended up with a restraining order, Ruby suspected.

Lou turned to anecdotal evidence. 'There's a girl at my office whose best friend's sister's mate met her husband through the personals,' she insisted. Ruby's head started to spin as she tried to work out the connection. 'Apparently she answered the ad for a dare and it turned out that the guy who placed it was a millionaire! Don't get many millionaire losers, do you, Martin?'

'You wouldn't have thought that a millionaire would need to advertise,' Ruby mused. 'I don't suppose many girls would say no to a date with someone that rich and successful.'

'Of course they wouldn't. But how would he know they weren't just in it for the money?' Lou pointed out. 'He placed the ad precisely so that the girls who answered wouldn't be blinded by his humungous bank account. It was the only way he could avoid the gold-diggers.'

'If it's true, it's a one-off,' said Martin.

'No! What about Mike Oldfield?' Lou countered. 'He was *addicted* to personal ads. Placed hundreds of the things until he was rumbled. Or would you call the millionaire composer of "Tubular Bells" a loser too?'

'Two-off,' Martin replied. 'Though it sounds to me like he had a problem.'

'The personal ads are full of people whose only *problem* is that they're too busy being successful in their careers to sort out their love lives,' Lou insisted. 'I read somewhere that several City firms are even taking out dating agency subscriptions on behalf of their staff as part of the benefits package. Happy home lives make for happier workers.' Lou pushed an open newspaper across the table towards Ruby. 'Take your pick, Rubes. How about a nice entrepreneur? International airline pilot? Millionaire racing car enthusiast?'

'Hmmmm,' Ruby pondered.

'Pounds or lira?' Martin smiled. 'Admit it, Lou. No normal, sociable person, with no obvious hang-ups or facial tics,' he looked pointedly at Ruby as he said that, 'should ever need to resort to a lonely hearts ad. There's the office, the gym, even the supermarket. Hundreds of ways to find the one you're after. If you can't chat someone up face to face then you probably shouldn't be allowed to mate in the first place.'

'Have you ever tried chatting someone up while you're on the Stairmaster?' asked Lou. 'Come to think of it, my dear, have you ever even seen a Stairmaster?'

Martin sucked his stomach in self-consciously.

'And how on earth can you tell who's single in the supermarket? Count the number of spuds in their basket? As for dating at work, we've all seen where that ends.'

Ruby cast her eyes downward.

'Do you mind?' she said. 'I haven't thought about *him* all weekend.'

'Except when you were dancing with Granddad, surely,' said Martin.

'Yeah,' Lou interrupted. 'Well, I know that I'm not going to have a workplace affair unless my firm change their equal opportunities programme to include that minority group we call the *attractive*. Personal ads are the only way forward. You specify exactly what you want. No danger of making a play for that guy with the pile of ready-packed meals for one in his basket, only to discover that he and his *boyfriend* have a finicky cat that will only eat Marks and Spencer's frozen lasagne. No need to do an extra twenty minutes on the Stairmaster just to impress the girl in the bright pink thong. And no danger of having to leave your job because your workplace paramour finished with you via two lines on your work group's electronic message board and humiliated you in front of the whole company.'

Ruby groaned heavily.

'Sorry, Ruby,' said Lou. 'Cruel to be kind. But come on,' she continued. 'We've run out of single friends to have round to dinner parties. Both of you expect me to sort out your love-lives when everything goes pear-shaped. I've had long nights of tears from you, Ruby. And long nights of tears from the women you've done wrong,' she reminded Martin. 'Ruby is always wishing that you would go for a girl who remembered to take her GCSEs. And Martin wishes that you, Rubes, would try dating someone who hasn't already been road-tested and rejected by his first wife. This is our chance to match each other up with the people we really think we should be with. We could even have a kitty as an incentive. Fifty quid each and the first person to write a successful ad pockets the lot?'

Ruby looked from Lou to Martin to see if he was wavering.

'Look,' said Martin suddenly. 'If any of us ends up even having an interesting phone conversation with someone we've met through a personal ad, then I'll happily give you my money.'

'You're on,' said Lou, sticking out her hand to shake on it. 'But this means you have to promise to give my scheme a proper chance.'

'Scout's honour,' promised Martin.

'He was never in the scouts,' Ruby pointed out.

Martin put his hand out anyway.

'What about you, Rubes?' Lou asked. 'Are you on for it?'

Ruby stuck her own hand out tentatively.

'I don't know. Can you promise you won't fix me up with a loser?'

'We promise!' chorused her friends.

'Then I don't see why not.'

The three pals performed a weird three-way hand-shake that looked as though it should have ended with them turning into crime-fighting super-beings.

'Right,' said Lou. 'I stand to make some serious money here. I'm going to start looking for someone for the pair of you straight away.'

'I thought we had to place ads,' Ruby pointed out.

'Place ads. Answer ads. The main point is that we choose dates for each other.' She patted Ruby on the hand. 'Don't look so worried.'

'I've got a nasty feeling I need to be,' she said.

'You don't,' Lou reassured her. 'This is going to be wonderful. We're going to have a fantastic summer. Martin and Ruby,' she concluded, low and serious, 'prepare to get lucky in love.'

6

On the drive back to London, Lou and Ruby risked carsickness to read every personal ad they could lay their hands on. Lou vowed to leave no stone unturned, answering every single ad from men under sixty on behalf of Ruby, unless the ad said that the guy in question was actually after another young man or 'required discretion' which meant that he was already married.

Every three-line advertisement made the guy who placed it seem so inviting. To a newly single girl like Ruby, the 'Encounters' page of *The Sunday Times* Style supplement was like the top layer of a box of chocolates freshly stripped of its cellophane at the end of a long, lonely diet. With the pick of the box, it was difficult to know which one to go for first.

'Do you think I'm the kind of girl who looks equally at home in a ball dress or a pair of Levi's?' Ruby asked as she hovered with the biro over an ad from a 'genuine country gentleman with homes in the City and Home Counties'.

'Ring it,' said Lou. 'If the marriage doesn't work out, he can live in the country one and you can stay in the town house with us.'

'Aren't you jumping the gun?' asked Martin, feeling a little left out as they trawled through the men while he drove.

'Your problem,' said Lou, 'is that you've got no imagination. No wonder you've never finished that novel.'

'Don't bring the novel into this,' Martin warned.

'Then stop being such a killjoy. And try to stick to the speed limit. What about this one for you, Rubes? Accountant with a poet's soul?'

'Sounds lovely,' she agreed.

But they were soon to discover that if the '*Encounters*' page was a box of chocolates, then it was a box full of those funny orange creams that even the dog won't eat.

You've got to know your enemy. How to sort out the wheat from the chaff. And Lou and Ruby didn't have a clue. Having ringed all the ads that interested them, and a couple for Martin too, the girls retired to Lou's flat to draft introductory letters and, more importantly, ring the telephone lines that accompanied each box number.

Each advertiser had one of these phone lines, where they could leave a short message to elaborate on the things they mentioned in their print ad. The calls cost premium rates, of course, but Ruby and Lou decided that a call to each of those lines was an investment they simply had to make. After all, if someone had a bizarre voice or said something a bit peculiar in their message, the girls would have saved themselves the cost of a stamp and hours of their time wasted writing a suitable letter.

Advertisements that didn't have a box number were dismissed out of hand. The girls determined that any man who didn't bother to record a telephone message must be one of four things: number one, he was too cheap. Lou had quickly noticed that while the telephone ads were free to place, picking up the messages left in reply cost as much for the guy who placed the ad as it did for the girls who rang to listen to him. Any man who balked at spending sixty pence a minute to listen to what might be the voice of the love of his life, was hardly likely to be lavish with the presents when he finally found her.

Number two, the man might be unnecessarily shy.

'What's wrong with being shy?' Martin protested. But Lou was ruthless on this point too. They were not after the kind of man who might need baby-sitting in a social situation.

Reason number three: the bloke wasn't able to make up anything sufficiently witty to say. Not that this stopped many men from leaving a message, as the girls would later discover.

Reason four was a terrible speech impediment.

'You can't help having a speech impediment,' said Martin when Lou announced that this was the fourth fatal flaw.

'Oh yeah,' Lou scoffed. 'I don't seem to remember your being quite so kind when you dumped poor *iccle Webecca from Wuislip*.'

Martin blanched at the memory of his ex.

'Got to narrow the field down somehow,' he back-tracked.

'Ring this one,' said Lou to Ruby.

She had found an ad that said, 'Could you be my muse? Sensitive writer, 32, seeks serious, sensual lady for friendship, maybe more.'

'Am I sensual?' Ruby asked.

'You've got ticklish feet,' said Lou.

47

'I guess I must be, then.'

'But are you a lady?' asked Martin.

Ruby tapped the number into the phone and listened impatiently to the long spiel about the service (delivered extra slowly to use up more premium rate time) before she could punch in the box number she was after. A £2.50 minute had already passed before at last she heard, 'Hi. My name is Davide.'

David-e. With an 'e'. Italian-style. Not just plain English David. Lou drew away from the earpiece she was sharing with Ruby to give a nod of approval. The writer's voice was at least suitably deep. No immediately obvious lisp or stutter. And Davide was exotic without being too pretentious.

'By now you'll have read my ad,' he said, 'and you want to know more about me.'

'Yes, please,' breathed Ruby. 'Lovely voice. I think we've found a good one here.'

'Where can I begin?' asked Davide. 'I could tell you I'm a published poet . . .'

'Poet!' snorted Martin. He was listening to the call via the extension line in Lou's bedroom. As a novelist in embryo, he had a general disdain for anybody who wrote anything that rhymed or scanned.

'But I have a day job as an editor . . .'

'He's an editor!' shouted Martin from the bedroom, as if they hadn't heard.

'We're looking for a date for Ruby!' Lou shouted back. 'Not someone to publish your non-existent novel!'

'Editor?' said Ruby worriedly. 'What if it's someone you know? What if it's John Simpson?'

Ruby had dated, very briefly, an editor from Lou's office who chucked her for being 'narrow minded' when she refused to use a dildo on him after their first date.

'His name's not Davide,' Lou reminded her.

'No. It's exactly the kind of name he might make up though.'

'What else can I say?' the message continued. 'I could tell you that I'm six feet tall.'

'Not John,' sighed Ruby with relief. 'He's only five feet eight.'

'And men never lie about their dimensions,' Lou commented.

'. . . I've got brown hair and eyes and some people say I look a bit like Hugh Grant. With the lights off . . .'

Davide laughed. Ruby tittered politely. Martin gave a room-shaking groan.

'But that would be the boring way to do it. So, to help make sure I make exactly the right impression on you in the short time that we have, I've decided to leave the rest of my message in rhyme.'

In rhyme? All three friends felt their stomachs contract in anticipation of the awful. Was he going to read out a poem?

Davide cleared his throat.

'Oh, God,' said Lou. 'He's really going to do it.'

'Here goes,' Davide began. 'O lovely lady, on the end of the phone, like me you've spent, too much time alone, but the wait is over, just leave me your number, we'll be in clover, sweet dreams in our slumber, I'll hold your hand, through winter, spring and summer, if you choose me as your lover, you'll never need another. O lovely lady, waiting by the phone, leave me your number, the lonely days are gone. Looking forward to meeting you, dream lady.'

And with a soft kiss blown into the receiver, Davide was gone.

Ruby put the phone down thoughtfully. Lou slumped into an armchair, hands clasped to her head in mock anguish. Martin joined the girls in the sitting room for a debrief.

'Oh, dear,' said Lou.

'Tosser,' said Martin plainly.

'He said he was six feet tall,' said Ruby. 'He's the *tallest* one so far.'

It was quite an issue for a girl who stood five ten in her stripy socks.

'He read a poem onto the line,' protested Martin. 'He used the phrase "lovely lady". Twice. And what's more, that poem didn't even scan!'

'Give him a chance,' said Ruby. 'I think he was very brave. And unusual.'

'I wonder where's he's been published.' Martin loaded the last word with sarcasm.

'At least he *has* been published,' Ruby retorted.

'Yeah, right! He probably prints his own eco-friendly, communist pamphlets and distributes them at Speakers' Corner. I bet his editing job is at *Lawn Bowls Monthly*. Plus, he had a funny voice,' Martin concluded his tirade somewhat weakly.

'He did not have a funny voice. Lou, do you think I should call the line again and leave my number?' Ruby pleaded. 'What should I say if I do? Should I leave my reply in rhyme too?'

'Oh, please,' Martin sighed. 'Like what? Dearest Dave,

My name is Ruby. Will you come and feel my boobies?'

A cushion went sailing across the room in the direction of Martin's fat head.

Lou paused and tapped her chin with a biro while she considered the matter for all of five seconds. 'No,' she determined, 'you shouldn't call that line again.'

'But he's young. He's tall. Ish,' said Ruby almost desperately.

'He's obviously a tosser,' said Lou.

'Thank you, Lou,' said Martin. 'Common sense prevails.'

'We can't waste our time replying to ads that make us feel uneasy,' Lou warned them both.

'But I didn't feel uneasy,' said Ruby. 'And I thought we were choosing for me this time.'

'We've already established that you're hopeless at sussing out men for yourself,' Lou reminded her. 'So we're going on *my* instincts here. Listening to that man made my skin crawl.'

'I know exactly what you mean,' said Martin. 'Did he honestly think that poem was a good idea?'

Lou recited a few lines in a passable impression of Davide's voice.

'OK,' Ruby admitted at length. 'He made my skin crawl too. He was terrible.'

'Then Davide is out,' said Lou decisively. She put a red line through his advert.

Unfortunately, it didn't get much better.

'Twenty-eight-year-old entrepreneur with Ferrari!' Ruby squeaked at one point. But when they rang the accompanying box number, Jolly 'Japester' (he used that word himself) Toby Jakes revealed with a hysterical giggle that he was in fact fifty-two years old and drove a Mini Metro.

'Got you to pick up the phone though, didn't I?' he laughed triumphantly. His laugh was so creepy that Ruby practically threw the phone back down.

Martin told the girls that he thought they were wasting their time. For every woman who found her multi-millionaire Mr Right via the personal ads, he reasoned, there were thousands more who had ended up going Dutch on a date with The Swamp Thing. And as for the ads they wanted him to answer . . . For heaven's sake! How could someone put 'GSOH' meaning Good Sense of Humour and make a reference to 'top sitcom' *Birds of a Feather* in the very same line?

He pointed out that none of Lou and Ruby's tales of small-ad success mentioned a man who discovered that his mystery advertiser had legs like a baby giraffe and the body of a super model combined with the brains of a cosmonaut. It soon became clear that the women who advertised in the personal ad columns were all fifty-something, 'been hurt before', looking for someone to 'love and cherish' them like the prize antiques they were.

Almost three hours later, Ruby put down the phone on yet another man who claimed to have the body of a professional athlete but finished each sentence with a death rattle that made it sound unlikely he could walk upstairs, let alone dribble the length of a football pitch. She had already dismissed the man who started his message with those magic words 'looking for commitment' but ended by saying that he was actually looking for a woman with whom he could populate Mars when the lizards from Uranus finally rose up and took over planet Earth . . .

'I don't think I could stand the responsibility,' she said.

A horrifying number of the advertisers were just looking for a bit on the side to rejuvenate lives deadened by bad marriages. Ruby pleaded the case of one guy who claimed to be separated, decree nisi pending, but Lou and Martin were firm. He did sound like a nice bloke, Lou agreed. But then so had Flett when Ruby first met him.

'Do you want to go through the same thing again? Pick some man up from the depths of divorce despair only to have him limp off after someone else as soon as he's regained his confidence?'

The words twisted in Ruby's gut just like a dagger. Who was Flett using his new confidence on now?

'This is hopeless, isn't it?' Ruby said. 'There's no one I like the sound of apart from the one getting a divorce. They really are all losers.'

'No!' Lou insisted. 'We've got to plough on. I mean, look at us. We're not losers! It'll be different when we place our own ads, I promise. Then, people like us will ring up and be gagging for a date because everyone else is so awful. Let's place ads this week. We could have our first blind date the Friday after.'

Ruby shrugged. 'Whatever. I've got to get home now.'

Martin agreed.

'I need to get some sleep before work,' Ruby continued. 'Not that I can sleep while I think about Flett the whole time.'

Lou rolled her eyes. 'Oh come on, you two! Let's write our ads now, while we're still thinking about it. This is a great idea.'

'Isn't that what New Labour said about the Millennium Dome?'

Lou couldn't understand why the others refused to get fired up by her plan. As far as she was concerned, it was brilliant. Her greatest idea ever. Writing ads for one another was the best way yet to ensure that everyone got the lover they deserved.

Growing up in Britain, you get ticked off for showing off so often that by the time you become an adult, you find it next to impossible to list your good points. That's why that classic job interview standard, 'What do you think your strengths are?' is such a nightmare for any self-respecting Brit. Ask any British person that question and they'll probably chew their nails for half an hour before saying, 'Well, I wouldn't steal pencils from the stationery cupboard,' when what they should have said is, 'I'm a creative team player with shit-hot leadership skills who could take this goddamn company to the top of the Nasdaq!'

Thus, describing yourself in a way that would make a person of the opposite sex want to jump your bones is practically impossible. It just isn't British. Consider these British responses to potentially leading questions in a chat-up situation.

'I hear you've written a novel . . .'

'Well, I was always quite good at typing so . . .'

'Is it true you used to be goalie for Manchester United?'

'Well, I do have rather big hands, so . . .'

Deprecate and shrug the compliments off. That's the British way.

And that's why the only way to get a halfway accurate report about a British person is to ask a British person's friend. While it's not acceptable under any circumstances to blow your own trumpet in this green and pleasant land, it is almost acceptable to play a horn concerto on behalf of your very best mates.

And that's what Lou intended to do for Martin when she placed her ad for him in *The Sunday Times* 'Encounters' page. She would make her friend sound like the best catch since Moby Dick. Only not quite so fat, of course.

Another Monday morning. The continuing effects of the post-wedding hangover meant that Lou was slightly late for work. Only fifteen minutes late, but it was enough to mean that the rush-hour crowds on the platform had all but disappeared by the time she got to the tube station. And joy of joys, when the train came, Lou found that she had a seat. She sat down and continued to work out the wording for Martin's ad in the margin of her *Guardian*.

Warm, witty writer? He'd like that one. *Super, sexy salesman?* Well, if she cut out the super and sexy bit, it would at least be factually accurate. *Silly, sarcastic charlatan?* Ruby would approve. *Looks a bit like Robbie Williams?* Nope. While Martin liked to think he looked like Robbie Williams, the perfect pop-star, Lou and Ruby knew that what his grandmother had actually meant to say was that he looked like *Robin* Williams, the aging American comedian.

While she tried to think of the perfect way to describe a thirty-something loafer, with the kind of floppy public school hair that some girls went crazy for, Lou glanced around the carriage at her fellow passengers. Opposite her, a girl in a suit that was slightly too tight and a pair of ridiculous chunky platform shoes read *Ms London*. Probably a temp, Lou decided. Next to her, a man in an Arsenal shirt and dust-covered jeans read the *Sun*. Builder, thought Lou, on his way back to the site after illicitly signing on at the dole office. And three seats on from him sat the woman Lou had mistakenly thought pregnant the week before. She wasn't reading anything, just staring straight ahead at nothing in particular with her mouth set in a half-snarl.

As though she sensed Lou's eyes upon her, the woman suddenly turned in her direction. Lou put up her paper like a fireguard and stayed hidden behind it for the rest of her journey.

But seeing that fierce woman again was actually strangely comforting. Because it proved to Lou that lightning could strike twice. If that woman had got into the same carriage as Lou again in less than the space of a week, then it wasn't entirely impossible that the dream lover might have done the same thing too.

Lou couldn't concentrate on Martin's ad any more. Once again, she felt the red-hot flush of lust tear through her body. Even the memory of that smile could affect her as strongly as if she had glimpsed the stranger across the floor in a sweaty nightclub. Lou fanned at her face with her newspaper. What a way to start a Monday! If only she could distil that effect into two lines and place a personal ad specifying *that* as what she wanted from a lover.

'The ability to make my knees go weak,' she scribbled in the margin.

7

For almost seven months, Martin had been able to sit on his creative urges and let his expensive laptop gather dust in a corner of his bedroom. But that Monday morning after Susannah's wedding, with Barry, head of ad sales for the entire International Magazines empire, bawling about the lamentable (i.e. empty) state of *The Satyr*'s back pages, Martin knew that he couldn't let another seven months pass him by. He had to get out of International Magazines before he was the man with no hair in the cheap shiny suit banging on about targets and deadlines.

'You are *shit*! The lot of you!' Barry had concluded the meeting even more eloquently than usual.

Martin's team exited the room with heads bowed low. Not even Lee's Dilbert desk calendar could cheer them up that day. It had become an office ritual, reading the new joke on Lee's Day By Day Dilbert calendar, like prisoners making a chalk line on the wall to mark the passing of another day in solitary confinement.

'What was wiv Barry this morning?' asked Mel. Martin knew that Lee had chosen Melanie from half a dozen applicants for her job because he thought she would brighten up the office. Six months on, the boys hardly looked at her legs any more, but Martin couldn't help noticing her grating Sarf Landan accent.

'Didn't get a shag last night,' Lee suggested thoughtfully.

'Then it's a wonder 'e's not like that every time we 'ave a meeting,' said Mel. 'I can't stand it 'ere much longer, Lee. I'm gonna leave if I have to go through that shit again.'

'Who will keep my spirits up when you're gone?' Lee asked her.

'You've got Martin,' Mel reminded him.

'Yeah,' said Lee. 'Martin will never leave, will you, Mart? Part of the furniture, our Martin. Isn't it time you got out on parole yet?' Lee joked. 'How long have you been here? Five years? Six years?'

'Seven years,' said Martin with a wince.

'That's longer than you'd get if you actually killed Fat Baz and done time for it,' Lee pointed out. Then he asked in a way that was almost concerned, 'You alright, mate? You've gone a bit quiet.'

'Yeah,' said Martin. 'Heavy weekend,' he added.

'Well, don't you go skiving off after lunch,' Mel admonished him. 'I'm fed up of covering for the pair of you while you nurse your 'angovers with all the best-looking female clients.'

'Not much chance of that today,' said Martin. That lunchtime he had a meeting with a client from a dating agency website that specialised in matching gay guys to their Mr Rights. Martin wasn't looking forward to it. He liked to do lunches when there was at least a vague chance of flirtation or conversation about football, and Mikey, from www.getyourrocksoff.com was clearly not going to be Mart's kind of girl . . . Even if he was wearing a fetching pink 'Sex Kitten' T-shirt and the tightest pair of jeans Martin had seen since 1981.

That said, Martin was surprised to find that he and Mikey actually had a lot in common. With the business quickly out of the way – a quarter-page colour ad in the October and November issues – 'just in time to catch the saddos who're gonna be on their own for Christmas' – they moved on to more interesting subjects. Before becoming a dot.com tycoon, Mikey had toured as a backing singer with a number of bands that Martin had actually heard of. 'I sang the voice of one of the lion cubs in The Lion King Four,' he added through a mouthful of roquette in balsamic vinegar.

'Great,' said Martin.

'Have you *seen* it?' Mikey asked.

Then they started to talk literature. Of sorts.

'I've got a mate who's a writer,' said Mikey. 'Not books, mind you. Screenplays. Much more money in that. Just sold some rights to Warner Brothers for a quarter of a million pounds.'

That made Martin look up from his coffee.

'You serious?' he asked.

'Absolutely. One minute he's working as a barman at The Fridge, next, they're flying him out to Hollywood. Got picked up from the airport in a limousine. He stayed in the same hotel that Richard Gere takes Julia Roberts to in *Pretty Woman*. You know, apparently there's a suite on the top floor of that hotel with a bloody carp pond in the middle of the living room. You don't want to know what he got up to in there, I can tell you . . .'

'What was the script about?' Martin interrupted, sensing that even if he didn't want to know what Mikey's friend had got up to in the indoor carp pool, Mikey was about to start telling him.

'Oh, this and that. You know. Dating.'

'Dating?'

'It's the hot topic, the studio executives said. Millions of people out there unable to *get their rocks off*.' Mikey laughed at the reference to his own website's name. 'All of them wanting to know that they're not alone in the world. All of them taking comfort from the fact that Meg Ryan always gets her man. In fact, she's up for the leading lady. Either her or Gwyneth Paltrow.'

'I'm impressed,' Martin told him.

'Neither of them do anything for me,' said Mikey.

'How did your friend get into it?' Martin persisted. 'Writing, I mean.'

'God knows. I was surprised. Didn't even know he could *read*. I suppose he's a very good liar,' Mikey smiled. 'I learned that when he ran off with my ex-boyfriend.'

'And he's still your friend?'

'No point holding a grudge. Besides which, he was also my dealer.'

'Oh.' Martin speared a chip and plugged it into his mouth before he could look surprised.

'You interested in writing, Martin?'

'I've dabbled,' Martin admitted.

'Got to be broad-minded if you want to be a writer,' Mikey observed. 'Explore a lot of different experiences.'

He leaned forward across the table. Martin leaned back in his chair. 'Yeah. I guess you do. Dating, you say? Hot topic.'

'The hottest,' Mikey pronounced lasciviously, leaning so much further forward that he knocked over the salt cellar.

Martin decided he wouldn't order that second bottle of wine after all.

But by the time he got back to the office, he knew what he had to do next. That night he would get his laptop out and start working on his novel again. If a part-time barman stroke drug-dealer could make it as a writer, then Martin definitely could. Lou's ridiculous dating pact would give him something to write about.

When Ruby came back from lunch that day, she checked her e-mail to discover two notes from John Flett. It came as something of a surprise to see his name in her 'in-box' once again. Since the day he informed her of the end of their relationship, she had had no correspondence from him at all.

One of the e-mails he sent now was entitled 'Press Release'. Fair enough. She had been waiting for him to get back to her with some more amendments to her thrilling release entitled 'Barrington Ball-bearings. A twenty-first century solution.' The other, intriguingly, bore the title line 'Dinner'.

Dinner? Was he inviting her? Ruby opened 'Press Release' first. 'Please find attached, blah, blah, blah.' She downloaded the file to read later. Now for 'Dinner'. Before she even opened the e-mail, Ruby was wondering whether or not she should accept his surprising offer.

Following one of many long conversations with Lou over the weekend about the unceremonious way in which she had been dumped, Ruby had promised her best friend that she would keep her dealings with Flett at twenty degrees below from that day on. Strictly business. She may have had to continue to work with him as his account manager but that didn't mean that she had to take any notice of his overtures if he decided that he wanted to be *friends* with her again.

'You can't be friends with someone who dumped you,' Lou was certain. 'Dumping someone is, by its definition, the very antithesis of a friendly act.'

That said, Lou had been certain that Flett *would* start to make friendly advances again. And soon. 'Nearly every dumper does,' she sighed. But what Ruby had to remember was that any casual invitation Flett sent her way was not a symptom of his having changed his mind about *her*. Lots of dumpers made friendly advances to the person they had dumped upon relatively soon after the event. It was about making the dumper feel better about himself. Not about making it up to the person they'd treated so carelessly.

'He'll probably treat you to lunch and think that's an end to it,' Lou told her. 'If you accept an olive branch you'll be absolving him of his terrible behaviour and confirming that he isn't a bastard after all. But he broke your heart. He is a bastard. So, don't do it.'

Ruby hovered with the cursor over the 'open' box on the e-mail. Lou's wise advice played like a soundtrack in her mind. Click. She opened it. Was there really any harm in accepting an invitation to dinner if . . .

To:	Ruby.Taylor@Hollingworthpr.co.uk
From:	JohnFlett@BarringtonBalls.com
Re:	Dinner

Imogen, darling.
Ivy booked for nine. Sure you can't get away from the Two-Faced conference any earlier?
J XX

Imogen! Who the fuck was Imogen? The bloody idiot had clearly sent the wrong e-mail to Ruby's address. Ruby stared at her screen until the words started to swim before her eyes. He *was* seeing someone else! And slowly, the realisation of exactly whom he was seeing dropped like an anvil at the back of Ruby's brain. Imogen. The Two-Faced conference. Oh, God. He was seeing Imogen Moss, Hollingworth's newest recruit. The new recruit who whipped the Two-Faced Cosmetics contract out from beneath Ruby's nose just three days after joining the company.

'They think she has the right look for the job, Rubes, I'm sorry,' said her boss at the time. And how could Ruby argue? She hadn't even combed her hair that morning. Imogen looked like she'd stepped from the pages of *Vogue*.

Ruby felt her eyes prick with tears almost instantly. It was as though she had received that initial Dear Jane e-mail all over again. Sure, she had guessed that a man like John Flett wouldn't simply have kicked her out of bed so that he could stretch out over both sides, but while she couldn't put a name to her replacement, Ruby had somehow managed to keep the full horror of Flett's probable new love at a distance. Now horror had a sleek blonde bob.

Ruby's vision was blurred as she looked out through the glass door of her office to the corner of the main room where Imogen stood, oblivious to the misery unfolding. Meanwhile, Imogen flicked up her bob with the casual insouciance of a 1980s Timotei girl and threw her head back to laugh. Ruby scrunched her hands into fists beneath her desk, so hard that her fingernails left dents in her palms for hours afterwards.

'Ohhhhh . . . aarrrrggggh!' Ruby couldn't begin to articulate her pain. 'Not her!'

Ruby suddenly felt as though she was mutating into a troll. She imagined her spine twisting as her shoulders slumped forwards to meet her knees. Her neck was shrinking. Her chin jutting out. Her boobs were going south to follow her self-esteem as it slithered its way to the floor and headed for the nearest available exit. She was deflating like a balloon at the end of a party. No one wanted to take Ruby home.

It wasn't long before the bile spreading throughout Ruby's limbs reached her fingertips. She opened Flett's wrongly addressed e-mail once again and forwarded it to Imogen, adding this personal note.

Fwd to: Imogen.Moss@Hollingworthpr.co.uk
From: Ruby.Taylor@Hollingworthpr.co.uk

Re: Dinner.

How could you??? Both of you??? Talk about
fucking Two-Faced. BTW, you can tell your new
boyfriend where he can stick his bloody ball-
bearings!

Moments later, Ruby had a chance to pass that message on herself.

'John Flett for you,' said the Australian receptionist Carina, putting the telephone down quickly but, Ruby convinced herself, not quickly enough to disguise the fact that she was sniggering about Ruby's parlous love-life.

In the time it took for Flett to walk from reception to her office, Ruby fixed her eyes on her computer screen, determined not even to look at the man until she had to.

But of course she looked up through her glass door at exactly the wrong time and saw him give Imogen what he probably thought was a discreet little 'see you later' wave.

'Hey, Rubes,' he said cheerily as he swung into her office like they'd never fallen out. Like they'd never been to bed!

'Good afternoon,' said Ruby in her most clipped tones.

'No need for formalities,' Flett joked awkwardly. He made to kiss her on the cheek. Ruby ducked backwards and glared at him.

'Busy day?' he asked.

'Very busy,' she said with hard-clenched teeth.

The sod was wearing the pink polo shirt she'd bought him! Oh, God. Ruby closed her eyes and had a flashback to the shopping trip. She'd quickly learned that outside the office, John Flett didn't have a clue about dressing. That Italian suit was a one-off. He'd been determined to buy the kind of clothes that shouldn't be seen outside the golf course. She had spent so much time and energy trying to persuade him to try something different. A pair of dark denim jeans instead of those corduroy combat pants that were unfashionable before he even got into them, perhaps? The polo shirt had been a compromise. It was still the duddy side of fuddy-duddy but the pink looked so good with his suntan.

'I bought you that shirt,' Ruby couldn't help exclaiming.

'I know,' he said. 'I thought I probably shouldn't wear it today but . . . Everything else is in the wash.' Flett balanced one buttock on the corner of her desk and looked at her earnestly. 'Look, I know this is difficult for you, Ruby. It's pretty difficult for me too . . .'

'Excuse me if I don't feel much sympathy for you,' Ruby hissed.

'But,' Flett ignored her last comment, 'we do still have a professional relationship to uphold . . .'

Ruby kept her eyes fixed on the piece of paper that now lay on the desk between them, the hard copy of the press release he had earlier e-mailed. Flett had a baby-boomer's distrust of cyberspace and liked to follow everything up the old-fashioned way. If only he'd stuck to writing letters instead of e-mails, Ruby sighed.

'I hope that you'll be able to work on the Barrington campaign with the same enthusiasm as you had . . .'

'Before you slept with Imogen,' Ruby whispered.

Flett cleared his throat. 'Imogen? What are you talking about now?'

'Imogen Moss. Of the Two-Faced campaign. Imogen of the other side of my office!'

'Nothing's going on with her . . .' he started.

'Oh, please. Save your breath. You know how when you get an e-mail there are usually a couple of options in the response box?'

Flett wrinkled his forehead. He didn't.

'One of them is reply and one of them is reply *all*,' Ruby continued.

'I don't understand.'

'No, clearly you don't understand e-mail at all! Or you wouldn't have copied your e-mail finishing our relationship to pretty much everyone in my office. Or sent your e-mail to Imogen inviting *her* to have dinner at The Ivy to me.'

Flett rubbed his eye nervously. 'You got that?'

'Yes, I did. I forwarded a copy to Imogen so you needn't worry about her missing out on your date.'

'Shit,' said Flett.

'Yes,' said Ruby. 'You are.'

'God. Ruby. I just . . . I, well, I don't know what to say.'

'Don't even bother,' she said, raising her palm to his face in a 'talk to the hand' gesture. 'It's quite nice to see you lost for words for once. I'll look at your amendments to the press release this afternoon. OK?'

Flett nodded. 'Sure. I'll, er . . . I'll e-mail you.'

Ruby smiled tightly, lifted the title page of the release and stared at the words until she heard him leave her office and close the door behind him. When the door clicked shut, she realised that she had been holding her breath. Now she took a gasp that turned into a sob. And the tears that had been making the words blur in front of her eyes suddenly rained onto that perfect first page.

'A team you can trust,' trumpeted the opening line. Pity Ruby couldn't say the same for the company's CEO.

Seeing John Flett exit Ruby's office at speed, Liz Hale, her fellow account manager, was soon by her side. Liz and Ruby had started working at Hollingworth at exactly the same time. That should have made them firm friends but Ruby was never sure whether Liz actually liked her. Lou suggested that Liz was just one of those women who had an unfortunate air of disdain even when she thought she was smiling. That afternoon, however, Ruby had no choice but to cry on Liz's shoulder.

'He's seeing Imogen?' Liz gasped when Ruby told her.

'Stupid bastard sent *me* an e-mail inviting *her* out to dinner.'

'Oh no. How could she be so two-faced?' Liz failed to hide a wry smile at her own pun.

'I'm going to have to kill myself,' said Ruby, only half-joking.

'Don't be silly. You'll rise above it,' said Liz.

'How can I rise above the fact that I've been dumped and I can't even hide myself away and not talk to the sod who did it? I don't want to work on my ex-lover's account. The only solution is for me to quit.'

'And work out a month's notice, during which time you'll have to work on his ball-bearings anyway?'

'I hadn't thought of that,' said Ruby.

'You're acting like a wounded animal here,' Liz told her. 'Lashing out, acting from your gut instead of your brain. I wouldn't be your friend if I didn't suggest that you took ten deep breaths and then considered how to find the best in this situation.'

Liz was a big fan of 'taking ten deep breaths'.

'I don't think your yoga breathing is going to make me feel better now,' Ruby snapped. 'There isn't any "best" in this situation at all. My ex-lover's new girlfriend works on the other side of this office. I can see her every time I raise my head.'

Liz continued regardless. 'If you can just apply yourself to the job in hand professionally, think how that will make you look. Everyone will be impressed by your dignity and tenacity at such a difficult time. This will all be old news by the time we get to the summer party . . .'

'The summer party?' Ruby looked as though someone

had rescued her from the *Titanic* with an inflatable raft and then burned a hole in it with a careless cigarette.

'Yes,' said Liz.

'I'd completely forgotten about that. I can't go to the summer party. Not now. What will everyone say when he turns up with . . .' Ruby swallowed painfully. 'Her and I turn up with . . .' she took another huge gulping breath. 'No one!'

'There, there,' said Liz, patting her on the arm. 'I don't suppose many people will notice.'

'Of course they bloody will. It's going to be a disaster!' Ruby was plunging back into the abyss without a bungee rope. 'I'm not going to have anyone to take to the summer party and he'll be there with Imogen and everyone else will be having a good time and I'll be sitting in a corner and I won't even be able to leave early because the damn party is going to be on a moving boat and the only way out is by swimming. Whose sodding brilliant idea was that one?'

'Well, much as I hate to remind you,' said Liz. 'It was actually *you* that suggested the river cruise at the first meeting we had back in February.'

'Nooooo!' Ruby buried her head in her arms and left a trail of snot all over Flett's press release. Back then, in the first romantic flush of her relationship with him, the idea of a cruise had seemed quite romantic. His arm around her shoulders as they watched the sun set over the Thames. A kiss as they sailed beneath Albert Bridge. 'Did I really suggest it?'

'I'm afraid you did.'

'Which means I definitely can't get out of it.'

'I guess not.'

'My life is such a mess.'

'Oh, come on, Rubes. It's not that bad. I'll be going on my own too.' Liz put her hands on Ruby's shoulders and squeezed tight in an attempt to be comforting. 'We could be each other's dates. How about that?'

Ruby lifted her head slowly and looked at Liz with an expression that was half grateful and half disbelief. 'Liz. That's so nice of you,' she snuffled. 'But, it's just not the same. Don't you see? I need to impress Flett, not get a sympathy vote.'

'What do you mean by that?'

'I mean, I can't go to the party with a woman. I've got to have a man. Otherwise he's just going to think that I'm another sad old spinster whose little black book should be in the ancient history section of the British Library.'

'In that case, Ruby,' Liz huffed, 'I don't know what more to say to you. The party's less than six weeks away. I wouldn't count on being able to find the man of your dreams in that short a time. I'd better get back to my desk.'

'Yeah. Sure. Thanks for the good advice,' said Ruby. But as soon as Liz had closed Ruby's office door behind her, Ruby gave her the finger with both hands. 'Thanks for bloody nothing, you old cow!'

Liz didn't want Ruby to be happy. That was it. She wanted Ruby to be single, like her, forever and ever and ever so that she had someone to moan with in the corner at every works do from now until they both retired to live with their pet cats in Battersea.

But the awful truth was, Liz was probably right. How on earth was Ruby going to get herself a new boyfriend in time to impress her ex and his new girlfriend at the party? Hire an escort?

Just then, Ruby's assistant, Katherine, poked her head around the door. 'Do you want a coffee, Rubes?' She paused, while Ruby tried to compose herself with a quick rake of her fingers through her hair. 'Are you OK?'

'I've never been better. No coffee, thanks.'

'Okey-doke. I'll just see if Emlyn wants some. Seeing as his temp assistant is off sick today.'

'Don't do it, Katherine,' Ruby said hopelessly as the girl skipped off hopefully in the direction of the Panter's lair. 'All men are bastards.'

If only she could stop herself from wanting one so much. Just then, the phone rang.

'Yes?' Ruby snapped.

'Who rattled your pushchair?' asked Lou.

'Oh, it's you.'

'Well, don't sound so bloody pleased to hear from me. Look, I'm ringing to say that I think we should still go for my personal ad idea. I've already written a really good one for Martin and I think it would be a laugh and I don't know why the pair of you won't give it a chance and . . .'

'Do you think we could have our first date within a month?' Ruby interrupted.

Lou was taken back by her sudden enthusiasm. 'If we get a move on,' she said, 'we could have one in a fortnight, punters permitting.'

'I'll write one for you this afternoon,' Ruby told her.

'What's made you change your tune?' asked Lou.

'Desperate times call for incredibly desperate measures,' said Ruby.

As soon as Lou hung up, Ruby was on the phone to Martin.

'What have you written about me? What have you said in my ad?' she asked. 'It's important, Martin. This isn't just a game.'

'Are we doing that personal ad thing?' said Martin.

'Yes, we're doing it!' Ruby snapped.

'Well, I haven't written anything at all yet. I've been busy.'

'What do you mean?' Ruby spat. 'You're never bloody busy! You sit in your office all day long playing Minesweeper.'

'I do not,' Martin protested.

'You know you do! You told me. How long does it take to write a couple of lines about one of your very best friends anyway? You're supposed to be the wordsmith! You want to be a writer. Well, I'll tell you something right now. You haven't got a hope in hell if you can't stick to a simple deadline.'

'Ruby,' Martin laughed. 'What on earth is wrong with you? If we're really going to do this ridiculous triple date thing, I'll do your ad today. In fact, I can feel the muse flowing through me right now. Desperately seeking . . .'

'If the word "desperate" or any derivative thereof appears in my ad, I promise I will cut your balls off with a rusty Swiss army knife!'

'Then don't act it,' Martin suggested. 'What's happened to make you so angsty this afternoon?'

'Flett just came in,' Ruby snorted. 'He's seeing Imogen from the office. I should have guessed. She's been giving me funny looks all week.'

'Maybe she was having trouble with her contact lenses,' suggested Martin.

'He's seeing her!' said Ruby in exasperation. 'He

admitted it. I know he's a shit, but I didn't think he'd turn out to be such a shit that he started seeing someone in my office.'

'That isn't very friendly,' Martin agreed.

'Anyway, they're going to be all over each other at the summer party and I've got no one to go with except Liz from the office next door. It's terrible.'

'That's terrible?' asked Martin.

'Of course it is!'

'Right. I thought you were going to tell me you've got three months left to live and have to have a vaginal orgasm before you die.'

'You're not taking me seriously, Martin. I can't go to the summer party with a girl.'

'Then take me,' said Martin. 'I'm always up for a party.'

'Oh, yeah. That'll really impress Flett, won't it?'

'OK. If you're worried that he'll think you're just dragging along a friend, we can pretend that we've fallen in love. But you will owe me big time for that particular acting job.'

'Martin, that is not what I'm worried about. I just know that he's hardly likely to be impressed by a man sooooo successful that the only designer gear in his wardrobe is a pair of Ralph Lauren socks.'

'Thanks a lot!' Martin snorted. 'Shall I write "money-grabbing" instead of "desperate" when I place your lonely heart . . .'

Ruby pulled her rape whistle out of her handbag and blew it down the phone. Hard. But as soon as she hung up she wished she hadn't been so angry. Martin was going to put her ad in *Loot* now. She knew it. She was doomed.

8

Fortunately for Ruby, Lou also knew Martin only too well and quickly warned him that if he scuppered their friend's chance of getting a decent date for the Hollingworth Public Relations summer party by placing her personal ad in a newspaper read only by flat-hunters and wife-swappers she would make sure that his date came equipped with her own pair of nutcrackers.

'Alright!' Martin exclaimed. He duly promised to place his ad for Ruby in the back of the *Financial Times* Saturday supplement. But Lou still groaned when he told her what he planned.

'I thought you'd be pleased,' he said. 'It's read by people with bucket-loads of money.'

'I know. But we're supposed to think of the publication most suited to the person we're writing the ad for. You know, think about a publication that the kind of person Ruby really *needs* to date might read. The demographic of the readership for the *Financial Times* is all wrong. You should know that, doing your job. *FT* readers are all stuffy, right-wing bigots whose idea of a good time is fox hunting or beating poor children with sticks.'

'Exactly Ruby's kind of man,' Martin pointed out.

'Yeah. Exactly the kind of man that has led her to the mess she finds herself in now. I was rather hoping that we might be able to persuade her to try something different this time around. You know, someone younger. Someone sensitive. Someone nice.'

'You mean a *Guardian* reader,' said Martin. 'Someone who cares about the environment and wears biodegradable sandals?'

'I just mean someone who isn't already married with kids. I'll have to help you sort through the replies,' Lou sighed with resignation. 'Otherwise this really will be a disaster for poor Rubes.'

'What makes you think I don't know what kind of man Ruby needs?'

'Just make sure you don't fix her up with another Flett. That's all I ask.'

'I will. But what are you going to do for me in return?'

'Find you a girlfriend who has already taken her A-levels,' Lou replied pithily. 'And passed them. Tell me exactly what you're going to say about Ruby in this ad of yours.'

Martin cleared his throat. 'I thought I might go with something like this: pretty, witty PR girl possessed of a fine pair of legs to match her glossy brown mane seeks lively and literate lover. If you could be the Darcy to my Elizabeth Bennett, please write with a photo to box number da-de-dah . . .'

A smile spread across Lou's face as she heard Martin describe their best friend so affectionately, though she was a little doubtful about the equine references. 'That's so sweet. And full of lovely mixed metaphors,' she added. 'Have you ever thought about being a writer?'

'Funny you should say that,' Martin replied.

Martin felt thoroughly guilty when he got home that night and saw the true, horrific extent of the layer of dust that had settled on the cover of his laptop during all those months of neglect; even Lou's smiley face and sarcastic 'Use Me' message had been all but obliterated by the passage of time. Martin didn't have a duster in the flat, so he pulled off one of his socks and used that instead. His socks were probably due for a wash anyway, he decided as he sniffed at one tentatively. He had been wearing the same pair since Friday.

With the dust wiped away, Martin clicked the laptop open as though he were opening a treasure chest and pressed the long-dormant 'on' button. The machine gave a feeble little fizz of indignation at being woken from such a long slumber and the screen flickered for less than a second before it went blank again. The battery, quite understandably, was as dead as Will Shakespeare. Martin would just have to run it off the mains . . .

He couldn't understand it. The adaptor wasn't on the shelf that had been the laptop's home since the day he snapped it shut in a fury after six hours spent staring at the tiny screen that yielded just four hundred faltering words. Neither was it in the drawer where Martin kept all his writing-related accoutrements: a copy of the *Writers' and Artists' Yearbook* (1988 edition), two sheaves of extremely blank white paper, two unopened ink cartridges for the printer and three A5 notebooks with narrow lines that hadn't had so much as a sniff of inspirational biro since he bought them.

Perhaps it was in the cupboard under the stairs, where Martin kept the Hoover, a broken toaster and a variety of other electrical knick-knacks. Including a hairdryer that once belonged to 'Webecca' who couldn't say her 'R's'. When Webecca arrived one Friday night, two months into their relationship, with that hairdryer and a newly purchased five-pack of knickers from M & S, 'because I seem to stay here more often than I stay in my own home these days,' Martin knew it was the beginning of the end.

With a shudder at the memory of Webecca's round, red face, Martin shoved the hairdryer back into a box of knick-knacks destined for a car-boot sale – if he ever managed to get up before midday on a Sunday – and continued with his search. Half an hour later, he came to the conclusion that the adaptor was clearly nowhere in the flat. And then he remembered.

'Oh, no. No, please.'

He stopped rummaging through the cupboard beneath the kitchen sink and sank back on his heels as the memory took more solid form.

'You'll weg-wet this,' Webecca had assured him as Martin legged it away from the house she shared with two other homemade hummus-eating postgrads in Brixton.

'I don't think I will,' Martin had replied at the time, unable to imagine a moment when he might miss Webecca's pudgy body or the clammy embrace of her hot little hands stroking his hair. He knew for certain that he would never miss the baby talk. 'Martin, I wuv you . . .' But his adaptor . . .

'Aaaaarrrgggghh!'

The Achilles heel he had never imagined.

Martin suddenly found himself having a moment of creative angst.

'What kind of laptop have you got?' he asked Lou over the telephone before she'd had a chance to say hello.

'IBM,' she said. 'Why?'

'Is that compatible with a Toshiba?'

'I don't think so. These machines are carefully designed so that you can't swap parts and save yourself loads of cash in the process,' Lou explained. 'Anyway, what's wrong with yours? Worn out through over-use?'

'Ha ha ha. I can't use it because the battery has run flat . . .'

'You just need to charge it . . .' Lou began.

'I know. But I don't have an adaptor.'

'Have you looked for it?'

'I loaned my adaptor to Webecca . . .'

'Oh, dear.' Lou couldn't help laughing. 'Oh, no.'

'It's not funny!' Martin protested.

'It is sort of divine justice though, don't you think? You were horrible to her.'

'She was a nutter.'

'I have to agree,' said Lou. Though she and Ruby had come out in Webecca's support immediately after the split, it hadn't taken long for the female fellow feeling to dissolve. 'But even a nutter has the right to be a little upset when you tell her you'd rather sleep with Saddam Hussein than see her naked again.'

'Did I say that?'

'That's what she told me you said to her when she called *me* in the middle of the night and tried to make me persuade *you* to take her back again. You still owe me for that, by the way. Three hours she was on the phone to me. Three bloody hours in the middle of the night.'

'Look, I'm sorry,' Martin muttered. 'I had no idea she'd do that . . . But do you think you could phone her now and ask for my adaptor back?'

'What!? That was a joke you made just then, right?'

'Lou, I'm desperate. I'll buy you a pint.'

'Darling, you would have to buy me a whole bloody brewery before I picked up the phone to your mad ex again.'

'She'll be over me by now,' Martin pleaded.

'Nope,' said Lou. 'I just can't take the risk that she isn't. Why don't you just send someone round to burgle it back? You could have them fetch your CDs while they're at it. And *my* CDs.' Lou was still faintly exercised by the fact that Webecca had helped herself to, and failed to return, a couple of Lou's own favourite albums that Martin had been borrowing at the time.

'Great idea,' said Martin dryly. 'Why has this happened to me? I just want to write. I'm foiled at every turn.'

'No, you're not. You could just do it the old-fashioned way,' Lou suggested.

'How's that?' Martin was confused.

'Pen and paper?' said Lou.

'That's so slow,' Martin protested.

'Sounds like it's your only option tonight, Shakespeare.'

Martin called three more friends before he gave up on the idea of borrowing an adaptor and admitted that Lou was right. Pen and paper was the only option unless he called Webecca. He took out one of the empty pads and wrote a date at the top of the page. As he did so, he had a sudden glimpse of a glittering future, in which his biographer would leaf through this pad and be grateful for the unhappy sequence of events that led to Martin Ashcroft having to write the early draft of his first great novel by hand.

Half an hour later, Martin was still chewing his pen. The biography fantasy had quickly lost its charm. So much for the connection between body and creativity being facilitated by the old-fashioned method of writing. Martin felt utterly stuck.

He glanced at the clock. It was eight o'clock already. He had three choices. He could continue to sit at the kitchen table and stare at a blank page in a notebook. He could go to the pub and have Lou and Ruby take the mickey out of him for his inability to get started on his magnum opus again. Or he could bite the bullet and call Webecca . . .

Webecca. Would it really be so hard? After all, seven months had passed since Martin ended their relationship. A whole football season had come and gone. The relationship itself had only lasted for two months, start to finish, which meant that, even using Ruby's worst case scenario break-up calculation that it could take up to twice as long as a relationship had lasted to honestly, truly get over it, Webecca should be over him by now. She probably had a new boyfriend, he told himself. Perhaps they could even be friends now. Laugh about the old times? At the very least they should be able to arrange the simple handover of their respective property without involving solicitors.

Convinced that she would at least treat him civilly, Martin dug out his little black book. It was rather smart as little black books go; a present from Ruby a couple of Christmasses previously, the little leather-bound address

book from Smythson was embossed with the legend
'Blondes, Brunettes and Redheads' on the cover. 'Not
that you're picky,' Ruby had observed.

Martin found himself turning to W for Webecca and
was momentarily confused not to find her number there.
She was under R, of course. Rebecca Roberts. What an
unfortunate name for a girl who couldn't say her 'R's'.
What had her parents been thinking? Ah, well, he supposed there was no way they could have known what
their daughter would grow up to sound like. But what
had Webecca herself been thinking when she decided to
study for a doctorate on 'Wacial DiscWimination and
MinoWity Wights'? Or chose to live in a street called
Wobinson Woad? At number thirty-thwee? It had given
Lou hours of fun, at least.

'Seven six four double *thwee* . . .'

'Webecca,' he said. 'I mean,' he cleared his throat.
'Rebecca? Is that you?'

'This is *Webecca Woberts*, yes,' she said primly. 'Can I
ask who's calling?'

'It's me. Martin. Martin Ashcroft? Remember?'

There was a sharp intake of breath at the other end of
the phone.

'Martin?'

'Yeah. Hi,' he said, lightly. 'How are you? Just thought
I'd give you a call and see, you know, how you're getting
on. What you've been up to . . .'

'Waaaaaaaah!' She answered his enquiry with a sob.
'I'm still on the *Pwozac*, you bastard.'

'Shit. Rebecca, I . . .'

'Don't apologise, Martin. What do you care? You
didn't *weturn* any of my calls. You didn't answer my

letters. You just cut me out of your life like I never mattered to you at all.'

'Rebecca, you know you mattered . . .'

'It's too late now, Martin. I had a nervous *bweakdown*. I had to leave the university and give up my PhD because of you. I spent *thwee* whole months at the *Pwiowy*.'

'The Priory?' Martin was actually vaguely impressed. 'You mean the place where all the stars go?' Webecca's parents were rumoured to be loaded. He almost asked if she'd met anyone interesting but decided it probably wasn't appropriate.

'*Thwee* months at the *Pwiowy*. Then another *thwee* months waiting for the *Pwozac* to work *pwoperly* and now, just as I'm starting to feel like myself again, you choose to phone me up and ask me how I am. Well, I'm not doing very well, actually and that's one *hundwed* per cent thanks to you.'

'I'm sorry,' said Martin. What else was he supposed to say? 'I had no idea.'

Webecca suddenly softened. 'Oh, Martin. Why did you do it? We had such a good thing when we were together. We were soul mates, Martin. I'd never felt so complete in my life and I know that you felt the same way.'

Martin didn't think it was a good moment to tell her that he had actually spent most of the time they shared together wondering how to tell her it was over.

'Is that what you've *wealised*? Have you come to your senses at last? You've been out all alone in the *weal* world and *wealised* that what we had was something special after all?'

'Actually . . .' Martin began.

'I knew this would happen,' Webecca continued re-gardless. 'Didn't I tell you that one day you would be back, begging me to *weconsider*? Well, Martin, I want you to tell me why I should. I was emotionally *cwippled* by our *bweak-up*. I lost almost two stone. At one point, the doctors thought they would have to put me on a *dwip*. And did you care? I *wote* to you *evewy* single day. I called you *evewy* night.'

And don't I remember, Martin thought.

'I even called your *fwiend*, Louisa. All I wanted was the chance to talk to you *pwoperly*. The chance to make what we had together work again. They told me I was being *widiculous*. They told me I should just forget about you. But I knew that this would happen. I knew that one day I would pick up the phone and hear your voice at the other end of it. And I was going to be *weady* to tell you where to stuff your empty apologies. You blew your chance at happiness, Martin. Our chance. Our one big chance. You don't deserve my forgiveness . . .'

'I know,' Martin interjected politely.

'But I'm *pwepared* to give you one more go. I know it will be hard. There are lots of things we need to talk about but I think that we can work *thwough* all the *pwoblems* we had and make our *welationship stwonger* for the time we've spent apart.'

'Rebecca, hang on,' Martin interrupted. 'I didn't . . .'

'Expect me to be so level-headed about this? No. I'm sure you didn't.'

'Rebecca,' Martin said hopelessly. 'I really was just calling to say hi.'

'What?' she said.

'And,' he took a deep breath against the sudden

pregnant silence at the other end of the line. 'To ask whether you've still got the adaptor for my laptop.'

'Your what?'

'My adaptor. You borrowed it before we split up. Remember? I need it back now. That's what I called you to say. And I've got your hairdryer. I thought perhaps we could do a swap? Over coffee?' he added, not wanting to sound as though he was interested in being her friend.

'Waaaaaaahhhhhhh!' Webecca began again. 'Waaaaaaaaaaaaaaaaaaahhhhhhhh!!!!'

'Oh, God.' Martin closed his eyes and prayed for the honking sobbing to be over quickly. Three minutes later, when it was clear that Webecca was neither about to stop crying, nor put the phone down on him, Martin knew he had no option but to put the phone down on her instead.

'Bye, Rebecca,' he muttered as he did it. He didn't think she heard. 'Bugger.'

Lou was right. A woman spurned is a woman who is never going to give back the adaptor for your laptop.

Martin was left with the other two options. Frustration at home. Humiliation in the pub. He sank back into his chair and let the waves of irritation wash over him. He would never write his novel. He was doomed to be stuck at *The Satyr* forever . . . Stuck in that office. Staring at that PC. Playing Minesweeper until his mouse-finger broke . . .

'Hang on a minute.'

Martin had a Eureka moment.

He grabbed his denim jacket, his tube pass *and* his security pass for the International Magazines building. Then he headed off to squeeze those ideas out of his brain and into Times New Roman Twelve Point at the office.

9

Though it wasn't Wednesday night, Ruby had demanded a crisis summit at the Hare and Hounds in view of that day's horrifying revelations. Lou had tried to calm her down over the phone.

'No, Ruby, I really don't think you can have someone sacked because they've stolen your boyfriend. I perfectly agree that it would be nice for you if you could, but I don't think it would go down well in the European Court of Human Rights.'

'But I feel so betrayed!' Ruby whined.

'Imagine how his wife must have felt when he started seeing you. Honestly, Ruby, these men never change their spots. He dumped his wife for a younger model. He dumped you for Imogen. He's going down the age range so rapidly that next week he'll dump Imogen for some girl who's still revising for her GCSEs. Then you can have him arrested,' Lou added, in a desperate bid to lighten the tone.

'That is not funny,' said Ruby.

'Ooops, there goes my other line,' Lou lied. 'I'll see you at the pub.'

Sometimes, Lou reflected, she felt as though Martin and Ruby viewed her more as a surrogate mother than a friend. Take that day alone. First she had to deal with

Ruby's Flett-related histrionics, then Martin – altogether more low key – but equally demanding as he expected Lou to come up with a solution to his adaptor problem other than waiting for the shops to open next day. He hadn't even properly apologised for leaving Lou to deal with the 'Webecca' problem first time round. Lou had to screen her phone calls for two months – home and office – after Martin's break-up with the girl and still he had refused to put her, and Lou, out of their misery. Sometimes, just sometimes, thought Lou, it would be nice to have someone that she could off-load on too.

That said, Lou didn't miss much about the men she had been with in the past. She certainly didn't miss the way her old boyfriends seemed to think that a month or so of super romantic chivalry bought them a year of her services, not only as a lover, but as a mother in the kitchen and, more often than not, as a secretary too. Lou shook her head with disbelief as she remembered taking a day of *her* leave to sit in one guy's flat, waiting for a plumber who never arrived to fix his ailing Zanussi. And when it turned out that the washing machine was beyond repair, he didn't rush out to buy a new one. Oh no. Instead, he started bringing his laundry round to Lou's, letting her get on with it while he flicked endlessly through the channels on her telly.

The departure of the last man from Lou's life had actually resulted in a marked improvement in her standard of living. Less washing-up and the ability to watch whatever she wanted, when she wanted to, without relinquishing the remote control to a being who hit the channel changer like a lab rat pressing the lever in its cage for snacks. No longer would Lou grab a carton of milk from the fridge only to discover that someone else had not only downed a whole pint since that morning but had thoughtfully put the empty carton back to remind her to get another one.

It would take someone extremely special to persuade Lou to give up that freedom again. Very special indeed.

But how would Lou recognise that person? The answer to that question, no matter who she asked, always seemed to be 'you will just *know*'. Well, Justin had seemed like a great catch when Lou first met him. Handsome, funny, in full-time and lucrative employment. It took a whole year for her to realise that he was also vain and irritating and viewed his full-time employment as altogether more important than hers – hence she was the one left doing his washing while he flicked through the channels.

Erica, who had the office next door to Lou's and seemed to have been single since the dawn of time, suggested that everyone should come with references from their previous lovers. 'You wouldn't dream of giving someone a job without checking their references,' she reasoned. 'So why should you sleep with someone whom you know next to nothing about?'

'Because none of us would ever get a shag again if our exes wrote us references,' Lou pointed out.

'Ah. Didn't think of that,' said Erica.

'References from your friends might be a good idea though.' And Lou explained the Lonely Hearts Pact to her colleague. 'I know both of them better than they know themselves. I'm sure I can find the right woman for Martin.'

'But do you think Ruby can find the right man for you?' Erica asked.

Lou's mind wandered briefly to the stranger on the tube. 'That I'm not so sure about.'

That night Lou took the tube down to Clapham to meet the others at the Hare and Hounds. Since the morning when she and her fantasy lover locked eyes over the idiot with the *Financial Times*, every tube journey had taken on new excitement. Whereas previously Lou might have travelled the length of the Northern Line in a packed carriage with her pelvis squished up against Joe Fiennes' buttocks and not noticed so long as she had a manuscript to bury her nose in, now she was acutely aware of the people travelling in every tube carriage with her. More to the point, she was acutely aware of the one person who wasn't sharing her journey.

There was little chance that the mystery commuter would be on the same tube train tonight but Lou's heart still quickened a little as she skipped down the stairs to the south-bound platform.

'This is ridiculous,' she reminded herself as she searched the length of the platform for that fleetingly familiar face, getting that nauseous, hollow feeling of anxious excitement when she saw a blond head bent low over the *Evening Standard*.

She couldn't quite believe she was allowing herself to get so worked up about a person whose name she didn't even know. Someone she had seen for less than a minute, for heaven's sake! Lou had never been the type of girl who believed in fate or love at first sight and all those fairytale endings and yet here she was, sure that she had glimpsed a soul mate and chewing at her cuticles (a nervous habit she had managed to give up only a year before) because she thought that she might have let the chance to find true and lasting love slip away.

Because her racing heart, her churning stomach, the way she had started taking the tube for even those short journeys she once would have walked in less time than it took for the train to arrive, all told Lou she must have fallen in love. And yet there were a million reasons why her stranger probably wasn't the one. Couldn't be the one, in fact.

'I'll *never* meet the one for me,' Ruby said dramatically, as she slammed her empty glass down on the table. 'I've had my last chance at love. I'm all loved out. I don't think I can ever bring myself to trust someone the way I trusted Flett again.'

'Nonsense,' said Lou. 'Just wait till those replies to your ad start coming in.'

'What's he put?' Ruby asked. Martin was safely out of earshot at the bar. 'You haven't let him put anything about me being desperate, have you?'

'I made sure he represented you accurately,' said Lou.

'Which is desperate,' Ruby confirmed.

Martin grinned as he arrived at the table just in time to catch the tail end of the girls' discussion.

'What kept you so late tonight?' Lou asked.

'I've been writing my novel,' said Martin proudly.

'Seriously?' said Lou excitedly. 'You resorted to pen and paper after all?'

'No. I went into the office and used my computer there.'

'So you didn't get the adaptor back?' Lou asked.

'You were right about Webecca.'

'She isn't over you?'

'Not hardly. She wants to send me the bill for her Prozac.'

'Are you kidding?' Ruby asked. 'You split up, what, seven months ago?'

'You were the one who said it takes twice as long to get over a relationship as the whole thing lasted in the first place.'

'Then I'm doomed until next September,' Ruby cried.

'Don't be silly. Life can turn around in a day,' Lou reminded them.

'Yeah. I could get knocked over by a bus tomorrow,' said Ruby gloomily. 'That would certainly shorten my recovery time.'

'Or you could meet the man of your dreams on the top deck,' Lou countered.

And then she told them. 'I saw someone I really fancied on the tube the other day. Not just fancied,' she added. 'Someone I felt I had a connection with. I wish I had plucked up the courage to speak before they got off the train.'

'You could have followed,' said Ruby.

'And been late for my editorial meeting? Don't think that would have gone down well.'

'I would have thought you supremely romantic and given you a promotion on the spot for being a joyful, spontaneous person,' said Ruby.

'And that's why you don't run a multinational publishing conglomerate,' Lou pointed out. 'Anyway, what's the real chance of a perfect stranger wanting to give you their phone number? If this person had stayed on the tube for one more stop, if I'd been able to find the courage to actually speak, I'm sure I would have said something stupid or spat all over them or something equally charming. I wouldn't have got a phone number. I'd have got a hard stare and a poke in the eye with the end of an umbrella.'

'No,' said Ruby. 'I don't think so. Wouldn't you be thrilled, Martin, if a girl asked you for your phone number on the tube?'

'It's every man's dream,' Martin assured them. 'You girls don't know how lucky you've had it, being the ones who get asked out all the time. Being of the sex that has to do most of the asking, I can tell you what a nightmare it is. You don't know fear until you're face to face with a woman you fancy, trying to find a line that will make her laugh out loud and not slap you.'

'See,' said Ruby. 'You should have gone for it, Lou. Men love being propositioned.'

Lou smiled and shrugged. 'I'm sure they do.'

'So. What did this gorgeous stranger of yours look like?' Ruby asked.

'Tall, fair-ish hair, wearing a dark blue suit. Slim.'

'That certainly narrows down the field of perfect strangers travelling on the tube during rush hour,' said Martin sarcastically.

'I can't think of anything specific about the way they looked. But I instantly felt we were *simpatico*. There was a moment when our eyes met and it was as if we'd known each other before. Forever.'

Martin began to play heartfelt chords on an imaginary violin.

Ruby was less cynical. 'You've come over all new-agey, Lou. You'll be believing your horoscope next and only dating men with the moon in Scorpio.'

'I'll never get that sad,' Lou assured her. 'But I feel pretty sad now, talking to you about this. If only London weren't such an unfriendly city we might have stopped and talked. Struck up a friendship at least.' She looked wistfully towards the door of the pub, as though the winds of fate might blow her stranger in. 'As it is, I don't suppose we'll ever see each other again.'

'You might if you make sure you catch the same tube every morning,' said Ruby excitedly.

'I do catch the same tube every morning. More or less. I'd never seen that particular person before.'

'You just mean you'd never noticed them before,' Ruby corrected. 'That's different. Now that you've established some sort of rapport, I bet you start to see them every day. All you've got to do is keep smiling and start saying "good morning" and before you know it you'll be one of those Underground love stories the *Evening Standard* runs every Valentine's Day to make us feel that London isn't such a heartless toilet of a city after all.' She clapped her hands together at the thought of it.

'Perhaps,' said Lou, 'but I doubt it.'

Later that evening, a slow smile spread over Ruby's lips as the perfect solution to the trouble she was having with writing Lou's ad formed in her mind. She'd been finding it difficult to think of a good way to describe Lou and next to impossible to imagine what kind of man her friend would really like. But now she had the answer.

In the back of *Time Out*, the London listings magazine, beneath the ordinary Lonely Hearts ads, is a column entitled Once Seen. Even before the personal ad pact, Ruby had made a habit of reading this column, where people would leave messages intended to jog the memory of someone they had met only briefly and longed to see again. Ruby loved it. The idea that someone might have glimpsed her across Waterloo Station and been unable to put her out of his mind ever since had her turning to the Once Seen column before she read anything else.

The possibility of finding yourself described in Once Seen was, to Ruby, as exciting as waiting for a sixth number on the lottery.

Ruby was decided. She wouldn't place an ordinary ad for Lou at all. Instead, she would place a Once Seen describing Lou and the mysterious Prince Charming on the Northern Line. She got quite excited as she imagined her plan succeeding and Lou's thrilled surprise at discovering her blind date was the person she already knew she fancied.

Ruby shared the idea with Martin as they caught the night bus back home.

'What will you put?' he asked. 'How do you know what she was wearing that day?'

'I'm guessing she was probably wearing what she wore to the pub that night. Did she come straight from work, d'you know?'

'I think so.'

'Can't you remember?'

'You're the girl. As a generalisation, we boys wouldn't notice if you turned up in a sack as long as we could see some cleavage.'

'Yeah.' Ruby recognised an accusation she herself had

made several times before. 'Well, could you see any cleavage?' Ruby had to ask.

Martin put his hand to his chin as he thought back to the evening in question. 'Nope,' he said. Then, as though he had just discovered Archimedes' principle again, Martin's eyes lit up. 'But she was wearing a miniskirt. I distinctly remember looking at her knees.'

'Martin!'

'I just can't help myself,' he sighed. 'Lou's got fantastic knees.'

Ruby glanced down at her own rather knobbly ones and pulled her skirt to cover them.

'You've got nice knees, too,' Martin insisted.

'You don't mean that,' said Ruby.

'OK, your knees are awful but your tits are fabulous. How about that?'

'You sod!' said Ruby, swatting him with her handbag. She pulled a disgruntled face but was secretly rather flattered. 'Are they better than Lou's?' she asked moments later.

'Better than most women's.'

'Only most?' echoed Ruby.

Martin sensed immediately that he might be about to make a faux pas equivalent to telling a girl that her bum did look big in that. 'Joking!' he assured her.

'What? Joking that there are better boobs than mine or that mine are better than most?'

Martin paled.

'Forget it,' said Ruby. 'It's not as though I care what you think anyway.'

'Then why are you getting so angry with me?' Martin asked.

'I'm not,' Ruby insisted. 'Like I said, it really doesn't matter whether you think I look good or not. In fact, I'd rather be one of the rare women that you don't find attractive.' She hoped she sounded dismissive but was frighteningly aware that she didn't. 'So we know she was wearing a miniskirt,' she said quickly to change the subject. 'I'll put this. Monday morning. Northern Line. You in the blue suit. Me in the miniskirt reading . . . What's she reading at the moment?'

'I dunno. Wild Geese or something like that?'

'*Wild Swans*,' corrected Ruby. 'That must be it. Doesn't exactly mark her out though. Everybody you see on the tube is reading it. Unless they're reading *Captain Corelli's Mandolin* or Harry Potter.'

'That's why it's perfect,' said Martin. 'You don't want to narrow her options down.'

'But there aren't any options,' said Ruby. 'I want to find her perfect stranger!'

'Oh yeah. Right.'

'What tube station did she say he got off at?' Ruby continued.

'Er. Northern Line, wasn't it? Camden Town? Put that.'

'OK. I will. What did you write for me, Mart?' Ruby asked as she snuggled up against him now. 'Where did you place my advert?'

'I can't tell you that. You know it's against the rules.'

'I've told you what I'm doing for Lou,' Ruby reasoned.

'Yeah. But you haven't told me what she's written about me, have you?'

'I swear I don't know or I would. Just pick me a good one. Swear you won't pick the worst of the bunch for the fun of it and I will make sure Lou finds you a princess,' Ruby promised.

'Then Prince Charming will be yours in return.'

Meanwhile, Lou found herself waiting at the tube station again. A train arrived. Lou stepped into a completely empty carriage. She chose a seat by the double-doors and checked the cushions for chewing gum before she ruined her trousers. No gum, thank goodness. But someone had left behind a copy of that week's *Time Out*.

Instinctively, Lou flicked straight to the personal ads. *Time Out* was one of the publications where she thought she might advertise Martin and his charms to an eager female population. She scanned down through Men Seeking Women, Women Seeking Men, Women Seeking Women . . . Then she came to a section she hadn't really noticed before. Once Seen.

There was just one three-line ad in this section:

> **Eurostar Ticket Office Waterloo 15/5.** You, brown hair, red trousers. Me, blue shirt, black jeans. You smiled. I dropped my coffee.

There followed a box number. A larger boxed message explained the purpose of the Once Seen ads. They were meant exactly for people like Lou and her Northern Line stranger. People who had shared a fleeting glance, an uncertain smile, and later wished they'd done something about it. Lou folded the magazine and slipped it into her voluminous nylon bag. Perhaps she'd place an ad of her own.

Next morning, the telephonist at *Time Out* took two personal ads for the following week's Once Seen column. The first, called in by a girl, who sounded bizarrely as though she wasn't sure quite where she had seen her perfect stranger, read:

> Wednesday morning, Northern Line. Me in
> black miniskirt, reading *Wild Swans*. You in
> the blue suit, blond hair. Would love to meet you
> again.

The second ad was another Northern Liner. Wednesday morning too. Shame that the second caller wasn't a bloke, thought the telephonist as she tapped the details of this second person into her machine. Wouldn't it have been amazing if the two ads had been placed by a girl and a guy wanting another chance with each other? That had happened once before. A French exchange student and a busker avoiding the police had bumped into each other on Victoria Station and got chatting while he helped her pick up her dropped books. They didn't swap numbers at the time – both too shy to ask – but three days later they both tried to place a Once Seen. Ellie the telephonist was able to put them in touch with each other straight away. The ads never even had to run. They sent her a card to thank her for arranging their first date. That was nice, that. She wondered if they were still going out . . .

Unfortunately, that morning's advertisers, both girls, obviously weren't looking for each other.

'I'll just repeat that back to you,' she told the second caller.

> '**Northern Line, last Wednesday morning**. Me in grey trouser suit strap-hanging, you in the blue suit leaning against door. Winked at me over man with *FT* before you got out at King's Cross. Wish I'd said hello.'

'When will that go in?' Lou asked.

'Next week's issue,' said Ellie.

'Do you think there's any chance it will work?' Lou mused.

'They often do,' Ellie told her. 'Don't forget to invite me to the wedding if it does.'

'Sure,' Lou laughed. 'You'll be first on the guest list.'

She put the phone down and smiled at the thought. A wedding? Little chance of that, Lou knew. But she still felt extremely excited. The future of her relationship with the perfect stranger was in the lap of the gods now. She'd done as much as she could do, bar spending her entire day travelling up and down by Underground until they found themselves in the same carriage again. Now all she could do was hope that her fantasy lover read *Time Out*, or at least knew someone who did. And pray that the stranger was actually a Londoner and not just someone on a fleeting business trip to London who usually lived in New York or Paris. And silently wish that they had been feeling the same way about Lou ever since; would recognise the way she had described their encounter, and not be absolutely horrified by the idea of a date with a girl glimpsed briefly on the Underground . . .

Meanwhile, Martin placed his ad for Ruby in the Style section of *The Sunday Times*. Despite Lou's reservations, Martin was convinced that *The Sunday Times* was the best place to introduce Ruby's obvious charms to the dating market. Lou was relieved that he hadn't used the *Financial Times* after all, but she still lobbied hard for the *Guardian*, beloved of soft-hearted lefties such as she thought Ruby needed for a mate. Martin, however, was firm in his opinion that the last thing Ruby needed was a vegetarian basket-weaver for a boyfriend. At least by advertising her in *The Sunday Times*, Martin felt he had some way of ensuring that the man he matched Ruby up with would be solvent. And these things did matter.

'Marxism is all very romantic,' he explained, 'but it doesn't pay for dinner.'

Lou had to console herself with the fact that she had at least managed to persuade Martin to do away with the horsey metaphors about good legs and a 'glossy mane', and Ruby's ad finally went into print like this:

> Summer is here! Don't spend it alone. Let this beautiful, vivacious, intelligent woman, 31, be your sunshine . . .

'What do you think?'

'Not bad,' Lou had to admit. 'I'll try and live up to it on the phone message.'

Lou had to record the accompanying telephone message, pretending to be Ruby. She knew that Ruby would probably have to do the same for her since, for many publications, one of the conditions of placing an ad was that you recorded a supplementary phone greeting.

There was no need to have Martin record a message to go with his ad, however. After careful consideration, Lou had decided that she wouldn't place Martin's personal in a newspaper after all. Instead, she typed his details into the database of an Internet dating agency called <u>pinacoladalovematch.com</u>, a homage to the Rupert Holmes song in which two estranged lovers rediscover each other through the lonely hearts and their mutual love of pina coladas and making love in the rain. When the ad was written, Lou scanned in the best picture of Martin she had in her collection. Unfortunately, it was five years old, but Lou felt it wouldn't be too misleading. He was aging remarkably well. She looked over the final ad copy.

> Why am I still single? Prince? No. Charming? Definitely. Good-looking, funny, affectionate male (31) seeks interesting, intelligent woman for friendship and fun. Maybe more.

'I can't wait to see how you've described me,' Lou told Ruby. 'Slinky? Sexy? Supercalifragilistic?'

Ruby shook her head wisely. 'I promise you will never guess.'

So, the lonely hearts had been placed. Each of the friends was secretly smug that he or she had written the personal ad that would finally usher true and lasting love into the life of the person they had been writing for. Ruby in particular was excited. It was as though they had each bought a ticket to a raffle with the best prize in the universe and this time she actually felt lucky. Yes, indeed. For some unknown reason, she was extremely confident that true love was waiting just the other side of the weekend. It might have been something to do with her horoscope, which promised 'big surprises' for that month.

The following weekend over brunch at the Café Rouge, the friends were able to assure each other that all of their ads had been published. While Lou and Martin debated the merits of *Supergrass* versus *Coldplay*, Ruby ploughed her way through every single newspaper she could lay her hands on. Was she the 'voluptuous brunette' in *The Sunday Times* or the 'shy but sexy animal-lover' in the *Independent*. What about the 'curvaceous cutie' described in the *News of the World*? She hoped to God she wasn't the 'damaged and dangerous damsel' she found advertised in the back of the *Sunday Telegraph*.

'Just think,' she said, stirring her cappuccino dreamily. 'Right now, somewhere out there is the man of my dreams. He's reading Martin's brilliant description of me while he eats his toast and Marmite. When he's finished his breakfast he'll pick up that phone. He'll listen to the message that Lou recorded for me and find himself intrigued . . .'

Martin and Lou shared a smile.

11

Martin's late nights at the office had quickly become a regular occurrence since the spotty boy in the computer shop informed him that it would take eight weeks for the out-of-stock adaptor he required to arrive. In any case, Martin found the office atmosphere strangely conducive to productivity once everyone else had gone home. Each evening at five thirty, he would pack up his tattered nylon record bag, leave the International Mags building by the front door and head for the café across the street. Once there, he would buy a cappuccino, sit two tables back from the window so that nobody looking in would notice him immediately and watch the doors of International Mags until Barry emerged at six o'clock sharp and rushed to catch his train home to Essex. When Barry was safely out of sight, Martin would head straight back into the office and resume work on his novel.

It was important to Martin that Barry didn't know he was staying late in the office night after night. Martin didn't know whether using the company's equipment for his own purposes would actually be a sacking offence, but he knew for sure that it would be a sneering one. He didn't want to have to explain himself and his creative ambitions to a Philistine like Barry Parsons. More importantly, he didn't want to open himself up to a more vicious version of the ridicule that Lou and Ruby had been affectionately dishing out for years.

The novel was going quite well though, Martin cautiously admitted to himself. In an early flurry of enthusiasm, he had bought a couple of books on the subject of writing from Amazon.com. The authors of those worthy books, who didn't actually seem to have written a *novel* between them, gave conflicting advice about what made a good novel great, but Martin at least picked up some tips about presenting a manuscript for publication.

The hero of Martin's own meisterwork, as yet untitled, was a bloke called Mark, an affable chap, trapped in a boring McJob, who harbours a secret crush on his female best friend. Throughout the story, the best friend, a girl called Ruthie, did her best to set him up with ultimately unsuitable women. At the end of the book, some sort of crisis would bring Mark and Ruthie together and make them realise what they really had beyond the friendship they'd always relied on. Martin wasn't sure what the crisis would be yet but he had already written the scene where Mark and Ruthie realise they've been in love with each other all along and share a passionate embrace beneath the fairy lights on Albert Bridge.

In fact, in the week after realising that Webecca would never give him his adaptor back, Martin had written what he considered to be seven great scenes. He could already see Hugh Grant playing his hero in the screenplay adaptation. He was a good-looking lad. But it was equally important, thought Martin, that the director chose someone who would bring out the intellectual quality in Mark's character as well as make him look good.

As for who would play the lovely Ruthie, Martin had initially plumped for Michelle Pfeiffer – he'd had a crush on the doe-eyed actress since seeing *Dangerous Liaisons*, aged seventeen, and thought she had the perfect mixture of serenity and vulnerability. But, lovely as she was, poor Michelle would probably be too old to play a thirty-something by the time the book was published and the film went into production . . . Into production! Martin gave himself a mental slap round the head for being so cocksure that anyone would even like his book enough to waste paper printing it. But it was good, he decided quietly. In fact, some of it was great.

Last job of each night, before Martin left the office after a writing stint, was to check the replies to Ruby's advert in *The Sunday Times*. The replies had started to come in almost immediately. Not that Martin was surprised that anyone would want to date his friend. He was, however, surprised at the number of men who seemed willing to date a person described in two lines in a national newspaper. There were three calls on the first night alone and many more during the week as the married men dialled in from the office.

And didn't some of them go on? Martin was glad it wasn't him who had to pay the phone bill as he listened to Hugh from High Wycombe drivel on about the responsibilities his 'exciting' job as an actuary entailed.

'I find my work very fulfilling and challenging,' he concluded, just as Martin was falling asleep.

If the lonely hearts game was all about selling yourself,

then most of the men who called Ruby positioned themselves firmly in the bargain basket by the checkouts with the broken boxes of biscuits and dented tins the second they opened their mouths.

Martin skipped through the replies pretty ruthlessly after the first couple of nights, instantly cutting from his list of hopefuls anyone who hesitated too long before speaking. Anyone with a voice he discerned to be more than a semi-tone above his own. Anyone with an accent too posh or too regional. Anyone who mentioned what car he drove . . .

Cars were a particularly sore point in Martin's life. Since Barry Parsons decided that Martin no longer needed a company car and his beloved Ford Puma was returned to the garage, Martin had been forced to drive his sister's old Fiesta. It was good of her to let him have it (her husband bought her a Ka for her thirty-fifth birthday) but it made Martin feel like an idiot. Ford Fiestas were girly cars (an image not helped by the extraordinarily permanent flower stickers that Marie had plastered all over it).

Martin did realise that there was something faintly hypocritical about his decision to disqualify men who mentioned the car they drove considering the fact that he had placed Ruby's ad in *The Sunday Times* precisely because he wanted to make sure she found someone solvent. But he justified it to himself by saying that there was a difference between being *successful* and being a *show-off* and mentioning the make and model of car you drove in the space of a two-minute recorded message to a woman you've never met before was definitely showing-off.

Flett had been a show-off, Martin remembered. And Ruby deserved something better than another Flett. Martin had hated the man from the first time he met him at one of Ruby's legendary dinner parties. Flett had been sitting in an armchair, pontificating about the importance of his bloody ball-bearings while Ruby rushed about the kitchen like a Stepford wife. He criticised everything Ruby put before him. The perfect, absolutely perfect, fish was, according to Ruby's new boyfriend, woefully over-cooked. The sauce was too full of butter. 'Got to watch your figure, sweetheart.' The potatoes were too hard.

Martin had to bite his tongue not to tell Flett exactly where he could stick his culinary expertise and resorted instead to countering each and every one of Flett's criticisms with a compliment. It was a strangely familiar experience, taking Martin back to Sunday lunch with his mum and dad and sister. Mum working so hard to please everyone. Dad shouting instructions from the carving chair.

Martin shuddered at the thought of Ruby ending up with someone like his dad. Someone who would chip away at her over the years. She deserved a man who would think himself the luckiest man in the world when Ruby smiled at him, not someone intent on making her feel grateful for crumbs of his time. The man Martin wanted for Ruby would be generous, funny and indulgent.

In short, what Martin wanted for Ruby was a 'good bloke'. Someone who wouldn't be taken in by all that 'Rules' rubbish either. Someone who wouldn't want to spend his life with a girl who always wore lipstick but never cracked a smile. Someone Martin would want to have a pint with. Someone he knew would take care of her. Someone a bit like him, in fact.

Lou checked that week's edition of *Time Out* to see whether her ad had been printed. And there it was. Right beneath the Once Seen title. Lou skimmed the words to check that nothing had been missed out or simply misspelled so badly that her perfect stranger wouldn't recognise her even if they did read the ad. It was exactly as she had dictated it.

But right beneath Lou's own ad was another that intrigued her. The person who had written this ad was referring to the same tube line on the same date. Even looking for another blue-suited lover.

'Good luck,' Lou murmured to her fellow Once Seener. 'Let's hope it works for at least one of us.

Three days later, however, there was nothing. Not one reply to Lou's appeal. Four days later, still nothing. A week later. Still nothing at all.

In contrast, by this time, Lou's Internet ad for Martin had attracted so many interested women that she was beginning to wonder whether she would need to take on a secretary to help her weed out the good ones from the girls who were clearly mad, bad or just too plain sad to consider.

'And even though he said that he wasn't leaving me for anyone else,' wrote Mary from High Barnet, 'when I went to the pub the following Friday he was already with another girl. Well, he must have been seeing her all along, don't you think? You sound like a nice bloke though,' she continued. 'I really like the way you described yourself in your ad. It makes me feel sure you'd never do anything so hurtful . . .'

Perhaps they should display the number for the Samaritans at the top of the pinacoladalovematch.com site thought Lou, as she deleted an e-mail from the next hopeless candidate. From fifteen replies down to two almost instantly. Finding the right woman for Martin wasn't going to be as easy as throwing dynamite into a fish-tank after all.

When the rest of that week produced no more hopeful dates, Lou toyed with the idea of going back through the replies the ad had attracted and deliberately picking out the worst of the bunch. It was strictly against the rules of the Lonely Hearts Pact to go for someone that you didn't consider in your opinion to be the *best* possible match for your victim, but as far as Martin was concerned, it was quite possible that the woman Lou considered to be the booby prize would be exactly the one he would go for.

Lou had never met such a hopeless bunch of girls as Martin's exes. Much as she wanted to be able to be kind about her fellow women, it was difficult to find much to be impressed by in the cohort of needy, clingy or downright pathetic creatures he was wont to fall in love with. It never failed to shock Lou that her friend Martin, who seemed to enjoy the company of intelligent women (i.e. herself and Ruby) so much, would so often end up with the kind of girls who thought that Nietzsche was an STD. Webecca, the PhD student, had been a rare exception to the rule. But she became an honorary 'Twit-girl' due to the fact that she was very good at hiding her intelligence in the company of men and Martin in particular.

'Insecurity,' Ruby had diagnosed one late night on vodka and Pringles. 'That's why Martin always goes for such thickos. It's a rare man who can see himself married to a woman he actually feels equal to.'

It was an idea that Ruby was clinging to at that moment. She had decided that Flett had ended their relationship because he was threatened by her intelligence. 'Men in our generation know, in a rational sense, that they should go for a woman who can hold her own in the boardroom as well as the kitchen, but, at a primal level,' she continued. 'In their mid-brains, there's still something that compels them to fight to be top dog. Look at the way Martin reacts when you beat him on the Nintendo.'

It was true that if either of the girls beat Martin on a computer game, or on the tennis courts, or even at cards, there would have to be rematch after rematch until Martin finally came out on top. If he managed to win in a 'best of three' competition, he would often risk defeat and make it 'best of five' just to increase the margin.

And Martin would probably be very happy indeed with the kind of woman that Lou couldn't have a conversation with, as long as that woman had longish hair and big breasts to distract him from her lack of conversational ability. Lou was about to admit defeat and pick out 'fluffybunny69@aol.com' who had talked about her new Burmese kittens, in response to Martin's request that e-mailers tell him something about their 'passions' . . . But no. This wasn't just about finding Martin a date he would like. It was about finding a date that would be good for him. There was still time yet.

Wednesday night at the pub quiz, Martin and Lou were able to confirm that their ads had received considerable interest.

'You had fifteen replies last night,' Lou told Martin.

'See,' said Martin. 'No woman can resist me.'

'Or man,' Lou told him with a smile. 'I assumed you wouldn't fancy a date with Simon from West Kensington. Straight-acting though he is.'

'Have I had many replies yet?' Ruby asked Martin eagerly.

'One or two,' said Martin dismissively. 'But no one I think suitable yet. I don't like the sound of any of them.'

'Martin, you can't just go ticking everyone off because you don't like them,' Ruby reminded him. 'You've got to consider what I might think too.'

'I bet he's just dismissing the ones with better cars than him,' said Lou perceptively. 'Or anyone taller or richer or . . .'

'You better not be,' Ruby warned him.

'I'm acting in your best interests,' Martin assured her.

'How about me?' Lou asked Ruby then. 'What kind of smorgasbord of talent has lined itself up for me to take my pick from next weekend?'

'Er,' Ruby looked down at her empty glass and swirled a solitary ice-cube around a little distractedly. 'I'm sure there will be replies soon,' she said at last. 'Though if there still isn't anything tonight I'm going to ring the paper and make sure that they've got the reply box set up properly.'

'You mean that *no one* has called or written to ask for a date with me?' Lou was surprised. 'No one at all? What did you advertise me as? *Desiccated old harridan seeking immediate marriage to toy-boy?*'

'Of course not,' said Ruby at once. 'It's just that you could say I wrote an ad that I know will only appeal to a very specific type of person – extremely specific in fact – so that when there is a reply I know that it will be exactly the right one. There'll be no question about that.' She nodded, confident that she had clarified the situation without giving too much away. Lou looked askance at such an odd explanation.

'OK,' Lou said finally. 'I have no idea what you're on about, but I trust you both to make sure that I'm not sitting alone at the bar eating peanuts while you two have the romantic evening of your lives at Suave.'

The restaurant they had chosen was supposed to be one of the hottest new eateries in town.

'Lou, you will have your date,' Ruby insisted. 'I swear on Martin's life.' She had her fingers crossed behind her back as she said that.

A week later, Ruby was beginning to get really worried. Lou and Martin were still expecting the date to go ahead that Friday evening and Ruby's appeal for Lou's handsome stranger had yet to elicit a single response. She was beginning to wonder whether she had made a terrible mistake . . . Forget wonder, Ruby *knew* she had made a terrible mistake. Lou's dream lover clearly wasn't the kind of man who read *Time Out* after all and, thanks to her stupid romantic optimism, Ruby had left it much too late to place another ad in a different paper as a contingency plan. Lou was going to be dateless. What a monumental cock-up.

Ruby decided that as soon as she got to the office that morning she would have to call Lou and come clean about her mistake. Perhaps Lou might be interested in one of the men who had replied to the ad Martin placed for Ruby instead? Under pressure the night before, and with Ruby twisting his arm up behind his back until he thought his shoulder might have dislocated, Martin had admitted that Ruby's ad had elicited fifteen replies. Fifteen! Not all of them could be terrible.

Just as Ruby was tying her shoelaces by the front door, the post dropped onto the doormat.

Bills. Bills. Bills. Ruby wandered back into the kitchen and put her Visa statement in a prominent position, propped up against the toaster, so that she would remember to pay it. There was an invitation from Clarins to try some new beauty product. Ruby scanned that quickly to check that they weren't offering a miracle, overnight 'be beautiful for your big blind date' treatment. They weren't. And finally there was a brown envelope. A big one. Ruby slit it open and another smaller envelope fell out.

She was momentarily confused as she looked at the address written in tidy hand on the crisp blue paper.

To The Girl of My Dreams, Box number 3567.

'Yes! Success!' Ruby punched the air triumphantly.

It was a reply to her ad in Once Seen.

Dear Beautiful Stranger, the letter began.

Do you believe in fate? I think I must do now! I'd never normally buy Time Out *but something steered me towards the newsagent's stand at the station the other morning and made me pick up a copy. And there it was. Your advertisement. I couldn't believe it. How many people are there in this city? Some say it's seven million. In that case, it must have been a one in seven million chance that I managed to find you again.*

I haven't stopped thinking about you since that morning on the tube. Your beautiful eyes. The way your smile lit up your lovely face and my grey morning. I spent all day at work cursing myself for my shyness. If only I had said hello. If only I had followed you onto the platform . . . But I was late for work. You know how these things are. Late for work! What a poor excuse!? I should have swallowed my fears and told you how I felt there and then.

But I didn't. And I thought that I'd never see you again. My anger at my timidity was overwhelmed only by the sadness I felt that we might never even get to be friends. It was a sadness that is only equalled by the joy and excitement I feel now!

So, here I am. My name, for your information, is Andrew. You know what I look like, of course. I'm thirty-three years old. I live in Tufnell Park and work for an Internet start-up company in Islington called www.A-syoulikeit.com. We sell cut-price theatre tickets. I like football and dogs. I speak bad French and conversational Italian. I'm not sure how enticing this sounds to you now, but I'd love to meet up and tell you everything else there is to know.

Please call me as soon as you get this letter. I can't wait a moment longer to see you again. Because if Cupid still exists these days, then he got me on the Northern Line that Wednesday morning.

With very best wishes,
Andrew

Ruby spread the letter out on the kitchen table and felt ever so slightly voyeuristic.

'A one in seven million chance.' Lou had really won the Lottery this time. Ruby felt exhilaration that she had found the perfect stranger mixed with a little twinge of jealousy that someone who had glimpsed her friend for mere seconds could obviously be so moved. Still, she gave a little jig of excitement as she double-locked the door behind her and clipped on down to the bus stop. Lou was going to be so surprised. So impressed. Ruby had found her stranger on the train!

12

Martin listened to the latest set of replies impatiently. What a bunch of tossers!

'Hi there, gorgeous,' began Robert from West Kensington.

How did he know that Ruby was gorgeous, thought Martin indignantly.

'I work as a lawyer and I drive a Porsche Boxster,' Robert continued quite seamlessly. 'But don't let that put you off. Ha ha ha.'

'Oh dear,' Martin muttered to himself. 'Wouldn't want Ruby to end up with a man who only has a two-inch penis. I'm afraid that you go to the back of the queue.'

The postal replies weren't much better. Used to dealing with insane fan letters to her authors, Lou had warned her friends that the old adage about green ink really did apply. Likewise, letters written on lined paper should always be regarded with suspicion. Martin didn't believe her at first, getting halfway through a letter written on tissue-thin lined paper in green biro and deciding that he was actually rather warming to the writer when he came to a passage about 'The Second Coming' which explained that the author was actually looking for a wife who would be willing to join him in a nuclear-proof bunker, with the intention of re-establishing the human race with her post-Armageddon.

'Shame,' Martin tutted, wondering whether this was the guy Ruby had already dismissed via his telephone ad weeks before. He decided to keep the letter for the post-mortem anyway. He might even write about it in his novel.

Almost all the letters left much to be desired. Martin soon realised those which weren't littered with misspellings were usually written by the over-fifties. And Martin was under very strict instructions not to choose Ruby a date who wouldn't understand her jokes about The Clangers (not that Lou or Martin really understood Ruby's jokes about the Clangers either). That left him with a very narrow age range, extending roughly two years in each direction from Ruby's median thirty-one.

But after listening to so many terrible messages, Martin very much wanted to choose a date from the letters rather than the phone calls to the accompanying number. He felt that a man who had taken the effort to write rather than phone was far more likely to be the kind of sensitive, thoughtful man that his dear friend deserved after her run-in with Flett and that other married loser before him. Martin was also biased towards anyone with a literary bent. Though poems were still out, *après* Davide.

Eventually, Martin settled for a man called Robin. In Martin's opinion, Robin's letter to Ruby was both sensitive and witty. While he said that he worked in the City he didn't mention the size of his bonus, which Martin took as a tacit signal that he must have had a substantial one. Robin hadn't enclosed a picture, as requested, but Martin knew Rubes wasn't lookist. In fact, she seemed to be grateful if the men she dated had two eyes looking in the same direction.

When he had decided upon Robin for sure, Martin

gave Lou the relevant details so that she could phone their victim, pretending to be Ruby with her very passable impression of Ruby's slightly rural Worcestershire accent, and arrange that Friday's date at Suave.

'Did he enclose a photograph?' Lou asked.

'No,' said Martin.

'Then I don't think you should go for him. If he didn't send a photo then he probably looks like a Gremlin.'

'None of the replies enclosed photographs,' Martin told her. 'Except for the guy from Peterborough who enclosed a photo of himself, one of his cat and one of his mother – whose bungalow he still shares.'

'Oh, God. Was he good-looking?'

'What do you think?'

'Robin it is then,' Lou sighed. 'Though Robin and Ruby sounds a bit twee.'

'Just phone him. It's either him or the tosser with the Porsche.'

'There was a reply from a man with a Porsche?' Even Lou, who pretended not to be impressed by such things, couldn't help exclaiming.

'He left a message on the phone line but forgot to leave his number,' Martin lied. 'Call Robin, will you?'

Lou agreed.

Though it wasn't strictly in keeping with the rules of the Lonely Hearts Pact, Lou also demanded that Martin show her Robin's letter, as a damage limitation exercise. In reality, despite his protestations, Martin was only too pleased for Lou's second opinion. Much as he hated the idea that there might be any area of life in which women were better endowed than men, he had to admit that he was worried he might have missed some subtle but extremely important clues in Robin's letter that a woman would pick up on immediately. In short, he wanted Lou to take partial responsibility if this Robin bloke turned out to be a psychopath.

'Do you think he's a psychopath?' Martin asked Lou outright when she'd read it.

'Who do you think I am? Bloody Cracker?' Lou asked. 'But I'm impressed that you're feeling so protective towards our friend. Unusually protective, I'd say,' Lou teased. 'You sure you want to set Ruby up with anybody at all?'

'I just don't want to be the one that set her up with an axe-murderer,' Martin blustered.

'I'm setting *you* up with an axe murderer.'

'Don't even joke about that,' Martin replied. 'Though I'd prefer an axe-murderer to a vegetarian. Have you picked one for me yet?'

Lou certainly had. In the end, there had been little competition for an evening with Martin. As Martin had suspected, most of the women who answered his ad seemed like members of a club for deranged ex-girlfriends who practised calligraphy in blood and castration in their spare time.

Nine out of ten e-mails that arrived at the bogus address Lou had set up on her friend's behalf went into way too much detail. Lou had endless sympathy for these poor tortured girls. Honestly, she did. But hadn't it occurred to them that it might be better to wait until the second date to pour out their hearts, rather than pour their hearts out in the first e-mail and scupper their chances of even getting as far as date one?

The girl Lou eventually chose stood out for two reasons. The first was the brevity of her note. Just her name and her vital statistics. That she was studying for an MA in Fine Art, that is. Not her hip-to-waist ratio. The second was the photo she had scanned in to accompany that note. Cindy Daniels looked every inch the art student. Her hair was twisted into a series of stubby dreadlocks that looked like unwashed paintbrushes, tipped as they were with bright pink and red and blue. She had a ring through her eyebrow and another through her nose. She was gazing straight at the camera with a smile that could only be described as dirty. Lou couldn't help but smile back when she saw it. Perfect. Here was Martin's girl all right.

Lou instantly knew Cindy Daniels would be a challenge. And she knew that Martin would be horrified when he saw her. She was a very long way from the groomed Jennifer Lopez-style lovelies that Martin usually lusted after, with their waist-length hair and lips so big that Ruby once wondered aloud if Leah's mother had stuck her to windows using her mouth as a suction cup to keep her out of trouble during shopping trips.

'I arranged the date by e-mail,' Lou told Martin. 'She sent confirmation this morning.'

'All fixed then,' said Martin simply.

And it was. The restaurant was booked. Three tables for two under three different names and three very different dates to spend the evening with.

13

The advertising department of *The Satyr* always had a slight party atmosphere on a Friday morning as the inmates of 'Stalag' International Mags looked forward to the weekend. Melanie bought the cappuccinos on her way into the office. Lee added the whisky for Irish coffee with a twist. Martin bought the cakes. And on that particular Friday, he was just biting into a doughnut with caramel icing when Barry Parsons wandered in.

'Hear you were in the office last night,' said Barry casually.

'Working on the Viking Vodka presentation,' Martin shrugged without looking up from his screen. 'Want to get it right.'

'After last month's figures, you need to get it right,' said Barry, picking up Martin's doughnut and helping himself to a bite. When he put the doughnut down again, there was slightly less than one decent mouthful left. 'My office in ten,' he said then, in what was obviously meant to be an intimidating manner.

'Sure.' Martin kept his eyes on the screen until he heard the door to Barry's office shut. When that happened, Martin put his head over the parapet briefly and checked that Barry really was out of his way before opening the computer file that contained his novel in progress. He ran the word count. Thirty thousand words so far. Martin planned to get a finished draft done by the end of the month. He'd already made himself a list of the agents he would hit as soon as he had the manuscript printed out. He'd use the machines at International Magazines to make copies of course.

In his wildest dreams, Martin imagined himself writing a list of acknowledgments for the front of the book and crediting Barry Parsons with making his life so miserable that he really had no choice but to write a best-selling novel and escape the rat race. That fantasy would sustain him through what he hoped would be his last couple of months in air-conditioned hell at *The Satyr* before he faxed his letter of resignation from Barbados . . . In the meantime, however . . .

' 'E's looking a bit pissed off this mornin',' Melanie observed of her boss. 'Says 'e wants you to go to 'is office straight away, Mart. I don't know what you done but it must 'ave been something terrible.'

'Good luck, Ashcroft,' said Lee, patting him on the back and saluting in the parody of World War Two camaraderie they adopted to lighten the atmosphere whenever it looked as though large chunks of proverbial were about to start hitting the fan.

'Tell Melanie that I love her,' responded Martin, playing the airman who would never return. Then he strode into Barry's office without looking back at his comrades.

'You've been late in the office every night for the past fortnight,' started Barry. 'I want to know what you've been doing.'

'Catching up with my workload, like I told you,' said

Martin. 'Getting ahead of myself so that I can organise my time better on a day-to-day basis.' Martin had practised for this moment since he first started using the office as his study after hours.

'Then how come your performance is still such shite?' Barry asked. 'You've had two cancellations this month. After I talked to you this morning, I called the guys from Viking to find out why they'd decided not to place their ads with us and they told me that you cancelled your meeting with them because you were ill and never called back to reschedule. When the fuck were you ill, Martin? You haven't been out of the office this month. You're spending more time here than ever before and yet you called them to say that you couldn't make the meeting because you were ill. I want to know what's going on with you.'

'I didn't feel ready to meet them at the time we'd scheduled. I didn't want to turn up at the meeting half-prepared and lose the sale because I didn't impress them.'

'So, instead, you lost the sale by just not bothering to follow up. You know what that looks like to me, boy? It looks like you're losing your touch. But since I know that you aren't losing your touch, what it also looks like is you deliberately not chasing up an account so that you can take it with you when you move to another mag. What's going on, Martin? Either you're up to something you don't want to tell me about or you're knocking off one of the cleaners.'

Martin almost laughed at that.

'While you won't tell me what your game is,' Barry continued. 'I can't bring myself to trust you and if I can't bring myself to trust you then it's not very clever of me to have you as my right-hand man. Who's got their eye on you, Martin?' Barry persisted. 'Nat Mags? IPC?'

Martin shook his head.

'Then you're telling me that you really are just a pile of shite and you can't even close a deal with a bunch of tossers like Viking who should cut their nuts off to get in the back of *The Satyr*?'

'I guess I must be,' said Martin, after giving the question some thought.

'What are you going to do about it?' Barry asked. 'I can't have any passengers on my team.'

Martin tapped his biro against his lower lip as though he was considering his options.

'If I want a tosser in charge of my mag, I can go across the street right now and give your job to that guy selling the *Big Issue*.' Barry nodded out through the window at the dread-locked crustie and his equally sad-looking dog who sat outside the office come winter, spring or summer. 'So, I'm asking you again, Martin. What are you going to do about it?'

Martin put his biro back into the breast pocket of his shirt and looked Barry straight in the eye. Time seemed to expand as the men stared at each other like a pair of belligerent bull elephants on the savannah. Which one of them would break for it first?

'You know what,' Martin said finally. 'I'm not going to do anything about it. . . .'

'Eh?' Barry's expression changed from anger to confusion.

'I've been meaning to tell you this for some time,' Martin explained. 'I'm sick and tired of working at *The Satyr*. I'm sick and tired of working for a man like you.

You can stick your crappy job where you keep your crappy brains. And that, if you can't work it out, is up your fat white arse.'

Barry's mouth trembled as he absorbed the insult and tried to find the words to rebut it.

'You're fired!' he shouted eventually.

'Didn't you notice me resigning?' Martin asked.

'I want you out of this building right now,' said Barry as his face grew ever redder. 'You're sacked. You hear me? You're finished at International Mags.'

'That was the point of my speech,' said Martin calmly.

'I've had enough of your lip.'

'I've had enough of your whole fat head. You, Barry Parsons,' said Martin, as he jabbed a finger in Barry's pigeon chest, 'are not the new Rupert Murdoch. You're not even the new Robert Maxwell, though you do give him a run for his money on the lard-arsed front. You head up the ad sales team for a poxy magazine called *The Satyr* and you don't even know what the bloody word means. You are going nowhere. In fact, you're not only going nowhere, you are safely there already, mate.'

Martin picked up his jacket from the back of his chair and prepared to leave.

'Yeah? Yeah?' Suddenly Barry was on his feet too and blocking Martin's exit. 'Well, what do you think you're going to do for your fucking living if you don't turn round and kiss my arse right now?'

'Something more dignified and exciting? Cleaning toilets?'

'Where the fuck do you think you're going?' Barry stuttered as Martin pushed past him and stepped out into the corridor. 'You've got one fucking chance to turn round and take back what you just said. One fucking chance to save your fucking job.'

'No thanks,' said Martin. 'I meant every single word.'

Seconds later, Barry was calling security.

Good as it had felt to tell Barry exactly what he thought of him, it soon became clear that Martin had taken Semtex to his bridges. Martin wasn't even allowed to go back to his desk to collect his belongings. Instead, Barry had Martin wait in the lobby of the office under the supervision of the least friendly security guard in International Magazines' employ – the one who looked like a bulldog chewing a wasp on a good day – while upstairs in *The Satyr*'s stuffy office Lee and Melanie quickly gathered together Martin's personal effects in a cardboard box.

'I'm really sorry, mate,' Lee said as he handed the box over in the lobby, beneath the blown-up version of the third issue cover – Kylie in the guise of a squirrel – that Martin loved so much.

'It's alright,' Martin said tightly.

'Did you try grovelling?' Lee asked seriously.

'It doesn't suit me,' Martin told him with a smile.

'Fair enough, mate,' said Lee. 'Look, your departure has come as a bit of a surprise,' he continued. 'No time to organise a leaving present or nothing. But we had a bit of a whip-round in the office. Buy yourself a drink.'

Lee handed over a jiffy bag with Martin's name scrawled upon it in Melanie's almost joined-up writing.

'Thanks,' said Martin. 'There'll be almost enough for half a pint of Strongbow if you and Mel both contributed.'

'Yer tosser,' said Lee, punching Martin playfully in the arm. 'I'll see you around.'

'Not if I see you first,' Martin replied with the old standard.

Lee patted Martin on the shoulder and trudged back to the lift, looking almost as broken as Martin felt.

'Fuck.' Martin smacked his hand against his forehead.

'Time's up,' said the security guard, using his bulk to intimidate Martin towards the door like a prison officer escorting his charge back to the cells.

'This is a great moment for you, isn't it?' Martin commented accusingly. 'Bet you spend your entire working week waiting just for moments like this when you feel like you're actually doing something. You'd love it for war to break out, wouldn't you? You don't feel like you're living unless you're picking on somebody else.'

'Out,' said the security guard without even looking at him.

'Fuck. Fuck. Fuck. Fuck . . .' Martin picked himself up from where the security guard left him on the kerb. Much as he had wanted out of International Magazines, he could not believe his bad luck. The idea had been that he would at least have a chance to go back to his office and retrieve his masterwork . . .

Martin Ashcroft, standing up for himself against Barry Parsons was suddenly Martin Ashcroft, thirty-one. No job. No prospects. And no novel.

Martin sank down onto a bench covered in bird shit and stared disconsolately at the detritus of more than half a decade spent chained to a desk at International Mags. His green plastic pen tidy. His oversized calculator with the extra big number keys. One postcard of a woman with a fat arse in a G-string – sent to the office by Lee from a stag weekend in Fuerteventura. Three chewed up biros. And *no* fucking novel. How could he have been so stupid!?

Martin dug out his mobile. Perhaps he could phone Lee . . . No chance. He knew that Barry would be in the office right now, searching for evidence that Martin had been working as a double agent for another publication, before getting one of the geeks from the IT support department to erase all trace of Martin's existence from International Magazines' infrastructure.

The very worst of it was the idea that Barry might actually read some of Martin's work before he deleted it. Martin groaned from the bottom of his stomach. He could almost see Barry's sick, smug smile spreading across his face like anthrax when he came across the words Martin had sweated over every night for the best part of a month.

Martin rattled the jiffy bag that contained his leaving collection. In fact, it didn't even rattle. Tight sods. Martin ripped open the bag. Might as well start his descent into homelessness via a six-pack of Tennent's Extra right now. He had never felt so much in need of alcoholic oblivion in his life. He glanced across the road at the crustie who sold the *Big Issue*.

'Spare me a quid, mate?' the crustie asked when they made eye contact.

'Could be the last time,' said Martin, dipping inside the envelope. 'I'll share whatever's in here . . .'

But the jiffy bag contained no money after all. Instead, Martin found a diskette, garnished with a Post-it note.

'Copied your contacts file,' Lee had written. 'You'll need this in your new job.'

Clever boy.

'Yes!' Martin punched the air. Because what Lee didn't know was that there wasn't a single address in the contacts file on Martin's hard drive. 'Contacts' was the working title of his novel. Glancing out from his office window, Barry saw Martin doing a lap of honour around the International Magazines' car park and felt sure that his suspicions were confirmed.

'The day is saved!' Martin shouted to the crustie. 'Let's go to the pub.'

While Martin toasted his success on escaping International Mags with his novel, Lou and Ruby were already getting ready for that evening's date at Suave.

Suave was one of the hottest new restaurants in London. At least, that's what it said in the month-old issue of *Time Out* in which Lou had first seen the restaurant reviewed, which meant that, by the time the trio got round to booking their grand blind date, just six months after the restaurant opened, Suave was already on its way back down the cool-ometer again.

Despite that, Ruby was still excited when she arrived at Lou's flat after work with three huge holdalls into which she appeared to have stuffed her entire wardrobe.

'I don't think you're going to be needing these,' said Lou, holding up a pair of shorts.

'I didn't think so,' Ruby admitted. 'But you're always hearing about people going on a blind date in London and deciding to elope the next day. I've got my passport,' she added. 'Martin might have set me up with a multi-millionaire yachtsman who insists on flying me to St Tropez tomorrow morning.'

'Or a ski instructor?' suggested Lou, as she happened upon Ruby's old salopettes.

They narrowed it down to three front-runner outfits. Leather trousers and a black slash neck top were discarded when Lou wondered aloud whether the restaurant had leather seats.

'Don't want your date to think that you're farting all night, do you?'

Lou pulled a little black dress out of Ruby's case next. 'What about this?' she asked.

'It's a bit boring, isn't it? A bit predictable.'

'Unlike this,' said Lou, digging out a bright cerise pink pencil skirt. 'When on earth was this fashionable?'

'Summer 2000,' Ruby said, regarding her fashion mistake with disgust. 'First nineteen eighties revival.'

'Whatever possessed you?'

'You, actually,' Ruby pointed out. 'Don't you remember telling me that I needed to inject some colour into my wardrobe? What are you wearing?' Ruby asked.

Lou nodded towards a stylish navy blue trouser suit that was hanging from the doors of her wardrobe ready to adorn Lou's long, slender limbs. The jersey material had an elegant drape that whispered expensive and Ruby was suddenly filled with loathing for the black dress that had served her so well in the past. At forty quid it had definitely been a bargain. But suddenly she felt it was showing its age, with the material getting a little more transparent with every wash and not in a fashionable way.

'I can't go to Suave in this,' Ruby sighed. 'They'll think

I'm one of the staff. Except that the staff will all be better dressed than I am.'

'Why don't you wear your DK dress?' Lou suggested.

'Haven't got round to dry-cleaning it since Susannah's wedding.'

In reality, Ruby had rather hoped she wouldn't have to. She had convinced herself that if she left the dress hanging in the breeze from her bedroom window for long enough, she would be able to get away with it. But that morning she had taken a tentative sniff at the crinkled skirt and had almost been knocked out by the alcohol vapour that still lingered on the expensive black crepe. She didn't even dare sniff the armpits. They'd done a lot of dancing that night.

'Black dress it is,' she said resignedly.

'It really suits you,' Lou assured her. 'Besides, you don't want to look as though you're trying too hard.'

Am I trying too hard, Ruby wondered? She stared at herself in the full-length mirror on the back of Lou's wardrobe door. She knew she looked presentable, but she had wanted to look *special*. After all, this was her one shot. There was less than a month left until the Hollingworth Summer Party. She had so much to do in that time. Apart from the usual – lose ten pounds, wax bikini line, have a facial – she had to convince Flett that he had been wrong to dump her for Imogen. And it seemed the only thing that might convince a man he had done the wrong thing in ending a relationship was to see the woman he had abandoned on the arm of another man.

'You look wonderful,' said Lou, as she clipped on a simple pair of silver earrings to complete her own effortlessly graceful outfit. 'Now where is sodding Martin?'

He turned up just before the taxi that Lou had booked for seven-thirty.

'Have you been drinking already?' Ruby asked him as a blast of alcohol vapour enveloped her when they kissed hello.

'One or two,' he said. Martin had actually spent most of the afternoon in the pub opposite the International Magazines Building, bribing the *Big Issue* seller with pints of lager so that he would listen to the plot of the Martin's book. Filthy, as the chap was called, had assured Martin that he had never heard a better idea for a best-seller and that losing his job was indeed the push that Martin needed to propel him to literary stardom. But there wasn't time to explain that now.

Lou was busy outlining the strategy for the evening. They needed to arrive separately, so that their dates didn't know they were part of a mass experiment. They needed to have get-out clauses and secret signals to let each other know if anything was going wrong. There would be a rendezvous at nine o'clock in the ladies' cloakroom so that they could update each other on their progress and set a time to split if things were going pear-shaped.

'Post-mortem at my house afterwards,' Lou added. 'I've bought a bottle of brandy.'

The taxi-driver pulled in as instructed, within view of, but not right outside, the restaurant's imposing frosted glass doors.

'Who's first?' asked Lou.

'I'll go,' said Martin, opening the cab door and heading for the restaurant at speed. All that lager had gone straight through him and he was on a mission to find the loo.

'Hey!' Ruby called him back. 'You forgot your share of the cab fare!'

'We'll get it later,' said Lou. 'Don't blow his cover. You ready for this?'

'I think so,' Ruby whispered.

Lou hadn't seen her look so worried since they took their finals.

'Don't worry,' she said. 'It's a blind date. How bad can it possibly be?'

14

Lou felt like a character in a police drama series as she sat alone at the bar and studiously ignored her friends. If only they had kitted themselves out with hidden headsets so that they could communicate with each other across the room without anyone noticing. As it was, the best they could manage in terms of high-tech spy equipment was to agree to set their mobile phones to vibrate and text each other from beneath the cover of the tablecloths if anything should go awry.

Which one of them would meet their date first? Lou hoped it was Ruby. Ruby was looking about her like a rabbit that knows it is within range of a fox but isn't quite sure where would be the best place to run to. She had drained her first double vodka tonic as though it was lemonade and was already on to a second. If she had to wait much longer, Ruby would barely be able to stand up. So much for making a good first impression.

Meanwhile, Martin was sitting at the other end of the bar, studying himself in the mirrored glass behind the optics. Lou couldn't help smiling. It was definitely a myth that men were less vain about their appearance than women. Martin's messy crop may have looked like a 'just out of bed' head to the uninitiated, but Lou knew for a fact that it was actually the result of hours in front of the bathroom cabinet with a pot of pricey styling wax. He was drinking beer from a bottle, she noticed. Hardly very sophisticated. Still, his date-to-be was a student. Lou could only hope that Cindy Daniels wasn't still drinking her choice of poison from a two-litre plastic jug.

Every time the doors to the restaurant swung open to admit another visitor, Ruby oriented herself towards the entrance with an eager smile. It was a busy evening. Though the celeb count stuck firmly at zero all night, the beautiful people who drifted in were still pretty impressive. Twice Ruby had been particularly excited by the latest additions to Suave's clientele. When a tall, blond man with the clean-cut, square-jawed look of a model advertising some rugged brand of aftershave actually smiled at her as he handed his coat to the cloakroom attendant, Ruby almost wet her knickers with anticipation. She was ready to do a lap of honour around the dining room and kiss Martin for scoring so spectacularly on her behalf. Unfortunately, moments later the gorgeous bloke walked straight by her to kiss a whippet thin brunette who had been nursing a mineral water in his absence.

'You looked straight past me,' the brunette complained.

'Forgot my glasses,' said the aftershave guy. He brought out a pair of wire-rimmed specs. 'There, I can see who I'm looking at now.'

Ruby sagged a little on her bar stool. Really, what chance was there that her blind date would be that gorgeous? The name Robin didn't bode well for a start. How many film stars could Ruby name called Robin? She came up with one, but that was a girl. The only male celeb called Robin that Ruby could think of was Robin Cousins, the champion figure skater who triumphed in the Olympics when Ruby was still at junior school. Robin Cousins. Ruby remembered the fuss that had been made of him. And sure, he could execute a triple salco with perfection, but even aged seven, Ruby had failed to find him alluring.

It was something to do with the hair, Ruby decided. There was something altogether too tidy about Robin Cousins' neat side parting. Serial killer hair, was what Lou called it, having noticed that every time you see a mug shot of a serial killer on TV, they look as though their mother has just smoothed their fringe down and had a go at a smudge on their face with a hanky. In fact, Lou theorised, the tidier the hair, the more likely the neighbours were to say, 'he seemed like such a nice man' when they found three lower leg joints in his fridge.

Ruby offered up a little prayer. 'God preserve me from a man with a serial killer fringe.'

She deserved to have a good time that night. There couldn't be many women in London who had had worse luck in the dating game than Ruby Taylor. Her long losing streak stretched right back to her first date, aged fifteen, when Paul Ferguson, the best looking boy in the school, asked her what she was doing on the night of the sixth form's Christmas party. Ruby was elated. She spent the money she had been saving for the school ski trip on a green silk blouse and a pair of black leggings from Chelsea Girl. She even persuaded her mother to let her use one of those 'Shaders and Toners' dye sachets on her hair. Chocolate delight, she thought it was called.

And Ruby was overjoyed to hear Paul say, 'Wow, you

look great,' when he opened the door to her on the night of the sixth form bash.

'Yeah, Ruby,' said Paul's girlfriend Charlie Baggott, who was standing right behind him. 'You should do your hair like that all the time. Thanks for offering to babysit tonight. I could have killed Paul when he said he might not be able to come to the party because he had to look after the kids.'

Ruby could only gawp as she watched the king and queen of her school head off for a night on the tiles while Paul's mother gave strict instructions for the care of Paul's two little sisters.

The date that never was had definitely set the tone. Ruby gazed down into her glass as her mind drifted inexorably back to John Flett. And, as it happened, Ruby wasn't looking at the door at all when her date finally did arrive. Instead, she was unattractively crunching an ice-cube when the barman gave a little cough to indicate that someone was standing right behind her.

'You Ruby?' the stranger asked.

'Yes. I . . . er . . .,' she still had the ice-cube in her mouth and a dribble of cold water escaped to run down the side of her chin. 'Whoops. Sorry.' She grabbed a napkin and spat the ice-cube out.

'Hi, I'm Ruby,' she started again. 'And you must be Robin.' She held out her hand to shake Robin's hand in greeting. He didn't respond in kind. Instead, he clutched his hands tightly around the neck of a plastic carrier bag and nodded warily. Ruby snatched her hand back and smoothed down her skirt as though that was what she had been intending to do all along.

Now that she had stopped being flustered, the reality

of the man who stood before her slowly began to take full and horrific shape.

'Everything alright?' Robin asked when he caught Ruby staring.

'Oh, yes,' she said. 'Everything's just, er . . . wonderful.'

He had better have a blinding personality.

Lou could only look on in horror from the other side of the restaurant. The only possible consolation was that Ruby's date was in fact one of those eccentric millionaires who dress like a tramp to deflect attention from the hoi polloi. He didn't look as if he could afford a copy of *The Sunday Times*, let alone be interested in reading it. But he had said that he worked in the City. Everyone who worked in the City was loaded as far as Lou could tell. Praying that this first impression of Robin was an unfair one, Lou gave Ruby a covert 'thumbs up' that went unanswered and went back to watching Martin. At the top of the stairs, a girl Lou recognised as Cindy Daniels was already scanning the room for her victim.

'Oh, my God,' Martin thought to himself. 'Lou has set me up with a Muppet!'

'You must be Martin,' said Cindy, extending her hand. As they shook, her bangles jangled a metallic cacophony. When she nodded at his suggestion that they might start with a drink, the waggling dreadlocks on her head that reminded Martin of the fibre optic lamp his grandparents had in their sitting room during the seventies. Was that a tattoo of a skull she had on her ankle beneath all those silver chains? She had a compass badly sketched in blue ink onto her bicep.

All in all, Cindy Daniels looked as though she might be more at home sitting halfway up an ancient oak tree, protesting against a bypass, than in that smart London restaurant. Her dress appeared to have been stitched together from the remains of half a dozen petticoats. She was as far removed from Martin's usual type as Swampy from Julian Clary. And yet . . .

There was definitely something about her.

'What are you having?' the waiter asked them both. He was grinning at Cindy as though he knew who she was. He wasn't bothered by her nose-ring.

'A negroni,' she said smoothly, swivelling back to face Martin on her bar stool. 'Do you need me to tell you how to make that?' she added over her shoulder when the waiter made no move towards the bottles on his shelf.

Martin was quietly impressed as Cindy rattled off the perfect cocktail recipe. The girl had a certain style.

'So,' she growled. 'I hope you're hungry.'

Martin stuck a finger into his collar to loosen it. He had a feeling that he was on her menu that night.

Lou was the last to be met by her date for the evening. By half past eight, she was actually beginning to think the unthinkable. She had been stood up. Stood up by someone who had never even met her and had time to get bored – the ultimate insult. Reflected in the glass behind the bar, she could see Ruby and Martin already at their respective tables, reading the menus, choosing their meals. She was starting to feel pretty hungry herself and the bowl of nuts in front of her, that the waiter kept refreshing, was hardly doing the job.

'Another one of those?' he asked, pausing in the act of polishing a glass and nodding towards her half-finished Cosmopolitan.

'I'll get it,' said a voice behind her. 'Assuming you are Lou.'

Lou turned and smiled in recognition.

'And you are?'

'Andrew. Andrew Norton.'

Lou nodded slowly. Appraisingly. Ruby really hadn't done badly at all. Andrew was taller than Lou. Not bad-looking, if you liked that rather straight, clean-cut sort of look. The clothes he was wearing weren't super-trendy but neither was he dressed entirely by Marks and Spencer. He looked as though he knew how to look after himself. Ate enough vegetables. Did enough exercise. He was the kind of boy your mother would love.

'I'm sorry I'm late,' he added. 'Visiting my auntie in hospital. Must have lost track of the time.'

My God, thought Lou. He's exactly the kind of boy my mother would love.

Andrew interrupted Lou's silent summing-up. 'Must say you don't look quite how I remember.'

'I'm sorry?' said Lou. How he 'remembered'? 'Have we met before?' she asked.

'Not exactly,' he said.

Lou looked at him uncomprehendingly.

'You really don't remember me at all?'

'No,' she admitted. 'I'm afraid I don't.'

'I look different above ground?' he quipped.

'You must do,' said Lou. 'Well. Shall we eat?' she suggested.

As they crossed the restaurant, Ruby made inquiring eyes over the top of her menu.

'One in seven million chance we would get together again,' Andrew was saying.

And then Lou realised.

'Talk about a lucky break.'

Ruby must have placed a Once Seen in *Time Out* and thought that this man, this person Lou had never seen before in her life, was her stranger on the train.

15

'I've got to come clean,' said Andrew to Lou. 'I answered your ad for a dare. My mate and I have got this stupid game going. Every week we dare each other to do something different. Last week I had to go to work with my underpants on over the top of my trousers.'

Oh, God, thought Lou. He was probably wearing Bart Simpson boxer shorts.

'Joke,' he said, looking suitably embarrassed. 'I really had to persuade a car dealer to let me test-drive a Ferrari. This week I had to answer a Once Seen ad and pretend I was the guy it referred to. I didn't expect to end up on a date because of it. I just had to try to convince the person who placed the ad that I was the man they fancied. I didn't think it would work but it was incredibly easy. I had some idea of what you looked like from the ad itself and then I just ad-libbed the bit about your beautiful eyes.'

'Well, you pulled it off,' said Lou.

'You really do have beautiful eyes though,' said Andrew.

Lou lowered her beautiful eyes to the tablecloth and shook her head in playful disapproval.

'I hope you don't mind too much,' Andrew said somewhat shyly this time. 'I know I'm probably not anything like the person you hoped I'd be but I'd be lying if I said I don't think we're going to have a really good evening. And I'd like to see you again. If you don't hate me for wasting your time.'

'I don't hate you,' said Lou. 'Why would I?'

'Perhaps you want to carry on looking for your real Prince Charming though?'

'My Cinderella,' corrected Lou. 'Prince Charming was the one who did the search. Remember?'

'Right. Of course. Well, do you want to carry on searching?' He gave her a smile that would have persuaded any red-blooded girl otherwise.

Lou ran her finger contemplatively around the top of her wine glass. 'No. I don't think so. There really isn't much point. The chances of me meeting the person I really saw on the tube that morning are far slimmer than you could possibly imagine.'

'But he might have written,' said Andrew. 'And you might not have believed it was him because I already had you convinced it was me.'

'Oh no. I would have known,' said Lou. 'You see, the thing is, Andrew, I haven't exactly been straight with you either. I didn't see any of the replies to my ad. My friend Ruby was supposed to choose a date for me,' Lou nodded in the direction of Ruby's table.

'That's your friend Ruby? Here in the restaurant?'

'Yes. But, ssssh! Don't attract her attention. She's on a date too. We had a dare of our own,' Lou explained. 'To find new lovers through placing personal ads. Me, Ruby and our other friend Martin.'

'Is he here?'

'Over by the kitchen door, sitting with the girl with dreadlocks.'

Andrew couldn't help gawping in the direction of Martin's date.

'All three of us were in on a pact. I wrote an ad for Martin, Martin wrote an ad for Ruby and Ruby must have written that Once Seen ad for me. Very clever. I told her I'd seen someone I fancied on the Northern Line and she tried to get us back together. I didn't expect her to think of something as subtle as that. The idea was that we would pick out the best match for each other from the suckers that applied to our personals and, hey presto, here we are tonight, seeing how well we did for one another.'

Andrew grinned. 'So why did you pick that thing she's sitting with this evening. Revenge?'

Lou cast a worried glance over her shoulder at Ruby.

'Martin was the one who picked him,' she said in her own defence. 'God, I hope he's got a sparkling personality.'

Ruby was ready to scream. When they made their lonely hearts pact, Lou and Martin had promised they would not deliberately choose the worst possible date they could find for her. They had sworn upon their respective lives. They were supposed to be beyond those college-style pranks now, where the person who locked tongues with the worst geek in the room would get a free kebab on the way home courtesy of the losers.

The lonely heart experiment was more serious than that. Ruby had pinned all her hopes on her friends' ability to see what she couldn't. To see what was right for her where she might be blinkered by such superficial concerns as lust and, she had to admit, desperation. She understood that she might not immediately fancy the person who would ultimately turn out to be her soul mate but personality could definitely not be considered a superficial concern. And it was hardly a superficial matter that her date that evening did not appear to have any at all. Add to that the fact that the shape of his head suggested a long-drawn-out forceps delivery.

If Robin was meant to be Ruby's Prince Charming, then he was clearly still in frog form. He didn't have serial killer hair but that was only because of the size of his bald patch. When the waiter asked whether he might relieve them of their jackets, Robin had flatly refused to be parted from his sensible padded parka, though he must have been getting sautéed inside it. Beneath the parka, Robin wore a pale brown suit and a white shirt so thin Ruby could see his chest hairs straight through it. When the waiter brought over the menus, Robin reached into his Sainsbury's 'Bag For Life' and brought out a pair of glasses held together with sticky tape.

Once they'd ordered their meals, Robin had nothing whatsoever to say to her, beyond complaining that the restaurant was awfully pricey. She had tried just about every conversational gambit going to get the evening swinging. From 'nice weather we've been having lately' to 'have you ever indulged in train-spotting?' Strangely enough, he hadn't.

And then the food arrived. The young waiter had looked nervous all the way across the floor, as he tried to juggle two hot plates and a bread basket. By the time he got to the table, a débâcle was almost inevitable. The waiter just about managed to set the plates down without an accident, but in doing so, he knocked the olive oil bottle flying. It bounced as if made of rubber on the Italian marble floor, spraying both Ruby and her monosyllabic date with expensive extra virgin.

'It's an old dress,' said Ruby, as dismissively as she could manage while she dabbed at the mess on her skirt.

'I thought so,' said Robin.

Ruby wasn't sure she'd heard right. The waiter glared on her behalf.

Robin had managed to escape the worst of the shower. At least that's what he thought. He tucked straight into his fish, cutting and eating as if he expected the plate to be whipped away again at any moment. He didn't look up from his plate until he was almost finished, giving Ruby plenty of time to take in the single droplet of olive oil that was oozing slowly across Robin's shiny head.

Would it be polite to tell him? Ruby wondered. The dollop had morphed from the shape of the Isle of Wight into Australia. Or was it more polite to pretend she hadn't noticed? Australia quickly became Italy as the oil headed for Robin's thick eyebrows. Perhaps she should just reach across the table and give his pate a quick polish with her napkin?

'I'm looking for a long-term relationship,' said Robin, when he finally finished eating. By that time, Ruby was just looking for the fastest way out.

A nine o'clock debrief in the ladies' room had been decided in advance. Martin had been invited too, but given the venue and the fact that he seemed to have come off pretty well in the blind date shuffle, the girls weren't surprised when he didn't get up and follow them at the appointed hour.

Ruby was there on the dot, like a greyhound from a trap.

She sat on the vanity bench by the mirrors and sparked up a cigarette while she waited for Lou to join her. She had been completely stuffed. She had given Robin every chance to redeem an appalling first impression but it was rapidly becoming clear that Robin's quirky dress sense was one of his more charming attributes. She recalled with a shudder how he had blown his nose on his napkin and then smoothed it back over his lap. By the time Lou made her own subtle getaway, Ruby was dragging on her cigarette like a death-row prisoner, sizing up the windows as a possible means of escape.

Lou didn't need to ask how Ruby's evening was progressing.

'We chose the wrong one, didn't we?'

Ruby nodded and exhaled a smoke circle.

'Is it just the way he looks?' Lou asked.

'You know I'm not lookist,' Ruby began. 'But when I have been out with men who are less than conventionally handsome in the past, Lou, it is because they have some other, definable quality that makes up for the fact that they must have hit every branch on the ugly tree before they hit the ground.'

'So, I take it he's not funny either?'

'Are we talking funny *ha-ha* or funny *peculiar*?' Ruby asked.

'I thought he'd be funny. The letter he wrote was really great. That's what swung it. I was sure you'd hit it off.'

'Perhaps I would have hit it off with the friend of his who actually wrote the letter.'

'He didn't write the letter himself?'

'No. Just like Cyrano de Bergerac,' Ruby laughed bitterly. 'Or *Cyril De Whatsit*, as dear Robin would say. Except that this time it's the ugly one who doesn't have any brains either and now I'm having dinner with him.'

Lou couldn't help smiling. 'Oh Rubes, I'm sorry. Still, at least you should get a free dinner for your pains.'

'I don't think so,' said Ruby.

'But he works in the City,' said Lou. The implication being that he was rolling in filthy lucre.

'As third in command at a *key-cutting* shop next door to Merrill Lynch,' Ruby told her.

Lou could only grimace.

'And as if that isn't bad enough, as I was getting up to go to the bathroom, he asked me if I wouldn't mind pinching a loo roll for him on the way back, seeing as I've got such a big handbag. He hasn't bought a loo roll in years, apparently. Or sugar. Or pepper. Or butter. Or salt. Why bother when restaurants have such handy, ready-packaged supplies?'

'Oh, God!' Lou spluttered. 'You're joking?'

'I only wish I were. When the waiter came round with the bread, he took one piece for his side plate and wrapped two more in a napkin for later.'

'Ruby, you're lying,' Lou snorted into her hand.

'I'm not. He'll be asking me to put the silver in my bag on the way out,' Ruby continued. 'Well,' she said, unhooking a half-finished loo roll from a holder in one of the cubicles. 'He can have his bloody loo roll but he needn't expect any other favours from me tonight.'

'You're not really going to steal a loo roll for him, are you?'

'Poor boy is going to need something to cry into when I leave him to pick up the bill on his key-cutting wages.'

'Attagirl,' said Lou. 'Better order some nice Beaumes De Venise with your pudding.'

'I think I will,' said Ruby resolutely as she stuffed the loo roll into her handbag. 'But how are you getting on? Is he?'

'No,' Lou sighed. 'He's not the one.'

'But . . .'

'He convinced you? I know. I can see why. But he answered for a dare. Said he just ad-libbed about my beautiful eyes in his letter. Clever of you though. Placing a Once Seen instead of an ordinary personal. If it had worked . . .' Lou was momentarily wistful.

'Would have been great. I can't believe the bugger conned me.'

'Doesn't matter. He's nice. Really nice.'

'That's not a very passionate adjective,' Ruby pointed out.

'Well, to be honest, I thought he was an idiot at first but I think I underestimated him. He's got GSOH.'

'Great shag, own helicopter?' quipped Ruby.

'If only. No, he's got a great sense of humour. We're having a surprisingly good time.'

'Perhaps I'll come and join you guys for pudding,' said Ruby. 'Because right now, I'd settle for good shoes, own hair. Even ghastly shoes and odd hair. I can't believe I've got to go back out there and face the dweeb.'

'You could escape through the bathroom window,' Lou suggested.

'Iron bars on the outside. Already checked. Are you going to want to stay for ages?' she pleaded.

'I'll make it an early one,' said Lou.

'Half nine,' Ruby bargained.

'It's nearly quarter past now. Nine forty-five.'

'Done,' said Ruby. 'Do you think we ought to get a message to Martin too? In case he wants to leave with us.'

'He'll see us going,' Lou decided. 'And if he wants to wind up his evening he can and meet us at home. I think he's big and ugly enough to get to the tube without being ravished by that little thing I set him up with.'

'Short, isn't she?' Ruby agreed. 'But don't think that means she isn't dangerous. I'm not sure I like the look of her.'

'Perhaps she's got little pointy teeth!' Lou replied with glee.

'She's not really Martin's type,' Ruby added authoritatively.

'Exactly. You know she's studying for a Master's.'

'Christ, she'll see straight through him!' Ruby joked.

'Do you think so? I've known some pretty intelligent women who were momentarily stunned by his boyish good looks.'

'Boyish good looks!' Ruby scoffed.

'Yeah,' said Lou slyly. 'A perfectly sane woman having a weak moment might think our friend Martin something of a catch.'

'What? A sane woman like Webecca?'

'She was never sane.'

'Or Gillian?'

'I must say, I was surprised at that one. Is the restraining order still in place?'

Gillian the personal assistant and sometime 'model' had gone about Martin's car with a can-opener.

'I think they'll be done by nine-thirty,' Ruby pronounced. 'Shortly after he tells her the story about the friend of a friend whose boyfriend made her suck on a courgette while they had anal sex.'

'That is *not* a first date story,' said Lou.

'It is if you're with Martin,' Ruby reminded her.

'I wonder who that girl was?' Lou mused.

'I don't know. But I've heard that story from at least four independent sources now. That girl certainly has a lot of friends.'

'OK,' said Lou. 'We better get back out there. Don't want Robin to rumble us.'

'I hardly care,' sniffed Ruby. 'In fact, I'm rather hoping he's already scarpered. I'd almost be happy to pick up the tab if it meant I didn't have to watch him pick at his teeth again.'

They peered out into the restaurant.

Andrew was studying the pudding menu intently. Robin was sitting at his table, reading the alcohol content on the bottle of Chardonnay, while extracting detritus from between his gappy yellow molars with his fingernails.

'Nine forty-five,' muttered Ruby. 'Don't forget.'

They touched knuckles together like fighters going back into the ring.

'You were gone a long time,' said Robin when Ruby sat back down.

'Diarrhoea,' she replied with a smile. 'Almost didn't make it.'

Why on earth had she thought that she might be able to find a man to make Flett jealous from a personal ad?

Ruby was right about one thing though. Martin and his date were ready to leave the restaurant by half past nine. But not because Martin had managed to scare Cindy away with his repertoire of appalling sex-related anecdotes. Not that he hadn't told any of them, either. Martin claimed that whenever he found himself in a one-to-one situation with an attractive, half-intelligent girl, he developed a very sophisticated and specific form of Tourette's Syndrome, whereby, instead of swearing and spitting at random, he would find himself utterly unable to suppress a story involving orifices and vegetables.

Cindy, that evening's date, had loved the courgette story.

'The funny thing is,' said Martin, thrilled at her response, 'the bit that really upsets people is the courgette.'

'Yes,' Cindy agreed. 'Strange choice. But not so strange when you think about it. I mean, if he'd asked her to bite down on a banana while he took her from behind, her teeth would have gone straight through at the first thrust. Too soft. Could have bitten her tongue off.'

'Er, yes,' said Martin, resisting an urge to cover his genitals. 'Sounds as if you've given the fruit and veg thing quite some thought.'

'Absolutely.' Cindy grinned a lazy feline grin and ran her fingertip around the rim of her wine glass until it sang.

'More wine,' Martin offered eagerly. They were onto their second bottle.

'Not here,' she murmured. 'Let's go somewhere a little,' she glanced about her, 'darker.'

'Darker? Yes. Like a nightclub, you mean? OK. I'll just get the bill.'

'You do that,' said Cindy. 'I shall be powdering my nose in the bathroom.'

She sauntered in the direction of the ladies'. Martin watched her go, transfixed by the sight of her black leather skirt clinging tightly to her gently curved buttocks. The way she swung her handbag as she walked was reminiscent of the flicking of a cat's tail. Cindy definitely wanted to play. As soon as she let the ladies' room door swing shut behind her, Martin did a furious thumbs-up for the benefit of Lou and Ruby. Both were pretending not to know him, of course. But the waiter noticed and gave him a curious look.

Martin glanced at his reflection in one of the restaurant's ubiquitous mirrors and decided that he wouldn't be going straight home after coffee that night. He looked pretty damn hot. What woman could have resisted him? By the time Cindy came back from the bathroom, bright-eyed and delicately wiping away the powdery foundation that had settled in the creases around her nose (she said), Martin had already paid the bill and ordered Cindy's coat.

'You paid!' Cindy purred. 'Oh, you good boy. You know what good boys deserve, don't you?'

'Tell me,' said Martin eagerly, leaping to grab Cindy's fake fur jacket from the waiter so that he could help her into it himself.

'Fondling,' Cindy whispered hotly. 'Every good boy deserves fondling. Didn't you do that rhyme at school?'

'Not quite like that,' said Martin.

'Then we are going to have to make up for some serious gaps in your education.'

Martin and Cindy were out of the restaurant by twenty past nine. By that point, Ruby was scowling at a skimpy *crème brûlée*, while Robin regaled her with a list of household items currently on special offer at KwikSave.

Lou had warned Andrew of the date's impending curtailment. He had called for the bill and gallantly insisted on paying it. A courtesy that Lou said she would accept only if she could do the honours next time.

'Of course,' said Andrew. 'It's my way of making sure that there is a next time.'

It was a very different story over at Ruby's table. When the bill finally arrived, Robin too snatched it up manfully. But not because he was intending to stick it all on his credit card. Oh no.

'I had the smoked salmon to start with and you had the deep fried Camembert with cranberry sauce. Then I had the chicken and you had the steak with frites. Your meal already comes to four pounds more than mine and that's before we've taken into consideration the fact that you had dessert and I didn't.'

'You ate half of it!' Ruby pointed out. In fact he had eaten most of it. As soon as she let go of her spoon for a second, Robin had snatched the *crème brûlée* from in front of her and practically licked the little bowl clean.

'But you had the broccoli that I didn't want.'

Robin split the bill item by item and seemed to be perfectly unfazed when the head waiter came across to find out how much should be put on each card. 'Thirty-one pounds seventy on this one and forty-three pounds on the other,' he said chirpily. Ruby, on the other hand, was mortified when she dug into her bag to find her purse as the waiter returned with their credit card slips, and accidentally sent the loo roll falling to the floor and unravelling across the tasteful wooden floor like a streamer advertising her cheapness.

'There's the loo roll *you* asked for,' she hissed at Robin, as loudly as she dared. But not even the dumb-struck waiter heard her. She was even too embarrassed to shift the embarrassment effectively.

'Thanks very much,' Robin bent down to roll the paper up.

The waiter placed their signed receipts back on the table with a pitiful glance in Ruby's direction.

'Have you got a pound or two? For the tip?' Robin asked when he surfaced from his loo roll hunting mission.

Ruby pulled out a fiver and placed it on the silver dish with an angry flourish.

'That's a bit much, isn't it?' Robin commented.

'Actually, Robin,' Ruby said steadily. 'It's only half as much as I want to leave. I thought you were going to match me.'

The waiter hovered expectantly.

'No,' said Robin. 'I don't think so. That's more than five per cent as it is. Coat please,' he barked at the waiter.

Ruby was lost for words. She just let her mouth drop open and stared at the cheapest man on earth. Even as they waited for their coats, he was transferring sugar sachets from the sugar bowl into his trouser pockets.

'Well, Ruby. It's been nice,' he said.

She was too shocked to disagree with him.

'But I don't think there's any reason why we should do this again.'

'What?' Ruby asked. Was he asking her for another date?

He wasn't. 'I mean, you seem all right and all that,' he continued. 'But I don't think you're really what I'm looking for. To be honest, I was expecting someone younger with longer hair. I'd take you for a drink somewhere to show there's no hard feelings, but it's getting rather late.'

Ruby's jaw hit the table this time.

'It's been lovely,' said Robin, retrieving the parka he'd only relinquished after the olive oil incident. And with that, he was gone, shuffling out into the night with his Sainsbury's 'Bag For Life' still clutched in one hand.

'Long-term boyfriend?' the waiter asked, as he helped Ruby on with her coat.

'Blind date,' admitted Ruby.

'Thank God for that. You had a lucky escape, girl. Here, you keep this,' he handed her back her fiver. 'Have a brandy or something on me. You deserve one.'

Safely outside the restaurant, Ruby sparked up another cigarette and headed for the tube station. Lou was already there, actually hanging on the arm of her date as though they'd known each other and perhaps even been together for years. They were laughing about something as Ruby drew nearer.

'Ruby, this is Andrew,' Lou grinned.

'I'm *not* the guy she fell in love with on the tube,' said

Andrew apologetically, 'but I'm trying my best to make up for it.'

'He's been doing a pretty good job so far,' Lou told her.

'Nice to meet you,' said Ruby, without taking the fag from her mouth. 'I'm sorry if you had to cut your evening short because of me. But if Lou had made sure that I didn't end up with a dork . . .' she spat.

'That's OK. Better to be left wanting more,' said Andrew with a longing look in Lou's direction.

Was Lou blushing in return? Ruby wondered. Andrew was pretty damn gorgeous for the kind of sucker who answered personal ads for a dare. Lucky cow! Wasn't it just Sod's Law?

'Martin left early,' Ruby observed.

'We noticed,' said Lou. Already using the royal 'we'! 'Wonder if that poor girl knows what she's letting herself in for?'

'Bit of an animal, your friend Martin?' Andrew asked Ruby.

'Well, yes. Though the only one that springs to my mind is a pig,' said Ruby.

'You sound almost jealous,' Andrew joked.

'Don't be ridiculous. I extend the dear lady he's taking home tonight my deepest sympathies,' Ruby sighed. 'You ready to go, Lou?'

'I guess this is goodbye,' said Andrew, frowning sadly. He lifted Lou's hand to his lips and kissed her lightly. 'I'll give you a call then?' he asked.

'Yeah,' said Lou. 'That would be nice.'

'Bloody great,' grumbled Ruby as they descended into the station. 'I'm the one who actually *needs* a boyfriend and you're the one who ends up with the gorgeous man hanging on your every word.'

'You're not seeing Robin again then?' joked Lou.

'He told me he wants someone younger. I've never been so humiliated in my life.'

'Not even when Flett sent the e-mail?'

Ruby grimaced.

'Brandy at my place?' Lou suggested.

'With a chaser of straight arsenic,' Ruby replied.

16

Cindy took Martin to a private drinking club in Soho. From the outside, it didn't look anything special. A plain black door opened off the street. There was nothing to suggest that it was anything other than another scruffy bed-sit flat whence prostitutes or drug-dealers plied their trade. In fact, next to the buzzer for the club itself some enterprising pimp had stuck a card advertising London's newest 'Brazilian Beauty' with her specialist massage skills.

Inside, however, the club was something else. It was decked out like a harem; the walls were dotted with brass mirrors and hung with bright swathes of silk that gave the impression of a sumptuous tent. There were no proper seats. Instead, the guests (who were admitted only after a fierce grilling from a maître d' dressed like a Mafia don with the incongruous addition of a fez) reclined on cushions around low tables littered with shot glasses and hookah pipes and lines of fine white powder that definitely hadn't been missed by a careless cleaner.

'Cindy!'

As Martin and Cindy walked through the room, almost every man there greeted Martin's date by her name. The girls were less friendly, but Martin guessed that could be attributed to jealousy. Despite his initial misgivings about her distinct eco-warrior style, he had decided that Cindy was very attractive. A seven out of ten, in fact. That was very good on Martin's scale. She would have been a nine if she hadn't been quite so short.

'Sit down here,' said Cindy, collapsing into a pile of cushions and dragging Martin down almost on top of her. Immediately she had hauled herself into a semi-upright position, Cindy made a grab for a sinister-looking hookah pipe on a nearby table and took a long, deep drag.

'What's in there?' Martin asked.

'What do you think?' Cindy smiled. 'The owner has an arrangement with the local plod.'

By this time, back at Lou's flat, the girls were sipping cocoa. After half an eggcup full of specially bought post-mortem brandy, Ruby had decided that it wasn't worth adding to her list of woes with a monumental hangover.

From time to time, she glanced up from yet another viewing of *Shakespeare in Love* to the clock in the corner of Lou's sitting room. It was a grandfather clock, much too big and grand for Lou's top floor conversion that had probably once been a maid's room. But Lou had fallen in love with it when she saw the clock in pieces at Camden Market and for about three days in every month it seemed to keep reasonable time.

'Is that right today?' Ruby asked her.

'Right as it ever is,' Lou replied.

'It's nearly midnight,' Ruby observed. 'Do you think he's coming back tonight?'

Lou shook her head. 'Obviously not. He must be doing well,' she said.

'Are you sure?' Ruby asked. 'I mean, what if he's not doing well? What if she's abducted him?'

'Ruby, that girl was barely bigger than a Barbie doll. He'll be fine. In fact, I bet he's having a whale of a time.'

Ruby nodded into her steaming cocoa.

'I still wish he'd call and let us know that he's alright,' she said with a frown.

'He's alright,' Lou insisted. 'Stop acting like his mother.'

'I'm not.'

'Are you jealous?' Lou teased.

'Get lost. Why would I be jealous of her?'

'Not her. I meant jealous of Martin,' Lou corrected. 'Because he ended up with a decent date and you didn't.'

'He might be having a terrible time,' Ruby reasoned.

'Looked like they were getting on pretty well to me. Instant attraction I'd say.'

'No,' said Ruby. 'He wouldn't go for that kind of girl . . . Would he?'

'I mean, why did you answer an ad?' Martin asked Cindy. 'You don't look like the kind of girl who would have trouble getting a boyfriend.'

'I don't,' Cindy assured him. 'But sometimes it's just too easy, yeah? Know what I mean?'

Martin wished he did.

'For example,' Cindy continued. 'Pick out any attractive man in this room. Anyone at all. And I've probably already had him.'

'Right,' Martin blanched. Perhaps *that* explained why none of the girls had been too friendly.

'But they're all the same,' Cindy yawned. 'They all think they're *so* bohemian and different with their art galleries and their acting projects and their exotic travel plans. Scratch the surface and they're all the same beneath. Trustafarians the lot of them.'

'Oh,' said Martin.

'Bankrolled by their mummies and daddies. I thought it would be more unusual to go out with someone *ordinary*,' said Cindy, rubbing her fingers over the knot at the top of Martin's tie. 'I thought, how about going for someone who doesn't pretend to have a creative bone in his body? Someone who has to advertise for a date because he's so boring? Someone who'll be so bloody grateful to have met me that he'll simply have to show me a damn good time.'

'I see,' said Martin stiffly. In more ways than one. Cindy's hand had slipped nonchalantly from his collar to his crotch. Not a creative bone in his body, eh? That was harsh. But there was something about the way Cindy gazed deep into his eyes as she spoke to him that made the uncharitable words seem sweeter. Something about the way she lolled on the cushions with the top three buttons of her shirt undone to show a bright orange satin bra . . . An orange bra!

'Not that you're anything like I expected, Martin. To be honest, when I walked into the restaurant tonight, I wondered whether I was going to be able to go through with it. As I was arriving, I saw a weird-looking guy walk in ahead of me, carrying a plastic bag. I thought that was my date and nearly doubled back.'

Martin felt a twinge of guilt when he realised that

Cindy was describing the man he had so carelessly picked out for Ruby.

'So when I saw you, I was pleasantly surprised. You're not bad-looking, Martin. Not bad at all.'

'You say the nicest things,' said Martin.

'I can do the nicest things,' said Cindy. 'Shall we get a cab?'

Outside on the street moments later, Martin hailed a black cab while Cindy twined herself around his body like a creeper. When a cab finally stopped for them, Cindy slid into the back seat, legs wide open, grabbed Martin by the collar again and pulled him in after her. It had occurred to Martin that the evening wasn't yet over, but he was still slightly taken aback when Cindy gave the taxi-driver her address before Martin had a chance to ask, 'Your place or mine.'

'My place,' she growled at him, then moved swiftly back to the business of sticking her slippery tongue down his throat.

'I-nnnnnnngh!' said Martin.

He didn't have a chance to get a word out all the way back to Cindy's house. She had her hand down the front of his trousers while he searched for the right change to give the taxi-driver, and by the time they reached the top of the stairs that led to the door of Cindy's rather grand-looking house near Regent's Park, she had unhooked his belt and was brandishing it like a whip across his buttocks, corralling him into the house like some poor calf to the rodeo.

The front door was still open when Martin's trousers finally dropped to the floor.

'Cindy!' he squeaked.

She pushed the door shut with a faintly balletic karate kick.

'Twelve-thirty,' muttered Ruby. 'How difficult would it be for him to text us?'

'He's having too much fun,' Lou sighed.

'At this very minute he could be bound and gagged and heading for some terrible humiliation!'

Lou almost snorted cocoa out through her nose at the thought of it.

'That sounds like Martin's idea of a *good* time,' she said smiling.

'I want to tie you up,' Cindy panted as she dragged him into her bedroom. 'Do you trust me?'

Martin nodded. It seemed the only appropriate response.

'There's nothing to tie you up to in here,' she said, as she continued to undress him. 'I've been waiting for a new bed to be delivered. One with a nice iron headboard. But there's been some sort of foul-up at the warehouse. Never order anything off the Internet, I say.'

'Right,' said Martin. He was a little distracted by her hand upon his penis.

'So for now,' Cindy continued. 'I'm afraid we'll have to improvise.'

Still holding Martin's family jewels with one hand, Cindy leaned over backwards with a yoga expert's grace, opened a drawer in her crowded bedside table and brought out a long red silk scarf. Martin smiled what he hoped was a devilish grin. He must have done something good in a past life after all. All his fantasies were coming true at once. A dominant woman. Silk scarves. Bondage. It was a cliché perhaps but a bloody fantastic one.

Cindy bound the red scarf lightly around Martin's eyes. Now this was what he called a really good blind date, he thought as her tongue flickered lightly over his nipples.

'Handcuffs,' she said suddenly.

'Handcuffs?'

'Yes. You didn't think I was just going to use scarves on you, did you?'

'Well, actually, I. . . .' He did.

'But they're so easy to escape from, you naughty boy. Where's the fun in that?'

Martin pulled the blindfold away from his eyes to see whether she was joking. Evidently not. She was already dangling a pair of pretty heavy-duty cuffs from her delicate manicured fingers.

'Got them from a real policeman,' she said with a grin.

'I see,' said Martin.

'Wouldn't believe what I had to do for them.'

'Don't tell me,' said Martin.

Handcuffs were an entirely different proposition from silk scarves. Entirely different. It took a great deal more trust to allow someone to tie you up using something from which there was little hope of escaping until your captor decided that they wanted to let you go. Somewhere in Martin's cerebral cortex, a tiny voice of concern squeaked briefly before the excited howling of his brain stem drowned it out.

'Should you really be doing this?' asked the faint murmur of reason.

'Sex, sex, sex,' grunted the brain stem. 'Sex with a woman. Sex with a woman is being offered to you on a great big silver platter!' Didn't matter how weird, to Martin's prehistoric animal brain.

But Cindy seemed normal enough anyway, didn't she? She had a Snoopy pyjama case on her bed, for heaven's sake. How dangerous could a woman who had a Snoopy pyjama case possibly be?

'I don't want you to escape before I've had my wicked way with you,' she said, clamping the handcuffs around one of Martin's wrists. She licked her full red lips and looked up at him through her thick black lashes like Princess Diana gone bad.

'Oh, go on!' yelled Martin's brain stem. 'She wants you!!!!'

'OK then,' said Martin. He held out his other wrist obediently.

'Oh no,' said Cindy. 'We need to cuff you *to* something.'

'I thought you said there wasn't anything to tie me to in here.'

'There isn't. We'll have to go into the bathroom.'

'The bathroom?'

'Towel rail,' explained Cindy. 'I could tie you to that.'

Martin followed her nervously into the hallway. She was buck-naked but for the tattoo of a plump red devil on her taut right buttock and didn't seem to care who saw. Martin held his boxer shorts nervously across his crotch for modesty's sake. 'Er, are you sure we should go into the bathroom?' he asked. 'What if one of your housemates wants to use the loo in the night? You do have housemates, don't you?'

The house was way too big for one girl. Besides which, Martin had seen a pair of wellies in the hall made for a pair of feet quite a bit larger than Cindy's.

'Relax. I don't have housemates,' Cindy assured him.

But the wellies?

'I live with my parents.'

'Parents!'

Martin's erection drooped as though it had been shot at.

'Chill out, Martin. They're cool. They don't mind me having people here. And they won't be back until tomorrow morning in any case. They're at the country house this weekend.'

'Great. Er, Cindy. Look. I've got to ask this. How old are you exactly?'

Cindy didn't really look as though she had been near a school in a very long time, but young girls and make-up. . . . It was almost impossible to tell a thirteen-year-old from a thirty-something these days. Martin didn't want to find himself in a pair of Metropolitan Police handcuffs for real!

'I'm twenty-seven,' said Cindy flatly.

Martin tried not to look too relieved.

'Come on.'

Cindy opened a door onto a vast bathroom. In the centre of the shining marble floor stood one of those double-ended Victorian bathtubs that could have accommodated a rugby team. When Martin made that observation, Cindy laughed, 'I already have.'

At one end of the bathtub, a contraption that looked like a gigantic birdcage turned out to be a shower.

'Spurts from all sides,' Cindy explained. 'Exactly how I like it.'

'This is amazing,' breathed Martin, taking in the full-size Roman statue of Venus that stood in the corner of the room, sans head, with a bale of towels draped over her outstretched arm. The room was lit by chandelier. It couldn't have been more different from the bathroom in Martin's flat with tiling so dirty Martin had assumed it was supposed to be yellow until Ruby bought him a canister of foaming, rinse-off Jif.

'This is the guest bathroom,' said Cindy. 'Step in.'

'What?' Martin was busy estimating the value of the oil painting of Florence above the fireplace. How rich must Cindy's parents be?

'Step into the bath,' Cindy told him. 'Stand under the shower.'

Martin did as he was told. Smiling a smouldering smile, Cindy relieved him off his pants and got him to link his hands behind his back around the central pipe of the shower contraption. He felt the cold handcuffs go on, just a little tight around his big wrists. When she had locked the cuffs shut, Cindy kissed Martin's fingers, sucking them in what he hoped was a small hint of pleasures yet to come. But she didn't get into the bath with him. Not yet.

'I've got to put some music on,' she told him.

'We won't be able to hear it from here, will we?' Martin asked. He was eager to get on with the action.

'Yes, we will,' said Cindy, as though it were obvious. 'There are speakers in the bathroom.'

Martin tried to locate them while Cindy went to choose a CD. She hadn't put his blindfold back on yet. Christ, her parents must be loaded, he thought. The house was incredible. Stuffed with antiques. A guest bathroom the size of a small swimming pool. And speakers above the loo were the ultimate in luxury. A surround sound experience while taking a . . .

Speakers that were suddenly playing Take That?

17

It was gone one o'clock. Lou had retired to bed, wanting to be up early to work on a manuscript next morning. Ruby lay awake on the lumpy sofa in the sitting room and stared at a cobweb hanging from the Designers' Guild lampshade. Still no word from Martin to let them know how his evening had gone. Lou was probably right that Martin wasn't in any danger from the pom-pom-headed midget she had set him up with, but Ruby still wished that he were back at Lou's house as promised to reassure her that he hadn't met the love of his life . . .

What?

Ruby caught her own mental meanderings and brought herself up short. *She didn't want Cindy to be the love of Martin's life?* Why would that be such a *bad* thing anyway? Ruby hoped that she wasn't becoming one of those women who thought that the whole world should be unhappy and loveless just because she was. She knew how unattractive that kind of anger could be. Liz Hale had been the scourge of young lovers for years, tutting loudly whenever she passed anyone indulging in a public display of affection and once making an office junior at Hollingworth cry when she suggested that said junior's new boyfriend had sent her flowers because he was shagging someone else.

Ruby would not allow herself to become a modern-day

Miss Havisham, wishing unhappy endings to every love affair. But . . . The awful thing was, she admitted to herself, she rather *preferred* it when Martin was single. She couldn't help it. When he wasn't single, he would slip from the radar, disappearing from her life for weeks on end or, worse still, insist on dragging his new squeeze to every social occasion. Wednesday nights at the pub quiz, boring though they sometimes were, would be completely ruined by the presence of some simpering lovely who didn't understand Ruby's jokes.

And Martin was *different* when he had a girlfriend. On his best behaviour at first, which meant that he was ninety per cent less funny than usual. Or soppy. Sickeningly so. Ruby winced at the memory of the first time she and Lou met Leah, the 'Hermes' girl. Leah and Martin had developed a secret language that involved him growling like a wolf at her and her making a sheepish 'baa' sound in return. Cute. Not. Ruby had been very glad when that particular relationship ended.

But she knew that they couldn't carry on like this forever. Lou, Ruby and Martin. An eternal triangle without the romance. Eventually one of them would meet the love of his or her life and settle down and perhaps get married and start a family and . . . There was no way they would all be limping to the pub quiz with their Zimmer frames in the year 2050.

As Ruby looked at the photograph of herself and her two best friends at their graduation ball, which Lou kept on her mantelpiece, Ruby felt sure that her real problem was not who Martin would end up with at all. Her problem was that she feared she would be the last one left single in this game of romantic musical chairs. She pictured herself five years hence, sitting at Lou's kitchen table, the spare part at Sunday dinner, nursing a vodka tonic while Lou cooked fishfingers for her beautiful twins. She pictured herself at Martin's house, watching Cindy cook supper while Martin amused *their* beautiful twins . . .

It was all too, too depressing. Would Ruby ever find her special someone? She felt as though she had spent her entire life searching for someone who would make her whole.

What Lou and Martin didn't know was that Ruby had pored over the personal ads for years. But not the dating ones. At least not the straightforward, *man with no teeth, lives with mother, seeks twenty-something Pamela Anderson lookalike with own Porsche* type that seemed to crop up so often. The personal ads Ruby liked to read were the ones with a much more specific target. *M. Harris seeks H. Johnson. Please apply to box number 555.* That kind of thing. She'd become addicted to them as a child.

Who were these mysterious people? How had they lost each other? And why was it so important for them to get back in touch now? Reading those ads, Ruby imagined all sorts of exciting scenarios.

Michael Harris, twenty-two, was heir to a vast estate. His mother disapproved of his mad affair with lowly miner's daughter Helen Johnson, eighteen and a half, love of his life. Now the old witch, Mrs Harris Senior, is dead – cracked her head open on an over-polished floor at the castle. Michael her son is a millionaire at last. He deserted Helen to avoid being disinherited but now he wants her back. To be his wife! Will she see his ad in the newspaper? Will they ever be reunited? And if they are, will she forgive him for letting money come between them in the first place?

The romance of it all. Ruby loved the idea of illicit liaisons, arranged by notes to a box number at the back of *The Times*. Added to that was the distant but compelling possibility that one day she would see her own name in the familiar black type. 'Would anyone knowing the whereabouts of Ruby Taylor please contact box number 370 to hear something that may be to their advantage.'

It wasn't quite as unlikely as it sounded. As a baby, Ruby had been given up for adoption. She couldn't remember when her mum and dad broke the news. It was as much a fact of life to her as was her friend Mary Jeapes' conviction that she had been dropped down the chimney by a stork. No, Ruby couldn't remember the day she found out she was adopted, but she did remember becoming increasingly convinced that she must be the secret love child of Shakin' Stevens and Princess Anne.

As far as Ruby was concerned, the mundane scenario of accidental teenage pregnancy and a young girl deserted by her feckless lover, was least likely candidate for the truth. Perhaps in an attempt to make her feel doubly 'special', Ruby's mother had told her that her natural mother and father wanted to get married but couldn't, because of circumstances *beyond their control*. To an eight-year-old girl raised on Ladybird fairy tale books where the princesses' dresses outshone anything designed since by Versace, 'circumstances beyond their control' could only mean the intervention of a wicked fairy stepmother. No gymslip mum but a princess had been compelled to give Ruby away. Perhaps they even left a changeling in her place.

When they found out that they had been robbed of their real daughter, Ruby's natural parents would want to track her down. They would contact her through the personal ads, of course. And Ruby checked them religiously until she was ten. After that, her preoccupation with being a minor member of the Royal family was replaced by a crush on Adam Ant and the peculiar realisation that she had reached that stage when she no longer wanted her favourite pop-star to be her secret dad.

Ruby didn't ever tell her parents what she was doing when she rushed up to her bedroom each evening with the back pages of *The Times*. She knew even then that she didn't want to hurt their feelings. They were happy to be able to tell Ruby's teacher that she was reading a broadsheet so early. From the age of ten until she hit eighteen, however, Ruby could honestly say that she never really thought about it. Being adopted, that is. She was still feeling largely indifferent when she left home to go to university. Not so her new friend Georgie, who was doing a degree on psychology and had been reading up on the effects of adoption on identical twins.

Georgie disguised her experimental interest in Ruby's predicament as genuine concern for Ruby's future mental health. When the break-up of a particularly intense first-year relationship left Ruby feeling as though she wanted to run back to her parents in Worcestershire and hide under the bed until she hit thirty, Georgie soon managed to convince her that her 'extreme' reaction to being chucked by a spotty engineering student, whose idea of romance was taking his chewing gum out before he kissed her, was not due to the hormonal highs and lows of puppy love, but a result of deep-seated psychological trauma caused by being given away at birth.

Ruby was only too happy to agree. Arriving at university in London, fresh from school where she had been a big fish, academically speaking, in a rather stagnant pond, Ruby was somewhat bewildered to find herself surrounded by other students who not only had five grade 'A's' at A-level but a dazzling array of other talents as well. Along Ruby's corridor in the halls of residence alone, there lived a girl studying molecular physics who had once played piano at the Royal Albert Hall. Jennifer, in the room two doors down, didn't know whether to finish her degree or join one of three international modelling agencies that were clamouring to have her on their books in time for London fashion week. Allegra had already *given up* modelling to concentrate on becoming a lawyer.

And rather than being inspired by her new acquaintances, Ruby fancied herself growing dimmer in their reflected glory. From being the cleverest girl in school, she had suddenly become the dunce. The talentless, rather plain-looking dunce at that.

So, the idea that her feelings of angst were down to something as glamorous as 'anxious attachment syndrome' caused by her early 'abandonment', as diagnosed by Georgie from her first-year psychology textbook, suddenly seemed as glamorous to Ruby as the eating disorders that seemed to be obligatory for all those girls from expensive private schools. When she heard about Ruby's adoption, Jennifer let Ruby help herself to a handful of chocolate bars from the secret stash she kept beneath her bed for moments of weakness between eating celery ('burns more calories than it contains, you know') and vomiting.

'Poor you,' sighed Jennifer, as though poor Ruby had been orphaned only yesterday. 'That's just too glamorous. You could be anybody's daughter.'

Favourite at that time was Mick Jagger.

'He gets around. And you've got the lips,' Jennifer pronounced. 'I'm thinking of having mine done,' she added, quickly segueing back to herself and her own supermodel fantasies.

Georgie had reawaken the fantasy princess and, when she should have been making notes on Jane Austen, Ruby found herself pondering once more whether she could in fact be the secret love-child of someone spectacularly famous. Was her father a film or pop star? Or even a high-ranking politician? Someone who would be only too delighted to welcome his long-lost daughter back into the fold and lavish her with gifts to make up for two decades of parental neglect? Perhaps she'd get a small flat in Chelsea like the one Jennifer had been given for her eighteenth birthday? She'd never turn her back on Mum and Dad, of course – they were the ones who had been there all along – but the idea that she might be the scion of some ridiculously rich and famous family sustained Ruby through half a term that would otherwise have been spent sobbing over that gangling ex.

The reality, of course, was anything but glamorous. Born as she was in the early seventies, Ruby had never seen her original birth certificate. A change in the law shortly after her adoption meant that she could apply to see it once she reached eighteen, but before that could happen, she would have to see a social worker. Ruby didn't mind too much. Actually, the fact that she had to see a *social worker* made it seem even more exotic. Almost as good as Jennifer's Harley Street shrink.

Ruby made an application, filling out the forms that would allow her birth certificate to be released by the council under whose auspices she had been adopted and, on the appointed day, she made her way to the offices of the local social services team. Climbing the concrete stairs to the reception, Ruby wondered for the first time whether this was such a good idea after all.

She was led into a room that looked like a primary school classroom and told to wait for 'Amanda'. The magnolia walls of the stark, square room were decorated with dirty child-sized handprints and posters about drug abuse illustrated by hollow-eyed models. The brown carpet tiles were patterned with trodden-in plasticine and littered with sad-looking toys; limbless dolls and wheel-free tow-trucks. If you didn't feel depressed when you arrived, Ruby thought, then you'd begging to be sectioned by the time you left this drab, cold room.

Ruby looked for somewhere to sit while she waited but could find only those three-quarter size chairs made for five-year-olds. She leaned against the radiator instead and looked out of the window onto the citizens of the city going about their business in the crowded street below. Another ordinary Monday. In a film-noirish way, it was the perfect backdrop to what Ruby assumed would be *the* defining moment in her life. She was about to find out who she really was. From this day forward she would never need to feel alone, unhappy or confused again. She would have, she had convinced herself, a feeling of identity so strong that neither heartbreak, nor the humiliation of coming bottom in the year-end exams could hurt her again. Knowing who she really was would make Ruby Taylor' life complete.

Amanda finally arrived, ten minutes late. She was a big woman and puffing loudly from the exertion of walking up the stairs when she leaned against the doorframe and practically fell into the room. Ruby couldn't have invented a more accurate cliché of a social worker.

She was wearing what Ruby could only assume was a kaftan, cut from an exceptionally ugly piece of brown batik print cotton. Around Amanda's neck hung half a dozen strings of multi-coloured wooden beads and her over-sized, red-framed glasses on a primitive looking cord. Her hair was red too. Henna red, except for a slightly greying inch of naked roots.

As she puffed her way across to Ruby, Amanda was preceded by a waft of patchouli oil that reminded Ruby of the 'ethnic' gift shop in her home town where she bought bangles as a self-consciously serious gothic sixth-former. Everything about Amanda screamed, 'I'm a woman of the world, you know. I *understand*.' Even the tight, lopsided curve of her lips, a bona fide 'half-smile', combined with a gentle incline of the head she had for Ruby. Sympathy in advance.

'Ruby Taylor?' Amanda smiled as she read the name from the top of her case notes. 'I'm Amanda Forbes Grant.'

Ruby stuck her hand out automatically.

'No need for such formalities here,' said Amanda, brushing the gesture away. 'Would you like to sit down?'

Ruby looked about her. In here? There were no chairs that could take even one of her bum cheeks. But Amanda nodded Ruby towards one of the children's chairs, before sitting down on one herself with a dramatic swish of her kaftan that brought to mind a hot-air balloon deflating as it lands in a field. Once settled, Amanda perched with the grace of one of the hippo ballerinas in *Fantasia*, while Ruby struggled to get comfortable.

'We're waiting for some slightly bigger chairs,' said Amanda. 'Funding.'

'Oh,' said Ruby.

'Never enough of it. You OK there?' She reached out and squeezed Ruby's hand.

'I think so,' said Ruby. 'If I don't move around too much.'

'I'm not talking about the chair,' said Amanda patiently. 'Are *you* OK, Ruby? *In yourself?*'

'I'm fine,' said Ruby.

'I'm sure you think you are,' said Amanda cryptically. 'Now. Where shall we begin?'

Ruby glanced down at the flat brown envelope that Amanda had placed on the Lilliputian table between them.

'Is that it?' she asked.

'Your birth certificate? Yes it is,' said Amanda.

'Can I see it?'

'Don't you think perhaps we should discuss some of the *issues* surrounding your adoption first?' Amanda asked.

'I don't think I've got any issues,' Ruby tried.

Amanda inclined her head again. 'Of course you have.'

'But I . . . I mean, perhaps I'd be able to articulate them more clearly once I've seen the certificate?' Ruby dissembled. 'Once I've found out exactly who my parents are.'

Amanda smiled. Ruby had obviously said the magic words.

'OK. Here you are then.'

Amanda picked up the envelope and handed it over. It felt quite thin. As though there wasn't much inside it. Which was exactly the case. Ruby opened the brown manila envelope to find just one slip of paper inside, light as tissue and almost as transparent.

'Is this all there is?' Ruby asked.

Amanda nodded.

A single piece of paper.

The name on Ruby's original birth certificate was Hope. Hope. When she saw that name written in light blue ink on the salmon pink paper, Ruby was pleasantly surprised. What a pretty name, she thought. And unusual too. She had harboured a secret dread that she would discover she had been called Sarah or Sharon. Something nondescript and commonplace like that. But Hope. That was lovely. Thoroughly different. Holding the birth certificate in her hands for the first time, Ruby looked at her birth name – Hope Mary Barker – and thought she felt a little glow of warmth in the pit of her stomach.

Hope. Her mother must have loved her to give her such a pretty name. Staring at those three little words, Ruby pictured the scene in the maternity ward. The beautiful young woman holding her newborn baby. In Ruby's imagination, Geraldine Barker of Greenwich (for those were the details under 'mother') told the nurse there was no word from the celebrity father yet but they were full of 'hope' that he would melt as soon as he heard he had a beautiful baby daughter with big, juicy lips, just like his . . .

'Quite a common name for adoptees,' Amanda the social worker interrupted suddenly. 'We see a lot of girls adopted in the seventies who were called Hope or Charity. Mary too. Biblical names. Given by the nuns who ran the Children's Society for the most part.'

'Oh.'

If there had been a glow at all, it was instantly extinguished.

'There's no name for the father, I'm afraid,' Amanda continued.

Ruby had noticed. There was just a short blue line where that should have been.

'And normally there would be some other documentation, like a letter from the mother, or at least some notes giving details of her circumstances when you were born. But in your case there doesn't appear to be anything more than the actual certificate.'

'What does that mean?' Ruby asked. 'Didn't she write me a letter?'

'Possibly. Though it wasn't compulsory. Probably got lost in the filing system somewhere. The adoption section at your City Council moved offices some time in the early eighties. A whole load of records that were supposed to have been moved to the new office with them ended up in a skip instead.'

'A skip?'

'I know,' said Amanda, screwing her face up in appropriate sympathy. 'Heads really should have rolled for that. Didn't your parents ever show you anything relating to your birth parents? They would have been told a bit about them prior to the adoption. They tried to match people from similar backgrounds. Make sure they knew what they were letting themselves in for,' Amanda added, in an attempt to make a joke.

'I haven't exactly talked to Mum and Dad about this,' Ruby admitted.

'I thought you'd say that,' Amanda nodded. 'You don't want to hurt them, right? Think they wouldn't understand?'

'I sort of hoped that you would be able to tell me everything I wanted to know and I wouldn't have to bother them,' Ruby said.

'This is as much as I've found,' said Amanda, jerking her head towards the certificate. 'Obviously I wasn't around when your case was being dealt with.'

'No, of course not. So . . .'

'So that's as much as I can actually tell you.' She leaned back and folded her hands over her hot-air-balloon stomach. The chair beneath her gave an ominous creak.

'Is it possible,' Ruby began, 'that the circumstances of my birth were extra sensitive and that the documentation is being kept secret somewhere? Perhaps there was someone,' Ruby hesitated, aware that she might be about to sound like a fool, 'famous, involved?'

Amanda gave her the 'pitying smile' from her range of useful facial expressions. 'I don't think so, Ruby,' she said with a shake of her head. 'This really is all the documentation relating to you in existence.'

Ruby held the scrap of paper more carefully after that.

'But we can talk about any feelings the certificate has raised, of course. How do you feel now, Ruby?' Amanda knitted her brows together in a trademark 'serious' expression. 'Are you disappointed?'

'Well, yes. Of course I am. And no. I mean, I've got my mother's name now at least and an address . . .'

'That address is almost twenty years old,' said Ms Amanda Good News. 'And it might not even have been her real address. Unmarried girls who got themselves pregnant in the nineteen-seventies were quite often sent to mother and baby homes as soon as the bump began to show. Their families would tell everybody that the girl had gone away to do a secretarial course and once the baby had been born and safely adopted, the mother would be able to go home again.'

'So, basically, this piece of paper is worthless?'

'No, Ruby. It's not worthless. It's a piece of your history, after all.'

'It doesn't feel like my history,' said Ruby quietly. 'This piece of paper could be anyone's birth certificate. I don't feel anything much when I look at it. I thought . . . I don't know . . . I thought . . .'

'Go on, Ruby.' Amanda looked pleased at the prospect of unearthing some emotion.

'It's stupid.'

'Nothing's stupid if it's what you're really feeling. Let it come to the surface.'

'I suppose I thought I would recognise something. Recognise her name. My name, even. I thought I felt a tiny bit of recognition when I read that but then you told me that all adoptees are called something like Hope and it immediately stopped feeling special.'

'Not all adoptees,' said Amanda. 'Just the ones who were named by adoption workers rather than given a name by their birth mothers.'

'Great,' Ruby shook her head. She wondered whether Amanda had gone on a special course to enable her to whip up a cloud around any fragile silver lining. 'That makes me feel so much better.'

Amanda smiled. 'You're reacting in a very natural way, Ruby. It's perfectly usual to have mixed feelings at this point. You're excited, you're angry, you're disappointed, you're sad.'

'I'm not sad,' said Ruby defensively.

'Oh, but you are. And it's OK to cry if you want to. It's really alright. You don't have to censor your emotions around me. I've seen everything, Ruby. You don't need to protect me from your feelings. I've seen people react in ways you wouldn't believe. One man got so emotional he even tried to hit me.'

Ruby resisted the urge to say that she wasn't at all surprised.

'It's a very difficult thing you're facing here. You can try to pretend that it isn't. You can try to put a brave face on. But, it's clear that you feel abandoned all over again, dear, and eventually your true feelings will surface. May as well have them come out now, eh? While I'm here to offer you a shoulder to cry on?'

At that, Amanda opened her arms, and, without getting up from her own chair, reached out like an octopus to pull Ruby from hers so that she suddenly found herself half on the floor and half-sitting on the older woman's squishy lap.

'Hey!' Ruby squeaked.

'Let it out,' Amanda demanded, pressing Ruby's head against her ample chest. 'Come on, Ruby. Let it go. Let the tears come now. Let them come. Cry for the baby you were.'

'But I don't feel like crying,' said Ruby, trying to free herself from the overly insistent embrace. 'Please let me go.'

Amanda continued to hold her too tightly.

'Let it out, Ruby. Let it out!'

'Let me go!'

Ruby finally managed to free herself. She sprang to her feet and made sure that she was as far as the door before she turned to Amanda and said, rather undramatically given what had just passed between them, 'I'm afraid I've got to go now. Tutorial in half an hour. Thanks for the birth certificate.'

'Ruby, you know you can ask to see me any time you want.'

'Thanks,' said Ruby. 'That's very . . . er . . .' 'Reassuring' was probably the word Amanda expected but it didn't seem quite right. 'Er, thanks.'

Ruby legged it down to the safety of the High Street and didn't look back.

Back in her bedroom at the halls of residence, Ruby hid the certificate complete with brown envelope in a shoebox beneath her bed. She didn't open the envelope again for almost a decade. Amanda's parting comment had been that while Ruby claimed she didn't want to talk about her adoption now, one day she might have an *epiphany* that would provoke her to take her search further. When the epiphany didn't happen at her twenty-first birthday or her twenty-fifth, Ruby assumed that it would never happen. Then Ruby became an aunt.

Ruby's sister Lindsay was three years her senior. She was Ruby's parents' natural daughter. Complications following Lindsay's birth meant that they were unable to have any more children of their own afterwards, hence the adoption. Mrs Taylor was determined to be a mother all over again. And now Lindsay was a mother too. Baby Lauren Joanna was born on the twenty-sixth of April, a fortnight before the John Flett goodbye e-mail.

Ruby saw Lauren for the first time on the Monday after Susannah's wedding – May Bank Holiday. It was a strange experience. She had been expecting the event to be somewhat similar to the day her sister introduced the family to her insane Border collie dog, Raffles. Ruby had been thrilled to meet the little puppy. Lindsay had spent a few moments introducing Ruby to Raffles and trying to make the puppy sit to command when Ruby gave him a biscuit (he preferred her finger). Then Lindsay had left Ruby and Raffles alone in the sitting room while she went to make a cup of tea and returned with two cups of tea AND a bottle of Chardonnay.

Raffles continued to race around the coffee table as though he were missing some vital part of cortical hardwiring, while the sisters relaxed into their usual Sunday afternoon pattern, talking first about Mum and Dad. 'Which one of us is going to have them when they finally go doo-lally?' Then Lindsay's effort at DIY, which basically involved sending her husband up a ladder and shouting at him. Then Ruby's love-life. Lindsay would listen endlessly to Ruby's complaints about her love-life, claiming she was torn between jealousy that Ruby was still out there and dating so many different, exciting men and enormous relief that she wasn't, as each *different* man turned out to be a bastard in exactly the same way as the previous one.

But the arrival of Lauren Joanna was entirely different to the arrival of Raffles the mad Border collie. No chance now that Ruby would be left to admire Lauren's repertoire of tricks while Lindsay uncorked the Chardonnay in the kitchen. The sitting room was full of other visitors for a start. Lindsay's mother-in-law had installed herself in the semi two weeks before the baby's due date but showed no sign of leaving now that Lauren had made an appearance. She would tell everyone with a martyred sigh that her daughter-in-law still needed her. Ruby's mother frequently wondered aloud how much Lindsay needed to have an old woman staring at her while she tried to breast-feed.

But mother-in-law was still there when Ruby arrived. As were both Ruby's own parents. Lindsay sat in the best armchair with the baby held firmly against her breast. All eyes were on her and the bundle in white cotton at her nipple. When Ruby walked into the room, she felt uneasy almost instantly. It was like a scene in some 1970s horror movie – Lindsay had just given birth to the spawn of the devil and all the attendant biddies were there to make sure that she didn't try to make a break for the sanctuary of the church with their new messiah.

'Here's Auntie Ruby,' said Lindsay in a peculiar little voice that Ruby didn't recognise.

'Auntie Ruby! Makes me sound about a hundred and twelve!' Ruby laughed.

'Old enough to have one of your own already,' Lindsay's mother-in-law observed.

Lindsay handed Ruby her baby niece. Almost as soon as the tiny creature realised that she was being handed to someone other than mummy her brow began to furrow, her peachy complexion darkened to magenta and she took a deep breath as though filling her lungs for a scream.

'She's going to cry,' said Ruby, preparing to hand her straight back.

'Just say something nice to her,' Lindsay suggested. 'Coo at her.'

'She looks like her daddy,' said Grandma Jones the mother-in-law.

'She looks like Lindsay did at that age too,' interrupted Ruby's own mother, Grandma Taylor. 'And me.'

And there it was. The family line. Ruby looked from her niece to her elder sister to her mother. Three generations of women with matching mouths and eyes and noses. Ruby remembered once reading a poem that said 'Family faces are a magic mirror' and at last she knew what that meant.

Back at home that night, Ruby dug out her birth certificate for the first time since her experience with Amanda the Patchouli Monster had made her want to rip it into shreds. Hope Mary Barker. The name was still there. Blue ink on pink paper. And no matter how much she felt like a Taylor girl, Ruby realised that if she ever had a baby it would have the Barker nose, not the Taylor one. Perhaps at last this was the time to get a better idea of what that nose looked like.

18

Ruby's adoption had been on her mind a great deal since that afternoon at Lindsay's house. And as she stared at the crack in Lou's ceiling, it was with her again. This time that old numb sense of loss was mixed up with the intense feelings of worthlessness that Flett's careless dumping and even the parting words of that thoughtless idiot Robin had provoked in her.

She couldn't sleep. Every time she closed her eyes, her last conversation with Flett started running like the adverts at the cinema. Or, if she managed to take her mind off him for a second, Robin's disappointed assertion that he was looking for someone younger and better-looking played instead.

Ruby flicked on the television, hoping that she'd be able to get absorbed in one of those bizarre Euro programmes they show late on a Friday night. But nothing grabbed her attention. She couldn't watch the horror movie on Channel 5 in case it kept her awake with fear. The only thing to do was read *Hello* and be reassured that even being rich and famous doesn't really protect you from heartache. For every celebrity wedding the magazine featured these days, there were at least two articles on stars who found themselves suddenly single again, eager to talk about their heartbreak from the 'sumptuous surroundings of their luxurious new home'.

Or a hotel room, depending how the divorce settlement had gone . . . Ruby pulled a new copy of the grown-up comic from Lou's overflowing magazine rack and began her search for celebrity solace.

That week's glossy cover bore the super-wide grin of Katrina Black – the only actress in Hollywood who could make Angelina Jolie look thin-lipped. Katrina Black was plugging her autobiography, a ghost-written tome en-titled *Little Black Book*. There had been lots of press surrounding the book's recent publication. It was sup-posed to be packed full of incredible revelations. Not least of which was the news that one well-known Tinseltown scion liked to wrap himself in cling-film beneath his hand-stitched Italian suits before spending the evening rubbing himself up against unsuspecting young women at film industry parties. Apparently, the point of the cling-film was to stop any embarrassing emissions from staining his threads, though, as most people quickly observed, that didn't explain why the actor wrapped cling-film around his *whole* body, ankle to neck. A double layer.

Ruby was as fascinated by the sexual peccadilloes of the rich and famous as the next girl, of course. But that wasn't why she too had been itching to get her hands on a copy of Katrina Black's biography. Ruby was interested in a rather different side of Katrina's private life because, in magazine and television interviews throughout her career, the actress had made no secret of the fact that she, like Ruby, had been given up as a baby. Katrina Black was the only other adoptee Ruby knew. Or knew of, at least.

The story had been told at least a dozen times before but only lately did it have a happy ending. When she first became famous, Katrina Black suddenly found herself prey to a particularly trendy crowd who quickly introduced her to drugs. Two high profile drugs-busts later – one of which ended in a pretty lenient jail sentence – Katrina booked herself into a rehab clinic in the Arizona desert and stayed there for as long as her filming schedule would allow. Six days, in actual fact, though the blurb for the back of the book made it sound much more dramatic than that. Anyway, during her time in rehab, Katrina decided, with the help of a therapist and a fellow inmate who had a Native American Indian spirit guide, that the root of her problems wasn't her sudden ascent to fame and her inability to say no to a nice line of coke at all. It was, she said, the *abandonment* she had suffered as a child. Her adoption had scarred her deeply, she claimed, robbing her of the ability to find balance in her adult relationships. And the only way to put those childhood traumas behind her and move on would be to obtain proper 'closure'.

Of course, the only way to obtain closure would be for Katrina to meet the woman who had given her up at birth and a whole chapter of Katrina's biography and most of the article in *Hello* was dedicated to her search for her natural family. She hired a private detective. She had her 'people' hunt through every birth, death and marriage record in the United States. She placed ads in every single newspaper in the country from the *LA Times* and *Herald Tribune* to a two-sheet freebie in the Appalachians. And, despite the money she threw at them, it was not the private detective or Katrina's entourage that reunited the actress with her *mom*, but a tiny ad in a Louisiana rag, whose biggest story so far that year had been about an alligator eating a pet poodle.

In true Hollywood style, the meeting was the subject of a documentary complete with perfect filmic moments. The megastar striding confidently down the modest street that she could have bought with the wages from one episode of her latest hit sitcom. Cut to the woman who had last seen her as a baby standing, already teary-eyed, on the front porch of her bungalow with the children she had given birth to (and not given away) since the first mistake she made.

That night in Lou's house, Ruby devoured the details all over again, looking for parallels to her own life. As Ruby guessed her natural mother must have been, Katrina Black's mother had been a teenager at the time she fell pregnant. Carlene Schmit claimed that Katrina had been conceived the first time she had sex, with a guy she had known and loved ever since she could remember. They made love the night before he enlisted in the army. Two weeks later he was killed in an accident during a basic training exercise. Gary Hobbs never knew Carlene Schmit was carrying his baby. She didn't know herself until it was too late to do anything about it. Not that she would have done anything about it, she claimed. She wanted to have Gary's child.

But things were different then, wrote Katrina's interviewer in the sugary style that peppered the whole article. *Only bad girls got themselves pregnant in those days and nobody wanted to help a bad girl, not even if she was carrying the child of the town's favourite son, a military hero, killed in action*. They glossed over the fact that Gary was killed while playing baseball with a grenade.

*Carlene had no choice but to give away the baby she so
wanted. They had just ten short minutes together after
the arduous birth – a twelve hour labour. Carlene held
her daughter in her arms and knew at once that her baby
was special, with a glittering future ahead of her.*

Who wouldn't say that about Katrina Black now,
Ruby thought a little cynically.

*But Carlene knew that she couldn't stand in the way of
Katrina's destiny. She knew that she would never be able
to afford the dancing lessons, the singing lessons and the
acting classes that would one day make her baby girl a
star. So she made the ultimate sacrifice. She gave her
baby away.*

'And it was the worst day of my life,' Carlene took up
the story. 'I felt as though something had been ripped
from me. My stomach felt empty. It was as though
someone had turned off the sound. I couldn't hear anything. I couldn't taste the food they brought to me. I
remember staring at the orange curtains of my hospital
room as the day turned into night.

'I thought I would cry for a week,' Carlene continued.
'But I knew, somewhere inside, that this would not be the
last time I saw my daughter. I knew that one day she
would come back to me. And I knew that I would
recognise her when she came.'

Carlene didn't seem bothered by the fact that she had
watched all of Katrina's movies and had been a huge fan
of the soap she starred in without realising that the girl
on the screen was her daughter. Perhaps it was the nose
job that had thrown her off the scent.

Whatever, she continued, 'And here we are, reunited at
last. At last I feel complete. My favourite daughter is home.'

Ruby looked at the photos that accompanied the eight-page interview and felt a little sorry for the children Carlene had borne since Katrina. They didn't have their half-sister's elegance, that was for sure. And though Katrina claimed to be inseparable from her newfound siblings, Ruby secretly wondered whether Katrina would really be happy to take the cross-eyed one along to a Los Angeles premiere.

The picture of Katrina and Carlene alone was somewhat better. Though their reunion had been recorded for posterity and the general American viewing public, there was no hint that the smiles were just for the camera. They looked into each other's eyes and, though there were sixteen years between them, their grins were mirror images. Magic mirror images, thought Ruby.

'No woman gives her baby away unthinkingly,' the actress concluded. 'The wound is deep on both sides. I'm just glad that I had the opportunity to heal that wound for both of us. I would urge anyone in the same position to do the same. Life is too short to be strangers.'

The article ended with a photograph of Katrina and her new beau, a rap star who had recently given up his 'gangsta' past and was currently 'rapping for God'. Without the strength Katrina drew from finding her birth mother, the interview explained, she might never have been able to find the true, adult relationship she so richly deserved. Discovering the true circumstances behind her adoption had given back to Katrina Black the self-esteem she had been unable to find as one of Hollywood's highest grossing stars. And finding self-esteem had enabled her to send out the right signals to attract her true love.

Ruby closed the magazine thoughtfully. Was that where she had been going wrong? Was she too carrying a wound so deep that it was still bleeding; attracting the wrong men into her life like sharks lured by the scent of death surrounding an injured fish?

It was very late. Ruby was still slightly drunk. She mocked up another ad for the back of *The Times*.

> Would anyone knowing the whereabouts of Geraldine
> Barker, formerly of Greenwich, please contact box
> number XXX.

She used the wording that Katrina Black had used in the ad that went into every single newspaper in the United States, substituting only the name of her birth mother and the city. Then she called up *The Times*' twenty-four-hour classified advertisement line and dictated the sixteen short words before proper consideration or cowardice could stop her.

Afterwards she felt a little odd. A little breathless. A little panicky. But she had done it. She'd really done it this time. She had finally placed the personal ad that might really change her life.

19

'Cindy,' Martin called, 'you're not seriously going to play that, are you? There's no way I can get down to it to a soundtrack by that bunch of nancy-boys.'

'Silence, slave!'

'What?'

'I said silence!'

Cindy reappeared in the doorway. She wasn't naked any more. Oh no. She was wearing a black cat mask and a matching leather bikini. In her right hand she held a long leather bullwhip. In her left, a huge purple vibrator. Her nipples poked through slits in the bikini cups. Martin's first instinct was to laugh.

'Shut up!' barked Cindy, underlining her order with a crack of the whip. 'You're in my kingdom now. I make the decisions about what we're going to listen to. In fact, I make all the decisions about everything to do with your puny little body from now on . . .'

'Puny?' protested Martin. He'd heard quite a lot of insults in his early days as a telephone salesman, but no one had ever called him puny. That wasn't fair. In fact, to his mind he was so far from puny that he'd recently considered a Slim-fast regime.

'I'm role playing,' Cindy explained patiently. 'Anyway, enough of your insolence,' she clicked back into dominatrix mode. 'Sing along with Mark and Robbie.

Make sure you stay in tune or I'll have to take my whip to you.'

'You are joking.'

Crack went the whip. She clearly wasn't.

And so Martin found himself singing along to Take That and Lulu's rendition of 'Relight My Fire' while Cindy, in her leather bikini, slid about the marble floor in front of him, pouting and posing and occasionally stopping to run the very tip of her bullwhip ever so gently across the top of his dick or hold the vibrator against his kneecap.

'You're not getting a hard-on!' she said accusingly at one point.

'I'm trying,' he promised. But this was hardly how Martin had expected to end the evening. Martin couldn't make up his mind whether it was erotic or just plain comical when Cindy bent over in front of him and gave him a front-row view of her crotchless leather knickers. When he stopped singing to gape at the spectacle, she snapped upright again and marched over to impress upon him how important it was that he didn't stop. And it turned out that she had put 'Relight My Fire' on repeat so it was always the same bloody song.

After six renditions of the dreaded tune, Martin decided that it was interfering with his enjoyment of what might otherwise have been a pretty incredible experience. He dared to ask Cindy if they might move onto something else. ' "I Want You Back", perhaps?' It was the only other Take That song he knew. 'Or how about you just uncuff one of my hands?'

'You'll get your reward when I say so!' was her answer.

Martin watched her wiggle back across the room to strike another pose by the open door.

'Please,' he tried again. 'My wrists are getting sore.'

'Insolence!' Cindy shrieked at him. 'You'll have to be punished for that.'

This time she turned the shower on. Martin was shocked by the sudden, heavy downpour but thankfully it wasn't too cold. However, it certainly dampened his ardour. Take That on repeat. A tepid shower. And a barking mad rich girl prancing about the bathroom in what, quite frankly, looked less and less like the outfit of a dominatrix and more and more like it belonged to the Village People's poodle.

Sod this, thought Martin. Not even he was this desperate to get laid. 'Cindy,' he said firmly. 'Uncuff me at once.'

'Never!' she snarled as she crawled across the bathroom floor in what Martin could only assume she thought was the style of a panther.

'I'm fed up of this, Cindy.'

'But I haven't finished!'

'I've got to go home,' he tried, going instead for the sympathy vote. 'My sister is on holiday,' he lied, 'and I'm supposed to be looking after her kittens. I forgot to feed them before I came out.'

Cindy didn't care. In fact, she cranked up the volume of the CD and returned to the bathroom for the big Lulu finale.

'Let me out of here,' yelled Martin.

'Relight my fi-i-i-i-re!' Cindy began to march about the bathroom floor in a strange showgirl goose-step, kicking her legs slightly higher than a Nazi but not quite as high as the *Folies Bergère*. High enough, however, that she managed to lose her balance and, with an ugly crack of skull on marble floor, went arse over tit and blacked out on the Ralph Lauren bath mat.

'Cindy!' Martin called. 'Cindy! Are you OK.'

He couldn't properly see how she had landed, chained as he was to the shower pipe.

'Cindy?' She didn't answer him. 'Cindy!!!'

Was she dead?

Martin twisted his hands desperately in an attempt to escape his soggy bondage. Take That were still playing and the shower was still pouring down on top of his head like some kind of Chinese water torture. 'Cindy!' He could just about see her legs if he leaned as far over as his bonds would allow him. She wasn't showing any sign of getting up. 'Cindy! This isn't funny now. Get up!'

No answer.

She must be dead, he thought. This was how these things happened. Sex games gone wrong. Who would believe he hadn't murdered her? Martin panicked and started to hyperventilate, despite the fact that it was pretty clear he couldn't have tripped her up from where he was standing with his hands cuffed behind him round the shower rail.

'Cindy!' he shouted. His voice was barely audible above Lulu's big crescendo. 'Cindy! Wake up, girl!'

Now it didn't seem like such good luck that there was no one else in the house. What time had she said her parents would be back? If they didn't come back until the following evening, Martin panicked, then he might well end up dead too. From pneumonia. The hot water had run out and the shower was starting to feel pretty damn frigid.

Martin groaned and slumped down as far as he was able. He could almost see his mother's face when they told her the news.

'A sex game, Mrs Ashcroft. A victim of his own depravity.'

The humiliation might well kill his mother too.

Though arguably, it could be far worse if Martin survived the night and Cindy didn't. There would have to be an inquest. He would have to explain in a court of law how he had come to be handcuffed to a shower rail with Take That's 'Relight My Fire' on repeat and a posh girl in a leather bikini lying dead on the guest bathroom floor. And that was before he explained how he'd met her in the first place!

'Cindy!' he shouted one more time. In a brief pause while the song ended and before it started again, Martin's worried voice echoed pathetically around the marble-tiled room. He tried to flick a bit of water from the bathtub in Cindy's direction, hoping that it might revive her if she was only slightly unconscious. When she still didn't move he started to pray. He hadn't prayed for a long time. Not since England was last drawn against Germany in the World Cup and it hadn't worked then either. But now he prayed much harder.

'Please, Lord,' he muttered. 'Look, I haven't known this girl for long and I know it doesn't look good, what with the leather and the whip and all that, but I think she's fundamentally a pretty nice person. A bit odd, perhaps, but who isn't odd these days, eh? Deep down inside, I know she's a good girl. And she's only young. Well, twenty-seven. She doesn't deserve to die. Please, let her live, Lord. I really do believe in you. Please let Cindy live, God. I know you can do that for me. I beg you, please send me a sign.'

The water in the shower was icy now. 'Relight My Fire' started for the fifth time since Cindy's slip and she still showed no evidence of resurrection. Martin was ready to give up and succumb to pneumonia. Just once more he offered up a little prayer. 'I know you can save her, Lord. Just send me a sign.'

Silence. (Except for Lulu).

'Oh, God,' Martin sobbed. 'Oh God, oh God, oh God.'

Suddenly, there was a patter of tiny feet. Or, more specifically, of tiny paws on marble. Martin opened his eyes, which had been tightly shut in prayer, to see a little white dog standing in the bathroom doorway. It looked at him quizzically, head on one side. No, thought Martin, it was looking at him *knowingly*. Was this the little white terrier of God?

Wagging its little white tail, the Bedlington terrier – that looked less like a dog than a lamb – trotted across the bathroom floor to where Cindy's lifeless body lay.

'Thank you, Lord!' cried Martin. 'It's a sign. Lick her face, boy. Lick her face until she wakes up! Or bark!' He encouraged the little canine. 'Go out on the street and bark until someone comes to see what's wrong. Go on, boy. Bark for me! You can do it!'

The little dog cocked his head to one side again as though he were pondering a solution.

'Go on, boy!' Martin shouted. 'Make like Lassie!'

And as if he understood, the terrier raced out into the corridor. Martin raised his eyes to heaven. 'Thank you, Lord. Thank you. Thank you for sending your heavenly angel dog to save this poor sinner. Thank you, Lord. Now if you could just help him find a passer-by and bring help to save us all.'

Help arrived sooner than even a miracle-worker might have managed; when the little dog reappeared moments later, it was in its owner's arms. The dog owner looked faintly familiar but this was hardly the moment for a 'haven't I see you before?' conversation.

'Thank you! Thank you!' Martin cried. 'I think she hit her head. Can you call an ambulance? I don't know how it happened but we've got to get her to hospital before her parents come home.'

'We *are* her parents,' said the woman holding the dog. Of course they were. How else had they got into the house? And now the woman was joined by her husband. He too, looked incredibly familiar as he stared in horror at the naked stranger in his bath.

'What the—' began Cindy's father.

'For God's sake,' cried her mother. 'We'll deal with him later. Let's get her off the floor.'

Between them, Cindy's parents managed to drag their daughter's flaccid body into a semi-upright position, the little dog yapping all the while. As they lifted her, Cindy started to moan. It didn't look good. She had a lump the size of a golf ball on her forehead. But at least she wasn't dead.

Cindy's mother dialled an ambulance on her mobile phone while her father flapped cool air across her face with the cat mask.

'Darling, wake up!' he cooed.

Meanwhile, Martin was still sitting beneath the cascading, bollock-freezing cold, shower. No one had bothered to switch off the Take That CD either.

Eventually, when she was convinced that the ambulance was en route, Cindy's mother turned the shower off. By the time the ambulance men arrived to cart Cindy off to hospital however, the key to the handcuffs was still nowhere to be found. With nothing but a hand towel to protect his modesty, Martin had to wait in the bath until the firemen arrived with their metal-cutting equipment. Just a hand towel; while the statue in the corner held enough fluffy bath-sheets to keep an Arctic expedition warm!

The firemen took forever thanks to a warehouse fire in Brent Cross. And then they had to wait for a plumber to turn off the water supply so that when the firemen cut through the shower pipe, they didn't flood the house.

Martin was finally freed from his bondage almost five hours after Cindy took her tumble, having been seen in his naked (and very shrivelled, thanks to the cold water) glory by a total of fifteen people other than the girl he originally took his clothes off for. It didn't take seven firemen to cut him free of course, but the fire chief had decided that all his boys should see the situation in case they happened upon something of its like in the future.

'It's good training,' he told them. Martin suspected that he was merely the light relief after a long hard night of fire-fighting. Then there were three plumbers, the three paramedics who took Cindy to the accident unit, both Cindy's unfriendly parents and the dog.

Understandably, all Martin wanted to do was slink off into the night and forget he and Cindy Daniels ever met. Unfortunately, that was not going to be possible. Oh no.

When the plumbers and firemen had gone and Martin was back in his clothes again, still shivering, Cindy's mother informed him icily that he would have to remain at the house until their lawyer arrived.

'Lawyer?' Martin exclaimed. 'But she's all right, isn't she? I mean, she's not going to die.'

'Cindy will be fine,' said her mother. 'No thanks to you. She has a mild case of concussion and will be staying in hospital overnight. But we'd still like you to sign this.'

'Sign what?'

The lawyer duly produced a ten-page thick contract from his briefcase with a flourish.

'I have no idea who you are, young man,' said Cindy Daniels' mother. 'Nor do I really wish to know. But I feel sure you know all about me.'

The way she said that phrase suddenly helped make the connection. That shocking red crop. Those steely blue eyes. Cindy's mother was Petunia Daniels, the actress. Which meant that her father was Benjamin Daniels, best Hamlet since Laurence Olivier. Star of the Royal Shakespeare Company and four times Oscar nominee. No wonder they had looked familiar. No wonder they wanted Martin to sign a document saying that even if the editor of the *News of the World* pulled his toenails out with a pair of rusty pliers, Martin would reveal nothing of what had gone on in their house that night.

Martin began to read the contract but was too tired and cold to concentrate. All he wanted was to go home. The last thing on his mind was selling his story to the tabloids. He wanted a hot bath and some warmer clothing. 'Look, Mrs Daniels,' he started, 'you don't really need me to sign this. I'm not going to say anything. I mean, what happened this evening is just as embarrassing for me as . . .'

'In consideration of your embarrassment,' said the actress, opening her cheque book, 'we'd like you to have ten thousand pounds. Name?'

'Er, Martin . . . Martin Ashcroft. A-S-H . . . But, you really don't . . .'

'Well, Mr Ashcroft,' Petunia interrupted him, 'I'll put my signature on this and you'll put your signature on that and I trust we shan't be hearing from you again.'

She handed Martin the cheque.

More than a little bewildered, Martin scrawled his name on the dotted line at the bottom of the contract. Petunia Daniels saw him to the back door of her house and bid him 'good morning'. Didn't even offer him the use of her phone to call a cab.

It wasn't until he got back to his own flat that Martin fished the cheque out and looked at it again. He toyed with the idea of going round to Lou's and letting the girls know how his bizarre night had progressed, but decided against it. That contract had seemed pretty stiff and he knew that both his friends had unscrupulous journalist pals who would be only too happy to share his secret with the *News of the World*. If there really was a secret to share . . .

It was as though he expected to find that the cheque, in fact the whole evening in the company of Cindy, had all been a figment of his overactive imagination. But there was the date, the amount (in figures and in words) and Petunia Daniels' signature. It was an ordinary cheque.

Nothing about it suggested that Petunia had been making a joke when she signed it.

Ten thousand pounds. Martin thought about his bank account. He'd just been paid. It wasn't empty. But he wasn't going to be paid again at the end of that month. Or maybe even the month after that. It shouldn't really take long for a salesman of his experience to find a new position. But that was providing Barry Parsons hadn't already rubbished him to every mag in London.

The cheque Martin now held in his hands was enough to cover the wages he'd lost until Christmas. He could live on ten thousand pounds for far longer than that if he reined in his lifestyle for a bit. How long would he have then? Six months? Twelve months? Ten thousand pounds was probably enough to live on in India for a couple of years. He knew a guy from college who'd been living in Goa since 1995 with no visible means of support.

Martin didn't want to go back to an office. Not the International Magazines office. Not any office. He wanted to write his novel. And the cheque in his pocket might just be a passport to time off. A sabbatical. A chance to finish his book and get it published and never in his life have to answer to a balding twat like Barry Parsons again.

Growing more and more excited by the second, Martin decided that via his unconventional meeting with Petunia Daniels, fate was giving him an almighty shove towards his ambition. He kissed the cheque. Talk about serendipity. Then he patted the pocket that contained the solitary diskette copy of his novel. His route to immortality. His destiny.

And it was empty.

20

Lou had never received a bouquet of flowers in her life. Sure, she'd had bunches of carnations picked up from a service station, but she had never before answered the door to find a little chap from Interflora staggering under the weight of half the Chelsea Flower Show. Her first instinct was to assume that he'd got the wrong flat. The doughy-faced girl in the flat downstairs, who wore her pearls even to go jogging in the morning, was always getting flowers from her equally chinless boyfriend. They must be for her. But no, these flowers really were for Lou.

'Once Seen, never forgotten,' Andrew had written on the card that accompanied them. Lou couldn't help smiling, despite the fact that one of the lilies was already shedding indelible yellow pollen all over her clean white T-shirt.

'For our second anniversary,' he explained when she phoned him to say thanks. 'Two weeks since our first proper date, you know.'

'You are such a romantic,' Lou said.

The day after their meeting at Suave, Andrew had called and invited Lou to join him for tea. It was a grey day – British summertime after all – so they planned to rendezvous in the Egyptian exhibit at the British Museum. When Lou arrived, five minutes late, Andrew was already standing in front of a huge, dislocated fist that must once have belonged to a giant statue of a mighty pharaoh. He hadn't seen Lou approaching, so she decided to hide behind a row of cat-headed goddesses and watch him for a while.

As she watched, she remembered something her mother had once said about meeting Lou's father. 'I liked the way he leaned against the lamppost,' Mrs Capshaw sighed, whenever she recounted the story of their first date. And Lou liked the way Andrew looked now, as he studied the giant fist while he waited for her to show up. Just hanging about. He looked relaxed. Not nervous. He was at ease in his own body, Lou concluded. That was nice. A teenage girl, sketching Egyptian arte-facts for a school project, gave him an appreciative glance. Andrew smiled back at her, but not in a seedy way. He stepped out of the way so that a father could lift his young son closer to the statue. Andrew laughed with the father as the little boy made his own fist, less than a hundredth of the size of the stone one. The two men shared a joke.

Lou nodded to herself as she watched him. Andrew was a catch alright. Good-looking, gregarious, generous. Fashionable, friendly . . . firm buttocks. He got a tick in every box on the ideal boyfriend scale.

'Lou!'

He had spotted her.

'We were just speculating on this guy's chances against Mike Tyson,' he said, nodding towards the granite hand. He took Lou's own soft hand and kissed it. 'Hello, you,' he murmured.

And Lou thought that perhaps it was possible to fall in love at *second* sight.

Since then, they seemed to have spent almost every spare moment together. Working as he did for an Internet ticket agency, Andrew was always able to get cut-price seats at the last minute for any of the West End shows. When they went to see *The Mousetrap*, Andrew managed to get seats in a private box. He brought champagne and expensive Belgian chocolates. He even had a floppy pink tea rose for the buttonhole of Lou's denim jacket.

He was indeed, the ideal boyfriend. And he would constantly marvel at the circumstances of their very first meeting. What were the chances that he would answer an ad for a joke and hit it off so spectacularly with the victim of his hoax? Surely they were even slimmer than the one in seven million chance Lou had of actually finding the real stranger she had fancied?

'Anyway,' said Andrew, 'your stranger is probably a tosser. He's probably got a girlfriend. Or a wife. And even if he didn't have, you probably would have hated him when you got the chance to talk. You're much better off with me,' he added with his most charming, little boy smile.

And Lou felt she had to agree.

More than a month had passed now since that fateful Wednesday morning on the Northern Line. Lou wasn't even sure she would recognise her stranger again. It had been a moment of madness, that was all.

'You are mad,' said Martin, when Ruby told him that she wanted to place another personal ad. 'The personal ad world is full of freaks.'

'And one very nice man with a Porsche who wanted to

meet me!' Ruby reminded him. In the aftermath of the dreadful triple date, the revelation that one of the guys who replied to Ruby's ad had a Porsche sent her into a frenzy. 'I still can't believe you sent me on a date with a man who split the cost of garlic bread when all along you knew there was a man for me out there driving a Porsche!'

'I didn't like the sound of his message. I mean, what kind of wanker phones up and tells you about his car within the first two seconds of describing himself?'

'The kind of wanker that at least has a car,' said Ruby. 'The nearest that Robin idiot ever got to a Porsche was cutting a spare set of keys for one. Besides, I don't know why you're so down on the system, Mart. You were the one who got a night of passion.'

'Yeah.'

Martin had neglected to tell either of his friends the true circumstances of his night on the tiles. Or rather, Cindy's night on the tiles and his night in the bathtub. He'd reread the contract Petunia Daniels sent him away with a dozen times since that Friday and it seemed that he only had to breathe the Daniels name in his sleep to have a lawyer jump on his head and smash his brains in. Much as he loved Lou and Ruby, he feared a law suit as big as New York if the truth ever came out in a real way, which would be the inevitable consequence of telling either of London's biggest gossips.

Neither had he told the girls about the missing diskette and the novel that was lost forever. It hurt just to think about that. The last thing he wanted was to have them offer solutions to what seemed like an insurmountable problem. A man to his very core, Martin was determined to suffer in silence.

'Where are you temping this week anyway?' Ruby asked.

'I'm doing a customer survey for McDonald's,' he told her flatly.

He was in a deep depression. And one that could probably have been alleviated by going on a long holiday costing roughly ten thousand pounds. Yep, two weeks after the Take That bondage incident, Petunia Daniels' cheque was still uncashed. He'd come close to cashing it once though.

He'd got a printout of his current account balance and been quite pleased with the three figure number until he saw the little 'd' after it. It was ridiculous to have a cheque for ten thousand pounds in his pocket and minus nine hundred in the bank. So he filled out a paying-in slip and joined the queue for the cashiers. As he waited in line, Martin wondered whether the cashier who served him would be surprised by the name on the cheque. How would she suppose he had come by a cheque for ten thousand pounds signed by one of Britain's most prominent actresses? Martin thought he noticed the old lady in the queue behind him trying to get a peek at his paying-in slip. Would everyone guess that it was a pay-off?

He didn't have time to find out that morning. Just as the old guy in front of Martin finished counting out a jam-jar full of two-pence pieces into neat little piles, the quietly industrious atmosphere of the bank was suddenly rent by an ear-piercing alarm. At first, both customers and cashiers looked up at the source of the noise with such bovine acceptance that Martin was reminded of a field of cattle remaining unmoved by the passage of a couple of low-flying fighter jets.

They were testing the alarms. That was the immediate assumption. It was only when the alarm refused to go quiet after almost a minute and a half, and the bank's manageress actually ran shrieking into the lobby, that anyone thought about evacuating.

'Get outside! Get outside!' she yelled. 'Everybody out.'

It took a few moments to persuade them. There was still no sign of smoke. But the sprinklers set into the ceiling of the lobby were now beginning to unleash a less than gentle rain. When a droplet splashed onto his paying in slip and smudged the neat way Martin had written his signature, he too decided it was time to go. Outside, a fire engine was already skidding to a halt by the pavement. Three firemen in their bright yellow helmets pushed through the bystanders all hoping to see a real fire.

By this time, the manageress was hyperventilating against a letter-box. The look on her face suggested that the situation must be very grave indeed.

'Move out of the way, folks,' said the man who had been driving the fire truck. The bystanders took two steps back and waited thirty seconds before they took three forward again. With the sprinklers now making like a monsoon inside the building, there wasn't much hope that particular branch of the HSBC would be open again that afternoon.

'Sod it.'

Martin sighed and stuffed the cheque and paying-in slip back into his record bag. Petunia Daniels wouldn't have to worry about going overdrawn that day. Or the next day. Martin just couldn't bring himself to cash that cheque. He had pride. He had integrity. He had . . . nothing.

Ruby didn't notice her friend's depression. She was on a mission; too caught up in her latest gargantuan effort to improve her love life. She hadn't applied herself to anything with such determination and tenacity since she and Mary Jeapes had done the 'I must, I must improve my bust' exercise, fifty times a day for two weeks aged eleven. Ruby was going to find that Porsche driver and she was going to meet him for a date. View to friendship and possible marriage . . .

Work was still hell. She didn't have to see Flett for a fortnight, thank God. But that was only because he was on his hols. Where he'd gone, she didn't know. But Ruby did know that Two-Faced Imogen had mysteriously booked the exact same fortnight off.

The summer party loomed like a title match. At the moment, Imogen was definitely the odds-on favourite to carry home the title of Hollingworth's queen. She had the man. And she would probably have a tan, to boot, after her fortnight wherever it was she had been.

Ruby confided her personal ad campaign to Liz, who suggested that she would be better off with yoga.

'What are the chances that the Porsche man will ring again?' Liz asked her. 'You need to find inner peace, Ruby. Not a boyfriend.'

'A boyfriend with a Porsche will give me all the inner peace I need,' Ruby explained, then she shooed Liz out of her office while she called through to *The Sunday Times* with her copy. 'Will Robert with the Porsche who left a message for Ruby please call again. Lost your number.'

'It won't work,' Liz said confidently when they met again by the photocopier that afternoon.

But – oh God – it did. It really bloody did! And miraculously, Robert with the Porsche was still single and still 'super keen to meet', as he said in the voicemail he left the very day the personal ad was published! Ruby wasted no time in arranging a date.

'How will I recognise you?' she asked him.

'I'll be carrying a dozen red roses,' he replied. 'And how will I recognise you?' he asked her. 'What do you look like, Ruby? You sound like a goddess.'

Ruby put down the phone on her chocolate-voiced dream-boy and swooned.

21

'I must not get too excited. I must not get too excited.'

Ruby forced down the rising bubble of anticipation in her stomach. It couldn't possibly be him. Why on earth would someone that good-looking – let alone someone that good-looking who also drove a *Porsche* – be answering Lonely Hearts ads? Yet there he was. Standing exactly where Robert had said he would be and carrying the requisite roses.

'Robert?' Ruby stuttered.

Robert turned vaguely in her direction as though Ruby had just sidled up to him wearing a filthy mac and hissed, 'Can you spare any change?'

She smiled her best smile while he looked at her blankly, his perfect lips set in a thin hard line. Oh God, she thought. It isn't him after all. Or if it is him, he doesn't fancy me. He's the wrong man. Or he's going to pretend I've got the wrong man because I'm clearly not the right sort of woman. There must be some other guy with serial killer hair waiting for me right around the corner. A guy this good-looking isn't going to . . .

'Ruby!' She had almost turned to go when Robert suddenly seized her hand and planted a smacker on the back of it. The thin line of his mouth was now an extravagant upwards curve. 'Contact lenses,' he explained, to excuse his previously vacant expression. 'Getting used to them.'

Ruby twittered nervously.

'Bit too vain to wear glasses,' he added, giving her a sheepish, but simultaneously highly alluring, grin.

Oh yes, thought Ruby, nodding helplessly. It would have been such a shame to hide those cheekbones behind a pair of frames.

'These are for you.'

He handed her the roses. And though she had been expecting to see a man waiting for her with a bunch of flowers, Ruby found she was suddenly inordinately thrilled. Not just one dozen red roses but two dozen. And not the kind of petal-bare bunches you find at the supermarket wrapped in a triangle of cellophane, either. The roses were wrapped in gloriously crunchy brown paper and tied in raffia – the Knightsbridge version of clear plastic wrap.

'Shall we?' he asked, opening out his arm so that she could thread her own through it. 'I don't know about you, but I'm starving.'

Ruby nodded again though she was suddenly too dizzy to eat. As they began to weave their way through the crowds at Leicester Square, Ruby felt herself physically open out like the buds she clasped in her hand. As he complimented her on the beige raincoat she had bought almost five years previously, she was sure she felt herself grow a whole inch taller in the warmth of his gentle flattery. When he told her that he had noticed her walking towards him and didn't dare think that she might be the girl he was looking for because she was so scrumptious, Ruby felt her face glow. She flicked her hair like it was the glossy tail of a dressage pony and not, for once, the hay such a pony would breakfast on. When Robert grinned at her, she knew her eyes were twinkling almost as much as his.

By the time they got to the restaurant, she had counted at least half a dozen girls looking enviously in her direction. She felt as though she had undergone a Hollywood makeover in the ten-minute walk from the tube station to the trendy, minimalist restaurant where Robert had booked a table.

Karma existed. And this was it. This gorgeous man in the expensive pink shirt that would have looked effeminate on any man less confident about his incredible animal attractiveness, was Ruby's reward for John Flett and Dave the accountant and Robin the key-cutter and every other toad who'd come before them. There was no question that Robert was more attractive than Robin, but Ruby's delight swelled to the size of a small cow as she decided that, yes, he was far more attractive than John Flett as well.

'I'm a criminal lawyer.'

And clearly more intelligent . . .

'Let me pull that chair out for you.'

And much more chivalrous . . .

'Champagne?'

And generous . . .

'Yes, please,' said Ruby.

Yes, please! Yes, please! Yes, please!

'Well,' he said later. 'That's the worst part over. I spent all day at work worrying that we wouldn't live up to each other's expectations. Didn't you?'

Ruby raised her eyebrows in surprise. To her subconscious, it didn't seem possible that this man could have fallen short of anyone's highest benchmark.

'You know,' Robert continued, 'apparently, we human beings can tell if we are attracted to someone within one fiftieth of a second. One fiftieth. Can you imagine how brief a moment that is? Whatever people say about first impressions and not judging a book by its cover, it's impossible to go back and write over the primeval feelings you have about someone as a result of the first time you saw them. Feelings of love can grow over time, of course . . .'

Ruby found herself unable to swallow her mouthful of *crème brûlée*.

'But if you're not physically attracted to someone within that first split-second moment of seeing them, you never will be.'

'What? Never?' Ruby asked.

'Never.'

Was he trying to tell her something?

He was.

'Which is why I'm so glad that my heart went out to you the moment we locked eyes.'

Ruby dropped her dessert spoon with a clatter. When she finished fishing it out from beneath the table, Robert was still leaning on his elbows, orienting himself across the table towards her, and staring at her with those milk chocolate button browns. It was one of those endless moments, when the world around you seems to fade out and all you can see is the face of the person you want to kiss.

'I can't believe you're single,' he murmured.

'Or I you!' Ruby replied.

'The last man to let you go must have been a fool.'

'Oh, he was,' said Ruby. 'I mean, we just weren't right for each other, that's all,' she spluttered, remembering Lou's instructions that she was to avoid saying anything even slightly bunny-boilerish at all costs. Keep it light. Keep it fluffy. But not Glenn Close casserole fluffy.

'This is one of those nights that I wish would last forever,' Robert cooed. 'I wish I could just whisk you off in the Boxster.'

It was the first time he had mentioned the Porsche that evening. So he definitely had one. Tick. Another mental box checked.

The waiter hovered with the bill. Just one more box to go. Ruby didn't expect Robert to spring for the whole of the check but, after Robin, she had decided that if he didn't at least make a show of attempting to be gentlemanly by refusing her share of the cash then . . .

'I'll get this,' Robert said, sliding his credit card inside the smart leather billfold with only the quickest glance at the total.

'Are you sure?'

'Of course I'm sure. It's my pleasure. Now I hope you'll let me drive you home.'

Ruby hesitated. The evening had gone perfectly. He seemed like an alright sort of guy. Forget alright. He seemed like the man of her dreams! All the same, said a sensible voice at the back of her head, she couldn't be sure that she wasn't being deceived. She had just one great telephone conversation and a fabulous evening at a restaurant to go on. It probably wasn't a great idea to get into his car but . . .

'I should get a tube,' she said, wishing she didn't have to. 'I live miles out of your way.'

'The whole point of a Porsche *is* those unnecessary miles,' he said.

Then they were strolling out of the restaurant together, arm in arm. He pressed the unlock button on his keyring. Across the street, a car that Ruby hadn't noticed as they walked to dinner that evening, sprang to life, headlights flashing like a wink when the alarm system disarmed. In midnight blue with a tan leather interior, it really was the most beautiful car she'd ever seen. Ruby had never been in a Porsche before. She'd never had a boyfriend with a car before! (Flett hadn't ever learned to drive, claiming that he was too intelligent to deal with the petty rigours of the Highway Code.) This was a moment for careful compromise.

'You could just drop me off at the tube station,' she suggested.

Next morning, the staff at Hollingworth couldn't fail to notice that there was something different about Ruby Taylor. It was as though the monsoon had ended and the sun was peeking through the clouds to encourage long dormant seeds to burst forth into extravagant multi-coloured blossoms. Especially pink ones. That morning Ruby was still wearing the rose pink top she had bought for the previous evening's date. With a neckline slashed down to the front of her bra, it was hardly office attire (though no worse than a pyjama top, which she had worn on a couple of occasions) and heads swivelled like windmills as she walked through the building to her desk.

Boy, did she feel good!

'Morning, Imogen,' she called as she passed the Two-Faced gang in their corner.

'Oh, er, morning Ruby,' Imogen replied, shocked into a stutter.

'Been somewhere nice?' Ruby asked her. 'You've got a great tan.'

'Majorca,' Imogen mumbled.

'Oh, really. Doesn't John have a villa there?'

Ruby knew that her greeting would be the instant catalyst for gossip but she didn't care. Let them gossip. Whatever they thought had changed her mood from black to fluffy pink with gold trimming, they didn't know the half of it. Lou had been right. Your life *could* turn around in a day. In an hour! In a perfect, explosive second!

'You look chirpy,' Liz commented as Ruby leaned languidly against the photocopier, fanning herself with a press release.

'I feel chirpy,' Ruby told her. 'I feel fan-bloody-tastic!'

'Do I take it that the date went well?'

'Well? Understatement of the year. Liz, you won't believe it. He's a lawyer. He's got his own flat in Islington. He drives a Porsche Boxster! He went to Cambridge. So he's intelligent as well as good-looking and charming and . . . ohmigod, he had such incredible manners. Even if he hadn't insisted on paying the bill – after ordering champagne and not just any champagne, but vintage champagne – I would have gone back to his place like a shot.'

'Oh, Rubes. You didn't . . .'

'I am in love!' Ruby exclaimed. 'So I did.'

'Well . . .'

'I know. I shouldn't get too excited. But I've got such a good feeling about this one. I mean, neither of us wanted the evening to end. I could tell that. We'd still be talking now if it weren't a work day.'

'Have you never heard of The Rules?' Liz asked.

'Who cares!' Ruby shouted. 'Liz, I am so happy I want to kiss Imogen. I've got my date for the party.'

'Have you asked him?'

'I have.' Ruby's chest was puffed with pride. 'And he said he'd be delighted. De-lighted! I can't wait till Flett sees him. Rob's got so much lovely black hair. Flett was always worrying about losing his hair. He is going to be green. Absolutely green!'

Ruby skipped to her own office. She even blew the Panter a kiss en route. And winked, to boot.

'What's up with her?' Emlyn asked Liz.

'Got laid,' Liz half-whispered. 'Through a personal ad.'

'Bloody hell,' said Emlyn. 'I might try one of those myself.'

22

'That's it. You've inspired me,' said Erica, later that week, when Lou told her about Ruby's wonderful date with Robert. 'I'm going to see if I can't find a personal ad boyfriend of my own. What do you think of this?'

Erica handed Lou a scrap of paper with her own draft ad scribbled upon it.

> Cat-loving vegetarian, 32, seeks sensitive soul with
> Pisces in his chart.

Lou read it aloud and nodded. 'Thirty-two?' was the only bit she queried out loud. Though she wasn't sure about the cat bit either. Or the Pisces part. She had vetoed every reply to the ad she placed for Martin that mentioned star signs or felines, flashing neon signals of desperation that they were.

'Do you think I should leave that bit out?' Erica asked. 'My age?'

'No. It's just that . . .' Lou began. Where to start? 'No, leave it,' she said. 'It's fine as it is.'

'Good. I'm going to e-mail this through to the paper right now,' said Erica. 'If I can get this to the *Guardian* by this afternoon it should make it into Saturday's edition. How quickly did you get replies?'

'Very,' Lou told her.

'Will you help me sort through mine? Assuming I get some of course.'

'Of course,' Lou nodded. 'And of course you'll get replies. Who wouldn't want a date with you?'

'Oh, thanks, Lou. It really cheered me up, you know. Hearing about you and Andrew. And Ruby and that lawyer bloke of hers. There are still decent men out there after all. You've found one. Here's hoping that I can.'

Lou nodded enthusiastically, choosing not to take the opportunity to remind her that while Lou had found Andrew on that first Lonely Hearts Club outing, Ruby had ended up with a man she would have crossed the street to avoid, and Martin hadn't been the same since his night with Cindy Daniels.

'So, how long is it now?' Erica asked.

'What?' Lou had gone back to examining the spreadsheet on her PC screen.

'You and Andrew? How long have you been seeing each other?'

'Er, nearly a month,' Lou calculated.

'If I can find a bloke half as lovely as Andrew I'll be happy,' said Erica.

'Yeah,' said Lou vaguely. 'Fingers crossed.'

Andrew. Lou still needed to call and let him know that she wouldn't be seeing him that evening. She hoped he wouldn't be too disappointed but had a niggling feeling that he would try his best to change her mind and get her to go over to his place. It was as though he assumed it was his duty to fill every spare moment in Lou's life now. She enjoyed his company well enough but it was getting to that point where she couldn't remember the last time she had spent a night alone. Or with her closest friends.

She'd been putting off the call all morning. Perhaps she'd just e-mail instead. When she opened her Outlook Express, it was surprisingly full. When she placed Martin's personal on the Internet, she had created a bogus e-mail address that would forward all replies meant for him straight to her. They were still coming in. Hairymary@hotmail.com probably needed to change her handle before she scored, Lou smiled wryly.

The replies had been amusing at first, but now they were just annoying. She needed to take Martin's ad offline again so that she didn't have to wade through badly punctuated love notes to get to the important stuff in her in-box any more.

Www.pinacoladalovematch.com was having a special 'summer loving' promotion. All new and existing users of the site would be entered into a grand prize draw to win a romantic weekend *à deux* in the European city of their choice, a flashing box trumpeted. Assuming they also found someone to go with through the personals, thought Lou unkindly.

She clicked her way through the site, following the links that would allow her to remove Martin's details from the database. When she had finished, she was directed straight back to the site's home-page. That week's 'hottest' new advertisers were featured in a chart at the top of the page.

'Ready, willing and abell,' said one particularly interesting headline.

The misspelling made poor Lou wince, but she clicked on the ad for the hell of it. According to the checklist that accompanied the illiterate blurb, this particular advertiser was just 21, a gorgeous slim blonde with a pretty substantial chest and an interest in stock-car racing.

'Yeah, right,' muttered Lou. Naturally, there was no photograph to prove it.

That was the problem with these Internet personal ads. With all personal ads, of course, there was no way of knowing how closely the blurb really matched the person it was describing but with e-mail personals the problem was even more extreme. With only words on a computer screen to go on, it wasn't even possible to know for certain the sex of the person you were communicating with after you'd exchanged a hundred e-mails if you never spoke on the phone. Every other week the newspapers carried a story about someone who had been misled by an online romance. There was nothing to stop anyone logging on as a beautiful woman when they were actually a small, dark and not terribly handsome man.

Why did they do it, Lou wondered. If you really hoped to meet someone, then there was little point telling a gay guy you were the man of his dreams when you were actually a girl. Did these people have a compulsion to dissemble? Or did they actually believe that they were the person they became on-line? Did it matter anyway? If you masqueraded as a person of the opposite sex, or scanned in a picture from a magazine instead of your own mug shot, who were you hurting if you never got as far as meeting face to face? Perhaps it was just a harmless way for people to explore those parts of themselves they couldn't freely admit to even amongst their closest friends.

Lou idly clicked back to the www.pinacoladalove-match home page and hovered with her cursor over

the 'browse the ads' option. Men seeking women.
Women seeking men. Men seeking men. Women seeking
women . . .

Briiing!!!

The sound of the telephone ringing brought Lou's
attention swiftly back to her office.

'Lou Capshaw.'

'It's Ruby.'

She sounded flustered. Lou instantly expected the
worst.

'What's up?' She prayed that Robert hadn't already
burst poor Ruby's bubble.

'I've had an answer to my ad,' she said.

'Another Porsche-driver?' Lou asked.

'Not that ad,' said Ruby. 'Another one.'

The letter arrived just as Ruby was heading out to work.
The plain brown envelope floated down on to the doormat right in front of her as she checked her hair one last
time in the hallway mirror. When Ruby saw *The Times'*
postmark, she turned the envelope over quickly. Then
she paused before ripping it open and held her breath.
She'd placed her lonely heart in *The Sunday Times*. This
wasn't a reply to that ad at all.

Caught up in the excitement of her budding new
romance, Ruby had almost forgotten that two-line request she had placed in such a hurry after her night on the
sofa at Lou's. She hadn't even checked the paper on the
day it was supposed to run. Didn't check that they had
printed her request word for word. *Would anyone
knowing the whereabouts of Geraldine Barker, formerly
of Greenwich, please contact box number 6789.*

Ruby sank down onto the bottom step. This wasn't necessarily a response to her advert, she told herself. It might just be a receipt for the money she had paid so far or a solicitation to place another one. But suddenly Ruby held the envelope as though it might contain a bomb. A time bomb.

In fact, she couldn't even open the damn thing on her own. She needed someone there with her. What if the letter inside *was* from her natural mother? What if it said, *I know who you are but I don't want to know any more about you than that*. It wasn't the kind of news Ruby felt she could handle on a Wednesday morning, alone, when she had to get to work.

So, the envelope travelled to the offices of Hollingworth Public Relations still unopened. And sat on Ruby's desk all day. Periodically, she thought she might be able to open it. Periodically, she made herself a cup of hot, weak tea with four sugars (in anticipation of shock) and laid the envelope out on her blotter with every intention of slitting it open to reveal the terrible secrets (or the invoice) inside.

But each time Ruby drank the tea and the envelope remained unopened. By four o'clock in the afternoon, she was feeling pretty jittery from all the sugar she'd imbibed. At half past four – the earliest she could possibly get away – she headed for her rendezvous with Lou and Martin.

This is what friendship is about, she reminded herself as she waited in their usual pub for Lou and Martin to arrive. There were very few people in the world that you could invite to the opening of an envelope (except most of Hollingworth's clients, as Liz frequently observed), who would actually be happy to turn up. But Lou and

Martin did. And when they arrived, Lou and Martin regarded the plain brown envelope with the due reverence its possible contents might accord it.

'My round,' said Ruby, getting up to go to the bar.

'No, mine. You sit there,' said Martin, pressing her gently back into her chair and dispensing with his usual sarcastic manner in an unusual display of compassion. 'Double vodka be strong enough to start with?'

Three double vodkas later the envelope was still intact.

'It's worse than getting your A-level results,' said Ruby with a nervous laugh as she prepared to rip it open at last.

'Can't remember that far back,' Lou told her.

'You do it, Lou. Open it for me.'

'Hand it over then.' Lou took the envelope and tore it open with one easy movement.

'No!' Ruby squeaked involuntarily. 'I'm not ready yet.'

'Too late,' said Lou. 'I've done it.'

'Is it,' Ruby closed her eyes tightly, 'an invoice?'

'It doesn't look like an invoice. There's another envelope inside here.' Lou pulled out a smaller envelope in eggshell blue. Airmail blue, in fact.

'What's the postmark?' asked Ruby, eyes still screwed shut against the revelations.

'America. It looks like Colorado,' said Lou.

'Colorado?' Ruby opened her eyes. 'How can it be from Colorado? My mother lived in Greenwich.'

'People move,' said Martin.

'Yeah, from Greenwich to Clapham. Not to bloody Colorado.'

'Do you want me to open this envelope too?' Lou asked impatiently.

239

'Yes. I mean, no,' Ruby shut her eyes again. 'Just give me a minute longer, could you?'

'Last orders at the bar!'

'Ruby,' Lou pointed out. 'We've been sitting here looking at the envelope for the best part of five hours. The contents will be the same whether you open it now or open it tomorrow or never open it at all. I think you should approach this like pulling off a plaster. The faster you do it, the sooner the pain goes away. If there's any pain to be had at all.'

'I always had to wait until my plasters got so old they just fell off,' said Ruby.

'Why doesn't that surprise me?' Lou smiled. 'After three?' she suggested. 'I'm going to count to three, then I'm going to rip this envelope open and start reading out what's inside it without stopping to draw breath first.'

'Lou . . .' Ruby began to whine.

'I'm starting the countdown now. One, two, three . . .'

Martin held Ruby's hands so that she couldn't cover her ears. With a rip like a fisherman gutting a salmon, Lou tore the envelope, shook the flimsy airmail paper out of its creases and began to read quickly in a low but steady voice.

> *13, Cherry Hills Road,*
> *Boulder,*
> *Colorado*
>
> *Rosalia.Barker@earthlink.net*

Dear Sir or Madam,
I am writing with regard to your advertisement in the London Times about the whereabouts of Mrs Geraldine Barker, formerly of Greenwich in London. Unfortu-

*nately, Mrs Barker is no longer with us, but I am her
daughter-in-law, wife of her only child Nathaniel (Nat).*

*I have recently been making a study into my husband's
family tree as a surprise gift for his fortieth birthday and
would be grateful for any information you can give me
about his mother's life in London before she immigrated
to America. I can be contacted via the above address and
e-mail. I look forward to hearing from you soon.*

   Yours faithfully,

   Rosalia Barker (Mrs)

Which part to take in first, Ruby wondered. My mother
is dead but I have a brother? Nathaniel Barker. Nat. Her
only child. Those three words signified a thousand
things. Nathaniel Barker didn't know she existed. Or
perhaps he knew Ruby existed once but thought she was
dead now too?

'This is heavy shit,' said Martin thoughtfully, when he
read through the letter for himself. 'You've got a brother,
Rubes. Did you know that?'

Ruby shook her head.

'This can't be right,' said Lou. 'It seems unlikely that
your mother would have moved to Colorado. Or died. If
she gave you up for adoption, then she was probably just
a girl herself at the time. And this woman says her
husband is nearly forty. How can he be your brother?
You're only thirty-one.'

'No. It's her,' said Ruby with a certainty that surprised
even her. 'Nathaniel and Hope. Both pretty biblical
names, don't you think? Perhaps I wasn't named by
nuns after all.'

'Eh?' said Lou.

'It's just something the social worker said to me.'

'Well, I think it's a mistake,' said Lou. 'This woman's got the wrong person.'

'I've got a feeling that she hasn't,' Ruby told her. She passed her hand over her forehead as though checking her own temperature. 'I feel really strange.'

'What do you want to do now?' Martin asked.

It was a good question.

'I don't know,' was Ruby's answer. 'This throws up a whole new set of problems, doesn't it? If my mother isn't around to explain the way things were when I was born, I'm not sure where to start. Perhaps I should just leave it at this.'

'What? And not find out if this bloke really is your brother?' said Lou incredulously.

'I read somewhere that siblings raised in separate families often find themselves inexplicably attracted to one another when they meet again as adults,' said Martin. 'You could end up having a torrid affair.'

Lou shot him a deadly glance.

'I didn't expect this,' Ruby murmured.

'Of course not. But the way I see it,' Lou told Ruby, 'you've got to take at least one more step. Just in case.'

'He might not want to meet me.'

'If I were your brother, I would definitely want to meet you,' said Lou. 'And much as I think it's unlikely that this Nathaniel bloke is anything to do with you, at all, I suppose you have to work on the assumption that he is. He's lost his mother. He thinks he's an only child. You might be his only family left in the world. Apart from his missus. This Rosalia girl . . .'

'On the other hand, he might just think you're after half his inheritance,' Martin added helpfully.

Ruby looked between them worriedly. Why did the worst case scenario always seem the most likely one?

'What were you planning to do?' Lou asked patiently. 'You must have thought about what you would do if your mother ever got in touch.'

Ruby cast her eyes downwards and grimaced. 'Of course I have. But I was sort of planning to try to see her from a distance. I thought I'd just get her address and go round there and try to get an idea of what she was like by looking at the outside of her house and seeing what she looked like when she left for work in the morning.'

'You were planning to stalk her?' Martin extrapolated.

'Not stalk,' said Ruby defensively. 'Just watch her for a bit before I made my mind up. But that was when I thought she lived in Greenwich. Not bloody Colorado.' Ruby took a big gulp of her vodka. 'I can't exactly just drop by someone there. And now she's dead anyway. My mother's dead.' She said it slowly and laughed nervously. 'My mother is dead.' It didn't sound right.

Martin instinctively took Ruby's hand.

'You don't know that she's dead,' he said. 'Not until you've written to this woman and explained who you really are and why you're looking for Geraldine Barker. It isn't impossible that you're looking for a different woman entirely. Barker's not that unusual a name. Neither's Geraldine. My mum's got three friends with that name.'

Lou agreed.

'And it is a bit unlikely that you'd have a brother so much older than you.'

'You might be right.' Ruby folded the letter back into its envelope and finished off her vodka. 'I need time to think,' she announced.

'We're here for you whatever you decide,' Martin reassured her.

'Whenever you want to talk about it,' Lou added.

Ruby looked at them with a half-smile. Her eyes were liquid behind tears that she was fighting to hold on to. 'Do you mean that?' she sniffed.

'You know we do.'

Lou took her other hand in a gesture of solidarity. 'Just don't do anything rash,' she added to Martin's promise. 'There's no need to rush into anything.'

'Especially if she's pushing up daisies.' Ruby's bottom lip trembled. She exhaled suddenly and loudly, as though releasing the pressure inside. 'What am I like? If my natural mother's dead, it's not as though I ever knew her.'

'You're still allowed to feel sad,' said Lou.

'Do you want to stay at my place tonight?' Martin asked. 'You don't have to be on your own if you don't want to. I can sleep on the sofa. I just put clean sheets on. And I've even got orange juice for the morning.'

'Sounds tempting,' said Lou. 'Can I come instead?'

As if someone had just flicked a switch, Ruby's face was wreathed in joy.

'Not often Martin gets that reaction when he asks a girl to go home with him,' Lou commented.

But Ruby wasn't reacting to Martin's offer at all. Instead, her gaze was fixed on the pub's front door, where a tall, dark-haired man was raking back his floppy public school locks with his hand as he surveyed the clientele.

'Robert!' Ruby called out to him. 'You made it!'

She dropped Martin's hand like dropping a used tissue in the dustbin. Lou and Martin oriented themselves towards the interloper as he swung into the pub with his pinstriped jacket slung casually over his shoulder. Robert Simpson. Sharp suit. Double-cuffed shirt. Brylcreem. Man at C & A personified.

'Hey, babe,' Robert air-kissed his new girlfriend hello. 'Did I miss last orders?'

'Yes,' said Ruby. 'But Martin hasn't touched his pint yet. You could have that. You do drink Special, don't you?'

'Sure,' Robert nodded.

Martin fought back the urge to protest as Ruby took his last pint and handed it to her new boyfriend. Then she got out of the armchair she had been sitting in so that he could make himself comfortable and sat down again on one of the chair's arms to snuggle up to him like a proper trophy wife.

'Martin, this is Robert,' said Ruby.

Robert made a cursory eyebrow gesture in Martin's direction.

'And this is Lou.'

He kissed Lou's hand.

'Sorry I had to stay so late at the office, Rubes,' Robert told her. 'Bloody knackered. Can't wait to get home to bed,' he added with a suggestive 'know what I mean' wink to Martin. 'Well, what were you guys talking about?' Robert asked.

Lou opened her mouth to tell him.

'Doesn't matter,' Ruby interrupted. 'It was all very depressing. How was your day, Robert? Do you think you'll win that case you told me about? The plumbing fraud?'

Robert squeezed Ruby's knee and launched into a diatribe about one of his clients, a con man who had fleeced a pensioner of her life savings by posing as a plumber and carrying out unnecessary repairs to her heating system. 'Bloody scrote's lying through his teeth, of course,' he told Lou and Martin. 'But I think I can convince the jury otherwise. The old woman can't remember what day of the week it is, let alone whether she authorised forty thousand pounds worth of repairs. Besides, if the old granny can't look after her money then she shouldn't be alive to keep spending it. Don't you think so, Martin?'

Martin winced.

'I didn't like him,' said Martin to Lou, after Robert had bundled Ruby into his midnight blue Porsche Boxster and whisked her back to his flat.

'Was it just the car?' Lou asked him.

'Of course it wasn't just the car,' Martin protested. 'That story. The dodgy plumber and the granny. He didn't give a shit. He doesn't care if he keeps a guilty man out of prison.'

'It's his job,' said Lou.

'I know. I just don't think I could do a job that involved hurting innocent people,' Martin tutted. 'God. Does that sound all superior of me?'

'It's OK. I don't like him either.'

'Seems sort of odd,' Martin said then. 'That someone that bloody confident about himself would have placed a personal ad in the first place.'

'We did,' Lou reminded him.

'I know. But . . . that was different. He drank my pint,' Martin tailed off in disgust.

Back at his flat that evening, Martin tried to remember exactly who it was that Robert reminded him of. That mannequin poise. The surface charm. The extravagant old-fashioned chivalry that didn't extend to refusing Ruby's seat when she offered it.

In the ten minutes that Ruby and Robert had remained in the pub after his sudden, swashbuckling appearance like a particularly bad parody of Zorro, Robert had monopolised the conversation. He presented himself like a wily fox, helping his chicken-shit clients evade proper justice. Robin Hood gone all awry. Ruby seemed impressed if no one else was, even clapping her hands with glee when he recounted yet another county court victory snatched from the jaws of defeat by his witty repartee. Since he rarely seemed to pause for breath, it was incredible that he managed to finish Martin's pint simultaneously. He never thanked Martin for that donation under duress.

Suddenly, as Martin lay on his back in bed and stared at the Chinese paper lampshade that was more grey with dust than white these days, the connection was made. Like Flett, Robert reminded Martin of his own father. And Ruby of Martin's mother in his father's presence. Twittering, twinkling; always orbiting her husband like a fragile, glittering star. Until such time as Martin's father decided that he needed even more reassurance of his attractiveness and started to date his teenage secretary instead.

That was why Martin had taken such an immediate dislike to him. When Robert acknowledged his presence with only the most cursory of glances, Martin had been reminded of the way his father dismissed him in public too. As a small boy, he thought he was the centre of his father's universe. Only later would Martin realise that as a small boy he had been the perfect accessory when his father went out on the pull. Women would always talk to a man pushing a pram or carrying a charming toddler. And a charming toddler wouldn't be able to tell Mum what Dad got up to in the park bushes.

Later, when he was almost as tall as his father and, said his mother, more handsome, Martin's father was quick to point out his son's faults to anyone who admired him. He'd say, 'He's normally so clumsy,' and ruffle his hair, when teachers praised Martin's skill on the tennis court or football pitch. From the outside, it looked affectionate. But subconsciously, Martin knew even then that his father was trying to keep him in his place.

He did that to Martin's mother too. Joking about her cooking and her driving until she was afraid to invite people over to dinner any more and could only drive Martin to visit friends if she didn't have to cross a roundabout to get there. As he grew older, Martin watched his mother start to fade in the glare of his father's insecurity. He knew she'd been different before. There were pictures in a photograph album from a time before his mother and father met. She'd travelled to New

Zealand with a girlfriend, long before gap year world tours were common. She was confident and fearless then. By the time Martin's father left them, there was no trace left of the young woman who had run away to see the world. That was when Martin was eighteen. Over a decade later, his mother still occasionally blamed herself for the way things didn't turn out.

Martin hoped he was wrong about Robert. He really did.

Perhaps he really was just jealous of Robert's success. The fast car. The exciting job. However immoral it seemed – trying to keep known criminals out of prison – there was no doubt that Robert's job made a real difference to real people's lives. By contrast, what was Martin doing? Temping in the post room of a direct marketing company, stuffing envelopes with a bunch of Antipodeans ten years younger than himself whose only aim was to save enough money to get to the next beer fest on the Continent.

Martin's grandiose scheme for escaping the rat race via a miraculous publishing deal seemed more ridiculous than ever now. In the days after he lost the vital diskette, Martin tried to remember as much of his book as he could. He'd scribbled down chapter outlines and even whole phrases. But there was so much he couldn't recall. And now, when he looked at what he had been able to salvage from memory, he wasn't sure that the rest was even worth remembering. Perhaps he'd been kidding himself that he had a talent at all.

Petunia Daniels' cheque was still pinned to the notice board in the corner of his bedroom but he felt sure now that he never would cash it. There was no novel to polish off after all. Nor would there ever be. He could still use the money to escape somewhere sunny, he supposed. But what would that make him? Petunia Daniels had earned that money by being an artist. She'd given it to Martin for being a joke.

'Surprise!'

Andrew was lucky that Lou hadn't done much karate practice lately, when he suddenly materialised from the shadow of her garden hedge as she wrestled with her key in the door.

'What are you doing here?' she asked him irritably, as he kissed her on the back of her neck.

'I was missing you,' he told her. 'I don't think I can sleep on my own any more. I'm too used to having you with me to cuddle up to.'

'Right,' Lou peeled his arms from around her waist and stepped into the house. He followed. 'Aren't you even going to wait to be asked in?' she said indignantly.

'Can I come in?' he asked. He was already closing the door behind him.

'You know, you really shouldn't turn up unannounced,' Lou admonished him. 'I might not have been alone. I might have been here with my other lover,' she raised an eyebrow.

'Why would you want another lover when you've got me?' Andrew asked, as he stuck his hand up Lou's skirt. Lou swiftly removed the offending hand and put the kettle on.

'Have you missed me?' Andrew asked, hovering behind her as she put camomile teabags into two mugs.

'I saw you yesterday,' Lou reminded him.

'I've missed you,' he said.

'That's nice.'

But it wasn't. Three hours later, Lou, like Martin, was staring at the ceiling above her bed. Beside her, Andrew was already sleeping deeply, with his arm slung possessively across her waist. They were the picture of love's young dream. But something really wasn't quite right.

That night, before he nodded off, Andrew had actually said the 'L' word. They'd just made love. Still on top of her, Andrew had raised himself up onto his elbows, looked down into Lou's eyes and told her that he loved her.

'I love you,' he said. Just those three words. Not 'I really love you,' in a jokey voice or 'I love you when you do that' or even just 'I think I love you'. Not any derivation of the phrase that actually detracts from it. Simply 'I love you'. Lou blinked back at him, uncertain how she should respond.

And now she was in her own bed, wondering if she finally understood that old boys' joke about preferring to chew your own arm off rather than wake up beside the person you'd gone to sleep with. Andrew had told her that he loved her and yet she didn't want him there. What was wrong with her? He was everything she had always claimed she wanted. Good-looking, intelligent, trustworthy. Utterly devoted. If she could love anyone at all then surely Andrew was the one?

Half an hour later, she was still no nearer sleep. Carefully, silently, as though she were a thief, Lou lifted Andrew's arm from her stomach. She slipped from the bed and padded towards the kitchen. While the kettle boiled to make camomile tea she fired up her laptop in the sitting room. While she was awake, she might as well get some work done. She'd check her e-mails first. The inbox flashed to let her know she had mail.

From: matchmaker@pinacoladalovematch.com
To: LC3@hotmail.com

RE: We've found your perfect lover!

Click on the link below to find out who fits all your perfect date criteria!

Checking behind her to make sure that Andrew hadn't got out of bed and started reading her mail over her shoulder, Lou clicked on the link.

Chris, 34, black hair, blue eyes. Works as a management consultant. Enjoys skiing, scuba-diving, going to the theatre. Looking for a woman who knows what she wants out of life . . .

Back at Robert's flat, Ruby sat up in bed wearing one of his T-shirts and started to tell him about that day's revelations.

'So,' she concluded, when she had finished explaining the ad in *The Times* and the letter and the Colorado connection, 'I don't know what to do. Perhaps he's my brother. Perhaps my mother and this bloke's poor dead mother just shared the same name. What do you think I should do, Rob? Should I forget all about it? Or do you think I should take this thing further? Lou thinks I should take it further but she also thinks that I should come clean about what I want from them now. I don't know about that. I don't want to scare anybody. And I don't want to have to have a relationship with someone I don't like just because we share genetics. I didn't expect it to work out like this. I thought my mother would still be living in Greenwich. I suppose she might be, if there's been some kind of mix-up. Where can I go from here?'

'Yeah,' Robert was already half asleep. 'Do whatever you feel like. Take it all the way, baby. That's what I'd do.'

'Would you really?' Ruby asked.

'Uh-huh,' said Robert. 'I would.' Seconds later, he was snoring.

23

Next morning, Robert sent Ruby off to work with a surprisingly indiscreet love-bite. It was much too hot to wear a polo neck sweater to the office, so Ruby had to turn her collar up instead, hating the fact that it made her look like a 1980s-style Sloane Ranger – she'd had to don her string of plastic pearls to keep the damn floppy collar in place – but secretly enjoying the attention her distinctly teenage badge of honour was attracting at the office. Especially at that morning's meeting with the Barrington Ball-bearings marketing team.

Every time she looked up from her notes, Ruby was certain that she'd just caught Flett staring at her throat. 'Yes,' she said inwardly. 'I already have another lover and he's far better at the job than you ever were.' Outwardly, she said, 'We *really* like the idea of a national ball-bearings' day for school kids, with engineers going into different schools about the capital to explain how important these little things are in all sorts of big machines.'

Flett nodded. His mouth set in a thin, hard line of disapproval.

'Anything else?' Ruby asked brightly when she saw that she had reached the end of her agenda.

'I think that's everything,' said Flett. He immediately began to pack his papers up.

'You're looking well,' said Ruby, drawing bizarre

strength from the disgusting evidence of her new love-life status on her neck. 'Been somewhere nice?'

'Majorca,' he said.

'Like Imogen!' Ruby trilled as though she didn't know they'd been together.

Flett gave her a narrow-eyed stare.

'Weather good?'

'Fantastic,' he muttered and for the first time ever, Ruby noticed that he really did do a strange thing with his tongue when he was agitated. Martin was right. It was disgusting! She had to bite the inside of her lip to stop herself from laughing out loud.

'We need minutes of this meeting with items for action as soon as you can produce them,' Flett said. 'Nice necklace,' he added, as he followed his team out of the meeting room.

'Up yours,' Ruby hissed beneath her breath, then she gave him the finger from behind the safety of a box file.

'Ruby! Can I have a word?'

Ruby's boss, Alan Hollingworth, was striding across the office towards her. Ruby blushed automatically and began to fiddle with her nasty plastic beads. 'I want to talk to you about the way you've been dealing with the Barrington account,' he continued.

Ruby's entire head was suddenly as red as her love-bites. 'I didn't mean to do what I just did,' she stuttered, referring to her impromptu one-digit gesture. 'But you know how it is. It's unprofessional, I know, but I . . .'

'What's that, Ruby?' asked Alan. He was flicking through the bundle of papers he was carrying to find something to give to her.

'Nothing,' she coughed. Perhaps he hadn't noticed after all.

In fact, he definitely hadn't.

'I just wanted to tell you how impressed I've been by your performance lately,' he said. 'I know you were disappointed not to get the Two-Faced campaign last year and you probably wondered how on earth you were going to raise the profile of something as boring as an engineering firm and those little silver balls, but as far as I'm concerned, you've done exactly that magnificently.'

Ruby could only nod.

'And professionally,' he added. 'I knew you'd rise to the occasion. You needed to be stretched.'

'Thanks,' Ruby managed.

'Of course, I'm not unaware of the situation between you and the CEO at Barrington,' Alan continued. 'I must say I would advise against forming such close personal bonds with clientele in the first place but, all things considered, you have even handled yourself in that matter with great dignity.' (Alan had been out of the office on the day when Ruby blubbed all over Liz Hale and the work experience girl.) 'And with a degree of maturity that shows just how far you've come since you began your career here as a graduate trainee all those years ago.'

'Thank you,' Ruby coughed again.

'And now I think it's time for you to take an even bigger role at Hollingworth PR,' he announced with a certain dramatic flourish as he finally handed her the sheet of paper he had been searching for. 'Ruby, I want you to go to Denver.'

'Denver?'

The sheet gave all the details. The International KFC RPM Group, of which Hollingworth PR had recently become a part, was holding its annual management conference in Denver, Colorado.

'I lobbied for Florida or Las Vegas,' said Alan. 'But the president wants it in this middle of nowhere location so he can go walking the Rockies straight afterwards.'

'Denver?' Ruby echoed.

'You won't have to do anything fancy. Just tag along with Mary.' Alan misinterpreted the expression of fear that passed over Ruby's face as professional anxiety. 'You'll need to leave for the States on Saturday morning. Greta will give you the itinerary. Just go out there and make Hollingworth proud.'

He patted her hard on the shoulder. 'There were those among the senior staff who thought you didn't have it in you,' he said, 'but I knew that you would turn out right. You're our rising star, Ruby. And now you're off to Denver. That's something to look forward to. Wish I could make the trip myself but I've got to be in Paris on Monday morning. Denver, eh? Makes a change from London for the weekend.'

He left Ruby in the corridor, fighting to draw another breath.

Denver. Oh, God.

Later that day, Ruby stared at the plane tickets for her trip as though they were her passport to outer space. The itinerary for the following week's conference of managers from the International KFC RPM Group Inc promised a packed programme of thrilling seminars and team-building exercises. Except on Sunday. Sunday's diary contained just two words. 'At leisure'.

'What can I do on Sunday?' Ruby had asked Mary.

'Anything you want,' Mary told her dismissively. 'I'll probably be nursing a hangover.'

'Where's our hotel?'

'Slap bang in the middle of Denver. You could get out and explore though. Meet some cowboys.'

Ruby didn't want to meet any cowboys. But the opportunity to meet certain other Colorado residents that presented itself to her now definitely hadn't escaped her notice. When Mary left her office, Ruby pulled open the top drawer of her desk and took out that eggshell blue letter with the Colorado stamp.

Later, she connected to the Internet and looked up www.mapquest.com. Sure, Boulder was in Colorado and so was Denver, but America was a big place. Ruby knew, in a snippet of info gleaned from pub quiz night, that California by itself was almost as long as the United Kingdom from Land's End up to John o'Groats. And Colorado was bigger than California, wasn't it? Just because Hollingworth were sending Ruby to Denver didn't mean that it would be practical, or even possible, for her to take herself to Boulder while she was out there. They might be a thousand miles apart.

She typed in the address of the hotel where the conference was taking place and then she typed in the address of the Barker family in Boulder. Moments later, the website came up with a neat little map, complete with distractions en route. Ruby blinked at the results in surprise. She entered the details again as a double check. But the answer was the same. Just thirty miles would separate her and the man who might be her long-lost brother. Thirty miles. To an American that was nothing. It would be like visiting a friend in Battersea when you live in Brixton. A day trip. Perhaps even the kind of trip you could legitimately make for just an hour in the company of someone you desperately wanted to see.

That afternoon's task had been to type up the minutes of the Barrington meeting for Flett but the minutes were forgotten as Ruby pondered the forthcoming trip. Was this incredible coincidence some celestial being's way of letting her know she *should* get in touch with Nathaniel Barker and his wife? Ruby checked a half-dozen horoscope sites for clues. She chewed a plastic biro into splinters. She doodled her way through a pile of Post-it notes. She tried to call Robert. He was out of his office.

With no one to stop her, Ruby began to draft an e-mail. Best to be vague, she had decided.

From: Ruby.Taylor@Hollingworthpr.co.uk
To: RosaliaBarker@earthlink.net

Re: Geraldine Barker

Dear Rosalia,
Thank you for your letter regarding Geraldine Barker, who was a friend of my family while she lived in Greenwich. I too am tracing my family's history and hoped that your mother-in-law might be able to fill in some of the gaps. By an amazing coincidence, I will actually be in Denver next week, on a conference. I will be staying at the Denver Best Hotel from Saturday until the following Tuesday. If it is convenient to you and your husband, I would love to visit you both while I am in the state.

Perhaps on Sunday afternoon? I look forward to
hearing from you.
Best wishes,
Ruby Taylor

Friend of the family? Incredibly vague. But Ruby figured
that she had all week to come up with a more plausible
story for placing that advert.

Meanwhile, Rosalia Barker sent her reply before Ruby
left the office that very afternoon.

From: RosaliaBarker@earthlink.net
To: Ruby.Taylor@Hollingworthpr.co.uk

Re: Geraldine Barker

Dear Ruby,
How exciting! We would definitely love to meet you.
Please come and join us for tea on Sunday afternoon.
We can do it English style! Our home is not very far
from the centre of Boulder. It's just a short drive from
Denver. Or perhaps we could come and meet you?
Please call as soon as you are settled into your hotel.
Looking forward to meeting you!
Yours truly,
Rosalia Barker (and Nat – though I want your visit
to be a surprise!)

'A surprise?' Lou bit her lip when she read the print-out
of the e-mail. 'Oh, Ruby. You haven't told her?'

Ruby answered in the negative and waited for another
sigh.

'Robert said I should go for it,' she said in mitigation.

'Does Robert know what you're actually going for?'
Lou asked.

24

On Friday evening, Robert pushed his salad around his plate listlessly as Ruby outlined her plans and fears for the forthcoming trip.

'Don't you like it?' Ruby asked him, when he finally pushed the plate to the centre of the table and abandoned it.

'Oh, no,' he said. 'It's lovely. It's just that . . .'

'What?'

'I don't know. Maybe I had a dodgy prawn sandwich at lunch. I don't feel so hot.'

'Oh, Robert.' Ruby instinctively reached across the table to touch his forehead and feel his temperature. Robert ducked away from her hand. 'Shall I ask the waiter to bring you some water?'

'You know what, I think I'd better go home,' he said.

Ruby felt herself sag with disappointment. 'I might have an aspirin in my handbag?'

'Ruby,' Robert interrupted her as she rifled through her fake Kate Spade. 'I don't think an aspirin is going to be enough to make me feel better. I need to go home and go to bed.'

Ruby looked up and bit her lip coquettishly.

'On my own,' he added. 'Just tonight.'

'Aw,' said Ruby. 'But I'm going away in the morning.'

'I know. But if this isn't food poisoning,' Robert

continued, 'if it's something like that gastric flu that's been going round, then the last thing I want to do is give it to you tonight so that you have to cancel that flight.'

Ruby nodded.

'I know how important it is to you to go to Chicago.'

'Colorado,' Ruby corrected him. He really must be ill.

Robert summoned the waiter. 'Can you walk to the tube by yourself?' he asked. 'I'm going to jump straight into a cab and go back to my place.'

'I'll be fine,' said Ruby. 'I could probably use an early night too.'

'To make sure you've got plenty of energy next time.'

Ruby blushed.

Ruby looked at her watch as she meandered sadly towards Leicester Square. She knew it wasn't Robert's fault that he was ill, but she had needed his company so much that night. She wanted someone to convince her that dropping in on the Barkers wasn't the worst idea since the Sinclair C5 and Robert seemed to be the only person who wasn't of that opinion. Martin and Lou had both been disapproving. That said, they had promised to stand by her whatever she chose to do.

She dug out her mobile and sent a text message to Lou. 'wot r u doing?'

Seconds later, she got a reply. Lou was in Holborn with some friends from the office. Why didn't Ruby join them? Why didn't she, indeed? Ruby turned and started heading in the opposite direction. Her route would take her back past Caruso's. As she trotted through the crowds she felt light with happiness again. When she spotted the sign for Caruso's swaying gently in the breeze, she couldn't help thinking how wonderful it would be one day to tell her children about those early dates with Robert.

'Your father and I met through a Lonely Hearts ad. We spent our sixth date mooning over each other at Caruso's. By that time, I already knew he was the one for me. I had fallen for his eyes, his mouth, his soft brown hair, his big strong hands which . . .'

. . . even now were cupped around the hands of a blonde girl that Ruby didn't recognise. Halfway past Caruso's huge picture windows, Ruby did a double take then stopped and stared. Robert, for it was he, was sitting right at the front of the restaurant, at exactly the same table he and Ruby had vacated less than twenty minutes ago, with his hands wrapped around the doubtless beautifully-manicured hands of a rather attractive blonde.

'Robert?'

Ruby gawped like a fish caught on the wrong side of the bowl. What should she do? Knock on the window? Walk on by and pretend she hadn't noticed? He was supposed to be ill. Had he lied to her? Who on earth was that girl?

But before she could take any action, Robert turned to admire his reflection in the window and jumped like Macbeth seeing Banquo's ghost.

'Look, I know this looks bad,' he began.

Ruby nodded.

'I'm not going to lie to you.'

'Thank you,' she said. 'Please don't.'

'I was on my way home to take something for my

stomach,' he began, 'but as I walked to the taxi rank I realised I was starting to feel better.'

'And . . .'

'Isobel was standing at the taxi rank too. A total coincidence. I haven't seen her for ages and it seemed silly not to go for a drink and catch up and by that time I was hungry again and so we came back here.'

Ruby nodded. 'Isobel? So that's her name. Can I meet her?'

All the time Robert was explaining this, Isobel had been glaring out at Ruby as though she was the one who should be angry. When Robert noticed, he took Ruby gently by the elbow and guided her a little to the left, to stand in a doorway out of view from the window.

'We're out of the rain here,' he told Ruby.

'We'd be out of the rain if you took me inside the restaurant,' said Ruby with a strained little laugh. 'Can't I come in and meet your friend? I could join you both for pudding.'

'You know what, darling,' Robert crooned. 'Perhaps some other time. I'd be more than happy for you to meet Izzy now but she's in a bit of a state. Just split up from her fiancé. Terrible man. Ran off with some other girl with less than a month left to go before the big day. We're discussing how Izzy might be able to get back the money she spent on a deposit for the wedding reception. I don't want to flaunt our happiness in front of her right now. Do you understand?'

What could Ruby do but nod?

'She's been crying and her face is all red and blotchy,' Robert continued.

'Didn't look blotchy to me.'

'I know,' said Robert smoothly. 'That's what I told her. I said, "Izzy, you look absolutely fine. No one will notice you've been crying." But she said, "Robbo, I don't think I can meet anyone new right now. I feel so fragile after everything Toby put me through." Personally, I think that meeting new people would do her the world of good. But . . . you know what some women are like.'

'Yes,' Ruby nodded again.

'So, I'll call you tomorrow, yeah?' Robert kissed her on the cheek and was preparing to move away.

'Yes,' Ruby said. 'Before ten o'clock. That's when my flight leaves, remember? Look, are you sure I shouldn't come in for a coffee? I don't want her to think you're going out with a lunatic. I gave her such a filthy look when I saw you sitting together in the restaurant. I'd like to explain . . .'

'I'll explain everything and arrange for you guys to meet each other at a better time soon. I'm sure you'd get on like a house on fire,' he added. 'Like cats and dogs.'

'They don't get on,' said Ruby.

'You know what I mean.' Robert glanced back in the direction of Caruso's somewhat impatiently. 'Look, I better get back in there. Don't want to find her crying all over a waiter.'

'No,' said Ruby.

'You,' said Robert, 'are a princess among women. There aren't many girls who would be as understanding as you are.'

'No,' Ruby murmured again.

'OK, sweet lips. I'll call you first thing. And I'll miss you like crazy while you're in California.'

'Colorado,' said Ruby one more time.

Robert kissed her full on the mouth. Then he was gone.

Ruby remained in the doorway to which he had led her for some moments, her brow heavily furrowed as she went over what he had just told her. It was certainly an odd state of affairs. Ruby couldn't imagine ever being so pissed off that she couldn't extend common courtesy towards the partner of one of her friends. But then, perhaps she *was* unusual. And though she had been dumped in some of the most horrible ways imaginable – starting aged twelve with Andy Squires, who had signalled the end of their relationship by snogging her best friend in front of her at the school disco, and ending most recently with Flett's bloody e-mail – Ruby had never been jilted. Could she really begin to imagine the pain of that? The humiliation of having to contact all those people who had been invited to the wedding to tell them that it had been called off? The embarrassment of having to close down your wedding list at Peter Jones?

Under those circumstances, Ruby had to agree, perhaps she wouldn't want to talk to anybody but her very closest friends either. Let's face it, Ruby told herself, she probably wouldn't even be able to get out of bed. Robert was right. Isobel needed space to recover. There would be plenty of time for Ruby to make her acquaintance in the weeks – perhaps, hoped Ruby secretly – years to come.

That said, surely there wasn't any harm in Ruby just poking her head round the restaurant door and saying hello. She wouldn't stop for coffee, wouldn't even sit down. But she did want Isobel to know that she wasn't a psychotic, ultra-possessive girlfriend who was out to stop Robert spending time with his female friends.

Hang on, said Ruby's conscience. Isn't that exactly what an ultra-possessive girlfriend would do?

'I won't be able to sleep tonight if I haven't let Isobel know that I'm not pissed off by the fact that he's spending time with her. I gave her such a filthy look when I saw them together in the restaurant. I need to explain . . .'

'Robert can do the explaining on your behalf,' said the conscience.

'Boys never remember to do that sort of thing,' Ruby continued. 'He won't have explained the situation properly and she'll go away with a terrible first impression of me. I don't want any of his friends to dislike me.'

'She doesn't want to meet you now.'

'I won't flaunt what I've got with Robert and make her feel bad for finding herself single again. God knows I've been there myself enough times. I'll just go in, introduce myself, and leave. Perhaps she'll even be cheered up to hear how Flett and I split. I could tell her about the Lonely Hearts Pact. She'd find that really funny. I know how to cheer a jilted girl up,' Ruby concluded. 'Robert is probably coming out with a load of old clichés. What a dumped girl really wants is *proof* that it isn't the end of her useful love life. There's life after heartbreak. I can prove that.'

'If you really think you want to . . .' said the little voice inside.

'I know I want to see him one more time before I fly to the States.' Ruby took a deep breath and stepped out of the shadows. 'Hi, Isobel. I've heard so much about you!'

She practised her opening line. 'No,' Ruby slumped back into the doorway. 'That's not right.'

Ruby spent five minutes practising her opening speech before she dare make for the restaurant again. By which time, Robert and Isobel were already stepping out for the tube station in the opposite direction. As Ruby got to the door and realised that they had already gone, she was just able to catch a glimpse of Isobel's blonde hair as Robert escorted her around the corner and out of sight.

The head waiter of Caruso's turned the sign on the restaurant door from 'Open' to 'Closed'.

Across town, Lou found herself in a dark and dingy nightclub with a gang of people from her office. John Simpson, the editor who had briefly raised Ruby's hopes that she wouldn't enter her third decade unmarried, was leaving Piper Publishing to work for one of the company's biggest rivals. This night on the town was to wish him well in his new job though Lou knew for a fact that she and Erica couldn't wait to see him leave so that they could fight over his newly vacant office with its view of the sluggish brown Thames.

As a general rule, Lou bailed out on these all-night leaving do's long before the party reached a nightclub. It never usually worked out. After the agony of splitting the bill twelve ways at a pizza restaurant, some bright spark would shout 'let's go dancing', then the group would wander out onto the streets of Soho like a twelve-headed monster finding reasons not to go to this club – 'too expensive' – or that club – 'can't go in there, I'm wearing trainers'. This particular night, however, eight people had managed to agree on a club called 'Poptarts' in a musty-smelling basement just off Oxford Street, and, despite their far from trendy attire and scruffy trainers, all eight had managed to get in.

Now Lou was in the ladies' room, waiting for a cubicle to become free. She couldn't help smiling as three girls stumbled out from behind one door, ostentatiously wiping their noses. She watched them in the mirror as they checked each other's nostrils for evidence of the Class As they had snorted off the back of a cistern.

'You've got a big white bogey!' one of them squealed. 'Don't waste it,' she added, 'it's the only kind of bogey you should eat.'

The second girl followed her friend's advice to the disgusted squeals of the third.

Suddenly, Lou realised that she wasn't the only person watching the three young women giggling at their own debauchery. Lou's gaze was drawn to the reflection of an older woman with short blonde hair that looked expensively highlighted and cut. She had paused in applying her lipstick to catch the three girls inane chatter. It wasn't long before the blonde caught Lou's eyes upon her too and returned her stare quite boldly. The woman's lips curved upwards, friendly but simultaneously almost challenging. Lou ran a hand nervously through her hair. The blonde looked as though she was about to say something when Erica collapsed into the room behind them.

'Oh, there you are,' Erica said with obvious relief. 'I've been looking for you all over. I can't stand this racket any longer. Call this music? Youth of today. Are we getting old, Lou? You don't fancy sharing a cab, do you? We can . . .' Erica paused, mouth open and turned slowly, as though she were a deer on the savannah sensing a predator behind her. Flicking her gaze briefly from Lou to her friend, the elegant blonde put her lipstick back into her handbag and turned away from the mirror, small smile still playing about her mouth like she'd heard a very private joke.

'What's up with her?' Erica half-whispered to Lou as the other woman stalked out of the cloakroom on extremely high-heeled boots. 'Did you see the way she was staring at you? I swear, everybody's out of their heads in this place. Looking for a fight. Or perhaps she was eyeing you up!' Erica laughed hysterically at that.

'Let's get a cab,' said Lou, rolling her eyes at Erica's suggestion.

In the cab back to North London, Erica was drunk and dreamy.

'If you meet the person of your dreams, your soul mate, then it's your *duty* to go after them,' she said. 'Whatever it takes. Whatever anybody else might think of you.'

'Sounds like you're talking from experience,' commented Lou.

'I am,' sighed Erica. 'My best friend from college married the love of my life, you know.'

'You're kidding.'

'I wish I were.'

'You never told me.'

'Can't stand to talk about it. They made me godmother to their first-born two years ago. All I could think of at the christening was that it should have been me that had his daughter.'

'And the stretch marks and the haemorrhoids and the varicose veins,' Lou added.

'Forget all that. It would have been worth it,' Erica said. 'Anyway, I sort of dropped out of touch with the pair of them after that, and last I heard, they were seeing a marriage guidance counsellor.'

'Oh.' Lou didn't know what to say.

'Too late now. I should have made a play for him as soon as Shelly told me she was interested. Could have saved them *both* the heartache. The world is full of people who end up walking down the aisle with the wrong person. Sometimes it makes me feel suicidal to think of Shelly ending up with the man I should have married while at the same time there's probably some poor cow on the other side of London starting to hate being married to Shelly's real dream man. All those happy endings gone awry just because nobody is brave enough to say what they really want when they want it. To risk a little bit of disapproval. To take a chance on love . . .'

The girls both looked into the distance, sagging beneath the weight of Erica's statement.

'So, it's like I said. If you think you've found the one, Lou, then it's your duty to make a proper go of it. To do everything you can to make it happen. Because if you don't, it might not just be you that you're dooming to a loveless life of heartache.'

'Gloucester Crescent,' said the taxi-driver gruffly.

'Ooops, here we are,' said Erica, opening the door and almost falling out onto the pavement. She thrust a tenner into Lou's hand. 'Will that cover my share?'

'I think so.'

'Remember what I said,' she concluded, wagging a finger in Lou's general direction. 'If Andrew's the one for you, then for God's sake, don't mess about. Get him up that bloody aisle double-quick. For both your sakes.'

'Yeah, yeah. See you Monday,' Lou smiled. Then she sank back into the deep black seat again, watching her own reflection in the rear-view mirror, wondering what that blonde girl in the cloakroom had seen.

25

Martin hoped Ruby was doing the right thing. He had
listened to her rationale for making this pilgrimage to
Boulder and made all the right noises in response, but he
couldn't help thinking that there were some things that
were meant to remain in the past. It was difficult for
Martin to imagine how his friend might have an attachment to someone she never really knew, but at the same
time, he knew only too well that the outcome of this
meeting, whatever it was, wouldn't leave Ruby un-
touched.

What worried Martin most was that the woman who
had written in response to Ruby's ad in the back of *The
Times* still didn't really know why Ruby was so keen to
meet her and her husband. When arranging the visit,
Ruby had merely written vaguely of 'family friends'. As
far as Rosalia Barker was concerned, the public relations
conference was the main purpose of Ruby's visit. Tea at
Cherry Hills Drive would merely be an interesting ex-
cursion in a previously planned trip.

Martin and Lou had both expressed the opinion that
Ruby should not turn up at Rosalia's house without
writing to her one more time first, explaining in full the
possible connection between them. That would have
been more sensible surely? And fairer too. Ruby thought
otherwise.

'This isn't something I can put in an e-mail,' she insisted.

Martin tried once more to persuade Ruby that it might be better if she took things more slowly even as she rang from the airport to remind him to water her plants while she was away. She could even send a note from the hotel, he suggested. But Ruby was not to be dissuaded. She just kept repeating her own view like a mantra. 'This is something that has to be done face to face.' Like breaking up, thought Martin.

Well, it worked in the movies. Long-lost families were reunited in an explosion of goodwill and happiness. The prodigal daughter returns to drink champagne. But still Martin couldn't shake the feeling of foreboding that had been his close companion since he promised Ruby that he wouldn't neglect her spider plants and wished her a safe journey from Heathrow. Families were difficult. Just because someone shared your genes didn't mean they would even necessarily like you. Martin at least knew that to be true.

Ruby was about halfway over the Atlantic when it struck her that she might be about to make one of her trademark huge mistakes. Mary was snoring beside her in Business Class. A nervous flyer, Mary had started necking champagne in the airport lounge. 'Mix a good half bottle of that with a couple of sleeping tablets,' she told Ruby, 'and a transatlantic crossing quite literally flies by.'

Ruby didn't take her up on her offer of a couple of knock-out pills, telling her that she wanted to enjoy the experience, look out of the window at the world passing by ten miles below. But by the time they were over Greenland, Ruby wished she had taken Mary's advice. The in-flight movies had long since lost their appeal. Nothing could distract her from the creeping fear that she had gone about everything absolutely wrong.

Ruby couldn't remember when her parents first told her she was adopted. It just seemed as though she had always known, in the way that everyone else at school knew they'd come straight from mummy's belly-button. Ruby could remember the day everyone in her class found out the truth however. Their form teacher, Miss Mayfield, had been talking to them about a junior school in Africa. The plan was to 'adopt' the school, sending the poor kids their old toys and unwanted books for Christmas. Elaine Roberts asked what it meant to 'adopt' something and for reasons known only to herself, Miss Mayfield thought it would be a good idea to illustrate her explanation using Ruby as an example.

The rest of the class were agog as Miss Mayfield told them that Ruby's 'proper mummy and daddy' had decided they couldn't look after her and asked for her to be given to someone who could. And no matter how carefully Miss Mayfield tried to explain that Ruby was now the Taylor family's 'real child', by lunchtime Elaine Roberts had dubbed Ruby a 'bastard' and told her that it was just a matter of time before someone from the local children's home came to take Ruby away.

The next few days had been hell. Ruby longed to ask her parents for confirmation that the children's home didn't have a place waiting for her but found herself unable to bring up the subject. By the third day, the news had reached Lindsay's form room. Kieran Pope told Lindsay that Ruby wasn't her 'real sister'. Lindsay landed a punch on his chin. Both the Taylor sisters were sent home at lunchtime.

Ruby's mother had to sit Lindsay down at the kitchen table and explain all about the adoption then. It seemed that it had been so much a fact of their lives that Mr and Mrs Taylor had forgotten to even formally go through the facts with their eldest daughter.

Ruby waited in the sitting room while her mother told Lindsay the real story. Even then Ruby's natural instinct was to wait for rejection, expecting her big sister to turn round and say that she didn't want to have Ruby in the family any more. Ruby was the cuckoo. Taking up space that she wasn't entitled too. But that wasn't how it happened at all.

When she had digested everything her mother told her, Lindsay said she was just relieved that no one would be coming to take her sister away. She went back upstairs to play with her Sindy dolls and never mentioned the incident again. Ruby was her proper sister. She would be forever. And that was that as far as the Taylor family was concerned.

And that's partly why Ruby felt like such a piece of shit as she crossed the Atlantic that Saturday. That very morning, as she waited in the Business Class lounge at Heathrow for her flight to start boarding, Ruby had called her parents with every intention of telling them exactly what she hoped to do while she was at the conference in Denver. But the right moment never seemed to present itself. Mrs Taylor was worrying about Lindsay and Lauren. Lauren had the snuffles and was keeping Lindsay and her husband up all night. Then she started talking about Mr Taylor's dodgy back. It was stopping him from enjoying his golf. And then she told Ruby about the teenage lad up the road they thought had been scratching the paintwork on the new Volvo. Ruby just couldn't find the right point in the three-minute conversation to say, 'By the way, Mum, I'm going to see my real brother.'

Anyway, there was still the chance that Nathaniel Barker might not actually *be* Ruby's brother. There didn't seem much point in upsetting her mother – and Ruby was sure that she would be upset – if it was going to turn out that Nathaniel Barker and his wife weren't related to Ruby after all. Lou thought Ruby should tell her parents anyway. Let them know that she was interested in finding out about her history at least. But though Ruby's mum and dad had always claimed that they would happily help her trace her real family, she'd never really been convinced.

So, the conversation passed without event. As the call came to an end, Ruby's mum just wished her a safe trip to America and said, 'we love you'. She only and always said that when either of her daughters was getting on an aeroplane. Just in case it crashes, Ruby supposed.

There's way too much time to think on the journey from Heathrow to Denver, Ruby decided. She wished she had somebody to talk to. Mary would be dead to the world until they reached the other side. Not that Ruby could realistically have opened up to her. She was still Ruby's superior, even if Ruby had now heard her snoring and seen her dribble in her sleep.

Ruby wished that Robert were with her especially. Though they had only been seeing each other for a couple of weeks at that point, she already felt that he knew her pretty well. He always seemed to say the right thing. It was mostly thanks to him that she had gathered enough confidence to contact Rosalia in the first place. Meeting Robert made Ruby feel as though the long streak of rejection, imagined or otherwise, that had been her life so far was over. If someone as fantastic as him could want her for his girlfriend, then why shouldn't Nathaniel Barker want her for his sister too?

As promised, Robert called Ruby on the morning of her flight to reassure her that everything would work out in the best interests of everyone involved. He told her that he would be by his phone – or at least by his mobile one – day and night until she returned to England, just in case she needed to talk . . . Except on Sunday night, when he would be at his sister's – he didn't think he could get reception at her house. And on Monday, when he would be at a reunion for people on his college course. But he would be thinking about Ruby even then, he said. He would be sending positive vibes in her direction. Ruby hoped that Martin and Lou would do the same. Though she knew they both thought she was mad.

Ten hours after take-off, the plane touched down in Colorado. Denver airport, with its tented white terminals, looked like a flotilla of ships sailing across the barren plain at the foot of the Rockies. The airport was in the middle of nowhere. The journey to the hotel took the best part of an hour. Mary managed to stay awake just long enough to claim her luggage. Now she was snoring in the back of the taxi as the outskirts of Denver passed.

Ruby had been to America only once before, as a teenager, when she went to New York with her mother and father and Lindsay. It should have been a dream holiday but Ruby was just sixteen then, and spent the entire time moping about the boyfriend she'd left behind at home when she should have been soaking up the experience. The wide-open spaces of Colorado couldn't have been more different than the concrete canyons of Fifth Avenue and Broadway but they still felt strangely familiar. Was it just because she had seen similar houses, stores and billboards a million times on television? Or was it, she wondered, some kind of tribal resonance? Had her mother walked along that sidewalk? Visited that cinema? Shopped in that mall?

'Been to Colorado before?' the cab-driver asked her jovially.

'It's funny,' said Ruby, 'but I feel I have.'

The *déjà vu* continued in the hotel, which was exactly as she had expected. Low, peach-coloured lighting in the lobby, hiding the wear and tear on chintzy sofas and cheap wooden coffee tables strewn with tourist information. One of those black boards with the plastic letters that attach with tiny studs announced the presence of the convention, along with the annual dinner dance of the Denver Dairy Farmers' Association. Once you stepped into the lobby you might have been in any hotel in any city in the world. Ruby's room was a beige box on the seventh floor with a view of a sad-looking car park.

But there was a small bunch of roses on the bedside table. At first, Ruby assumed that the hotel had sent roses to all the guests, or at least the ones attending the KFC

RPM Group convention. But the card told her otherwise.

'Welcome to Denver,' said the neat blue hand. 'We're so excited to meet you. From Rosalia and Nathaniel Barker.'

When Ruby opened the window to get some air, the car park seemed to lurch up towards her. Later, Ruby wondered if she should have called and cancelled that afternoon rendezvous. She could have said that the convention was over-running and she wouldn't have Sunday free after all. Ruby could even have sent Rosalia an e-mail – she had her laptop with her – pretending she had never left London at all. As Ruby looked at the bunch of joyful yellow roses on the bedside table, she still had her hand on the lid to a veritable can of worms.

26

'Would you answer this ad?' Lou asked Martin. They were having brunch *à deux* in the Café Rouge.

'Which one?' Martin asked.

Lou spread out the 'Soulmates' section of the *Observer* on the table before him and circled Erica's two-line ad for his attention.

> 'Cat-loving vegetarian, 32, seeks sensitive soul with
> Pisces in his chart.'

Martin wrinkled his nose. 'Cats? Horoscopes? Wrong side of thirty? Uh-uh. Not for me.'

'I thought so,' said Lou. 'Erica from my office placed it. I hope she isn't going to be disappointed.'

'Why should she be? You asked for my *personal* opinion. It's perfectly possible that a cat-loving, vegetarian Pisces may be calling her box number right now,' Martin pointed out.

'Yeah, but is that what she *needs*?' asked Lou.

'You're not proposing another pact?' Martin joked. 'You know how well that worked.'

'You never did say what happened between you and Cindy,' Lou smiled. 'Did I do right there?'

Martin looked about himself nervously. 'It will come out in my memoirs.' Then he looked at his watch. 'Two o'clock. That makes it seven in the morning in Colorado.'

'You've worked out the time difference!' Lou exclaimed.

'I knew it anyway,' Martin blustered. 'What time was she supposed to be going to see them?'

'Not until the afternoon.'

'Do you think she's OK?'

'She hasn't called. That's always a good sign. Besides, if she isn't OK, I don't suppose we'd be the first people she calls any more. Apparently, Robert told her that she should call him day or night if ever she needed a shoulder to cry on.'

'That's good of him,' said Martin sarcastically. 'Seeing as he is supposed to be her boyfriend and all.'

'Perhaps he isn't just a Porsche-driving wanker after all. Perhaps he has a sensitive heart beneath that brash exterior.'

'Yeah,' Martin looked unconvinced.

'God, I hope she's met her Mr Right,' Lou sighed. 'It seems like ever since we've known that girl, Ruby has been in a dreadful relationship, recovering from the ending of a dreadful relationship, or trying to throw herself straight into a new one.'

Martin nodded.

'OK,' Lou asked him suddenly. 'Truth or dare. Have you ever wanted to get it together with Ruby yourself?' She fixed him with her piercing blue eyes.

Martin almost spat out a mouthful of cappuccino in surprise.

'You know I already did,' he said. 'In Freshers' week.'

'Yeah but what happened after that? Why didn't you two start going out with each other after your night of hot passion?'

Martin shrugged. He wasn't about to tell Lou that Ruby had taken his virginity then sent him away with threats that she would tell everyone he was a premature ejaculator if he mentioned what had gone on between them. 'I don't know,' he said. 'I guess we didn't know each other well enough to make it work.'

Lou shook her head dismissively. 'And then?' she asked.

'Then we became friends and pretty soon we knew each other *too* well to sleep together again.'

'Is that possible?'

'You know it is. You don't want to sleep with someone once they've given you a blow-by-blow account of their sex life with someone else.'

'I see. So you didn't know her well enough and then all of a sudden knew her too well?'

'I suppose so. Besides, Ruby's always telling me how well I prove the "all men are bastards" rule. She always sides with my ex-girlfriend in any break-up. She wouldn't risk being anything more than my mate.'

'But you *would* want to be something more than her friend?' Lou probed.

'I didn't say that,' Martin protested.

'OK,' said Lou, folding up her paper. 'I think I've finished with the witness, m'lud.'

'What do you mean by that?' Martin asked irritably.

'Nothing. Oh look, saved by the boy.'

The door to the café swung open to admit Andrew, dressed in a smart blue suit.

'Hey, man,' said Martin. 'Didn't anybody tell you it's the weekend?'

'We're going to see my parents,' Lou explained.

'Though you really didn't have to go so far as wearing a suit,' she added to Andrew.

'I wanted to make a good impression,' he told her. 'It's important to you.'

'Not that important,' Lou assured him. 'My mum will be impressed if you've washed in the last fortnight.'

'It's the Stepford husband,' Martin cracked.

'Shall we go?' Andrew asked. 'We don't want to be late.'

'They'll be expecting it of me,' said Lou.

'But not of me,' said Andrew.

Lou hadn't taken anyone to meet the parents for a very long time indeed. In fact, she hadn't brought anyone home at all since she was still at school and boyfriends had to pass inspection by Mum and Dad before they were allowed to cross the threshold of her bedroom. Then, the bedroom door had to be left ajar to ensure she got up to no naughtiness. The result was that after years of listening out for the footfall of her parents on the stairs, Lou had developed the supersonic hearing of a bat. She could also make love in absolute silence.

Back then, Lou's parents had begged her to concentrate on her A-levels rather than her love-life. Now, they begged her to concentrate on her love-life rather than her career. They'd been giving her the 'nearly thirty' line since she celebrated her twenty-first. And when Lou called her mother to say that she would be coming over for Sunday dinner and would like to bring a friend, she could almost hear the relief in the old lady's voice.

But perhaps Lou's mother was right to be so concerned with settling down.

Following Andrew's surprising declaration of love, Lou had convinced herself that she was wrong to react so negatively. She pinched a copy of a pink-covered book about Commitment-Shy Women from the PR office at work and read it from beginning to end. Much as she scoffed at self-help books – unlike Ruby, who was always reading 'Women who do too much something or other' – Lou had to admit she fitted the profile. Her early love-life had been littered with men who didn't seem to want her as much as she wanted them. That, the author of the book explained, was because Lou had actually been deliberately picking men that she couldn't get close to. Now she had met someone who was ready to commit to her, she was reacting so strangely because Andrew had unwittingly hit upon the real problem. It was Lou who was afraid of commitment and marriage and all that entailed. Not the unavailable men she had chased after all her life.

And Lou did want marriage and babies, didn't she? She felt sure at least that she wanted a family. As an only child, she had had an idyllic childhood. She was the centre of her parents' universe, wanting for nothing from tennis lessons to a pony of her own to so much real, unconditional love it almost suffocated her at times. There was no doubt she had grown up with a sense of true security, but also a heavy sense of the responsibility of carrying forward the family line. Her parents assumed she would have children. Lou had assumed she would have children. Even if she couldn't see herself with a baby, she had often imagined raising a daughter of her own, looking and sounding just like her . . .

Of course, having children didn't necessitate being

married, but Lou definitely couldn't imagine doing it on her own. And now Andrew had come into her life, talking long-term commitment right from the start. By the time Lou finished reading that book about Commitment-Shy Women, she thought she had diagnosed her problem *and* found the answer. She was almost thirty. It *was* time for her to grow up and settle down. If the only people she ever allowed anywhere near her heart were perfect strangers glimpsed once on a packed rush-hour tube then Lou might be dooming herself to growing old alone.

So, in the end it was fear that made Lou take Andrew to meet her parents. Fear that she was sabotaging her own happy ending by turning her nose up at Mr Absolutely Obviously Right. Because he was right. Wasn't he?

And of course the day went wonderfully. But the drive back to London that night found Lou closing her eyes and pretending to sleep so she wouldn't have to get into conversation.

Lou's parents had loved him. He'd made her mother laugh. He'd promised her father that he would help him build a barbecue before the end of the summer. When Lou's mother told her that they made a fantastic-looking couple, Lou found herself transposing their heads onto her cousin Alice's wedding photo.

Then the fantasy crashed like a needle skittering over an old record.

It wasn't right. It never would be right.

Andrew squeezed her knee and gazed at her as though she were the only girl in the world.

How on earth was she going to tell him?

27

A combination of time-zone confusion and nervous anticipation meant that Ruby was awake at five o'clock the morning after her arrival in Denver. The previous evening, the conference delegates had gathered in the hotel's western style ranch-themed restaurant for a welcoming drinks party followed by an extravagant dinner at which Ruby found herself sitting next to her opposite number from the Dutch office of Hollingworth. His English was as bad as her Dutch and they spent the entire meal smiling inanely and saying, 'It's good here, yeah?' 'Yeah, it's good.'

Meanwhile, Mary had hooked up with her own opposite number from the new public relations and advertising agency in New York that was the latest jewel in the International KFC RPM Group's crown. Used to her superior in full 'ice maiden' mode about the office, Ruby was a little embarrassed to watch Mary snuggling up to Todd Barnhardt like she was a school girl and he was captain of the football team. However, Ruby was grateful that Todd's attentions kept Mary from noticing that her junior left the fray during coffee.

On the journey to Heathrow, which now seemed a million years ago, Mary had promised Ruby several 'all-night networking sessions' with a wink. Ruby had been dreading them, picturing herself stuck in the hotel bar until Mary drank enough to pass out. An 'all-night networking session' with Mary, legendary for her business prowess *and* her somewhat unladylike alcohol consumption, was as inviting as an audience with Stalin in the days when the first person to stop applauding him would be shot. Ruby had heard rumours of Hollingworth staff finding themselves blocked from promotion for drinking orange juice when Mary was on a bender.

Thankfully, Mary hadn't seemed terribly interested in Ruby's plans for that Sunday either but said that she should hire a car or take a taxi to wherever she wanted to go and stick it down on expenses. 'Even as far as Boulder?' Ruby asked. Even as far as Boulder, Mary confirmed. KFC RPM were paying.

That morning, Ruby had room service bring her breakfast as soon as they were able. Though she had hardly made a dent in the steak she had found herself faced with at the welcoming dinner, Ruby was suddenly ravenous; hardly surprising since according to her body it was actually time for lunch. What would be going on at home right now, she wondered. She thought of Robert travelling in the Boxster to his sister's house for a barbecue. He obviously thought a great deal of his sister. He seemed to visit her at least once a week, sometimes more often and had once even cancelled a date so that he could dash down to help her with some baby-sitting crisis or other. Ruby wondered when she would get to meet Robert's family herself. Would she like them? Would they like her? Would she be good enough for a successful lawyer like their son? Would she be good enough for the Barkers?

When Ruby phoned Rosalia Barker to make arrangements for that day's meeting, she was overwhelmed by the woman's warmth. By this stage, Ruby had managed to convince Rosalia that Geraldine Barker had been a neighbour of Ruby's parents in the early seventies and she was keen to know if Geraldine had left behind any photographs of her parents from that time. Rosalia was only too pleased to make the Barker family album available to her new friend.

'Here's hoping we can do one another a favour,' she said. 'There are lots of faces in photographs from those days in Greenwich that my husband can't put a name to. Perhaps some of them are your folks.'

'Perhaps,' Ruby agreed.

Between five in the morning and ten which was when the taxi would arrive to take her to Boulder, Ruby went through almost as many outfit changes as she would for a date. The nerves were much worse though and by the time reception called Ruby's room to say that the taxi was waiting for her outside the hotel, Ruby had worried the cuticle on her left thumb so much it was actually bleeding.

'Have a nice day,' chirped the bell-boy as Ruby scuttled through the lobby.

She was so anxious that she didn't even hear him.

The Barkers' whitewashed house at number 13 Cherry Hills Drive was like something out of a movie; one of those Disney films where an almost perfect family adopt a lovable dog or alien who makes their lives complete.

Ruby had the taxi-driver drop her off on the other side of the street and just stood there on the pavement for a moment, taking in the wide flat boards that made up the walls, the pink gingham curtains hanging in swags at the open windows, the even brighter pink flowers in the pots that lined the windowsills and flanked the stairs up to the front door like a legion of little floral soldiers.

The place even had a picket fence and one of those metal postboxes with a flag that the mailman raises so the people inside know when they have a letter without having to step out of the house. From the front gate hung a faux rustic wooden plaque in the shape of a smiling sun. 'Welcome to our home', the plaque announced. 'All who enter beware', said another wooden sign sticking out from one of the flower-beds. 'You'll never want to leave!' It was cheesy beyond description, Ruby thought. But nice. Friendly. Really friendly. Just as Rosalia Barker had been on the phone.

Ruby took a deep breath and reached out for the latch on the gate. As she did so, the door to the white house opened and a woman, about her age, perhaps a little older but not by much, stepped out onto the porch with a pair of secateurs and began to prune her flower boxes.

Ruby froze, as though she had been caught breaking in. But at first the woman didn't even see her. She was humming to herself, flowing easily from one flower box to the next, dead-heading her geraniums as though she were miming the mundane task at the beginning of a ballet about gardening. Eventually she turned to look at Ruby as though she had sensed her gaze upon her.

'Hey there!' she called across the garden with an enthusiastic wave. 'Hey!'

Ruby stepped out from the shadow of a tree. Rosalia

Barker was already racing down the garden path to meet her, abandoning her pruning shears and stripping off her gardening gloves as she went.

'Are you Ruby?' she asked.

Ruby nodded. Rosalia took Ruby's shakily proffered hand in both of hers and shook it energetically. 'How are you?' she asked. She smiled so broadly that it seemed impossible that she hadn't recognised at once the family connection with the stranger who stood in front of her. 'I'm so glad to meet you at last. Come in. Come in! I was just tidying up the flowers for your visit. Can't stand to have shrivelled petals on my plants,' she explained. 'Makes the place look so untidy, don't you think? Do you like to garden, Ruby?'

'I don't have one,' Ruby told her.

'That is such a pity!' Rosalia exclaimed. 'My husband is always telling me that you Brits have the best gardens in the world. Tells me everything else about the country is pretty crummy, of course. But your gardens are supposed to be just lovely.'

'I suppose they are.'

'I'd like to visit,' Rosalia confided. 'But Nathaniel doesn't really want to go back there.'

'That's a shame.'

'I'll work on him,' Rosalia assured her. 'And we'll be there before you know it. Come in, come in.'

She led her visitor indoors.

While Rosalia went to take off her gardening apron, Ruby sat on the very edge of a white wicker-framed sofa in a living room that confirmed Rosalia's liking for neatness went far beyond her tidy plants. A small pile of issues of the *National Geographic* was aligned exactly with the edge of the coffee table. Every plant pot sat squarely on a doily to protect the varnished surfaces beneath.

'You need a drink?' Rosalia called from the kitchen. 'I just made iced tea?'

'Iced tea would be nice,' Ruby confirmed.

She peered around the room. The blinds were pulled down to save the carpet from fading in the brutal glare of the sun. There was a framed verse from the bible on top of the mantelpiece. That one about the lilies in the fields. And some photographs. Rosalia and a tall man in ski gear. Rosalia on her wedding day, holding a bouquet of pink roses and grinning so much that she was fit to burst with joy. Rosalia and her husband . . .

Ruby picked up the little silver frame that had pride of place on an occasional table and squinted at the groom with his arm around Rosalia's waist. He had dark hair. A suntan. Ruby had never been able to get a tan like that. Did they look alike? Not at first sight. She had the frame almost against her nose as she looked for similarities. Then Rosalia returned from the kitchen, still grinning, with a tray loaded down with iced tea and three glasses. Ruby jumped as though she had been caught stealing again.

'Isn't that frame the sweetest?' Rosalia asked warmly. 'It was a gift from my husband's mother on our wedding day. It's a family heirloom.'

My family, Ruby thought.

'Did you find your way here easily?' Rosalia asked, as she poured the tea into two of the glasses and made sure her guest got a slice of fresh lemon.

'Er, yes,' said Ruby hesitantly. 'I got a taxi.' She was still on goldfish mode.

'And what do you think of our beautiful state?' Rosalia continued.

'It's lovely,' said Ruby blandly. 'The mountains are so big.'

'They are pretty big, I agree,' said Rosalia. 'Especially when you're skiing down one of 'em. My husband loves to ski the steepest hills you ever saw. He's such a sporting daredevil.'

Ruby nodded. She certainly wasn't. She hadn't worn a pair of trainers since her last day at school. Perhaps they weren't related after all.

'Sweet enough for you?' Rosalia asked as Ruby took a first sip of her tea.

Ruby nodded again. Though it was horrible. She hated the stuff. Couldn't understand why the Americans seemed to have such an aversion to making tea properly, piping hot, with milk.

'So,' Rosalia sprang up from her seat as though she had ants in her pants and started to dig around in the top drawer of a bureau. 'Before Nathaniel comes back from Home Depot, I want to show you what I have on the Barker family so far. I started my search on the Internet,' she explained. 'Barker seems to be a relatively common surname back in England but I was lucky enough to know the parish where Nathaniel's maternal grandparents were born and their church had just put all of its resources on-line. Can you believe my luck?'

She sat down again, right next to Ruby on the sofa this time, and opened a box file marked 'The Barker Family Tree' in neat black marker pen.

'I've always been fascinated by history,' Rosalia continued. 'I know you Brits think we Americans are crazy the way we keep on. But we're all so jealous of the way you can trace your families back for generations and generations. My grandparents came over from Europe during the Second World War and that's where my story ends. But Nathaniel . . . well, you'll see how much stuff I have here.' Rosalia took out a photograph. 'This is Nathaniel's great-grandfather,' she said, handing Ruby the black and white photo of a man in a naval uniform. 'And this is his great-grandmother.'

Seeing Ruby's eyes narrow as she studied the photograph of a young girl with wavy blonde hair, Rosalia assumed that the room was too dark and flicked on a table lamp to help her.

'Better? Paternal side,' Rosalia explained. 'Nathaniel doesn't take after them at all. Not physically. He favours his mother.'

'He does?' Ruby's voice came out in a croak.

'Oh, yes.' Rosalia continued to dig on through her box of documents. 'It's really quite incredible. Let me show you.'

Ruby could only gape as she watched Rosalia produce birth certificates, marriage certificates and death certificates like a magician pulling rabbits from a hat. 'That's his mother's birth certificate,' she said, casually adding another document to the heap on the coffee table. Ruby picked it up and read the name. The name that had been printed under 'mother' on her own birth certificate. His mother's place of birth also matched that given on the scrap of paper that Amanda the Patchouli Monster handed over to Ruby almost ten years before.

'Where is it?' Rosalia muttered, not noticing how hard Ruby was gripping Geraldine Barker's certificate. 'I had it the other day when I went to get those copies done. Ah yes, here it is.' Rosalia sank back into the cushions and pulled a photograph from an unprepossessing brown envelope with a final magical flourish.

'This is my husband as a baby with his mother. She was twenty-three years old at the time.'

Ruby's hands were shaking as she took the photograph to look at it herself. The young woman was holding her baby on her hip, with her other hand she gestured towards the camera, trying to encourage her little boy to smile. Nathaniel Barker glared at the photographer suspiciously. One little fist was clenched around the leg of a well-loved teddy bear. The other grasped a handful of his mother's blouse, determined not to let her go.

Ruby felt her throat begin to close. Her eyes pricked.

'Wasn't she beautiful?' Rosalia said brightly.

Wasn't she?

The family face. The magic mirror. Ruby's parents had a dozen photographs like this from her own childhood. She'd hated having her photograph taken too. Always scowling at the camera like her brother. Still scowling at the age of twenty-three, when she looked almost exactly as Geraldine Barker had done.

'You know,' said Rosalia, looking at Ruby appraisingly. 'You favour her a little too. Isn't that funny?'

Ruby nodded, keeping her eyes cast down so that Rosalia couldn't see the glitter of imminent tears.

'What happened to her?' Ruby asked. 'When did she die?'

'Last fall,' said Rosalia sadly. 'End of October. Malaria. Can you believe it? She went to Bangladesh with a group of missionaries from our church and got ill when she came home. We thought she just had the flu, or something. She insisted on carrying on like normal, taking food to the old ladies she used to cook for when their families couldn't help them. Helping out at Sunday school. Then one night she just collapsed and died of liver failure. It's typical of Geraldine to have caught her death when she was doing her best for other people,' Rosalia added with a rueful little smile. 'Still, God always takes the good ones.'

'She sounds like a lovely woman.'

'Oh, she was,' said Rosalia emphatically. 'Always doing something for people less fortunate than herself. Old people. Young people. Especially babies. She couldn't see a baby in trouble and not try to do something about it. Used to cry like a waterfall when she saw those abandoned kids in the Balkans on TV. And when she found out about the babies in that orphanage in Bangladesh, there was no way any of us were going to stop her heading right out there to save them.'

Ruby handed the photograph back. Rosalia sniffed loudly as she took it. 'I'm sorry. I was very close to my mother-in-law,' she explained. 'Incredibly close. So,' she clapped her hands together then as though to dismiss the sombre mood. 'Let's hear more about you. Your parents were from the same town as Geraldine? Did your mother know her before she was married?'

'Not exactly,' Ruby began. Wasn't the real story obvious yet?

Deep breath. Ruby put her iced tea down.

'Rosalia,' she said. 'I haven't been entirely honest with you.'

As the real story tumbled out, Ruby almost felt as though she had left her body and was floating by the ceiling, watching herself tell Rosalia about her adoption and watching Rosalia's trusting eyes grow so wide they might pop out of her head.

'Oh, sweetheart,' Rosalia muttered over and over. 'That's terrible.'

Rosalia was lost for words as Ruby described her afternoon with Amanda the Patchouli Monster at the social services office and the emotions that had accompanied the discovery of her birth mother's name. It was the first time Ruby had really spoken about that afternoon to anyone and she was surprised by how much it still hurt to think about it. That stupid comment that she might have been named by nuns because her natural mother couldn't be bothered. Ruby was unable to hold back the tears.

When Ruby had finished talking, Rosalia put her arm around her shoulders and hugged her close. She stroked her hair, cooing and whispering soothingly, like a woman well used to baby-sitting, though she had no muchlonged-for children of her own.

'Darling,' she said eventually. 'My heart goes out to you. You've had a terrible time. But there's clearly been a misunderstanding.'

'What do you mean?' Ruby asked.

'My husband's mother married at the age of twenty-one,' said Rosalia patiently. 'She had just one child, my

Nathaniel. Her husband was killed in a car wreck before she could have another one.'

'But look.'

Ruby wiped her nose on her sleeve and dug into her bag for her birth certificate.

'Geraldine Barker,' Ruby pointed out. 'And the birth place is the same too. Look. Mother's place of birth, Sheffield. That's what it says on Geraldine's own birth certificate. You can't tell me it's all a coincidence.'

'It could be,' said Rosalia.

'But I even look like her,' said Ruby, picking up the photo of Nathaniel and Geraldine again. 'And,' Ruby went back into her bag for a baby photo she had lifted from her parents' house a few weeks before, 'I used to look like Nathaniel too.'

Rosalia chewed her lip as she took in the undeniable resemblance of her husband as a child to this young Englishwoman at the age of two.

'I just don't see how it can be possible,' Rosalia exclaimed.

'But it's not *im*possible,' said Ruby.

Rosalia could only shrug at that.

'Please,' Ruby begged her. 'I don't see how there can be any other explanation. Your mother-in-law was my mother.' She took the other woman's hands in a beseeching sort of gesture.

'You'll have to talk to my husband,' Rosalia said, subtly extricating herself from the hold. 'But I promise you, he's never mentioned anything like this and Nathaniel always tells me everything.'

As she said that, outside the house, a well-loved station wagon pulled up against the kerb. A guy in a blue checked shirt with a baseball cap shading his eyes from the sun jumped out followed by an excited looking black Labrador. If Nathaniel Barker had ever considered himself to be British, he looked every bit the American now. Rosalia looked nervously towards the door as she heard her husband's key turn in the lock.

'He loved his mother,' Rosalia said quietly. 'Be careful how you tell him all those things you've said to me.'

The Labrador preceded its master into the sitting room.

'Elvis!' Rosalia exclaimed, as the Lab wished her hello with his tongue. 'Get down, boy.'

The dog immediately turned his attentions to Ruby.

'Honey,' Rosalia called to her husband, who was taking off his boots in the hall. 'We have a visitor. From England,' she added a little more quietly.

Ruby stroked the dog's soft ears. Its goofy canine face was strangely comforting.

Nathaniel Barker stepped into the room, tucking his baseball cap into his pocket.

'From England? Have we met before?' Nathaniel asked as he reached out to shake Ruby's hand.

'Not exactly,' said Ruby.

Rosalia looked nervously between her husband and their visitor as Ruby prepared to tell the story one more time.

'You're lying.'

Nathaniel Barker didn't want to know.

'You're talking bullshit!' he raged.

He didn't see how it could be possible that his mother, a god-fearing woman, a practising Christian and leading member of her church, could possibly have had a child out of wedlock after his father's death.

'Don't you think I would have noticed?' Nathaniel asked his would-be sister. 'I would have been eight years old when you were born, for chrissake. I would have known if she was having another baby.'

He refused even to look at Ruby's birth certificate and closed his eyes when his wife showed him the photograph of his mother again and tried to make him admit to the similarities between his beloved old mum and the young woman, this stranger, who stood before him now.

'You have made a mistake,' was all he said, while he pointed Ruby towards the door.

The promised lunch party didn't happen. While her husband headed out into the garden to take his anger out on a hedge with a pair of brutal looking clippers, Rosalia called Ruby a taxi to take her back to Denver.

'I'm sorry. I'm sorry,' the besieged housewife said. 'I've never seen him get so angry before.'

'It's OK,' said Ruby, wondering if her legs would take her when she stood up again.

Less than three hours after she had left, Ruby was back at her hotel. She was still shaking as she called the airport and had them put her through to the British Airways desk. There was a flight leaving for the UK late that night. She was supposed to be in Denver for another three nights but after Nathaniel's outburst, the whole city suddenly seemed a strange and sinister place. Ruby wanted to be home again. She wanted to be in the arms of someone who loved her. When she had finished making arrangements to change her flight, Ruby finally burst into tears.

She left a note at reception for Mary (who was still asleep after a hard night getting to know her colleague from New York), claiming a family crisis had sent her hurrying back to London. It wasn't entirely untruthful, she supposed. Then she asked the receptionist to call her another taxi. There was one already waiting in the street outside the hotel.

'Have you enjoyed your stay in our city?' asked the receptionist as she prepared Ruby's final bill.

'Let's just say the natives haven't all been that friendly.'

'Oh, I'm sorry,' said the receptionist automatically. 'Have a nice day,' she added, as she handed Ruby her receipt.

Ruby dragged her trolley case disconsolately through the lobby to the taxi waiting outside. Behind the desk, the telephone started ringing again, but Ruby was already settled into the back of the cab and drawing away from the front of the hotel by the time the receptionist connected the 'English girl' that the caller was after with the English girl who had just left the hotel without saying 'you have a nice day too'.

'It's urgent,' said Nathaniel Barker.

'But sir, she's already in the taxi.

'Well, go and get her.'

'I can't do that, sir. I'm not permitted to leave the desk unattended.'

Nathaniel hung up.

Despite the tailwinds, the flight back to the United Kingdom from Denver seemed to take much longer than

303

the flight that had taken Ruby out there. Ruby took an aisle seat. She didn't want to see Denver from the sky this time. She didn't ever want to see Colorado again. She had spent the evening crying in the ladies' room of the departure lounge as bad weather conditions had delayed her flight into the early hours of the morning. When the plane finally left the tarmac, she felt nothing but relief.

Across the aisle, a honeymoon couple clasped hands. The new bride sighed. 'I want to live there forever.' Ruby was just anxious to be home.

Halfway through the journey, the in-flight entertainment system showed a film that Ruby had been keen to watch since she first read that the leading lady had been cast. Katrina Black, the actress who had written so movingly about her adoption and her successful search for her birth parents, was playing the ditzy heroine in this movie about a girl with amnesia who doesn't recognise her husband.

But when the movie came on, Ruby closed her eyes and tried to sleep. In reality, she knew she was angry with Katrina. Jealous that her story had the happy ending Ruby felt she'd been denied. Katrina's half brothers and sister had welcomed her into their family and were only angry that they had waited so long to meet her. But of course they *would* be happy. Katrina Black was a famous actress. Ruby Taylor was an account manager in a second rate public relations company who would probably get back from this terrible trip to discover that she didn't even have a job after running out on the conference. Katrina was the prodigal daughter, returning wreathed with the halo of fame. Ruby brought back nothing but the shame of an extra-marital liaison that no one wanted to admit.

'Ladies and gentlemen,' the captain interrupted the entertainment programme. 'I'm sorry to have to report that due to a prior incident at Heathrow, our flight this evening will be diverted to Manchester airport . . .'

Ruby snapped awake.

Manchester?

28

'I've chosen him!'

Erica pounced on Lou as soon as she arrived at the office on Monday morning.

'Chosen what?' Lou asked.

'My date! My ad went into the *Guardian* supplement on Saturday and the Soulmates section of the *Observer* yesterday morning and by last night I'd already had three replies!'

Lou raised an eyebrow.

'I didn't like the sound of the first two,' Erica continued breathlessly. 'Both were a little bit wet.'

'Pisces?' Lou suggested.

Erica tutted at that. 'Very funny. But the third one sounded lovely. A really great voice. Deep. Well-spoken. Educated.'

'That's good,' Lou agreed.

'I called him back as soon as I got his message and we talked for half an hour. I can't believe how easy it was to chat to him. I thought it would be really awkward but he put me at my ease. His name is Bob. He works for a law firm in the City – represents lots of asylum seekers apparently. He said he really likes cats – would have one himself if the lease on his flat didn't forbid it – and he's almost a vegetarian. Well, he only eats organic meat and free-range eggs.'

Lou nodded. 'That does sound worthy.'

'Oh, piss off, Lou,' said Erica, giving her a playful slap on the arm. 'You're supposed to be excited for me.'

'I am. When are you meeting him?'

'Tonight.' Erica bit her lip. 'At The Engineer in Primrose Hill. Eight o'clock, assuming he can get away from the office on time.'

'Are you excited?' Lou asked.

'I'm absolutely terrified. What if he doesn't think I'm attractive?'

'Why shouldn't he?'

'But he sounds gorgeous. He said he looks like Richard Gere.'

'And you believed him?'

'I live in hope,' Erica sighed.

'He probably means he's the same height as Richard Gere,' Lou suggested. 'Richard Gere's a midget, so I've heard.'

'He is?'

'Stands on boxes for all his kissing scenes.'

'But Julia Roberts . . .'

'She's probably a midget too. Look, don't worry about tonight. Richard Gere or no, he'll definitely be enchanted by you.'

'Wish I'd had time to hit the Jolene,' Erica said, examining her feather-light facial hair in the mirrored section of her powder compact. 'How is it possible that I didn't notice this horrible hair on my chin until it's grown almost as long as an eyelash. It must have been growing for a week.'

'Another of life's great mysteries,' said Lou.

'So. Is your friend Ruby back from the States yet?'

'Not due back till Thursday morning.'

'Have you heard from her?' Erica asked. 'Found out how she got on with her meeting?'

'Not a word.'

'No news is good news, I suppose,' Erica suggested.

'Yeah. I'm sure she would have called if anything went really wrong.'

Ruby had watched the last case come off the luggage carousel. It wasn't hers. Now, she found herself utterly alone in an empty baggage reclaim area. The carousel she had been watching so avidly for the appearance of her little blue trolley case, came to a halt with a mechanical sigh.

'Hey!' Ruby called to a man wearing overalls who was pushing a mop disconsolately across the other end of the hall. 'Where's my luggage?'

'What?' The man cupped his hand to his ear.

'My luggage,' said Ruby, scooting up to his end of the hall with her empty airport trolley. 'It didn't come off the conveyor belt with all the other stuff.'

The man in overalls looked at her blankly.

'What's happened to it?'

He shrugged and carried on sweeping.

And that was about as helpful as anyone was going to be that night. The woman on the lost luggage counter had only just started working at the airport and claimed she had never actually had to deal with a lost luggage case on her own to date. She couldn't help now. Her manageress was on a fag break. By the time the manageress came back from her fag break and confirmed that she couldn't help either – Ruby would have to contact the airline directly – Ruby had missed the bus chartered to take the diverted Denver passengers back down south to London Heathrow.

'Catch a train and get the airline to reimburse you,' the lost luggage manageress instructed. Ruby took a compensation claim form and made her way to the airport's rail station. But the information screens showed no trains for London in the foreseeable future.

'What time's the next train for London?' Ruby asked a passing station worker.

'Tomorrow,' he said.

'You're joking, right?'

'No,' said the station worker. 'I don't do jokes.'

'Then what am I supposed to do about getting home?'

'You should have got a plane that arrived in the morning,' said the station worker. 'Or one that landed at Heathrow.'

'My plane was supposed to land at Heathrow,' Ruby informed him.

'What you doing here then?'

'You tell me.' Ruby clenched her fists to stop herself from giving him a v sign. Not that it would have made any difference. The station worker was pretty much inured to the contempt of the British public after five years' spent walking that platform.

Ruby trudged back to the terminal. At least having lost her luggage meant she didn't have to carry it around with her. She found a payphone, since the battery in her mobile phone was flat, and dialled Robert's number. Her lip was quivering as she waited for him to pick up the phone. She knew that as soon as she heard his friendly voice the floodgates would open. But she wanted to hear Robert's voice. She needed to know that someone thought she was worthy of his love and affection.

The phone rang five times before the call was passed to an answer machine.

Ruby put the phone down, then picked it up and dialled again. She knew that Robert often let his machine pick up calls when he was actually in his study, working on something brought home from the office. If she called again, he would know that something serious was up and pick up the phone himself.

Five rings. The answer machine kicked in once more.

It was a Monday evening. Ten o'clock. He wouldn't be out at this time. Ruby knew that much because he would never come out with her on a Monday night. Monday nights were sacred, reserved for preparation for Tuesday morning's progress meeting.

Robert's message ended.

'Bleep.'

'Robert, it's me,' Ruby whispered to the tape machine. 'I'm back. Well, I'm at Manchester airport. I had to get a flight to here instead of Heathrow. Something about an incident there causing diversions. I wanted to come home early. Everything went wrong. Oh, darling, I've really missed you. I wish so much you were in to take this call.'

She sniffed loudly.

'I don't know how I'm going to get home,' she continued. 'I've missed the last train from Manchester to London tonight. This has turned out to be such a disaster. I should have listened to Lou and Martin. Oh, Robert, I . . .'

His answer machine gave a beep to signal that Ruby had run out of time.

Who else could she call? She couldn't ring her parents. They would only want to know why she was back from Denver early and even the slightest hint of concern in her mother's voice would be bound to set the waterworks off. Ruby would phone Lou, but she couldn't remember her number. That was the danger with programming numbers into the SIM card of your mobile and not bothering to learn them off by heart. Lou had moved only recently and Ruby wasn't even sure if the area code was 0207 or 0208. She did know that Lou was ex-directory, having taken her name out of the book following a disastrous love-affair with a guy called Magnus who claimed he heard messages from God.

There was just one person left.

'Martin?'

'Ruby! How's it going?' He sounded pleased to hear from her. 'It's nearly half-ten at night here. What time is it where you are?'

'Half-ten,' said Ruby flatly.

'But I thought . . .'

'I'm not in Denver any more. I'm in Manchester.'

'Is there a Manchester in Colorado?' Martin asked sleepily. He'd nodded off in front of the telly.

'Manchester, Cheshire, dimwit. I'm back in the UK.'

'Oh, what? Why?' Martin asked. 'Did you . . . ?'

'I met up with Rosalia Barker and her husband but he didn't want to know me!' Ruby tried to stifle a sob. Too late. Before Martin could say a single comforting word, Ruby was snuffling and snortling into the phone, the tears were streaming down her face and she could hardly breathe for crying.

'Ruby, Ruby, Ruby,' Martin tried to break through to her.

'And now I'm in Manchester and I can't get back to London until tomorrow morning. There aren't any trains and I'm going to have to spend a night in an airport hotel and I can't even get hold of Robert and I feel sooooo lonely.'

'Ruby,' Martin said soothingly. 'Where are you again?'

'I'm in the airport. In Manchester.'

'Don't bother checking in to a hotel,' said Martin firmly. 'I should be able to get there in three hours.'

'Eh?'

'Just work out which terminal you're in and call me on the mobile when you know. Then find yourself a nice quiet place to have a cup of coffee and wait for me. I'll be with you as soon as I can. I've done it in three hours before. Might not take so long now. I don't suppose there's much traffic.'

'You're coming up here?' Ruby was confused.

'That's what I said, didn't I? Look, it's going to be OK, Rubes. You can tell me everything that happened on the way back to London. Only thing you have to do is buy me a cup of coffee at a service station to make sure we get back into town without me falling asleep at the wheel.'

'Martin, I . . .'

'Save the extravagant thanks for later,' he said.

'I owe you one.'

'It's what friends are for.'

Moments later, Martin was rummaging through a pile of rubbish on the kitchen table looking for his car keys and wondering what on earth he had put himself up for. It was eleven o'clock at night. By the time he got to Manchester it would be two in the morning. By the time they got back to London it would be six o'clock at the earliest and at nine o'clock he was expected at the offices of Manpower to take a variety of psychometric tests that would allow a temp controller ten years his junior to fix him up with a job so far below his capabilities that he would fuck up in two days out of boredom.

'Fuck it,' said Martin, simultaneously finding the car keys and deciding to ditch the interview. Another day spent putting off the resumption of his far from glittering career would hardly make a difference now.

And miraculously, his sister's Fiesta, which never started first time, did start first time for the first time ever. That had to be a sign. As did the fact that all the traffic lights between Chalk Farm and the M1 turned green at his approach. In no time at all, Martin was bombing up the motorway, ticking faceless Midland cities off a mental list. Three hours soon seemed like a pessimistic estimation. If he didn't get stopped for speeding, then he might make it to Manchester in two.

Meanwhile, Ruby sat at the edge of a deserted coffee bar. Half the tables had chairs stacked upon them, so that the cleaners could move easily between them with the floor polisher. She was nursing the same small cappuccino she had been nursing for the past two hours. She hadn't even had enough money to pay for that one cup of coffee after using up most of her change trying to get through to Robert again. Midnight, one o'clock, half past one passed and he still wasn't picking up the phone. When she tried to buy a coffee with only eighty pence to her name, the cashier had taken pity on her and rung up the expensive cappuccino as a slightly cheaper can of Diet Coke.

'Won't you get into trouble?' Ruby asked her.

'I don't give a *sheet*,' she said. The cashier was French. 'I'm going back to Biarritz next week. Is too wet here. Too *mee*serable.'

Ruby nodded in agreement.

'You OK?' the girl asked then. Ruby's eyes were somewhat pink.

'I'm fine,' said Ruby. 'Long flight. Just tired.'

'You are staying *here* over the night?'

'I'm waiting for my friend to pick me up. He's on his way from London.'

'From London? That's a long way. He's a special friend,' the girl observed.

Now, seeing Martin walk across the terminal floor to find Ruby, the French girl smiled a complicit smile. 'He's gorgeous,' she mouthed. And Martin did look pretty dishy. Tired. Dishevelled perhaps. But dishevelled really suited him. Always had done.

'Found you!' he said.

'Martin,' said Ruby. 'I'm so sorry.'

'Don't start with sorry. Come here.'

He wrapped his arms around her. Ruby was instantly in tears again.

'Come on,' Martin cooed. 'You're almost home now. Tell me all about it on the way back to London.' He led her out to the car park with one arm around her waist, carrying her hostess bag with his free hand.

'It's got wheels, you know,' Ruby pointed out to him.

'What do you think I am?' asked Martin. 'Some kind of pouf?'

29

'Ruby,' said Martin. 'I know this isn't going to make up for what you've been through this last couple of days but I want you to know that I think of you as a sister. I mean, not as a sister exactly. But I love you just as much as I love my real sister. If I had a lifeboat with four spaces in it, you would definitely be in there with Mum and Marie.'

Ruby continued to gaze out at the streetlights strobing past as they headed into London. Though Martin had assured Ruby she could talk about her experiences in Colorado until his ears bled if she wanted to, she hadn't said that much at all since they got out of the airport car park. At one point, she was so quiet that Martin thought she must have fallen asleep through tiredness. She had spent most of the last three days in the air, after all. If anyone deserved to get jet-lag . . . But Ruby's eyes were wide open, watching the motorway traffic stream silently by.

'You don't need Nathaniel Barker, Ruby,' Martin tried again. 'You've got this far without him. You've lived for thirty years not knowing that you even had a half-brother. You didn't miss him then.'

Ruby still didn't say anything.

'It doesn't matter what he thinks of you anyway because he doesn't really know you,' Martin continued.

'If he did know you then I'm sure he would be happy to tell the world that you two are related. He'd be really proud. If I found out I had a half-sister like you, I would be completely . . .'

'It's just the story of my life, isn't it?' Ruby interrupted. 'My mother gave me up for adoption. Every man I've ever loved since has dumped me. Not even my fucking brother wants to know me now. I'm always the fucking reject.'

Martin was shocked by the vehemence of her sudden exclamation.

'He'll probably come round,' Martin said cautiously.

'Why should he? John Flett didn't come round, did he? Dave the accountant never wanted me back. I've had just about as much rejection as I can take.'

'Ruby, I'll never reject you,' Martin reiterated. 'If I wasn't driving, you know I'd give you a hug right now.'

'Hmmmph,' Ruby snorted. She took the empty cigarette packet she had found in the Fiesta's untidy glove-box and began to shred it into ugly confetti.

'It's alright for you and Lou,' she continued. 'You know what it's like to be loved unconditionally. You don't know what it's like to lie in bed at night and worry that your mum and dad are going to send you off to a children's home because you failed your maths test. You don't know what it's like to feel that you've got to be a good girl because your parents didn't have to choose you from the reject pile. They did you a favour. You've got to be so grateful. I've spent my whole life being grateful for fucking crumbs of affection.'

'Ruby, that's not the way it really is,' said Martin reasonably. 'You know that your parents love you no matter what you do. Your dad drives a six-hour round trip every winter just to bleed the radiators in your flat!'

'I know,' Ruby snapped. 'I know. But there's a little part of me that doesn't know. A tiny little part of me I can't quite bury, that is always watching their faces for a flicker of disapproval. A part of me that could never take the piss like my sister did just in case they asked to un-adopt me again. And that little tiny part of me takes every single slight and rejection I've had in my life and feeds on it until it drowns out all the sensible, rational parts of my brain with its constant fucking worrying.'

She pinched the top of her nose in a desperate attempt to stave off tears.

'Oh, God. I'm sorry,' she said. 'This is the last thing you need. You've come out here in the middle of the night to fetch me from bloody Manchester. You got out of bed and drove for three bloody hours. You don't need to hear me going on and on and on about how bad my life is and . . .'

'Stop,' said Martin.

'I'm trying,' said Ruby, thinking that he was asking her not to cry.

'I mean, stop saying sorry. I wouldn't have come to pick you up if I didn't want to. I told you that you could talk about this as much as you need to and I meant it. You don't have to be grateful to me, Ruby. You and Lou are my best friends. I love you unconditionally and I just feel honoured that I can be here for you.'

'You don't mean that,' Ruby started.

'Can I hear the stupid part of your brain talking again?'

Ruby sank back into the passenger seat.

'You know what,' Martin told her. 'Other people's families aren't the Walton-esque fantasy you seem to assume they are. Just because you're brought up by your natural parents doesn't mean you're any *less* likely to get fucked up. Bloody hell, there were years when I just *wished* that my mum and dad would turn round and tell me that I was adopted. It would have made a lot of fucking sense.'

Ruby gave him a sidelong glance.

'I'm sorry,' he said. 'I didn't mean to belittle the way you're feeling but . . .'

'I understand. It doesn't matter.'

'What I'm saying is, you had a *happy* childhood, Ruby. Really you did. You were loved. You really were loved. You still are.'

'I know. I know,' she muttered.

'You've got a family. You've got friends. You've even got a new boyfriend and he seems alright,' Martin choked out those last few words. 'What are you looking for, Ruby? What else is it that you think you need?'

Ruby shrugged. 'I think it's just that I've spent my whole life trying to prove that Mum and Dad were right to have adopted me.'

'Everyone who knows you knows they were.'

'Yes. But don't you see that the real proof of that would have been for my natural family to look at me as I am now and agree that I've made a success of myself and that they didn't give away the runt of the litter. I wanted them to confirm that it wasn't *me*. It wasn't *my* fault.'

'You were a baby, Rubes. How on earth could it have been your fault?'

'I don't know. But I needed to hear that circumstances

beyond their control made them give me up and have them fall madly in love with me now. I wanted to know that if things had been different they would *never* have let me go. I wanted them to want me to be part of their family again. Nathaniel Barker didn't even want to listen.'

'But it must have been a shock for him,' said Martin playing devil's advocate. 'You turning up on the doorstep like that. He didn't know he had a sister, Ruby. He's got a lot of things to work out for himself now. He probably feels like he's been lied to. He's got to come to terms with a whole new version of his mother for a start. Perhaps he even feels guilty that his mother didn't give him away too.'

'If he feels so guilty, why doesn't he try to make it up to me?'

'Guilt doesn't always work like that,' said Martin. 'Sometimes, knowing that you've done something bad to someone who didn't deserve it just makes you end up hurting them even more. You remember that temp at International Mags that I went on one date with?'

'Which one? There's been a couple.' Ruby smiled.

'The gorgeous one. Veronique.'

'The one who didn't fall for your charm?'

'She didn't give me the brush-off,' said Martin defensively. 'I know that you and Lou find that hard to believe but the fact is, she really liked me.'

'And you liked her, didn't you?'

'Yeah. Yeah, I did. But then . . .'

'What? What went wrong?'

Martin took a deep breath and spewed the real story out. 'She told me she had a colostomy,' he said.

Ruby stopped shredding the cigarette packet and looked at her friend's shadowy profile.

'And I know that it shouldn't have mattered to me but it did. I just didn't want to sleep with her after that and so I tried to pretend that we weren't going to have sex there and then because I wanted to wait and make it special. And after that I had to start avoiding her in the office. And she was just so lovely and she couldn't understand why I didn't want to see her and she started to make me feel so guilty that I told my boss she'd forgotten to do some paperwork that I was supposed to have done myself and he terminated her contract.'

'Martin. That's horrible!'

'Yeah. I know. But you see what I mean about guilt making you react in strange ways? I should have been nicer to her. Perhaps I should have told her what the problem was. But I did everything wrong because every time I saw her face I was confronted with the evidence of my own shittiness. My own inability to deal with real life. The kind of shame I feel about getting Veronique the sack is probably the way your half-brother feels about telling you to get lost too.'

'No,' said Ruby mercilessly. 'I don't think it's the same at all. What you did was just a crappy masculine reaction to the thought of physical imperfection. God help you if women ever decided not to give a man a chance because there was something slightly unsavoury about him. Not that a colostomy is unsavoury.'

Ruby pressed her hand to her mouth. Martin thought she was going to cry again. But instead she gave a loud, giggling snort. 'Oh God. I'm sorry! That poor girl! Certainly puts my cellulite into perspective. I can't wait to tell Lou.'

'You mustn't tell Lou,' Martin pleaded. 'It's bad enough putting up with all the Hermes jokes. I only told you because I thought you'd understand! I thought it would help you feel better.'

'Now we know why you kept referring to your love-life as a bag of shite!' Ruby was half-crying, half-giggling now. 'I'm sorry, Martin. I'm sorry. I guess I am a bad person after all.'

'Alright!' Martin groaned. 'Let's leave it now, shall we?'

Ruby shook her head at him ruefully.

'At least I made you smile,' he said.

'You're going to hell, Martin Ashcroft. You do know that, don't you?'

'You laughed,' he reminded her. 'You're coming too.'

They reached Ruby's flat at quarter to six in the morning. They had driven through the dawn and turned into Ruby's street just in front of the milkman.

'Nightcap?' Ruby suggested.

'Just the one.'

As they walked up to the front door, Martin wrapped his arm around Ruby's shoulders.

'You cold?' he asked her, hugging her close.

'Not any more,' she said.

They stopped for a moment on the steps. Ruby looked up at Martin. Her eyes were still glittery from crying, her eyelashes still wet and spiky. It was a far better look than she'd ever managed with a mascara wand, Martin thought. He smiled a shy, closed-mouth, half-smile down at her pink, blotchy face.

'Thanks,' she said, wrinkling her nose to stop the tears again.

'What for?'

'For driving all the way up to Manchester. For listening to me dribble on about my neuroses and for trying to understand.'

'You deserve better,' he said simply. 'I wish there was something I could do to make you realise that. And them . . .' he added.

Ruby shrugged, knowing whom he was referring to at once.

'Who needs two families anyway?' she said bravely. 'It's bad enough having to do one set of relatives at Christmas.'

'Too right. Two lots of relatives. Two lots of sprouts,' Martin pointed out. 'Though, I don't suppose they have sprouts for Christmas dinner out there, do they? Or you could end up with three lots of sprouts! Two Christmasses and one Thanksgiving!'

'Martin,' Ruby stopped him with a finger on his lips. 'I don't want to think about them at all. As far as I'm concerned, Colorado never happened. Agreed?'

'Agreed.'

'Thanks.' They still didn't move any closer to the door. 'For everything,' Ruby added almost nonsensically. Then she stood up on tiptoe and went to kiss him on the cheek. Just a friendly kiss.

But it lasted a bit longer than usual because as Ruby kissed Martin on the cheek he pulled her in for another hug and she ended up with her lips almost squashed against his. When he let her go again, she stumbled back feeling just a little flustered. She thought he might be blushing too.

Half an hour later, Martin left to drive back to his own place. Ruby stood in the middle of her empty sitting room and surveyed the old sofa with its tidy cushions, the polished coffee table, the invincible cheese plant that Martin had forgotten to water after all. On the mantelpiece stood a framed picture of Ruby with her mum, dad and Lindsay, taken when they came to see her graduate. Ruby picked the frame up and gave it an affectionate little polish with her sleeve. She remembered how worried her mother had been about the dress code for such an event. Should she wear a hat? Or was that just too much? It wasn't a church service after all. It had been so important to her that she didn't let her youngest daughter down. In the end Mrs Taylor plumped for the light blue suit she had worn to Lindsay's wedding. No hat, which was a good thing because the wind was blowing gale force. Ruby's brother-in-law Steve must have taken the photograph. He was a wonderful bloke. Lindsay was lucky to have found such a husband. Ruby felt lucky enough just to have him as a brother-in-law.

Ruby studied her father's proud smile and felt another wave of tears behind her eyes. This was her real family. Not a man from Colorado who refused to acknowledge the possibility of her existence but the three people who flanked her in this photograph, the fantastic man who had taken the shot and the tiny baby with the Taylor' family nose who had yet to be born when it was taken.

As soon as it was a decent hour, Ruby would call her mum and her sister. Find out how her niece was getting on. And as she replaced the photo in pride of place on the mantelpiece, Ruby felt something like relief. At least now she wouldn't have to put them through the pain of finding out that she had gone in search of her natural family. Nathaniel Barker had spared the Taylor family that sticky problem. It was probably for the best that he didn't want Ruby in his life.

On a shelf in the corner, the answer machine was flashing to show one message. Ruby pressed 'play'.

'Hey, baby. Are you back home yet? Sorry I wasn't there when you called from the airport. I've been in the office,' he added, which was odd, since Ruby had remembered on the drive back from Manchester that he was supposed to be at a college reunion that night. 'Hurry on over whenever you like, sweet-lips. I've been missing you too, too long.'

Robert.

Ruby's frown melted away.

Somebody loved her after all.

30

Lou noticed instantly that Erica was wearing exactly the same outfit she had been sporting when she left work for her big date the night before.

'You didn't?' Lou murmured.

'I know. I know. I shouldn't have done. It goes against everything they say in The Rules. But for heaven's sake, Lou. I've got to get it when I can. I'm thirty-seven . . .'

'I thought you said you were thirty-two!' Lou exclaimed.

'Thirty-seven and a half,' said Erica proudly. 'And I don't have to answer to anyone but myself and if I want to spend the night with a man I've only just met, then I'm bloody well going to.'

'You've changed your tune.'

'He's changed my life!'

'So quickly?'

'Well, quite slowly really,' Erica said with a saucy smile.

'Erica! Pur-leese. I've only just had my breakfast.'

'I know! And I know that I've ticked you off in the past for falling into bed too quickly, Lou, but that's partly because you're such a vulnerable soul.'

'Thanks.'

'I, on the other hand, know that it really doesn't matter if he never calls again.'

'You don't mean that.'

Erica bit her lip and suddenly looked like a teenager getting a serious attack of angst over her very first love. 'Too right I don't! I'll *die* if he doesn't call me. I have to see him again!' She fell into a mock swoon.

'He must have been amazing,' said Lou.

'He was. Right from the very start. Having said that he wouldn't wear a carnation because he didn't want everyone to know we were on a blind date, he turned up with a *huge* bunch of roses.'

'Tesco Metro? Marks and Spencer?'

'No way. They were definitely from a proper florist. All wrapped up in brown paper. Look at this,' Erica reached into her handbag and brought out her diary. She had carefully pressed one of the beautiful pinky-orange rosebuds against the page for the day of the big date.

'My God, that's soppy,' said Lou.

'I know. But whatever happens next, I want to be able to remember last night for the rest of my boring little life.' Erica sat down on the chair on the opposite side of Lou's desk and leaned over as if to impart a secret. Lou leaned towards her so that their heads were almost touching over the desk tidy.

'What on earth did he do to you?' Lou asked excitedly.

'I don't know. Nothing. I mean, everything. I can't even begin to tell you. But I think I had an orgasm,' said Erica. Then she covered her mouth as though she had just uttered a terrible curse. When she took her hand away she was chewing her lip nervously again.

'Well, that's good, isn't it?' asked Lou. 'But what do you mean you "think" you had one?'

Erica leaned forward once more. 'I mean, I don't know

if that was what I had because I've certainly never had anything quite like that before now. I thought I had, but after last night, I'm just not sure. It was just so . . . Oh, I shouldn't be telling you this, Lou.'

'Erica, I'm not going to tell anyone else if that's what you're thinking.'

'I know you wouldn't. I'm not even sure if you want to hear it yourself. But I've got to tell somebody. I need to make sure that it *was* an orgasm and not just some strange kind of fit.'

Lou stifled a giggle with the result that it came out as an indignant little snort.

'What's so funny?' Erica asked.

'Nothing's funny,' said Lou, quickly recovering herself. 'Tell me what it felt like and I'll put your mind at rest.'

'Well,' Erica took a deep breath. 'He went down there and er . . . You know, I never would have asked him to do it. I just couldn't believe my luck when he did it of his own accord.'

'Did what?' asked Lou.

'Don't make me say the word,' Erica begged her. 'Anyway, it started like a tickle in my lower regions, then it felt as though I was going to sneeze, only from my nnngh,' she grunted and pointed coyly beneath the desk, 'and not from my nose. And then I thought I was going to wet myself and finally I couldn't help screaming.'

'Yup,' said Lou with a guffaw. 'That was an orgasm.'

'Thank God for that,' said Erica. 'I thought I'd gone epileptic.'

Ruby decided to lay low at home until Wednesday morning. Thankfully Alan seemed happy with her explanation that family problems had brought her home in a hurry.

'Everything sorted out?' he asked, in a sincere enough tone but one that let Ruby know that he didn't really want the gory details, much to her relief.

Ruby nodded.

'Well, hope it won't stop you enjoying Friday's party.'

Friday's party. The summer party was just two days away now. The girls in the Two-Faced Cosmetics team were running a sweepstake on who would get too drunk to think and sleep with Emlyn 'The Panter' Cruickshank by accident. They were supposed to be keeping it a secret from the man himself, but the waves of hilarity emanating from Imogen's desk – for it was in the top drawer of her desk that the book of bets was being kept – and the fact that the laughter stopped abruptly whenever the Panter was in the vicinity, had inadvertently alerted him to the mischief afoot. Not that he was offended. The fact that none of the odds on the office girls were longer than fifteen to one probably gave him a great deal of confidence in his dubious attractiveness.

'You're down at eleven to one,' Liz informed Ruby.

'Oh, please,' said Ruby. 'I know what that man has in his socks. Besides,' she added, 'I'm attached.'

Liz raised a haughty eyebrow. 'So, he's still coming to the party, this new boyfriend of yours?'

'Absolutely.' Ruby nodded. 'You bringing someone along? Your cat perhaps?'

Liz pursed her lips in irritation. But Ruby wasn't bothered. She was very much looking forward to the party. It was almost impossible to remember how inconsolable she had been at the thought of attending that party just over a month ago, when John Flett was still the centre of Ruby's existence. She shrugged off Liz's suggestion that Ruby was just 'papering over the cracks' with the wonderful Robert. He was a fantastic boyfriend but he was also a real soul mate. He seemed to know exactly what she needed. The previous evening, his response to Ruby's explanation of the Nathaniel Barker predicament was a simple 'Fuck him.' Yeah, Ruby thought. 'Fuck him, indeed.' No point going over and over what had happened in Colorado . . . especially as Robert wanted to go to sleep.

With Robert's support, Ruby felt she could get over this latest rejection *and* rub John Flett's nose in the shitty mess he had very briefly made of her life. The Hollingworth party couldn't come soon enough.

The following Friday morning was like the last day of term at the Hollingworth offices. The back of every door was adorned with someone's sweetie-wrapper party dress, just waiting for five o'clock and the rush for the ladies' room to come.

When Ruby arrived that morning, Imogen was already holding her dress against her, showing her assistant and 'office best friend' Janine what she was planning to wear that night. 'And a pair of these,' Imogen added, holding up what appeared to be a pair of leg-warmers.

'Very *Kids From Fame*,' said Ruby as she passed.

Imogen looked at her blankly. She was too young to remember.

Never mind, thought Ruby. Wondering whether Flett would 'get' Imogen's retro eighties chic or be transported back in horror to the start of the man at C & A phase he had yet to entirely leave behind him. Forget witty references to a decade that invented the puffball, thought Ruby. She was going to go for *timeless* elegance. In the garment bag draped over her arm was a beautiful new silk dress by Nicole Farhi; its skirt as red and delicate as an extravagantly fragile poppy. It had cost a fortune but Ruby didn't care. She was going to have a fabulous evening. She was going to look her best ever and spend the night draped on the arm of a wonderful man, while Flett attempted and failed to keep up on the dance floor with his 'bastard daughter of Bananarama' girlfriend. He would see Ruby looking serene and sophisticated and utterly better off without him. Not that Ruby was worried what Flett thought any more . . . .

'Ruby, it's Robert.'

'Oh, hi,' Ruby trilled. 'I was going to call you in a minute to let you know the plan for tonight. We've decided to have a few cocktails in the American Bar at the Savoy before we go on to the boat. Isn't that a great idea? Thought it would be nice to start the evening with a spot of sophistication even if we'll all be under the table by half past eight. It's a free bar all night once we're at the party . . .'

'Ruby,' Robert interrupted.

'Yes?'

'I don't think I can come to the party tonight after all. Something important has come up.'

'What?'

'Something to do with the case I've been working on. I don't think I'm going to be able to get away from the office until nine at the earliest. I'd say that I'll join you later on, but of course, I can't. Not unless I swim out to the middle of the Thames in my dinner jacket,' he laughed feebly.

'What's come up?' Ruby asked. 'Isn't there someone else who can take care of it for you?'

'Not really. It's some new evidence pertaining to next week's big case. It could make all the difference. I don't want to promise you that I'll be at the party and then have to let you down.'

Ruby felt her mouth go dry. 'It would make all the difference to me if you could be at the party,' she tried.

'Yeah, Rubes, I know that. But for my client, it's going to make all the difference too. The difference between freedom and prison. I can't let him down. Or his wife. Or his children,' Robert added as the killer blow.

'Perhaps you could join us at the Savoy for an early drink,' Ruby persisted. 'Then go back to the office straight afterwards.'

'Ruby, I'd love to,' he said soothingly. 'But I've got meetings until seven o'clock in any case.'

'So you can't get away for even half an hour?'

'Not even half an hour. Look, I'll call you later,' he said to placate her. 'You never know. I might be wrapped up earlier than I'm expecting. How about that?'

'OK,' Ruby put the phone down slowly and looked ruefully at the red dress hanging on the back of her office door. Katherine, her assistant, popped her head round the door moments later.

'Rubes,' she wheedled, 'd'you mind if I pop out for a few minutes? I forgot my mascara and I need to buy some more for tonight.'

Ruby waved her away dismissively.

'Rubes,' Katherine began again. 'Er, d'you know if Emlyn's going to be at the party on his own tonight? Not that I want to know for any particular reason . . . Some of the other girls are . . .'

'I don't know,' said Ruby flatly. 'But you do know that you're the favourite at two to one?'

'What?'

'You're the favourite to get your knickers off for the Panter,' Ruby snapped. 'Just try and have some dignity tonight, that's all.'

Katherine backed out of the room. Mouth gaping.

Ruby was too pissed off to care. She couldn't believe it. Why did he have to work late *tonight*? A Friday night. The night of the summer party? Ruby's fantasy romantic evening on the pleasure boat was sinking.

Because she couldn't go on her own. She was over Flett. Make no mistake about that, she assured herself. She knew she never wanted to have him near her again. But she also knew that she would need to be so far over him that she couldn't remember his birthday (January 15th) before she would be happy to see him smooching with Imogen while she didn't have a smoochee of her own to snuggle into when she wanted to avert her eyes.

'Aaaaagggghhhh!' Ruby stabbed a biro into her mouse-mat. 'Why tonight?' She knew she ought to try to be understanding but it simply wasn't fair. She *needed* Robert to be at this party. She *deserved* it, after everything that had gone wrong for her over the past few weeks. But he was abandoning her to stay late at the office on behalf of some criminal. Some drug-dealing low-life scum who made OJ look innocent, whose lovely wife probably couldn't wait for him to go inside so that she could shag his best mate and whose pre-school children were probably out nicking cars already anyway. 'No, no, no, no, no.' Ruby snapped her pen in half.

'You alright, Ruby?' Liz Hale was observing from the open door.

'Fine.' Ruby brushed her hair back. 'Robert just called to say that he's not feeling well. I'm not going to come to the party tonight after all. Going to go round and look after him,' she lied.

31

Lou was only too happy to let Ruby come out with her and Andrew that night.

'Though it's going to be a bit couply,' she warned. 'We said that we'd go for a drink with Erica, from my office, and her new man. Do you mind?'

'It'll cheer me up,' said Ruby. 'Besides, I don't mind coming out with couples when I'm not technically single myself. At least when you're telling each other your funny little anecdotes about how you met and what he said to you last week, I can talk about Robert.'

Lou winced. 'I don't tell "funny little anecdotes" about Andrew, do I?'

'No, you don't,' Ruby admitted.

'Phew. Look, you shouldn't let yourself get too angry with Robert. After all, I don't think you can argue that wanting to impress your evil ex-lover is more important than staying out of jail is to Robert's poor client. And his wife. And his children.'

Ruby rolled her eyes.

'Imagine how you'd feel if that man went to prison because Robert was out partying with you,' Lou continued.

'The thing is the bugger probably deserves to. Robert never seems to represent innocent guys. But I know you're right. It's just that I've looked forward to this so much. I wanted to be able to walk into that party with my head held high and not care if Flett is with Imogen because I've got a much better man of my own now.'

'Ruby, you don't need a man to help you hold your head up in front of Flett. Or Imogen. What's she got that you haven't?' Lou asked then.

'Sun-tan. Thin thighs. My ex-boyfriend,' said Ruby.

Ruby went straight to the pub in the clothes she had been wearing all day. She hadn't put any make-up on that morning, in an attempt to make the most of the effects of the previous night's face-pack in preparation for the Hollingworth party. It didn't seem worth putting on any slap to meet Lou and eco-friendly Erica. In fact, according to Lou, Erica had once said that make-up was a symbol of man's suppression of the female gender and melted all her lipsticks into a big red blob in the shape of a penis to express her disapproval.

Which was why Ruby was surprised to see that Erica was definitely wearing lipstick when she came into the pub that night.

'Hi!' And she was breathless and excited in a decidedly girly way. 'Bob's going to be another half hour or so,' she explained to Lou, Ruby and Andrew. 'He works so hard. But I can't complain. Not when he's working for next to no money at all on behalf of those asylum seekers.'

'What does he do?' asked Ruby.

'He's a lawyer,' said Erica, unable to disguise her pride. 'Specialist in human rights.'

'Amazing. My boyfriend's a lawyer too,' said Ruby.

'Oh, really?'

'Yeah, but he's more into the big bucks criminal side of things.'

'Oh, well,' said Erica, as if that made him one of the bad guys too.

'He's working really hard at the moment,' Ruby confided. 'We were supposed to be going to a party tonight but he's just had some evidence come in that might save one of his clients from prison. I could hardly insist that he comes to my works do instead when some poor bloke's liberty is on the line. He did say he would call later on though. He might still be able to join us.'

'You don't want the lawyers to spend all night talking shop,' said Lou.

'Or football,' said Andrew. 'Since that's all we men ever talk about.'

'What do you do, Andrew?' Erica asked.

'About what?' Andrew quipped.

Lou squeezed his hand beneath the table. Perfect answer. Perfect guy.

'You know what,' said Ruby magnanimously, when she and Lou were alone in the ladies' later that evening. 'I think I was wrong about your friend Erica. She's really all right. A girl's girl.'

Lou raised an eyebrow in amusement.

'No, really. She is. She's quite a laugh. I hope this man of hers turns out to be a decent bloke,' Ruby continued. 'Doesn't it strike you as statistically impossible that we've all got lucky through personal ads? First you with Andrew, who really is great, Lou. You should hang on to him.'

Lou nodded thoughtfully.

'Then me with Robert. Now Erica with her Bob. That's three out of three. There just aren't that many decent single men floating around without good reason. I hope Erica's bloke doesn't turn out to be some kind of weirdo who gets his kicks from answering Lonely Hearts. Or a married man pretending to be single. Erica doesn't deserve that.'

'She's usually pretty level-headed about things,' said Lou. 'I think she'd sniff a chancer out. He can't be married, anyway.'

'What makes you say that?'

'He's willing to meet her friends, for a start. Married men don't want to meet your friends in case you have someone in common who knows his wife.'

'Aaaaah!' Ruby nodded in understanding.

'It's an even better indicator of marital status than a white gap in a suntan where a wedding ring should be.'

'I once met a man who told me that he had a pigmentation anomaly on his left hand that just made it look as though he'd taken off a wedding ring.'

'Was that true?' asked Lou.

'Of course it wasn't.' Ruby sighed. 'Well, at least Robert has neither of those traits. I checked his hands on the first date and he's already met you and Martin and he would have met loads of my friends at the party tonight if it wasn't for that case coming up.'

Lou narrowed her eyes. 'Are you sure he has to work late?' she teased.

'Yes, I'm bloody sure. He would have come along to the party as soon as he finished. Except that if he doesn't finish before eight then he can't. Because it's on a boat.'

'What time does it start?'

'Leaves the mooring at seven-thirty.'

'You could still go, couldn't you?'

'I don't know,' Ruby admitted. 'I don't want to go on my own.'

'Oh, Ruby. Why not? Much as I fail to understand the way you seem determined to bundle up your self-esteem and hand it to the first man who smiles at you, surely meeting Robert has given you enough confidence to go to the bash and enjoy yourself without him having to actually be there?'

'Flett won't believe he exists if he doesn't see him.'

'What do you think Flett's going to think if you don't show up at all? "Ah yes. That'll be because she's at home shagging her brand-new boyfriend?" Your absence won't make Flett any more convinced that he was wrong to dump you. If you go along looking fantastic and spend the whole night dancing like a wild thing, on the other hand.' She gave a little shimmy in demonstration.

'Lou, I know it sounds pathetic, but I really don't think I can. It'll put me off my rhythm if I have to share a dance floor with Flett and Imogen doing some kind of smooch.'

'Won't it be a laugh to see her having to cope with his appalling lack of rhythm while they do it?' Lou suggested.

Ruby allowed herself a small smile as she remembered dancing with Flett on their first proper date. It was a good job that Ruby had got to know and love his personality first. When John Flett took to the dance floor, it was less Saturday Night Fever than a nasty case of St Vitus' dance. Much as she adored him, Ruby could only dance with Flett if she kept her eyes firmly closed and blocked out the shocked faces of the people around them as they watched the sophisticated businessman hear 'Come On Eileen' and start making like a chimp being prodded with electrodes.

'Robert dances like a dream,' Ruby mused. 'At least, from what I can gather when he's waltzing me from the front door into the bedroom.'

'Purleese,' said Lou. 'You're making me sick.'

'What about you? You're all loved up. You've got a lot to thank that stranger on the train for.'

Lou paused halfway through applying her lip balm. 'Yeah. To think I was stupid enough to believe that someone who smiled at me on a train could be my soul mate, eh?'

'Stupid or not, it got you the wonderful man you're with right now. I think that shows just how clever fate really is.'

'Was Andrew really the only person who replied to the ad?' Lou asked.

Ruby nodded. 'Yep.'

'Oh, well.'

'Lou,' said Ruby. 'You can't tell me you're disappointed that you ended up with Andrew instead of someone you never even spoke to? The man on the train almost certainly wouldn't have lived up to your expectations if he had answered the ad. He might have been married. Or had a speech impediment. Or a penchant for wearing ladies' underwear in the sack.'

'Who wears ladies' underwear in the sack?' asked a booming voice from one of the cubicles which had been shut for the duration of Lou and Ruby's conversation. Now the newly married Susannah Foreman emerged, zipping up her too tight chinos over her belly-button ring and smoothing her T-shirt (a tight red number which had 'Manteaser' written across it in 'Malteser' style script) across her ample chest.

'I thought it was you two,' she told Ruby and Lou. 'So, spill the beans. Ladies' knick-knacks in the boudoir?'

'There are no beans to spill,' said Lou. 'How's married life?'

'Oh, you know. Just got back from our honeymoon. Bloody hot out there in Tanzania.' Susannah's face was still lobster red to complement her outfit. She and Winky had been on a safari. Winky was the kind of bloke who somehow looked right in a pith helmet.

'Did you enjoy the wedding?' Susannah asked.

'Oh, yes,' said Lou and Ruby dutifully.

'Did you score?'

'Nope,' the girls shook their heads.

'Well, you can't say I didn't lay on enough choice for you!'

Ruby and Lou both smiled tightly as they remembered the rowdy rugger buggers and the lecherous grandfather of the groom. 'We're both fixed up now, anyway,' said Ruby. 'Through Lonely Hearts ads. Just like you!' she added.

Susannah whacked Ruby on the back as if she'd just scored a try at a rugby international. 'Good girl! It's the way forward, if you ask me. I couldn't believe my luck when I bagged Winky. Though I did have a few false starts.'

'You did?'

'Oh, yeah,' Susannah told them. 'I can laugh about it now. Loads of married men looking for a bit on the side. Weirdos who still live with their mothers.'

Ruby nodded in recognition at that.

'Lots of men who seemed quite promising on paper but who turned out to have been advertising themselves in the way an estate agent describes a Balham broom cupboard as *bijou*.'

'I definitely had one of those,' said Ruby, remembering Robin.

'And one really disappointing experience with quite a good-looking bloke who turned out to be a personal ad junkie.'

'Do they exist?' asked Lou.

'Oh, yes. Though I think it's just a polite way of describing a sex addict who preys on vulnerable girls. He said he would take me out for dinner one evening but tried to get rid of me as soon as the first course had been cleared away so that he could meet another advertiser for coffee. Didn't even have the decency to meet the girl in a different restaurant. I saw him sitting in the window with her as I went past in a taxi.' She shook her head at the memory. 'Well, at least he didn't get into my knickers. I nearly gave up after that,' she confided. 'But Finty – I think you met her at the wedding – persuaded me to advertise one more time. And this time I got my Winky.'

Lou and Ruby cooed appropriately.

'So you've got a personal ad bloke too?' Susannah said to Lou.

'I suppose I have.'

'Glad to hear it,' said Susannah. 'I told Winky you weren't a lesbian,' she added to Lou and Ruby's horror. 'Honestly, men assume that just because you turn down a tongue sarnie with a man who's already vomited up ten pints, you must be gay. I've won a tenner thanks to you, Lou.'

'Oh, great!' Lou exclaimed.

'I'll buy you a drink to celebrate.'

'I think you'd better.'

When Lou, Ruby and Susannah got back to the table, Erica was looking sheepishly excited. 'He just called to let me know he's on his way,' she said, waving her mobile as if that proved it.

'Where's he coming from?' asked Ruby politely.

'Near Old Street,' said Erica.

'Hey!' said Ruby. 'That's where Robert's firm's based too.'

'He's going to call again as soon as he's parked,' Erica explained.

Erica's mobile played 'Für Elise' to let her know she had a call but when it rang again this time, Erica answered before Beethoven could get to the end of the first bar.

'Hello!' she said briskly, immediately softening into a giggle when she realised that her new man was making the call. 'Where are you now, you sexy beast?'

Ruby and Lou shared the kind of 'aah!' look reserved for the newly in love and small fluffy puppies.

'Just three minutes away? Where did you park the car? Yes, that's a good idea. Have you put the alarm on?'

Oh, the fascinating conversations people have on their mobile phones, Lou thought. Even stranger was why everyone else stopped talking to listen.

'Are you sure it's not single yellow lines there? They don't matter after six o'clock? Well, I guess you are the lawyer, Bob! Yes, of course I'm excited about seeing you. I've been looking forward to this all day. Mmm-hmmm. Yes, I know. Where are you now? Just outside the bar? Can you see me yet? Yes, it is very busy but if you stay on the phone I can guide you in.'

'Like air traffic control,' joked Andrew. 'How big is your new boyfriend's nose?'

'No, I'm not on my own,' Erica explained to her caller. 'That was Andrew. Lou's boyfriend. Yes,' she laughed. 'I'll tell him your nose is absolutely perfect! Best nose I've ever seen. We're sitting towards the back. On the left side. No hang on. My left. So that's your right as you come in . . . I'm wearing a black top. Yes, of course I'll recognise you. How could I forget you, Bobby?'

Lou made an irreverent gagging motion with her fingers in her mouth.

'What's that? Oh yes, Lou was just teasing me for being so soft. Yes, I've been here with Lou all evening. We came straight from work. And met up with her boyfriend Andrew and her old college friends Susannah and . . . Where are you now? You must be really close to us! Shall I stand up so you can see me better? What's that? You'll have to shout. Sounds like you're losing your signal . . .'

Lou saw him first, her face automatically adopting the cartoon 'shocked' expression – eyebrows up, mouth wide open – as she recognised the smooth, handsome features and the curly black hair that framed them so well. She didn't know what to do. Grab Ruby and run? Grab Erica and run? Gesture at him madly until he ran away from them first? Too late. The crowds had parted around him. Erica and Ruby were turning to greet the latest addition to their party simultaneously. Four eyebrows went up in a delighted hello!

'Hi!' said Ruby. 'You made it!'

'Darling!' said Erica.

'You!' said Susannah.

'What the—?'

Ruby's Robert, Erica's Bobby and Susannah's Rob froze with his mobile phone still pressed against his ear.

'Robert!'

'Bobby!'

'Rob!'

He just turned on his heel and ran.

'Come back here, you bastard!' shrieked Susannah.

The personal ad junkie had taken one too many hits.

32

Winky, encouraged by Susannah and emboldened by four pints of Special, was all for chasing Robert out into the street and giving him what for on behalf of all three women he had wronged. Luckily for Robert, he was in the Boxster and out of harm's way before Winky managed to lever himself off his bar stool. He didn't even try to talk his way out of it. He just cut off his call to Erica and fled the bar like the rat out of hell that he was, leaving Erica and Ruby to digest the unhappy facts.

Susannah told them in very unflattering terms what she felt Robert had seen in them. 'He's a sex addict. He wants easy sexual encounters. No commitment. He knows that the kind of women who place personal ads are vulnerable, insecure types who won't take too much encouraging into the sack. He probably expects to be able to shag on the first night and never have to call them again.'

Erica and Ruby were green as they each remembered their first date assignations.

Under the circumstances, Lou didn't think it would be such a great idea if Ruby went to the works' summer party after all. But Susannah insisted. 'Get back on the horse, my girl.' And suddenly finding the 'go to hell' chutzpah that had been missing for her whole life, Ruby told Lou that nothing was going to stop her from catching that party boat now. She changed into her Nicole Farhi and applied make-up in the ladies' room while Erica leaned against the Tampax machine in shock.

'Ruby,' Lou reasoned. 'Do you really think you want to go to this party?'

'Less than an hour ago you were telling me that I should,' Ruby protested.

'I know. But that was before . . . You're really angry, Rubes. If you're going to get drunk and disorderly, wouldn't you be better off doing that here with us instead of in front of your work colleagues?'

'But there's free booze. You go to the party, girl!' said Susannah, whose answer for everything was more alcohol.

With her head now on the hand drier, Erica groaned. 'How could I have been so naive?'

'Are you OK there?' Lou asked, briefly switching her attention to the other injured party.

'Hey!' said Ruby indignantly. 'You're supposed to be *my* best friend.'

'Oh come on, Rubes. Erica's a victim in this too. How was she supposed to know that her Bob was your Robert?'

'And my Rob,' Susannah reminded them. 'He must answer every single ad placed in London. What a freak! He's probably impotent.'

Erica and Ruby's faces registered similarly anguished expressions. And Ruby had to agree that there was no way Erica could have known her new boyfriend had already promised himself to every other thirty-something looking for 'friendship maybe more' within the M25 but that still didn't make her feel better.

'Why don't I send Andrew home?' Lou suggested. 'Then we girls can go for a drink together and bitch about the bastard you've both had a lucky escape from.'

Erica nodded resignedly.

'I'm not going to sit here moping about that shit,' said Ruby. 'I've got a boat to catch.'

'Go, Ruby,' said Susannah. 'Hit the champagne and forget all about it.'

'I'm going to,' Ruby assured her.

And with that, she was gone.

Ruby managed to grab a taxi right outside the bar and made it to the river in time, arriving on the jetty just as the deck hands were pulling in the rickety bridge that had connected the pleasure boat to the shore.

'Hang on!' she shouted. They paused in their rope hauling and helped her across. As the taller of the two placed his hand in the small of Ruby's back to make sure she didn't lose her footing and tumble backwards into the petrol black water, he gave her a dazzling smile.

'I feel better already,' she murmured, as she straightened up and attempted a sashay into the cabin where the party was already in full flow. Unfortunately, since she had downed two bottles of Metz on the taxi ride over, it was inevitable that she caught her toe on a badly placed rope and nearly entered the festivities head first.

'Enjoy your trip,' shouted the guy who had winked.

'I could sue you for leaving that rope laying about like that,' she reprimanded him.

'Don't spoil that pretty face with a frown,' he said.

Ruby fluffed herself up again. 'OK,' she said. 'I won't.'

Three deep breaths. In for a count of ten. Out for a

count of ten. Liz 'the yogi' Hale would have been proud. Ruby gathered herself on the threshold of the party.

'What you waiting for?' one of the deck hands cried. 'Do you want us to announce you or something?'

'Cretins,' Ruby muttered. She'd forgotten about the wink and the smile now. She brushed down the skirt of her red dress and tucked one side of her bob back behind her ear. Behind the door to the main cabin, all sorts of horrors might await her. Flett and Imogen might already be snogging to 'their song'. Ruby's late arrival would pretty much guarantee that all eyes would be on her as she entered.

She glanced longingly back towards the shore. Perhaps Lou had been right. The reality of Robert's duplicity probably hadn't even sunk in yet. It would almost certainly hit her like one of those big iron balls they use to demolish buildings as soon as she saw John Flett and his itty-bitty girlfriend. Drinking yourself back to happiness might work for Susannah and Winky but it had never worked for Ruby before. She felt a sudden, overwhelming urge to go home and hide out beneath the duvet. But the jetty was already thirty feet away. Too far to jump. Too far to swim. Especially in pure silk Nicole Farhi. No way out this time. Ruby stepped into the fray.

'Ruby! What are you doing here?' The first person she bumped into was Liz Hale. 'I didn't think you were going to come along tonight because Robert . . .'

'I don't have to have male company every time I go out,' said Ruby archly. 'Why should I miss the party of the year just because I don't have a date with a penis?'

'Quite,' said Liz. 'Isn't that what I said to you all along?'

'I know. And I'm sorry about earlier,' Ruby told her.

'Apology accepted.'

'When it came down to it, I couldn't bear the thought of staying in to watch the telly instead and missing out on someone making a complete and utter tit of themselves. Who are the contenders tonight?'

'Alice Martin has been knocking them back all afternoon. She went for lunch with Mariel Cooper.' Ruby and Liz both rolled their eyes at the name of the client who had big shares in Johnnie Walker. 'I give it until nine o'clock before Alice is heaving her guts up into the Thames.'

'Lovely,' said Ruby sarcastically. 'And . . .'

'He's here,' said Liz, knowing at once whom Ruby was referring to. 'He was chatting to Alan a few minutes ago but I don't know where he's got to now.'

'Perhaps he jumped overboard when he saw me coming,' Ruby quipped.

Liz looked concerned. 'Look, Ruby. You're not . . .'

'Don't worry!' Ruby said defensively. 'I'm here to have a good time, not a fist-fight with the man who dumped me by e-mail. Or his girlfriend. I'm beyond that now.'

'Have you seen what she's wearing?' Liz asked. 'I had a pair of legwarmers like that when I was twelve.'

'Retro-eighties chic is all the rage,' Ruby informed her. 'Provided you can't remember it the first time around.'

'Well, I think she looks ridiculous.'

Ruby nodded, wishing she could agree. Unfortunately, much as Ruby wanted her to look like a refugee from *Flashdance*, Imogen looked as though she had stepped from the directional fashion pages of *Vogue*. The leg-warmers were a witty addendum to a surprisingly stylish outfit. It was eighties chic MTV-style. The only possible consolation would be if Flett had donned a kung-fu style bandanna and rolled the sleeves of his jacket up à la *Miami Vice* to complement his new young lover's look.

He hadn't.

Ruby caught her first glimpse of Flett that evening as she and Liz queued at the bar for warm white wine.

'So, what made you change your mind about coming?' Liz was asking at the time. 'I must say, I'm really glad that you've come to your senses. You shouldn't have to go into social exile just because one of your clients . . .'

Ruby jabbed Liz hard in the ribs as Flett sidled up beside them.

'Ruby,' he nodded curtly.

'Jonathan,' she replied briefly, before turning her attention back to the barman.

'That's a lovely dress,' he said. 'Very sophisticated. It suits you.'

'Thank you,' said Ruby, rewarding him with a half-smile. 'That's a . . . nice shirt,' she said. He was wearing the pink polo shirt. Again! 'Pink suits you.'

'Johnnie! Have you got me that glass of wine yet?' Imogen shouted. 'I'm absolutely gasping!'

'Run along, Johnnie-boy,' muttered Ruby under her breath as Flett scuttled back towards his new girl.

'See you later?' he said as he went.

'You handled that really well,' said Liz, giving Ruby a congratulatory pat on the back. 'How do you feel?'

'I feel fine,' said Ruby, tightening her grip on the brass

rail that ran around the bar. 'Why should I feel any different?'

'Well,' Liz pontificated then, 'he may not be here tonight but Robert is obviously having a positive effect on you.'

'Positive effect?' Liz stepped back in horror as Ruby's face crumbled from sophisticated, serene composure to the 'tragedy' mask of historical theatre. 'Oh, Liz! My life is a disaster!'

Liz's eyes widened desperately as she heard the first line of that overly familiar tune.

'Robert isn't here tonight because he's been seeing someone else! He answered an ad in the *Guardian* that was placed by one of Lou's workmates.'

'Nooooo!' said Liz appropriately.

'When I thought he was going to be working late tonight, I decided to go for a drink with Lou. She was supposed to be on a foursome with Andrew and her workmate Erica's new man. Turned out that Erica's new man was my old one!'

'Ruby, that's just awful!'

'He's a personal ad addict. My friend Susannah went on a date with him almost two years ago.'

'Can I help you?' asked the barman.

'Two dry whites,' Ruby managed to sniff before carrying on with the tears.

'What did you say to him?'

'I didn't get a chance to say anything at all! He saw me sitting next to Erica and made his escape before either of us could grab hold of him and punch . . . his . . . fucking . . . lights . . . out!' She gulped agonisingly between each word, finishing on a rib-racking sob that drew the attention of everyone within a ten-metre radius.

'Here's your wine,' said the barman nervously.

'Thanks,' said Ruby.

'Is that everything?'

'No,' she said. 'I'd better have another two as well.'

'Ruby!' Liz began in a warning tone. 'You can't just drown your sorrows . . .'

'Oh, for fuck's sake,' said Ruby. 'I was getting two for me and two for you. You know what the queue for the bar will get like later on. I can have a couple of glasses, can't I? Without turning into a blubbering wreck?'

Liz was kind, or cowardly, enough not to tell her that she had already achieved the blubbering part without the assistance of Sauvignon Blanc.

'Let's sit down over there,' said Liz, pointing to a suitably dark corner, 'and you can tell me all about it properly.'

'I don't want to spoil your evening too,' said Ruby, forgetting her previous diagnosis that the only thing stopping Liz Hale from committing suicide was the fact that even her non-existent love life seemed preferable to Ruby's endlessly humiliating one.

'I'm your friend,' said Liz. '*Your* pain is *my* pain.'

'That's nice,' said Ruby. 'I mean, it's not nice. Oh, you know what I mean.'

The barman placed the second round of white wine on the bar in front of them.

'That it?' he asked again. He indicated with a subtle gesture of his eyebrows the fact that Ruby had already drained one of the previous two glasses.

'One more,' said Ruby, raising a finger. 'Each.'

'Ruby . . .' Liz began. 'Do you really think you should have any more wine?'

'You're right,' said Ruby. 'I shouldn't. Barman, make mine a double vodka.'

Oh dear. Months later, Ruby would still be unable to recall what really happened on the night of the Hollingworth party. Not even under hypnotic regression. Martin and Lou had always teased Ruby for her inability to truly let go under the influence of alcohol. She'd never had a blackout or sudden memory loss such as Lou was prone to on a weekly basis during their college years. Ruby had never even thrown up, leading Lou to suggest that Ruby's refusal to truly let it all hang out while drinking alcopops was reflected in her extremely low hit rate with orgasms.

But that night, on board the incongruously named good ship *Primrose*, Ruby broke through all her previous barriers. Two bottles of Metz, two glasses of wine, three double vodkas and all on an empty stomach. Pretty soon, Liz Hale was just a shadowy blur with big red lips that seemed to be moving twice as fast as the words that were getting through Ruby's ears. The combination of alcohol and the movement of the boat had set up a sine wave undulation in her stomach. But her worries were starting to fade and go fuzzy at least.

'I feel like dancing,' she told her shoulder to cry on.

'I think you should stay sitting down,' said Liz sensibly.

What did Liz Hale know? Ruby hauled herself to her feet and crossed the dance floor, zig-zagging as if she was trying to escape from a crocodile. Imogen and John Flett were bopping energetically to that Buck's Fizz Eurovision classic 'Making Your Mind Up'. When it got to the part in the song where the two blonde bimbettes generally lost their skirts, Ruby suddenly found that she was leaning too far forward to remain upright. She made a grab for the nearest thing to stop her fall. She heard a ripping noise. Someone was shouting.

All black . . .

33

'Recorded delivery,' said the postman, thrusting a clipboard towards Martin's chest. Martin hesitated instinctively. Recorded delivery could only mean bad news. Probably the kind of bad news that his bank manager charged twenty pounds per letter for. The HSBC were the only people Martin could imagine would bother writing to him in this way. The night before he had stuck his cash card in the hole in the wall and actually prayed until the machine spat some cash out. He must have hit his overdraft limit by now. He had been writing cheques all week in the knowledge that they might turn out to have more bounce than Tigger.

The postman cleared his throat. 'Do you want it or not, mate? I haven't got all day.'

'What? Sorry.' Martin scribbled his signature.

'Signature there,' said the postman impatiently. 'You've got to print your name in that box. Never mind. That'll do.'

He handed the envelope and a few other items over, tutted and walked back up the path slamming the gate shut behind him. Martin wondered whoever got the idea that postmen were cheerful. Perhaps it was the early mornings. What time was it? He could barely focus on the clock in the kitchen, so gummed with sleep were his eyes.

Seven a.m. Martin looked at the plain white envelope with his name and address set squarely in the middle in neat, Times New Roman. Seven a.m. On a Saturday morning. It had better be good news, thought Martin. But how likely was that? No one ever sent good news by registered post. Still, if it was his bank manager, he did at least have a contingency plan. The cheque from Petunia Daniels, still un-cashed, was pinned to the note board in his bedroom.

Best have a fortifying cup of tea first, he decided. While the kettle boiled, Martin listened to the messages on his answer machine. The first was from his sister, asking if he wanted to join her and her family in Bournemouth over the next bank holiday weekend. 'I don't think so,' said Martin to the empty room, imagining three days being used as a vaulting horse by his niece and nephew. The second was from Webecca. 'Martin, I weally hope you're not sitting there ignoring this message . . .' He skipped straight to the next one.

'Martin, it's Lou. Calamity. Can you believe that Ruby's man turned out to be Erica's man as well? He's one of those sex addicts who trawl the personals for victims. Erica's crying on Andrew's shoulder but Ruby thinks she's OK. She's gone to the Hollingworth party on her own. Bloody Susannah Foreman was encouraging her. She probably is OK. But I'd be really grateful if you could go round and check on her at some point tomorrow morning. You live much closer than I do. Make sure she hasn't done anything stupid. Thanks, babe. Mwah. Mwah.'

Martin played that message again. Ruby's man turned out to be Erica's man? Did this mean Ruby and Robert were finished? It had to.

'Yes!' Martin balled his hand into a fist and made a footballer's victory gesture. 'Yes. Yes. Yes.' It wasn't all bad news that morning then. He'd go and see Ruby as soon as he was dressed. Take her for a coffee. If he still had any money . . .

'Oh, sod it,' said Martin as he ripped the ominous envelope open at last. The news wasn't going to get any better if he left it unread.

He was halfway down the densely printed page before it hit him that the missive wasn't from his bank manager at all. He sat down at the kitchen table and started again. The letter was printed on the thick creamy notepaper of Euphemie Gilbert at the Wilson Gilbert Literary Agency.

Back when he started his novel Martin had sent two chapters and a synopsis to just about every agent in the *Writers' and Artists' Yearbook*. And he thought he'd counted all the knock-backs in, everything from *Dear Mr Ashcroft, Mr Tyler regrets that he is not taking on any new clients at the moment*, to *Dear Mr Ashcroft, I regret that I am unable to put my weight behind such a derivative piece of writing*. That one hurt the most, but Martin had kept it in any case, convinced that before too long there would come a day when that particular agent would have to eat his own clichéd words.

But Euphemie Gilbert? Martin couldn't even remember having sent his script to her.

Dear Mr Ashcroft,
How thrilled I was to read such an exciting manuscript! she wrote. *I find it hard to imagine that a writer of your calibre doesn't already have representation, but if that is not the case, I wonder if you might care to meet me for*

lunch to discuss your literary future. How glad I am that I took heed of Petunia's assertion that yours is a rare and wonderful talent!

Petunia? Martin rubbed his eyes. Perhaps he wasn't awake yet after all. Perhaps this was just another cruel and unusual dream like the one in which Cameron Diaz declared undying love for him and bought him a Porsche 911 to prove it. Who was Petunia? The only Petunia he knew was Petunia Daniels and she would hardly be the first to sing his praises. Would she?

Euphemie continued:

I have taken the liberty of printing out a copy of your work in progress to show to my colleagues here at the office. How close are you to finishing the novel? Everyone is enormously excited at the prospect of meeting you, including Simon Dunford, Petunia's own agent, who would like to talk to you about film rights immediately.

Martin's chin hit his chest.

Petunia Daniels. The missing diskette.

And, sure enough, there among the rest of the post that the jolly postman had delivered that morning was a note on one of Petunia Daniels' personalised Smythson correspondence cards.

Dear Mr Ashcroft,
I fear that I have utterly underestimated you. I hope you will forgive me that, meeting you as I did under such extraordinary circumstances, I failed to offer you the hospitality and respect you deserved. I'm sure you will understand that in the past Cindy has met many young men who, rather than seeing her for the wonderful

creature she is, see beyond her to an opportunity to meet her parents. I'm afraid that I assumed the worst of you – hence the rather embarrassing little matter of the contract – and my compulsion to read the material stored on your diskette.

By the time I reached the end of the first chapter, however, I knew that you have a real talent for story-telling and the fact that you chose not to bank the cheque with which I tried to pay you off, was a further reason for me to review my opinion of you. I can only hope that the name and address you gave for our silly little contract was your real one and apologise for having treated you so shabbily. If this note does reach you then perhaps you will see your way to allowing me to repair some of the damage caused by joining us all for dinner at your earliest convenience.

Best wishes,
Petunia Daniels

Martin raced out the house without grabbing a jacket. It was spitting with rain but he hardly noticed. It was as though the letter he clutched in his hand emitted enough heat to make him immune to the elements. He was grinning like a loony and he knew it. As he passed the old wino who always sat outside the tube, the old man raised a can of Special Brew in a toast.

'Good morning to you, young gentleman.'

'It is indeed a fabulous morning,' said Martin, as he raced on past. Then he stopped. And for the first time ever he dug into his pockets to find some change to give the homeless man. After all, Martin thought, he was going to make it. The evidence that he was about to get his big break was still clutched in his sweaty palm. He could afford to be a little magnanimous.

Martin pulled out what he thought was a note. It was a note, but not a banknote. Just the note his upstairs neighbour had pushed under his door to let him know that the bass on his stereo was set too loud. And a fifty-pence piece.

'I take American Express,' said the wino hopefully.

'Switch?' asked Martin.

The wino shrugged and accepted the coin.

'I'm sorry,' Martin told him. 'I did want to give you more. I would give you more except I haven't got any cash on me at the moment. I've just got an agent.'

The wino looked at him blankly.

'An agent for my writing. Euphemie Gilbert at the Wilson Gilbert agency wants to represent me. She represents the best people in Britain.'

The wino nodded. 'You trying to sell your house then?'

'No,' said Martin exasperatedly. 'A novel. Look, just remember this face. When I pick up the Booker Prize I'll be back with a crate full of Special Brew. You,' Martin assured the wino, 'are looking at the next big thing.'

Martin grinned all the way to West London. When he got to Hammersmith he dipped into the newsagent stroke off-licence that never stuck to the licensing laws and bought a bottle of chilled champagne. He nearly bought the sparkling Chardonnay. But only nearly. The Chardonnay was cheaper, sure, but this was the biggest day of his career so far. His big break day. And the last day he even needed to think about a future where spending thirty quid on a bottle of plonk instead of ten quid might leave him with nothing but baked beans to live on at the end of the month.

Martin was so buoyed up by the time he got to Ruby's street that he even bought her a bunch of flowers from the shop on the corner. In fact, he bought two bunches and then had to discard half of them, because they'd clearly been sitting outside the shop in a green bucket for the best part of a week. Even the ones he salvaged looked as though they would be dead by that evening. But it was the thought that counted. And he felt sure that his news would be much more exciting than roses to his dearest, most wonderful friend.

Martin rang Ruby's doorbell impatiently. He couldn't wait to tell her. He couldn't wait to tell her. This should take her mind off that idiot Robert. Where was she?

Thirty seconds later, during which Ruby had made no signal that she might soon appear at the door, Martin jabbed the doorbell again. 'Come on,' he muttered. 'Answer it.' He pressed the buzzer three times, then stood back from the door and looked up at Ruby's windows with what he thought was a particularly appealing smile on his face. Where were your friends when you needed to spew your good news all over their breakfast table?

'Ruby!' Martin shouted up.

'Shurrup!' came a voice from an open window across the street. 'Some of us are trying to sleep.'

Martin looked at his watch. It was only just past eight o'clock. Pretty bloody early for a Saturday. But . . .

'Ruby!' Martin shouted again. Defiantly. Then he looked about him furtively to see if any hulking great Hammersmith resident was preparing to throw something at his head. No sign. One last shout. 'Ruby! Open the door, will you! It's Martin.'

A small cloud of worry passed through his mind then. Perhaps she really had done something stupid as a result of being chucked for the second time in a month. Perhaps she was out cold on the kitchen floor having washed down twenty aspirin with some floor cleaner.

'Ruby!!!!'

He rattled her door, hoping he wouldn't have to kick it in.

Finally, he heard the sound of the sash window to Ruby's bedroom groaning open as though it had been painted shut and left that way in 1973. Ruby's head emerged, like a tortoise at the end of a long winter inside its shell. She blinked, even in the distinct lack of sunlight – it was still British summertime – and had to shade her eyes in order to be able to see who was shouting up at her.

Martin held the flowers aloft. 'Happy Saturday!' he chimed. 'I brought you these. And this!' He held up the champagne bottle. 'I tried to get Lou to come over and join us for breakfast but she must have gone to stay at Wotsit's. I couldn't get hold of her. Can I come up?'

'What? Oh.'

Ruby looked behind her, into the bedroom, as though she were surveying the damage. 'I, er, I suppose so.'

'Well, don't sound so pleased to see me.'

'Hang on,' she said. 'I'll open the door.'

Ruby drew her head back inside her hovel and moments later the entry-phone buzzed to let Martin know that he could come in. He bounded up the shabbily carpeted stairs, two at a time. He was going to sweep her into his arms and give her a great big hug and . . .

'Look at the state of you,' he said when Ruby opened the door of her flat to him. 'Big night at the Hollingworth party? You look like somebody rode you hard and put you away wet,' he added with a wink.

Ruby went crimson.

'Lou told me about Robert,' Martin continued. 'He isn't worth it, you know. He did you a favour getting out of your life and this time next year you'll be laughing about it. Anyway, the news that I have for you is going to cheer you right up. You remember that . . .'

'Martin,' Ruby said, gesturing in the direction of the figure now looming behind her. 'This is, er . . . This is Emlyn Cruickshank.'

'Eh?' Martin stuck his hand out automatically to meet Emlyn's own extended hand. Emlyn Cruickshank wasn't a particularly big man but he was much too big for Ruby's stripy pink towelling dressing gown, which gaped at the front to show his Wylie Coyote print boxer-shorts.

'Emlyn from work,' the Panter clarified. 'You've probably heard a lot about me.'

'Oh, yeah,' said Martin. 'I've heard all about you.' Then he tossed the flowers onto the Formica table that Ruby had been meaning to replace ever since she bought her flat, and added, 'I didn't mean to interrupt anything. I'll come back later.'

'Nope. You're all right. I'm done here,' said Emlyn, in a way that Martin found altogether too proprietorial. 'Done here?' It made him sound like a vet, taking his leave after fixing some poor cow's udders.

'Won't you stay for a cup of tea?' Ruby asked. Desperately, it seemed to Martin. What on earth was she doing with this bloke?

'Breakfast? Toast?' Ruby continued in a twitter. 'I haven't got any bacon in the house but if you hang on here I can just run down to the shop and get some. Won't take me two minutes. Streaky or back?'

' 'S'alright,' said Emlyn. 'Told the boys I'd meet them down the Slug to watch the rugby today. Better put some clothes on first though. Eh?'

Emlyn ambled back into the bedroom.

'Is that?' Martin asked.

'Don't say it, Martin,' Ruby warned, closing her eyes against his angry expression.

'It's the one with the athlete's foot, isn't it?'

'I think that's gone now,' Ruby pleaded.

'How do you know? He didn't take his socks off.'

'No?'

'You mean you didn't notice?'

Martin knew he had looked pretty bad at several junctures in his life but he had never, never been seen by another man while wearing a girl's fluffy dressing gown and a pair of grey, mid-calf-length socks with holes in the big toes of both of them.

'How drunk were you last night?' Martin asked.

'Not very,' Ruby lied.

'You only just found out about Robert and Erica.'

'I don't want to talk about that,' Ruby warned.

'Lou was really worried about you. Well, I'll have to tell her you're clearly going through an extended period of grieving.'

Ruby squirmed. But before she could say anything in her defence, Emlyn reappeared in the doorway to the kitchen. His suit fitted him only marginally better than the dressing gown had done.

'Bit embarrassing to have to go to the Slug in my work clothes,' he said. 'It'll make the boys wonder what I've been up to.'

'I'm sure you'll have a great time telling them in blow-by-blow detail,' said Martin sharply.

'Martin!' Ruby was anguished.

Perhaps it had sounded a little more sarcastic than he meant it to but Martin stared Emlyn straight in the eye as though he really was expecting a fight. Emlyn looked back at Martin like a dopey Labrador that can't decipher the words in the message but knows that it has been delivered belligerently.

'I'll call you,' Emlyn said to Ruby eventually. Then he kissed her on the top of her head and left.

'Martin!' Ruby whined as soon as the door shut behind her latest man. 'What did you have to say that for?'

'Well, he will, won't he?' Martin spluttered. 'He'll go straight down the pub and tell all his mates that he slept with you last night. He may even invite them to sniff his fingers for evidence. See how many of them recognise the smell.'

Ruby's mouth dropped into a horrified 'O'.

'I just don't understand you. Yesterday you were all about Robert. Robert this. Robert that. Robert was the love of your life. Then Robert turns out to be a wanker. And last night you slept with some other twat. No wonder you can't get a man and hold onto him. You're faster than Speedy Gonzales when it comes to getting your knickers off. Do you think that earns you any respect? "Hi, I'm Ruby Taylor. Fly me." '

The harsh words hung between them like breath in freezing air.

'Piss off,' Ruby said suddenly. 'How dare you speak to me like that?'

'Ruby, I'm sorry.' Martin said almost immediately, snapping back to friendly concern as though he'd woken from a trance.

'Piss off,' she said again. 'Where do you get off on being so bloody horrible to me?'

'Ruby, I didn't mean to be horrible,' said Martin, desperate to regain lost ground. 'I just don't understand why you think you need to be with that sort of guy. You just slept with a man that you once claimed made you physically sick! What's going on in your head that makes you think you have anything to gain from letting an idiot like that, who's laid half your bloody office, get into your bed too?'

'Get out,' Ruby persisted. 'Get away from me.'

'But I brought you these.'

Martin held up the flowers again but Ruby pushed them back at him.

'I don't want your crappy flowers. Go away.'

'Ruby, I came round here because I wanted to tell you . . .'

'Just fuck off. I don't want to hear anything you've got to say to me. You don't know what it's like. You don't understand what it's like to be me.'

Three quarters of an hour later, Martin stormed out of the tube station at Chalk Farm again. This time, he didn't have a smile for anyone. Especially not the wino.

'All right mate?' the wino called after him. 'You sold that house yet?'

Martin dropped the flowers he had bought to make Ruby's day into the wino's lap.

'Rather have the champagne,' he said.

'Piss off,' said Martin. 'Buy your own.'

Back at his own flat, Martin sat down at his own Formica-topped table, cleared a space in the week's accumulated free papers and pizza leaflets, and plonked the champagne bottle on top of his super-important letter from Euphemie Gilbert.

'Bollocks,' he said. Ruby hadn't even given him a chance to tell her his news. He read the first couple of lines of the letter through the distorting green lens of the bottle. Didn't seem quite so impressive now. He was really fucked off. Really really fucked off. And he wasn't really sure why he felt quite so bad. Or perhaps he was. And he just didn't want to admit it.

Across town, Ruby sank back down onto her unmade bed. The fitted sheet had come away from the mattress during the previous night's exertions. First, she lay on her back and stared at the ceiling. The dusty pink paper uplighter. The yellowing plastic of the ancient light fitting. That was depressing enough. Then she rolled onto her side and brought her knees up to her chin in a foetal position. Halfway through that manoeuvre she felt a peculiar, squishy sensation beneath her calf. She put her hand down to find out what she was laying on and found herself holding a condom, neatly tied in a knot to prevent leakage.

'Happy fucking Saturday,' she murmured to herself, sitting up and staring at Emlyn's little present in disgust. How had she ended up sleeping with the Panter? She had a vague recollection that he'd held back her hair as she vomited her guts into the river while the boat came into dock. They'd shared a taxi home and then . . .?

Holding the open end of the johnny between her thumb and forefinger, she stretched the condom like a catapult and aimed for the bin. It sailed clumsily through the air to land on her dressing table, knocking the little china dog she had inherited from her great-grandmother at the age of six to the floor. She knew without looking that the dog would be broken.

'Happy fucking life,' she half-shouted. Then she burst into a sob.

34

Andrew was still sleeping when Lou awoke. The sun was streaming in through the flimsy white curtains that looked fantastic with the Zen theme she had chosen for her interior decoration but were bloody hopeless at keeping out the light even during the British summer months. Moving super-slowly and carefully, anxious not to wake the man sleeping so soundly beside her, Lou slipped from the bed and made her way to the bathroom.

How was it possible to be with someone and yet still feel so utterly alone? How was it possible to be with someone as wonderful, warm and kind as Andrew and yet still wonder if love would ever find you? Love *had* found Lou, as Ruby and Martin kept reminding her. There was nothing Andrew wouldn't do to make her happy. Not just flowers, great restaurants, all the obvious boyfriend stuff, either. Earlier that week, when Lou complained that she didn't have time to come out because she had too much housework and homework to do, Andrew had insisted on doing the ironing for her, while she marked up a manuscript that had come in late.

There was no question that Andrew was the most fantastic bloke she had ever had the good fortune to go out with.

Lou stepped into the shower and let the jets pound down onto her head, standing there until the hot water

ran out and the steam disappeared and she was starting
to feel almost shivery. But she didn't want to get out of
that cubicle. She didn't want to go back to the bedroom
until she knew that Andrew was gone. And she knew that
the likelihood of him having decided to gather his clothes
and split the scene like a guilty one-night-stander was
absolutely zero. Nil. In fact, he was knocking on the
bathroom door right now.

'I need a pee,' he called in to her. 'Are you OK? You've
been in there for ages.'

And though Lou felt as though she would rather jump
from her bathroom window than open the door and
smile at him then, she managed it.

'Needed to wash the smoke out of my hair,' she said.
And she even pinched his bum as they dosey-doed in the
doorway. Not that she wanted him to act on the flirtatious gesture. But he deserved it. Because he was a great
bloke and she knew she should be grateful to have him
and perhaps, one day, if she just let herself believe that
someone that fantastic might really be the one for her,
she'd get over it and they'd live happily ever after like
Susannah and Winky.

'Fuck.'

That was what love was supposed to be about. Susannah and Winky, slobbering all over each other like he
was a deer and she was a salt lick, entwining their limbs
like a creeper and an apple tree, only just able to let each
other out of sight for long enough to go to the loo. True
love was not furtively checking your e-mail, while your
other half is in the bathroom, to see if you've got a
message from someone you met through a cheesy on-line
dating agency. True love shouldn't be disappointed when

Chris the Management Consultant writes with the news that an old girlfriend is back on the scene.

Still wrapped in a damp bath towel, Lou collapsed backwards onto her bed. 'Fuck.' She couldn't do this. She couldn't keep pretending. Not a single day longer.

There is never a right time to break someone's heart. And anyone with even a microgram of sensitivity in his or her body will agonise for an age over that timing. Only problem is there's always some reason not to make someone unhappy. The day a relationship ends, if that relationship was at all important to the suckers involved, becomes as important an anniversary as a wedding day or birthday.

Obviously, the average person doesn't want to kick someone they once loved while that person is down. It starts early. At school, you don't want to chuck someone when they're revising for those important exams, then you don't want to upset them while they're waiting anxiously for the results, and then, when they get the results and they're dreadful, you feel obliged to stick with them through the re-sits.

But it's not just the hard times when someone is down that become obstacles to making your getaway. After times of bereavement, unemployment and general un-happiness, those events that should be happy ones also make some times off-limits for the eager would-be dum-per. Christmas, birthdays, Easter. All impossible. A clever person with a sensitive lover that they sense is not quite as into them as he or she used to be, could stave off the inevitable for years by carefully spacing out those crucial dates.

Which is what Andrew seemed to be doing right now. Every time he called Lou at work, he seemed to have set another milestone that she knew she would have to pass before she could be free of him without thinking she'd ruined his life.

'My boss has invited us over for dinner,' was the latest one.

'What? Both of us?' Lou didn't think dinner parties with the boss happened outside seventies sitcoms any more. They certainly didn't happen at her office. 'When?'

Andrew named a date that was almost a month into the future. 'I hope you don't mind,' he said. 'But I've sort of said yes on your behalf already. If you don't want to though, I can tell him that you've got other things on. But they're all dead keen to meet you. I guess they've heard so much about you.'

Lou suddenly had that freefall feeling of nausea that usually accompanies being chucked. It wasn't how she should feel. Doesn't everyone want to hear that someone adores them so much they can't even shut up about them while at work?

Lou made a quick mental calculation. If she accepted this dinner invitation and held off ending the relationship until a decent time after that date, then she and Andrew would have been seeing each other for almost three months by the time she told him 'This isn't working out'.

'I don't think I'm doing anything,' she said grudgingly, 'but I wish you'd asked me first.'

'I know,' said Andrew, but she could hear the grin in his voice and she knew that he hadn't really sensed her unhappiness at the situation at all. So much for her other great idea, which was that she would simply become increasingly distant until *he* dropped the axe on their relationship instead; saving her the guilt and salvaging maximum self-esteem for himself from the fact that he technically did the ending.

There was no point asking Ruby or Martin for advice on this matter. Ruby had never ended a relationship in her life. Never seemed to be able to hang in a relationship for so long that she got bored before the bloke did. Or, if she did get bored first, Ruby was always too scared that there would never be a replacement to risk making herself voluntarily single. And Martin was no more successful at perfecting the art of severance. He had a string of ex-girlfriends who couldn't quite believe that he'd finished with them, who continued to ring him for months after the definitive event, until he ended up sleeping with them again or got a restraining order. And she knew what her mother would say.

'Louisa Capshaw, you do not know what's good for you!'

So? thought Lou. Bran is good for you. Apples are good for you. But they're boring. Andrew was emotional fibre. What Lou Capshaw wanted was someone who would give her a heart attack.

When Andrew finally left the flat to play five-a-side football with his mates, Lou called an immediate conference with hers.

'Martin,' she said, when he answered the phone. 'What are you doing?'

'I'm asleep,' he said.

'Then you're sleep-talking. Can you come out for brunch with me and Ruby?'

She heard Martin roll over in bed as though all his bones were aching.

'Heavy night?' she said.

Martin snorted.

'Are you on your own?'

'Very much so,' Martin told her.

'Are you ill?' Lou asked.

'Just sick at heart.'

'What's that? Shakespeare? Why don't you come for breakfast with the girls?'

'Think I'll give it a miss.' Martin hung up.

'What?'

Lou dialled Ruby.

'Yeee-ssss,' Ruby answered shakily.

'Not you as well?'

'What do you mean? As well?'

'Did you have a good time at the party last night?'

'I had a terrible one!'

'I thought so. Come out with me,' Lou suggested. 'I think I might need cheering up too this morning.'

'I can't get up,' said Ruby.

'What is wrong with the pair of you? I just got the same bullshit from Martin.'

'Ask Martin,' Ruby snorted. Then she too hung up the phone.

Lou pulled on her denim jacket and headed for the tube station. She was going to go to Ruby's flat and drag her out of bed. Martin, she knew from years of experience, was best left alone when he had a hangover. But it sounded as though Ruby was moping about Robert and the only cure for that was a twenty-four-hour-long moan. Lou already figured that she would be on the receiving end of the mammoth whinge at one point or another. Might as well get it out of the way a.s.a.p. And it would take her mind off the Andrew conundrum.

Half an hour later, Lou was gliding smoothly down an escalator at Leicester Square station, hoping to catch the Piccadilly Line west. She was reading the posters that flanked the walls, finding distraction in the disgusting warts fashioned from chewing gum that adorned every picture of an attractive model. She'd given up scanning the Underground crowds for her dream lover now. At least, that's what she told herself. In reality, perhaps she was working on the principle that if she stopped looking, the stranger would find her again. A variation on the platitudes her mother had spouted throughout Lou's adolescence that you shouldn't 'look too hard' for love.

Lou was almost at the bottom of the escalator when it happened. She heard a shout come from somewhere behind her but before she could properly turn round to see who was trying to attract her attention, the escalator came to a sudden, lurching halt and a middle-aged guy, who had definitely eaten more burgers than bran flakes in his time, slumped against her with his full, dead weight and sent her crashing down the final three steps.

Kieran Dunmore had suffered a first, minor heart attack that would shake him into pledging a serious life change as he lay in a hospital bed that night. Lou Capshaw, who had broken his fall so spectacularly and possibly saved his life in the process, also had time to do some serious thinking. There wasn't much else to do as she waited for the overworked accident and emergency staff to get round to seeing to her badly twisted ankle.

In the event, Andrew arrived to keep her company before any doctor did. He'd run from the tube station to the hospital and nearly ended up a patient himself as he skidded across the highly polished floor of the waiting room to her side.

'Brought you these,' he said, kissing her hello and handing her a pile of magazines.

'Thanks,' Lou took the new reading material gratefully. She had already devoured the waiting room's supply of tatty *Readers' Digest*. 'What have you brought me?'

'*Marie Claire. Cosmopolitan. Time Out.*'

35

'Martin!' Petunia Daniels trilled, 'I'm so glad you called.'

'I just wanted to thank you,' he said, 'for passing my manuscript on to that agent friend of yours.'

'She's tremendously excited,' said Petunia. 'Says there's something of the young Martin Amis about you, my dear.'

'Oh.' Martin hoped that was a compliment. He'd never actually read any of the author's books, just the interviews about his extravagant dentistry.

'So, when are you going to come to dinner so that I can make up to you for being such a witch last time we met? Cindy is anxious to see you again too.'

'She is?' Martin was surprised.

'Yes. You made quite an impression on both of us. How about this evening? We're having a few pals around for an informal supper. Perhaps you'd like to join us?'

Martin hesitated. The plan for that evening had been to go to the cinema with Ruby and Lou. Martin guessed he probably wasn't invited to that any more.

'If you're sure it's OK with you,' he told Petunia.

Perhaps the knock she received to her head had had a lasting effect on Cindy Daniels. Martin hardly recognised the vision in a pink floral sun-dress that opened the door to him that evening. Even Cindy's hair was suddenly the kind of colour one might expect to find in nature rather than on the head of a plastic gonk hanging from the rear-view mirror of a Ford Escort. Her dreadlocks had been cut away to leave behind a neat blonde crop like Mia Farrow's.

'Cindy?' Martin asked just to confirm that it wasn't her less-evil twin.

'Hi, Martin,' she said, dropping her eyes to the floor in a gesture that Martin took to be embarrassment. Then she looked up at him from beneath her lashes with that gaze like Princess Diana on acid again and he knew that she hadn't been replaced by a fembot. Beneath that bizarre Laura Ashley exterior, Cindy Daniels was alive and ready to give some poor bloke a kicking.

'Nice dress,' he said, for want of something better.

'It's Chloe,' she told him.

'I'm sorry?'

'Chloe the designer. It's the "Good Life" look. Based on the seventies sitcom of the same name. More ironic chic, you could call it.'

'Right,' said Martin, nodding as if he got it.

'How are you?' she asked.

'Fantastic,' he said.

'I like your book,' she said then. 'I like artistic men.'

'I thought you were bored of them,' Martin observed.

'I hardly had the chance to get bored of you, did I?' She locked eyes with him meaningfully.

'Martin!' Petunia Daniels appeared in the hallway behind her daughter just before Cindy had time to fly at their guest and rip his clothes off. 'Come in! Come in,' she trilled. 'It's so good to see you.'

She kissed him warmly on both cheeks. The greeting

couldn't have been more different from the way she had last dismissed him. 'Darling, we're so excited to have you here with us this evening. There are lots of people simply dying to meet you. Do you know Andrew Greenwood?'

'The director?' Martin gasped.

'That's the boy.'

'Not personally.'

'Fenella Anderson is here too,' said Petunia, referring to the actress who had been her closest rival throughout her career. 'Now darling,' Petunia whispered, 'you really mustn't take too much notice of her. She's only been here for half an hour and she's already drained my Bombay Sapphire. New bottle this morning.'

'Yeah, and you had half of it with lunch,' mumbled Cindy.

Petunia chose to ignore her daughter. 'Come on in. Everybody's waiting. Let me take your coat. This way, Martin. Deep breath,' she instructed as though Martin were about to step out onto the stage on opening night.

Martin obliged. And it was a good job he did because he quite forgot to breathe again as Petunia ushered him into the sitting room and introduced him to four faces he had hitherto only seen on television. (Plus Cindy's father. And Martin really didn't want to think about the circumstances under which they had previously met.)

Fenella Anderson patted an empty space beside her on the big squashy sofa. 'Well, hello there young man,' she purred, white teeth gleaming. 'Why don't you sit here?'

'Or here, if you're scared,' commented Andrew Greenwood dryly. The openly homosexual director flashed a predatory grin no less frightening than Fenella's in Martin's direction.

Manda Prost and her husband Christian Lovegrove, London's hottest young actors, looked on in amusement from a red velvet chaise. Martin put his hand to his chin to check for dribble. The last time he had seen Manda Prost was when a sneak preview of her *Satyr* cover had been circulated round the advertising department at International Mags. Manda Prost with the bottom half of a fox was something to behold but there was no doubt, thought Martin, as he watched her cross her legs and let her chiffon skirt fall open to reveal a good furlong of thigh, she looked even better without a bushy red tail.

'You're familiar with Manda and Christian, I presume?' asked Petunia.

'Yes,' Martin croaked.

'Hi, Martin,' said Christian Lovegrove. 'Loved your book. It's a Catcher in the Rye for the twenty-first century.'

'Fabulous,' Manda agreed. 'We've warned Euphemie that if we don't get first refusal on the film rights, she'll be straight off our Christmas list.'

Martin could only look at her. It didn't seem appropriate to speak. With so many famous faces in the room, Martin felt as though he was a member of the audience at a very small performance, not a guest at the same dinner party.

'I'll be taking ten per cent too,' announced Cindy loudly. 'Since without me, none of you would have met this delicious man in the first place.'

'How did you meet?' asked Manda curiously.

Martin glanced nervously in the direction of Benjamin Daniels, whose expression was suddenly like a cloud over a Test match. Thankfully Petunia chose that moment to clap her hands together and announce, 'To the dining room, everybody! Dinner is served.'

As Petunia Daniels fussed around her guests, dishing up a gazpacho she had made from scratch that afternoon, Martin realised he was having one of those 'if they could see me now' moments. He was sitting between Manda Prost and Fenella Anderson, while Cindy sat opposite and gazed intently at him. Martin glanced down to either side of him. Fenella's long black skirt had a split to the thigh and as she sat down she revealed her left leg almost as far as her French knickers.

On Martin's right, Manda Prost was also showing a fair bit of leg. Even when it was fully wrapped around her, Manda's chiffon skirt left very little to Martin's overactive imagination. The outline of her G-string was clearly visible through the see-thru red material. Despite that, during the second course, Manda seemed to find even her flimsy outfit too hot and let her skirt fall apart so that she was showing even more thigh than Fenella.

Petunia was serving asparagus. Martin stared in dismay at the vegetables when his plate was placed before him. He remembered something about the correct way to eat asparagus being with one's fingers. But that didn't seem possible. The spears were dripping in butter.

'What's the matter?' Cindy asked, noticing he wasn't eating. 'Don't you like it?'

'Makes your pee stink,' commented Christian.

Martin looked about the table anxiously but none of the other guests seemed in any hurry to start eating and show him the form. Then Manda picked up one of the floppy green spears. She popped one end of it into her mouth then let it drag out over her soft red lips as she sucked off all the butter, giving Christian a particularly dirty wink as she did so.

Martin bit his lip. Manda had picked up her asparagus with her fingers, but it seemed that her method of eating was more about foreplay than manners. Besides which, Manda was a film star. She was allowed to get away with bad manners because she was so sexy.

Then Fenella did the same. She licked the butter off one of her asparagus spears like the kind of French madam every public schoolboy dreams of losing his virginity to. In fact, it looked a little comical. Martin wondered whether she was just trying to keep up with Manda. At least she didn't wink. Unlike Cindy, who, sensing that her first dibs on Martin might be endangered by the other ladies at the table, set about her vegetables as though she was auditioning for Deep Throat.

Fenella had placed her slender hand on his thigh. She rested it there quite naturally and continued to talk to Benjamin without missing a beat as she slowly inched her way up towards Martin's flies.

'Coffee, Fenella?' asked Petunia.

Fenella took her hand away from Martin's crotch to take an exquisite little espresso cup from her hostess. Meanwhile, Manda, whose left hand was suddenly free again now that she had finished her cigarette, brought it to rest on Martin's right knee. She too continued her intense conversation across the table as she slid her hand imperceptibly closer to Martin's family jewels.

'Don't you think so, Martin?' Christian asked suddenly.

'What?' Martin jumped back to attention.

'Marlowe is more passionate and intense than Shakespeare. His Edward the Second . . .'

'Red hot poker,' said Fenella. 'That'd give you a shock.'

Almost as big a shock as Fenella got when she went to put her hand back on Martin's crotch and found that Manda had beaten her to it. The two women's fingers almost entwined for a second before they both realised and withdrew quite abruptly. Thankfully, they were both such professional actresses that above the table, no one saw the merest flinch.

Meanwhile, Martin was growing hotter and hotter. The blush that had started when Fenella first touched his knee, had become the kind of beetroot flush his mother dreaded during her menopause. Martin took a gulp of water to cool himself down and dribbled rather inelegantly onto the tablecloth when Benjamin asked for his opinion on some TV actor's portrayal of Piers Gaveston.

'Didn't see it,' Martin managed to splutter.

'Shame,' said Benjamin. 'Quite incredibly erotic.'

As was the sensation that Martin found himself experiencing now. He dare not look down to see who was massaging his balls this time. Instead, he pulled the tablecloth so that it covered his lap and tried to concentrate on the conversation going on around him. Across the table, Cindy had slid lower in her seat. Her Dangerous Diana gaze had been replaced by an impossibly naughty smile. When Martin looked at her she licked her lips and said 'Do me too.' At which point Martin realised that the 'hand' massaging him so expertly was in fact Cindy's naked foot. She had kicked off

her hippy thongs and was playing with him with her pink
painted toes.

'Shall we retire to the other room, ladies and gentlemen?' asked Petunia.

Everyone agreed it was a great idea. Cindy let her foot
slip from Martin's lap and got up to follow her mother.
Martin, however, couldn't stand up.

'Something the matter?' asked Benjamin when he
noticed that Martin wasn't following.

'Just savouring my coffee,' said Martin helplessly.

'Bring it with you,' said Benjamin.

Martin limped into the room where the evening had
started. And of course, the only place left to sit by the
time he arrived was a gap on the big squishy sofa between
Manda and Fenella. As Martin approached, holding his
jacket awkwardly over his groin, the two women smiled
like a couple of cats that have just figured out how to
undo the latch on the birdcage. Meanwhile, Cindy
watched from the chaise like the pampered Abyssinian
that would be waiting in the garden if poor birdy
managed to get out past these Siamese twins.

'Let me take that jacket,' said Petunia.

Martin gave an anguished squeak as Petunia snatched
at his one good jacket. The three witches shared a
knowing look.

'Wife-swapping!' Andrew Greenwood exclaimed suddenly.

'At it all the time round these parts,' elaborated
Christian.

'Martin, come with me,' Cindy said suddenly, rising
from her languid pose on the chaise to lead him out into
the hallway. 'You can help carry the card table.'

'What are we playing?' asked Fenella.

'Strip poker!' Manda suggested.

'Yes, please,' said Andrew.

Outside in the hall, Martin was starting to sweat. 'Is that the time?' he asked without even looking at his watch. 'I should go. The tube stops at half eleven.'

'Get a taxi,' said Cindy. 'Or stay. There's plenty of space in my room.'

'I . . . I . . .'

'I promise there won't be a re-run of last time,' she said, as if that were the only thing on his mind. There was also the question of his not having been to the gym for a month. Let's face it, he'd only ever really been regularly for a fortnight when he was nineteen. Then there was his underwear. He knew that his suit looked OK, but underneath! He'd been meaning to buy some new pants for months but of course, he hadn't bothered. In fact, he'd almost bought into that girly superstition that says that if you wear your worst possible underwear, members of the opposite sex will be only too keen to help you take your clothes off. It was Murphy's Law of dating, up there with not shaving your legs before a first date (for the girls, that is).

'Come on,' said Cindy, pressing him up against the velvet embossed wallpaper (not Indian restaurant embossed, you understand). 'You look fantastic tonight.'

'Cindy, could you do that in your bedroom?' Petunia tutted as she walked through the hallway with a plate full of petits fours. 'Do that?' She made it sound as though Cindy were a five-year-old setting up a gymkhana for her dolls on the hallway floor.

'God, I fancy you!' Cindy exclaimed.

With that, Cindy went for the kill. She pressed her mouth against Martin's and forced his lips open with her tongue. After the initial shock, which reminded Martin of first trying to breathe using a mouthpiece when learning to scuba dive, there was nothing he could do but relax into it.

Except that every time he closed his eyes, he thought he could see Ruby.

'Forget her,' he told himself. It could never have worked with Ruby.

Cindy was mad as cheese, that was certain. But at least he would never be bored.

36

The last thing Ruby wanted to do was revisit the most recent part of her love life. She didn't care if she never saw Emlyn Cruickshank again. In fact, she didn't want to go into the office at all. She toyed with the idea of pulling a sickie on the Monday morning after the party. But that would be much too obvious. Instead, she limped in late, the back way, punishing herself by using the stairs instead of the lift to her seventh-floor office so that she could make it to her cubicle without passing any of her colleagues en route.

What a terrible weekend she'd had. If she had felt bad on Saturday morning, then Sunday proved to be even worse. She'd gone round to Lou's flat first thing to commiserate with her about her heavily bandaged ankle and to tell her everything that had happened since Robert became the latest man to blow her fantasy world to pieces in that bar. Martin had beaten her to it. His bicycle was leaning against the front wall. Lou was resting on the sofa, so Martin got up to answer the door when Ruby knocked. He looked at her as though she were there to sell him dishcloths.

'Martin,' she said pleadingly as she followed him down the hallway. 'I'm sorry about yesterday.'

'Doesn't matter,' said Martin shortly. 'I've forgotten about it already.' He didn't even bother to sit down with the girls again, just picked up his jacket and said that he had better be on his way to lunch.

'You are not going to guess who he's having lunch with!' said Lou excitedly as soon as they heard the door shut. 'You remember that girl I set him up with on the blind date? Only turns out she's Petunia Daniels' daughter! Martin went for dinner at her house last night. He claims that Manda Prost tried to feel him up under the table.'

Lou paraphrased Martin's story from the moment he left Suave with the dread-locked Daniels' daughter, through the extraordinary events in her bathroom to the letter from the literary agency dropping onto his doormat. 'Can you believe the bugger didn't tell us who Cindy really was because he thought we would go to the newspapers and do a kiss and tell and he would end up with a lawsuit?'

Ruby shook her head. Though thinking back to Saturday morning's flare-up in her kitchen, it was clear that there was a lot she didn't know about Martin.

'And he didn't say anything else about Saturday morning?' Ruby asked Lou suddenly.

'Like what?' said Lou.

'Nothing.'

When Martin reacted so badly to Emlyn's presence in her flat, Ruby had allowed herself a little fantasy that he might in fact be jealous. That clearly wasn't the case. Why would he want to be with her when he could have Manda Prost feeling him up under the dinner table? When he had a lunch date with Cindy Daniels? Martin could only feel sorry for Ruby. He mixed with the glitterati and now his novel – the one he hadn't even told her anything about – was set to make him famous too.

'So, are you going to tell me what happened at the party?' asked Lou, voice full of concern.

'Sorry,' Ruby was a million miles away. Not with Flett. Not with Robert. Not with Emlyn. 'To be honest, I can't quite remember.'

Unluckily for Ruby, there were plenty of people queuing up to tell her exactly what had happened after she took to the dance floor on the good ship *Primrose*. The last thing she could recall was lurching towards Flett and Imogen, losing her balance, the sound of something ripping . . .

'Not Imogen's dress?' Ruby asked Liz, peeping out through her fingers as though that might save her from the horror.

'Mine,' said Liz flatly. 'I tried to get between you. I thought you were going to punch her.'

'And then?'

'Emlyn carried you outside. And you vomited all over his jacket. I suppose that's why you felt obliged to take him home with you.'

'Does everybody know?' Ruby asked.

'Everybody,' Liz confirmed.

Katherine, Ruby's assistant with the long-time crush on the Panter, was barely speaking to her.

When she fired up her computer, Ruby's e-mail box was already full to bursting. Emlyn had sent several, entitled with such discreet headlines as 'About last night' and 'You were great.' Ruby deleted them straight away. But all morning he kept sending more.

Ping! Another e-mail.

From: Emlyn.Cruickshank@Hollingworthpr.co.uk
To: Ruby.Taylor@Hollingworthpr.co.uk

Re: Are you ignoring me?

Well, are you?

Ruby sighed. It was the twelfth e-mail he had sent since nine that morning. Was she ignoring him? *Why* was she ignoring him?

Ruby peered over the top of her PC in the direction of Emlyn's glass-fronted office. He was standing up at his desk as he took a phone call. Ruby hadn't really looked at Emlyn in a long while. Perhaps he didn't look so bad, after all. He was tall. He had all his hair. He had a nice enough smile. Good straight teeth. Perhaps he did have an unusually low hairline, one that in crueller moments she had described as 'Neanderthal', but at least that gave him a good position to start receding from. By the time he was fifty he might almost look OK.

'Let's do lunch,' his next e-mail begged.

'I'll meet you at Pret A Manger,' Ruby replied. 'You leave the office at 12.30 and I'll leave ten minutes later.'

It was a bit late for that kind of damage limitation, but it made Ruby feel better. Sod Flett. Sod Robert. Sod Martin. She was going to have a fling with Emlyn Cruickshank. And at 12.40 she was almost excited as she left the office and sneaked down to the sandwich bar. Perhaps this had been inevitable all along. Perhaps she and Emlyn were *meant* for each other. Until the athlete's foot revelation, she had definitely considered him fanciable. Now, she was smiling almost nervously as he joined her by the BLTs.

'How do you feel this morning?' he asked.

'Fine,' she said. 'Even a hangover that big couldn't last forever.'

'I'm sorry I left so abruptly on Saturday. That bloke who came round . . . Was he . . . ?'

'No,' said Ruby decisively. 'He was just a friend.'

Was, being the operative word, she thought.

'So,' said Emlyn.

'So,' said Ruby.

'So, I think we can safely say that we took Friday night's team-bonding exercise to its ultimate conclusion.' Emlyn laughed at his own joke. 'You really were great,' he said, suddenly quite serious.

'Was I?' Ruby blushed and fiddled nervously with a lock of her hair. 'Well, thank you. I thought I made rather a fool of myself on the boat.'

'Er . . .' Emlyn couldn't deny it. 'I meant after that.'

'Of course . . .'

'Though when you lurched onto the dance floor, I think everybody was hoping you'd give John Flett what for.'

'Really?'

'The guy's an arsehole, Ruby,' Emlyn told her. 'Trust me, everyone was rooting for you. Even Imogen.'

'Imogen. But she . . .'

'Finished their relationship later that night. It was the first time she'd seen him dance and she decided that she couldn't bear to sleep with a man who danced like her granddad.'

'You're joking.'

'That's what she said to Alice this morning. It was the way he danced combined with that pink polo shirt that he's always wearing. She said it was like going out with Nick Faldo's dad.'

'The pink polo shirt! Yes!' Ruby was unable to hide her glee.

'Added to that,' Emlyn began, before sucking in his bottom lip as though the condition might be catching, 'she couldn't stand that weird thing he does with his tongue.'

'What thing?'

'This thing.' Emlyn tried to touch his nose with his own tongue. 'Every time he gets agitated or thinks he's made a good point.'

'Yes!' Ruby balled her fist. 'There is a God. Excuse me,' she added, in response to Emlyn's rather worried look.

'So,' Emlyn paused. 'I was wondering . . .'

'Yeeeeessss?'

'Look, Ruby, I understand that Friday was an emotional night for you and perhaps I shouldn't have come home with you when you were obviously in such a vulnerable state and you might think perhaps . . .' He hesitated. 'Look, you can say no if you want to and I promise I won't hold it against you, but I've been wondering whether you might like to . . .' He cleared his throat. 'Do it again some time?'

Ruby paused just long enough for him to panic.

'Not just have sex, I mean,' he added hurriedly. 'But go out somewhere. Properly. The two of us. On a date. We could go to the cinema. I'd like to see *L'Appartement*. Have you ever seen that film? It's on at the Riverside

Studios. It's subtitled. It's French, you see. But if you don't like subtitles we can see something else . . .'

'Yes,' said Ruby.

'Is that yes, you don't like subtitles?'

'No, it's yes I'd like to go on a date with you. As long as you're not asking because you feel that you have to. If you're just asking because you feel that you ought to in case I'm upset by the idea of a one night stand then . . .'

Emlyn grinned at her.

'Ruby,' he said sincerely. 'I have wanted to go on a date with you since I first started working at Hollingworth PR.'

'Do you really mean that?' she asked.

'Don't you remember my bungled attempts to chat you up over a sandwich before?'

Ruby nodded. She wondered whether she should tell him now the real reason she had managed to resist him.

'I was very jealous when I heard that you'd started seeing Flett. And worried too,' he added. 'I'd heard he was a ladies' man and I didn't want to see you get hurt. When he ended it I almost whooped with joy across the office but decided you probably wouldn't appreciate that. I was going to bide my time until I thought you were starting to get over him, then I was going to invite you over to my place for dinner and see whether anything happened. But by the time I was ready to ask you out, you'd already started seeing that Robert guy.'

'Well, that turned out to be pretty short-lived,' said Ruby with a sniff.

'Can I ask what happened?'

'Buy me dinner and I'll think about it.'

'So,' Emlyn grinned. 'When do we have our first date?'

'What about tonight?' said Ruby.

'I normally play five-a-side football on a Monday night,' Emlyn began, 'but they won't miss me this week. *L'Appartement* isn't on this evening though. So we'll have to see something else. Or go bowling? What about that? Have you ever done it?'

'Bowling?' said Ruby. 'No. I haven't.'

'Then let's go bowling tonight. You'll love it. Great fun. And I'm pretty good if I do say so myself.' He looked at his watch. 'Better get back to the office, I suppose. You ready?'

'I think so. Perhaps we'd better go back separately. We don't want everybody to be talking about us.'

'It's a bit late for that,' said Emlyn. 'I collected thirty quid on Imogen's book this morning.'

'You what!?'

'I'm joking. Damn,' Emlyn muttered.

'What?'

'I forgot to go to the chemist. I don't suppose you could go there for me on your way back to the office, seeing as you've got ten minutes left and I haven't.'

'Of course,' said Ruby. 'What is it you need?'

Emlyn cast his eyes down towards the table shyly. Ruby waited for him to say 'condoms'.

'I think I know,' she said, impressed at her own maturity. 'Featherlite suit you?'

'Eh?' Emlyn looked at her uncomprehendingly.

'Durex. Featherlite?'

'Oh, no. I mean, yes. If you want to. But what I really need you to pick up is this.'

He handed her a scrap of paper onto which he had scribbled the name of a fungicidal cream. 'For my athlete's foot. Large size if they've got it.'

He kissed her wetly on the mouth and was gone, leaving Ruby to push away the remains of her avocado and pine-nut wrap in horror.

She held the piece of paper as though she might contract the infection from that. Athlete's foot. He'd had it – unless he'd spent long periods in remission since their initial conversation on the subject – for the best part of three whole years. Ruby's memory scrolled backwards to Friday night. Was Martin right? Had he kept his socks on in bed? Oh, no. Suddenly, Ruby had a very clear image of Emlyn Cruickshank wearing her dressing gown and a pair of greying tennis socks. She scrolled forward to that evening's date. Bowling! A date that would require her to wear communal shoes. Communal shoes that might only moments before have been on the sweaty feet of the person with the second worst case of athlete's foot in London.

The fatal flaw! Ruby took a sip of her tea and retched. She couldn't share shoes with anybody. And she definitely couldn't sleep with someone who might want to take his athlete's feet into her bathroom afterwards. How on earth was she going to get herself out of this one? Feign death?

'Ruby just called in,' said Liz Hale to the Panter moments later. 'She said that she was taken ill with terrible stomach cramps while having lunch. Didn't see much point in coming back into the office. She's gone straight home. Said you'd understand.'

Across town, Lou was also doing a sickie. Hers was legitimate however. While Ruby went home to read

Hello and navel-gaze, Lou found herself in another waiting room. This time to see her GP, who would be supervising the recovery of her ankle from now on.

Andrew had been a star, of course. He actually carried Lou, all nine and a half stone of her, up three flights of stairs when they finally got back from the accident unit. The next day he had done her shopping, filling the trolley with extravagant goodies to cheer up an invalid as well as all the boring stuff she'd asked for. He told her he was available every night to sit at her bandaged foot and peel grapes.

And because of all this, Lou tried harder than ever before to fit him into the vision she had for her future. Because of this, Lou hadn't even looked at the Once Seen column in the back of the issue of *Time Out* he'd bought for her on the day of the accident, but left the magazine pristine and unread for the next unhappy visitor to A & E. The fantasy was over. It had to be. No more scanning the tube carriages for her stranger. No more surfing the net for another one. Lou had to work with what had been given to her in the real world.

Lou was surprised to find that she was momentarily relieved by her decision. But hours later the relief was all but gone. She wanted to be single again and she didn't know how she was going to manage it. How ironic that Andrew had come into her life as the result of a joke when getting rid of him was proving to be such a serious matter?

Lou didn't like to disappoint people; that was the problem. When she looked back over the relationships she had had in the past and examined them more closely, she saw that she was almost as bad as Ruby when it came to picking the wrong partners and failing to deal with the situation effectively. Sure, Lou had finished a relationship before, but never in a particularly adult way. She had never found the courage to say, quite simply, 'This isn't working out.' Instead, she had to come out with the 'It's not you, it's me,' line.

When ending her relationship with Mad Magnus, the psycho she had momentarily mistaken for a creative type, Lou had gone to the ridiculous length of convincing him that it was she who was mentally unstable, so that he wouldn't feel so bad to have lost her. Magnus, who saw angels at the bus stop and claimed he could see people's animal familiars if he stared into their eyes for long enough, still occasionally rang and suggested that Lou might like to see his therapist.

Lou reasoned that it was easier for her ex-boyfriends to hear, 'I think I want to become a nun,' than 'I simply just don't fancy you.' But the problem was that still left room for hope. After all, what man can resist trying to steal a twenty-something woman from Jesus? Or convincing a girl who claims to be unsure of her sexuality that she really does want a man?

Lou's break-up methodology so far had been the relationship equivalent of trying to rescue a fly with a broken wing from a spider's web. There was no point. It was cruel to be *that* kind.

That afternoon at the doctor's surgery, appointments were running almost forty minutes late. Lou shuffled in the uncomfortable plastic seat she had chosen because it was the furthest away from the man with the frightening cough. She had read every dog-eared issue of *Woman's*

Own on the table. She didn't feel like reading the manuscript she had been carrying around in her bag for most of the week. (A good sign that she probably shouldn't suggest that Piper's publish it.)

'Mr Edwards to Dr Rushdie's surgery,' announced the intercom.

The young man who had been sitting next to Lou got up to go to his appointment and dropped an issue of *Time Out* onto the pile of magazines as he passed.

Lou hesitated for all of thirty seconds before she snatched the magazine up. It was an old issue. Almost a month old. The issue that came straight after the one in which she and Ruby had placed their fateful Once Seens. Lou felt her heart start to quicken as she flicked through the well-read, tattered pages.

Next morning at the office, Lou opened her desk diary and drew a big red star on the page for a Friday three weeks ahead. She would be single by the end of the month.

37

Erica had quickly resigned herself to the single life again after discovering Ratbag Robert's voracious appetite for the lonely-hearted. A month after that humiliating night in the bar, she really was able to laugh about it.

'I suppose he must need a lot of practice to be that good in bed,' she conceded with a sigh. 'And at least I know *I'm* still in working order now. As does the woman in the flat downstairs. She knocked on the ceiling to complain about the noise of my vibrator.'

'Bloody hell,' said Lou.

'Yeah, when I met her in the hallway, I told her it must have been the washing machine vibrating against the fridge.'

'Too much information!' Lou laughed.

'Can you read this?' Erica let a manuscript plop onto Lou's untidy desk. 'Euphemie Gilbert sent it round last night. It's brilliant. I read it in one sitting. She's trying to set up an auction and wants an opinion on it by Friday.'

'What's it about?' Lou asked.

'It's like *Four Weddings and a Funeral* without the sad bits. It's romantic comedy from the man's point of view. I laughed so hard at one point that I almost choked to death on a Hob Nob I was eating at the time.'

'That's good,' Lou agreed.

'It's extremely feel-good. I promise you'll believe there

are still good men out there when you've finished reading this. Shame it's only fiction,' added Erica.

'Who wrote it?'

'He's called Matthew Carter. And apparently he's young and gorgeous and single. Well, dating some It girl,' Erica sighed, 'but he hasn't been with her long.'

'You're not falling in love with him because of what he's written here, are you?' Lou knew only too well that the authors who wrote the sweetest things often turned out to be the biggest pains.

'I hope we get it,' Erica concluded.

She left Lou flicking through the pages for good bits.

Ruthie smiled a little sadly but it was a start. A smile. One day, Mark thought, I'm going to tell her how difficult it's been for me to watch her get so hammered by love . . . One day I'll tell her how I've wanted to punch the lights out of just about every man she's fallen for. I wish she would believe me when I tell her I know what's good for her. She's always chasing after some arsehole when everything she needs is here at home . . .

Nothing funny about that. But it was sort of sweet and raw. Lou sighed. She wrapped two big elastic bands around the manuscript to keep it in one piece and put it in her bag for later.

Brriiiinnnnggg. Her telephone jolted her out of her reverie.

'Lou Capshaw.'

'Lou, it's Andrew. What are you doing tonight? I know it's a Wednesday and you usually do that pub quiz thing but . . .'

'I'm not doing anything,' Lou said. The pub quiz gang was no more now. Ruby and Martin both claimed that they didn't have a problem with the other but still seemed hell-bent on avoiding the old threesome. Ruby claimed she had to work extra hard to make up for her summer party débâcle. Martin was always claiming that he had to be elsewhere too. Cindy Daniels knew an awful lot of people who threw an awful lot of parties.

'I'm going to come over and cook for you,' Andrew announced. 'All you have to do is make sure I can get to the sink through those piles of washing-up you never get round to doing.'

'Andrew,' Lou started to protest.

'No buts,' said Andrew. 'I want to give you a really special night.'

When he put the phone down, Lou opened her diary and pencilled him in for that evening. She flicked through the next couple of days. Thursday morning, physio. Monthly sales meeting that Thursday afternoon. Friday. Big red star.

'Doing anything special this evening?' Liz asked Ruby.

'Nope.' Ruby smiled ruefully. In the corridor right outside her office, Emlyn was helping the new temp to un-jam the photocopier. He'd soon got over losing out on the woman he'd apparently waited so long for, Ruby tutted.

At least she no longer had to put up with the knowledge that someone else in the office was sleeping with Flett. Emlyn was right. Imogen had indeed called an end to the relationship. In fact, she had asked that all Barrington Ball-bearing meetings be taken outside the office from now on so that she didn't have to bump into him.

Imogen was secretly dating Evan Flanders, the unfeasibly rich and handsome chairman of Two-Faced. It was supposed to be very hush hush, since he was still in the process of divorcing his childhood sweetheart wife; but a picture of the new happy couple had appeared in the tabloids that week.

'I don't know how they found out that we were going to be at The Ivy,' Imogen moaned to her friend on the features desk at the *Daily Mail*.

Flett had started e-mailing Ruby with a vengeance after the Hollingworth summer party and his dumping. He begged her to come out to dinner and talk about the Barrington campaign. Lou warned Ruby to stick to lunch within spitting distance of the office.

'Do you think he wants me back?' Ruby asked.

'Of course he wants you back. Imogen has dumped him.'

Ruby allowed herself a tiny smile at the thought but was surprised at how little comfort the idea gave her. Her stomach didn't seem to want to do that somersault thing it always used to do when she heard Flett's name any more. The gaping hole she thought he had left clearly wasn't quite as big as she thought. As for Robert, he had merely been a filthy port in a terrible storm. Her night with Emlyn was an aberration. Even remembering that Sunday afternoon in Denver didn't hurt so much now. Not since the letter arrived.

When Ruby saw the envelope postmarked Colorado on her doormat, she felt her stomach rise towards her throat expectantly. What would be inside this time? Another tract about the evil of mankind like the one Nathaniel had pressed into her hand as he escorted her from his premises? She almost tore the damn thing up without even bothering to read it.

Dear Ruby, the letter began. This time it wasn't in Rosalia's neat hand.

Since you left my house a month ago, I've been giving a great deal of thought to the news that you brought to me. I fear I have been an irrational man and that I sent you away with hatred ringing in your ears when I should have welcomed you to the family like the long-lost sister you are.

Because your mother is my mother, Ruby. I can remember the day you were born. We were living near Portsmouth at the time, but Mum and I moved back to Greenwich, where Mum lived before she was married, to stay with her sister during the last months of the pregnancy. It was so she could have you without anyone in our hometown knowing what had been going on.

As you know, my father died when I was just five years old. Three years later, our mother met another man, who promised that he would marry her. But I was the problem. He didn't want to inherit another man's son. He met another woman, with no children and no baggage and quickly married her instead. Shortly afterwards, our mother discovered that she was pregnant with his child. She tried to tell him but he didn't want to know.

Things were tough then. We had no money. I was old enough to go to school while our mother went out to work but if she'd kept you, she would have lost her job. She'd already lost her husband – the man she loved. She was suffering the loss of her lover too. She didn't think she could manage the pair of us alone and made the decision to give you up for adoption so that someone better prepared to look after you might.

But our mother was a courageous and loving woman. I know that she loved you and, had circumstances been different, I have no doubt that you and I would have grown up together all our lives. She did what she thought was best for both of us, Ruby. The sense of shame I picked up around the time of your birth was not to do with our mother's morality, or lack of it, but the ignorance of people who never read the parable about casting the first stone.

And I forgot that too when you came to my house all those weeks ago. I blamed you for our mother's unhappiness. I saw her go into a decline during her pregnancy and after she left you at the hospital. The only way she could escape the memories was to emigrate to America, forcing me to leave behind the only life that I had known. I hated you for that. I blamed you because I had to leave my school, my friends, even my country. But you were just a baby. The hypocrisy of British society in the 1970s was what made our mother so ill with unhappiness she couldn't bear to stay there, not you.

So, that's the true story. I hope that you will be able to forgive me for denying what I knew and treating you so badly that Sunday afternoon. Our mother never had a second chance to meet you though I know she spent her whole life wishing that she could. I can only pray that you will give me a second chance instead. Rosalia has almost finished the family tree now. There is a place for you. We hope to hear from you as soon as you get this letter.

With love,
Your brother, Nat

Sitting at the kitchen table with the letter in front of her, Ruby felt like a shipwrecked sailor washed up on shore at last, pummelled by alternate waves of relief and unfathomable sadness. She read the letter again and folded it away before she blurred all the words with her tears. She'd call Nat Barker as soon as it was a decent hour in Denver. And at some point, she knew, she would have to call her parents and Lindsay and Steve and tell them what had been going on these past few months. Right then, however, she held the telephone in her hand with her thumb poised over the button pre-programmed with someone else's home number. Martin's.

Martin was the only person who knew the full story so far and she wanted to tell him what Nathaniel had written. But she couldn't. She hadn't spoken to Martin in almost a month. Lou said she had hardly heard from him either. He'd moved on from their friendship. He didn't seem to need them any more. No more pub quiz for Martin. Where was he that evening? On a date with Cindy Daniels and her celebrity-offspring friends?

At three o'clock in the afternoon, Cindy Daniels was still snoring on her back. She had a thesis to write before the end of the month and spent those waking hours when she wasn't snorting coke, fretting that she would never get the work done. Actually sitting down and getting the work done didn't seem to have crossed her mind.

Martin was fretting too. It was only three days since Euphemie Gilbert had sent his manuscript out to four of London's top publishing houses. She had warned him not to expect an immediate response but every time the phone rang, Martin felt sure he was going to lose his guts all over the carpet with excitement. Every caller got short shrift, even his mother – though he did tell her that he had to hurry her off the line, leaving it free for Euphemie Gilbert's call.

In theory, he had someone to keep him company during the interminable wait, but Cindy's wasn't the company he wanted. He would have liked to have passed it with Lou and Ruby. If the news was good, then he supposed that Cindy would be an adequate person to drink champagne with. But if the news was bad . . .

Sex with Cindy Daniels had turned out to be everything Martin expected and quite a few things he never would have imagined. But when they weren't in bed together they were on different planets. Sure, Cindy took him to lots of A-list parties, but Martin soon discovered that a night at the hottest club in London could be more tedious than a night at the Hare and Hounds when every tabloid-familiar face concealed a stranger. It was also getting just a little wearing that nine out of ten people Cindy introduced him to were ex-lovers – men and women. And it was clear that Cindy subscribed to a 'never say never' approach where these exes were concerned. Her mobile phone was constantly vibrating with text messages requesting her attention. Martin knew it was only a matter of time before Cindy added another new love interest to the numbers on her SIM card.

The telephone rang. Martin dived from the bed to grab the handset, accidentally kicking Cindy in the back as he did so.

'Martin!' Euphemie purred. 'Piper Publishing are interested! The editor's someone called Lou Capshaw. I think you'll like her. She's a very nice girl.'

It had taken Lou minutes to guess the genesis of the work. Mark and Ruthie. The only things Martin had changed in the story were the names of the characters and his own. Matthew Carter was a pen-name. But thankfully, Erica had been right. Lou loved the story. And not just because she knew the lovelorn pair involved.

Since Erica's workload for that autumn was already almost too much for her, the girls decided that they would recommend that Piper made an offer on the book immediately, with Lou as potential editor, and call Martin in for a meeting. Lou was looking forward to seeing Martin in her offices and to finally admitting face to face that she was quietly impressed by his talent. But first there was another altogether more important meeting to arrange.

38

With half an hour to go before the big date, Ruby paused midway through putting on her make-up and stared at her reflection.

'You look a mess,' she told herself. The effect wasn't helped by the fact that she had only properly made-up one eye and, even as she berated herself for not quite making the standard, she blinked so that a neat little semicircle of wet mascara spots appeared on the top of her cheek.

'Arse.'

She started to rub the dots away with a cotton bud but only succeeded in turning a neat row of specks into a big dirty smudge that looked like a black eye. A battle scar. The conversations in the pub during which Lou, she and Martin had reassured each other that they didn't look a day older than when they first met seemed ridiculous now. Ruby looked her age, she told herself, suddenly more dissatisfied than she had ever been with her skin and her hair and her stupid, ill-fitting clothes. When she walked down the street these days she was invisible to a whole generation of people. She felt much closer in attitude to the students who crowded around her favourite bookshop than to their tutors. But the students didn't even see her. To them, she was a grown-up. Perhaps it was time to act accordingly.

Abandoning her make-up, Ruby lay down on her bed.

The phone rang.

It was Lou.

'Ruby! What are you doing, picking up the phone?'

'I'm sitting on my bed.'

'You'll never get there in time. You're supposed to be in Battersea. In that bar.'

'What's the point?' Ruby asked.

'What? What do you mean, what's the point?'

'Lou, I'm not going on this blind date,' she said firmly. 'I've decided that I've got to get off this sodding dating roundabout and sort my stupid life out.'

'Really? Sort your life out?' Lou echoed. 'That's great, Rubes. And I'm glad to hear it. Really, I am. But you haven't got time to do it tonight. Are you dressed yet?'

'Of course I'm dressed.'

'What are you wearing?'

'Jeans. Black T-shirt.'

'For goodness' sake. That's not a date outfit. Put something sexy on, quick. Put on that black dress you like. The one with the boat neck.'

'Lou. Are you receiving me?' Ruby asked. 'I'm not going on this date.'

'Yes, you bloody are.'

'You can't make me.'

'Wanna bet?'

'Lou, just forget it. I know you think you're acting in my best interests and I'm grateful for what you're trying to do for me but . . .'

Briiiiiiinnnnng.

'Oh, dear,' said Ruby with relief. 'There's the doorbell. Gotta go. Speak to you later.'

Ruby put the phone down. Saved by the bell. For once she'd be glad to see Jehovah's Witnesses. All she had to do once she got rid of the God-botherers was to pull the phone lead out of its socket and ignore Lou's calls and . . .

'Ruby, look at the state of you!'

Lou stood on the doorstep. She bustled past into the flat as fast as her almost recovered ankle would allow her.

'I knew you would do this to me. I knew it. I've gone to all the trouble of finding you a perfect date and you're still sitting at home in your jeans with fifteen minutes to go before you're meant to be on the other side of London. Put that black dress on. I'm calling a cab.'

'Lou, I . . .' Ruby tried to stand her ground.

'Just do it. Just this once. Trust me, Ruby. I have found you the man of your dreams. You have so much in common with this guy. He's gorgeous, sexy, good-looking . . .'

'How do you know he's good-looking?'

'He scanned in a picture when he last sent an e-mail.'

'Can I see it?' Ruby asked sensibly.

'Forgot to bring it,' Lou replied. 'Look, stick the dress on. Do your make-up. It won't matter if you're a little bit late. I've done such a good PR job on you he'll probably sit there and wait for you all night.'

Ruby stood firm in the hallway, making no move to get changed.

'Lou, I'm serious. I'm changing my life. And the first fundamental change I have to make is to my attitude to men. I'm not chasing after love any more. My desperation has brought me nothing but trouble and heartache. I'm going to learn to live without love and then it won't matter so much if I don't ever find it. I've got to learn to be a whole person within myself. I don't need a prop.'

'Oh, for crying out loud. Why do you have to see the bloody light now!?' Lou clutched her head. 'Don't do this to me Ruby. Not tonight. Give me one more chance. Put the dress on.'

They were in Ruby's bedroom now and Lou was rummaging through the wardrobe.

'Will you get out of there? I didn't ask you to place another ad for me. And after the Robin and Robert fiascos, I would have thought you might have known better. I'm not putting myself through it again.' She shook her head. 'I'm staying in.'

'I can't let you do that.'

Lou grabbed the bottom of Ruby's T-shirt and started to yank it off over her head.

'Lou!'

'You don't know what's good for you!'

'I finally do know! That's the point. Get off my T-shirt.'

Ruby yanked the T-shirt back down.

'One more for me, Rubes. I went to all the trouble of placing another ad. It took me weeks to think of the right wording and I was so careful when I sifted through the replies . . .'

'Well, thanks very much, but that's not exactly my fault,' Ruby reasoned. 'You're not going to guilt me into this. I'm living for me, Lou.'

'Someone else could be living for you, too. Just this

416

once. Never again.' Lou fell to her knees. 'Please, Ruby. Please. Ow!'

'Watch your ankle. God almighty,' said Ruby as she helped her friend straighten back up. 'Anyone would think this blind date was George Clooney.'

'Better. I promise you. Your blind date is perfect. I hear Clooney's a bit of an arse.'

Ruby shook her head. 'It's still too late. You've ambushed me on the way back from Damascus. I've seen the truth about myself at last.'

'You're seeing life through your blue-tinted spectacles,' Lou replied. 'Oh Ruby, I know these last few months have been a disaster. You've met some awful men, you had all that trouble with your natural family and you've fallen out with Martin. But that doesn't mean you've got to become a nun. You're thirty-one for heaven's sake. Your boobs still defy gravity and you're not ready for a cat. The most unattractive trait a person can have is a lack of hope, girl. There's nothing to live for but love, Rubes. You were the one who used to say that.'

'Lou.' Ruby sighed. 'Will you cut the Dawson's Creek philosophy? Did you talk to him?'

'I did.'

'What's his voice like?'

'Plums in honey!' Lou was delighted. Ruby was softening like butter in the sun. 'I'll call you that cab. Put your dress on.'

'Do you think I should wear the black?'

'You'll look a million dollars . . .' Lou was frantically dialling for a car before Ruby had a chance to change her mind. 'Hello? Yes. Can I have a taxi from 17 Blandfield Avenue . . . top flat.'

'I can't believe I'm doing this,' said Ruby as she disappeared into the bedroom.

'Ten minutes. She'll be ready.' Lou hung up on the cab firm. She hugged Ruby tightly once she was safely in that little black dress. Then she held her at arm's length to get a better look. 'Not bad,' she said encouragingly. 'Girl, you are da bomb.'

'Well, if this date bombs, you're ancient history, Lou Capshaw.'

'It won't bomb.'

'Will you come in and wait with me?' Ruby asked.

'Are you kidding? I don't want to cramp your style.'

The excitement that Lou had whipped up on the cab ride to Battersea quickly evaporated to be replaced by cold, clammy fear when Ruby walked into the bar on her own. It was almost empty. Suddenly, the copy of *Captain Corelli's Mandolin* that Ruby had tucked under her arm for identification purposes seemed to scream blind date. *This girl is waiting for a blind date.* Which was ridiculous, Ruby tried to tell herself. Plenty of people carried books with them in London. You really never knew when you might get stuck on the tube and want something to take your mind off the wait.

But there was no one else with a book in that bar. In fact, no other patron was sitting alone. The other customers divided neatly into three couples and one group of five girls who had clearly come straight from the office to celebrate somebody's birthday by getting right out of their heads.

'What can I get you?' the bartender asked cheerily.

'Er, I don't know if I'm actually staying yet,' said Ruby

pathetically. 'You haven't, er, seen a man with a book have you?'

The bartender cocked his head to one side.

'What does he look like?'

'Like this,' said Ruby, holding up her copy of the book. 'Blue and white cover. Exactly the same as this, in fact.'

'I meant the man,' smiled the bartender. 'What does he look like?'

'Oh, I . . .' Ruby blushed. 'I don't . . . Average looking, I suppose.'

The bartender nodded wisely, convincing Ruby that he was onto her too.

'Perhaps he's late,' he suggested.

'Yes. You might be right. I suppose I'll have a . . . an orange juice.'

Ruby perched nervously on a stool up at the bar. The bartender placed her glass in front of her and swapped her five-pound note for two fifty-pence pieces.

'Four pounds?' said Ruby incredulously.

'Freshly squeezed,' said the bartender.

Ruby certainly felt as though she had been juiced.

She looked at her watch. According to Lou, the date had been set for seven-thirty. It was almost ten to eight. The door of the bar swung open, momentarily admitting the noise of the traffic outside as two laughing girls stepped in from the street. One of them merely raised her eyebrows in the direction of the bartender to send him scurrying to get her usual. He turned up the sound system en route between vodka bottle and cranberry juice. The two new girls leaned against the bar next to Ruby and engaged the bartender in conversation about 'the other night'. The bartender's eyes flashed at the cranberry juice girl and he performed a nifty manoeuvre with his shaker to impress her. Feeling suddenly invisible again, Ruby picked up her glass and moved to a table by the wall.

Ten minutes later, Ruby had looked at her watch fifty times. Eight o'clock. How long should she give him? She'd given him too long already, hadn't she? She'd been stood up. She'd spent a tenner on a taxi ride, four quid on an orange juice, got something unidentifiable but sticky on the skirt of her favourite black dress and what for? She'd been stood up.

'Lou,' she jabbed an SMS message into her mobile. 'I've been stood up. U R so dead.'

'Just hang on,' Lou sent a message back. 'He's tall, dark, handsome and hung like a donkey. So he says.'

At which point someone who fitted that description (well, the first three parts at least) wandered into the bar and looked about him as though he were searching for someone who would be recognisable only from the novel she carried tucked beneath her arm.

Ruby felt her cheeks colour pink at once. He was lovely. He looked friendly. He looked almost as nervous as she did, which was extremely endearing. When he had looked about the bar for a couple of minutes and still didn't seem to have spotted her, Ruby chanced a little wave.

He gazed somewhere beyond her. Literally a *blind* date.

Perhaps he was short-sighted. His slightly scrunched up, squinting expression suggested he needed glasses but was a little too vain to wear them. Ruby picked up her book and opened it out ostentatiously. He sat down on a stool at the bar and reached into his bag to bring out a copy of the *Evening Standard* and a book of his own . . . yes! It was *Captain Corelli*.

Ruby twisted to take a last good look at herself in the mirror that was hanging behind her. She checked her hair for dandruff, her teeth for spinach. Not that she had ever really eaten spinach in her life.

Meanwhile, the man that Ruby was sure she must have been sent to that bar to meet was flicking through the pages of the novel, glancing up occasionally when the door to the bar swung open. It was very dark in the corner where Ruby had chosen to seat herself. Her target squinted at the cocktail menu. She was obviously going to have to go to him or their date would never get started.

Taking a deep breath she got to her feet and prepared to cross the floor. As she drew closer she turned on a megawatt beam. Lou was right, this man was an angel. His eyes may have been useless as far as long-distance vision was concerned, but weren't they a beautiful blue? As Ruby walked across that bar, the disillusionment and cynicism that had been gathering like a cloud above her head all day were suddenly and absolutely dispelled.

He was just a foot away from her now. He glanced at the book that Ruby held in front of her like a choirboy carrying a bible and then looked her straight in the eye. Ruby squeezed a couple more kilowatts out of her beam.

'Hi,' she said.

'Hi,' said the stranger.

'*Captain Corelli's Mandolin*,' said Ruby, holding the book out towards his face.

The stranger shied away from the proffered novel, then

peered at it closely as if to confirm the title and nodded. Ruby checked him over eagerly as he did so. Serial killer hair? She didn't think so. In the seconds it took for the stranger to look from the book to Ruby's face again, she had convinced herself that she could make a go of it with this one. Love was worth one more shot after all. In fact, she decided, as the stranger's smile became slightly quizzical, love was worth throwing herself at this man's feet for. His eyes, his lips, his hair . . .

'Er,' said the stranger.

'Yes?' said Ruby eagerly.

'What can I get you?' the barman asked her man.

Ruby looked at him expectantly, waiting to state her own preference. White wine or orange juice? Which should she have? What if he didn't drink? She didn't want him to think she was a lush. But she could definitely have used a spritzer to help her loosen up. Perhaps she'd have an orange juice this time and a spritzer next time round, depending on whether he bought alcohol for himself or settled for a soft drink.

'Two bottles of Becks, please,' he said.

Ruby pulled a little face. She was impressed that he was the type of man who liked to take charge but she hated Becks and wasn't it a little presumptuous of him to assume that she wanted alcohol anyway? Best not to mention it this time, she decided. Wouldn't want him to think she was a difficult sort of woman. Hang on, though. Perhaps she should take a stand at this point. The way you were with someone at the very start of a relationship set the tone for later on. She of all people should know that. If she hadn't been so willing to please Flett, if she hadn't agreed to everything he suggested just to make him like her, he might have found her a bit of a challenge and actually liked her more.

Ruby bit her lip and got ready to tell him. 'I'm sorry,' she said. 'But I don't really like Becks.'

'Don't you?' asked the stranger.

'No, I don't. I prefer white wine.'

'Really.'

'Yes. Always have done.'

'Oh.' He looked from Ruby to the bottles on the bar and back again. The barman had already opened them.

'It'll be OK just this one time,' Ruby said accommodatingly.

'Right,' said the squinter. 'Er, enjoy your book,' he added, getting to his feet and taking the beer to his best friend, who had finally arrived, and commandeered a table by the door.

It took nanoseconds for the tears to come.

Leaving sodding *Captain Corelli's Mandolin* in a puddle of beer, Ruby fled for the door. The sum total of her embarrassment was increased momentarily when she tried to push the heavy glass door when she should have pulled it, but then she was out on the street. And headlong into someone's chest, knocking him onto his backside on the pavement.

Almost simultaneously Ruby and Martin's mobile phones chirruped to announce the arrival of a new SMS.

'Do U like pina colada?' was the text message Lou sent to both.

39

Lou paced her living room. It was a mistake to agree to let Andrew come to her place. She should have insisted that they meet on neutral ground. But of course, she couldn't insist on that without Andrew wanting to know why she was so keen not to have him in her kitchen. She tried saying, 'Let's just go for a drink.' But Andrew had insisted, 'I want to cook for you.' And then Lou knew she couldn't tell him she didn't want him to cook for her without saying why over the phone. Or by fax. Or by e-mail. She had considered both those methods during the long day at work.

Now, with ten minutes to go before Andrew turned up (absolutely on time, of course) with a bag full of groceries to turn into some delicious expression of his love, Lou rehearsed her speech. Should she wait until he had finished cooking? No, of course not. She would have to tell him before he started, otherwise she would forever be the girl who had eaten his romantic dinner and then dumped him over coffee. In any case, she hardly felt like eating anything with the weight of the imminent ending on her mind.

'Andrew,' she rehearsed, 'there's something I've got to say to you. Sit down.' She'd cleared all the rubbish off her armchair so that she could sit there and he could sit on the sofa. 'I just want to say how much I've enjoyed being with you these past couple of months.'

'It's not you. It's me,' she tried.

God, no. She berated herself. She couldn't use that line. Even though it really was her and not him, everyone thought that line really meant, 'It's not *me*. It's definitely *you*.'

There was still a part of her that thought perhaps she shouldn't do it at all. In Andrew she had all the raw ingredients for a perfect life. Here was a grown-up, good-looking, solvent, generous, warm-hearted man who adored her. A man who adored her even when she knew she looked like the Loch Ness monster's little sister and had a terrible temper to match. It didn't take a huge leap of the imagination to see Andrew standing at the top of the aisle, looking back at Lou walking towards him with a grin as wide as the English Channel. She could see him painting the nursery yellow; pushing a pram that contained two lovely brown-haired twins (one boy, one girl); presenting her with an eternity ring on their tenth anniversary, taking the twins to school, teaching them how to play football on long, summer holidays in Tuscany, giving the daughter away at her own wedding, cosying up to Lou on the veranda of their perfect house as their retirement stretched ahead of them – a long straight road of well-planned for, financially comfortable and perpetually sunny days.

'Oh, God.' Lou poured herself a vodka tonic. That night she had sent Martin and Ruby out to find their perfect future, and here she was, preparing to let go of hers.

She remembered something that an old boyfriend had said to her. One that she didn't want to let go of at the time. *One person can't be happy enough for the two of us*. And that was it in a nutshell. It didn't matter how wonderful Andrew was and how much effort he was prepared to put into their relationship. While Lou didn't feel the same way, his love was only building a tower without foundations.

She had to end it and she had to end it that evening. Even if she did have to end it with a real stinker of a line.

'Taste this.' Andrew advanced towards her with a spoonful of the sauce he had created so lovingly. He held one hand beneath the spoon to catch any drips and even blew on it to make sure that it wasn't too hot for her.

Lou shook her head.

'Go on,' said Andrew. 'It's delicious.'

Lou forced herself to smile and took a mouthful.

'What do you think?'

It was a little hot. It burned her tongue. But she nodded.

'It's, em, great.'

'It should be,' he said. 'Because I put all my love into it.' He stared at her intently as she licked her tingling lips. 'Oh, sod it, Lou,' he burst out suddenly. 'I can't wait any longer to say this.'

'Say what?' She was horrified.

'I'm crazy about you. I have been since the first day we met. Within a second of meeting you I felt like we'd known each other forever and I do want to know you forever, Lou. Forever.'

'Oh God,' Lou couldn't stop her expression of anguish escaping that time. But Andrew misinterpreted.

'I can tell by your face that you feel the same way,' he

laughed, misreading her horror for the shock of delight. 'Well, why don't we do it?'

'Do what?' Lou asked him. Though even as she asked him, she feared she already knew. Please, don't let him be about to ask me to marry him, the voice inside her screamed. Please don't ask. Please don't ask. Please don't ask. The second of silence that followed gaped like the bloody Grand Canyon.

'Move in with me,' he said at last.

Well, at least it wasn't the other 'M' word. Lou felt her body collapse in relief. She sank down into the sofa, closed her eyes and put her head in her hands.

'Lou? Are you OK?' Andrew put the spoon down, carefully, to avoid staining the work surfaces, then hurried back to see how she was feeling. Lou didn't know whether to laugh or cry or hug him or punch him or what.

'You didn't think,' he began. 'Oh, Lou. Have I disappointed you? Did you think I was going to ask you to . . .' It turned out that even Andrew couldn't say the 'M' word. 'Well, I'm sure that we will,' he said. 'One day. It's just that . . . We haven't known each other very long. I think it would be more sensible to live together first, don't you? See how we get on. I mean, I am absolutely committed to you, Lou but, you know . . .' He stumbled. 'I've never asked a girl to move in with me before.'

Lou shook her head.

'Oh, come on, Lou!' Andrew exclaimed, still thinking that she felt slighted by the proposal that wasn't forthcoming. 'You can't expect . . .'

'Andrew,' she stopped him. 'I don't want to marry you.'

'And that's OK by me,' he said, taking both her hands. 'But move in, yeah? Your place or mine?'

'Andrew,' Lou interrupted again. 'I don't want to move in with you either.'

'Why not?'

'It's not you, it's me,' ran the autocue in her mind. 'Or how about "I love you but I'm not *in* love with you"?' Another corking line. 'You could try, "I'm not ready for a relationship right now" or "I've been hurt before and I just can't commit." ' In the event, none of those lines came out of Lou's mouth when she opened it.

'Are you saying you don't want to be with me at all?' Andrew pre-empted. 'Are you trying to tell me it's over?'

Lou nodded. 'That's right. And it's because I'm a lesbian.'

Did he believe her? Lou would never know. Andrew didn't hang round long enough to need convincing. He just pulled his coat on over his apron and went storming out of the flat, streaming expletives behind him. Lou didn't even blink for a minute or so afterwards. Had he really gone?

Strange thing was, Lou thought, as she sat alone on her sofa, watching tomato sauce drip down the wall (he'd thrown the pan across the sitting room), he didn't try to make her reconsider. Despite the fact that moments earlier he had been telling her that she was the one for him, albeit on a semi-permanent trial basis, he hadn't asked for a proof, or a proper explanation, or even a second change. He had literally seen red and picked up the pan. Now she was seeing red all over her previously Zen white interior.

Lou took a sip from her glass of wine and laughed. All that time looking for the fatal flaw and being unable to find one and getting herself all tied up in knots because she simply couldn't think of a good reason not to be with Andrew. Now she had one. Who would have thought that the perfect man could throw such a spectacular tantrum?

It didn't matter. She'd never have to put up with it again. Because at last Lou had silenced one nagging voice; the little voice in her head that said that what *she* wanted – what she really, really wanted – in a lover, was the only opinion that counted. Not the opinions of her parents, her friends or her work mates. Not the opinion of the old lady across the street who told her, 'You've got a real catch there,' when Andrew helped her up the stairs with her shopping bags. Lou had listened to the voice inside and was finally going to act on it. Andrew wasn't right for her for one fundamental reason. He could never be the stranger on the train.

> Wednesday morning, late in May. Northern Line.
> You in the grey skirt suit, poked your tongue out
> at the bloke reading *FT*. Me, in the blue suit, gave you
> a wink. Will I ever see you again?

Lou had found her Once Seen that afternoon in the doctor's surgery while she waited for a check-up on her ankle. She kept re-reading the two-line ad in *Time Out* all day, just in case she had hallucinated it. Now, certain that Andrew had finally gone home and confident that she could plug the telephone back into its socket again without him calling up to ask if she really meant what she'd said, Lou rang the number that accompanied the advert.

'Hello,' said Lou, when her call was finally answered. 'I'm responding to your ad in the back of *Time Out*. The Once Seen?'

'Oh, hi,' said the girl on the end of the line. 'You don't want me then. You want my flatmate, Alex. Alex! Alex!' She put her hand over the receiver but Lou could still make out her muffled words. 'There's a woman on the phone says she's responding to your Once Seen.' The girl came back on line. 'I do hope you're the one,' she said conspiratorially. 'We've had all sorts of weirdos ring up. You wouldn't believe the number of people who thought they recognised themselves. I said it was a mistake to put a telephone number. Alex was just about ready to give up. It was all quite a long time ago . . .'

'I'm definitely the one,' Lou interrupted.

'Then you know what you're letting yourself in for, don't you?' said the girl. 'You remember Alex exactly?'

'Oh, yes,' said Lou. 'I definitely remember Alex.'

Alex. So that was the stranger's name.

'What's your name?' asked the flatmate brightly.

'Lou. Short for Louisa.'

'Well, nice to talk to you, Lou. I'm Hannah, by the way, in case we actually get to meet up! I do hope so. I'm desperate to know what Alex had been raving on about these past few months. OK, Lou. Here comes your dream date!'

Lou clutched the telephone receiver tightly as she listened to the phone at the other end being passed over.

'Hello?' said Alex.

Lou was silent as she let the sound of Alex's voice

caress her ear after all this time. The slight Northern accent. She hadn't expected that.

'Hello? Are you still there?' Alex asked.

'I'm here,' said Lou.

'You're the girl who ended up in the lap of that *FT* bloke?'

'That's me.'

'I hope you didn't think I was laughing at you,' Alex continued. 'You know I was laughing *with* you, of course.'

'I knew that,' said Lou.

'I wish I'd spoken to you.'

'I wish you'd spoken to me, too,' Lou murmured.

'But it isn't always easy,' said Alex. 'You know how it is. You can never be quite sure how it's going to be received. Talking to a stranger on the train.'

'I've thought about you a lot,' said Lou. 'I even placed a Once Seen myself.'

'I hadn't even heard of them until a few weeks ago. And when Hannah told me, I didn't think anybody really replied to them. You wouldn't believe the number of people I've had calling up and claiming to be you.'

'Hannah told me.'

'I think they're just chancing it. Makes a change from answering a normal personal ad, I suppose. Own up pretty quickly as soon as they hear my voice, though.'

'You've got a lovely voice,' said Lou.

'Thank you. But it doesn't take long for them to realise that I'm not the man they thought I was.'

'That you're not a man at all,' Lou echoed.

'And that's OK by you?' Alex asked.

'That's OK by me,' Lou told her. 'At last.'

40

'Do U like pina colada?'

Martin, who had grown up to a soundtrack of Barry Manilow, courtesy of his mother, had to explain the significance of the joke to Ruby. On the way to the bar that evening, he had an inkling that he was about to become the victim of a Lou Capshaw set-up but he'd gone along with it anyway. Now that Cindy had moved on to a hairy-backed sculptor called Louis, he didn't have much to occupy him of an evening any more.

He feigned annoyance at Lou's big prank but was secretly delighted when Ruby agreed to join him for one more drink. One drink became four and they were still there when the barman announced he was closing for the night.

Turfed out of their comfortable chairs, Ruby and Martin decided to walk until they could find a taxi to take them north of the river. But there were no taxis south of the river to pick them up. Every black cab that passed had its light turned off or, if it did have its 'for hire' sign illuminated, the driver was on his way home to Peckham and didn't want to have to go north again.

'My feet are killing me,' Ruby groaned, as they walked steadily northwards, growing less and less confident that their cab would ever come.

'Take your shoes off,' Martin suggested.

'No way,' said Ruby. 'There's all sorts of shit on the street. Dog shit. Broken glass.'

'You could just look where you're walking,' said Martin.

'If you were a gentleman you'd carry me.'

'I would carry you,' he assured her, 'if you were a lady.'

Ruby limped on.

'Ow!' she exclaimed, as they neared the Thames and the entrance to Albert Bridge. 'I think I've just broken the skin on my ankle.' She sank down onto a bench. 'I can't go any further.'

'We've just got to get north of the river,' said Martin. 'Then we'll be able to get ourselves a cab.'

'I'm not moving,' she said. 'You get a cab and bring it back here for me.'

'Don't be ridiculous,' Martin sat down beside her. 'Let me have a look at your foot.'

Ruby held her foot out towards him and let him take her shoe off. Cinderella in reverse. Even in the orange glow of the street lights, Martin could see that her toes looked angry red where the thin fake snakeskin straps had rubbed and chafed in the short walk from the bar to the riverside.

'Am I bleeding?' she asked him pitifully.

Martin cupped his hand around her heel. The back of her ankle was indeed wet with blood.

'What do you buy such bloody stupid shoes for anyway?'

'To look attractive,' Ruby said. 'To get a man.'

'A woman wearing trainers who can actually walk is

far more attractive than someone limping in stilettos.'

'Yeah, right.'

'Here.' Martin started to untie his own trainers. 'You wear these and I'll go barefoot.'

'They'll be too big for me,' Ruby began to protest.

'You've got big feet,' Martin reminded her. 'They'll probably be too small. Do you want the socks too?'

'Are you kidding?' said Ruby, wrinkling her nose at the thought.

'I haven't got athlete's foot,' he promised her, reading her mind.

'That wasn't what I was thinking,' Ruby lied.

'Just put my trainers on and let's get across this river. I'm actually quite keen to get home.'

Ruby slipped her feet into Martin's Pumas reluctantly. They were, as she had dreaded, still very warm. But Martin was already halfway across the bridge in his socks by now carrying her snakeskin sandals. Ruby tied the laces as tightly as she could and slopped out onto the bridge after him until they were walking side by side.

'So, does this mean we're friends again?' Ruby asked him when she drew near. They'd spent the evening in the bar indulging in fairly nasty banter. It was what they'd always done when they *were* friends but Ruby wanted to make sure.

'We're friends,' said Martin abruptly. He didn't want to get all psychological about it. 'Do you know that if enough people walked in perfect time over this bridge,' he said to change the subject. 'It would set up a sine wave that could break the bridge in half. That's why there are those notices telling troops to break their step.'

'Would it really happen?' asked Ruby.

'I don't know. Let's try it now. Walk in time with me. One, two, three, four . . .'

They linked arms and headed out over the river. Ruby wondered what the people who passed them in their cars must think they looked like. Martin in socks, carrying a pair of girly sandals. Ruby in a pair of trainers so big, it looked as though she was wearing false feet at the end of her skinny legs.

'Ow!' Suddenly Martin broke step and hopped onto his left foot. Frowning with pain, he brushed a piece of gravel from the bottom of his sock. 'That hurt,' he said. It was a total understatement.

'Do you want your shoes back?' Ruby asked.

'You need them more than I do.'

'No. You need them. I can limp in my sandals.'

'You can't limp in your sandals,' Martin said huffily. 'Just keep walking. I'll catch you up.'

'That's very gentlemanly,' said Ruby.

'I'm just being a good friend.'

'You've always been a good friend to me,' said Ruby, suddenly serious. 'Even when I thought you were being horrible to me, I can see now that you were just concerned. I've taken you for granted,' Ruby added. 'I mean, when you think about how we met it's a wonder that you ever wanted to become my friend at all.'

'What do you mean?' asked Martin suspiciously.

'I mean, I was so nasty to you, after we slept together that night in Freshers' week. I don't know why I was so nasty, except that I was confused. I'd never slept with anyone before and you were so confident and I was sure that you would tell everybody and I was just trying to protect myself from the jokes and . . .'

'What?' said Martin. 'What did you say?'

'I thought you'd take the piss if you found out I was a virgin.'

'But it was my first time too,' Martin blurted.

'Why didn't you tell me?'

'You seemed to know what you were doing.'

'But I was following your lead.'

'Maybe we were both naturals,' Martin laughed.

'I agonised over that night for three whole years!'

'Three years? I still agonise about it now!'

'Think how good we could have been if we'd practised,' Ruby mused.

Martin nodded.

'Is your foot better yet?' she asked.

'It's getting there. If we just rest here for a moment longer.'

Martin leaned against the side of the bridge and looked down into the water swirling by below. He thought about his novel. His characters Mark and Ruthie standing side by side in this very spot. The fairy-lights twinkling on the candy-coloured struts that towered above Martin and Ruby now were reflected in the river like the sparks from a firework. Their own reflections looked back at them like strangers. Like people who didn't know each other too well to fall in love.

'Don't we look strange,' commented Ruby.

'You are strange,' said Martin, giving her a gentle pinch on the arm.

Now they turned from the river and looked into each other's eyes. And suddenly it was as though they hadn't known each other for a decade. As though there was still much to discover. Much to find exciting and fall in love with.

Martin took Ruby's chin gently and tipped her face up towards his.

'Have you ever wanted to kiss me?' he asked her.

'Do I have to answer that question?' she replied.

'There's a bit in my book where the hero asks this girl if she's ever wanted to kiss him and she tells him that she has but he's much too scared to act on it,' said Martin. 'So they don't get it together and they both end up with people they don't really like.'

'That's a pity,' said Ruby.

'I'm going to cut it out,' he told her. 'Put in a happy ending instead.'

'Can there be a happy ending?' Ruby asked him.

'If we want it,' Martin confirmed.

Ruby felt herself leaning towards him then. Closing her eyes. Puckering up her mouth . . .

Epilogue

'Out the way, girls!' said Ruby. 'Wide load approaching!'

Lou and Susannah made way for the blushing bride.

'Gorgeous dress, Ruby,' Susannah assured her.

'Shame I can't say the same for this one,' said Lou, holding out the skirts of her peachy-pink delight.

'Bridesmaids always pull at the reception,' reminded Alex, coming up behind Lou in the ladies' room and planting a kiss on her collar-bone.

'Not in front of my relatives, please,' said Ruby.

'What? The born-again Christians from Colorado?' Alex asked.

'No. Rosalia and Nat are extremely open-minded,' Ruby told her. 'I meant the old aunts on my husband's side. You'll get them all excited,' she added with a wink.

'Erica's pulled,' whispered Alex. 'Someone from your office called Emlyn Cruickshank?'

'Oh no,' said Ruby. 'Tell her to make sure he keeps his socks on in bed.'

'His socks?' said Susannah.

'Don't ask.'

'How are you feeling?' Lou asked the bride then. 'Is this everything you wanted?'

Ruby looked at the women surrounding her now.

Ruby thought of the people who'd been in the church that afternoon. Her mother and father. Lindsay, Steve,

Lauren. Rosalia and Nat. She thought of the speech her father had made for her at the reception. So full of unconditional love that it made her cry into her champagne. She thought of her husband's sister, Marie, standing in as his best man and managing to be funny without resorting to dirty jokes. She thought of Lou, insisting on making a chief bridesmaid's speech and making up for the lack of smut in spades.

And then she thought of her new husband. Martin. Smiling like a loony as she walked up to the altar. Wiping a sneaky tear away as they finally took their vows. Telling everyone at the reception that he'd loved her since he first saw her . . .

'This is everything and more,' she said. 'It's everything and more.'